After an eternity of formless floating

she felt a hand gently stroke her forehead. She opened her eyes. The room was exactly as she had left it, the fire an ever-changing glow in the semi-darkness, the rug thick and warm under her, Ben's dark eyes reflecting the flames. She almost expected some fundamental change to have occured.

She smiled lazily up at him "Pretty wild," she said.

He smiled too. "You always were."

Perhaps, though this had certainly been a first. She supposed that was the power that Ben had always had with her: a direct link with her animal desires. It wasn't as though he manipulated her. But whatever he did naturally seemed to have some fundamental connection to her own inner embers. Other men might painstakingly set down paper and kindling and ignite a slow flame in her that would, in time, burn as brightly as any. Ben's very essence operated on her like gasoline poured on a smoldering log.

Dear Reader,

When two people fall in love, the world is suddenly new and exciting, and it's that same excitement we bring to you in Silhouette Intimate Moments. These are stories with scope, with grandeur. These characters lead the lives we all dream of, and everything they do reflects the wonder of being in love.

Longer and more sensuous than most romances, Silhouette Intimate Moments novels take you away from everyday life and let you share the magic of love. Adventure, glamour, drama, even suspense—these are the passwords that let you into a world where love has a power beyond the ordinary, where the best authors in the field today create stories of love and commitment that will stay with you always.

In coming months look for novels by your favorite authors: Maura Seger, Parris Afton Bonds, Elizabeth Lowell and Erin St. Claire, to name just a few. And whenever you buy books, look for all the Silhouette Intimate Moments, love stories *for* today's women *by* today's women.

Leslie J. Wainger
Senior Editor
Silhouette Books

IMRL-7/85

Alexandra Sellers

The Old Flame

Published by Silhouette Books New York
America's Publisher of Contemporary Romance

SILHOUETTE BOOKS
300 East 42nd St., New York, N.Y. 10017

ISBN: 0-373-07154-X

First Silhouette Books printing August 1986

America's Publisher of Contemporary Romance

Printed in the U.S.A.

Books by Alexandra Sellers

Silhouette Intimate Moments

The Real Man #73
The Male Chauvinist #110
The Old Flame #154

ALEXANDRA SELLERS

used to force her mother to read to her for hours. She wrote her first short story at the age of ten, but as an adult, she got sidetracked and didn't get published until she was twenty-seven. She also loves travel; she wrote one book in Israel and began another in Greece.

I can’t even think of his name.

—sung by Billie Holiday

Chapter 1

"Aw, c'mon, she asked for it."

"They all do."

All the men laughed. Sondra, the only woman at thc table, sat unsmiling, unmoved by their masculine amusement.

"If she had been shot and paralyzed, would you say she had asked for it?" she asked calmly, in some part of herself hating them, and yet in another, completely untouched by it all. The part they saw was the calm and untouched side.

This reference to another case, much in the headlines, sobered two of the men somewhat, but Blake Roebotham made a very good living defending rape cases, and he was not about to admit the parallel. Crumpling the plastic wrap that had held his cafeteria sandwich, he stuffed it into the empty Styrofoam coffee cup and prepared to stand up.

"The difference is," he pointed out just a little less magnanimously than he would have done for a jury, "that my client didn't carry a violent weapon."

Sondra felt suddenly very lonely, as she often did when she was the only woman among men. She stiffened her spine for the argument that she did not want to make. She wanted to ignore this bait. But it had to be said. Men couldn't keep on getting away with these attitudes without challenge. "All men carry a violent weapon at all times, if they choose to use it that way," she said coolly.

Blake Roebotham was standing now, hitching his black robe back off his shoulders in a self-consciously casual way that he was—more obviously than he knew—hoping made him look rakish. Looking directly at Sondra, he gave vent to a remark so snide and vulgar that he lost the masculine participation of most of the other men at the table, who frowned their disapproval. But they did not say anything, and the wiry-haired barrister waved and went on his laughing way.

No one at the table said anything for a moment, and then two of the men began to mutter about the time. Sondra reached for the remains of her own lunch and dropped it on the nearest tray. Then the three lawyers stood up together.

"Christ, Ben," Sondra said to the man nearest her. "Couldn't you have given me someone a little easier to stomach than Blake Roebotham on a rape case my first time out?"

She meant it, but of course she didn't expect Ben Glass to understand that, and he didn't. He looked at her with an amused smile in his dark eyes. "Hey, come on, Sondra, you know you love a good fight."

That was true. She enjoyed her work, probably more than most people; she had been a good defence lawyer, and she intended to work just as hard now in the Crown Attorney's office as a prosecutor. But Blake Roebotham's tactics didn't fit her definition of a good fight. She knew that the major thrust of any defence of a rape case was to challenge the credibility of the victim, but Blake Roebotham was one of those men who actively *enjoyed* his psychological public rape of his client's victim. There was a kind of slavering of the mental chops that Sondra found disgusting and that, she knew, both sickened and terrified the victim in this case, who had suffered a three-day confinement and repeated rape by a man who had also mentally tormented and terrified her. Sondra, who knew that every grimace of pleasure on Blake Roebotham's face as he questioned her reminded Laney Meredith once more of her time in that prison, and that, on some level at least, Blake Roebotham knew exactly what he was doing, would have given a great deal not to have to go into this particular courtroom every day.

But there was no point trying to make Ben Glass understand that. He had laughed at Roebotham's sexist drivel five minutes ago, and she couldn't be certain that her own assignment to this case hadn't been deliberate tactics against her on *someone's* part. Perhaps the male powers that be in the Crown Attorney's office, Ben Glass included, had thought that a little of Blake Roebotham's brand of psychological rape at the beginning would be just what she needed to keep her in line during her stint as a Crown Attorney.

Sondra knew Roebotham had a reputation for being almost as offensive to any woman Crown involved in the prosecution of one of his clients as he was to the plaintiff; everybody must know of it. And since Sondra was considered a bit of a maverick as a lawyer, it was possible not everyone in the rather conservative Crown office had been overjoyed to hear that she would be joining the staff. They might not mind at all seeing Blake Roebotham put her in her place.

She could forgive Ben Glass—if only just—if he wanted to see someone take her down a peg or two. There had been a kind of antagonism between them for years that was not entirely limited to—or explained by—the rivalry between Crown and defence on the many cases they had fought. Come to that, probably *she* wouldn't have minded seeing *him* put to rout by another woman lawyer, either. And besides, it was an attitude that she had met all along the line as she and other women of her generation had stormed the male bastion of the law.

What she couldn't forgive was this: if her total inexperience of rape cases and her newness to prosecution after nearly ten years of defence cost her this case, not only would a very dangerous man go free, but his victim, her witness for the prosecution, would be psychologically destroyed.

She couldn't forgive Ben Glass for running that risk. He should have let her cut her prosecutor's teeth on a couple of small, unimportant cases first while she got into the swing of things.

There was also the fact of what it would do to *her*, professionally and psychologically, to lose an important case to a creep like Roebotham her first time out.

All of which meant that Sondra was taking the case personally. She found she took it home with her at night to an alarming degree, wasn't sleeping well and was not in any way detached—on the inside—from the sleazy sexist attacks she was getting from Blake both inside and outside Courtroom 417. On the surface, Sondra could always look calm. But inside she was still churning with fury at Blake Roebotham's last, foul crack, and she was aware that she was blaming Ben Glass for it.

"How's it going, Sondra?"

They had lost the other lawyer somewhere in the halls, and Sondra had been striding along at Ben Glass's side, lost in thought, almost forgetting he was there. Now his quiet voice calmed her inner turmoil. Whatever else you could say about Ben Glass, he was a brilliant intellect and a very, very astute lawyer. No question at all that *he* was heading towards the Supreme Court of Canada one day. And for the first time in her career, Sondra reminded herself, Ben Glass was her ally, not her adversary, in court. It would take her a little while to get used to the idea, but she could begin right now by asking for his help.

"Frankly, Ben, I just don't know," she admitted matter-of-factly. "I guess you know this is my first rape case, and the plaintiff has been very remote on the stand. Very distant and emotionless. I can't be sure how the jury is taking it, and I can't be sure she won't suddenly crack under cross-examination. And how it'll influence them if she does."

They reached the escalators that led from the basement of the courthouse, where the cafeteria was, to the upper floors of offices and courts. Sondra leaned against the moving rail and looked worriedly at Ben Glass, one step below her as they moved slowly upwards.

He had what most women would call an interesting face, she supposed: thin, dark and intense, his intellect apparent in the shape of the broad forehead and the expression in his black eyes. He wasn't tall—one step's advantage meant she had to look down to meet his eyes, but certainly the first impression one got of the deputy Crown was not one of lack of height. No, the first impression was also the most lasting—intensity and intellect.

She had locked horns with him many times in court, and each time it had been an experience. The courtroom always seemed to crackle with that something extra, when they were fighting, that made it seem almost a personal battle.

Their most recent case had been similar to many others: Ben Glass had taken her client apart like a lobster—cracking the shell in some places, delicately prying into others—until it had been obvious to everybody that his alibi was a fabrication—neat and professional, polished, even admirable in its manufacture—but nonetheless manufactured. Ben had done it by playing very astutely on the pride of her client in having had the really rather incredible brains and moxie to have concocted the alibi so brazenly.

Sondra had won the case on an appeal under the new Charter of Rights and Freedoms by virtue of a technicality—the question of whether the police had had reasonable grounds for arresting her client in the first place. It wasn't a victory she was particularly proud of, but she had enjoyed the battle of wits with Ben Glass. And, of course, between lawyers there could be no ill will over the nature of her appeal. In this far-from-perfect legal system, such tactics were an everyday, expected occurrence.

"Would you like me to drop in for a while this afternoon and tell you what I think?" he was offering now, and what she might lose in excitement she was likely to gain in other ways, Sondra reflected.

"Yes, would you?" she said smiling. It was an offer she'd been hoping for. "I'd appreciate it."

He nodded. "I've got a meeting with a witness at two-thirty, but it shouldn't take more than half an hour." Although Ben Glass wasn't in court that week, he was very busy preparing the Crown's case in an upcoming murder trial. Sondra repressed the little voice that urged her to tell him not to bother. It wasn't for herself; it was for Laney Meredith. And she had as much right to Ben's expert advice as the murdered man, and certainly would benefit from it more than he could. A conviction in this case, Sondra was sure, would go a long way towards rehabilitating Laney Meredith. "I'll come up as soon as I can," he told her.

Sondra looked at her watch as they got off one escalator and moved towards the next, suddenly feeling the tension that had been with her all morning as a very physical presence. Two-twenty. She moved her shoulders uncomfortably inside her black legal robes. "Thanks, Ben."

"Are you free for dinner tonight, Sondra?"

She stumbled in surprise, automatically reaching for the moving plastic handle of the escalator in front of her. When she gained her footing, she turned to see Ben Glass standing at the foot of the moving staircase, looking up for her answer. His office was on this floor; he wasn't going any higher.

Now what was this? Was this Ben Glass trying to relive old times, or was this her new boss extending the welcome mat? She was new to the Crown office, and she'd been busy preparing this case almost since day one. There had been little time for examining the social functioning of the place. How buddy-buddy were they in there?

Meanwhile, Ben Glass was getting step by step farther away from her, and other people had got onto the escalator between them. No way now to feel around for clarification. "I'm not sure," she temporized, bending around the people below her to find Ben's line of vision. "How about drinks instead?"

He nodded and waved and was gone. Thoughtfully, Sondra turned and straightened. Was it possible Ben was interested in her after all these years? He couldn't be. Too long ago, and too far away. Besides, he was married. He'd got married years ago. And he wouldn't be likely to invite her so openly to something that he intended to be clandestine.

That was another problem women moving into a man's world hadn't solved yet: how to decide when an invitation from a colleague was a move and when it wasn't. In fact, how to stop the question from crossing your mind at all. Or perhaps other women *had* solved it. Perhaps part of her consciousness was still stuck back in an earlier generation.

Or perhaps part of her mind was caught up in the past. Ben Glass was as attractive as ever. And she had always been a pushover for brains.

At the top of the escalator, Sondra turned down a long corridor labelled Courtrooms 417-421 and opened a glass door with Witness Room painted on it neatly in black.

Laney Meredith, hollow-eyed, stunned and motionless, as always, sat on a small sofa next to her mother. Her eyelashes barely flickered as Sondra entered her line of vision.

"Hi," said Sondra, in a carefully calculated mix of optimism and calm. "How are you?"

"I'm all right," said the girl, a tiny seventeen, pretty and delicate, in a voice as cool and distant as the moon.

"He's being very rough on you," Sondra said. "But you're doing fine, just fine." In fact, she didn't know if that were true. One of the difficulties she was finding here on the other side of the fence was an inability to read how the jury was taking the testimony of this shell-shocked girl. Did they understand the reason for her remote lack of emotion, or did they find her cold, uninterested, calculated?

She was amazed at how much difference it made just having to put her case on first. Of course, she had known life would be different as a Crown Attorney. But at the moment she felt it was like going in blind, this business of being on the attack from the start. For the first time Sondra could see firsthand what Crowns had often maintained—the position of the defence was a bit of a luxury. You could sit back and observe and evaluate the case against you, attack it when and as you could, and you didn't have to proffer your defence till all the evidence against you was already presented.

But, of course, the defence complaints still held good from this side of the fence: Sondra found it a novel experience to have the police on her side instead of being as obstructionist as humanly possible....

"He's going to keep you all afternoon, Laney," Sondra said of the defence attorney, who in spite of her intentions had somehow become "he" in their conversations, in much the same way as Laney's attacker had become that same, unnecessary-to-name "he"—he the attacker, the powerful, the victimizer; he the man whom all women recognized. "I'll do what I can about getting an early recess. You've been through enough for one day. Think you can hold out for another two hours?" She wasn't telling Laney yet that she had no doubt that Blake Roebotham would keep her over into Monday. Time enough for that when today had been got through.

Laney nodded distantly. "Yes," she said in a disembodied voice exactly like a shrug, the same voice the jury had been hearing. "I'm all right."

"He'll try to make you angry this afternoon," Sondra told her matter-of-factly. A businesslike tone was the only thing Laney Meredith responded to. When she heard sympathy or too much fellow feeling, she closed up too tightly to take in even basic information. "I don't know on what angle, but he'll try to get you angry and then trip you up—trick you into making a perfectly ordinary admission that he will then make sound damaging." She didn't tell her that a show of anger might cause her to lose sympathy with the jury, which historically tended to disapprove of any show of anger or bitterness on the part of rape victims, God alone knew why. She didn't tell her because too many instructions could make a witness seize up on the stand, and Laney was already far too reserved. For all she knew, anger would be an improvement. For all she knew, Laney didn't have the jury's sympathy to lose. "There's not much you can do about it except count five before you make any answer all afternoon,'' she finished.

Laney had heard this advice before and wasn't doing too badly at following it. But Blake Roebotham had fifteen years of experience in just how to badger an already shattered woman into a furious statement that he could use to great effect with the jury, while Laney was a novice on the stand. It was just one of the injustices of a legal system that Sondra knew needed to be dismantled and rewritten from the ground up.

''I'll be all right,'' Laney said dully. Sondra managed to keep herself from shaking her head, wondering again if that lifeless tone was setting the jury's teeth on edge, or if, like herself, they could see where it came from. ''Thank you,'' said Laney as an afterthought, while Sondra smiled and lifted a hand at the door.

She moved down the corridor to the door of the lounge reserved for women Crown Attorneys. She had five minutes before the two-thirty court session. As always, the jury was the great unknown in this business. A judge was harder to fool, easier to read; the machinations of a jury were almost always a mystery. The jury in this case was nearly equally divided between the sexes—seven women and five men. Sondra had managed to swing that, but since historically women jurors were as likely to let a rapist go free as men were, she had no idea whether that had been the right thing to do. She knew Blake Roebotham had watched her attempts to get more women among the twelve with something like glee. He had even aided her. Probably he had a technique specially geared to a predominance of women on the jury, and of course under these circumstances he would find a victory even sweeter, showing Sondra that he was able to turn women against their own sex.

But her woman's instinct told her times were changing, that some, at least, of the women on the jury would see through the defence's shabby tactics and the woodenness of the plaintiff; that they would look at the defendant and put themselves in the place of his victim, at his mercy in that horrible basement, and hold out for the conviction that he deserved.

Sondra breathed deeply as she washed her hands and combed her hair, trying to find her own calm centre in the whirlwind. She had laid a little trap for Blake Roebotham this morning. With luck he would put his foot into it this afternoon.

It had been a risk. It had meant leaving a dramatic piece of information to be drawn out by the defence attorney, knowing that if he did *not* bring it out, she herself wouldn't be able to bring it out on re-examination.

The case needed drama to keep the jury interested. The evidence that Laney Meredith had given them had been robbed of most of its human interest by her severely emotionless delivery. And Sondra knew that her only hope of drama with this witness had been to let the defence draw out evidence that he wasn't expecting. But still, it was a risk.

If she was reading Blake Roebotham right, he was gearing up for a real attack on her witness this afternoon. Sondra would have to be quick, protecting Laney from harassing questions, making his unreasonable hostility and her witness's vulnerability obvious to the judge and setting the stage for her request for an early adjournment.

If she were quick enough, she might be able to cut the ground from under Roebotham just as he was building for his big end-of-the-day crusher and come out of it with a four-thirty adjournment and the image of a harassed victim left for the weekend in the minds of those twelve good people and true.

She wondered whether Blake Roebotham would second-guess her intention and start his climax early. A four-thirty adjournment was within reason, four o'clock was not, unless the witness got hysterical. And she couldn't see Laney Meredith doing that. After the brutality she had experienced at the hands of the man who now sat facing her through every word of her testimony, Blake Roebotham's brand would only make her go colder and more distant.

She wondered if Roebotham knew that, too. Almost undoubtedly, after fifteen years of meeting every conceivable kind of victim response on the witness stand. He must have browbeaten and harassed a dozen women who had taken the violence completely to heart, the way Laney Meredith had done. He would judge very nicely how far he could drive her.

Well, she would have to play it on her feet. She had done that often enough before. If he started early, maybe she would let him carry on past the four-thirty adjournment request he would be expecting from her and building for, and into anticlimax. Let the jury see his tactics exposed. Point them out, if possible—the tactics of a man who, just like his client, cared for nothing but himself and his pleasure.

Sondra felt a sudden burst of urgent protectiveness towards the girl—so young and so damaged—of whom the Crown, in its wisdom, had seen fit to appoint herself the champion.

That much at least was fitting, she thought: that it should be a woman standing up to plead a woman's cause—every woman's cause—against this incredible, mindless violence of the male half of the human race. If she'd had to make the choice between sitting helplessly by and watching the case, as the jury must, or arguing it herself, Sondra would choose the active role every time. At least, inexperienced at prosecution or not, she could do *something*.

Nevertheless, it was a strain. More of a strain than she had felt in a courtroom for many years—since her first years as a junior lawyer, in fact.

And even so, this was a very different feeling than the one she had felt then. She had been nervous then, but it had been more a kind of stage fright. She could never remember feeling in a courtroom this combination of black dismay, fear and deep-rooted helplessness before, but it gave her a ruthless determination to win—by any methods at all.

God damn all men, she was thinking in sudden violence as she gripped her battered black briefcase and strode across the hall to Courtroom 417. God damn them all.

Chapter 2

Laney Meredith had been waiting for a late bus that Friday night when Hughie Macomber happened by in his bright red muscle car. It was cold and sleeting, and she had just missed one bus and had at least twenty minutes to wait for the next, and on his third attempt, Laney Meredith had decided to trust the friendly, persuasive young man who had promised to drive her straight home.

Once she was in the car, his puppyish friendliness had changed. He told her that he had a gun in his belt, that he belonged to a notorious gang, that he was their hit man, and that if she did not give in to his demands she and her parents would be "dead meat" by morning. Then he drove her to a parking lot deep in an industrial area, raped her and left her there. Fifteen minutes later, just as the lights of an open doughnut shop with people inside came into the frozen, weeping, limping girl's view, the red muscle car had returned with a roar. Forcing Laney Meredith into the car again, Hugh Macomber had then driven her to the empty house of a family he had known was away and locked her in the basement.

He had kept her there for three days in complete terror, going and coming at odd, unpredictable intervals, leaving her for long periods without even access to a toilet. On the third day, Laney Meredith found a screwdriver that someone had left on top of the furnace. With that, her heart beating in terror, she had managed to force her way through the two locked doors between her and the rest of the house, wrapped herself in the nearest blanket and run for help to the neighbours.

This was the girl who, Blake Roebotham was convinced and meant to convince the jury, had "asked for it."

The first thing he had done this morning when she had turned the questioning of Laney Meredith over to him had been to pick up the lawyer's movable lectern aggressively and move it closer to the witness stand. Sondra knew that this was a tactic devised to frighten the witness with a threatening physicality that would remind her of her attacker, and so make her more nervous and her testimony less effective. That was the sort of defence Blake Roebotham ran.

Nor had he waited to go on the attack verbally. He had been loud and hectoring all morning, alternately demanding that Laney Meredith speak louder and that she repeat herself, and loudly doubting her word. He obviously had no reason to change that attack this afternoon. Sondra sat back to watch and listen, planning what strategy was available to her, waiting for her chances.

"Now, Laney, let's get back to the basement," the defence lawyer was saying in a loud, no-nonsense tone. Sondra knew that the unnecessary loudness and the cold lack of feeling in that voice must be terrifying her witness deep inside. And there could be nowhere on earth that Laney would want to "get back to" less, even in memory, than that basement. But there was nothing Sondra could object to. She had to trust that the jury would see this psychological rape for what it was. "You said you wanted to escape from my client. Isn't that what you said?"

"Yes."

"Well, then—" Blake Roebotham paused as though this point had puzzled him for some time "—why do you think it took you three days to escape from the Millers' basement?"

Laney blinked as though trying to focus. Sondra counted a pause five seconds long. "That's when I found the screwdriver," said the lifeless voice.

"That's when you found the screwdriver. Had you been looking for it for three days?"

Pause. "No."

"Oh, you hadn't," Roebotham repeated in nicely calculated surprise. "Do you mean you weren't looking for a tool to help you, or you hadn't been trying to escape during the previous three days?"

"At first I tried to escape, but then he came back and took away my clothes and...after that I didn't try anymore."

"Oh. Now why was that? Would that be because you were in fact quite happy to stay in that basement and wait for my client's visits?"

"No."

"Well, then, why do you think you stopped trying to escape? I mean, a basement—I know my basement is where I store my tools—one would think that a basement would give you lots of opportunities for making an escape. Did you *search* the basement during that three days?"

"No."

"Really. Why not?"

"I couldn't search the basement. I was locked in the furnace room."

"Did you search the furnace room?"

"I looked for something to put on."

"And did you find something?"

"I found a piece of old towel. He took it away after."

"And then, with your modesty restored, did you resume your search for a way of escape?"

"It wasn't modesty. It was cold. I was freezing."

"It was cold. Now that strikes me as odd. Haven't you just testified that you were in the furnace room?"

"Yes."

"Well, this was February, wasn't it? A bitterly cold February, if your testimony is to be believed. And you were in the furnace room! Wasn't the furnace keeping the place warm?"

"No. It was cold."

"Well, now, as I understand it, the Millers were away on vacation. The house wasn't vacant, was it? Just locked up for two weeks. One would presume they didn't want their pipes to freeze while they were away. And yet you say the furnace wasn't working?"

"I didn't say the furnace wasn't working. It wasn't keeping the basement warm."

"Oh, so it *was* working!" His tone thanked her for making a difficult point clear.

"It came on sometimes."

"I see. Well, about how often did it come on?"

He must be running into danger here, Sondra thought, scanning the faces of the jury. Surely all these people, in these days of more and more expensive heating fuel, turned down their home heating when they were away. And surely they knew that the temperature that would keep the water pipes from freezing and bursting would not keep a naked human being warm.

And if they didn't, she had two witnesses who would make the point clear later on: the police sergeant who had taken the temperature of the basement the day Laney escaped from it and the doctor who would tell them that the girl had in fact suffered from exposure in the basement.

"I don't remember. Not very often."

"So you were pretty cool down there," he said as though it had been a minor discomfort. No response. Laney Meredith had not needed the prompting from Sondra not to volunteer a comment unless a direct question was asked her by the defence attorney. She never agreed or disagreed with any statement, or had to restrain herself to keep from commenting. Between questions she simply wasn't there; she was somewhere deep inside herself.

"Were you?"

Laney blinked at him. "Were you?" he repeated aggressively.

"I don't understand the question."

"Were you cold in the basement?" Roebotham asked, hiding any chagrin he might have felt over this tiny evidence of loss of control of the questioning.

"Yes. I was freezing."

"And did my client know this?"

Pause. "Yes."

"Did you ever tell him you were cold?"

Pause. "I don't remember."

"You don't remember. Well, is it possible you did *not* tell him?"

She shrugged. "Maybe. I think I told him. He knew, anyway. I didn't have to tell him."

Blake grinned at the jury. "If only men could read all the women's minds that they're expected to read, there'd be a lot less divorce in the world!" he joked. A couple of the male jurors grinned agreement.

Sondra let him have the joke. If she wasn't mistaken, more than one of the *women* jurors was infuriated by the remark.

Having achieved his purpose, Blake whirled to confront the witness again. "So would it be fair to say that for most of the time you spent in the basement, you were more concerned with the lack of heat than with getting out?"

Pause. "I was concerned about both."

"But isn't it a fact that you only discovered the screwdriver because you were tinkering with the furnace to try to get more heat out of it?"

Sondra became aware that she was biting her lip. Oh, how carefully she had laid this trap, and here it was about to spring, and she wanted it sprung so badly she didn't know how she had sat still during the past five minutes. She could see Blake Roebotham gearing up. She knew where he thought he was going: he was getting ready to suggest that, if only Hugh Macomber had supplied her with heat, Laney Meredith would not have worried about escaping at all. That in fact she would have been quite happy to be subjected to three days of terrorization and rape if only she had been a little warmer.

"No."

There was a sound of moving air that meant someone had come into the courtroom. Sondra hoped it was Ben Glass. She wished every man in the world could be present for what was coming next, and especially all those who laughed at the sort of jokes that Blake Roebotham had been cracking over lunch.

Blake Roebotham blinked, and this time it was real, not feigned, surprise. "No? But didn't you tell my learned friend only this morning that you had found the screwdriver while you were attempting to tinker with the furnace?"

Yes, she had. Oh, yes, she had, and Sondra had very, very carefully left the subject of the furnace right there. She risked a backward glance and saw Ben Glass's dark head already tilted in the close attention that was his trademark.

"Yes."

Now Blake Roebotham was frankly puzzled, but he did not yet smell the trap. He smelled only a discrepancy in the girl's story that might be turned to his client's advantage somehow.

"Well, tell us which is the truth, Laney. Were you tinkering with the furnace when you found the screwdriver or not?"

Tell him, Sondra prayed silently. Tell him just as you told me. Let that accurate little mind that has been reduced only to facts without feeling not forget this one fact....

Laney gazed at a point somewhere to the right of the defence lawyer's head. "I was tinkering with the furnace when I found the screwdriver, but I wasn't trying to get more heat from it. I was trying to get it to blow up."

The gasp from the jury was small but audible in the silence. Blake Roebotham was very surprised, but it wasn't in his nature to be affected by this stark statement of human despair. He was planning how to move out of this corner.

Sondra could feel him groping for his lost footing, could feel his dismay at achieving what had been his goal—the courtroom had now heard the first sign of emotion in Laney Meredith's voice, but it hadn't been the emotion he wanted to elicit. On the words "blow up," they had all heard the reflection of the deep and sickening despair that this young girl must have gone through in order to decide what she had decided in that cold basement.

He tried to repair the damage by storming through, deliberately misunderstanding, banking on her reluctance to come any closer to that awful moment of decision he had just uncovered. "I *see*. You were going to blow up the house in order to make your escape?" he asked, shocked, as though the property were more important than the human suffering going on inside of it.

He didn't want her to answer that, of course, it was a rhetorical question, and after only the briefest of dramatic pauses, he opened his mouth to carry on. But Laney wasn't intimidated.

"No. I was locked in the furnace room. I thought if it exploded it would kill me."

Hearing it, the jury breathed as one person. Now, if not before, they must surely understand what had caused that lifeless voice, that frozen lack of emotion. Laney Meredith had gained more credibility in the past two minutes with her bleak, unvarnished truth than any amount of wily questioning could take away from her now.

Blake Roebotham had blundered again. Now his task was to make them forget what they had heard as soon as possible. His voice became suddenly louder, more aggressive.

"Isn't it a fact, Laney, that when my client arrived in your basement hideaway, you used to run to him and hug him?"

"Yes."

"You couldn't wait for him to unlock the door, isn't that right?"

"Yes. He was warm." More emotion was showing through Laney Meredith's distant voice. No one could miss the sickening self-hatred of a person who had been forced to turn to her tormentor for this basic human necessity.

"Now am I right in assuming that at this time you had no clothes on at all?" Somehow he made it sound as though that had been through Laney's own choice.

"Yes."

"So if you were running to hug my client every time he arrived, wouldn't he be justified in assuming that you liked his company, and that perhaps you didn't really object to his attentions?"

"No."

"Could you speak up, please? The jury is having difficulty hearing you." Sondra knew the badgering tone was deliberate and calculated. Watching the jury, however, she was almost sure Roebotham had calculated wrong.

"No."

"No? You ran to the door each and every time the man arrived, didn't you? You were, by your own admission, completely naked. You clutched at him and pushed yourself into his arms and held on for dear life! Didn't you?"

"Yes."

"And yet you say he couldn't mistake those actions for affection?"

"No. He knew I was cold. He always brought a blanket with him and took it away when he left."

Again the jury all breathed in simultaneously. At last Blake Roebotham seemed to realize that he could not storm his way out of the trap Sondra had laid for him. She had drawn out only the barest bones of what had gone on in the basement during those three days during examination-in-chief, and he suddenly seemed to realize that it was a potential minefield.

Belatedly, he jumped ship, too late to keep the jury from the personal interest they suddenly found themselves taking in the girl in front of them.

"Now, Laney, this morning you identified some clothing you were wearing on the night you were picked up." He moved to the table where the clothing still lay. "All this is your clothing?"

Laney Meredith nodded. "Yes."

"I see what you called your blue jumpsuit here, and a scarf, and a pair of socks, and a pair of winter boots. Is this everything you were wearing that night when you were standing waiting for the bus?"

"No, not everything," she responded in a small voice.

"What else were you wearing?"

"I had on a wool toque and mitts."

"Oh! And what happened to them?"

"He—they fell off in the parking lot."

"I see," said Blake Roebotham in vigorous good humour. "What parking lot would that be?" He made it sound as if there were dozens involved in this case.

"The one where he raped me."

"Oh, they fell off. Now, before you set off on your walk—your long, cold walk back to civilization, as my learned friend described it for us this morning—did you try to find your mitts and your hat?"

Pause. "No."

"You didn't? But wasn't it a very cold night, Laney? Haven't you testified that the reason you got into my client's car was because it was so cold and sleeting?"

"Yes."

"Yet on such a cold night you didn't stop to pick up your woollen hat and mittens before setting off on that famous trek back to civilization?" No response. "Did you at least look for them?"

"No."

"Why do you think that was, Laney?"

"I never thought of it."

"You never thought of it. On a night that you have testified was so cold and inhospitable that you accepted a ride from a total stranger in order to escape from it, you subsequently never thought of picking up your hat and mitts to put them on."

It was not a question. Laney made no response. It was obvious Blake Roebotham had intended to make her angry and was not pleased about having failed. But he went on with hardly a beat lost as though he had expected no response.

"Now, as the mitts and hat you say you were wearing that night aren't here in court, Laney, we're safe in assuming, aren't we, that the police never found any evidence of them, either in the parking lot or in my client's car or anywhere else they might reasonably have been expected to be if you were telling the truth?"

"I don't know."

"Well, don't you think my learned friend would have showed them to you and asked you to identify them in court, along with all this other damaging evidence against my client?"

"I don't know."

Unable to get a rise, Blake tried a more accusatory tone. "Isn't it a fact that you weren't wearing a hat and mitts at all that night, Laney? Isn't it a fact that it wasn't cold weather that induced you to get into my client's car that—"

"Oh, Your Honour, I object," said Sondra with quiet precision. "The weather that night is a matter of public record. It was miserable and sleeting, with a temperature well below zero. We can call someone from the weather office to establish this as a matter of record, and my learned colleague can take issue with the weatherman if he wishes, but not with this witness, please. She is not qualified in any case to state more than what she has already testified to—her perception that it was extremely cold and miserable and that it was sleeting."

The judge looked amused. "Well, Ms. Holt, he hasn't actually got to the point of challenging her weather report," he said kindly, with the unstated message that he saw what she was after, but she'd have to be more careful how she got it. "He's entitled to try to bring out what the witness's response to the weather was. Carry on, Mr. Roebotham."

"Thank you, Your Honour," Roebotham said graciously, with the air of a man who would not suffer such unwarranted intrusions between himself and the truth so calmly forever. He returned to the attack as though the interruption had never been.

"Isn't it a fact, Laney, that you had a *prearranged date* with my client that night to be picked up at that bus stop? And isn't it a fact that that was why you didn't bother to wear a hat and gloves on such a cold night?"

"No. I was waiting for my bus."

"Now, Laney, is that everything you were wearing that night?"

Pause. "I think so."

"Think it over for a moment. I see this blue one-piece kind of jogging outfit here that you call a jumpsuit. And here are socks, and boots, and a long scarf, and a coat, a sheepskin coat, and I guess this is your handbag. Now, is that everything?"

"Except for my toque and mitts, I think that's everything."

Sondra sat still, masking her emotion behind a poker face. She had warned Laney that this question would be coming, had told her not to forget. That was the problem with a witness who had suffered such trauma. Laney's mind was letting her forget what she could not bear to remember. Sondra would have to work hard to pull this one out of the fire.

Blake Roebotham, casually bending over the exhibits table, whirled suddenly. "Laney, why weren't you wearing any underwear that night?" he demanded sharply in an accusatory tone that would better have suited a cop challenging a criminal.

Laney, thank God, was unmoved by the suddenness of the attack. "I was wearing underwear, too," she said with the simple detachment that had characterized so much of her testimony so far. A detachment that saved her from any consciousness of how Roebotham might construe this change in testimony. "I thought you meant my outer clothes."

"Could you speak up, please?" he said in a hectoring voice, almost shouting. "The jury can't hear you."

Sondra bit her lip. It was ugly, but she had no choice but to let him go ahead. He had the rope. Now let him hang himself with it, she prayed.

Blake Roebotham was famous in legal circles for his "underwear" tactics in rape cases. He could probably have done this line of questioning in his sleep. No matter what the relevance to the case, Blake Roebotham could always be counted on to bring up the question of what underwear the victim was wearing. He had said more than once that it was because the jury expected a discussion of underwear in a rape case, and far be it from Blake Roebotham not to satisfy their longing. This reduction of the jury to the status of lip-licking audience, and a criminal trial to a sideshow, however, was only part of the reason for what he did.

It was partly also, Sondra knew, because the public discussion of her intimate apparel often shamed and upset the victim and thus affected her credibility with the jury; partly because it allowed Blake Roebotham to say the word "panties" in a way that he hoped would titillate the male members of the jury and lead them to look at the victim as no more than a sex object; and partly because, by reducing the crime to the discussion of what underwear the victim had put on and why, the defence lawyer hoped to leave the impression in the jury's mind that the victim had somehow been planning to meet some man, somewhere, who would do to her what Blake Roebotham's poor sucker of a client had been enticed to do.

If the underwear of the victim did not fit in with this projected scenario, Blake Roebotham had been known to invent some that did. More than once he had described lacy and enticing underthings before the jury and asked the victim if that wasn't what she was wearing. Her denial not unnaturally confused the jury, and generally, one could assume, made its members doubt the victim. But Sondra could at least make sure he didn't try that one this time.

"I was wearing underwear," Laney repeated herself, for the first time looking steadily at the defence lawyer instead of gazing with blank eyes in his general direction.

"You have just testified under oath that everything you were wearing that night was here on this table."

"I didn't think you were asking about what I had on underneath."

There was the tiniest flicker of something like anger behind Laney's calm brown eyes. It was the first time she had answered a remark that wasn't a direct question. Don't get angry now, Sondra begged her silently. Don't lose them now. She got to her feet.

"If the Court please, the witness has *not* testified that everything she was wearing is on the table. She has testified as to her toque and mittens."

Blake nodded graciously as though Sondra were splitting hairs, but *he* didn't mind. But of course that subtle and seemingly unimportant contradiction of Laney's testimony had been calculated and deliberate, and he had been hoping to have it go unchallenged.

And her interruption had served the additional purpose of interfering with Blake's buildup, giving Laney a much-needed breather.

"Now, Laney, is there anything else you didn't think I was referring to that you were wearing that night?" Blake asked with cynical solicitousness.

Pause. "I don't think so. But maybe I've forgotten some things."

"Well, let's try to be specific. Were you wearing a sweater?"

"No."

"Were you wearing a watch or jewellery?"

"No, I don't think so."

"Well, it looks to me as though there isn't much more you could have been wearing, is there?"

"I guess not."

"So it was only your underwear you happened to forget to mention," Roebotham suggested helpfully.

But either Laney had withdrawn again into the distant reaches of herself, or she wisely was not going to be drawn into any more unsolicited responses.

"What was that?" demanded Roebotham irritably. "Can you speak up, please? The jury can't hear you!"

"I didn't say anything," Laney explained gently.

There was a titter from the courtroom. It was probably more a nervous response than a sign of amusement, but it nevertheless was a sign that the mood was not entirely with the defence lawyer.

"I asked if it was only your underwear you forgot to mention."

Sondra stood up. "Oh, Your Honour, I object," she said in an unhurried voice. "That question has already been asked and answered. The witness has testified that she was wearing underwear, and that through a misunderstanding of the intent of my learned friend's question she omitted to mention it. It was a perfectly natural mistake that anyone might make."

The judge repressed a smile. "I think the point has been established, Mr. Roebotham," he said. "Perhaps you'd better take another line of questioning."

"When you were in the Millers' basement, Laney, were you wearing your underwear then?"

"At first I was. Then he took away all my clothes."

"So when you made your heroic escape, you were in fact completely naked." Pause. "Were you?"

"Yes."

"Speak up, please!"

"Yes."

"You didn't find your clothes in the Millers' house?"

"No."

"And how were you finally reunited with them?"

"The police found them."

"I see. Now I confess to being a little puzzled, Laney. If I had been the policeman who listened to your story, and then I had gone searching and had found all your clothes except your underwear, I might be just a little curious as to what had happened to that underwear. When the police showed you all these clothes they had found, did they ask you whether you had been wearing underwear at the time?"

"Yes."

"And what did you tell them?"

"I told them I was wearing underwear."

"And weren't they a little surprised—" Blake moved in even closer to the witness stand, obviously feeling his oats, feeling there was something here and ready to make a show of it for the jury "—weren't they a little surprised that there was no underwear among all these clothes they had found?"

"No. They found some underwear."

Blake Roebotham jerked his head back in surprise, but it was too late; the trap had sprung. "What?" he demanded, recovering fast. "Can you speak up, please?"

"They did find underwear with my clothes."

"They did? Did you say they did?" Now he was expressing mock surprise, standard defence attorney surprise, in an effort to convince the jury he was not surprised at all.

"Yes."

Sondra bit her lip. He plainly did not know whether to run with the ball or drop it. Run with it, she begged him silently. Maybe I can bring this thing back in line if you run with it now.

"And did they show you that underwear and ask you to identify it?"

"Yes."

"And why hasn't it been introduced in evidence with all these other things?"

"I don't know."

Sondra let him hang there just long enough for the jury to see that he was taken aback and not sure where to go next, and then slowly volunteered, "If the Court please, I would like to assure counsel for the defence that the underwear found by the police is going to be introduced in evidence later in the Crown's case."

He couldn't leave it there now, of course. There was no way for him even to know that he should.

"Is this witness going to be called on to identify it?" Blake Roebotham demanded.

"No. It was not entered in evidence by means of this witness because, due to the nature of the mental torment she has undergone, it was extremely distressing for her to attempt to identify her own underwear. She was unable to make a positive identification of it."

Those who could read him knew that Judge Arthur McVean was secretly amused at this obvious baiting of a trap. Sondra had appeared before him many times, and it was obvious that he understood, if Blake Roebotham did not, that she was trying to engineer something. "Well, let's save that evidence until it's brought out before the jury in the proper way," he said dryly. "I think this witness has testified as far as she can as to her underwear."

But Blake had deemed it time for some show of righteous anger. "Well, with Your Honour's permission, if the underwear is going to be submitted as evidence, I would like it to be shown to this witness! If the jury is meant to take a certain pair of panties as incriminating my client, and if the witness is unable to identify those panties, then my client is entitled to have the fact brought out. It seems as though the prosecution has devised this method of ensuring that the defence's hands will be tied with regard to questioning this witness on her inability to identify an important piece of evidence against my client!"

Sondra had to lower her eyes for a moment in case Roebotham, reading triumph in them, should back off. When she looked up again, Judge McVean was looking at her. "Well, Ms. Holt?"

It was now or never. She said dryly, "Counsel for the defence knows very well that it is within his powers to recall this witness later on for the purpose of questioning her about any relevant exhibit. However, he has accused the Crown of tying his hands, which was certainly not my intent. I can bring in this evidence now, Your Honour," she said calmly. "It will mean putting on our police witness out of order at this point, but that will be only for the purpose of testifying as to the underwear. If Ms. Meredith will stand down for a moment, I'd like to call Sergeant—"

"Oh, I don't see any need to bring on any witnesses out of order," Blake Roebotham said loudly as though suddenly seeing the position he had been manoeuvred into. "Let's just have this witness shown the articles in question and endeavour to identify them."

That was ridiculous and he knew it. She had already said that Laney couldn't identify the underwear. Evidence couldn't be brought in without being in some way connected; Blake himself would be the first to scream if she tried. So far the only connection any underwear had with the case was that the police had found some in Hugh Macomber's closet. If Blake wanted to show that underwear to this witness, its credentials had to be established first.

But he had been hoping to make the jury feel the Crown was being obstructionist. He was grasping for anything now, trying to shore up the breach he knew he had made in his own wall. Sondra was hard-pressed not to laugh in his face. This must be the first time in his entire career that the victim's underwear had exploded in his face.

"If the underwear is to be introduced, it can only come in through the police witness," Sondra said, allowing a tinge of impatience to colour her tone. "My learned friend knows that very well. Do I understand him to say that, having made an issue of this exhibit, he now no longer wants it introduced at this point?"

He didn't, but he would look like an absolute fool with the jury if he backed down now, and he knew it. He *had* to take up the challenge, but Sondra didn't make the mistake of thinking he was happy about it.

"No, let's get this underwear into evidence," Roebotham said aggressively, making points where he could. "Let's see what exactly is at the bottom of all this!"

"Counsel for the defence knows very well that the only thing at the bottom of it is the orderly presentation of the Crown's case," Sondra returned calmly. "However, we are perfectly willing to change that order in this instance."

"Is your police witness in court, Ms. Holt?" asked the judge.

She made a show of looking into the body of the courtroom. There were only a few spectators—Laney Meredith's mother, Hughie Macomber's family, a reporter, one or two others and Ben Glass.

Ben Glass caught her eye as she did so. There was a smile behind his eyes as he looked at her, and for a moment it caught her off guard. Then she remembered that Ben Glass was on her side now.

She had seen him in the courtroom audience a few times since he had become deputy Crown, usually when one of his juniors was in trouble and he was stopping in to listen to how the case was going so he could offer advice. She had learned to look for the sight of Ben Glass in the courtroom as confirmation that she had the prosecution on the ropes.

There had never been approbation in his eyes when he looked at her then. It was something of a shock to see it now.

"Not at this moment, Your Honour, but he is in the building. It will only take a few minutes to locate him."

"Well, let's call him," snapped Blake Roebotham impatiently as though he was having to put up with deliberate delaying tactics.

By all means, let's call him, Sondra agreed silently. And when the jury has heard his testimony, maybe in future you won't be quite so eager to grill women about their choice of underwear on the stand. Maybe you'll take pains, if you know how, to be a little less predictable.

Getting the testimony of where and how Laney Meredith's clothes were entered into evidence while Laney was still testifying was exactly what Sondra needed to underline her witness's integrity for the jury, to counteract the emotionless style of her delivery by putting the full weight of police confirmation right behind every single thing she was telling them.

Sondra smiled warmly at Blake Roebotham. Your penchant for underwear, my learned friend, she was thinking, is going to convict your client.

Chapter 3

Ben Glass picked up his drink and saluted her with it. "Here's to the good old days," he said, watching her.

Sondra blinked. The good old days? Just how far back was he referring to? For at the look in his eyes, Sondra herself was suddenly remembering long-ago and far off days, and they weren't days she cared to remember—or have remembered—now that she and Ben were colleagues.

So she smiled distantly and, lifting her glass in acknowledgement, agreed dryly, "The good old days. Do I take it you're already regretting the loss of an adversary?"

"I like storms," Ben said softly.

She could not hold his gaze. She would never have believed she could be so weak, but that word conjured up a memory that was as unexpected as it was shattering. The memory of the day when Ben had said to her, "Being with you is like being in a storm. If you can ride it out till the storm exhausts its fury, there's perfect calm."

And he would know, because in those long-ago and far away days, she and Ben Glass had been lovers. And she remembered with unwelcome clarity the day he had said that, as they lay exhausted in tangled sheets in the aftermath of their lovemaking, while he had lazily stroked her cheek and hair. It had been a very intense affair.

But it had also been brief, and there had been many stormy days between them since then in the courtroom, and that, too, was over now.

And she was quite sure it was that that he was referring to. He couldn't possibly be trying to dredge up memories of an old affair. She herself hadn't thought of their days as lovers in years.

"I don't know about liking storms," she said lightly, "but I'll miss our courtroom battles."

"Oh, yes?" pursued Ben, cocking his eyebrow, and she had the distinct feeling that he was laughing at her.

"Losing to you was no shame," she pointed out, determined to ignore any subtext. "And winning was a real victory."

There was no question that Ben Glass had been a worthy adversary. Going into court against him had always meant she had to be that much more aware, had felt that much more alive.

"There are other places to win and lose than a courtroom," Ben said, a suggestion that made her gasp. Her eyes flew to his face, and he looked serious; he looked as though he were remembering that he had lost her.

"No question," said Sondra. "But I'll still miss you. Especially if it means I'll be going up against men like Blake Roebotham instead." And if she wanted to get off an uncomfortable subject, that name was the way to do it.

"Ah, Blake's not so bad," said Ben with male tolerance. "He certainly played things wrong this afternoon. Tell me how you engineered the business of putting your police witness on in the middle of the cross-examination of the plaintiff."

He took up the new topic so readily that she knew for certain he hadn't been trying to flirt with her. Sondra made a mental note to keep a tight lid on her imagination in future.

"Blake Roebotham—" Sandra smiled without mirth and took a long pull of her own drink "—is too smart for his own good. If he hadn't jumped on his old standby underwear tactic as a way out of a little trap I'd left for him, the underwear would have waited until I put the police witness on in the proper order. And the jury wouldn't have learned that the clothing was actually found in the defendant's closet until then. It's probably our most damaging piece of evidence. Thanks to Blake's penchant for the sleazy, we've now got it established that the plaintiff's testimony is backed up by some very solid proof even before she's finished testifying. Now they're going to know they're hearing the truth from her."

"Surely the defence knew where the girl's clothing was found?" Ben asked.

"Of course they did. But we weren't about to tell them she couldn't identify her own underwear, were we, now? I knew Blake would notice the omission. In fact, I counted on his penchant for underwear in this case. But I must say I never expected even him to go so far with it. So the plaintiff forgot to mention her underwear—he still shouldn't have gotten so carried away. It was a mistake I could take advantage of."

"Yes, it was," said Ben in some satisfaction. "I guess you threw him. It'll do him good to see what I've been up against all these years. He needed a firsthand taste of the Holt technique."

She wondered idly if Ben had taken some razzing for the number of times he had lost cases to her.

"Blake's problem," she said in some satisfaction, "is that he's got into a rut. He doesn't feel he's cross-examined a victim until he's grilled her about her underwear. He's too predictable. I haven't finished with that underwear yet. I'm going to make him sorry he ever heard the word."

"Do I take it you engineered the whole thing? That you somehow managed to get the girl to refuse to make the identification of the underwear for the sake of courtroom tactics?"

She raised her eyebrows, but it didn't surprise her that he suspected her hand behind the trap. That was the way things worked in the legal system. You said to your witness something like, "Now, if you're not sure, absolutely *sure*, it would be better to say so before we get to court. If there's any doubt *at all* in your mind..." And somehow the witness picked up the idea that it would be a good idea to remain a little doubtful on the subject till she could pick up further clues on what was expected from her.

Sondra, like every experienced defence attorney, knew that that kind of thing went on in the Crown office every day of the year. No question that she herself would learn to engage in such tactics as an art form. But this time she had not had to. She shook her head.

"She refused to identify it, Ben. We could hardly get her to look at it, and she flatly refused to identify it. Everything else, no problem. The underwear, found in the same closet, obviously hers, too, no way. The shrink says it's her attempt at control over what happened, that if she can deny the underwear she can deny—inside—that it happened to her at all. Also there's the ugly fact that it's torn and bloody, as you saw, and the rest of her clothing isn't." Sondra made a face. "He cut it off her with a knife, if you can believe it.

So no doubt it's the starkest reminder of what she went through." God, what a nightmare it must have been in that basement. She doubted if Laney had told them even half of it.

"She just sat there, saying, 'I can't be sure. It's a very common brand, isn't it? I can't be sure it's mine.'"

Ben wrinkled his brow. "I don't understand. If she'd already testified to that fact—that he cut it off with a knife, why the hell was Blake asking her if she was wearing underwear?"

Sondra smiled grimly. "She hasn't testified to it yet. That's where I took my risk. I was sure when we introduced the underwear through the police witness that Blake would ask if Laney Meredith had identified it. And then he'd insist on recalling Laney Meredith to show that she couldn't. Or so I figured. And *then* I was going to bring out how it had got torn and bloody."

"Mmm," commented Ben. "Interesting manoeuvre. Risky, too. Why did you want to do that?"

"Because what happened to her during those three days is just a never-ending horror, and I wanted to impress the jury with that fact. I wanted them to see that there's no way we can go through every single minute, but that if they asked about any one minute, they'd get another horror story they hadn't heard before." She took a sip of her drink, her eyes narrowed in anger, not at Ben, but the world. "Was it so much of a risk? I mightn't have risked it with anyone else. With Blake I didn't think so. I figured it was as good as a sure thing."

In fact, she'd have bet heavy money on him going after the underwear issue one way or another. She couldn't have known that he'd do it in a way so completely to her advantage, and on a Friday afternoon just in time for the police officer to bring out his damning testimony before adjournment; that had been a gift of the gods.

Sondra grinned. Blake's cross-questioning of the police sergeant had of course been brief. The clothes had all been rolled together in a bundle in Hughie Macomber's closet, underwear included. It was wiser not to have that information repeated before the jury too often.

"He'll bring out his big guns for the victim now, of course," Sondra muttered now, almost to herself. "He'll sit and dream up some method of attack he can use Monday morning, and he'll go on about that underwear for two hours, till everyone is sick of the subject and he thinks it's lost its impact."

The distaste in her voice was so strong that Ben responded again, "Blake's not so bad."

Which only another man could say. Sondra looked at him. "Oh, but he is, Ben. When are we going to recognize the significance of what men like Blake Roebotham do? He's part of a masculine system that backs up rape as a permissible reinforcement of the second-class status of women. He makes it *okay*, whether his client gets off or not. What he does to rape victims on the stand is his way of partaking in the rape."

Ben looked at her in astonishment. "Is that really the way you see it, Sondra?"

"Oh, yes," she said. "Oh, yes."

"It's just legal tactics. Everybody does it."

"To rape victims."

"What?"

"Show me one jewellery store owner who, in testifying about a robbery, is asked what sort of display he had set out and whether it wasn't made particularly enticing just to invite the robbery. Show me the defence lawyer in this murder case of yours who'd dare to suggest that the victim 'asked for it.'"

"Come on, Sondra, isn't that analogy a bit extreme?"

"Think about it, Ben." But she knew he wouldn't; there weren't many men in the world who did, she supposed.

"Sondra, men haven't been thinking about much else for the past ten years. Don't you think it's a little extreme?"

She looked at her watch. "It's late," she said. "I have to go."

Ben didn't move. He simply watched her from those dark eyes. "When are we having dinner?" he asked levelly.

She bent to pick up her handbag. "I'm sorry, Ben. I'm not available for dinner these days."

"Got a man friend?" he asked.

After a beat she lied. "Yes." In the last couple of years there hadn't been room for much of a private life, but she had a funny feeling it wouldn't be politic at this juncture to admit it to Ben Glass. "Is that relevant?"

Ben smiled slowly at her. "Not very," he said. "How long is he going to last?"

"Who?" she demanded irritably, knowing.

"Your man friend. You don't give any of them very long, I understand."

She felt angry, not least because of the cat-and-mouse attitude he had adopted with this questioning. She looked balefully at him. It was as though he were deliberately trying to provoke her. Why? "Who do you understand that from?" she demanded.

"One or two who've had their walking papers before they were expecting them."

"Like you?" The moment she said it she felt that he had deliberately goaded her into making the reference to their past, that it was what he'd been pushing for. Well, now it was out in the open, something she would have liked to pretend had never been between them. Irritably she bit her lip. What did the man want?

"Like me," he agreed easily. "In some ways. Not in others, Sondra."

"Such as?"

"Well, the ones I know were pretty upset about the treatment."

"Well?" She was furious. How dare he rake through her past like this?

"But I don't get mad, Sondra. I get even."

She blinked and set her bag down on the table with a thump that rattled the glasses. "Are you crazy?"

"No," he said, smiling the sort of smile she'd seen him use in court when he thought he was getting a defendant on the ropes.

"Then I am," she told him. "Are you trying to say you've resented the breakup for—what is it?—something like seven years?"

"No," he returned. "Are you trying to say there hasn't been something between us for seven years?"

"For God's sake!" she said disbelievingly. "You're married, aren't you?"

"I was married for two years," he said. "I separated three years ago, and my divorce came through a while back. Are you sure you didn't know that?"

Now that he said it, she thought she remembered hearing that his marriage had gone on the rocks. But that was hardly the point. "And was there something between us all through your marriage?" she asked sweetly.

"I never thought so, I admit," returned Ben Glass. "My wife did, though. If there was one point she never shut up about for two years, it was her jealousy of you."

"Me!" Sondra was thunderstruck. "My God, Ben, we hardly spoke to each other outside the courtroom!"

"She came to watch one of my cases early in our marriage. You were defence attorney. It was your first biggish case. It was an important one for me, too. Don't you remember it?" He paused for a moment. *"Regina v. Pinchin and Pinchin."* All criminal cases in Canada are Regina versus the accused. Regina, being the Latin for queen, signifies that a crime against one of The Crown's subjects is a crime against The Crown, in the same way that in the U.S. all criminal acts are deemed to have been committed against the people. "Our first time as opponents. Apparently we generated a lot of electricity. My wife never forgot it."

Sondra smiled reminiscently. "Yes, I remember. God, I had to be on my toes!" It had been exhilarating. "I won," she reminded him.

"Yes. My wife accused me of letting you win."

Abruptly Sondra's smile died. "You never did!"

He laughed. "Damn right I didn't. I was grimly determined to win that case, any way I could, and I told her so. But I slipped up when I thought Sarah would accept that fact without asking why."

She laughed outright. "Don't tell me you told her you were hoping to get back at me for unceremoniously dumping you?"

"I didn't, but after that she always felt there was something between us. I tried to tell her it was strictly professional rivalry."

"Which it was!"

"Was it, Sondra?" He looked at her, and a little frisson of physical excitement rushed up her spine to her scalp. "Then what is it now?"

"Ben..." she said warningly.

"As long as we were adversaries in court, Sondra, we could control this. Courtroom hostilities can be a great outlet for sexual tension." He beckoned to the waitress for refills of their drinks, and she disappeared towards the bar before Sondra could protest. "What did you think we were going to do about it now?"

"What did you?" she countered irritably.

"I thought we'd start by having a drink to the old days," Ben said imperturbably.

Just in time she remembered the old rule of counting five before responding. Sondra covered the pause by watching the arrival of the waitress and then taking a long sip of her drink. When Ben did not jump to fill the silence, she said at last, "Very brief and long-dead days. Hardly even a corpus delicti. Not worth the honour, surely?"

"Ah, but some corpuses are more delicti than others," Ben pursued lightly.

In spite of her intentions, the air was crackling with something like electricity. How had he managed that? she wondered irritably.

Sondra leaned on one elbow. "All right, Ben," she declared matter-of-factly. "What is it you want?"

"Very easy, Sondra." His voice was very lazy all of a sudden. "I want to go to bed with you again."

Her drink splashed onto her fingers as she sat up suddenly. "Are you out of your mind?" she demanded.

"Maybe. Interested?"

"In what? Starting up where we left off?" she demanded in disbelief.

He shrugged. "Well, we could give it a try and see where chance took us. If we didn't like it, we could quit again. You're older now, of course, so this time I'd expect a little more finesse if you decided you didn't like it." He paused. "But then, I'm older, too. I have every intention of making sure you do like it."

His eyes were dark, almost black. When he looked at her, they conjured up some very sexy, very confused memories.

Ben Glass had been quite a lover, in every sense of the word. He had known how to engage her on every level: intellectual, emotional and physical. It wasn't because she hadn't liked his lovemaking that she had left him, and she was quite sure that he knew it.

She had been just starting out in law then; she had met Ben not long after she was called to the bar. He had been a young lawyer with several years' experience, ambitious to have a judicial seat someday. Even then his massive intelligence had been the most obvious thing about him, and it was that that had first attracted her to him. She had learned later, not too much later, that there were other things for which to value a man. The discovery had left her weak.

And threatened. She had broken things off before there had been a deep involvement, so there could be no hard feelings. At least, she supposed there couldn't. But she had not made any explanation, had never discussed with Ben her fear of seeing her hard-won legal career scuttled by sex before it could properly begin. She had merely called things off.

Not long after, Ben Glass had moved into the Crown office. It was a natural move for someone who was ambitious. Her subsequent battles with Ben Glass in court had always been marked by fireworks and what the judges called "personalities," and sometimes by what had seemed like real hostility.

Yet she admired him, and she was sure he admired her. Ben Glass's intellect took a back seat to no one she had ever met. His handling of a case was always probing and precise, and his great forte as a Crown, in her opinion, was his unequalled ability to pinpoint and then manipulate a witness's worst character faults.

She had said to him bitterly once, "So because my client is an arrogant son of a bitch, he does seven years for importing." There had been no question that her client had been guilty of possession, and maybe even trafficking. He had been "uncooperative" in naming others involved in the case, and had arrogantly dared Ben to go ahead when he had threatened to charge him with importing—which, unlike the other charges, carried a minimum seven-year sentence.

Ben had gone ahead, and her client's native arrogance, skillfully brought out by Ben, hadn't done him any favours with the jury. But that was the system. She knew she couldn't blame Ben for the system, no matter how easy a target he was.

Remembering the fireworks now, she looked into Ben's eyes and felt the racing of her own heartbeat. They would be together much more now that she was a prosecutor than when they'd been on opposite sides of the fence. He was right. What *would* happen to that electricity now that they were no longer adversaries?

He sat looking into her eyes, watching the memories flood her mind. When she returned to the present, he said, "Have you really been walking in and out of my office these past weeks without feeling a thing, Sondra? Be honest."

"I've been nervous," she said. "It's new to me, and then you plopped this case on me before I had a chance to get my bearings." It was true; she had been nervous. But she was glad he hadn't asked her what she was feeling right now.

"Nerves," he repeated. "You're fooling yourself, Sondra. You have to be fooling yourself. Every time you've bent over my desk to ask me something I've been . . ."

Suddenly he thrust back his chair and got to his feet. "Talk isn't going to get us anywhere," he told her harshly. "You could argue your way out of a Soviet spy trial." He put one determined hand on Sondra's arm, and she stood up, too, but it was without volition. His grip on her didn't ease as they threaded their way through crowded tables to the exit. And Sondra was concentrating too much on walking without stumbling on suddenly shaky legs to try to shrug him off.

In the small, dark-panelled foyer, he stopped. He said, "Let's just try an experiment. Let's just see who's right before we do anything else."

He took her other arm in his grasp and turned her to face him. Sondra thought wildly, unbelievingly, He can't be going to kiss me in the foyer of The Open Arms! But his lips, just a little above hers, parted, and his eyes were dark, and there was a sudden clamour in her blood. She wanted him to kiss her, here or anywhere, and to hell with who might see.

His mouth covered hers, and she trembled as though an electrical connection had been made. She felt his hands leave her arms and encircle her, and she was being pulled against his body, where she felt the stirring of his flesh and the churning response of her own.

Involuntarily, her lips parted in invitation, and then, with no tentative exploration to warn her, his tongue was deep in the hungry hollow of her mouth. Her knees melted, and she heard the responsive moan in her throat and knew that the sound could not have escaped him.

Her hand went to his hair, just as the door was pushed inward on them from the bar. His lips left hers, and his arms fell away. As another couple walked through, they stood there and tried to control their breathing. Thank God it was no one they knew; the woman gave them a smiling glance and turned her head with the obvious intention of minding her own business. The man didn't even look their way.

"Who's right?" Ben challenged her quietly when they were left alone. He was looking down at her with eyes that were full of a passion she remembered from long ago; a passion that had stirred her to the roots then, but which until ten minutes ago she had been determined would have no more power to move her.

She was wrong, but did she want Ben to know that? Was there any guarantee that seven years had given her any more ability to deal with such a shattering sexuality than she had had before?

When she didn't answer, Ben opened the street door and guided her out into the evening. It was nearly dark; she was surprised at how long they must have spent over drinks. Not far along the curb, he bent to open the passenger door of his car, and then stood looking at her, and the force of his determination was such that she didn't think to protest, but simply got inside.

In another moment, he had climbed in the other door and slid the key into the ignition. For an instant, in the light of the street lamp, Ben looked into her eyes. Then, without a word, he pressed the engine into life and pulled out into the evening traffic.

Chapter 4

For a few minutes he drove along the expressway that bordered the north shore of Lake Ontario, then he turned north. The sun had set, and the beams of the headlights of the cars that swished by them got steadily brighter as dusk turned into night.

Neither of them spoke. Sondra was feeling a strange, peaceful willingness to have these few minutes of her life decided by someone else. Where they were going now didn't really matter to her. She assumed it was to Ben's home. What they did when they got there was something she would decide only when she had to.

She rolled down the window and let the wind stream over her face and hair, smelling the night. Ben drove well, fast and smoothly, and at this hour the traffic was light.

She didn't know where he lived, but she was faintly surprised to discover it was so far out of town. They were well north of the city now, alternately passing through farmland and the small bedroom communities that serviced the city to the south.

If she'd been guessing, she would have imagined that, like herself, Ben Glass would have an apartment in town, not too far from the courthouse. But she was content to wait for whatever happened. Perhaps he had a favourite restaurant out here in God's country. She had been working hard all week, and being in a car at night always relaxed and soothed her. Sondra lay back, enjoying the change in the scents borne to her by the wind as they moved from city to country.

She opened her eyes because the sound of the engine changed, noticing the dashboard clock with shock. They'd been driving north for an hour and a half! Surely *nobody* commuted daily from this distance! Where on earth was Ben taking her?

She said, "Have I been asleep?"

"I think you dozed a little." He was braking, and the high whine of the engine descended to a growl. "Hungry?"

She was, which was hardly surprising. Sondra peered out at the nondescript roadside café that he was parking in front of. "Is this place the find of the century or something?"

Ben glanced over. "It's not bad. Good truckers' food."

How bizarre. All this way for food that wasn't bad? Well, she was too hungry to question the sanity of it. Sondra pulled down the sun visor and examined herself in the mirror attached to the back of it.

Her smooth blond hair had been thoroughly ruffled by the wind and by the headrest as she slept. She snapped open her bag and impatiently pulled a brush through the tangles, but her makeup could stay as it was. She didn't wear much anyway, and whatever was left would pass muster in a roadside café.

When she closed her bag again, Ben shut off the interior light and they got out. "Chinese and Canadian cuisine," read the sign, and Sondra choked back a laugh. If there was one sign in rural Ontario that was the kiss of death on any hopes of a decent meal, that had to be it.

"I don't *believe* that you have driven nearly two hours to get to a place like this!" she protested in amusement, but Ben merely smiled and opened the door.

"It's better to stick to the Canadian," he informed her, which went without saying. "Chinese" food in rural Ontario had little, if anything, to do with the land of Mao and his ancestors, and often even less to do with good taste.

But the place wasn't bad. She had the sense to order a simple hamburger and fries and coffee. In this sort of restaurant, "Canadian cuisine" never meant sourdough bread or deep-fried Oka cheese or even French-Canadian pea soup—unless it came out of a can. Wherever the hamburger came from originally, north of the 49th parallel it passes as Canadian. As do "french" fries, of course.

Over the meal they talked shop. Sondra was happy to leave any more controversial subject alone. She had the feeling that Ben had some purpose in mind—though how it could be gained by bringing her to dine in a place that didn't even have a liquor licence, she couldn't imagine. But *she* didn't have to fall in with whatever his purpose was. She had made no promises, and her being here couldn't be construed as one.

So she discussed her lineup of evidence with a real appreciation of Ben's expert advice, and never let her mind wander to the subject of just what Ben thought he was doing.

Which, as it turned out, was a mistake. Because once back in the car, instead of turning around and heading back to the city as she had expected, Ben pulled out of the parking lot and continued north.

"What are you doing?" Sondra demanded, startled. "Where are you going *now*?"

"Where I've been going from the beginning," Ben answered imperturbably. Then he laughed. "Have you been imagining I brought you out here for the sake of feeding you a mediocre hamburger and weak coffee?"

Sondra had to laugh, too. "I admit I thought it a bit bizarre."

"'Bizarre' is an understatement."

"Well, where are we going, then?"

"To my place. I assumed you knew."

Sondra looked around at the almost unrelieved blackness that surrounded them. They were far from the bedroom communities now. "Do you really live so far out of town, Ben?"

"On the weekends, I do. We're almost there now."

He turned off the highway onto a dirt road, and now, without the lights from the odd passing vehicle, the world outside was pitch-black. His headlights created a pocket of brightness that illuminated a not very smooth road crowded on both sides with forest and thick undergrowth. She knew that the trees must be a blaze of autumn colour now, but the night and the artificial light robbed them of much of their glory.

They were in cottage country. He must spend weekends at his cottage. Which accounted for his previously inexplicable change into casual clothes at the office. Sondra felt a little flicker of anger. She said, "You took a fair bit for granted, didn't you, bringing me all this way without telling me? I told you I had a dinner engagement."

She felt rather than saw the movement of his head as he glanced at her. "If you'd asked, I'd have told you, Sondra. When you hadn't protested after the first half hour, I figured I was safe in assuming that the dinner engagement wasn't of pressing importance. You could have asked me to stop anywhere along the line."

She bit her lip. True enough. "It's already nine thirty," she said. "How much farther?"

"Only a few miles, but it's the slowest part of the journey. Another twenty minutes from here, counting the boat ride."

"The boat ride!" She turned to face him in indignation. "Are you out of your mind? When are you planning on taking me home again?"

He was concentrating on pulling into the parking area of a small marina called Mike and Marg's. He must be negotiating from memory, because in the pitch-black nothing was visible except the spotlighted marina building in the distance. After he had parked, he reached over her knees to open the glove compartment and push a button. She heard the trunk pop open. He still hadn't answered her.

She put her hand on his arm. "Ben," she said determinedly. He looked at her. "When are you planning on driving me home?"

He looked at her for a long moment in which all she saw was moonlight reflected in his eyes. "I'm planning on Sunday night," he told her simply. "But I'll take you back tomorrow if you insist."

He opened the door and stepped out, leaving Sondra gasping like a beached fish. Tomorrow! Sunday! She grabbed for her door handle and came around the car towards him, loaded for bear. "You arrogant—!" she screeched. "What the hell are you trying to pull? Tomorrow? You'll take me home tomorrow? You'll take me home right now!"

Ben lifted a duffle bag and a box of groceries out of the trunk and banged down the lid. He looked at her calmly. "No I won't," he said. "That hamburger and coffee set me back four-fifty. I'm not taking you home till I've seduced you."

A hoot of laughter escaped her, and she leaned against the car as laughter shook her frame. Ben's lips twitched, and he bent and picked up the duffle bag. "Here," he commanded, handing it to her. "Carry this."

He hitched the box of groceries under one arm, taking a flashlight out of it and shining the light on the path in front of them. If it could be called a path. "Slow down!" Sondra demanded after a moment. She slipped her handbag under her arm and reached for his arm with her free hand. "My shoes weren't designed for this!"

Obediently, he slowed down. Sondra was still being hit periodically by giggles. They used to laugh a lot, she remembered suddenly. Ben had an understated sense of humour that got her every time.

And he was smart. Too smart. He knew she didn't want to face another two-hour drive back to the city at this hour, but she would have insisted on it if push had come to shove. She had the funny feeling he had known exactly how to make sure it never came to a showdown, to allow her curiosity about his place, and her fatigue, to overcome her annoyance at being outmanoeuvred.

So long as he didn't outmanoeuvre her right into bed, Sondra thought wryly. She intended to take lots of time making up her mind about that.

His shoes made a hollow sound, and the flashlight's glare showed the wooden slats of a pier. After a moment, Ben stopped and handed her the flashlight. Then he bent down and unzipped the roof of a small cabin cruiser. "Climb in," he invited.

A few moments later they were heading out of the harbour towards the blackness of the lake beyond. "You can't get to the cottage by road?" she asked. She had to work to keep the excited laughter out of her voice. She was enjoying this adventure; it appealed to her innate craziness to be abducted like this. What had she been facing tonight? A meal by herself, some shopping for necessities and then a weekend of work on *Regina v. Macomber*, trying to second-guess what that bastard Blake would try on Monday. Life was too short! she thought suddenly. But she wasn't about to communicate all this to Ben.

"It's on an island," Ben explained.

"That sounds nice. How many cottages altogether?"

"Just one. It's a small island. I own it."

"Fantastic! You spend your summer weekends here? You *are* lucky."

"Many of my weekends all year round. It's winterized. In the winter I come out by snowmobile."

"My God, Ben! Isn't it lonely in winter?"

"I like the solitude after a week in town. I like having the best of both worlds. Besides—"

He broke off in order to concentrate on navigating the entrance to a narrow channel, and by the time they had got past the buoys and markers he seemed to have forgotten what he was about to say. He pointed out the location of his island on the large-scale map of the area by the glow of a small dashboard light. But Sondra could finish the sentence for him. He meant that he brought company along on his weekends, of course. And why not?

"Ten minutes," he told her as they passed another large buoy that rang its bell as it swayed in the choppy waves.

As the boat hit the open water of the larger lake, it began to bounce against the waves with teeth-jarring thuds. The whole boat was shuddering. "Choppy tonight," Ben remarked, slowing down so that the prow settled into the water.

"What's that mean? A storm?" Sondra asked.

"No, not necessarily. Georgian Bay gets pretty rough at times."

After another few minutes, the boat picked up speed again, and then a dark shape rose up directly in front. "Is that it?" Sondra asked when the boat didn't alter course.

"This is it," he assured her, cutting the engine back and edging expertly up to the short pier. "Think you could jump out with the bow rope?"

Sondra kicked off her shoes and, unzipping the canopy, hiked one foot up on the gunwale. When the boat kissed the jetty, she took the rope and jumped neatly ashore into a wind that buffeted her powerfully from all directions.

It was pitch-black out here, and the white bow light wasn't making much difference. This was quite a wind. "Where the hell's the mooring pin?" she hollered, her voice torn from her by the wind that was blowing her hair wildly around her face and her pleated skirt up around her hips. With one hand, she clutched the rope; the other futilely alternated between pulling her hair out of her eyes and trying to beat her skirt down. She couldn't see a thing standing in front of the bow light like this. It was blinding her. Where the hell was Ben?

Ben was laughing as he killed the motor. "Just hang on to the rope," he instructed her. "I'll be there in a moment."

He leaped nimbly up beside her, and she felt his hand grasp the rope. His other hand closed unexpectedly at her waist. "You must have the sexiest legs in the Ontario Bar," he said. "I don't know many sights more erotic than that of a woman's skirt being blown up around her waist in a high wind. Especially if she's wearing stockings instead of panty hose."

She jerked away from him, feeling her own melting at the tone of his voice, but he caught her to him again. She could feel the tension of the muscles in his arm around her back as the boat pulled on the rope he held.

"Shall I kiss you again to remind you that you want it as much as I do?" Ben asked. And when the wind blew her skirt wildly up at the back, suddenly there was heat, and then the touch of his hand on her thigh.

She gasped audibly, frozen into immobility as his fingers stroked the sensitive flesh between her stocking tops and the elastic edge of her panties. She was standing spread-legged for balance on the dock, and there was no resistance when his hand slipped from behind between her parted thighs.

And all the time the bulge of the muscles of his other arm, resisting the pull of the boat on the waves, was pulling her against him and away, against him and away, in one of nature's rhythms that reminded them both of another.

He was hard and aroused; he must have got that way just looking at her as the wind blew up her skirt. She could feel his shape pushing against that sensitive hollow of her flank between her hip and where he held his hand. His fingers slid lightly back and forth, drawing heat and wetness from her in a response she could not deny.

"I want to make love to you, Sondra," he growled against her ear. She felt his hand slide up her hip to the upper elastic that held the delicate cotton and lace, and then it was inside, sliding downwards again, his fingers against her naked flesh. She moaned. It was all too sudden. She hadn't been expecting this kind of approach at all. "I want to kiss you," he said. "I want to taste you. I want to put you down on the dock right now and taste you in my mouth."

Every word was an assault on her flesh. If she hadn't remembered so clearly what he meant, and how much he meant what he said, she might have had more control. But every word was attached to memories that made her weak with desire. And all the thought she was capable of was that a man who would kiss her in the foyer of The Open Arms was capable of anything at all on a deserted dock in the middle of Georgian Bay.

Meanwhile, the wind roared in the trees, and her skirt blew erotically against her thighs and back as Ben abruptly slipped his fingers inside her and nearly lifted her off her feet.

The gasping moan was torn from her throat, and she clung to him for balance, feeling drunk as her head fell back. Pleasure slitted her eyes, and his, as he watched her. His thumb, from memory, found her centre and traced circles around it, and her body obediently began the delicious climb towards release. She no longer cared herself where they were, or when. She only wanted the pleasure he gave her, with every cell of her being.

When he felt the involuntary pressure of her body against his hand, his thumb slipped away and instead the heel of his hand pressed against her. She could feel herself in his grip, between fingers and palm, and now he rocked and half lifted her in the rhythm that became more powerful and more urgent as her own desire did.

The pleasure built in her as he watched her face in starlight and moved his hand in response to what he read there. The wind blew her hair and her skirt in its own wild caress, and she lay back against his arm or the wind—she was no longer sure which—and pressed against the heat and strength of his hand, and cried aloud as she reached the peak and leaped off into the storm.

"Seven years wasted," Ben said roughly, holding her as she floated gently to earth. "Lie down on the dock. I haven't tasted you for seven years, and I'm doing that before you get away from me again. Lie down."

Chapter 5

The moon was fat and heavy on the horizon, engorged and red. It sailed close over the blackness of a distant horizon, and its ever-changing light rode in shards on the tossing water. The wind was wild and getting wilder with every moment.

"I told you to lie down."

His voice came to her from the silvery darkness, next to her ear, and Sondra started. The bow light was quenched now, the pretty little cabin cruiser made fast for the night while she had stood stupidly watching the moon make its appearance.

"Ben," she whispered in protest, for he could hardly have meant it. She needed time to collect her scattered wits, to try and understand just what the past ten minutes meant, and where she wanted to go from here. But there was a kind of raw urgency in him, a determination that was almost anger.

In the darkness she felt his hand at her waist again, and then her skirt slipped over her thighs and fell with a swoop to her feet. In something like fear she stepped back, but now the wildness of the wind was in him, and he held her in a grip that was unbreakable. "Sondra, lie down," he said hoarsely.

The wind now had full access to her thighs and hips as she stood almost naked on the dock. Moonlight picked out the gloss of her stockings, emphasizing the darkness above. Her black cotton panties absorbed all light, and Ben's gaze as well, as he sank to his knees in front of her.

There was moonlight on his curling black hair, but the sight of his head below her was suddenly shut out by the sudden heat of his mouth enclosing her, making everything black with pleasure. She clutched at him for support, her fingers threading through curls that were suddenly as sensuous as silk to her touch.

"Ben, my God, *Ben*," she protested, but her only answer was his fingers against her inner thighs, inexorably pressing her legs farther apart, and his tongue against her centre, demanding more access.

She felt the heat in her thighs, her knees, her stomach and breasts, and even her own mouth, burning and tingling along every nerve into her brain. It disturbed her vision, her hearing, her balance, turning all her senses to its own rough necessity.

When she fell he caught her and lowered her to the dock with rough impatience. Then his firm hands were at her hips again, and this time she felt the cloth of her panties being pulled away from her body, down her thighs to her ankles in one ruthless sweep.

Now the heat of his mouth was doubled, and his tongue could move where it willed. With gentle, burning insistence, it found its way to the heart of her, and Sondra writhed and moaned under the expert demands of this intimate kiss.

Underneath her, the dock rose and fell under the relentless pressure of the wind and the waves. She heard the wood groan and creak, heard the water breaking against the rocks of the shore. Above, trees swayed in the wild wind, black against the moon and the night sky, dancing and bending in their half-willing response to its force, moaning a little in protest and acceptance, even as Sondra's throat produced the same involuntary noises.

He had forgotten nothing about her. He had even learned more. When she tore at his hair, he did not relent. When she writhed under the pressure of his mouth, he rode with her without stopping that gentle fury of his mouth's caress, which was now a life necessity to her. When she cried aloud and pressed up against him with a body suddenly gone wild, he increased her frenzy and his own with a pressure and a passionate wildness that within seconds drove her senseless into pleasure.

The wind tore her passionate cry out of her open mouth with an intimacy like a kiss and blew against her heated, heaving body, and rocking her wooden bed in a rhythm that matched her own.

"Ben!" she cried again. "Oh, God, *Ben*!" Because the sweet heat that melted her was pleasure that was almost torment. It flowed from her centre like liquid honey, till she felt its sweetness in every nerve, every cell, felt its heat ripple up her abdomen to her breasts, felt its honeyed darkness enclose her brain in sensation.

Her rhythm broke up into uncontrollable tremors, and then her body stilled. When the last shiver shook her, the last muscle quieted, Ben lifted his head and looked at her.

"I've missed you," he said.

Slowly she sat up, feeling drunk and unbalanced. Under her thighs her hands encountered the fine wool of her skirt, and she struggled to her feet and picked it up. Her panties were still around her left ankle. Wordlessly, she pulled them on, pulled the skirt over her head and buttoned the waist. Ben took a couple of steps and then bent over. "Your shoes," he said, and she heard the light clatter of them on the dock.

She slipped her feet into them as he picked up the groceries and the duffle bag with one arm and the flashlight with the other. Her first coherent thought was, Thank God they were Princess Di heels and she didn't have to worry about them going down between the boards.

"This way," Ben said softly, and the flash illuminated the steps hewn into the rock that formed the island. With legs like jelly, she followed him into the trees, following the light into blackness.

A generator came on with the lights as Ben flicked the switch inside the door. Sondra looked around. It was a small cottage, but it looked very cozy, very comfortable. A huge stone fireplace dominated the main room where they were standing, with a sofa, easy chairs and a thick rug in front. A picture window filling most of one wall looked out over the lake; she could see the moon, higher in the sky now, and changing its red for silver.

In front of the window sat a huge desk, with papers and a typewriter and an untidy pile of books and papers both on it and beside it. In the silence she could hear the wind and the water.

"The kitchen's in here," Ben called, and she turned with a start to find herself alone. Through a doorway she heard the bustle of unpacking and followed the sound. The kitchen was modern rustic, decorated in pine and copper, with a glass breakfast nook facing the same direction as the picture window in the main room. He must have spent a fortune on the place, she was thinking. She wouldn't have disdained a kitchen like this in her city apartment.

"You call this a cottage?" she asked lightly. She was feeling uncharacteristically ill at ease. "It's very beautiful."

"Thank you. It started out as a cottage, but I've been upgrading it for quite a while now. I intend to retire here someday. I'm planning on taking a year's sabbatical soon. I want it to be ready for that."

"Won't you feel isolated out here by yourself?"

Her handbag was on the table beside the grocery box; Ben must have tossed it in there after she had leaped ashore. She picked it up without a word. Had he really been so collected throughout what had happened? That wasn't a very pleasant thought.

Ben finished unpacking the groceries. Most of them appeared to be perishables; the cupboards and fridge had certainly been well stocked before the new additions. With a little shiver, Sondra thought that there was enough food in the place to last months.

"There are some permanent people down in the cove. In the summer we get families, and in spring and fall, fishermen. By the time winter rolls around, the permanent residents say, you're quite happy to be isolated for a few months."

"But... what would you do here alone all day?"

"Write."

"Pardon?"

"I'm writing a book. If it's successful, I'll take the sabbatical to write another." He picked up the kettle. "How do you feel about a cup of coffee?"

"A book! What sort of book?" In her sudden interest, her nervousness fled unnoticed. "A legal text?"

Ben laughed. He was spooning instant coffee into two mugs. "A crime and adventure novel about the drug trade."

She looked at him. "I should be surprised, but I'm not." There had always been something different about Ben; he was too complex a man, and too intelligent, to fit into one mold comfortably.

"No?" He put the coffee things on a tray and poured boiling water into the cups. "Shall we sit in the lounge?"

There was something quizzical in his gaze as he looked at her, as though the memory of what had happened on the dock was never very far from his mind. Sondra was suddenly conscious that she must look a mess.

"Where's the washroom, please, Ben?"

Two bedrooms and the washroom led off a short corridor on the other side of the lounge. Sondra examined herself critically in the mirror. She certainly wasn't as cool and serene as she was famous for. Her shoulder-length blond hair, usually so immaculate, looked like a bird's nest. Her cheeks were still pink with the telltale flush of sexual excitement, and her cool grey eyes seemed somehow darker. She supposed it was the result of enlarged pupils, which the psychology magazines said made you seem sexier because dilated pupils meant you liked what you were looking at.

She supposed that meant she liked looking at Ben. Or at least that he would think so. It would be hard to come staggering in from the dark without having dilated pupils, though, Sondra told herself irritably as she pulled her brush through her hair.

He had her at a disadvantage, and she didn't like it. She rinsed her face and hands, tied her hair back and brushed down her beautiful grey pleated skirt, which just might be permanently ruined, and the delicate grey cashmere sweater that matched it. Then she stared at her reflection in the mirror.

What was she going to do now? She had been willing to come with Ben because she had been quite certain of being able to control both him and herself in any sexual duel. But she hadn't been expecting a sudden sexual advance like the one on the dock. She had been expecting a few kisses and lots of time to make up her mind as to what she intended to do about Ben's sudden declaration of interest.

A soundless laugh shook her. Had she really been expecting "lots of time to think" from Ben Glass? Either she had a short memory, or she was fooling herself. Nothing in their brief affair seven years ago should have encouraged her to think his sexuality easily tamable. He had swept her off her feet then as easily as he had done ten minutes ago.

And he would do it again.

She felt the heat return to her cheeks at the sudden image the thought conjured up in her brain. Turning abruptly, she put out the light and opened the door. She had been without a man for too long; that was her problem. She'd been working hard these past two years; she'd excluded too much from her life.

But that didn't mean she had to take on Ben Glass as a lover. He was too unpredictable to fit the tidy mold she expected men to occupy in her life. If ever there was a man who was obviously destined to spill out over the edges and into her life, she was with him right now.

And he had lighted a fire in the fireplace and turned out all the lights except for one lamp; and there were two snifters of a rich, dark brandy on the little table between the two easy chairs in front of it. With a civilized I'm-in-control-of-myself smile, Sondra sank into one chair and picked up a glass.

Waterford crystal. She held it out towards the fire, where Ben knelt encouraging the blaze into roaring life, and watched the flames through the liquid.

"Your coffee got cold," he said, standing up and picking up his own glass. He raised it in salute, a dark smile in his eyes. She suddenly remembered his toast of a few hours ago—to the good old days—and she knew that that smile was now underlining just how good the old days had been.

Suddenly wondering how dilated her pupils might be, Sondra dropped her lashes. Her heart was thudding; her womb was contracting with the memory of what had happened on the dock. When she looked up, he was watching her, and her gaze locked with his. In that moment she knew another affair with Ben Glass was inevitable. It had been a foregone conclusion from the moment she agreed to drinks with him tonight. She had simply been exercising her female prerogative to be blind up to the last possible moment.

Ben saw the knowledge in her eyes, and his smile deepened. She let him have his victory, then dropped her eyes again. There was no point in letting him read too much there.

If Ben understood how brief their renewed affair was going to be, if he knew that in that second of capitulation she had also decided the question of how long he would last, and that the answer was three months, he might be angry.

She had learned that men didn't like to think that a woman entered a relationship with eyes wide open to the knowledge that it wouldn't last. They wanted her to be wholehearted, drowning in the possibility of permanence, no matter what their own attitude might be.

Sondra took a sip of the warming brandy. It went straight to the knot of excitement in her abdomen, bathing it in liquid fire. Anticipation crept up her spine, and her head fell back against the high curve of the chair as her languid gaze met Ben Glass's black-eyed sexual intent. His pupils were dilated, too, she noted lazily, excitement melting in her limbs. He wanted to undress her right now.

If he wanted to, he just might, she realized with another stab of anticipation. Ben Glass wasn't like other men. Those long-ago and faraway days of their brief affair were suddenly close and sharp in her memory, and her body shivered at her thoughts.

Three months, she told herself silently. They might just be the most exciting three months of her life.

Chapter 6

The taste of his kiss was brandy and woodsmoke. The brandy was on his tongue, the woodsmoke on his skin and hair and clothes. Sondra breathed deeply and sighed her pleasure at the heady charge on her senses.

He was bent over her in the chair; only their mouths touched until she lifted her free hand to his chest and clenched her fingers in the soft wool of his sweater. It was one of those kisses that is meant to be short until it deepens and lengthens and takes on a life of its own. Ben broke away at last to set down his glass and, taking it from her helpless hand, hers, too. Then he sank down onto the thick rug on the floor behind him and drew her out of her chair and down on top of him.

The fire sparked and spat, and his glossy black curls, and his eyes, reflected flames. She lay stretched along the length of his body as his arms wrapped her tightly and held her head down for his kiss.

Expert. Oh, expert. Deep and passionate and knowing. It sent shivers over her skin and scalp so that her hair seemed alive with nerves under the touch of his fingers, and her flesh quivered.

His sudden arousal was hard and uncomfortable against her body, pressing her thigh and pelvic bone with a painful urgency. She shifted against him, seeking an easier position. She had a sudden mental image of Ben Glass naked, and the memory of the sight, the touch and taste of him made her stomach hollow.

He lifted her hips and pulled her skirt up out of the way, then placed her squarely on top of him, pulling her legs a little apart to fall around his hips. Now the pressure was exactly where her body wanted it, and she couldn't stop the little grunt of satisfaction in her throat as he settled her against him.

Hearing it, he smiled. She felt it in his kiss and lifted her head a little to look down at him. Smiling up into her eyes, he placed his hand over her bottom and slid it around and down between her legs, and the heat of his fingers permeated the cloth of her panties and reached the melting core of her that was already ready for him.

She began to press rhythmically against him. It was involuntary, the self-directed motion of her hips seeking fulfillment. Lightly, his fingers pressed and encouraged her.

Meanwhile his tongue, deep in her mouth, was thrusting in hard, sure strokes, melting her with its suggestiveness. She had never in her life been aroused so quickly to urgent demand. When his tongue withdrew and their lips parted, she said, "Ben." And he could hear it in her voice.

He was beyond smiling. His dark eyes were alive with heat. He said softly, "Shall we go to bed?"

But she didn't want to be slowed down now, to slide from this peak of rough and urgent excitement that had come on her so swiftly. Her body was demanding his with a clamour she scarcely recognized.

"Ben," she begged. "Ben!"

His eyes widened and then narrowed as his passion broke the bounds he had set on it. With one swift, violent motion, he rolled over and swung her with him, so that now she lay on her back under him, pressed into the thick fur of the carpet; and now it was his body that had a life of its own, pressing hard against her with a demanding urgency.

His hand was at work between them, undoing his trousers, working his flesh free. She felt the pressure of the fabric of her cotton panties as he pulled on them, and then, finally, erotically, his flesh found hers and drove home with one powerful, urgent thrust.

She felt the cry driven from her throat as his body reached its depth in her, pushing pleasure into every cell. For a moment they were motionless as they looked into each other's eyes, reminding each other that now her body enclosed his, and between them something had been forever changed. Then the unimaginable pleasure of his masculine presence in her swept to her brain, and her head fell back, and she was distantly aware of the warmth of flames on her face as her body lifted to meet another powerful stroke, and another.

It was a rough, urgent mating. He had become aroused as quickly and violently as she and had already lost control. There was no time for finesse or subtlety; he could only drive into her, over and over, hungry for the pleasure that he knew he could find in her body, hungry for the proof that his body gave her pleasure.

His wild urgency fed her excitement unbearably, and when she felt the last line of his control snap, and his body's sudden surge to completion in her, her body heaved in response, taking his pleasure as the trigger to her own, so that it fired up in her all at once, like the shower of sparks that erupts in a blazing fire when a log tumbles from the precipice.

After an eternity of formless floating, she felt a hand gently stroke her forehead. She opened her eyes. The room was exactly as she had left it, the fire an ever-changing glow in the semidarkness, the rug thick and warm under her, Ben's dark eyes reflecting the flames. She had almost expected some fundamental change to have occurred.

She smiled lazily up at him. "Pretty wild," she said.

He smiled, too. "You always were."

Perhaps, though this was certainly a first. She couldn't ever remember just ripping the bare minimum of clothes off like this, an animal that didn't care how or where but only for immediate gratification of the rawest desire she could ever remember experiencing.

She supposed that was the power that Ben had always had with her—a direct link with her animal desires. It wasn't as though he manipulated her. But whatever he did naturally seemed to have some fundamental connection to her own inner embers. Other men might painstakingly set down paper and kindling and ignite a slow flame in her that would, in time, burn as brightly as any. Ben's very essence operated on her like gasoline poured on a smouldering log.

"Not just me," she protested. "What is it?"

"Other than the obvious?" he asked with a grin, then stopped smiling as he looked down at her and stroked the hair from her forehead. "I don't know any more than you," he said. Something in the way he said that made her wonder if it were true. "But we're both seven years older now. Let's not run away from it again, okay?"

There was something about that that made her uncomfortable, and Sondra smiled absently and pushed herself to a sitting position. Her skirt was crushed up around her waist, her underwear nearly destroyed. One shiny, smooth nylon was thickly laddered from her ankle all the way to the elastic that clasped her thigh.

Pulling down her skirt, she said, "I certainly hope you've got some clothes to lend me tomorrow."

Ben was taking his trousers off. In fact, he was taking off everything except his snug maroon shorts, which went very nicely with all the curling black hair on his thighs and abdomen. He seemed to have no physical shame, but of course with a body like that he didn't need much, Sondra thought, wondering if her pupils were dilating now. He wasn't your standard *David* figure by any means, too slim for that. But she liked his lean-hipped, lean-muscled look. She hoped his jeans would fit her, but of course she could survive in a shirt or something if she had to. "Bound to be something around," he said. "Are you going to insist on going home tomorrow, or will you stay the weekend?"

She shook her head. "I've got work to do for court Monday. I've got to be home."

"Could you work here? Have you got the stuff with you?"

She shook her head again. "I left my briefcase in your car, remember?"

Ben threw his clothes onto one of the chairs and stood up. He really was almost beautiful in the firelight. His eyes were so dark looking down at her. "Hell, that's easy enough. We'll take the boat back in the morning and pick it up."

Sondra looked around. The cottage was extremely pleasant. Except for the crackling of the fire now and again, and the wind still blowing in the trees, she couldn't hear a sound.

Besides, if she stayed here, Ben would be a sounding-board when she was planning her courtroom strategy. He could give her lots of necessary advice on the transition from defence to prosecution.

And besides, she wanted to make the most of the three months.

She stood up on legs still unsteady from lovemaking. "Sunday afternoon?" she asked.

"You got it," said Ben, with a little nod of his head. He picked up her hand. "Now what do you say to a nice hot bath?"

"I'm putting a shrink who examined Laney Meredith on the stand," Sondra said late on Saturday afternoon. "What order do you think would make best use of her testimony?" She was curled up on the sofa, her briefcase on the little table pulled up in front of her. There was a fire blazing in the hearth, and by turning her head only a little she could see Ben at his desk, facing out over an expanse of the lake. In the distance several dark green islands dotted the water, with here and there a touch of red to remind them of the coming autumn.

It had been a wonderful day. They had awakened to beautiful weather at dawn and, not wanting to miss it, had got up and dressed and gone down to the boat in a few minutes. There hadn't been another boat out on the lake except for two fishermen anchored in a pretty cove, waiting for a bite in the silence.

Ben's motor was relatively quiet, but he had steered well clear of them, knowing they would resent it if he came too close and scared the fish. Then he had headed out across the lake at full throttle, the wind whistling in their ears, whipping Sondra's hair around her head.

On the way back, her briefcase safely collected, he had taken her on a longer route down some quiet waterways, impressive for their beauty. Up close, the inroads the autumn was making on the trees were more obvious. In spite of the summer heat, the year was dying. Birds were gathering to plan their routes south. Many cottages were already closed for the year, their inhabitants, who had spent the summer there, already back in the cities, in the schools.

It was tremendously beautiful. Sondra could almost see wanting to spend a year here alone, a few kindred spirits dotted here and there on this lake and others, watching the fall turn into winter, the lake freeze, and only your own chimney giving any sign of human occupation.

And then the long, slow melt, the arduous Canadian process of winter turning into spring...for a writer it might very well be ideal.

They had returned to the cottage with huge appetites, and the smell of woodsmoke from the chimney was already home to Sondra. Together they had made a breakfast of which, on a normal morning, she might not have eaten a mouthful. But here she had eaten her full share of the bacon and eggs, fried potatoes, toast, honey and drip coffee.

Later they had gone swimming, and Ben had taken her on a walking tour of his tiny island. They had lazed in the hot sun, swum again, and now they were ensconced for the evening, the fire alight, the sun low on the horizon, Ben at his desk in front of the window, Sondra by the fire. Geese honked as they flew low over the water; higher up, a cluster of smaller birds swooped and banked, practicing their formations, choosing appropriate leaders.

Ben swung around in his chair. "What's she going to testify to?"

Sondra consulted her notes. "Basically the signs of trauma in Laney Meredith's personality since the attack, and, most importantly, why Laney is refusing to identify her underwear."

"Bad luck getting a woman," Ben observed. "I wonder who managed that? Who have you got—Clarkson? McDougall?"

They were the usual court-appointed women psychiatrists, Sondra knew. "No," she said, glancing at her notes again. "We got somebody different. For the moment I can't remember why...Zimmerman. Andrea Zimmerman. Oh, I remember now."

"I don't know her. Is she a new one?"

"She's Laney Meredith's own psychiatrist. This is her first court appearance."

"Was the girl under psychiatric care prior to the rape?" Ben asked in surprise.

"I don't think so...no, her mother got her to a shrink right away, though. She was examined by one of the usual court psychiatrists, too, last spring. Who is it?—Dady, Michael Dady. But he was out of town last week, and anyway Dr. Zimmerman is very impressive. I decided to go with her."

"Go with Dady," said Ben. "If he gets back in time."

"Mind telling me why?" Sondra bridled a little. She didn't like the sound of that "bad luck getting a woman."

"A male shrink in a rape case carries more weight with the jury. You've already got most of your case resting on the testimony of a woman. A slightly hysterical woman at that. Juries don't like to believe women. Back her up with a male professional."

Sondra stared at him. "Jesus Christ, Ben! This is 1986! And Laney Meredith is *not* hysterical!"

"She's not normal, either." He lifted his palm towards her. "I'm not *on* the jury, Sondra. I just try to predict the people who are. Juries have a built-in prejudice against women in a rape case. In *any* case, but particularly in a rape case. They're very aware that it's one woman's word against one man's. You know all this, Sondra. It's the woman they listen to more skeptically. The chances are they'll carry that same skepticism over onto any woman professional in your case. You're going to need credibility from whomever is going to be telling the jury that a woman is psychologically incapable of identifying her own underwear for whatever reason. Get a man to do it."

She was furious. "In a case where I have one very qualified and one only moderately or inadequately qualified person, you're telling me to use the less qualified person because he's a man?"

Sensing her anger, he lifted his hands. "It's not an order, Sondra. It's my advice. Whoever this woman is, you say she isn't experienced on the stand. You know what Roebotham's like with women. Is she going to be able to stand up to him?"

"I've talked to her twice. She is extremely capable and intelligent."

"That isn't what I asked. I asked, will she stand up to the kind of stuff Blake Roebotham is going to throw at her?"

"This is my first prosecution, Ben. What kind of stuff, exactly, is he going to throw at her?"

Ben lifted his hands again. "It depends on the woman. Is Dr. Zimmerman a feminist? If she is, he'll lead her into more and more extreme statements till she sounds rabid. Then he'll suggest, just subtly enough for the jury to pick up, that she'd testify to anything to get any man locked away for rape. He's got a technique for women, Sondra. You've got to recognize the fact."

She breathed in deeply. "His technique, as you put it, is contempt. That's his entire technique, Ben. He tries to make the jury share that contempt. That's all. But you'll have noticed that I have seven women on the jury."

He scratched his chin. "I noticed," was all he said, but she knew he felt she had made a serious mistake.

"I think those women are going to get angry if Roebotham tries that kind of sexist crap on them."

He raised his eyebrows and shrugged again. "Traditionally that isn't what happens in rape cases."

"Traditions are changing, Ben. Women are more protective of one another than we used to be. We've spent the past two decades, nearly, learning the real facts about rape. Some of us at firsthand. And women aren't—"

He broke into what seemed likely to become a diatribe. "Okay, Sondra, I understand that the shrink you are going to put on is going to be a woman. That's your decision, and let's leave it at that. What did you want to ask me about the order?"

She bit her tongue. She was angry, very angry, but she had the distance to see that much of her anger was disappointment with Ben Glass. She desperately wanted him more aware, more in tune with an issue that was so important to her.

But few men were. She said only, "I can put the shrink on right after Laney's finished testifying. I'm pretty sure I'll be bringing out more on that underwear on the redirect, so the doctor's testimony then would just reinforce the idea that the underwear is hers, but she can't accept it psychologically. Or I could save her till the end, which I'd prefer to do if her testimony is going to be strong enough, because then we leave the jury with a recap of all the worst bits... You know, it's an opportunity to show them the underwear again, remind them, after all the boring technical stuff, that we're talking about a real crime with real blood..." She faded off, thinking, and they were both silent for a bit.

"Just remind me again what other witnesses you've got," Ben asked after a few minutes of thought.

Sondra consulted her file. "Okay, I've got the neighbour whose house she ran to after escaping. She'll testify to the girl's physical condition, and also to the fact that the accused was seen hanging around the Miller house, if not actually going in and out. There's Mrs. Miller, who'll testify that he had no business being there. We think her son may be called by the defence, by the way, to testify to giving the accused a key to the house so he could go in and feed his rabbit or something.

"There's the cop who responded to the call and took the girl to the hospital. He took down her story. There's the cop who took over the investigation, took down the Franklin statement, arrested the accused and searched his home. That's Dykstra, who was on the stand yesterday. There's..." Rooting through the file to make sure of not missing anyone, she gave him a quick but thorough rundown of the case, and all the time he listened closely, his eyes intent, his intelligence so obvious she wanted to throw down the file and go and kiss him.

When she was finished, he looked out over the lake, his brow serene, his eyes narrowed in thought. She waited in silence. "I'm going to have a problem giving you advice on this, Sondra, because of our difference of opinion as to the sex of your psychiatrist. If it were Michael Dady you were putting on, I'd say put him on last, because you know Roebotham won't likely be able to shake him. That way you get all the technical confirmation out of the way and finish up with the emotional impact, as you've said. Dady's not the best at putting that stuff into laymen's language, but he's pretty good.

"If you're going to put on a woman, and that woman an unknown in terms of any court track record, with Blake Roebotham as an adversary, I have to advise you what I think. And that is that you should put her on early in your case. That way, if Roebotham blows her away, the jury has time to forget it.

"My best advice to you, since obviously there are good reasons for using the girl's own shrink—if Roebotham weren't defence I'd have less argument with it—is to put *both* psychiatrists on the stand. Zimmerman early in the case, and then Dady last, to pick up any pieces—in case there are pieces to be picked up."

And of course to give masculine credibility to the whole enterprise, Sondra added for him silently. Still irritated, but hiding it, she thanked him for the advice, made notes and added them to the file.

It was her first rape case. God, she thought all that stuff had gone out with the ark! Was it really still operational? What irritated her more than anything was the fact that she probably ought to follow Ben's advice. This was her first prosecution as well as her first rape case. His experience must be invaluable.

Yet her instincts were all the other way. *She* felt that the woman psychiatrist would *add* to the victim's credibility. A woman telling others what a less articulate woman had felt—what any woman must feel after such an assault on her person and her personhood. How could a man have more credibility in such an instance?

Ben had gone back to work. Sondra gazed at his dark head bent over his desk, outlined by the light of the dying day. He was intelligent, brilliant. But he was a man.

A man with brains and a great deal of experience urged her to do one thing.

All her instincts pointed the other way.

Which should she listen to?

Chapter 7

That night, for reasons she didn't really understand herself, she wouldn't make love with Ben. She simply felt no desire for him.

She didn't realize it until, coming out of the bathroom with nothing on but the baggy, faded, blue-and-white flannelette pyjama top he had loaned her, she walked straight into Ben's passionate embrace and involuntarily went stiff.

He sensed it immediately, breaking away to put his hands on her upper arms and look into her face. "What's up?"

Sondra shook her head, amazed herself at the immovability of her body's inner rejection of him. It wasn't going to be stirred, neither by his kiss, nor the pleasant masculine scent of his skin, nor by the sight of his well-shaped naked chest that was so warm to the touch.

"I don't know," she said, and it was only half a lie.

Ben put his arms around her again, but now the response had reached her brain—she did not want him to. Calmly she placed the flat of her palm against his chest. Even so, the feel of that dark, springy hair was pleasant under her fingers. With a quizzical lift to one eyebrow, he let her go.

"Ben," she said, "is the bed in the other room made up?"

"Probably. Why?"

"I think I'd better sleep there tonight."

"Why?" he asked, not demanding, not angry, just wanting to know.

"I'm not going—I don't want to make love tonight."

"Oh." He dropped his hands from her arms and crossed them over his bare chest. He was wearing the flannelette bottoms that matched her top, which made everything that much more intimate somehow. "Any particular reason?"

Anger, it had to do with anger, but that was the closest she could come to any connection. "No particular reason." She shrugged. "Just—not in the mood, I guess."

"It's not your period, is it? Because I really don't—"

Shaking her head, she cut him off. "No, it's nothing like that, Ben. I just don't—"

His brows snapped together suddenly in thought. "This isn't anything to do with our conversation earlier tonight, is it? Are you angry with me for what I said about that woman shrink?"

"I'm not exactly thrilled with the advice you gave me, Ben, but this is not a form of punishment, if that's what you mean."

By mutual consent they moved to the armchairs in front of the fire. "Good," said Ben. "What I said to you, Sondra, was simply tactical advice. It has nothing to do with my own attitude to women."

She had to smile at the naiveté of that, but she let it pass. She gazed into the bright embers of the fire. "All right, I understood you to mean that."

He caught her hand and held it, and their clasped hands swung between the chairs for a moment. "Let's go to bed," he suggested quietly after a moment. "We don't have to make love, but I'd like to hold you."

She wasn't sure how she felt about that. In some ways that seemed more of an intimacy than sex. Lying there, being held in the dark as she fell asleep—that wasn't quite part of the scenario she had envisioned last night when she had decided Ben's term of office would be three months. That was too much like living with someone, like being married.

"If you don't mind, I'd rather sleep alone, Ben," she said after a moment.

"And if I do mind?" His voice was just slightly gruff.

She looked at him. "Then I'm sorry, but I do want to sleep alone."

He inclined his head in acquiescence. "Can't argue with that," he observed with a rueful smile.

"Good night then." Sondra stood up and looked down at him, willing him to let her go, not to try to press her.

Ben was gazing at the fire, where a few tiny flames still flickered up among the embers. He looked up and smiled. "Good night, Sondra," he said. "Sleep well."

His eyes went back to the flames, and she left him there. It was an hour before she went to sleep, but she didn't hear Ben move in all that time.

"Sleep well?"

"Very well," Sondra told him cheerfully. "You?"

"Pretty well, once I got to bed. I started working after you went to bed. I was working till four o'clock."

"Working?"

"Writing. I finished a chapter."

So that's what he had been doing. Not hearing him move, she had imagined him sitting there staring at the flames for an hour. It had made her uncomfortable without knowing why. She demanded in surprise, "Do you often work that late?"

"Often enough. Nighttime on the lake is peaceful, often mournful. Last night the loons were crying. Great atmosphere."

Sondra took a sip of coffee, feeling intrigued. "Do you let anyone read your work while it's in progress?"

"I haven't so far." Ben was at the stove, wearing a truly disreputable pair of old jeans and a baggy track jacket. The weather had turned cold in the night; this morning there was the scent of autumn in the air. "Sunny side up?" he asked her, breaking four lovely brown speckled eggs into a pan of spattering butter.

"Yes, please. Would you let me?"

"Read the manuscript in progress?" He shrugged. "I suppose so, if you're interested." He laughed suddenly. "Did you want to read last night's efforts, by any chance?"

Sondra wrinkled her brow. "Sure, if you like. Why?"

"No reason really." He laughed again as he concentrated on spooning hot butter over the eggs. "What time do you want to go back today?"

Sondra yawned and stretched and looked out the window. Yesterday's quiet lake was rather rougher this morning, and the sky was a more rarefied blue. Somehow the autumn colours on the other islands stood out more clearly today.

"Fall has arrived," she observed, half to herself. The kitchen was warm and welcoming, and even the sound of the electric generator in the distance was somehow pleasant. If the truth were known, she didn't want to leave. When she had agreed to stay with the proviso that they go home Sunday, she had imagined an after-breakfast departure, giving her plenty of time at home to be sure she would be ready for Blake Roebotham tomorrow. But now, faced with the choice, she preferred to spend the extra hours here.

"When do you normally leave?" she asked.

"Depends. The weather looks good, and there isn't that much traffic back to the city this time of year, so I'd probably leave late. Sometimes I go back early Monday morning. But you have a heavy day tomorrow. If we leave about four, you'll be back by eight at the latest. How does that seem to you?"

She nodded absently as he slid two beautifully fried eggs and some Canadian back bacon onto her plate. "You're lucky, having this place." She smiled at him. "It's really perfect, isn't it?"

"As close as I'll ever come, I imagine," he agreed.

The breakfast was delicious. Afterwards they went for another ride in the boat, and he took her to a nearby shore that was part of a very large island, where they took a lazy hike through an uninhabited section. The scent of autumn—her favourite scent—was strong on the air, but the honking of geese overhead was a strong reminder that the season would not last.

After a light lunch, they both sat down to work again, but an hour was all Sondra needed before she felt comfortable with what was likely to happen tomorrow. She had a feeling that Blake Roebotham would keep the plaintiff on the stand for most of the day, but she had contingency plans if he did not. First, a list of the points she must cover again on re-examination, to make sure that Blake had not succeeded in confusing the jury where he wished to. Then she had to make up her mind who was to follow Laney Meredith on the stand, and familiarize herself with the statement, and what points she had to draw out for the jury.

She had originally decided to follow up Laney's testimony with the police sergeant the jury had met on Friday, giving his complete testimony, how he had got the name and licence number of Hughie Macomber from the neighbours Laney had run to, how he had gone to the suspect's home to make the arrest. But now the jury had already heard the most pertinent details the officer had to offer in the case. And Ben was advising her to follow up Laney's testimony with the psychiatrist.

Well, she couldn't decide that now. She was going to wait and play it by ear. A lot of it would depend on how Laney responded to Blake's continued cross-examination on Monday. Sondra might need the psychiatrist's supportive testimony immediately afterwards anyway.

Maybe she would use a documentary film method, Sondra thought, if the witnesses were going to be available in the proper order. She would follow Laney's journey from the basement to the neighbour's house. Maybe Monday she would put on Aleria Franklin with her graphic description of Laney's condition on that freezing winter morning when she had come sobbing and pounding hysterically on the back door.

That was pretty convincing confirmation. Let Blake Roebotham try to make out that she hadn't been involuntarily confined in that basement once that evidence was in front of the jury!

It was three o'clock when she stopped, without having made many final decisions, but a good deal more familiar with the case and the direction it should take. Ben was still working steadily at his desk by the window. Sondra closed her briefcase, then gazed absentmindedly out the window for a few minutes before going to the bedroom to change.

No doubt Ben wouldn't mind her wearing home the clothes she'd been using over the weekend, but there really wasn't much point. She hated wearing crumpled clothes, but the skirt wasn't too bad, and wearing Ben's clothes home would be a message that she expected to see him again. And that was taking something for granted, and she never did that with men, or allowed them to do it with her.

Sondra regarded the gaping run in her stocking with distaste, but bare legs would be worse. Well, there was only the boat trip, and then into the car and home. No one was likely to see her. Besides, she should wash the jeans and shirt.

So she changed quickly into her own clothes and threw Ben's jeans, which had been snug over her hips and loose at the waist, into the washer that sat in an alcove off the kitchen. The generator out in the trees immediately racketed into life to provide the electricity, and a few birds squawked their indignation at the noise as Sondra wandered back into the sitting room.

Ben was up getting himself a fresh cup of coffee from the pot. "Finished?" he asked her.

"Yes. Are you?"

He glanced back at the desk. "Not really. I'd like another half hour. Do you mind?"

It wasn't much after three, and she was in no hurry. "Can I read last night's chapter?" she asked, suddenly very curious to know just what he was writing.

Again the amusement flickered behind his eyes. "Sure," he said with a grin. "Why not?"

He moved to the desk and flipped over a pile of pages, pulled off a few sheets and handed her the rest. Sondra headed back to the fire with them, and silence settled over the room once more.

It wasn't possible to pick up the thread of the plot, nor could she tell who the man and woman were whose lives she suddenly found herself involved in. But there was no mistaking what they were doing: they were going through some very interesting, rather barbed preliminaries prior to deciding whether to give in to a rather fierce mutual sexual attraction.

Ben wrote in longhand, and the strong, full-looped writing required concentration. Sondra was in the middle before she quite realized what she was reading, and by then she was caught.

Both the man and the woman seemed to have a chip on their shoulders over some previous circumstance, and were obviously angry, both with each other and with the fact of their sexual attraction towards the enemy. They were mentally circling each other, looking for the weak spots, each trying to hide their own sexual vulnerability from the other.

It was like watching two cats with lashing tails. She began to want something to happen, to clear the air of all the heavy electricity being generated. She felt that tension in her own stomach and realized she wanted to jump at this angry, baiting man and claw his face.

Fortunately the woman did it for her, only whether she was leaping to claw his face or to pull him into a savage sexual embrace was not known either to her or to the man, or to Sondra. The man's response was just as savage, just as equivocal, and when he finally clamped his mouth down on the woman's, Sondra's little gasp was the first breath she had taken for some time.

Now all the energy of their anger went into the wild sensuality between the two, and the writing was powerfully, almost brutally, frank, and the effect on Sondra predictable. The man was getting an angry satisfaction from giving the woman a tormenting sexual pleasure, and the woman was getting her own satisfaction through showing him every response openly, making him tremble with the effect of his power over her till he too was helplessly inflamed and could only fall on her with a despairing cry and complete the union.

Because the language of the writing had so much of Ben in it, it reminded her of Friday night. She couldn't help attributing the man's sexual feelings to Ben, imagining that these powerful descriptions of the man's sexual need were his own. And it was easy to put herself in the place of the woman, and imagine Ben doing those things to her, filling her ear with the rough eroticisms that were involuntary expressions of his own need.

By the time she got to the end of the chapter, she could feel her own sexual melting, and she set down the last page and looked up to find Ben's eyes squarely on her. He had been watching her read, and she had no idea for how long.

And then came understanding, and it hit her so hard it took her breath away: he had written this last night, after she had resisted him sexually and gone to bed alone.

The fact that this ferocity might in fact be the level of his own sexual need of *her* was suddenly and unbearably exciting.

For one long moment they stared at each other across the room, her eyes widening to take in the whole sight of him. Something powerful stirred deep in her, and she suddenly felt as though she would, in this moment, memorize every muscle and every eyelash of his being.

He did not move towards her, though she felt he must; and after an eternity had passed in one timeless second, he opened his mouth.

"Ready?" he asked.

Sondra blinked. "What?"

"It's nearly four o'clock. Ready to go home?"

Her hand went to her throat. "Oh! Oh, yes, I'm ready when you are."

He showed his teeth in a grin. "I believe it," he said softly. "But there's a storm blowing up out there, and we should get out of here while we can."

Before she could respond to that, he got to his feet and moved over to the fireplace, pulling the screen away from the hearth and knocking the almost dead embers into smaller bits. Sondra stood up shakily.

"There's a box in the kitchen," he told her. "Could you pack the perishables in it to take back with us?"

"Yes, of course."

He was acting as though there were nothing at all in the air between them as he moved purposefully off towards the bedroom, unzipping the track jacket as he went. Taking a deep breath, Sondra strode to the kitchen and began banging tomatoes and lettuce and a carton of milk into the small cardboard box sitting on the table.

When Ben joined her only a minute or two later, he was wearing the trousers, shirt and sweater he'd had on Friday night. With a quick glance around the kitchen, he touched a few switches, then picked up the carton and his duffle bag in one hand and the green garbage bag that held their weekend's refuse in the other.

"Got everything?" he asked.

Sondra ran into the bedroom for her purse and the jacket she had borrowed for the weekend. The weather was too cold to go without it, but she would leave it in the boat.

At the last moment she remembered the clothes in the washer. She'd been so involved with the book she hadn't noticed that the machine had stopped. She stepped into the alcove, calling, "I've just got to throw your stuff in the dryer," and suiting the action to the word.

The dryer didn't respond when she pushed the button. She pushed it twice more. "Ben!" she called, turning around, and jumped a little to find him right behind her. He was looking at her in dry amusement. "The dryer won't work," she informed him in a lower voice.

He grinned. "No, because I shut down the generator. There wasn't any need to bother washing the clothes, Sondra. I could have done it next week."

"Well..." She looked around nervously, concentrating on the problem with an unnecessary intensity because Ben was so close to her and she could swear he knew what effect he was having on her in this claustrophobic space. "Well, what are we going to do with them now?" she demanded, her voice going high. "We can't just leave wet clothes here to mildew!"

He was laughing at her. "We have two choices, I guess," he said, highly amused. "We can hang them out on the line, or we can take them with us."

"Oh. Well, which do you prefer?"

"Frankly, my dear, I don't give a damn."

"Will they...will they be all right on the line?" God, he must think her a total fool. But she preferred to have him think her foolishly concerned with an old pair of jeans and a shirt than to know that what she wanted to say was, "Could we make love once before we go?" And she could not control this unfamiliar nervousness that was making her babble so stupidly, making her see these wet clothes as an insurmountable problem.

"Well, no one is likely to steal them."

That was true. Yes, well, perhaps that would be better than carrying them all the way to Toronto. "Pity you don't have an indoor line," she muttered. "Then..."

Repressing an amused oath, he strode to the back door, dropped the garbage bag he had been carrying along with everything else, opened the door and waved to the outdoor line. "Will you hang the damn clothes up, woman, and stop dithering?" he demanded with a grin.

He locked up as she did so, and she met him around the front. It was nippy outside, and clouds were scudding up.

"Here, let me carry that," she said, reaching for the garbage. "Do you take this back to the marina?"

He grunted acknowledgement as he slammed and locked the door, and as they stepped out of the protection of the house the wind caught them. It was a cold, strong wind, nothing like the one that had been blowing on Friday night, and Ben grunted.

"Good thing we're leaving when we are. This is likely to get rough."

In fact, there were whitecaps on the waves, and their journey back across the lake was a series of rapid, violent thuds that seemed determined to shake the teeth from her head. By the time they had dumped the garbage and packed their few things into the car, the rain had started.

In the passenger seat, Sondra shook her long hair free of the drops. "It's nice, the rain," she said, smiling. "I like storms when I'm inside, safe and dry." In cars they sometimes made her nervous, but she wasn't nervous now.

"You like making love in the rain, don't you?" Ben said, guiding the car down the rainswept road to the highway.

"I—what?" She'd never made love in the rain in her life! That might be all right in the tropics, but lying out in even a summer rain in Canada was likely to give you a head cold, in her opinion. So whatever adventurous woman he was remembering now, it wasn't her. And she felt a stab of fury, quickly suppressed, at the thought that he couldn't keep his women separate in his memory.

"It's just something I remember about you. I was thinking that if it weren't for your case tomorrow we could be listening to the rain and making love right now. You'd have liked that, wouldn't you?"

Oh, *indoors*! That was different! Yes, she remembered that afternoon, too. Seven years ago. She looked over at him with a little smile. He was teasing her quite deliberately. He had probably known exactly what was wrong with her when she was dithering over the wet clothes. "Yes, I'd have liked that," she told him frankly. "If you'd asked me, I'd have wanted to stay. Isn't that why you gave me that chapter to read?"

He grinned at her, and it was a challenge. "Did you like it?"

She held his gaze and smiled. "It was pretty sexy," she said finally. "I'd like to read the book from the beginning. You're a real writer, aren't you?" Thank God for that, she was thinking suddenly. How would she have handled it if the writing had been amateurish?

"Ah, but no one is a writer without inspiration."

"And I inspired that scene?"

"Maybe you should stick around permanently."

"Are there many sexy scenes in your book?"

He looked at her. "There will be if you stick around."

She laughed, enjoying the look in his eyes and how it stirred her. "But will they go down on paper?"

"We might institute a rule that you would have to say no on Saturday nights so that I will make love between the pen and paper instead of to you."

The frank admission that the scene on paper was born of the desire she stirred in him was a heady wine. She found herself wondering whether she could stir him now, if she wanted to, and how far.

"I wouldn't want to waste the time," she told him without thinking, because she knew, if he did not, that their time together was limited. She wondered with a sudden wistfulness what he would write when she left him.

There was a crack of laughter from Ben. The car slowed suddenly, and his hand came out to her chin, to turn her face to his.

"That's rich, coming from you," he said, and there was a dark, fathomless shadow in his eyes that she did not understand. "Considering you're the woman who hasn't minded the waste of seven years."

He turned back to the road again, but the shadow she had seen in his eyes was now over her heart. It was the shadow of yearning, of a need she recognized, but had never been able to name.

Sondra shifted uncomfortably in her place. She did not want to name the need.

Chapter 8

"Now, Laney," said Blake Roebotham with withering contempt. "I think the jury would like to hear exactly why you got into my client's car on the night of February eighth. Could you tell us about that?"

"It was cold. He said he would drive me home."

Laney Meredith was looking worse than she had last week. She wasn't standing up to the stress of being on the witness stand at all well, Sondra noted with a professional eye. Sondra herself was going to have to be on her toes. There was a fine line, sometimes a dangerously fine one, to be drawn between preventing opposing counsel from harassing the witness, and leaving the impression with the jury that the witness had something to hide. She would have to tread delicately here, because what some witnesses could stand up to, Laney Meredith very well might not.

"I see. And did you have any particular reason for believing what he told you?"

"I don't understand the question."

"Let me put it another way. Had you been driven home by Hugh Macomber before?"

"No."

"Had you been out with him before?"

"No. I'd never met him."

"Yet you got into the car with him on this night, a young girl alone, on no more than the promise of a stranger that he would drive you straight home?"

"Yes."

"I see. Would you mind telling the jury why?"

"I trusted him."

"Do you normally trust strange men in cars who make you promises, Laney?" he asked with bright interest.

The witness shrugged. "I don't know," she said slowly. "I haven't met that many."

Blake let a little anger show. "Well, the ones you *have* met, Laney. Do you normally trust them?"

"No, I guess not."

"Just my client. You trusted him."

"Yes."

"Yet you didn't know him? You hadn't been with him before?"

"No."

"Laney, are you telling the jury that just this once you went against your natural grain, the natural grain of any young woman, we might imagine, and climbed into the car with a total stranger?"

"Yes."

"So you don't make a habit of climbing happily into closed cars with strange men?"

"No."

"How many times have you done this in the past, do you think?"

"I've never done it before."

"And my client just happened to be the lucky one, is that it?" Blake pursued sarcastically. Someone on the jury seemed to suppress a snicker, which was exactly the reaction he wanted. He sent the faintest flicker of recognition and encouragement towards that brother in the jury box.

"Now, what was it about my client that caused you to change your habits so drastically that night? Was it because he's so handsome?"

"No."

"No, he isn't really very handsome, is he? Unless, of course . . . have you ever had a black boyfriend, Laney?"

"No."

"What would your mother say if you came home and introduced a black man as your boyfriend?"

Laney shrugged. "She wouldn't say anything. My mother's not prejudiced, if that's what you mean."

It was the longest statement the jury had heard from her all morning, and they sat forward in unconscious interest.

"So if you'd wanted to, you could have brought Hugh Macomber home and introduced him?"

She wrinkled her brow. "But I didn't know him."

Sondra repressed a smile. Well done, she thought. A lot of witnesses would have walked right into the hypothetical at that point, and found the trap had closed around them.

Thwarted, Roebotham decided on a quick frontal assault. "Didn't you, Laney? Isn't it a fact that you knew Hugh Macomber quite well, that you had had liaisons with him in the past, and that you were afraid to take him home to your mother because of his colour?"

"No. I never knew him."

"Well, let's just run over this again. You were standing on the corner waiting, as you say, for your bus. Is that right? And a car came up with a total stranger in it, and he offered you a ride. And you simply climbed in the car and drove away. Is that what you want the jury to believe?''

''I said no at first.''

''Never mind how many times you protested, Laney,'' he said aggressively. ''The fact is that you got into the car and drove away, isn't that so?''

''But—''

''Is that substantially the truth?'' he shouted.

''Your Hon—'' Sondra began calmly, but Laney Meredith had forgotten the rule of counting to five, and was answering already.

''No,'' she said firmly.

''No?'' Blake repeated in theatrical amazement. ''Are you telling us now that you *didn't* get into the car?''

''It's not substantially the truth,'' Laney said with quiet firmness, and Sondra blinked in admiration and sank back into her seat. Let Laney handle it her own way.

Blake had lost his momentum. He tried to recover it with bluster. ''Then you had better tell us what is!''

''It's not substantially the truth if you leave out that he kept driving away when I said no and coming back a few minutes later. And he kept telling me how cold it was and that I could trust him and he would drive me straight home. He promised me he wouldn't hurt me.''

Blake bowed to her, sarcasm in every line of his body. ''Well, thank you. I see the jury and I will have to revise our definition of *truth* if we're going to listen to you much longer,'' he said with heavy meaning. ''However, I think they may have their own ideas on the subject.''

''Your Honour, I object,'' said Sondra. ''This witness has not in any way altered her statement of what went on before she got into the defendant's car. There is no need for my learned friend or the jury to revise their definition of truth on her behalf. It is improper for counsel for the defence to suggest that she has altered her statement."

"The question is what is substantial," said the judge. "But I think the facts themselves have been clearly enough outlined to the jury, Mr. Roebotham."

Blake nodded acquiescence. "Now, Laney," he said, moving over to the table of exhibits. "I refer to these clothes that you identified for the jury on Friday as being the ones you were wearing on that night." He flicked the blue jump-suit with a finger. "We've heard from Sergeant Dykstra where this clothing was found. We've also heard that he found some underwear at the same time."

He turned to the underwear, which had been entered in evidence on Friday afternoon. Laney Meredith had not been in the courtroom then, and this was the first time in quite a while that she would be faced with the sight of the under-wear. Since she had first declared herself unable to identify it, she had virtually refused to look at it. She was visibly withdrawing now.

"Now, Laney, I show you what looks like the remains of a brassiere and a pair of panties. Have you seen these items before?" Blake was saying with deliberate callousness as he approached the witness with the torn and blood-stained garments in his hands.

Laney Meredith hung her head. "Yes," she said softly. "They showed them to me."

"Who exactly do you mean by 'they'?"

"The police."

He was holding the underwear in the air for all to see, and it was obvious that this was a painful humiliation for the seventeen-year-old. Sondra bit her lip in fury, knowing that it was a deliberate technique on Roebotham's part.

"And did the police ask you to identify these items as your own?"

"They asked me if I recognized them."

The once-white underwear was torn to ribbons and smeared with blood. The memories it conjured up in the girl's mind were the memories that she might never be free of for the rest of her life, Sondra knew. Yet there was nothing she could legally object to in what Blake was doing. In the male-dominated system of law, it was all perfectly fair and legal to make the victim of this horrible crime suffer over and over in the name of a fair trial for the accused.

"And did you recognize them?"

Her voice sank. "No," said Laney quietly.

"Could you speak up, please? The jury can't hear you!" Blake demanded loudly.

"No, I didn't recognize them."

Blake looked puzzled. "Yet you identified all this other clothing as your own, did you not?"

"Yes."

"Speak up, please!"

"Yes."

"Well, now, Laney, I wouldn't blame the jury if they were confused at this moment. *I'm* confused, I confess. We all heard Sergeant Dykstra testify on Friday that this clothing, which you claim as your own, was found in the bottom of my client's closet all rolled up together with this underwear, which you admit is *not* yours. Do you have any explanation for that, Laney?"

"No."

Roebotham pulled on his earlobe. "No, it would be hard to come up with any explanation to cover that discrepancy, I imagine," he remarked, almost amused.

"Your Honour, I object. This witness is under no obligation to 'come up with an explanation' for any imagined discrepancy raised by my learned colleague. *She* is not on trial here, though the jury might be forgiven if they had begun to wonder. It is my learned friend's client, the accused in this case, who will be required to account for the presence of this clothing in his closet, not this witness."

"I think that point is well-taken, Mr. Roebotham," said His Honour. "This witness is hardly to be held accountable for the presence of women's underwear, which she does not identify as her own, in the accused's closet."

"Now, Laney," said Blake quickly, "were you *wearing* any underwear at all on the night in question?"

"Yes, of course."

"I beg your pardon? Could you repeat that, please?"

"Yes, I was wearing underwear."

"I asked you to repeat what you had said. Did you say, 'Yes, of course' you were wearing underwear?"

"Yes."

"Well, now, Laney, as I recollect your testimony on Friday, there was no 'of course' about it. When I asked you if there was anything you were wearing that night that had *not* been entered in evidence, you testified, I think, as to a hat and mittens, isn't that so? You didn't mention underwear at all."

"I didn't know you meant underwear, too. Everybody wears underwear."

He was getting her rattled. The sight of the underwear, still being waved in everybody's vision with every gesticulation Blake Roebotham made, had unsettled her, as Sondra had known it would. She got to her feet.

"Your Honour, this point has already been gone over. My learned colleague has been told several times by this witness that she was wearing underwear on the night in question. The jury is well aware that she forgot to mention it when he first asked. My learned friend is belabouring the point."

"Well, Your Honour, if I am, I think it's a point that will stand belabouring. There is a discrepancy with regard to the identification of this clothing, and my client is entitled to get to the bottom of it."

"Yes, I think this needs clarification for the jury to understand these exhibits, Ms. Holt," the judge ruled. "Carry on, Mr. Roebotham."

"Now, Laney, how certain are you that the clothes you identified as your own really are yours?"

"I'm certain. They're mine."

"Yet they were found rolled up with this underwear, which is not yours, according to testimony the jury has already heard. Isn't that so?"

"I object. The witness is being asked to testify to something she cannot know from her own knowledge."

"Objection sustained."

"Did you make this blue jumpsuit yourself, Laney? Or did you buy it?"

"I bought it."

"Were there others identical to it on the rack when you purchased it?"

"I don't remember. Probably."

"Are there any particular markings on this jumpsuit that helped you identify it as your own?"

"I just know by looking at it."

"Let me repeat the question. Are there any particular markings on it that helped you identify it as your own?"

"I don't think so. Just the general—"

"Just answer the question, please. There are no *particular* markings on this jumpsuit? You haven't got your name embroidered on it or anything of that nature?"

"No."

"And what about the coat? Is that an individual item, or is it a mass-produced coat that you bought off the rack?"

"I bought it off the rack."

"So there may be thousands of women wearing a coat identical to this one in this city."

"I guess so."

"Is that true of the boots, too?"

"Yes, but . . ."

"Yes. So in fact there is no particular identifying mark you can point to on any of these items found in my client's closet that will back up your claim that they are yours."

"But they were all together," she said, confused.

There was a brief, triumphant pause. Then Blake's voice dropped. "They were all together. Exactly. Would you say, therefore, that the fact that these clothes were all together was a significant factor in making the identification of them as the ones you were wearing that night?"

Not seeing the trap she had walked into, Laney shrugged. "I don't know. I know they're my clothes."

"If the blue jumpsuit had been found with a coat you didn't recognize, would you have been able to identify it so readily?"

There was a pause while she stared at him. "I—I think so, yes."

"You think so. Well, the jury isn't going to convict my client on what you think, are they, Laney? Now, you've already admitted there were no distinguishing marks on the jumpsuit, haven't you?"

"But—"

"Have you admitted that there were no distinguishing marks on the jumpsuit?"

"Yes, but—"

"So it was of material significance to your identification that all these clothes were shown to you together, isn't that so?"

"I—I don't..." She was on the ropes now, and Blake knew it.

"Isn't it a fact, Laney," he shouted, going in for the kill, "that because all these clothes you thought were yours were shown to you together, you identified them as your own? Isn't it a fact that the presence of a coat like your own with a jumpsuit like your own had the effect of allowing you to think that both were yours, whereas if you had been shown the items individually, you might not have been able to make a positive identification?"

She was so confused and cowed now that Sondra could see she scarcely heard, let alone understood, the question.

"I—maybe." Her voice went up rather pathetically at the end, as though she instinctively wanted to placate his anger. Sondra wondered how many times Laney Meredith had tried to placate Hugh Macomber's rage, to be cowering so visibly now.

Suddenly Sondra was trembling with her own fury. She got to her feet, interrupting Blake's next hectoring question. "Your Honour, I object to this browbeating. This witness has gone through enough and should not be subjected to this treatment at the hands of the defence counsel."

Blake received a reprimand and bowed to the judge.

"How did you reconcile the fact, then, that the *underwear* found with this clothing was *not* your own, Laney?" he demanded in a quiet, low voice that made the jury sit forward in interest.

"I don't know what you mean."

"Well, let me put it another way. You have testified before the jury that the presence of *all the clothes together* was a significant factor in your identification of them. Yet this underwear—" he lifted the hand holding the torn and bloody cotton "—that you have testified was *not* yours was also found with the clothing. Now, doesn't that cast a doubt on your identification of the clothing? The jumpsuit was sufficiently like your own to reinforce the identification of the coat, and the boots and all the rest. But presumably this underwear was *not* sufficiently like your own, in that even the presence of *all the other items of clothing you identified as your own* was not enough to allow you to identify it. Isn't that so?"

"No..." Laney said tentatively, confused, and then more firmly, "No."

"Your Honour, I object," said Sondra in a quiet but carrying voice. "The witness has not testified that the underwear is not her own. She has said that there are not sufficient particular identifying marks on it to make a firm identification possible. My learned friend should refrain from putting words in the witness's mouth."

"Objection sustained."

Blake turned sarcastically on Laney. "You have refused to identify this underwear, have you not?"

"Yes, but—not because it wasn't like mine. It was."

Blake smoothly ignored that pitfall. "Tell me, did my learned friend, the Crown Attorney, talk to you about this underwear before the trial?"

Laney blinked. "Yes."

"Did she ask you to try to identify it?"

"Yes."

"Did you get the feeling that it was important that you get up on the witness stand and unequivocally claim this underwear as the underwear you were wearing that night?"

"She said I should try to look at it and see if I could identify it."

"Did she say your case against my client would be materially weakened by your refusal to identify this underwear?"

"Oh, Your Honour, I object. My friend is trying to put a conclusion before the jury as to the strength of the case against the accused. He should save that for his summation."

"I think you can rephrase that, Mr. Roebotham."

"Of course, Your Honour. Did the Crown Attorney tell you it was important that you identify this underwear, Laney?"

"Yes, she did."

"And did the police say something of the sort, too?"

"Yes."

Blake shook his head admiringly. "And yet, in spite of all that pressure, both from the police and from the Crown Prosecutor—" he made *prosecutor* sound like the equivalent of *KGB colonel* "—you stood your ground and refused to identify the underwear, Laney. That must have required strength of mind, because I know that the Crown Prosecutor can be a very forceful woman when she chooses. You must have been very certain in your own mind, therefore, that the underwear was *not* yours in order to stand up to her like that. I'm not sure I'd have the courage." He laughed lightly.

"Your Honour—" Sondra got furiously to her feet.

"Please refrain from personalities, Mr. Roebotham." The judge spoke without waiting for her objection. "Your comments about Crown counsel are inappropriate."

"I withdraw anything that might reflect on my learned friend's competence and good faith," Blake said instantly with a gracious smile and bow, knowing the damage was done. "Now then, Laney, if you had been left to your own devices, wouldn't the presence of this strange underwear in among the clothing you were asked to identify as your own have cast some shadow of doubt on your certainty that this other clothing was your own?"

"No."

He smiled skeptically, too shrewd to let her make any explanation of that. "I see. Your Honour, I have no further questions of this witness."

Sondra glanced at the courtroom clock, but she knew without looking that it was just time for the noon recess. She heard the judge point it out and declare the adjournment with an impassive face, but inside she was far from impassive.

She had been far too sanguine about her ability to handle the problem of the underwear. She should have known that Blake Roebotham hadn't got his reputation for nothing. Yet she had not expected him to be able to turn it into anything quite so damning.

And now the jury had the whole noon recess to ponder the question of whether any of the clothes were Laney Meredith's. And there might not be a hell of a lot of repair work she could do. Even if Laney Meredith had now seen the light and was willing to identify the underwear, Sondra couldn't allow it. The last thing she needed now was a wavering witness.

Sondra turned to the law student who had been assigned to her for the case. "When the jury has gone, grab Laney for us, please. And stop looking like a kid whose balloon had just been broken. All that stuff was just flimflam."

She wasn't sure whether she was talking to bolster his courage or her own. She had two hours to work out a way to destroy the effect of a very damaging morning, and she needed all the courage she could find.

It was beginning to look as though Ben was right, though perhaps not for the reasons he had stated. She'd better get that shrink on the stand as soon as possible after Laney had finished testifying.

"And find out if Dr. Andrea Zimmerman can make herself available this afternoon instead of tomorrow. If she can't, subpoena her," Sondra ordered flatly. "We need her."

Chapter 9

"I should have known it would backfire. I should have known he didn't get his reputation over nothing."

Ben raised knowing eyebrows at her. "It's not over yet, and I'm quite sure you haven't won your last trick. If you have, Roebotham's getting off a lot easier than *I* ever did."

Sondra laughed in acknowledgement. "No, this is just my regulation despair before the storm," she admitted. "I have to hit the depths before I start to crawl up the other side."

He looked interested. "Really? Did you go through this kind of thing when we were up against each other?"

"Whenever you gave me real trouble, I did."

He threw back his head and laughed. "I wish I'd known it! God, sometimes it was my highest wish just to know I'd given you one truly bad moment. You were always so calm under fire."

She smiled mock smugly. "I play great poker, too." Then she sobered. "How the hell am I going to pull this one out of the fire, Ben? I can't let her suddenly renege on her refusal to identify the underwear, even if she wants to."

Sondra had just spent half an hour with her witness, calming her and reassuring her, and outlining the tack she would be taking when they went back into court this afternoon. Laney Meredith had been more distraught than Sondra had yet seen her, and it was a testament to Blake Roebotham's undoubted skill that he had shaken her up thoroughly but had abandoned the questioning in time to avoid any pathetic outburst that might have had the jury thinking him a real brute and swinging back to sympathy with the witness.

Now Sondra had to make her calculations based on the fact that she had a very shaky witness whose emotions might well be out of control by the time she took the stand again.

"She's now totally unpredictable," Sondra said unhappily, half to herself.

They were in Ben's office, and she had a pad on her knee and was making notes while she bolted a lunch of a cardboard sandwich and coffee.

"You know what really makes me mad?" she said suddenly. "I didn't like your advice yesterday about the woman psychiatrist, and I'd made up my mind to follow my instincts and put her on last. I wanted to show you how wrong you were. But now she's got to go on next and testify about this damned psychological block about the underwear. My instincts don't have to shout about *that*. So nothing gets proved."

Ben looked at her. "I don't need any proof of your legal instincts, Sondra," he said. "You're miles from having to prove anything to me. What are you talking about?"

"Oh, not about my skills," she explained, faintly embarrassed. "About women. About the credibility of professional women with a jury."

"If I'm out of date, I'll be delighted to have it proven to me," Ben said slowly. "But if you ask me for advice, Sondra, I can only give you what my experience has shown to be the best advice in any particular instance. I play by the odds and take chances where my nose tells me to. What I will never give you or anyone is advice that's motivated by what *should* happen. Of course juries should give the testimony of women the same weight as that of men, but the question is, do they? That's all."

He was right. She was being uncharacteristically irrational. Even if she had, quite justifiably, done it her way and pulled off a conviction, it would have proved nothing, except that her instincts in this particular case had been sound. Sondra looked uneasily at Ben. It wasn't like her to get up on a soapbox, or to take things like that advice personally. Something was getting to her on this case, and she didn't know what. Was it Ben himself? Was it her now violent dislike of Blake Roebotham? Whatever it was, she had better stamp on it before she destroyed her own case.

"Ms. Meredith, the counsel for the defence this morning asked you whether there were any particular identifying marks on the clothing in evidence that had allowed you to identify it as your own. Can you tell the court, please, what you understood him to mean by the term 'particular identifying mark'?"

"Well, he said, was my name embroidered on it. I thought he meant a name tag."

"I see. So you did not understand that a particular identifying mark can mean any distinguishing mark of any nature that helps you identify it as your own?"

"No."

"Do you understand it now?"

"Yes, I do."

"Now, I am going to show you the blue jumpsuit, which you have identified quite clearly as the one you were wearing on the night of your abduction, and ask you, Ms. Meredith, if there is anything about it that sets it apart in your eyes from the other jumpsuits manufactured to this design."

"Yes, this button came off once, and I sewed it back on with white thread. All the others are sewn on with blue thread."

"Now, which button has the white thread?"

"The one second from the top."

"And which button did you repair with white thread when it came off?"

"The one second from the top."

"I see. Now, did you understand, at the time when my colleague put his question to you, that this white thread on the button second from the top was in the nature of the 'particular identifying mark' he asked you for?"

"No, I thought he meant my name."

"Now that you know what a particular identifying mark is, are there any others on this jumpsuit that you can tell us about, that helped you to identify this clothing as your own?"

"There's a little purple stain on the leg here where I was eating a grape Popsicle once and it dribbled onto my knee. And I tried to get it out with a little bit of Javex, so there's a little white mark around it where the colour was bleached out."

"So, looking at those two identifying marks, you have no hesitation in stating that this jumpsuit is yours and was the one you were wearing on the night of the attack?"

"That's right."

"Now, Ms. Meredith, are there similar identifying marks on the other items of clothing that you have testified were the ones you were wearing that night?"

"Yes, there are."

"I show you the coat that you have previously identified. Can you tell the jury about any particular marks that helped you positively identify this coat?"

"Yes, the pocket is torn a little here."

"That's the seam of the right pocket you're referring to, where it is joined to the coat at the bottom?"

"Yes."

"Anything else?"

Laney examined the coat. "The manufacturer's tag is missing. I ripped the tag out because it was always standing up inside the collar and tickling my neck."

"I'm going to show you the boots, too, Ms. Meredith, so the jury will understand that there is no question about your identification of your clothing. Is there any particular distinguishing feature about the boots that enabled you to identify them?"

"The heels are worn down on the inside. I always wear down my heels on the inside because of the way I walk."

"I see. Now there was no question whatever that the handbag was yours, was there?" The handbag hadn't been found in the closet, it had been found in the glove compartment of Hugh Macomber's car, but that wasn't stopping Sondra. The jury didn't know it yet.

"No. It had all my things in it."

"Now, what things would you be referring to?"

"Objection, Your Honour," Blake interposed. "The witness has already spent some time identifying all the contents of the handbag for the jury. It's really unnecessary to go over them all again."

"Your Honour, counsel for the defence himself cast doubts on that identification by misleading this witness as to the nature of distinguishing features. In the light of the testimony extracted from the witness as a result of this confusion, the jury has a right to have the real evidence placed before them again."

"Objection overruled."

Sondra took her time over the identification of all the exhibits, telling Laney Meredith not to rush herself, but to be absolutely certain, using the time to calm the witness, to relax her and build up the confidence that Blake had spent the morning destroying.

When she was satisfied, she turned to the judge. "Your Honour, as I stated on examination-in-chief, we intended to call this witness for additional testimony subsequent to the testimony of Sergeant Dykstra..." She had to make it clear that this was examination-in-chief and not re-examination, because she would be bringing out new information now. She didn't expect any problems, but she was new to this, and you never knew with judges. When she got over the hurdle without a hitch, she breathed with relief.

Then she motioned to the underwear. "Now, Ms. Meredith, I would like to ask you to do something that I know is extremely difficult for you and that we have previously tried to avoid for that reason. I would like to ask you to examine this underwear, which has been entered in evidence as Exhibit G, and tell me whether there are any distinguishing features that are similar to the underwear you were wearing on the night of February eighth."

With a horror that was visible to all, and which Sondra was sure the jury could not miss, Laney Meredith stared at the underwear exhibit as Sondra approached her. Then, with a deep, shaking breath, she reached out and took the bra and panties in her hands.

"Is there anything on those tattered remnants that seems familiar to you, Ms. Meredith?"

"The...the brand—the manufacturer's tag is attached to the elastic."

"What is the manufacturer's name?"

"Dici."

"And is there anything you can tell us about what underwear you commonly buy?"

"I always buy Dici."

"Now, is there anything on the underwear that describes the size of the items?"

Her hands were trembling as she looked over the exhibit for the first time. "The underpants are size small."

"How do you know that?"

"There's a little tag here with a black S on it."

"What size of underwear do you wear, Ms. Meredith? I am sorry that we are forced to go into such personal details—" she flicked a look at Blake Roebotham as though it were all his fault "—but I think the jury needs to know."

"I wear size small."

"Is there anything that would indicate the size of the bra?"

"There's a tag at the clasp. It's thirty-two A."

"And what size of bra do you normally buy for yourself?"

"Thirty-two A."

"Is there anything else that shows a similarity between these two pieces of underwear and what you yourself commonly buy and wear?"

"They're white, cotton and Lycra. They're the kind I mostly buy." God, she was doing marvellously. Far better than Sondra had dared hope. What courage she had in spite of everything.

"And were you wearing underwear similar to this on the night you were attacked?"

The girl was suddenly shaking visibly, the bloody underwear trembling in her hands. "Yes, yes I was."

"Ms. Meredith, are there any distinguishing features about this clothing that would let you positively identify this as the underwear you were wearing that night?"

"No, I'm sorry, no," she whispered pitifully. "It's just underwear, isn't it? It was almost new, it was only a few weeks old."

The jury was sitting forward, sympathy on most of their faces.

"Now, Ms. Meredith, I know this is very painful, but you have testified that when you were being held prisoner, the accused at one point came in and took away all your clothes. Can you tell the jury, please, whether at that time there was any blood on your underclothes?"

If she was held together at all, it was with twine. Laney stared at a point over Sondra's head, and she was looking into hell. "Yes," she whispered. "There was blood. My blood."

It must have chilled anyone who heard it. Sondra's pause wasn't theatrical, but because she could not for the moment speak.

"Can you tell the jury, please, how the blood got there?"

"When... when he came back, he had a knife. He made me take off my clothes and then he cut—" Her voice failed.

"Take your time, Ms. Meredith. The jury understands that this is enormously difficult for you."

"He cut my underwear off with the knife, and he—the knife cut me, too, in a few places. Later I—I wiped the blood off me with the underwear. When he took my clothes, he took that, too."

"Thank you, Ms. Meredith. Just one thing more. When you say 'he,' would you tell us, please, to whom you are referring?"

"To him," Laney said, going suddenly still and cold and frightened, and staring down into the defendant's box. She didn't point, which made it all the more chilling.

"You are looking in the direction of the defendant, Ms. Meredith. To be absolutely unequivocal for the record, could you please point to the man you have been referring to?"

Obediently Laney lifted her hand and pointed, and the jury let out a collectively held breath.

"It's the defendant, Hugh Macomber, whom you have pointed to, Ms. Meredith, is that correct?"

"Yes, that's correct," she said with quiet conviction.

Sondra paused and glanced through her notes. "Now, Ms. Meredith, I want to clarify some points that were brought up by the counsel for the defence. When you were in the basement, you have testified you were very cold. Is that right?"

"Yes. I was freezing."

"Now, did you tell the defendant that you were cold?"

"I think so. But I don't remember whether I said it in those exact words."

"Did you ask him to bring you a blanket or some clothes because you were so cold?"

"Yes, I begged him. Over and over."

"And did he bring you anything to keep you warm?"

"No."

"Now, you testified, did you not, that when the accused entered the furnace room where you were being held prisoner, you used to run to him and cling to him?"

"Yes, I did."

"Did you do that because you liked the accused, Ms. Meredith?"

"No. I hated him."

"Then would you tell the jury why you ran to him as you did?"

"I was so cold. He was warm. Sometimes he let me inside his coat and wrapped his arms around me. He was very warm."

"Now, Ms. Meredith, will you tell the jury, please, whether there was any possibility of the accused mistaking this need for warmth to stay alive for any sort of affection you might have for him?"

"No," she said, clearly and distinctly, and with absolute distaste. At long last Laney Meredith was coming alive. "He couldn't possibly have thought I liked him. He knew I hated him. He knew I only needed warmth. That was why he did it, why he kept me so cold. He used to laugh about having a surefire way to make girls . . . make them . . ."

Staring at the accused, she couldn't finish. Sondra said, "That's all right, Ms. Meredith. I think the jury understands.

"Now, just so there is no possibility of error, can you tell us, please: before he stopped his car at the bus stop where you were standing on the night of February eighth, this year, had you ever, to your knowledge, seen the defendant before?"

"No. Never."

"Thank you, Ms. Meredith. That's all."

It was Blake Roebotham's turn at recross-examination. He got lazily to his feet in his place, disdaining the podium, looking as though nothing Laney Meredith had said in the past hour had any significance at all.

"Laney," he said, "do you think your coat is the only coat in Toronto with a torn right pocket?"

"I don't know."

"You've stated that you wear your heels down on the inside, Laney. Are you pigeon-toed?"

"A little bit."

"Pigeon-toed people commonly wear their heels down in such a fashion, don't they?"

"I don't know."

"Do you think you're the only pigeon-toed person in Toronto, Laney?"

"I don't know. I guess not."

"Is it possible that some other pigeon-toed woman bought a pair of boots exactly similar to your own and wore down the heels on the inside?"

"I guess it is."

"Laney," he said, "can you positively identify the underwear of Exhibit G as what you were wearing on the night of February eighth?"

"No."

"And would you agree that we do not normally show people that we hate them by running excitedly up to them and hugging them for all we are worth?"

"Not normally, no," Laney said calmly, and it was as though, suddenly, she were years older than Blake Roebotham in wisdom and experience, as though she suddenly saw him as a posturing child. With a pang, Sondra thought, She's grown up all at once. She's begun to come to terms with it. There's a part of Laney Meredith now, a scarred and sad part, that is as old as womanhood itself. Now she can begin to heal.

She was seventeen, but she was older than any man in the room, and she knew something they would never know. Poor Laney Meredith, Sondra thought, we all come to it sometime, if we are women, but not all of us so early. It's not fair, and it's not right, but that doesn't mean it will ever change.

She felt the tears prick her eyelids, and blinked them impatiently back. She ought not to let the case get to her like this. She had to stay detached or she would trip up.

From a great distance a voice said, "Is that all your questions, Mr. Roebotham?"

"Yes, Your Honour."

"The witness may stand down," said Judge Arthur McVean. "You may call your next witness, Ms. Holt."

Should she call the psychiatrist now, or had Laney's testimony this afternoon already saved the day? Could she risk saving Dr. Zimmerman to the end as she'd originally planned? Playing for time, Sondra riffled blindly through her papers. Her notes were blurring before her eyes. What was the matter with her? What on earth was the matter with her?

"Are you ready with your next witness, Ms. Holt?"

She got to her feet, and suddenly, by sheer force of will, her head cleared, and her cool command returned. "Yes, I am, Your Honour. I'm going to recall Sergeant Dykstra of the Metro Toronto police for his full testimony now, if the Court please. Call Emmanuel Dykstra, please."

As she turned her head, a familiar shape caught her eye, the shape of Ben Glass, hunched forward attentively, taking everything in. She threw him a smile, feeling warmed by his interest, and he nodded and showed no sign of being about to leave. She was glad he was there. Had he been there most of the afternoon? That was real friendship, because his own case was coming up for trial very shortly.

She was hugely grateful. This meant she'd be able to get an outside opinion as to how her re-examination had gone.

Another gaze caught her eye, and this one was far from friendly. With a start of rueful surprise, Sondra found herself the object of a very annoyed pair of eyes belonging to Dr. Andrea Zimmerman. Oh, hell. They had subpoenaed her away from her office this afternoon, and now she wouldn't be called.

As the Court waited for the arrival of Sergeant Dykstra, Sondra bent down to her junior. "Go and tell Dr. Zimmerman that we apologize profusely, but she won't be needed this afternoon, and we'll let her know when we want her to testify."

As Sergeant Dykstra strode through the doors of the courtroom, she saw the junior earnestly whispering to the indignant doctor. Oh well. That sort of thing happened all the time with witnesses. Dr. Zimmerman wasn't the first, and she wouldn't be the last. Sondra felt sorry for the patients who had missed out on this afternoon's therapy, and sorry for the doctor's lost income.

But it was just one more injustice in the system, and there was nothing Sondra was likely to be able to do about it. And she had to concentrate on what she *could* do. Ignoring the doctor's fulminating glare, she turned to her witness.

"Sergeant Dykstra, you've already been sworn," she began.

Chapter 10

Sondra stretched languorously, a sense of total physical well-being seeping into every cell. Beside her in the soft lamplight, Ben's naked body was a creation of light and shadow. Lazily he stroked her flank, her stomach, cupped one full breast in his well-shaped hand.

"Mmm," she murmured appreciatively, stretching again under his touch. He bent and kissed the swell of her breast, brushed the still-erect nipple with his lips, then lay back and drew her into his embrace.

Resting her cheek on his chest, she could hear his heartbeat, powerful and rapid, trying to slow. Her hand strayed through the dark, curling hair on his chest as he held her in his arms.

There seemed no need of speech. Odd, how easy it was for them to be together after so long. Her predominant feeling was one of comfort, the comfort of being with someone she knew well and could be easy with. Yet half an hour ago she had been almost unbearably excited by his mere presence.

Sondra pondered the question idly. In her experience the two feelings didn't usually exist side-by-side for the same man. Either he excited you or you were comfortable with him. Never both.

"Will you stay the night?" Ben asked softly, kissing her forehead. His voice was attractively husky with the aftermath of passion, and she enjoyed the sensation of its vibrations through her body.

Smiling, Sondra shook her head as awareness of the future slid into her head to replace the sensuous glow of the present. "I can't, Ben," she explained ruefully. "I want to get up in my own home in the morning with everything I need right there. Roebotham scares me, frankly. I want to be on my toes every minute in that courtroom."

She pushed herself to a sitting position beside him, and Ben tucked one arm behind his head and looked up at her. He was amazingly attractive, Sondra thought involuntarily, her heart thrilling a little as she watched him. Especially to anyone who was a pushover for brains. His intelligence shone out of his eyes.

"You were certainly on your toes today," he told her admiringly. "It was remarkable the way you finally got your witness pulling with you instead of being a dead weight. That was a powerful session this afternoon."

Sondra glanced appreciatively around the bedroom in the half-light. Ben had a gorgeous apartment, and though of course she didn't like it as much as her own expensive, smartly decorated condominium, there was nothing she would fault on taste or comfort. The master bedroom was pleasantly masculine, subtly sybaritic, as though it had been designed with unconscious sexual symbolism in mind.

"Yes, I don't really know what caused it. I think it had something to do with the way Blake kept attacking her. It was as though she came to a point where she had the choice of lying down and dying under the attack, or taking back control of her own life by accepting what had happened. She's got a lot of courage. When it came to it, she refused to let Blake Roebotham do to her what Hugh Macomber did to her in another way."

"You really have a hate on for Blake," Ben observed lazily. "Do you really think he's as sinister as all that?"

She looked at him. "You don't see it, do you? You really don't see it."

"Sondra, I see that he's a damned successful defence attorney who happens to run a little close to the wire—morally, not legally—from time to time. But then most of us do. I see no reason to hate him for it."

Sondra sighed. Gone was her warmth and comfort of a few minutes ago. Gone the sweet feeling that she had known Ben Glass for a lifetime and would know him for another. She didn't even think of arguing. This was something that no woman could explain to any man—or none that she had ever known. Men were a club when the chips were down. A club where each member defended the other against outside attack without question.

Anyway, at the moment she didn't have the strength to stick to her guns, and she didn't want an argument. She just wanted to get home. So she smiled perfunctorily and said lightly, "Yeah, well, I guess it's personal between me and Blake. I don't like him."

"Frankly, he's not my closest buddy, either," Ben admitted. "But he's a damn good defence attorney."

"Well, it's getting late," Sondra said, letting that pass. "I guess I should—"

Ben reached up and gently pulled her down into his warm embrace again. "Before you go," he said softly, "I want to ask you something. Do you...."

She was stiff in his embrace, and feeling it, Ben raised himself on one elbow and looked down into her eyes. "What's the matter?" he demanded in concern. It seemed it was the first moment he had sensed any change in her.

"Nothing's the matter," she denied with faint irritation. "Why?"

"Your eyes have changed colour," he said suddenly. "They've gone as cold as icicles. What brought this on?"

But she didn't want him peering too closely into her feelings. She shrugged. "I want to go home. I've got court in the morning. Why don't you just say what you want to say and forget the colour of my eyes?"

He released her and sat up, shaking his head. "It'll keep," he said. "Would you like a cup of coffee?"

Her instinct was to say no, but she was driving, and they'd had a heavy meal and the coffee would jolt her alive... God, how many reasons she could invent for ignoring her own instinctive wants, Sondra realized impatiently. "Yes, all right, Ben," she said.

The shower was quite enough to jolt her alive, of course, but when she emerged from the bedroom dressed and ready, Ben had a tray laid with cups and a steaming carafe in front of the stone fireplace, and had tossed another log onto the remains of their earlier cozy fire, which flickered and glowed in the friendly room, and it was beyond her to turn it down.

They sat and talked platitudes and a bit of shop. *What happened to the comfort?* a little voice inside her wailed, but Sondra sternly held back the hand that would have reached out and clasped Ben's then. Comfort was a short-lived thing, she reminded herself sternly. Women who looked for security with men were looking in the wrong place. The only security was within yourself. And she wasn't going to let herself compromise what she knew to be truth for the sake of recapturing those few minutes of heart's ease she had felt with Ben earlier.

"I probably won't see you before court tomorrow," he said when the coffee ritual had run its course and she was at the door. "I've got some appointments. Good luck, Sondra. And don't mistake—just because I don't hate Blake Roebotham doesn't mean I don't want you to wipe the floor with him. You've got this case going your way. I want to see you win it."

In light of her doubts earlier in the case, that was at least good to hear. She suddenly wanted to ask him whose decision it had been to assign this case to her and whether there were others in the Crown office who were not so concerned that she should win. But that was another conversation, and she was already at the door.

"Good night, Ben," she said, when he had kissed her.

"Good night, Sondra. See you tomorrow."

He closed the door as she set off down the hallway, and the sound of its shutting ricocheted unpleasantly down her spine. In the instant before she forced the feeling from her mind, it was as though she were being shut away from something essential, like water, or food. Something that she needed in order to survive.

Tuesday turned out to be a slow, gruelling day, during which the jury spent much of the time being excused so various points of law could be argued on the *voir dire*, and information placed before the judge for a decision as to whether it could properly be brought out before the jury.

Blake was no slouch when it came to the new Charter of Rights and Freedoms, or forensic detail, Sondra discovered. She was caught unawares by two of his appeals to the Bench—one that certain evidence she wanted to submit was tainted by improper police procedure, and one—regarding forensic testimony that the blood on the underwear was of the same rare type as Laney Meredith's blood—on the far-fetched grounds that the lab work was too sloppy for the evidence to be admitted. He felt labelling the blood slides wasn't sufficient. He wanted some technician to testify that the sample had been taken, had gone straight under a microscope and the results carried directly into court, all in the same hot little hand.

Fortunately for Sondra, because the blood type was important for establishing that the underwear found in Macomber's closet really was Laney Meredith's, Judge McVean was satisfied to question the forensic witness about the labelling techniques and whether they had been properly followed for the two specimens in question.

Of course, that didn't mean that Blake Roebotham couldn't question the witness again in front of the jury, and he made great play with how casually the slides were numbered, how many floors there were between where the specimens were taken and where they were examined, and how many different hands they passed through "before the results were offered to the jury as evidence."

"And if any one of those individuals screwed up, if you'll forgive me for the phrase, anywhere along the line, what would that mean in terms of the evidence before the jury?" Roebotham demanded righteously.

The witness, who was not easily rattled, raised an eyebrow. "That would depend on how they screwed up," he said dryly, and evoked a titter in the court.

"How many different ways are there of screwing up in the lab?" Blake asked in theatrical surprise.

"Well, you could drop the slide and break it, and that would mean starting over again with another slide," the witness outlined calmly. "Or you might get the numbers wrong and that would mean a reconciliation of all the specimens that had come into the lab that day. Or you could lose the specimen altogether."

"Or," Blake jumped triumphantly into the silence, "presumably you could assign a result to the wrong specimen altogether."

"Yup," agreed the witness without heat. "But whatever you read in the papers about medical laboratories, that doesn't happen very often in a police laboratory, and I've never heard of that sort of thing happening where we didn't find it out and correct it before it got into evidence."

"Well, of course, if it had happened, you wouldn't have heard about it, would you?" Blake pointed out dryly. "No one would know."

Sondra never knew what sort of effect this kind of argument had on the jury. Nor did anyone, she supposed. But she knew what effect it had on her: it bored and irritated her. Yet she had to remain at even greater attention than usual, because the technical aspects were not her forte, and she had to be sure nothing slipped by her through ignorance.

On redirect, she asked merely, "Mr. Billings, presumably in a police laboratory the consequences of any mistake are likely to be graver than in an ordinary medical laboratory. Would you say that the technicians who handle the tests and evidence in the police laboratory are aware of the added importance of accuracy in their work?"

"Yes, I think so. No one wants to think a criminal has gone free, or an innocent man been convicted, because they weren't accurate in their lab work. We're aware of it constantly, I would say."

"Was the blood specimen you examined as Laney Meredith's in fact blood you took from Laney Meredith?"

"To the best of my knowledge and experience and belief, it was."

"And was the specimen you examined as being taken from the underwear in Exhibit G actually blood that came from that underwear?"

"Yes, it was."

"And were those two blood samples both Type B, Rh negative?"

"Yes, they were."

"Thank you, Mr. Billings. That's all."

She got most of the evidence she wanted before the jury. But she was as exhausted by the end of the day as if she had lost every argument. At this rate, she would hardly last out the week, and fortunately she wouldn't have to. One of the points Blake had raised in the absence of the jury was the fact that he had to appear for another case on Thursday and Friday, so tomorrow was her last day for the week.

Striding back to her office at the side of her student assistant at five-thirty that afternoon, Sondra was aware of wanting two things: a long, hot bath and the company of Ben Glass over dinner. In that order.

But what you want you can't always have, Sondra told herself. If she didn't take it easy, Ben could become a habit difficult to break.

Anyway, she told herself that evening as she relaxed in her elegant tub, one out of two wasn't bad.

Aleria Franklin, the Millers' next-door neighbour, testified that she knew Hughie Macomber to speak to, that he was a friend of Matthew Miller. She had noticed Hughie Macomber "hanging around" the Miller house several times that weekend, and she had spoken with him to tell him that they were away on vacation. Hugh Macomber had said that he knew it, that Matthew Miller had asked him to feed his rabbit during his absence and otherwise keep an eye on the house.

"Did you have any further conversation about the rabbit?"

"Yes." Mrs. Franklin looked down at Hugh Macomber in the accused's box. "I told him the house was too cold for an animal. I said I had all Monica's plants because she wanted to turn the heat down, and I pointed out that we were having very cold weather and maybe the rabbit would die."

"And what did Mr. Macomber answer to that?"

"He laughed. He said it was all right. He had the rabbit in the furnace room, and it was warm enough."

Sondra paused as though to read her notes, letting the callousness of that sink in. Then she lifted her head. "Did you let it go at that?"

"No, I did not. The weather was so cold that week it caught everybody by surprise, and I asked him if he wanted to put the rabbit in our house...."

Sondra let her answer lengthily to every question and waited for Blake to object. Every word that came out of the woman's mouth showed the defendant as cruel and callous in his disregard of his victim's most basic human needs, as well as a fluent and unprincipled liar. When Blake objected to conclusions drawn by the witness, or on other grounds, he merely underlined the damaging testimony. The judge might tell the jury to ignore a certain comment, and the court reporter to strike it from the record, but mostly the damage was done as soon as Mrs. Franklin spoke, and Blake knew it.

"Now, Mrs. Franklin, I ask you to turn your attention to the morning of the eleventh of February this year. Did anything unusual happen on that day?"

"Yes, it surely did."

"Can you tell the jury about it, please?"

Taking her instruction quite literally, Aleria Franklin turned towards the jury, drew in a deep breath and began to speak in a low, indignant voice, as though she knew each member of the jury personally and was speaking to that one alone. "I was sitting at my kitchen table, it looks out on the backyard, about ten o'clock. I work shift, and I wasn't due in till noon. I was drinking a cup of coffee when I saw something move out of the corner of my eye. When I turned my head, there she was, running and staggering through the snow, barefoot, bare-legged, wrapped up in a purple cloak. I was so surprised I just sat there for a moment, and then she fell down, and I saw that she was totally bare naked, and the purple cloak was a blanket. A minute later she was screaming and banging on the back door, and I jumped up and opened it, and she just fell into the room, screaming, 'Help me, oh, God, please help me....'"

The witness seemed to falter at the memory. "How did her condition appear to you?" Sondra prompted gently.

Her condition was dreadful, and Mrs. Franklin described it to the jury with gruelling accuracy, her eyes filling with tears at the memory. She had wrapped the sobbing, shivering girl in an electric blanket and a quilt and given her a hot water bottle as well, but she had continued to shiver for a frighteningly long time. When the police and her mother arrived to take her away, she was still shivering fitfully.

"Did you know the girl's name when she came running to you for help?"

"No, I never knew her. I never saw her before."

"Did you have cause to learn her name, Mrs. Franklin?"

"Yes, I did."

"Is the girl you helped, and on whose behalf you called the police on February eleventh of this year, Laney Meredith, the plaintiff in this case?"

"Yes, she is."

"Thank you." Sondra sat down, well satisfied with the impact of her witness on the jury. If they had had any doubts about what Laney Meredith had suffered in the Miller basement, or if Blake had succeeded in raising any suspicions that she had been there voluntarily, the chilling description that they had now been given of her condition must have blown those suspicions to smithereens.

On cross-examination, Blake surprised her by asking, "How well did you know the defendant when you spoke to him about the rabbit?"

"I knew him by sight. He was with Matthew a lot."

"Did you know him by name?"

She paused. "Yes. I think so."

"So when the police asked you who you had seen on the Miller property, you gave them my client's name immediately?"

"Oh!" she said. "No, now I remember, I asked my children what was the name of Matthew's friend."

"And they gave you the defendant's name, and you relayed it to the police?"

"No, the police were there. They were there when the kids came home from school at lunchtime. They waited for the kids to come home, and I asked them then."

"And did you subsequently identify the defendant for the police?"

"What do you mean, identify him?"

"Did you see him in person and say, 'That's the man'?"

"Yes, I did."

"Was the defendant in a police lineup at the time?"

"No, he was just sitting there, and I came in and I recognized him and said so."

"Was Hugh Macomber the only suspect in the room when you saw him?"

"I guess so. There were other men around, but I think they were police."

"Was he the only black man in the room?"

"Yes, he was."

"Did they ever ask you to try to identify any other man as the man you had seen in the Miller backyard?"

"No, just the one."

"Did you ever see Hugh Macomber enter the Miller house, Mrs. Franklin?"

"No, I never did."

"Did you ever see him coming out of it?"

"No, he was just hanging ar—"

"Just answer the question, please. Did you ever see my client coming out of or going into the Miller house while the Millers were away on vaçation between February second and February sixteenth of this year?"

"No, I didn't."

"Thank you. No further questions."

Mrs. Franklin's neighbour, Mrs. Miller, was not such a damaging witness, but her testimony took its toll. She testified that she had not been aware of an agreement between her son and the defendant allowing the defendant to enter the house in the family's absence, that her son did not keep any pet, that when the family had got home the police had pointed out damage to the lock on the back door, that the lock had certainly been undamaged when they left on vacation two weeks earlier. She also testified that she had turned the heat down to the barest minimum that would keep the pipes from freezing during their absence, and that the furnace had a heat pump that forced the hot air into the upper floors of the house, so that the main part of the house was always warmer than the basement.

"Mrs. Miller," Blake said, "do you know of your own knowledge that your son did *not* give my client a key to your house?"

"My son wouldn't give anyone a key without asking me or his father about it."

"I repeat, do you know of your own knowledge that he did not?"

"I'm sure he didn't, but I don't *know* it in the way you mean."

"Thank you. Now, Mrs. Miller..."

"I can't figure him at the moment," Sondra confided later to Ben Glass. "I thought I knew what his defence was going to be, but today he challenged Aleria Franklin on how certain she was that it was Macomber she saw skulking around on the property next door, and now he seems to be leaving open the possibility that Hugh Macomber had a key to the Miller house and therefore wouldn't have had to break in. What do you think he's doing?"

Ben considered. "I think you're putting on a tough case and you've got him worried. So he may be abandoning a single line of defence for a scatter attack on your evidence."

If Ben were right, it meant that Blake could now see that his line of defence, the old standby that the victim was willing before and only changed her mind afterwards when her family started asking questions, was in danger. So he was now challenging all the testimony, hoping to convince the jury that none of the testimony was completely sound.

Sondra nodded her agreement. "Yes, that's what I would have thought, if it were anyone but Blake Roebotham. But

I don't want to be too quick to think I've got *him* on the run."

Ben looked suddenly thoughtful. "You're right," he said. "If anyone would be shrewd enough to try to make you think you already had him beaten, in the hopes that you'd get careless, Blake would be the man." He looked at her. "You're quite right. Don't underestimate him."

Sondra yawned and stretched. "Thanks, Ben," she said. "God, I'm tired! I never thought I'd be grateful to Blake Roebotham for anything, but I must say I'm glad to have the four-day weekend ahead of me, rather than two more days in court. If you don't mind, I won't be in again till Monday."

Ben opened his mouth as though to say something, then closed it. "No, go ahead, Sondra. This case seems to be taking its toll on you."

"Yeah, isn't it just?" She laughed. She wasn't enjoying the battle of wits the way she usually did, and it was exhausting her in a way that was new to her. "Probably I'm expending too much energy in personal hatred of Blake Roebotham."

Ben grinned. "I'm not walking into that one." He hesitated. "Sondra, would you like to go up to the cottage this weekend? I could let you have the key. You could go up tonight or tomorrow and have a couple of days to yourself. I'll be going up Friday."

She took a deep breath and sat up. "Oh!" she exclaimed, liking the idea enormously. "Oh, Ben, heaven! Just what I need! How do I get to the cottage from the marina? Is there a map?"

"There is. But unless you're experienced on Georgian Bay, you'll have trouble following it. If you like, I can phone Mike and Marg to let them know you're coming, and they'll take you out. They run a taxi service. It means you'd be at the cottage with no transportation except the canoe till I get there. But there's a CB radio in the kitchen, and Mike and Marg monitor Channel Thirteen twenty-four hours a day."

"I'd love it!" Sondra said. "You're sure you don't mind? You won't want to be alone to work?"

He smiled at her. "You don't stop me working, remember?"

She returned the smile and the sharing of a sweet memory. "Yes, and I mustn't forget our Saturday night bargain."

His forehead creased in a frown. "What Saturday night bar—oh, *that* Saturday night bargain! Ah, well, that won't be necessary this weekend. Those two characters don't get together again for another four chapters, and in between it's all action."

Sondra smiled sweetly, shaking her head. "Sorry," she told him. "I have a contract. My union would frown on—"

"Your union!" Ben shook his head. "I have enough evidence on your union to break it in two and put all the top brass behind bars for twenty years. And believe me, I will."

"You do that very well," Sondra told him. "Have you thought of writing for the movies and casting yourself as the corrupt deputy Crown?"

"Of course I have," he said, smiling. "Don't change the subject."

"I haven't changed the subject. I've reserved decision."

"Fine. Remanded for decision till Saturday night. It's going to cause quite a wrinkle in my plot if the decision goes against me."

"Ah, well, what's flexibility for?" Sondra shrugged.

"I just hope you have a nodding acquaintance with it," Ben said. They were laughing quietly, enjoying the nonsense after a long, too-serious day.

"With what? Flexibility?"

"Ummm," Ben agreed, his eyes alight.

Sondra drew her dignity around her. "That's for me to know, and for you to find out," she told him. But Ben got the last word.

"I'll look forward to the finding out," he said with a meaningful smile.

Chapter 11

Sondra didn't realize how much the case was getting to her until she arrived at the cottage and felt the sudden wild swing of her own unwinding. The place was cold, and Mike showed her how to turn on the central heating and a few other mechanical gadgets, then offered to light a fire for her in the grate.

But she suddenly couldn't wait to be alone. Thanking him, she ushered him out the front door and waved him off for the shortest length of time consistent with politeness, and then closed the door with a sigh of relief.

Alone, with no responsibility to anyone for two days. No one could phone and make demands on her. No one would turn up unexpectedly. Sondra's control began to slip as she realized it, until she was leaning against the door helplessly shaking.

To give her hands something to do, she crossed to the fireplace, knelt down and took sheets of old newspaper that had been stored in a pile in an antique pine box. Crushing the paper, she tossed it onto the grate. There was kindling there and everything, and she was expert at laying a fire. Her shaking fingers laid the pale, thin kindling sticks efficiently across the wadded newsprint. Then she stood and reached for the tall box of matches on the stone mantlepiece and set the paper alight in a dozen places.

Calmly, she fed bits of bark and tiny twigs into the blaze until it had a good grip on the pile of kindling, then set the large pieces of wood down in the centre of the blaze and watched as they caught and flared up.

Then, sitting on the floor in front of the roaring, comforting fire, Sondra dropped her face into her hands and burst into tears.

Oh, God, it was so ugly. It was all so ugly. This whole corrupt, theatrical setup designed to foster the ends of justice—what a farce! And never had it been so obvious to her as during this case. Her head was filled with sudden images of Blake Roebotham tearing into the victim of this ugly, vicious crime, with an expression of thinly veiled pleasure on his face as he did so.

Justice? Who got justice in the end? Nobody, nobody at all, least of all the victim! Jesus, why had they given her this case? Whose idea had it been? Who knew about her and how murderously difficult this case and Blake Roebotham would be for her? Who had wanted to compound the pressure of her first prosecution by adding to it the ugliness of her first rape case? By piling on the cruel expertise and utter consciencelessness of Blake Roebotham?

It was the feeling of helplessness that was killing her, really, touching the bottom line, over and over again, the line that said almost any woman was defenceless against almost any man who was determined to rape. All her life she had hated that feeling of helplessness. She had spent her life determined to be strong, determined never to be helpless.

She was strong in this case. She was running a very effective prosecution. She had a great deal more damning evidence, anyway, than most rape cases provided. And the circumstances surrounding the rape surely engaged the sympathy of the jury. Yet still there was this constant running battle with her own despair, her own childish, helpless panic.

Still, there was the feeling of guilt. God, she felt guilty just looking into Laney Meredith's eyes, seeing the horror one human being could bring on another in this world. She felt those eyes as an accusation of *her*—why hadn't she stopped this horror from happening to Laney Meredith? Why hadn't she been there?

Oh, God, that was ridiculous. Yet she couldn't stop it being how she felt. She couldn't stop hating herself every time Blake Roebotham won a point in Courtroom 417. And she couldn't stop feeling absolutely driven to win this case, in a way she hadn't felt since her earliest cases, a pressure that was with her now in almost every waking moment.

The sobs that marked the momentary breaking of the pressure shook her frame for a long time. When she next looked up, the fire was blazing away, throwing its heat at her. Sondra dried her cheeks shakily, feeling the relief that this release had brought, then leaned back against the chair seat and stared into the flames. What an interesting load she was carrying—paranoia and megalomania and God knew what else. No wonder she had felt the pressure to be unbearable.

She knew what the problem was now, though. Funny how you could hide something so obvious from yourself. She must be an expert at sleight of mind. And if she could joke about it, maybe she'd be able to relax a little in court from now on.

Can it be twenty years? she wondered, counting. More like twenty-one. So long ago. What had been happening then? Was it the year the Beatles came over from England and went on the *Ed Sullivan Show*?

Unbelievable. Those names were the great sunken ships of the past; approaching them was like coming on an underwater wreck and seeing the faint shape of what it had been, distorted by the encrustations of time....

Ed Sullivan. Really big shew. Really big shew. God, could it be so distant? The U.S. involvement in Vietnam scarcely even begun? Sondra laughed shakily. Had there ever been a time before Vietnam? She had been so wrapped up in that once; it had seemed like her whole life. The era of Yorkville coffee houses and bearded American conscientious objectors and protest had seemed to mark her birth to world consciousness, so that she could remember very little of what went on before. Like a butterfly, unable to remember its previous incarnation as a caterpillar, or the long days of sleep in the cocoon...

Looking at it now, she could understand something that hadn't been clear before: that those days of wild protest had followed her parents' divorce when she was fifteen. That was why what went before had seemed like a cocoon, and why she had been so determined to forget it, to find it irrelevant.

It had been the year that Karen had gone off to college, too, leaving her suddenly alone in a too-quiet house with her unhappy mother.

Of course, that wasn't when she had lost Karen. That loss had occurred three years before, when she had failed Karen so desperately and their relationship had never recovered. When Karen moved out it was just underlining the emptiness....

Funny, how it could all suddenly be so sharp. How it could all be in focus, just like that, all the reasons why this case was so difficult for her, and Blake was making her so angry...

It was no longer a question of wondering what the hell was wrong with her. Now she wondered how she had held herself together during the past week. She recalled thinking at some point that Laney Meredith was held together with twine. She laughed mirthlessly. She, too, had been held together with twine during this case. Only she had not known it.

Ben arrived late Friday afternoon. Sondra was sitting out on the island's highest point, a rock that sat about twenty feet above the water, when she saw a boat heading directly for the island. At such a distance it wasn't possible to identify the boat, but she knew quite clearly that it was Ben.

She was glad he had got away early. She hadn't been expecting him till nine or ten tonight, but she had had enough of her own company; she wanted the comfort of another human presence. A friend's presence. She told herself that any friend would have done, but it was a lie. It was Ben she wanted to see.

She scrambled over the rock and through the trees and arrived on the dock as he cut his engine and glided in. Smiling, the setting sun bright on his hair, he tossed her the painter and shouted hello. Together, with quick expertise, they made the pretty little cruiser fast. Then Ben picked up his duffle bag and a bag of groceries, and they set off for the house.

"Gorgeous day," he observed. "Has it been like this since you arrived?"

"Mmmm, fantastic," she agreed. "A bit chilly, but sunny and beautiful the whole time." But of course chilly weather was to be expected now. Last weekend had been the exception, not the rule. Sondra hadn't even brought a swimsuit.

As though picking up on her thoughts, he asked, "How's the swimming?"

She laughed. "Swimming! It's been too cold. I've been wearing a jacket. Were you hoping Indian summer would continue?"

He grinned at her as they entered the cottage, then looked around with the pleasure of a man returning home. "I like fall swimming," he said, dumping the groceries in the kitchen and then striding through to the bedroom with his duffle bag, holding her hand on his arm so that she would come with him.

He looked around at the evidence of her habitation of his bedroom with satisfaction, and that was the first moment she realized he had wondered if she would have put her things in the other bedroom. As perhaps she should have, Sondra told herself, feeling stricken. Maybe she was taking too much for granted.

But the light in his eyes as he looked into hers told her she was not.

"Well," said Ben, dropping his duffle bag and beginning to pull off his jacket, "I like swimming in this weather. How about joining me? It's invigorating."

A burst of laughter escaped her. "I believe it would be!" she told him. "No, thanks. Besides, I didn't bring a suit."

He looked at her. "There's nobody on the lake. You don't need a suit. Come on, Sondra." He continued to undress as he spoke. "Be brave. I promise you, it's an experience."

Oh, well, what was life for, if not to gain experience? With a laugh of surrender, Sondra turned to the chest of drawers where she had put her clothes. She was feeling uncharacteristically light-headed, quite unlike herself. But what did it matter? "I'm not going in naked, not in this weather. I'll wear a T-shirt."

"That's probably a good idea. Maybe it's a little late for nude swimming."

"Maybe," she agreed dryly.

The water was freezing, and every bit as invigorating as he said. But after a minute or two, it didn't seem so bad. "I suppose one could get used to it," she admitted, striking out at Ben's side towards the middle of the lake.

"Sure you could," approved Ben. "Cold is mostly a state of mind, anyhow."

They were not in the water long. Much less than halfway out into the water that divided them from the neighbouring island, they turned and started back. It was cold, all right, but Sondra discovered she was really enjoying herself. It wasn't the sort of cold that crept into your bones and made you feel sick, although it might if she stayed out longer. It was more a kind of all-enveloping cold that made her feel as though her body were part of the lake.

And then she got out of the water and remembered why *she* did *not* like fall swimming. "Ben!" she shrieked, standing in open-mouthed amazement as the light wind caught her. "My God, I'm *freezing*." Within seconds her teeth were chattering.

Ben laughed uproariously. "Don't stand there, stupid, *run*," he called, tossing her one of the towels they had dropped on the rocks.

Gratefully she clutched the thick terry cloth around her and set off up the rocks towards the compellingly welcoming vision of the cottage, Ben at her side.

"You *lied* to me," she accused him between bouts of shivering laughter. "I'm an *icicle*!"

Ben opened the door and allowed her to pass through. "How was I to know you'd climb out ten feet away from your towel?" he demanded, still laughing.

"Well, I expected the air to be cold, but not *that* cold," she muttered darkly. "It was like being on an ice floe!"

Ben, shivering now himself, was already taking long strides towards the bathroom. "It doesn't behoove a Crown Attorney to indulge in wild exaggerations," he told her. "Anyway, the best part is just beginning."

"And what's that?" she demanded suspiciously, following in his wake.

Ben bent to put the plug in the tub. "Now we take a hot bath and get warmed up again," he told her, his mouth twitching. He turned on the taps. "Come here."

She had to say one thing—she was feeling alive in every pore. Ben might be crazy, and she might have the mother and father of all colds tomorrow, but that swim had been invigorating.

"It's September, not November," Ben said, taking the towel she was clutching around herself. "You're not going to die yet."

As the tub filled, he stripped off her T-shirt and underpants, then rubbed her body and head vigorously with the towel, bringing the warm blood to the surface and causing a pleasantly sensual contradiction between warm and cold in her skin. His arms were leanly muscled but strong, and she enjoyed the buffeting as much as the returning circulation.

"Get in," he offered when the tub was nearly full. When she was in, he stripped off his swim trunks and slid in behind her, his legs encircling her and his chest against her back. The water level surged up, and the drain began a frantic gurgling. The tub was slightly larger than normal, and Ben lay back and pulled her with him. "To think that for another thousand bucks I could have had a double tub," he observed mildly. "If you're planning on sticking around, I think I'll get one installed."

"Don't rush me," she said in a Groucho Marx voice, relaxing back against his chest in gentle pleasure, because now was not the time to start discussing her three-month time frame, and anyway, she was indulging in a lazy dream of sticking around Ben Glass forever.

Which was ridiculous, but it didn't hurt to dream.

Ben was rubbing the soap into a lather between his hands, and then he picked up her right arm and began to soap it with long, sure strokes. When he moved down to her hands, the stroking changed metre, and he rubbed the suds into her knuckles and between her fingers and massaged her palm with those long, strong fingers that were looking more and more sensual to her.

Left arm next, and then his soap-slicked hands slid underwater and moved competently over her breasts and stomach, massaged her shoulders, her neck, her flanks, straying firmly to the extent of his arms' reach and finding the curling little nest of hair between her thighs.

His touch was delicate, teasing, but very knowing, and Sondra made a little noise of pleasure in her throat as she felt her eyelids droop. After a moment his hands slid away to her flanks again, and she knew why: she could feel his body hardening against the small of her back.

Lazily she moved to a sitting position, then turned to face him on her knees, and they smiled knowingly at each other.

She bent down and kissed his body and had the pleasure of hearing the breath catch in his throat. His flesh was warm, with water and with the blood that pulsed underneath, but she knew that her mouth was even warmer, and she parted her lips and took him into that heat, shocking both of them with the suddenness of the sensation.

He lifted his hands and touched her head. "Not too much," he warned gently. "Not now." But she only grunted acknowledgement, using her knowledge of him to tease and excite him with her tongue and lips and from time to time, very gently, with her teeth. When she felt his body rise instinctively, searching, she moved into that long, stroking rhythm that she knew it demanded.

"Stop now," he said after only a moment of that, during which his body had swelled in her mouth to a hardness that made her tremble. "Sondra, no more."

She ignored him. Immediately his hands clenched in her hair, and he tried to stop her. Then, after another moment, his hands in her hair clenched for another reason, and she heard him moan and felt the heaving of his body in the same instant, and tasted the musk on her tongue, and smiled inside.

When his shudders subsided, she gently lifted her head and exchanged a smile with him. His eyes were half-lidded with pleasure. "Bad," he said, but the pleasure in his voice belied the word. "You weren't supposed to do that."

"According to whose game plan?" she challenged softly, still smiling with the pleasure his pleasure had given her.

"Mine," he admitted. "But I like yours. What else is on it?"

"I don't know," she confessed. "I play by ear. But I think we get out of the tub now before it gets cold."

"Mmm," he grunted, savouring the languorousness in his limbs. "Maybe I can move."

Still kneeling between his legs, Sondra rinsed the last of the soap from her skin and got out of the bath. "Shall I draw you some hot water till you're ready to move?" she asked, not waiting for his answer, but suiting the action to the words as she spoke.

Ben watched her as she bent over the taps, the lazy satisfied look slowly leaving his eyes, to be replaced by a more urgent one. "Come back here," he ordered quietly, but she knew the languor had settled in his limbs, and the tone of his voice was an empty threat.

She shook her head, already wrapping herself in a fresh, warm towel.

"I'm getting a drink," she said, smiling down into his eyes, unable to hide her satisfaction over the effect she had had on him. "Would you like a drink?"

Ben looked at her steadily, a challenge in those half-lidded eyes that promised the evening wasn't yet over. "Yes, all right," he said after a moment. "If you want to be under the influence, that's all right with me." He reached for the soap. "There's some white wine in the bag. I intended that for this evening. Among other things."

Wondering just what else he might be intending for the evening, Sondra escaped to the bedroom, where she towelled her hair and body dry and slipped on her white terry robe.

Then she went to the kitchen and unpacked the groceries. A thick, luscious-looking steak, bacon, fresh vegetables and half a dozen ears of the season's last corn. If nothing else, he had intended to eat well this weekend, she thought.

By the time she had opened the wine and returned to the living room, Ben, in a deep maroon-coloured bathrobe, his wet hair curling against his head, was stoking up the fire.

He turned and watched as she entered, the bottle in one hand, two glasses in the other, trying to hold closed the front of her bathrobe, which had suddenly worked itself loose.

"Very nice," Ben observed as she set the bottle and glasses down on the little table.

"Nice wine," she said softly, pouring the two heavy crystal glasses full.

"Is it?" Ben whispered hoarsely, slipping his arms inside the robe and around her back, pulling her to him as their lips met in a kiss. "I chose it because it matches your hair."

She looked up, laughing. "What?" she demanded in disbelief.

"Silky, pale and golden," he told her, nuzzling.

"Very dry, too, I see."

"Don't be so unromantic," he commanded, pulling her down onto the sofa beside him. He handed her one glass and took the other, and they lifted their glasses to each other.

"Here's to great sex," said Sondra with a smile as Ben watched her over the rim of his glass. He wasn't smiling.

"Here's to great love," said Ben, and drank.

But though Sondra held the glass to her lips, she did not drink. She couldn't. She was choking with an emotion she did not recognize. And her throat was closed as surely as if a hand squeezed it.

He cooked the dinner, a delicious steak, with an exotic salad, and potatoes baked in garlic butter. They ate as twilight stole over the lake and the first stars appeared, and there was a peace in her heart that she was new to.

It had to do with the look that had been in Ben's eyes ever since his toast to love at the fireplace, and the fact that there was no one in whose eyes she had ever before wanted to see that look.

It wouldn't last, of course. But she could enjoy it while it did; and she would enjoy, too, the times of melting in her own heart as her eyes registered the shape of his head in lamplight, or the movement of his hand against a backdrop of trees and lake and sky.

She would never afterwards remember what they talked about while they washed the dishes together in the warm, friendly kitchen, or later, as they sat wrapped in each other's arms in front of the fire. Nothing serious, nothing important, she knew that much. But it was all wrapped in a special glow that softened every word, gave every touch and look a deeper significance.

In the silence, once, a flock of geese flew squawking overhead. They listened till the sound receded in the distance, and then Ben said, "Winter's coming."

It seemed profound. "Yes," she said with a little shudder. "I hate winter." She didn't, always, but somehow in that moment "winter" seemed to signify more than just cold temperatures and snow. The world was a harsh place, as cruel as the harshest winter, and sometimes she was afraid of what lay ahead for the human race.

"It's all a question of being ready for it," Ben said, and she wasn't sure that he was referring to merely another Canadian winter. Had he heard the echo of a deeper despair in her? "Storing up what you're going to need."

"What do you store up against nuclear winter?" she asked, because only here and now, only in Ben's arms, was it suddenly safe to let the despair show.

"Love," said Ben. "We store up love. It's the only thing that's safe."

She had never thought of love as *safe* before, but in Ben's arms, just here and just now, she could believe it. Just here, and just now, it suddenly seemed the safest thing in the world.

Soon, but not too soon, he stood and drew her up after him, and, still closely wrapped in each other, they went into the bedroom. He slipped her robe off gently, slowly, without a word, and lifted the blankets while she slid between cool sheets. Then, in the faint starlight that glowed through the window, he undressed himself, and then his warmth was beside her.

He loved her slowly, gently, less with passion than with love, as though to show her that passion was only one expression of love, empty on its own. She responded with a tearing need that frightened her, her body rising to his touch with a mewing cry that she had never before heard herself make.

Except perhaps seven years ago, a distant memory suggested, but that was long ago and far away, and she did not want to remember that this was the feeling she had run from.

His hand was a hand of fire, writing letters of flame on her soul, and the message was one that had been waiting for her since before time. Flesh was gone; there was no flesh, only dark, vast spaces that ignited a shower of shooting sparks wherever they brushed together.

This was beyond sex; it was union. But when his body entered hers at last, she knew that sex was the passage to this union, that the acts of their bodies reflected what went on light-years away, and yet here and now, in another region that was her part of the universe, and his.

The building pleasure that his body made in hers was a pleasure not only of the flesh, but of their entire being, hers and his, that in that distant realm were now one. And as it peaked and exploded in and around them, she found a truth that she had been seeking through eternity, and captured it, and brought back . . . only the faintest distillation of its essence.

"I love you," she whispered when she was Sondra again, and he was Ben. "I love you," said Ben. And though the words did not express what they had learned, and what they knew, they were the only words that came close.

Chapter 12

During the night the weather broke, and they awoke in the morning to a dark sky and the sound of heavy rain being driven against the windows.

"That doesn't sound as though it's about to let up," Sondra observed, stretching in her warm cocoon as Ben stood by the window looking out.

"It doesn't look like it, either," he said. "I think it's a day around the fire for us."

They made a simple breakfast and ate it without speaking very much—rather to Sondra's relief, because this morning she felt sluggish and uncommunicative. Then, after Ben had made a roaring fire in the grate, by quiet mutual consent they settled down to work, Ben on his book and Sondra in front of her briefcase.

She faked it for a while, but her heart wasn't in it. She had only one more witness to put on the stand before she rested her case, and that was Dr. Zimmerman, who was again not very happy at having to abandon her patients at short notice to sit in a courtroom. Sondra had assured her that she would be called first thing Monday and would be through probably before lunch, but she could understand the doctor's skepticism and ire.

She also knew what testimony she hoped to get from the doctor and basically how she intended to get it, and there wasn't much more to be done. She had spent Thursday evening and a lot of Friday working on the case already, including giving a great deal of thought to whether Blake would put his client on the stand, and how she would approach him in cross-examination if he did.

After half an hour, she gave up on her briefcase and wandered over to the bookcase against the kitchen wall. Unlike the usual run of cottage bookcases, it wasn't filled with damp and moth-eaten tomes from unknown authors circa 1928 and 1951. It was a real library of what looked like well-read hardcover and paperback novels, a legal text or two, and a fair amount of philosophy, poetry and literature.

None of which she wanted to read at the moment. In sudden decision, she turned back to the room. "Ben?" she asked tentatively, hoping she wasn't driving an entire train of thought from his head. "Can I say something?"

Rather abstractedly, he turned. "Sure, go ahead."

"You said I could read your manuscript in progress. May I read it now?"

If he had been less preoccupied, she wondered, would he have said yes? Maybe not, but he was, and he did, turning to pull open a drawer and extracting a dauntingly thick sheaf of typescript from it. "There you are," he said. "Mind if I don't stop to talk?"

She shook her head, taking the pages from him with a smile and a brief, "Thanks." He turned away instantly as his other world reclaimed him, and with more than a little excited curiosity, Sondra sank down on the sofa, pulled the comforter snugly around her and settled in to read.

The hours passed away in companionable silence, while the wind gusted heavily against the cottage, carrying the driving rain against shingles and glass with a violent thrumming that let up only at odd, brief moments.

They kept a friendly fire going all through the day.

Ben's book was heavily and intricately plotted, a fast and suspenseful story about an aging West Coast hippie marijuana grower who ran afoul of mafia's trafficking in hard drugs and, of course, couldn't go to the police about it. He had a couple of moments of facing unexpected, sudden death—two of which were much more imaginatively contrived, Sondra felt, than the Mafia could manage—but it all made for exciting reading.

The major twist in the plot was that the imaginative murder attempts weren't contrived by the Mafia at all, a fact that Jude, the hero, figured out after a while. That meant two lots of people were after him, and he didn't know who the second lot was.

In spite of almost constant danger, and in spite of the fact that a prime suspect in the imaginative attempts to do away with him was a woman named Jennie towards whom he felt a powerful sexual attraction, the man wasn't without a sense of humour, and towards the end Sondra was alternately sucking in her breath in shock or fear, and then expelling it in laughter. Then came the typed copy of the scene she had read last weekend, between Jude and Jennie, and there, abruptly, the writing ended.

She sat up in dismay, it occurring to her for the first time what it meant to read a work in progress. It meant she would have to wait for the outcome to be written before she could read it! Opening her mouth to let out a wail of dismay, she looked over to where Ben was engrossed in his writing and stifled the reaction. He would be stopping soon enough for something to eat anyway. She would ask him to tell her the ending over dinner.

And she might as well cook it. Stacking the manuscript pages neatly on the little table, Sondra got to her feet and moved quietly to the kitchen, and for the next hour was involved in concocting a meal, all the while imagining various endings for the story. When the meal was nearly ready, she stood in the doorway for a moment, watching him work.

"Ben?" she asked tentatively. Never having been in close quarters with a writer before, she half expected a growl of annoyance.

But he merely finished the word he was writing and looked up. "Dinner ready?" he asked. "Smells delicious."

"Ten more minutes," she told him. "Is that all right?"

"That's fine. I'll just finish this, and then I'll come."

He was as good as his word; he was ready to eat while the food was fresh and hot, a fact Sondra appreciated. She had taken trouble with the meal, and she would have hated having to keep it warm.

"It's an exciting story," she told him as they ate. "Is it nearly finished now?"

"About a third to go. Did you enjoy reading it?" He asked as though he really wanted to know, and so she told him how exciting it was to read and how impatient she was to know the ending, which was true. She didn't tell him that it was really a man's book and that his female character was rather too shallow to catch women readers.

She did tell him that she found his hero's philosophizing fascinating. "Are you publishing this under your own name?" she demanded.

"If it gets published at all, yes. Why not?"

"Well, your hero makes some pretty liberal statements on the subject of marijuana, wouldn't you say, for the alter ego of a Crown Attorney who's prosecuted some notorious drug cases?"

He grinned in acknowledgement. "Maybe my alter ego knows I need a breather. I can't speak out in public, as a Crown, to say that I think the laws need reforming, but they do. I think Jude is quite right when he points out that, however addictive it may be, marijuana doesn't kill people the way drunk driving and drunken blackout murders do. Nor does it—so far as we know—cause lung cancer."

Sondra sighed. "Oh, well, our generation is out of date, really, isn't it? Everybody's getting into these awful hard drugs nowadays. Is that why the delineation between Jude with his B.C. marijuana fields and the Mafia with their cocaine and heroin is so sharply drawn?"

"I am interested in making the point about the contrast, I admit," Ben said with a grin, ironically eyeing the glass of the legal drug she had poured for him before he lifted it for a sip. "But I really just wanted to write a good adventure yarn as a second string to my bow, and as a way of providing me with a year or two of sabbatical. Let's face it, the law is a pretty tame companion, year in and year out. I want to live a little more fully."

"And have you got a publisher interested yet?"

"One American publisher has been encouraging, but with a first novel they said they'd wait to see the complete manuscript before committing themselves."

"But you have written a legal text, Ben. In fact, two."

"First *novel*, Sondra. The two legal texts to my credit got me the polite response. I doubt if a first-time *author* would have got even that much."

"Oh. It sounds difficult."

He grinned. "I really don't know. What I do know is that the book is far from sold, and its being good is not going to be any guarantee of anything."

"Well," she said, laughing, "if you appear on Peter Gzowski, Ben, tell him from me to put his guests in seats that make them appear a little more comfortable. They always look as though they're waiting outside the principal's office!"

"Peter Gzowski's show went off the air some time ago, Sondra," he told her with exaggerated care, repressing a grin. "Could you be thinking of Phil Donahue?"

"Wrong!" she carolled. "He's got a new show now. I read it in the *Globe* just the other day. But I have to admit," she said grinning, "I didn't know his old one had gone off the air till I read that about his new one. I don't like talk shows much. I probably haven't watched one since 1978."

"That would account for it, certainly," Ben agreed, swirling the wine appreciatively around on his tongue. "I remember 1978. It was a good year."

He held his wineglass up, propping his elbow on the table, smiling questioningly into her eyes. "Yes?" he prompted.

"Vintage," she agreed, feeling the answering smile twitch the corners of her lips. "A very good year."

"'The fundamental things apply, as time goes by,'" he quoted softly, and she remembered how the song from *Casablanca*, the original cut from the movie, had been issued as a single that year, and how much, being an old movie buff, she had loved it, with Bogie saying right in the middle, "'Here's looking at you, kid.'"

Ben repeated the toast and drank, and there was a sudden, sharp pang in her heart, and she thought, Was it necessary to run away from this? Have the past seven years really been wasted as he said?

And that brought her up with a sharp shock. Waste? She had never applied that word to any part of her life before, and she wasn't starting now. Some people, Ben included, might think that abandoning the emotions for the sake of a sense of personal security and independence was a waste, but *she* did not.

She had chosen career, though it had been more instinctively than consciously done, and she had chosen well. She was well on her way at thirty-three. By fifty she intended to be either federal Attorney General, if she went the political route, or a Supreme Court Justice, if she did not. Both paths were still open to her, though she seemed to be tending towards the latter. Politics was just as interesting, but a good deal less savoury, than she had imagined when she was starting out. Sondra remained involved with a federal party in her riding, and the day might come when she began to push for the nomination, but she was beginning to wonder. The law had its moral problems, too, but at least as a judge she could hope to effect changes to the system rather than fighting *within* it as she did now. And surely, no matter how desperately the system needed revising, there would not be so much compromise along the way in justice as in politics?

Ben's dark face swam back into focus, and she awoke with a start. He was smiling quizzically at her. "You've been gone a long time," he observed. "Were you making those nasty frowns in 1978?"

Smiling, she shook her head. "1998," she confessed. "But it started out in 1978."

"You move very fast," he said admiringly. "No wonder you got away from me so easily."

Looking at Ben, she thought suddenly, You're not content with the here and now as I am. You're not content to leave the past behind. You can't help mixing the past with the present. It's the way you live. Maybe you're mixing the future in, too, right at this moment.

But I can't live that way. I started leaving the past behind when I was twelve years old, because it was the only way to survive, and now it's such a habit I can't live any other way.

She wanted, suddenly, to warn him. To say, don't put me in the picture you're making of the future. Don't think of me as the same woman you knew seven years ago. I'm the eternal caterpillar, Ben, and soon I'll be wrapping my life with you in a cocoon, and then everything will change. I'll change, and I won't remember this.

She felt tears prick her eyes, and she forced them resolutely back. There's no use crying about it, she told herself. It's the way I am.

All at once she seemed to be looking at Ben through the wrong end of a telescope. No matter what I said to you last night, Ben, she wanted to tell him, the present is all I have to offer. And I've been a fool, and taking a fool's chances. Because the present won't satisfy you now any more than it did seven years ago. Seven years ago I moved fast enough to get away. What are the odds that I'm slower now, especially where you're concerned, and that this time it won't be so easy?

This time the butterfly might get her wings scorched.

"Dr. Zimmerman, could you tell the jury, please, what your professional specialty is?" Sondra asked when the doctor's credentials had been established.

"Yes, the bulk of my practice is work with children and adolescents who have been sexually molested."

"Is Laney Meredith your patient, Doctor?"

"Yes, she is."

"When did she first come to you for treatment?"

"I saw Laney for the first time on February fourteenth of this year. Her mother brought her to me for a preliminary interview."

"Did Mrs. Meredith tell you at that time why she was bringing Laney to see you?"

"She said that Laney had suffered repeated rape and confinement over a period of several—"

"Objection. What the plaintiff's mother told this witness isn't binding on the defendant," Blake interrupted.

"Sustained."

"After that first interview, did you see her again?"

"Yes. Laney became a regular patient with me."

"And how often did you see her?"

"Once a week for an hour."

"How long did that go on, Doctor?"

"Laney is still my patient. Her experience was an extremely traumatic one, and she is still working to come to terms with it."

"Could you tell us, in layman's terms, the nature of the psychological trauma Laney suffered as a result of the events of February eighth, ninth and tenth this year?"

Andrea Zimmerman might not be experienced on the witness stand, but she had a plainspoken way about her that had none of the consciousness of superiority that Sondra had run into with many a medical witness who was more experienced. She did not speak like God handing down a commandment, but human to human, and in Sondra's opinion the jury had to respond favourably.

The terms Dr. Zimmerman chose to describe Laney's personality trauma were easy, lay language and had the effect of making the tragedy seem much more immediate than distant medical terminology would have done. That kind of testimony was the bane of a lawyer's life, but Sondra knew from experience that it wasn't entirely deliberate. Many modern medical doctors had real and actual difficulty speaking in ordinary language to ordinary people. She looked around as she returned to her table for some notes, wishing Ben were here to hear this, but his murder had finally come to trial this morning.

"Dr. Zimmerman, at my request, did you have cause to make a particular examination of Laney Meredith?"

"Yes, I did."

"What did that entail, please?"

"As I understood it, Laney was unable to make a positive identification of the underwear found with her other clothes by police. You asked me to examine her in an attempt to discover whether that inability was rooted in her trauma. I examined Laney both physically and psychiatrically."

"And what was your opinion in that regard?"

The psychiatrist took a breath and rested her hands on the wooden barrier in front of her. "Well," she said, "on the one hand, Laney's refusal to positively identify the underwear was understandable from the point of view that the underwear was relatively new, was of a popular brand, plain white in colour and had no particular marks on it that she would recognize.

"On the other hand, she showed signs of extreme discomfort and distress when presented with the items of underwear. She wouldn't touch the items and could scarcely be brought to look at them. In my opinion, that sort of distress is caused when an individual who is inwardly denying something is faced with the facts that make denial impossible."

"What do you mean by denial, please, Doctor?" asked Sondra.

"In layman's terms, I mean the attitude a person adopts when something is too painful to face. Most of us, for example, deny the death of a loved one when it first happens, especially if the death has been sudden or unexpected. In one part of our minds we know the death is a fact. Yet with another part of us, we keep expecting to see our loved one, or hear their voice. We turn to tell them something and discover with renewed pain that they aren't there. It is a psychic defence pattern to deny knowledge that is too difficult to accept all at once."

"I see. And Laney Meredith is experiencing denial with regard to the events of February eighth and subsequently?"

The doctor's testimony on that point was clear and emphatic. Laney couldn't accept all at once the dreadful fact of what she had gone through in the basement. So her psyche was protecting her by denying inside what she had experienced.

The underwear made denial impossible. It was a vivid reminder of the truth. So Laney's psyche made the simple choice: she refused to accept that the underwear was hers.

Hearing the testimony, Sondra was struck by the enormous leap forward Laney had taken during her own testimony towards learning to accept what had happened. They had all watched the transformation. If only the jury could make the connection, could understand how much courage the girl had shown that day....

Blake Roebotham was speaking in an undertone to his assistant, Sondra saw. She glanced at the doctor. She might be annoyed at having to abandon her clients today, but there was no doubt she was an ally. The warmth of her regard for her patient and her anger at the attack were obvious.

Sondra said quietly, so that her tone would not alert Blake, "Dr. Zimmerman, you've examined the underwear yourself?"

"Yes, I have."

"And you've heard Laney Meredith's description of how her own underwear was cut off her with a knife?"

The doctor clenched her jaw. "Many times."

"Dr. Zimmerman, what do you think are the chances that two sets of underwear of identical size and brand and degree of newness could be discovered cut and stained with blood in this way?"

"I suppose it depends on how many women Hugh Macomber has raped and terrorized in this way," she said flatly.

Suddenly awake to what was being said, Blake leaped to his feet, frothing in indignation. "Objection, Your Honour! That comment is entirely gratuitous! It is prejudicial to my client! I move that it be struck from the record."

"It is so ordered," said the judge to the court reporter. He turned to the jury. "The jury will ignore the last statement of the witness. Confine yourself to making statements of your own knowledge, Doctor."

"Yes, Your Honour."

"Doctor, what is your professional opinion with regard to this underwear?" Sondra asked, hoping the doctor would once more take the ball and run with it. She was not disappointed.

"In my opinion, there can be no doubt that the underwear in question was the underwear Laney was wearing when she was raped and that, as she learns to deal with and accept what happened to her, she will also be able to accept this very graphic reminder of her helplessness at her attacker's hands."

God, she was brilliant. *She* should go into politics, Sondra thought. And it was exactly twelve twenty-five. "Thank you very much, Dr. Zimmerman. Your witness," she added to Blake.

Blake rushed to his feet, hoping the judge would not notice the time until he had got in a question or two. In no way did he want to send the jury out to lunch mulling over this testimony without challenging it.

"Dr. Zimmerman—" he began, but it wasn't his lucky day.

"Mr. Roebotham," said Judge McVean, "since it's within minutes of the time for noon adjournment, I think this is a natural place to break." He looked at the bailiff. "Court is adjourned till two-thirty."

As the jury left the room, Blake wandered over to the Crown's table. "Is this your last witness?" he said, arms akimbo on his hips as he stretched and screwed his face up in a yawn.

"Yes," she said, trying not to let her dislike get the better of her. It wouldn't hurt to tell him that. "We should rest our case this afternoon."

Blake nodded thoughtfully, his chin and jaw pushed out. "Interesting witness. Very self-possessed. Wonder if she loses it in bed?"

He had turned to Sondra's male junior and was ostensibly making the grinning remark to him, but Sondra knew exactly how the remark was intended. She wanted to slam the lid of her briefcase, but she didn't. Blake thrived on knowing he'd scored a hit. And it was one of those comments that would be dignified by any response at all.

"Ready?" she asked her junior, who was torn between his boyish pride at having been included in the male clique by Blake Roebotham and his faint consciousness that there was something wrong in that kind of comment. He got to his feet eagerly.

"Yup!" he said.

She nodded coolly to Blake when she left, not trusting herself to speak.

Chapter 13

Oh, not *now*!'' Sondra muttered in exasperation, and at her tone the others at the table, Ben and her junior and Ben's junior, turned involuntarily in the direction she was looking. Blake Roebotham, with two other men in tow, was coming their way.

Ben frowned at her, just as though she were a schoolgirl talking out of turn, she told herself angrily, and in return she stared coldly at him.

''You have your opinion. I have mine,'' she reminded him evenly. ''Did you by any chance think that made my opinion invalid?'' She was aware, as she spoke, that, as a man, Ben was taking a little of the heat that ought to be reserved for Blake Roebotham, but tough! She'd taken enough of other women's heat from men in her day.

Ben looked startled. ''What?'' he said. ''What's the matter?''

Blake's party was already pulling out chairs, and Blake was chatting enthusiastically with everyone at the table, of course not excluding Sondra. She sighed inwardly, waiting for it, knowing it wouldn't be long in coming. It wasn't.

"So, did Sondra tell you all about her little tame psy-chi-a-trist?" Blake began as soon as there was a pause in the conversation. He said it that way, all the syllables separately, and the impression it left was that of a general all-round putdown.

Ben was immediately interested. "No." He looked at her. "How did she do?"

"Oh, well! Very well!" Blake answered for her. He clapped his hands and rubbed them together. "I'm looking forward to sinking my... teeth into her this afternoon. Yes sir, I am looking forward to that."

Nothing she could say. No way she could think of to call him on it. Everybody at the table had got the innuendo, and they would all respond to it as men first and as human beings not at all.

"This afternoon, eh?" said one of Blake's buddies, laughing obsequiously. Sondra made a mental note that he must be hoping to be made a partner in the firm. "That's fast work even for you, isn't it, Blake?"

"Speak to my procurer here," Blake said magnanimously, indicating Sondra. "She arranged this for me." He laughed. "Unfair practices, Sondra. You know my tastes too well." He turned to the others. "See, now I have to make a choice. If I screw the good doctor on the witness stand..." He shrugged, leaving their imaginations to complete the idea.

And they were all smiling the bland, silly masculine smiles that men routinely put on in such conversations, and Sondra was aware of a sickening loneliness and an overriding fury. This she was not going to let pass, whatever the cost. She tossed the remains of her sandwich onto her tray; she wasn't hungry anyway.

"Blake," she said without heat, "I resent your attitude, your comments and your implications about my witness, who is a professional woman at the top of her profession. In my opinion, it is your obligation to respect that, in exactly the same way as you expect respect—as a *professional*—regardless of anyone's personal opinion of your self, your methods or your morality." She stood up, her hands on her tray, looking straight at him. "You in particular should be very careful about letting the personal into professional judgements, in case it should lay you open to judgement by the same attitude."

"Touché!" she heard someone murmur mock-admiringly, but before anything more could be said, she picked up her tray and left the table. Emptying her tray into the trash bin, she discovered she was shaking with reaction. God, she despised him. There wasn't a human being alive on earth for whom she had such contempt and hatred.

Yet she was aware that the basis of his personality was weakness. If he did not feel himself fundamentally weak, he would not need the constant reiteration of masculine superiority to convince himself of his strength. What he was basically hoping to prove was that, no matter how weak he felt himself to be, he was still stronger than fifty percent of the population, simply because he was a man.

And the others at the table—was it in their interest as men to have one among them carrying the banner in this way? Sondra shook her head. She only knew that the deep and abiding fury she was feeling wasn't directed at Blake Roebotham at all. Her outburst just now had scarcely mitigated it.

And that was because the fury was directed at Ben. Ben, who had sat there like all the others, grinning at her as she spoke, letting Blake get away with the mental equivalent of rape—against her, against Dr. Zimmerman, against all women.

"Dr. Zimmerman, are you a follower of Sigmund Freud?" Blake Roebotham asked as court reconvened.

She paused. "Well, in some respects everyone in psychiatry and psychotherapy is a follower of Freud, in that Freud was a pioneer of the psychoanalytic method. However, much has been discovered in the field since his day, and although I have great respect for him as a pioneer in my field, I am not a *disciple* of Freud. I disagree with some of his theory, and in particular his conclusions with regard to the psychology of women."

"Thank you, that's a very full answer. Much more thorough than a simple yes or no, if a little less enlightening." Sarcasm just brushed the tips of his words, like gilt on scrollwork. A flicker of irritated comprehension crossed the psychiatrist's face.

"Should I restrict myself to yes or no answers?" she asked gently. "I'm sorry if that wasn't clear. No, I am not a disciple of Sigmund Freud."

Jesus, Sondra wondered admiringly, did she *know* she sounded just like a mother? Could a knack like that possibly be unconscious?

Blake looked down at his notes, and Sondra was almost sure the doctor had got to him. She sat forward, suddenly feeling like a spectator at a hockey game.

"Were you required to study Freud's theories during your psychiatric training?"

"Yes."

"Is that a requirement for any psychiatrist?"

"It was in my day. I believe it still is."

"So you are familiar with Freud's theories?"

"Fairly familiar. I've been practicing for over twelve years, and I imagine I've forgotten a certain amount."

"Tell us, if you will, Sigmund Freud's theories on the subject of female rape fantasy."

Sondra stood up. "If the Court please, what's the purpose of this line of questioning? This has no bearing whatsoever on the case, or on this witness's previous testimony. My learned colleague's questions should be limited to the exploration of what has been brought up in examination-in-chief."

Blake raised tolerant eyebrows. "Your Honour, this witness is testifying as an expert in psychiatry. She has made comments about certain psychiatric theories as part of her testimony. The defence is entitled to explore her credentials as a psychiatrist and to bring out other theories that might have a bearing on her patient's behaviour."

"I'm going to permit a few more questions along this line for the moment, but let's not get too far afield here, Mr. Roebotham."

"Thank you, Your Honour. Dr. Wasserman?"

Someone in the court tittered. The doctor looked tolerantly down at the defence lawyer. "My name is Zimmerman," she explained kindly as though to a thick child who was doing its best.

"Yes, of course, Dr. Zimmerman. I apologize."

She smiled expectantly and said nothing.

"Could you outline for us Dr. Freud's theories on rape?"

She opened her eyes at him. "As I explained, I am not a Freudian, and furthermore, just at the moment there is a great deal of controversy on the subject of what his theories were at the end of his life."

"Well, what were they at the beginning of his life? Or I suppose I should say, at the beginning of his career in psychiatry? Can you tell us that?"

"At the beginning of his career Freud accepted that the rapes his women clients told him about were factual."

"What?" Blake demanded, obviously surprised.

"Freud accepted what his patients told him with regard to incest and child rape," she repeated.

"Well, now, I'm no psychiatrist, Doctor, but isn't it a well-known fact that Sigmund Freud said that almost all women's stories about rape were pure fan—"

"Your Honour, my learned friend is quite right. He is not a psychiatrist, and he is not entitled to testify as a psychiatric expert. He's not entitled to testify at all unless he's sworn as a witness," Sondra interposed coolly.

"You'll have to find another way at getting at what you want, Mr. Roebotham," the judge agreed.

"Dr. Zimmerman, did Freud ever change his mind about the theory you've just outlined?"

"Yes, he did. There's evidence now that he changed it twice, once to disagree with his early beliefs, and then later, before he died, it now appears he began to question the theory of his middle years and returned to his earlier belief."

"During his middle years, as you call them, what percentage of rapes did Freud think were the products of the complainant's own fantasies?"

"Because of the overwhelmingly high incidence of such stories among his patients, Freud found it difficult in his middle years to accept them as factual. At that time, he theorized that most of such incidents were based on fantasy," Dr. Zimmerman said. "However, recently there has been reason to believe that at the end of his life Freud was coming to question his own theory. That's a highly controversial issue among Fr—"

"Thank you, Dr. Zimmerman, just answer the question. Now, is it possible that a patient could lie to her own psychiatrist?"

"Yes, of course it's possible."

"Does that happen often?"

"With some patients it happens in the initial stages... I wouldn't say it happens often, no."

"Have you ever been lied to by a patient, Doctor?"

She paused a moment. "Not that I can recall at the moment. There are different ways of lying, of course, but I can't recall an outright material lie. It doesn't happen very often."

"But it does happen?"

"Yes, of course it does. I imagine it happens in courtrooms, too. Whenever you deal with people, you are dealing with a human element."

"Thank you. Try to restrict yourself to the question, if you will, Doctor. We don't want this to take all day." He fixed her with a look. "Dr. Zimmerman, could Laney Meredith be lying to you?" he demanded suddenly.

She wasn't rattled. "About what?" she asked with interest.

"About her story of being raped by my client!"

"Are you asking for my professional opinion as to whether my client has been lying to me for eight months?"

"No. I am asking you whether the possibility exists that she could be lying."

"As a professional with many years' experience, I do not believe that she—"

"I'm not asking for what you believe now. I am asking for the possibilities. Isn't it *possible* that your client is lying to you?"

"Under the theoretical conditions that anything is possible, I suppose it is, but I don't—"

"Isn't it possible, Dr. Zimmerman, that your patient was quite happy to be in Hugh Macomber's company until she found she had to explain to her parents where she had been and with whom, and out of fear she started lying and has been lying ever since?"

The psychiatrist looked at him coldly. "Do you want a professional opinion as to human possibility, or a discussion of mathematical possibility?"

"I want to know what is possible in this case."

"In my professional opinion, in human terms, what you suggest is impossible. I don't think I am qualified to discuss *mathematical* possibilities, Mr. Roebotham."

Sondra felt like cheering.

"Dr. Zimmerman, are you a feminist?" Blake asked, startling the courtroom and the witness with this sudden change of subject.

She thought for a moment and then smiled. "You'll have to define that word for me before I can answer you."

"Are you married, Dr. Zimmerman?" Blake asked without pausing.

"No."

"Have you ever been married?"

"Yes, I have."

"And how did your marriage terminate?"

"Oh, Your Honour, I object. This is irrelevant," Sondra said. "What bearing can this witness's marital status possibly have?"

"What's the purpose of this line of questioning, Mr. Roebotham?" the judge asked.

"Your Honour, this witness has just testified in human terms. It strikes me that her own human condition must have a bearing on that judgement. My client has a right to try to show bias on the part of a witness."

"Bias!" Sondra repeated in surprise. "What sort of bias is my learned friend hoping to show against *this* witness?"

"Your Honour—"

"If you're going to be discussing what bias you hope to show, we'd better have the jury excused," ordered the judge.

When the twelve had filed out, Blake began, "Your Honour, the attitude of feminists towards the subject of rape is well-known, and not everyone agrees with their beliefs. This witness's testimony has been very telling against my client. She has stated unequivocally that the plaintiff is telling the cold, stone truth. My client has a right to show a possible feminist bias, stemming from rabid, lock-up-all-men-whether-they're-guilty-or-not, antirape sentiments."

"Your Honour..." Sondra, torn between amusement and outrage, restrained herself with a superhuman effort, because an emotional outburst on the part of counsel would only irritate the judge and prejudice her position. "This is about as farfetched as any barrel-scraping it's been my privilege to hear. This witness is a professional and has testified as a professional. To suggest that any personal opinions she holds would influence that testimony with the purpose of deliberately frustrating the ends of justice is an extremely serious allegation. And my learned colleague has no grounds whatsoever for such a suggestion."

"Mr. Roebotham, have you any grounds for making the suggestion?"

"Well, Your Honour, the witness is a woman and therefore part of a segment of the population that has expressed itself recently as being in revolt against the establishment...."

Some people in the courtroom began to laugh.

"Quite," said the judge dryly, not without amusement. "I don't think this line of questioning is justified, Mr. Roebotham. The witness is, as Ms. Holt has stated, a professional woman. I think we have to rely on her impartiality before the court."

The jury came back in while Sondra was still metaphorically shaking her head over Blake's stupidity. Was it the product of masculine rage, or did this kind of tactic actually *work* with some judges? God help justice if it did.

When the jury was seated, Blake stood looking at them sorrowfully, as though apologizing for his inability to uncover the evidence he knew they should have from this witness. He sighed deeply.

"No more questions."

Sondra got to her feet. She had to kill the impression he had given the jury, of the witness's secret bias. "Dr. Zimmerman, I think it's important to clear up any possible misapprehension left in the jury's mind by my learned friend's questions of a moment ago. So would you tell the jury, please, do you know the defendant in this case, Hugh Macomber?"

"No, I don't."

"Had you ever seen him before you entered this courtroom?"

"Not to my knowledge."

"Have you ever spoken to him?"

"Never, to my knowledge."

"Dr. Zimmerman, as far as you know, do you have any connection with the defendant in any way?"

"None at all."

"Did you know Laney Meredith before she became your patient in February, Dr. Zimmerman?"

"No."

"Do you have any relationship or connection with her other than the professional patient-doctor relationship?"

"No, I don't."

"Thank you. Now, Dr. Zimmerman, my learned friend asked you some questions concerning Dr. Freud's theory of rape. You mentioned, I believe, that modern findings dispute some of Freud's theories."

"Yes, that's true, particularly in the area of the psychology of women."

"Would you say there have been significant modern findings with regard to rape?"

"Yes. In the years after Freud, it was the received wisdom that in the vast majority of cases either the rape was a product of the patient's fantasy or the victim had been a willing participant. It was believed that true rape almost never happened. But we know this is simply not true. It is now estimated, for example, that one in three women in North America has been sexually abused as a child. It was the enormity of the statistics that originally caused Freud to doubt the facts. But we know now that these statistics are, sadly, the reality."

"Dr. Zimmerman, in your professional opinion, is there any chance that what Laney Meredith has told this court about her experiences could be the product of her own fantasy?"

"Based on everything I know, my past experience and my experience with this patient, I am absolutely convinced that it was not, and that this rape took place in the manner she has described it to me and to this court."

"In your professional opinion, is there any chance that Laney Meredith was a willing participant in the gruesome treatment she was subjected to by this defendant?"

"None whatsoever."

"Thank you. That's all."

"Mr. Roebotham, have you any more questions of this witness?" the judge asked.

"No, Your Honour."

"You may stand down, Doctor," he said.

"That's the prosecution's case, Your Honour," Sondra said. She looked up at the clock. "Just in time for adjournment," she added with a smile.

"Court is adjourned until tomorrow at ten o'clock," the judge intoned.

"All rise!" commanded the clerk, and everyone shuffled to their feet as the judge departed. It was the end of another working day.

Well, almost. Back in her office, as she was taking off her robes, she looked up through the glass to see Ben striding along towards her.

"Hi!" she said, mustering a friendly smile.

"How's it going?" he asked. They both sat down, she behind the desk, he in front of it.

"We rested our case this afternoon. I don't know. It looks pretty good to me. Unless Blake has something up his sleeve, and I don't know what that could be, they'll have a hard time talking themselves out of a conviction on this one."

He smiled. "Good. I've been keeping something from you because I thought this case was getting to you a little, and I thought you could do without any added pressure."

She grinned and sighed. She had known all along that her workload had to be heavier than this—taking on one case and being occupied solely with it to its conclusion. The Crown office was a great deal more pressured than that. "Thanks for breaking me in easily," she said good-humouredly. He had been right; she was feeling far too involved in Laney Meredith's case. It would have been too much pressure to have been trying to prepare another case last week.

But now, the major part of her work was over. There was nothing she could do during the defence's case except to stay alert and look for his witnesses' weak spots.

"Thanks for the breather," Sondra said, meaning it. "Which case am I getting now?"

Ben laughed. "Ah, sweet naiveté. I love to see them come into the Crown office with stars in their eyes, expecting reason and order and a human work load! And only a year later, their youth gone, their vitality all but destroyed..."

"Which *two* cases am I getting now?" Sondra interrupted with a laugh.

"They stagger out, rushing back to the calm waters of private practice as though to a beach in Miami—a little crowded, perhaps, but still, a vacation."

"Three?" she queried faintly.

Ben straightened up. "Let's just say that you are now considered a full-fledged member of the Crown team, and as such, will be assigned cases routinely in your turn. And as your initiation—" he lifted his hand, and she saw for the first time that he held a piece of notepaper, which he handed to her "—you can ask Mary for the files on these. They're all in various stages of preparation. Only one of them, I think, has a trial date set. *Regina v. Tilley.* That's theft over two hundred. The—"

He stopped, because Sondra was gazing at the paper in silent shock. "Is this serious?" she asked faintly.

She had expected to build up a reasonably heavy caseload over time; she knew they were overworked in the Crown office, but she certainly hadn't bargained on having everything dumped on her at once. How long would it take her to familiarize herself with this lot? And how much time would she have on some of them?

"Sadly, it is. I did warn you we had a heavy caseload. However, it isn't as bad as it looks, Sondra. At least two of them, possibly four, won't come to trial because they'll plea bargain. Most of them have had some work done by your predecessor on the case. In most cases that's John Loundes.

Only the last on the list—Crowther and McFadden, is it?—is completely cold. Tilley is pretty well ready to go. It's really a question of your familiarizing yourself with it before you go into court, or so I understand."

Which was about the state she had inherited *Regina v. Macomber* in. Most of the preparatory work had been completed by a Crown Attorney who had left to go into private practice.

"Am I inheriting John Loundes's caseload then?" she asked.

Ben half shrugged. "A lot of it, you are. But of course a few of his cases have been completed by others during the past couple of weeks. Some were put over, of course."

"And to think I always thought Crowns had more fun!" Sondra sat forward and dropped the paper on her desk. "All right, thanks, Ben. I guess I'd better at least have a look at the Tilley file before I go home tonight." She looked up again. "How's your own case going?"

The trial Ben had begun today was the murder case. It was likely to run for weeks and would be very much in the public eye. It was the sort of murder that made people angry and indignant—the cold-blooded shooting of a jewellery store owner who had already given the thieves all they asked for, and who had apparently been shot as some sort of macho lark.

He grinned. "We're selecting the jury, at the moment."

"Does this mean the book takes a back seat now?" she opened her eyes in mock horror at the sudden thought. "Do you stop writing weekends when you're prosecuting a case? Does this mean a wait of weeks before I get to read the next chapter?"

He laughed. "Are you kidding? This is when I need the relaxation most. The only thing that drives a case I'm working on out of my head is Jude's troubles." He looked at her meaningfully. "Well, there are other things. Are we having dinner tonight?"

His look stirred something in her, sharpened the memory, never very distant from her mind, of the weekend and the disturbingly profound feeling she had experienced, of loving Ben Glass. Sondra dropped her eyes and breathed deep.

The list of her cases was under her hand. She focussed on it, fighting for control. If he was going to affect her like this, the affair was going to have to be over long before Christmas. Three months would be too dangerous.

"Not tonight," she managed to say, feeling how hard her heart was beating in opposition. No question where her heart would have led her. It was almost choking her.

If there wasn't a proverb that said, "If you lead with your heart, someone will trump it," there should be. Calming herself with a deep breath, Sondra looked up. "Thanks, Ben, but I have things I want do."

Chapter 14

The next night her answer was the same, but this time, instead of leaving her with a friendly warning not to work too hard, Ben remained in his chair, gazing at her.

"Are you deliberately avoiding me, Sondra?" he asked quietly, and because it was too close to the truth she responded with anger.

"Give me a break, will you, Ben?" she demanded irritably, putting her hands to her temples. "I've had a lousy day, okay?"

That much was true. Blake Roebotham had begun to put on the defence's case today, and among the witnesses he had called had been a sixtyish, self-righteous, Freudian woman analyst who had examined Laney Meredith and had been quite certain that she suffered from "rape fantasy, Oedipal problems, father projection and unconscious seductiveness" among other things, which had all conspired to "put her into a situation" with the defendant of which she had subsequently been "unable to handle the consequences."

It didn't help that she made Sondra furiously angry in a way that she could not recall ever having felt towards a witness before. What a betrayal, of truth, of right, of her own sex! How did the woman justify it with her conscience?

Yet she had to repress her anger in order to effectively challenge the psychiatrist. Anger of that sort was only self-defeating with the jury. The trick was to let the *jury* feel the anger. If she showed her own, it would only exorcize any feelings of anger the testimony might otherwise arouse in the jury.

Never had that task been so difficult. Sondra had been biting her lip through the entire cross-examination, forcing herself to challenge the woman's testimony calmly, leaving it to the jury to observe the contradictions inherent in what she was saying.

"Now, Dr. Radcliffe, the jury has heard you testify that 'there is basically no such thing as rape.' Would you say the same thing is true of murder?"

Dr. Radcliffe smiled superciliously. "I am afraid that it doesn't work that way. The case is very different for rape than for murder. On a conscious level, of course, rape often exists. I'm not saying it doesn't. But what we look at in our profession are the unconscious drives that may cause..."

She simply tied reason up in knots as far as Sondra could see. But would the jury see it that way? Or were they just looking, as so many rape juries apparently did, for an excuse to let the defendant go free? Would this woman's anti-woman testimony allow them the easy way out? They could find Hugh Macomber guilty on a lesser charge—of "forcible confinement," perhaps, and go away with a sense of having achieved a reasonable compromise, ignoring the truth that within a few weeks or months an unrepentant, unchastised rapist would be back on the street with a ticket to attack any woman whose "unconscious seductiveness" practically begged him to do so?

The witness made her so angry, she could sense a haze forming in front of her eyes. At one point in the cross-examination, she felt her hands curl instinctively, and realized with something like shock that she wanted to strangle the woman.

Oh, God. This issue was just too close to her heart. Sondra had sat in the courtroom thinking of the caseload Ben had dumped on her last night, and hoping that none of them had anything remotely to do with rape.

"Isn't a hard day all the more reason to take a break?" a voice asked, and she jerked aware and found herself in her own office, with Ben on the other side of her desk.

She took a deep breath, feeling a stirring inside her, an unfamiliar desire to tell this man all her troubles. But he was the enemy, wasn't he? Sondra reminded herself sternly, thinking of the way he had sat there and let Blake talk and joke in that revolting way, grinning, *enjoying* it. What would *he* understand of her troubles? No more than Blake Roebotham himself.

Yet she had this instinctive feeling for Ben that was none the less powerful for being at odds with her conscious judgement. And it was instinct, in the end, that dictated her response to his repeated invitation to dinner. After that woman's horrible testimony today, Sondra felt friendless and alone.

"All right, you're right," she capitulated with a smile. "But I've got to put in an hour or so here first."

In the end it was more like two hours. Ben had work to do, too, of course, and both of them were too tired at the end of it to want to eat in a restaurant.

"How about going home and ordering in?" Ben suggested. So eight-thirty found them at his elegant kitchen table, laying out little cartons of rice and ribs and the little plastic bags of soy sauce that a nearby Chinese restaurant had sent up.

"I didn't know I was so hungry!" Sondra exclaimed, sinking her teeth into the meat of a delicious honey-garlic sparerib and her chopsticks into a carton of steamed snow peas at the same time. "I must have forgotten to eat lunch today! Did I?"

"I didn't see you in the cafeteria," agreed Ben, digging in just as hungrily. After that there was silence for a few minutes as they silently ate their way through half the food. When the edge was taken off their appetites, they began to chat again about nothing in particular. Then Ben made coffee, and they took their cups in and sat in front of the fire.

"I love fireplaces," Sondra observed quietly, enjoying the sparking noises of the logs and the mesmerizing flames. "But I hardly ever use mine, you know? There never seems to be the time. And if there is, when I'm alone, it hardly seems worth it. Just about the only time I use my fireplace is when I have friends in, and even then only during the winter."

"That's not really surprising, is it?" Ben asked.

"I don't know. Why not?"

He took his arm from around her shoulders and leaned forward to put his coffee cup down on the square table that sat in the middle of his three-sides-of-a-square sofa. "I think it's difficult to make a place feel like a home when you aren't sharing it with anyone. Even a cat can make a place feel more like home. Sitting in front of a fire all alone sometimes just underlines the loneliness."

She supposed that was true, though she didn't want to admit it. Sondra had always been self-sufficient, and of course there was a price to that. Sometimes you were alone when you didn't choose to be. But line that up against the number of times couples were together when they would rather be alone! Everything had a price.

On the weekend, when she had told Ben she loved him, that had been a dangerous moment. It was at moments like that—and like this, if the truth were known—that Sondra wondered if she wouldn't rather change the price of solitude for the price of togetherness, wondered if a man like Ben wouldn't be worth the price.

She knew he was going to kiss her, and she suddenly wanted the touch of his lips and his body with a hungry ache that food would never assuage. Startled by the suddenness of her own need, she bent forward as though she had not noticed his slight movement, picked up her nearly empty coffee cup and drained it.

"Is there any coffee left?" she asked, getting to her feet and picking up Ben's cup, too. "Do you want some more?"

"No, thanks," Ben answered with a little smile. "You go ahead. There's some in the pot."

Her stomach didn't want it, but her hands and mouth did, and it might serve to keep her brain clear. Sondra poured her cup full and came back to the fire, feeling calmer and less likely to fling herself into Ben's arms and cry out her troubles and her need of him.

"How's your case going?" she asked, sinking down in her place beside him, because it would have been ridiculous to change seats now; it would be obvious, and the last thing she wanted to be was obvious.

"We finished jury selection late this afternoon, and I made my address before we adjourned. They look like an intelligent bunch, and as we've got a good case, that should operate to our advantage. Your day wasn't so good, I take it."

Sondra rubbed her eyes, and mascara came off on her fingers. So much for tearproof makeup. "The woodsmoke is making my eyes water," she said inconsequently. "Yeah, it was lousy. Blake put on this absolutely *horrible* Freudian woman. I couldn't believe I was hearing what I was hearing. I just felt this primitive fury, Ben. I wanted to claw her eyes out."

"That sounds typical Roebotham."

"She testified that Laney Meredith had unconscious sexual desires for her father—who's been *dead* since she was ten, by the way—and that she projected those desires onto Hugh Macomber because he was in a father-position that night, offering her *protection*, if you can believe it, and that when it 'went wrong' she felt betrayed—oh, Christ, I can't remember half the garbage we had to listen to!"

"Who was she?" he asked.

"Her name is Radcliffe," Sondra began, "and she's—"

"Oh, yes, Radcliffe. We know her of old," Ben said flatly. "Blake likes to use her in this kind of case."

"You know who she is?" Sondra demanded indignantly.

"Yes, he's had her on the stand before. As I said, anything that's not your simple, straightforward rape is a signal for Dr. Radcliffe to be brought in."

She felt betrayed. "You could have warned me!" she accused, dismayed to hear how close her voice was to cracking.

He blinked at her. "Come on, Sondra, you know how to deal with hostile professional opinion! I'd have mentioned her if I'd known you didn't know her by reputation. I just assumed you did."

He looked at her in concern. "Did she do your case a lot of damage?"

Sondra shook her head. "I don't think so," she said, "But—" She stopped and gazed into the fire. No way to tell him what Dr. Radcliffe had done to her personally, how churned up and angry she still felt over that cold-blooded, uncaring, *evil* opinion that the attack that had nearly destroyed Laney Meredith at the age of seventeen had somehow been her own choice, her own fault.

"But?"

Sondra shook her head. "Oh, nothing. It just irks me that a woman whose profession is supposed to be *caring* can so callously blind herself to the facts. I wish I'd thought to ask her how many times she'd testified in rape cases and whether she had ever accepted any woman's accusation of rape. That would have shown her theories up for what they are!"

"There is a difference of opinion on the subject of rape, Sondra," Ben pointed out reasonably.

"Sure," she agreed without heat, damping down her furious anger. "There's always been the 'she asked for it' school, ever since Joseph and Potiphar's wife. There always will be. But most women don't swallow it, Ben. Most women know that 'there but for the grace of God, go I.' And it is deeply and thoroughly sickening to hear a woman who denies that clear and frightening fact."

"Is that how you feel?" he asked in surprise.

Indignantly, she replied, "Of course it's how I feel! It's the way it is!"

He sat looking at her in silence, absorbing it. "You always seem so strong and self-sufficient," he said at last.

"I am strong and self-sufficient," she told him. "That doesn't mean some lunatic with something to prove isn't going to leap out of a doorway at me someday."

"Nobody leaped out at Laney Meredith," Ben pointed out. "She got into the car."

"And I am twice Laney's age. What does that prove except that now she knows better than to trust plausible villains, a lesson I learned when I was twelve?"

"Do you trust me, Sondra?"

This unexpected personalizing of the conversation was a breath of fresh air on her overheated feelings, and she laughed lightly, feeling the weight of her bitterness ease a little.

"About as far as I can see you," she told him with a grin.

"I see," he said soberly, as if he were hearing God's truth, and she'd thought she was joking, but maybe she wasn't. "Why not? Is it something about me in particular, or do you just have trouble trusting men altogether?"

She dropped her head in her hand. How on earth had they got onto this? The last thing she wanted was a discussion of their relationship and where it was going, and that looked to be where Ben was heading now.

"Oh, I don't know, a little of both, I think," she admitted. "What difference does it make, Ben?"

"It makes a big difference to me. I want you to trust me. I think I'm trustworthy where you're concerned. I've watched the way you go through your men—it's happened to me once already—and I don't want it to happen to me again. And I'm afraid it will happen unless we can head it off early. Right now, for example."

She sighed. "Ah, Ben," she said, feeling very tired. "What is it about men that makes you want a woman to cling until *you* call it quits? What's that old song—'you don't want me, you just want me to go on wanting you'?"

"That's not the way it is, Sondra. I thought I'd made that clear."

"No?" she asked disbelievingly. "How is it, then, Ben?"

He lifted his hand and gently cupped her cheek. He said slowly, "I love you, Sondra. I've loved you for a long time. I want to marry you. I brought you home tonight to ask if you'd consider our moving in together."

She couldn't have been more shocked if the ground had opened up at her feet. She jerked awkwardly back from his touch. "No," she stated flatly. "No way, Ben. You know what I'm like. You knew when you started. Don't try to change the rules in the middle of the game. Don't try to change *me*." She felt immediately guilty. My God, he was proposing, after all. He had said he loved her. She hadn't been able to soften her first, instinctive reaction, and she wished she had.

"I'm sorry," she said quietly. "I'm really sorry, Ben, if you love me. But you did know. You can't say you didn't know what I'm like."

"Sondra, on the weekend you told me you loved me."

"Yes, and it was true, Ben. But it makes no difference."

"It has to. If love doesn't make the difference, what does, Sondra? What is there, in all the world, that matters?"

In a low voice she said, "What matters to me is that I run my own life, and I depend on no one for my happiness."

"All right." He leaned forward and took her hands gently in his. "Tell me why you don't want to let me make you happy."

"That isn't what I said!"

"Oh, yes, it is. You made a specific statement there, as well as a general one, whether you know it or not. You do not want to depend on me for your happiness, and I want to know why."

She looked at him in sudden hostility. "Why do you want me dependent on you for my happiness?"

He shook his head. "It doesn't have to be that way. You don't have to give up your autonomy in order to love someone. But you do have to trust. Without trust, there's no love."

Goaded, she protested, "There's no love where you don't care for someone's essential self, either, Ben! It's only selfish need and sex. The fact is that I understand that, and you and all men wish I didn't! I don't pretend, and that's what bothers you!"

He looked straight into her eyes. "What makes you think I don't care about your essential self?"

"I don't think. I know. You have no respect for me as a person, as a woman, as an individual. You only see something that you want."

"That's not true. Why do you think it's true?"

"Come on, you all belong to a club. You have no respect for women as women. You respect me as a lawyer. I know that. But I'm more than a lawyer. I'm a human being—a particular human being, a *woman*. And when you belittle women, you belittle me."

"I do not belittle women," he said flatly.

She laughed. "The words may not actually pass your lips, but there's always one man who says it for you, isn't there? I haven't stormed the male bastion of the law all these years without learning how it works!"

"What are you talking about, Sondra?" he asked in real confusion.

"I'm talking about sitting at a table of men where one man is making repeated and consistent attacks on women—and therefore on *me*—and the others do nothing but grin and keep silent. I'm talking about being expected to 'take it in good part,' still, in this day and age, as if the women's revolution had never taken place. I'm talking about language that, if used against a black person at the table, would have every single one of you screaming in outrage! I'm talking about being all alone against the world, Ben, whether you're there or whether you're not! And that's not my idea of love."

He was silent for a long time, staring into the fire. Then he said, "Whenever Blake Roebotham has attacked or insulted you personally, Sondra, I've always said something."

"I'm a woman, Ben. When he attacks women the way he does, he attacks me personally. He attacks my essential self."

"Blake doesn't mean half of what he says," he began helplessly. "If you could only see it the way other men see it—he's harmless. He—"

"He is not harmless, Ben. His hatred of women exudes from his pores. Sometimes it's so tangible I think I can smell it. And other men, you included, use him for your own ends."

"Now, come on!" he protested. "How do you justify that?"

"For a start, he is a very able lawyer who turns all his talents to helping rapists go free. If that isn't other men using him, I don't know what is. And from where I sit, what he does in our little lunchtime engagements is to vent a communal hatred of women that the rest of you are too civilized to express for yourselves. So you sit there and listen to one of your number do it, and everybody feels better—except any woman who happens to be listening."

"I don't buy it," Ben said irritably. "I don't buy it at all. All right, Blake goes on about rape victims a bit. I don't like it, frankly; I never have, but I see it as basically harmless. He has to operate on the assumption that his clients are innocent, Sondra, or he couldn't represent them properly."

"Blake knows damned well that his clients aren't innocent. The only assumption he operates on is that they have a right to rape women."

"A man is innocent until proven guilty," he reminded her. "And no one knows what percentage of rape charges are simple malice."

She laughed. "Ben, you've got to be kidding! *Malice?* Where have you been for the past fifteen years? You know perfectly well that most cases of rape aren't even reported! No one knows how many women are raped every year, because most women simply won't go through what Blake is putting Laney Meredith through! You *know* that!"

"That doesn't alter the fact that there is such a thing as nuisance charges—"

"There are nuisance charges in all crimes, Ben! The rate for it is about two percent! And it's been shown over and over again that there is no reason to believe that the ratio of nuisance or malice charges in rape is any higher than for any other crime. In fact, when you consider the doubt with which the cops treat the women pressing rape charges, chances are that *fewer* than two percent get through the system to the courts. A lot fewer!"

He looked at her. "What percentage of women do you think experience rape?"

"I don't know. I don't think anyone knows for sure. I do know this—that one out of every three women in North America has probably been molested *as a child.* That much they do know."

He was quiet, looking back into the fire. "If that's so, how is it I've never met one?" he asked quietly, but she knew he was shocked. "Except in the course of my work, as witnesses for the prosecution, I have never met a woman who was raped. I don't know how many people have. Have you, Sondra? Other than the Laney Merediths, I mean. Can you name me one rape victim you know *personally*?"

"You've got to be kidding," she said. Did he really believe what he was saying to her?

"No, I mean it, Sondra. Name me one. Just give me one name."

She looked at him incredulously. Was it possible he really believed what he was saying? Did he really think that because they didn't tell him about it, it had never happened to the women he knew? She took a breath. If men needed educating, she could start right here.

"Karen Elizabeth Holt," she said, clearly and concisely. "My sister. You've met her, all right. And if I'd been five minutes earlier that night, Ben, I'd be adding my own name to the list."

Chapter 15

They gazed wordlessly into each other's eyes. The fire spat and crackled, and a log fell in on the others in a shower of sparks. Ben dropped his eyes and shook his head helplessly.

"My God," he muttered. "I'm sorry. I'm really sorry. I had no idea."

Saying it aloud had burst some invisible control inside her, and she felt the tears hot in her eyes. "I'd like to know something," she said, not accusing, just flatly asking. "Whose idea was it to assign the Macomber case to me? I just want to know."

He looked startled. "Well, I—it was mostly mine, I guess. It was John Loundes's case before he left and it had been kind of hanging there because everyone was too busy to take it on. We were going to ask for a remand when it came to the court date, but then you came aboard and it seemed a better idea to go with it. You were experienced, and even though it would be your first prosecution, we thought—I thought, and Rajiv agreed—we thought the benefits of not having another delay would outweigh the drawback of your inexperience as Crown."

"Did you think I had a chance of winning the case?"

"What? My God, of course I did! I thought you had an excellent chance! I still do! If anyone can take on Blake Roebotham and make him eat dirt, it's you, isn't it?"

"And that's what you wanted to see me do? Make Blake eat dirt?"

"What do you think I wanted?" he asked, his brows drawn together in real perplexity.

"I don't know. It crossed my mind that—that Blake was a tough assignment, and it was a big case to throw at someone new to prosecution. I thought—I wondered if maybe someone wanted Blake to teach me a little lesson, take me down a peg as a woman, so that I'd be easier to handle."

"Good God," he whispered. "You don't trust anybody, do you? Do you really think our conviction record is so good we can afford to throw away a case for the sake of some private sexism? Do you really think any one of us would be so bloody-minded as to do that to you? To anyone?"

"Ben," she said, "when I was with Lawlor and Bellamy—" that was the big, famous firm she had first taken a job with after she was called to the bar "—they had a tradition of an annual conference dinner. It was at a different location every year, but the first year I worked there, someone decided the dinner would be at The Greenleaf." The Greenleaf was a famous and exclusive men's club, one of only a few in the city. "Women aren't allowed in the front door there, Ben. They can't walk up the front steps and in the front door. I was the only woman lawyer in the firm. The partners asked me if I would mind using the servants' entrance to get into the club because they had got the club to agree to seat me in the private room booked for the dinner. I missed the annual conference that year. Was that all in the course of business, do you think?"

He said, "If I tell you that nothing like what you suspected crossed my mind, or anyone's in the Crown office, will you believe me?"

The tears were suddenly hot on her cheeks. "Yes, if you tell me so, I'll believe it."

"I'm telling you so. It was a decision made between me and Rajiv." Rajiv was the Chief Crown Attorney. "It was mostly my idea. I thought you'd give Blake Roebotham serious trouble, and I have been rooting for you from the beginning, Sondra. I always will."

She gulped on a sob. She had not understood how the suspicion had preyed on her mind until now, when it was proved false. And there was something endlessly comforting in the knowledge that Ben was "rooting for her." "Thank you," she whispered.

"Tell me about your sister," he asked softly.

Sondra stared into the flames as though seeing there the images that had haunted her for so much of her life. The bright quick flame that had been the sister she loved and admired...

"My sister used to baby-sit for the neighbours," she began. "The Wileys. They lived a few houses down from us. She was fifteen. I was twelve. On Saturday nights, if she was baby-sitting, my parents used to let me go over and keep her company. It was more fun that way. That Saturday night I was going to go over, as usual, but I—we wanted to watch different things on TV at eight o'clock.

"So I decided to watch my program at home and go over to the Wileys' at nine. My parents were out that night, and I fussed around locking up and making sure the lights were out. Then I went over.

"I rang the bell and no one answered, and then I heard funny noises through the window, and I... I was suddenly really scared, and I didn't know why, and that's when I noticed that Mr. Wiley's car was in the driveway. And I thought something had happened to one of the kids, and I just opened the door and went in.

"He was on the living room floor with Karen, and his hand was over her mouth and she was screaming in her throat. He looked up, right at me, and then he stood and did up his clothes while I just stood there with my mouth open. I was so stunned. I didn't know what to think or do."

She paused, trying to calm her erratic breathing, trying to ease the need for tears in her throat. "And he walked by me to the door and said something about what a pity I'd missed the party. I don't know. I never quite heard. But it was a threat. I knew that. I've never been so scared of anyone in my life as I was of Mr. Wiley then.

"It sounds slow in the telling, but it was all happening so fast. The next thing I knew he was out the door and the car was driving away, and Karen was lying there all curled up and choking and calling my name....

"We didn't know what to do. We were so scared. My parents were out, and we didn't think to call them where they were. I wanted her to come home, and you know what? She said she couldn't leave the kids in the house alone. There's a lesson in there somewhere. He walked out of the house, leaving the girl he raped, *knowing* that she would feel responsible for his children! I've hated him for that almost as much as for what he did to Karen."

She was silent for a long time. "Did you call anyone?" Ben asked at last, and her thoughts came out of the flickering flames and focussed.

"No, we were too scared. And Karen—all she wanted was a bath, so I helped her to bathe, and then I ran home as fast as I could, because she was scared to be alone, and got her some clean clothes to put on. Hers were ripped. She didn't want to touch them . . . we didn't realize we were destroying evidence. We didn't think about that at all.

"When the Wileys came home, he was grinning all over his drunken face. He tried to pay Karen, but I made him give the money to me. I knew she didn't want to touch anything he'd touched, didn't want to take anything from him. He asked if we wanted him to walk us home, and we didn't answer. We just got out of the house and ran as fast as we could home."

Her throat ached with tears, but she wasn't shedding any now. She was as stony-faced now as they had both been, facing her parents when they came in and telling them what had happened.

She felt a hand on her hair, and her stomach clenched because otherwise she might cry aloud.

"What happened?" he asked gently. "What did your parents do?"

"They didn't call the police. They explained that—that we had—that there was no evidence to stand up in court, that I would probably be considered too young to testify. They said it wouldn't serve any purpose except to embarrass Karen in front of everybody. And then—the next day my father called my sister and me, and we all walked over to the Wileys' together. I was terrified. I didn't want to go, but I was too scared to say so. Mr. Wiley was in his backyard, getting ready to barbecue, I think. He had one of those white chef's hats on, I remember. And my father walked up to him and said, 'My daughters have a message they want me to deliver, Jack,' and then he kicked him as fast and as hard as anything I have ever seen, and Mr. Wiley grunted horribly and doubled over, and then my father just beat the living hell out of him.

"I'd never seen my father do anything remotely violent before. It terrified me, watching that. It made me feel good for Karen, but it was terrifying to watch my father. He was so changed suddenly. He beat him so hard his hands were black and blue for ages afterwards. Jack Wiley never got a chance to lift a hand. He was immobilised right from the start. Once he said, 'Ray, I can explain,' but my father just kept on punching and kicking him. His hat was on the grass. I'll always remember his white chef's hat lying on the grass afterwards, and his face a bloody mess.

"When my father was finished—he was exhausted, breathing as though he were dying—he said, 'If you go near either of my daughters again I will kill you.' And I could hear from his voice that he meant it, and I was never so terrified in my life. Then he turned to Karen and me and said, 'Does either of you have anything you want to say or do? You can kick him if you want,' and we both just shook our heads, and all three of us turned and walked back home."

She looked up, released at last from the visions in the fire. "My sister wasn't ever really herself again, and neither was I. She used to be so much fun. She was so alive. Afterwards she was much more subdued. I knew I was different, too, but I wasn't sure how. I suppose, looking at it now, what I felt was my own loss of trust."

"How is your sister now?" asked Ben.

"Oh, she's all right as far as it goes. She's a producer for the National Film Board. She won an award last year for a documentary on child molesting."

"Did she ever fall in love? Didn't she get married?"

What did that prove? "Oh, she's been married for years. It works well. He's a reporter. You know Douglas MacCready? That's Karen's husband."

Ben's eyebrows narrowed in interest. "But you've never married," he pointed out.

"No. I never wanted to."

"What was your parents' marriage like?"

Sondra took a deep breath. At this rate she'd have told him her entire life story before midnight. Well, he was asking. It wasn't as if she'd pushed it on him.

"I thought it was happy. But when I was fifteen they got a divorce. My father left us. I'd always been closer to my father than my mother. I hated him going. It meant there were only the two of us, my mother and me. Karen was already at university."

The fire had burned down till it was only log-shaped ashes, glowing red in the cracks. "Sondra, did you by any chance think I knew this when I gave you the Macomber case? Did you think *that* was why I gave it to you?" Ben asked in a hoarse voice.

She caught her breath. "Not really," she protested quietly, not meeting his eyes. "At first I—I wondered. Just now, when you told me the decision was mostly yours, I knew you wouldn't have done it for that kind of reason." She took in a deep breath. "But going through all that in court every day, finding how difficult it was for me, sometimes I got a little paranoid."

Ben leaned back, then flung himself forward and to his feet, as though trying to throw off the heaviness of the atmosphere. He moved the fire screen and tossed a new log onto the glowing embers.

"You know what strikes me most about what you've told me, Sondra?" He turned, his back to the fire, and smiled gently down at her. "It seems almost as though *you're* more haunted by the past than your sister is. In the normal course of events, I would expect Karen to be the damaged one, yet from what you say, and how you say it, and from what I remember of Karen—which may not be accurate after seven years—*she* seems to have recovered her equilibrium. Possible?"

Was it? As flames licked up the sides of the sweet-smelling pine log, Sondra's eyes were caught and held, seeking truth in that ever-changing light. And distantly she knew that unless she found the truth of what she was and what had made her what she was, this relationship with Ben was doomed. The past would smother her love as well as his, and fear would continue its rule over her life.

She began slowly, "Those are the three things that stand out in my childhood: the rape, the beating, the divorce. Each time I felt like a tree being struck by an ax. That's the only way I can describe it, Ben. Those are the things I always remember. They stand out as ugliness against a background of pleasant, ordinary things that was the...really the main theme of my life."

"What was the worst part of your sister's rape, for you?" he asked, coming to sit beside her and taking her hand firmly in his, and for the first time she knew what she had never allowed herself to accept: Ben was totally trustworthy, and she would be safe with him. That understanding might disappear with the rising sun tomorrow, but just here and now, for this one moment, deep in herself, she could see the truth, and how she had been running from it in fear.

"Guilt," she said at once. "Oh, God, I felt so guilty! I knew that if I'd been there it might never have happened. If I hadn't been so pigheaded about wanting to watch that damned television program, or if I'd hurried instead of dawdling the way I did when it was over...or if I hadn't stood waiting at the door but had just walked in—oh, I went over and over what I did that night, how easy it would have been to have done something different and saved my sister!"

Ben pointed out, "You might not have saved your sister. You might have got raped yourself."

"*Yes*, yes, I know that!" she almost sobbed. "And it would have been *better*, don't you see? I would rather he had hurt me than her! I would! She was so—oh, God, Ben, her face, when I went over to her! It was as though he'd killed her. I've never seen such eyes in my life! It haunted me. I dreamed about it for years, that awful, *unspeakable* look in Karen's eyes, and the noises she was making. She was whimpering, and there was nothing I could do to make it right! Nothing! And I stood there wishing it had happened to me instead! I really did! If it meant I didn't have to see that look in her eyes, I'd have given anything!"

Without realizing it, she had begun to cry. She turned into his shoulder and felt his strong arms wrap about her with such sureness, then she began to howl in release. "You don't—oh, God, if you knew what it's been like, seeing that same look in Laney Meredith's eyes, as though part of her was killed and she knew it—oh, God, and Blake's face! It gets the same look on it as Jack Wiley's had when he passed me in the hall. It's just—*sickening*! Ben, you—you think he's harmless, but he's not. Whatever he is, I don't know what, but what Blake Roebotham is, is the root of this whole thing, why men rape. Maybe he's never done it himself, and never will, but in his head, he—oh, God, I hate them, I hate them all, the men who do that to women!"

She was nearly incoherent. She wasn't sure he could understand, but the relief of saying it was tremendous, and of being able to cry out her helplessness to him instead of being forever strong and capable, as she had been for so long. Abandoning herself to the newness of it, she clung to him and wept and wept her sense of loss, and he held her, comfortingly, as she had not allowed herself to be held for twenty years....

How much that night had destroyed for her, as well as for Karen. All her sense of security seemed to have gone up in smoke during that one minute when she stood in the hall and saw what a child's father could do to another child. She had known such things happened; she had been taught never to talk to strangers from the time she could walk. But that was *strangers*, and this was Mr. Wiley, who laughed and played with his children and had barbecued hot dogs for all the neighbourhood kids last month!

"I asked my father if he would ever do that to my friends," she whispered hoarsely when the terrible bout of crying had passed. "He said no. He said he would never hurt anybody like that, that Mr. Wiley was sick inside. He had something wrong with him, and we had to realize that we lived in the sort of society that didn't do anything about men like him. He said, 'Don't ever think this society is perfect, Sondra. It's filled with problems. I'm sorry you had to learn it so soon, but make no mistake, you would have had to learn it someday. It's the way we are.'

"I wanted to believe him. I *did* believe him. But he had beat Jack Wiley up, and I had never seen him raise his hand to anyone before. Not even when Goliath bit him and drew blood."

"Goliath?" asked Ben with a grin.

She smiled through her tears, for the first time in what seemed an age. "Goliath was our dog. At first his name was Davy. He was supposed to be a medium-sized mongrel, but he just kept growing. He wasn't very bright, and he used to chew up our shoes and slippers all the time. We had to hide them from him.

"One day he didn't notice my father's foot was in the slipper, and he just...started to chew on it. My father let out a yell they heard at the neighbours'. It was a bad bite. He dripped blood all over the carpet. He was furious. He had to have tetanus shots and everything, and he limped for a week after." Sondra began to giggle. "It was pretty funny, though it was a while before Dad thought so." She sobered. "Most people would have kicked the dog, or hit him, when they felt him biting, don't you think? But he didn't. He hollered, and Goliath let go. Goliath was just as surprised as Dad was, we always said."

"Your father sounds like a very kind man," said Ben.

"Yes, he does, doesn't he? I think he was. Looking back on it, I think he felt that beating up Jack Wiley was the only way he had. I don't think he enjoyed it, or anything. But for me, coming so soon after what Jack Wiley had done, the violence was really...frightening. And I never really knew why he took us along to watch it."

He looked at her in surprise. "Never? Not even now?"

"I—well, I haven't thought about it for years."

"Well, as a man, I think I understand your father and what his motives were. Don't you see that he was trying to give both you and Karen your sense of personal power in the universe back? He was trying to exorcize your sister's feeling—and yours—of being a helpless victim, of wanting to see the man punished. Karen obviously couldn't get her revenge herself unless she shot the man. Your father acted as her agent. He allowed her an outlet for her anger. How did she react to the man's beating?"

"We've never talked about it."

"Well, maybe you should. She was older than you. She had been physically hurt by the man. Maybe it worked for her."

She had a quick vision of her sister, married the day after she graduated from university, still married to the same man nearly fifteen years later, a thriving feminist who had been a leader in the women's movement throughout her marriage, handling her career and her man with dexterity, and now, only recently, preparing to take on motherhood for the first time as well.

No one, least of all Sondra herself, had ever noticed that there was a material difference in the brilliantly successful lives of the two sisters. Her career success had masked the terrible emptiness of her emotional life. Sondra had friends; there was always some man to bring home for Christmas; her name got in the newspaper with satisfying frequency. No one saw underneath to the crippling sense of isolation, of fear to trust. She was highly intelligent. She masqueraded well. She had even fooled herself, telling herself that a serious involvement with a man would endanger her career.

It was always the men she had liked most who got dumped the earliest, she saw, and Ben had had the shortest run of all. Sondra looked up at him now, more grateful than she would ever be able to express that he had come back for a second try. She wanted a second chance.

She loved him; there was no question of that. She had loved him seven years ago; that was why she had panicked and thought of losing her career in the demands of love and marriage.

She loved him. But could she really love anyone? Did she know how? Knowing what she knew, would it ever be possible for her to love and trust any man?

Chapter 16

Blake Roebotham put his client on the stand as the last witness for the defence on Wednesday. The line the defence was taking had been obvious for some time. With all the corroborative evidence putting the accused at the scene of the crime, it was really the only line he could take; that Laney Meredith had been a willing participant in her own confinement and rape.

Matthew Miller, the friend in whose basement Hugh Macomber had kept Laney Meredith locked up, had already testified that the defendant had told him he had a girlfriend, but had nowhere to take her, and that at Hugh's request he had given him his house key before he had gone on vacation with his parents.

"How long have you known Hugh Macomber, Mr. Miller?" Sondra had asked conversationally as she got to her feet when it was her turn at cross-examination. She knew the young man was lying; she had to find a way to break down his story for the jury. And she had to do it on her feet.

"About a year."

"Is he a good friend of yours?"

"Pretty good," said Matthew.

She smiled at him, instinct telling her to try honey first. If Blake had scared him with stories of how gruelling her questioning would be, it might just catch him off guard to use the friendly older sister approach.

Or mother, she reminded herself wryly, since Matthew Miller looked scarcely out of his teens.

"Would you call him your best friend?"

His eyes instinctively sought out those of Hugh Macomber in the dock, and in them was a mixture of hero worship and fear. *Okay,* thought Sondra. "I guess so."

"Do you look up to him a lot, Matthew?"

"I guess so," he responded in faint bewilderment. Where was the terrible harpy he had been promised would descend upon him?

"How old are you?" Still the conversational tone, as though she were one of his mother's friends taking a friendly interest in him at a big get-together.

"Eighteen. Just turned."

"I see. Do you know how old Hughie is?"

"He told me he's twenty-three."

Sondra was nearly certain now. Matthew Miller's character was not strong. A more powerful, determined character, enhanced by a little hero worship, could have a field day twisting this boy around his fingers. "Do you go to school?"

Blake got lazily, unhurriedly, to his feet. "Your Honour, fascinating as this biography may be, I don't think it has any point. My learned friend is getting far afield here."

"This witness has testified that he is the defendant's friend. My learned colleague knows I am entitled to bring out the nature of that friendship," Sondra said with a tolerant smile. She didn't say, *to show bias*, because she didn't want to spook Matthew Miller.

"If she is trying to show that this witness is biased, I think she's going the long way around," Blake said with emphasis.

"Objection overruled," said Judge McVean. "The witness may answer the question."

The court reporter picked up the paper coming out of the top of his machine and read back the last question. "Do you go to school?"

Matthew had picked up Blake's warning message. "Yes, I go to school," he said warily. "I graduate next year."

"Are you going to college?"

"Yes, ma'am."

"Does Hugh Macomber go to school with you?"

"No, ma'am, he doesn't go to school at all."

"So what do you think you have in common with him, Matthew? What makes you friends?"

Matthew shifted uncomfortably behind the stand. "I don't know. We just are."

"Do you look up to Hugh Macomber, Matthew?"

"Yeah, I guess so. A little bit." But he wasn't looking in the defendant's direction. He hadn't known he would have to answer questions about *himself*.

"If he asked you to do something, would you do it?"

He shrugged. "I guess so. It depends."

"Would you disobey your parents for him?"

"I don't know. He never asked me to do that."

Sondra glanced deliberately over at the jury. "He never asked you to disobey your parents?"

"No, ma'am."

"Did you have your parents' permission, then, to give the key of your home to any friend you wished to?"

Matthew understood now. Panic flared his nostrils momentarily. "No..."

"So you did, in fact, disobey your parents because Hugh Macomber asked you to?"

Matthew dropped his eyes. "I guess I did."

"That's pretty serious, isn't it? Giving a friend a key without telling your parents? He might have stolen something, mightn't he?"

Matthew was looking a bit lost. "I guess so."

"And you might have been charged with being an accessory to that crime. Did you know that when you gave your friend the key?"

It was obvious he did not know what to answer. Because, of course, he had never given the defendant his key. "Yes," he decided at last. "But he wasn't going to steal anything."

"But he could have. Isn't that right? He had two weeks to do whatever he wanted to in your parents' home. With your key, he *could* have cleaned out the entire house. Isn't that so?"

"I guess so," Matthew said sullenly.

"So you were willing to take some pretty serious risks at Hugh Macomber's request. You were willing to do what he said in defiance of your parents."

No answer.

"What about committing perjury, Matthew? Were you willing to defy the law for your friend, too?"

Blake leaped to his feet in a show of righteous anger, and was overruled.

"I don't know what that is," Matthew said when he was instructed to answer the question.

Sondra gave him a stern but loving older sister look. "Perjury means telling lies on the witness stand, Matthew. Would you do that for Hughie if he asked you?"

His liquid eyes were suddenly big and round. "No...no, I'm not lying."

"Matthew, do you know what the penalty is for committing perjury?"

"No..."

"It's imprisonment. Did Hugh tell you that when he asked you to testify in his defence?"

There was no answer, but the jury was free to see the way the witness's eyes were drawn unwillingly to the face of the defendant, resting on it in mute horror.

"Did he tell you that getting up on the witness stand to tell lies is a crime with serious penalties, Matthew?"

"No." Now the voice was hoarse.

"Did you know that your friend Hugh was willing to have you sacrifice not only high school and college for his sake, but also your freedom?"

His eyes came back to her face and fixed there.

"Are you sure Hugh Macomber is as good a friend as you think he is, Matthew?"

Matthew Miller swallowed and did not speak.

"No more questions," said Sondra.

Blake Roebotham got to his feet with a little extra noise than usual, trying to draw the jury's interest away from the stricken face of the witness.

"Matthew, have you committed perjury here today?" he asked in high good humour, his manner indicating what answer he expected to get.

The dark eyes sought a saviour. "N-no."

"So there would have been no reason for my client to warn you about the consequences of perjury, would there?"

"No."

"No. All my learned friend's threats are meaningless if you are telling the truth, aren't they?"

Matthew did not respond, and after a split second Blake carried on as though he had expected no response. "Now, I'm going to ask you again, just so there's no doubt in the minds of the jury: did you give Hugh Macomber a key to your parents' house before you went on vacation?"

"Yes," he said, flicking a challenging look in Sondra's direction, as though under the force of Blake's personality he had suddenly realized that no one could prove him a liar except himself and Hugh Macomber, and that Hugh Macomber would never do so. "Yes, I gave him a key."

"And did he tell you the reason he wanted a key was in order to have someplace to take his girlfriend?"

"Yes, that's what he told me."

And suddenly, before her eyes, the pleasant, basically honest face changed. It was one thing to do a favour to save a friend, Sondra reflected. It was another to rejoice inwardly in flouting the law of the society you lived in. In Matthew's face she saw that he had taken the step that might now put him forever on the wrong side of the law.

As he stepped down, she saw him glance unhappily towards Hugh Macomber, and she thought, There's still a basic honesty in you, my young friend. And if I get a conviction in this case, I am going to come after you with a charge of perjury, or let you think so. And I'll let you sweat about it for a couple of weeks. I'll let you think about your friend off in prison and face what it would mean to you to go there. And when you are thoroughly terrified, I'll tell you I'm dropping the charges and give you a lecture instead. Maybe that will straighten you out.

After that there had been a pause, which Blake had covered by riffling through his notes, but which Sondra knew from long experience as defence attorney meant he was trying to decide whether he should rest his case now or go through with putting Hugh Macomber on the stand in his own defence. A jury with even moderate intelligence must have seen through Matthew Miller. Hugh Macomber was in trouble.

After a few moments Blake raised his head. "Your Honour, I am now going to call the defendant, Hugh Macomber...."

Hughie Macomber had already proved himself a plausible charmer the night he had convinced Laney to get into his car, and he set now out to use the same charm on the jury.

He had known Laney Meredith for some time, he told them sweetly. He had been sexually intimate with her several times before the night of February eighth. She had been afraid to introduce him to her family because he was black, an immigrant, and she thought her parents would be angry. So they had been reduced to meeting on the sly.

On the night of February eighth, he had met her as planned on the way home from a school friend's house, where she had been doing homework. They planned to have a couple of hours together before he would drive her home. But Hughie had that week been given the key to the home of a friend whose family had all gone on vacation. They could stay there for the weekend, with no one any the wiser. Laney could phone her mother and tell her some story to account for her absence.

At first, Laney had agreed. They had gone to the Millers' house; they had made love; and then she had got frightened. She had demanded that he take her home.

This was where Hughie Macomber had made the mistake that would haunt him all his life. He loved Laney. He wanted to be with her for a few days instead of having only a few stolen hours in the back of his car. So he had taken her to the basement and locked her in, not listening to her pleas that she be taken home.

He had kept her there for the weekend, visiting her whenever he could, whenever he wasn't working or at home with his mother and brothers and sisters. She had always seemed pleased to see him; he thought she had got over her fear and wanting to go home. He had been going to come to her that Monday to take her home when the police had arrested him at his job. He had been shocked to hear that the charge was rape. He had never raped anybody, and that included Laney Meredith.

"Your witness," said Blake Roebotham.

Sondra got to her feet, slipped her hands into the pockets of the trousers she was wearing underneath her black robes and stood looking steadily at Hugh Macomber for several long moments. Then she glanced at the jury, and back at the defendant, as though it was obvious they all agreed that here was an unprincipled, unrepentant villain who had just proved by the words out of his own mouth that he deserved no quarter.

"Mr. Macomber, how old are you?" she asked coolly.

"Twenty-three. Ma'am," he added suddenly, with a slight nervous glance in Blake Roebotham's direction.

Sondra's eyebrows came together quizzically. "Did Mr. Roebotham instruct you to call me that?" she asked, letting the dry amusement show through her tone.

"Excuse me? Ma'am?" He blinked soulfully at her.

"Did Mr. Roebotham point out to you that it would make you seem like a nice, polite young man if you would remember to call me 'ma'am' on the stand?"

His mouth opened. "Uh, I... no," he replied, his voice curling up questioningly at the end.

"Did you call Laney Meredith 'ma'am' when you were trying to pick her up that night?"

"No," he said slowly, thrown off stride a little. He glanced at Blake Roebotham.

"Why are you looking at the defence attorney? Are you hoping he'll instruct you how to answer?"

He fixed his eyes on her. "I'm not looking at the defence attorney," he denied irritably.

"Ma'am," she prompted.

"Ma'am," he supplied automatically. The jury tittered.

"Is that how Mr. Roebotham used to remind you to be polite to me?"

"Mr. Roebotham never told me to be polite." It sounded like a lie, and it wasn't the first he'd told by a long way.

"He never told you to call me 'ma'am' at the end of your answers to impress the jury with your good manners?"

"No, he didn't."

"Well, fine, Mr. Macomber. Then as long as you wouldn't be breaking any instructions from your counsel, let's make a deal: you don't bother to pretend a polite respect for the law, and I won't bother to pretend I believe the story you just told the jury. Okay?"

"Oh, Your Honour, this is deliberate provocation of a witness!" Blake called lazily, standing half out of his seat. "I appreciate my learned colleague's tactics, but really—" He lifted his arms in casual, sarcastic good humour.

Sondra received a small reprimand, but her point had already been made.

"How old were you when you came to this country, Mr. Macomber?" she asked.

"I was eleven. Ma—" he began, and stopped in the middle of the word.

"Were you educated here?"

"Yes, I was."

"How far did you go in school?"

"I went to Grade Twelve."

"Grade Twelve," she repeated admiringly. "Did you graduate?"

"Yes, I did."

"So you're hardly unintelligent, then, Mr. Macomber?"

He didn't reply.

"Was it cold in the Millers' basement?"

"It was a little bit on the chilly side," he admitted.

"A little bit on the chilly side. We've heard police testimony to thc effect that the temperature in that basement on the Monday morning that Laney escaped was six degrees Centigrade. That's about forty-two degrees Farenheit. What country were you born in, Mr. Macomber?"

"Jamaica."

"That's a pretty warm country, isn't it?"

"I guess it might be."

"I guess it might be," she agreed dryly. "Canadians go down to Jamaica in winter to get away from the cold here, don't they?"

"I guess they do."

"How did you feel about your first experience of a Canadian winter back when you emigrated from such a hot climate at the age of eleven?"

"It was cold. I was freezing all the time." He grinned at her, trying to bring her under his charm, but Sondra didn't return the smile, and as with so many who are used to getting their own way, her refusal to find him charming made him sullen.

"Had you ever experienced a temperature of six degrees Centigrade before you came to Canada?"

"No."

"And now, only twelve years later," Sondra said admiringly, "you think of such a temperature as only 'a little bit chilly'! You seem to have adapted very well! I think most Canadians would consider an indoor temperature of six degrees more than a little bit chilly, especially if they had to stay in it for very long."

He did not reply.

"But, of course, it wasn't as cold for you as it was for Laney Meredith, was it?" she pointed out. "You were wearing clothes all the time, weren't you? And you brought a blanket along to keep you warm while you raped her in that freezing basement. Isn't that so?"

It was a two-pronged accusation, and he was caught in it as she had hoped he would be, not knowing whether to deny the blanket or the rape.

"I didn't rape her," he said after a damning pause. "She's lying about that."

"But you did take all her clothes. And you did bring a blanket with you and take it away each time you left, didn't you?" she stated flatly.

"She never said she was cold," he said sullenly.

"Well, now, we've heard from the doctor who examined Ms. Meredith after her escape that she was suffering from exposure, and that if you'd left her in the basement another ten to twelve hours she might easily have died. We've heard him testify that under such conditions her lips would have been blue, that she would have been shivering uncontrollably, that her teeth would have been chattering. Did you observe all these symptoms in your prisoner when you visited the Miller basement that Saturday and Sunday?"

He paused. "I don't remember."

Sondra left that to the good sense of the jurors.

"Where did you meet Laney Meredith?"

"At the bus stop."

"Which bus stop?"

"The one at Jane and Keele."

"And how did you go about convincing her to get into your car?"

He suddenly realized the trap he had walked into. "That's where I met her that night. *Before* I met her at the coffee shop," he countered triumphantly.

"I see. Did she tell you about her family, who were so opposed to her dating a black man?"

"Yeah, she talked about them a lot."

"What's her father's name, Mr. Macomber?"

"I—I don't think she ever told me that."

"But she did tell you how opposed he was to her dating you?"

"She told me he *would be* against it. She never said she told him about me. She said he was real strict."

"So it would come as a surprise to you to hear that Laney Meredith's father died when she was ten years old?"

Hugh Macomber's eyes slid around the room, looking for inspiration. "Maybe it was her uncle, her mother's boyfriend, somebody like that," he said.

"How many sisters and brothers does Laney have?"

His eyes focussed on the middle distance. "Uh—she never told me that."

"Well, who did she talk about in these long sad chats you had about her strict family?"

"She talked about her mother."

"Does she live with her mother?"

He was by no means unintelligent. It was obvious to Sondra now that he was trying to remember Laney's testimony of last week, looking for clues in anything she might have said. "Yeah, she lives with her mother."

"Alone?"

"She never told me that," he said evasively.

"Well, it seems as though she didn't tell you very much. What did she tell you about her mother? What's her mother's name?"

"If she told me, I forget."

"Is there anything she told you about her mother that you remember?"

He thought a moment. "I don't think so."

"So you don't remember her telling you that her mother was a racist? You told us a few minutes ago—"

"Yeah, she told me that. I remember that. That's why she couldn't take me home."

"Is *your* mother a racist, Mr. Macomber?"

"My mother? No. She likes Canadians."

"So she wouldn't have objected to your dating Laney Meredith?"

He knew it was leading somewhere, but he couldn't see how to avoid the pitfall. "No," he said uneasily.

"Well, then, why didn't you take Laney home to *your* place and introduce her to your family? You've complained about how terrible it was to have to meet and make love in your car. You testified that you lost your head at the thought of having a place to take your girlfriend at last. If it was that important to you, why didn't you just take her home?"

He struggled to find an answer, and his dismay was obvious, Sondra hoped, to all.

"I—we have a very small apartment," he said. "I was ashamed to take her there."

There was a gasp from the body of the court, where a neatly dressed black woman, surrounded by several bright-eyed children, all clean and neat and obviously respectable, sat looking at her son with shocked eyes.

"You were ashamed of your family?" Sondra pursued.

He hung his head guiltily. "Yes, ma'am," he admitted.

Sondra turned coolly to the courtroom. "Is this your family I see in the court?"

"Yes."

"Can you point them out for the jury, please?"

"Oh, Your Honour, I object. The defendant's family isn't on trial here!"

"The defendant," Sondra argued, "has testified that his family shamed him so much that he preferred to sit in cars and freezing basements rather than take a friend home to meet them. The jury has a right to judge whether that was a reasonable response...."

"Objection sustained," ruled the judge. But the jurors were all gazing at Hugh Macomber's family, especially the woman whose eyes were so bleak as she looked at her son.

"Well, then, Mr. Macomber, can you tell us just what it was about your family that made you ashamed to introduce them to a friend?"

"Not my family," he said sullenly. "The apartment is too small."

"How many bedrooms are there in your family's apartment?"

"Three."

"And does it have a living room?"

"Yes."

"A dining room? A kitchen?"

"Not a dining room. A place to eat off the kitchen."

"A bathroom?"

"Yes."

"Is it, in fact, a fairly ordinary three-bedroom apartment?"

"I guess so."

"Is it kept clean?"

Everybody in the courtroom was aware of Mrs. Macomber's eyes staring at Hughie, daring him to besmirch her reputation as a housewife. He shifted uncomfortably.

"Yes, my ma and sisters keep it real clean."

"Is it comfortable?"

"Yeah, except it's crowded."

"Well, how many people live in it?"

"Me, and my ma and my sisters and brothers."

"How many sisters and brothers do you have?" Sondra asked in theatrical wonder, pointing up the absurdity of all this.

"Three sisters and two brothers."

"Is that seven people altogether then? You and your mother and five other children? Your father doesn't live with you?"

"That's right."

"And you want the jury to understand that you preferred to take a girl you liked very much, according to your own testimony, to the freezing, unfurnished basement of a friend's house rather than to your own home? That you preferred to stay out with her in your car, where both of you, according to your testimony, were unhappy, rather than sit on your own sofa at home? Is that what you're asking the jury to believe, Mr. Macomber?"

"Well..."

"Isn't it the truth that you had never spoken to Laney Meredith until the night you so conveniently saw her standing in the freezing rain at the bus stop? Isn't it the truth that you decided to take advantage of her being alone and young and vulnerable? Wasn't it her very youth and innocence that made you think of her as a likely victim? Isn't the real truth, Mr. Macomber, that you stopped and spoke to Laney Meredith with the express purpose in your mind to get her into your car with promises of good faith and trustworthiness, and then drive her somewhere secluded and rape her? Isn't that the answer that clears up all these contradictions in your testimony?"

"No. Ma'am."

"Had you ever raped anyone before Ms. Meredith?"

"No. I swear I didn't."

"She was your first victim, then. Was she your last?"

"I—" He paused, and his eyes went hard as he saw the trap he'd been led into. "And I never raped her, neither. I never had any victim!"

That was how they spent Wednesday afternoon, and much of Thursday morning. Sondra went through his testimony piece by piece, line by line, lie by lie, trying to expose the contradictions, the obvious lies, the unremorseful arrogance of the man who thought he could talk his way out of his terrible crimes.

For Sondra it was not as difficult as she had feared. She had been frightened of her own emotions, worried that they would get out of control, and that she would attack the defendant just a little too bitterly, making him pitiable and driving the jury over to his side. It was a fine line, but she stayed on the right side of it; and she couldn't help wondering more than once how much she was aided in that by the fact that she had expressed so much bitterness already to Ben on Tuesday night, and could question Hugh Macomber without feeling she was also getting back at Jack Wiley.

She had no real trouble. Instead of the emotional ordeal she had worried about, it was a battle of wits, and Hugh Macomber was not really a match for her. His story was too full of holes, and she had so much more experience.

Still, she might prove his guilt and yet not get a conviction. Juries were unpredictable, most especially in rape trials. Proving his guilt to the satisfaction of the judge did not mean proving it to the satisfaction of the twelve people in the jury box. That was why rapists' lawyers almost invariably chose trial by jury rather than trial by judge alone.

Nevertheless, she felt she exposed him, and she knew that Blake would never have risked putting his client on the stand if there had been any other way.

And there was only so much she could do. In the end, it was up to the jury, in the exercise of their conscience, to decide. She couldn't decide for them.

She finished her cross-examination just before noon on Thursday, and Blake's redirect was brief enough. After lunch they and the judge would address the jury, and then it was out of her hands entirely.

But she wanted a conviction. She had never so desperately wanted to win a case. She wanted it so badly now that she didn't even bother to try to eat any lunch. She went to her office with a cup of black coffee, and once again marshalled all the points she wanted to make, all she wanted the jury to remember and consider.

And then, too soon, though she was impatient for it, she stood at the frail lectern, her notes in front of her, and gazed into the faces of the jury that would decide the fate of Hugh Macomber, and possibly of Laney Meredith, too.

This one is for you, Karen, she promised, and for Laney, too, and for me, and all the women who have suffered and need protection and never get it. This time we're going to see justice done.

She glanced down at her notes again, then looked up, and smiled briefly. "Ladies and gentlemen of the jury," began Sondra Holt in a steady, calm voice, "it is not only rape that you have heard described during your long days of patient listening to the proceedings in this court. It is rape under the most cruel conditions, rape accompanied by threats, violence, physical and mental cruelty, and deliberate terrorization of a young woman of the tender age of seventeen. A young woman who, before this attack, as you have heard, was a virgin...."

For all of us, she was thinking. For every woman who has suffered and cried alone...

Chapter 17

"Ladies and gentlemen of the jury, have you reached a verdict?"

"We have, Your Honour."

"On the charge of aggravated sexual assault, how do you find the defendant? Guilty or not guilty?"

"Guilty, Your Honour."

Hugh Macomber let out a high, eerie cry that scraped down the spine like chalk on a blackboard, and behind him, his mother sobbed once as though she had been struck, and then buried her face in her hands and wept.

Judge Arthur McVean, unmoved, demanded silence.

"On the charge of kidnapping, how do you find?"

"Guilty."

"On the charge of forcible confinement, how do you find?"

They found Hugh Macomber guilty as charged on all counts against him.

Sondra sat looking at the jury, breathing deeply. A couple of the women nodded at her in a kind of recognition of what they had all gone through in this courtroom, but no one was really jubilant. There were no broad congratulatory smiles, just the acknowledgement of an unwelcome responsibility that had been carried out to the best of everyone's ability.

It had been a long wait. Sondra had never experienced one that seemed longer, though many juries had actually stayed out far longer. It was Friday noon, and she had been considering going to lunch when the word had come that the jury had reached a verdict.

Now the postverdict formalities ran by her ears as though a distant radio were playing, and at last she heard the judge say, "Sentencing this afternoon at three o'clock." Then he rose and they all rose, and it was all over but the shouting.

She stayed on her feet and strode to the door without looking once in Blake's direction. It wasn't a question of *personal* triumph, no matter how much she might despise him. It was a question of seeing justice done, to the limited extent that that was possible within the present system. With any other defence counsel she would have looked over after the verdict, but she wasn't going to accept Blake Roebotham's value judgement about what had gone on here.

Ben was the man she wanted to see. Ben was the one who would understand what this meant to her. And as she entered the office, she heard his voice, and took a couple of running steps towards it before she caught herself.

He looked up as she rounded the corner. Nearly everyone was there, secretaries and Crowns, and Rajiv Rамataursingh, and they all broke into applause. It died down as she approached, and then they were saying "congratulations" and "knew you could do it." She smiled and thanked them, but she had eyes only for Ben.

"What was it? On all counts?" he asked for them all, because they'd heard only the briefest of reports.

"On all counts," she breathed, only now beginning to believe it, and she broke into a broad grin at the relief from all the tension she had been living with for weeks past.

"What a coup!" said a secretary. "I'll bet Roebotham is one surprised lawyer today!" And there was a certain personal satisfaction in her tonc that made Sondra wonder if she too had felt a personal interest in seeing Blake Roebotham get his comeuppance at the hands of a woman. Not that Blake had never lost a case before—he had lost his share—but everybody knew that there had been a real personal antagonism between him and Sondra in this one, and that Blake had pulled out all the stops in his defence.

"Lunch?" asked a voice. "Are we going to lunch?"

Sondra smiled. "Just give me five minutes," she said. "I want to phone the plaintiff." She strode into her office and closed the door, then sank into her chair and stared at the phone. They had won. Laney was sitting at the other end of that phone, waiting to hear, and now she could phone and tell her that the jury had believed her, that they wanted her attacker punished.

"Hello?" said a quiet voice that she recognized at once.

"Laney?" said Sondra. "This is Sondra Holt, from the Crown Attorney's office."

"Yes," said Laney. "They've reached a verdict."

That was all she said. It was as though she could not bring herself to ask directly what that verdict had been. And Sondra understood clearly, for perhaps the first time, how much more than important—how *crucial*—this verdict was to Laney Meredith's ultimate recovery. How desperately she needed to know that she had not gone through all that torment in court, on top of everything else, for nothing. For the sake of knowing herself a fool to have tried, to have thought her integrity of person might be important to the society of people in which she lived.

"Laney," she said quickly, "the jury has found Hugh Macomber guilty on all counts against him. The sentencing will—"

She heard a muffled sob, and then the cool, distant witness of a few days ago was breaking down in howling sobs of release and gratitude. "Oh, God," she tried to say. "Oh, God, is he going to go to prison? Will they put him away?"

"There was no recommendation for mercy from the jury. I think he'll get at least two years, probably more. But you can hear it for yourself, Laney. The sentencing will be this afternoon at three o'clock. You can be there."

"Oh, God."

"You have a right to be there. He was inhumanly brutal to you, Laney. You're entitled to your revenge."

Was that what her father had told her sister? Had it been prompted by what she was feeling herself, right now? A desire to protect and defend the defenceless? There was so much to understand.

"Maybe I'll come," said Laney. "I—I can't think right now."

"Three o'clock in Courtroom 417," said Sondra.

"All right."

She hung up then and leaned back in her chair. She had a strong feeling that Laney ought to come. An inner conviction that she needed to be present when society told her she had all the rights that Hugh Macomber had denied her.

It was an inner conviction that it would help Laney get over the trauma. It *must* be what her father had felt, when he wanted his daughters to witness the punishment of Jack Wiley.

She had been too young to understand. But she understood now. He had done what he felt was right, and that was all any of us could do.

It was becoming the accepted thing that Ben and Sondra went to lunch together, and today was no exception. A couple of the other Crowns joined them, and they went, as usual when they were actually in court, to the cafeteria in the basement. Sondra had plenty of time before three o'clock, and she could easily have found someone to go out with had she preferred. But the others were all arguing cases—Ben in particular had work he wanted to do over the noon recess—and she wanted to be with her fellow Crowns in this small celebration of her victory.

And with Ben. Since the night when she had got out all that repressed anguish over Karen and her father, she felt closer to Ben than ever. For the first time, she seemed to feel love as a real thing, a powerful force within her. She wanted to bc ncar him.

As luck would have it, Blake Roebotham was dircctly in front of them when they joined the cafeteria lineup. Sondra imagined, looking at his face, that he would have liked to avoid their company at the moment, but pride would not allow him to seem to be running away from her. So they all sat down at one table.

He started a few minutes later when he had finished what was on his plate. Making a business of picking up the little creamer carton, he said as he added the cream to his coffee, "Well, so my client joins the long stream of poor suckers who pay the price for women who can't make up their minds, eh, Harvey?" Harvey was the young lawyer who had hopes of making partner this year. He grinned and shook his head in helpless resignation over the futility of trying to get justice for rapists.

"So, whaddya think he'll pull?" Blake asked Sondra aggressively. "What does the plaintiff want him to get? Will anything less than ten years soothe her zest for revenge?"

For the first time in these matches with Blake, Sondra felt sad rather than angry. She felt how his attack hurt her, reminding her of her feeling of dreadful helplessness on the night her sister had been hurt and she had done nothing to help.

Feeling like this, she could see the futility of challenging Blake Roebotham on his own ground. He was hurting her, and she did not want to pretend that he was not. She looked at him sadly, and shook her head.

"Blake," she said quietly, "rape is such a horrible crime. Please don't."

That was all she was going to say. If he didn't shut up, she would just leave quietly. She had no stomach for tough-minded defence today.

"Lay off, Blake, okay?" She heard Ben's quiet voice beside her, and a little of the pain she had carried alone for so long eased.

"Yeah, Blake, you lost fair and square," said another voice. "Your client is guilty. Don't take it out on Sondra."

"You're going a bit overboard, Blake," said a third voice simultaneously. It belonged to a man who a mere two weeks ago had sat at this table grinning mindlessly over one of Blake's sickening attempts at a joke.

Sondra looked around in startled wonder. Except for young Harvey, there wasn't one mindless grin at the table. What had happened? He had been no worse today than usual. What had changed? Not that she had won the case; that was ridiculous. Was it because Ben had opened the way? Yet these men weren't sycophants; they were hardly out to please Ben the way poor Harvey had to please Blake.

Whatever had made them defend her, she felt the results deep in her heart. For the first time, sitting with a table of men, she didn't feel alone. For the first time, she didn't feel the automatic armour slide into place, protecting her from abandonment.

She looked around. They were all eating as usual, including Blake. It was as though nothing much had happened, and she gazed at their faces and felt a sudden burst of affection that made her want to take them and the whole world in her arms and burst into tears.

Ben's hand squeezed hers on the table, and she turned her eyes to his. Maybe he could tell her; maybe he could explain this odd male ritual of challenge and surrender that she had just observed, but which they all seemed to have taken part in unconsciously. She would ask him.

Judge Arthur McVean wasn't a hanging judge. He always took extenuating circumstances into account and listened closely to the presentencing statement of the accused, especially if there were signs of real remorse.

But he could be strict when he felt the occasion warranted it, and to those with experience, Sondra included, it was obvious from the first few moments of his beginning, that he felt severity was warranted in the case of Hugh Macomber.

"On Friday, the eighth of February," he said after outlining the guilty man's early history, "you persuaded Laney Meredith to get into that bright red Camaro of yours. She was minding her own business..." Sondra kept her eyes on the judge, but she wondered how Laney Meredith was feeling at this moment. She was glad the girl had come. To her it seemed a sign of returning health, of a renewed sense of self, that Laney Meredith cared that the man who had done such evil to her was being punished by the society she was part of.

"Because this seventeen-year-old girl got into your car, you terrorized her."

Was that how Karen had felt, watching their father beat up Jack Wiley? Had she taken a satisfaction from it that Sondra herself had somehow been unable to partake in? Had knowing that her father valued her enough to take justice into his own hands helped her to heal?

"Not satisfied with what you had done, you came back for her, and this time you brutally forced her into your car. You took her to an empty house, a house in which the owners had turned the heat down to just above freezing..."

Why hadn't it worked for her? Why had that backyard beating somehow only compounded the fear and helplessness she had felt? Had she been too young to understand properly what was going on? Had she seen her own father's violence as a separate thing, unconnected to what had caused it?

"Not content with that, you took away all her clothes. When she refused to take off her underwear, you took out the knife that you had already used to threaten her, and you..."

It had done the opposite of what her father had intended. It had made Sondra feel alone, unprotected. It had made her feel that from now on she must be unwaveringly strong in order not to be hurt by the world.

"Miss Meredith, in my view, has a lot of spunk, a lot of intestinal fortitude..."

She had never shown weakness. She had been afraid to be humanly weak or vulnerable; she had been afraid to let herself need anyone.

"As I see it, my primary obligation is to sentence you to a term that will let all other men with your ideas understand..."

Loving someone meant you needed them. Loving meant showing the one you loved your weaknesses as well as your strengths. Love meant sharing fears and failures as well as successes.

"Society will demand a substantial term of imprisonment, both as a punishment for the ugly and unconscionable acts you have committed, and as a deterrent to others who..."

She had shown herself openly to Ben only twice. Once, involuntarily, when he had made love to her with such loving passion that she could not hide herself from him and once, on Tuesday night, when she had chosen to tell him about the past that haunted her.

"Therefore, Hugh Brian Macomber, your sentence is as follows..."

Those two moments had changed her irrevocably. In those moments she had seen the real depths of her love for him, always hidden from herself, and from those moments she knew there was no going back.

"...on the charge of forcible confinement, two years. And finally, on the charge of aggravated sexual assault, six years. The sentences shall run concurrently..."

Hugh Macomber's cry was sudden and dreadful in the total silence of Judge McVean's courtroom. It chilled Sondra to the bone.

"...you shall now be taken...to a penitentiary..." She heard, and she thought involuntarily of where he was going now, and what would happen to him there. He would get no help, no rehabilitation. He would be almost as brutalized and degraded in a federal prison as Laney Meredith had been at his hands, and what good would that do anyone? In the normal course of events, he would get parole in two years and would come out angrier and more violent, probably, than when he went in.

"Don't ever think this society is perfect," she heard her father say again as Hugh Macomber was handcuffed and led away weeping from the last freedom he would know for at least twenty-four months.

"All rise!" shouted the bailiff, and Sondra stood with the rest in the ritual respect for the law as the judge left the bench and the court.

Her part in the thing was over. She had no control over what happened now. She had done the best she could, what she had had to do. She had played the role assigned to her in the play of events that marked humanity's puny attempts to make the world a better place.

Just then Matthew Miller, looking stricken, crossed her line of vision. Sondra's eyes narrowed. Oh, yes, my fine friend, she thought in sudden good humour. And then there's you.

There's always something one human being can do, Sondra thought. Hugh Macomber is a lost cause, perhaps, but... Matthew Miller isn't.

"I guess you know I won my case," Sondra said.

"I read it in this morning's *Globe*," Karen replied, and Sondra could hear her smile. "Congratulations."

"Thank you. I earned it," she said with feeling.

"You sound as though it was more than just another case. Was it especially important to win your first prosecution?"

Sondra laughed lightly. "Well, it was, but what made it especially important to me was you."

"Me! What did I have to do with it?"

"It's the first time I've ever done a rape case, you know. Half the time I wasn't sure whether I was prosecuting Hugh Macomber because of what he did to Laney Meredith, or... or..."

"Jack Wiley because of what he did to me?"

"Yeah."

"Yes, I know what you mean. Filming those kids last year, I kept seeing us. It's like an emotional purge."

"Yeah. Do you mind being reminded of it? Do you mind if we talk about it?"

There was a short pause. Then Karen said gently, "It isn't me who minds talking about it, Sondra. It's you."

"I—what? What do you mean?"

"Only that I've tried to bring it up a few times in the past, and that you could never bear to have the subject discussed. You always said it was for my sake, but I've been talking about Jack Wiley for years now. I couldn't have lived with it if I hadn't learned to look at it, at what happened to me and what it did to me. But I've learned never to bring it up with you."

"But I—Karen, I don't remember anything like that!"

"Do you remember last year—two years ago now, I guess, when I was doing the film?"

"Yes, of course."

"Well, all during that time, how much did we talk about what I was doing, what I was finding out?"

"Well, not very much, but I felt it was a rough period for you, that it was a difficult assignment and if you—"

"It was a purging for me, all right. And it was difficult, but it wasn't a subject I wanted to avoid. Sondra, I came to terms with what Jack Wiley did to me a long time ago. But something like that never goes away. It's like a spiral. On every curve, you meet it again, in some other area, and come to terms with it again."

"God, how depressing!"

"It's not. It's really not. I don't carry it around with me. I just confront it when it comes up again. Listen, did you ever hear the story of the two monks and the naked woman?"

"No. I don't think so."

"Two monks were walking one day, and they came to a river, and a naked woman was sitting there. She came up to the first one and asked him to carry her across the water. This monk got very angry and indignant and called her names and said she was perfectly capable of walking across the river herself.

"The woman went to the second monk and asked him to carry her across, and he picked her up and went across the river with her. On the other side he set her down, and she thanked him, and the two monks went on their way.

"Now, after about five miles, the first monk, still fuming, turned to the second, and said, 'There was no need to do it, you know. She only asked to be provocative. She was perfectly capable of crossing that river under her own steam!'

"And the first monk looked at him and said, 'Are you still carrying her? I put her down five miles ago.'"

Sondra laughed involuntarily. "What is that supposed to mean?"

"In your efforts to avoid Jack Wiley, you've been carrying him with you all these years."

Sondra drew in a sudden, painful breath.

"I've learned to face what happened, Sondra. Sometimes it seems like a daily part of my life; I run into memories every five minutes it seems, some days. But you find that when you face something like that, it loses its power over you. It's there in my life. But I'm—it doesn't have any power over me anymore."

Sondra found she was near tears. "Well, then, I'd—I'd really like to talk about it with you someday soon, if that's all right. All that business about Daddy beating him up and all that—that's a problem for me. Could we talk about it sometime?"

"Sure. Do you want to come over tonight? I'd really like to hear how it affected you. I've often wondered just what you went through. It can't have been easy. Did you feel guilty because it was me and not you?"

"Oh, God, did I! How did you know?" She couldn't tell Karen she still did. Perhaps she would have the courage for that face-to-face.

Karen laughed a little, not unkindly. "It is a fairly common human response. It's called survivor guilt."

It was a mental shock to hear that the terrible secret she had lived with for so long was so common it even had a name! She'd thought she was alone in the feeling! She'd thought she felt that way because she really *could* have done something to prevent what had happened to her sister!

"You really couldn't have done anything to stop it, you know," said Karen, as though reading her thoughts. "He was drunk and very scary. If you'd been there, I don't think it would have made any difference. When you came through the door, I tried to scream at you to run, but he had his hand over my mouth. I was really scared he'd get you, too."

"I never knew you felt that way," Sondra said, feeling the track that one burning tear made on her cheek. "I—didn't you ever blame me?"

"Never. Are you kidding? Never once. You were only twelve. I was just so grateful he didn't get to you. When I was shooting that film, there were young kid victims whose eyes—I just looked at those eyes and thanked God your eyes had never looked at me like that."

It was more than she could stand at the moment. She breathed deeply. "I can't talk anymore over the phone. Tonight then?"

"My place," Karen said. "Doug's away on location. I'll feed you."

Yes, thought Sondra, hanging up the phone. Her heart was beating in a powerful mixture of fear, nervous anticipation and a flooding relief. You'll feed me. You always have. In more ways than one.

Chapter 18

Did you have a good talk with your sister?'' Ben asked.

He hadn't gone to the cottage this weekend. He had too much work to do on his murder case, and Sondra had been feeling emotionally exhausted and confused and had wanted the comfort of her own home around her.

It was a pity, though, because this looked like the weekend the fall colours would be at their best. So they had agreed not to work today, Sunday, and they were now driving north on the back roads, windows open on a beautiful fall day, admiring the colours.

''I know one thing I'd miss on a South Sea island,'' Sondra had said, revelling in the crisp, autumn scented air that streamed into the car. ''The change of seasons.''

''Not to mention the fallout from French atom bomb testing,'' Ben agreed with a grin.

She'd protested, ''You're feeling cynical today. You're letting that murder get to you.''

"I have seventy-eight witnesses lined up," he had pointed out. "It's hard not to let numbers like that get to you."

They had put the radio on after that, a station playing Sunday morning golden oldies, Bob Dylan and early Beatles and "I Can't Get No—Satisfaction," and the silence between them had been companionable for several miles until Ben had broken it with his question.

Sondra took a deep breath. "Oh, yes," she said. "Good, but very difficult. When I think what I've been carting around with me for twenty years...I'm glad we talked. I haven't trusted anyone for twenty years, do you realize that?"

"I knew there was something you were running away from."

"What, even seven years ago?"

"No, not then. Then I just accepted that what I thought was very special just somehow wasn't special to you. But then I watched you, and there was no doubt it was a pattern. As soon as things threatened to get serious in any relationship with you, suddenly the man was out in the cold."

Foolishly, she felt her cheeks go pink. "You watched me?"

"Not at first. At first I just took my ticket to ride and tried to put you out of my mind. It was after my marriage failed, and there you were, still heart-whole, that I began to watch you. I told myself that I was still fond of you, of course, but that the real reason I watched you was out of curiosity. I was wrong, of course. But it took me a long, long time to admit it to myself."

"Why did it take so long?"

He laughed a little and reached to turn down the radio. "Because I am not a masochist, I hope. I'd fallen in love with you once and been burned. You hadn't changed in any way that made me think that a second attempt would be any more successful than the first. I spent three years watching, waiting for something to happen...waiting for you to see."

She looked at him in amazement. "See what?"

He shrugged. "Oh—that the world is not your enemy, I suppose. That you are not an island unto yourself."

Karen had said something like that to her last night as Sondra had lain against her shoulder sobbing out her guilt and remorse and pain. "Nobody does it alone, honey," she had said then. "We're not here on God's earth to do it alone, don't you see? That will destroy the world, just as it's been destroying you. We're *meant* to work together. We're meant to find our place in the whole human tribe. We're all one huge organism, Sondra." She had brushed the damp hair away from Sondra's forehead. "You have to learn to share your pain, too."

Her breath trembled in her throat as the memory of last night's tears almost overwhelmed her. "Yes, I do see that," she croaked, her voice suddenly failing her.

He smiled gently. "I know you do. That was what I finally realized—that I had to take the chance. When you came to work in the Crown office, we were in much closer quarters, and it was still there between us. *I* knew it was still there, even if you wouldn't see it. We were drawn to each other, Sondra. One day you walked down the hall where I was standing, and you absolutely, unconsciously, swerved over to where I was so that you almost had to brush past me. If you'd had paint on your feet, you'd have created a straight line with a broad U-blip in it. And I was standing at the bend of the U."

She was amazed. "Really? *Really?* I never...I just..." She broke off. She needed him, but she hadn't wanted to know it. What work she must have done, unconsciously, to cut herself off from any recognition of this powerful feeling.

"No." He nodded. "And suddenly the waiting was worse than the fear of rejection. I was being a coward, standing on the sidelines when I could get in the ring and fight for what I wanted. I knew there was something. And I knew I was being a fool if I didn't try to make you feel it, too."

She was crying silently because of the newness of the feeling of being loved. It wasn't the same thing as *knowing* you were loved. Not at all. That stayed in the head. That was how she had accepted that her father still loved her after the divorce—in her head. That was how she had felt Ben's love seven years ago. It had never reached her. But it was reaching her now, and this sense of human sharing, of release, of the knowledge that she need not be alone, was almost too powerful to bear.

Ben had pulled the car off the road into a deserted picnic area under a huge bower of oak trees. He took her wordlessly in his arms and simply held her, and she cried out her release from solitary confinement in great gulping sobs.

When they subsided, he got out of the car and came round and opened her door and extended his hand. "Come," he said.

The day was warm and the grass was dry, and they lay on a hillock looking up at the brilliantly coloured roof of leaves, yellow and orange and brown and patches of brilliant fire-red. It was soothing to the spirit, and just on the edge of consciousness, Sondra was thinking, If I am part of the human organism, then I am part of this, too. It can't just stop at humanity—either we are all isolated individuals, or we really are all One, all part of some greater, unimaginable whole.

Maybe the mystics could imagine it. Maybe that was what they were talking about when they spoke of enlightenment and universal consciousness. Maybe there was a way to get up above the world somehow and see all the connections between things that looked separate here on earth. Maybe they really saw it in some way, through some other sense.

She was seeing things through a different sense right now. She was seeing with the heart what with the head alone she had never been able to see.

"You know," she said, "Karen said last night that Dad talked to us about what we could do. He and Mom and Karen discussed the choices she had, and she said I was there. They decided on Daddy beating up Jack Riley. But I don't remember any of that. All I remember is the shock of seeing my father suddenly being violent."

"I suppose to a child of your age it was all just talk. Sometimes I think we grossly overestimate how much a child understands of ordinary human conversation. Anyway, you would still have been in a state of shock, wouldn't you?"

"I guess so." She stared entranced at how the sun sparkled and flickered through this incredible bower of leaves. "Ben," she said with a soft urgency.

"Yes, my darling?"

"I really do love you, you know. I know that now. I really do."

And then the sunlight was a halo around his head, and there was the sweetness and solace of his lips joined to hers.

They had lunch in a little restaurant on the edge of Lake Simcoe that was near enough to a couple of towns to stay open all year round. The cooking was good, if plain, and they felt very lazy afterwards.

They rented a small motorboat and spent an hour on the lake. Then the wind blew up suddenly, and the weather changed. They got in the car and started for home just as the first raindrops hit the windshield.

Later that evening, by the fire, she asked what she had been meaning to ask since it had happened.

"Why did everybody jump to my rescue the other day with Blake, Ben? Why did you? Was it just because of what I'd told you?"

The wind gusted loudly, and rain burst suddenly and violently against the windows. She smiled, feeling safe from the storm.

Ben said, "I want to tell you about a man I knew, a convict. He was my client when I was in private practice, and I'd lost the case and he'd been sent up. I forget what for. And then he came out on parole and did a break and entry or something. Instead of just revoking his parole, they wanted a new trial. I think because his sentence was nearly over by the time he did this new job. The details aren't important.

"Anyway, I was new and this was a minor case, so I pulled it, and here I was in the position of prosecuting a guy I'd been defending eighteen months before. It was pretty weird, but he was philosophical about it, and we got very relaxed and had a few very free talks while his trial was pending.

"He said to me that one thing he really hated about prison was the fact that whatever cell you got put into the walls were always covered with pinups. Everywhere he looked, he was met with pictures of naked women, in the one place where he was never going to be able to see the real thing, or do anything about the feelings those pictures aroused in him.

"He told me he hated it. He said he loved women, he loved sex, and to be constantly reminded of what he couldn't have was a real torture.

"I was young, pretty green, especially about what prisons were really like. I asked him why didn't he just tear the damn pictures down? And he looked at me, a little surprised, and said simply, 'The other guys wouldn't stand for it.'"

Sondra wrinkled her brow. "What?" she asked, perplexed.

"Yeah, you see, Sondra, you don't know. No woman knows. But I understood what the situation was right away. In fact, I was embarrassed that he'd had to tell me. I should have known at the start."

"Know what?"

"That the other men in the prison population wouldn't allow one of their number to live in a cell that wasn't decorated with pinups. He'd have been on the outside, don't you see? It's a male thing. It's being part of the group. Of course, in a prison, the whole thing is much more extreme. Probably he'd have been beaten up—considered a fag, whatever. But it is a microcosm of the real world, Sondra.

"Men learn early, often even before their teenage years, to toe the line in the male club unless they want to be totally ostracized. It happens to every man somewhere along the line. Maybe he's sitting with a bunch of friends, and a girl they know walks by, and one of the group—usually the leader because he's the tough macho one—starts talking crudely about her. And maybe he doesn't like it. Maybe talking about a friend like that behind her back offends him. And maybe he'll even protest just that once.

"But most likely not. Most likely the rest of the guys will be laughing and joining in, and suddenly the choices yawn in front of him: he can be true to himself and be ostracized, or he can shut up and be part of the male club.

"And once you make that choice, it just gets easier and easier to block that stuff out, to stick a grin on your face and let it all go by. And your macho heroes, like Blake, carry on all through high school and university, and right into life, leading the pack. And maybe he knows, or maybe he doesn't, I've never figured it out, that the pack isn't really with him, most of them. They have just taken on protective colouration as a habit."

"That's disgusting. My God, didn't it at least change during the women's revolution?" Sondra demanded.

"For some men it did, and for some it's changed back again. I read a column in the paper the other day where the male columnist was going to town on what he called 'self-righteously sensitive' men, 'guardians of the morals of lesser men than they,' who talk about health foods and think that there are certain topics of conversation not suitable in the presence of children. As far as this columnist was concerned, men who enthuse about parenting and homemaking are embracing this wimpy life-style because they are failures as men in the marketplace where it really counts."

"*When* did you say you read that?" she demanded.

"Last week. It is alive and well, the male club, don't ever think it's not. And a lot of the time, Sondra, we knuckle under to it unconsciously."

"And that's why Blake gets away with what he does."

"That's why. Frankly, I don't even notice Blake anymore. Or I didn't until you began to point things out to me. I didn't want to listen to you, Sondra. Underneath I was blocking out everything you were saying about him. But you persisted, and because I love you, you finally got through to me. And then of course I saw what was really going on, and I had to challenge him."

"But once you challenged him, the others did, too. Why did they all jump on him that day?"

"Well, to be honest, I think you caused that."

She looked at him. "I don't see how. He'd been going on at me for weeks, and no one had complained." She remembered the sense of her own isolation, then, with an immediacy that was painful.

He stroked her hair and then her cheek in the soft firelight, and she was reminded that the storm was outside and she was here in the warmth.

"You might not like what I'm going to say. But, Sondra, whenever Blake went on the way he did, you always seemed up to his weight. You were so tough. It was as though you hung out a sign that read, 'I can handle this.' It was as though you might resent any man thinking that you would need support or protection."

She gasped. "But that wasn't true at *all*!"

"No, I know it wasn't. Maybe I even knew it then but didn't want to face it because of what it would mean. But, you see, in the unwritten rules of the male club, it's okay to protest if there is a woman present who—who needs the help. That's the best way I can explain it. And it never seemed to actually *upset* you, if you see what I mean. It always seemed as though you were challenging Blake on...on some kind of *political* grounds. Can you understand what I'm saying? It doesn't put me—or any of us, really—in a very good light, but that's the way it is."

"All right," she said.

"And after you told me how much Blake upset you, I looked back on my own behaviour, and I realized I'd been ignoring what was going on, that I'd wanted to avoid knowing it because...because it meant a confrontation of a particular sort, and I'd let your strength be my excuse not to take Blake on. I made up my mind to change that, not to let him get away with it again.

"Last Friday, when you won your case, I would have challenged Blake no matter how capably you were handling him yourself.

"But you yourself reacted differently on Friday. For the first time, instead of striking back, Sondra, you were vulnerable. You let your feelings show. Your whole tone of voice was different. And that's why not just I, but every man at the table, suddenly jumped into the breach. You were vulnerable. You took what Blake was doing out of the political realm, and suddenly most of the men present were forced to recognize what was actually happening: Blake was attacking you and hurting you. Most men, to give us credit, won't go along with it when the situation isn't being effectively disguised anymore."

"Strange," she said, shaking her head. "It's not because I was weak, is it? That's what I thought you meant, but that's not it, is it?"

"No. It had nothing to do with weakness, although of course men will jump to protect weak women, too. It was because you—you stopped playing it Blake's way. Because you were admitting he hurt your feelings instead of pretending so well that he didn't that everyone could pretend to themselves they believed you."

"Funny. That was the first time I really let *myself* know that he was hurting my feelings. I've always been so afraid to be helpless, to let myself see when I'm being hurt. You feel so strong, don't you, when you're pretending you can't be hurt? And that day the battle was just too much for me, after all that had happened. I just didn't want to pretend anymore."

He smiled at her. "Feelings are our Pandora's box, you know. You can't just let out the good ones. Either they're all locked up, or they're all free, good and bad, comfortable and uncomfortable."

"Yes." She reached an arm around his neck and gazed into that dark, intelligent, beloved face. "I couldn't have loved you if I hadn't remembered all that hurt. I know that. I've had my love all locked up along with everything else." She smiled as thunder rumbled in the distance. "I'm glad you came after me. I'm glad you stopped waiting, Ben."

He kissed her upturned lips with gentle passion. "We've both had a lot to learn," he said. "You know, the other night I was reading through my manuscript from the beginning, something I haven't done for a while. And I realized that Jennie isn't a person. She's not real. She's the sort of stereotyped woman Blake Roebotham would want to read about."

She couldn't stop a little laugh escaping from her throat. "Did you know?" he asked.

She nodded, smiling. "I thought when I read it that it was more a man's book. I enjoyed the adventure, but it was hard to relate to Jennie as a woman."

"Were you going to tell me?"

"I might have. I thought maybe you were deliberately writing it that way, as a masculine adventure."

"No," he said. "I knew the book was wrong somehow. I could feel it. It wasn't coming right. That's why I was reading it over, to see where I'd gone wrong. And the problem was Jennie had died on me. She'd given up because I'd made her do and say so many things that weren't her character. I wasn't listening to what Jennie felt any more than I was listening to you. And it was only after listening to you, and accepting what you told me, that I could see I'd been treating Jennie the same way."

She smiled. "You talk about her as though she's a real person."

"She is a real person. You won't understand until you've done it yourself. She may not be flesh and blood, but she's real. She's a part of me as surely as Jude is. And I've learned lately that we ignore any part of ourselves at our peril. It isn't just you who's had to change, Sondra. I've had to take a long look at myself these past weeks. Maybe if I'd done that seven years ago, I wouldn't have lost you then. Most men are brought up to ignore what women tell them. But we don't have to go on like that. We can change."

She kissed him, because that was as painfully honest as any discovery she had made. "Thank you," she said. "What are you going to do to bring Jennie back to life?"

"Oh, just go back and rewrite her the way she wants to be written. That part won't be hard. What's hard is realizing how much of the stuff I've written just recently may not fit once she's functioning properly."

She stared at him in mock horror. "You mean that sex scene is going to get the chop? You can't! That's my favourite scene in the book!"

"You like that scene because you think what Jude is doing to Jennie is what I wanted to do to you that night when you slept alone, and it gives you a sense of pow—"

"Well, isn't it?" she challenged softly.

He looked down at her, a sexy smile deep in his dark eyes. "What I wanted to do to you? Well, some things were, I guess."

He was teasing her, but two could play at that game. "Which things, for example?"

The look in his eyes deepened into desire. "Do you want me to show you, or tell you?"

She was lying across his lap, stretched out on the sofa, leaning against his propped-up legs as he held her in his arms. Under her waist now, she felt how easily she aroused him, and the pressure of that flesh against her and what it meant was like lightning along her nerves. She wanted him with a passion as sudden and quick as his own, a passion of fainting intensity.

She returned his look without knowing it. "Both," she said hungrily, and the game was no longer a game.

His hand was against her neck. It moved, and she felt the strength of tightening arm muscles, as he ripped her shirt open down the front, exposing the roundness of her pale breasts and darker nipples, in one powerful stroke.

As Jude had done, with Jennie.

She gasped in sheer erotic excitement, and he bent his head to kiss her breast, as Jude had done with Jennie. Her nipples came hungrily erect, and she pressed his head more firmly against her flesh, desperate for his touch.

As Jude has done with Jennie, he was suddenly trembling with a need greater than he could control, and he tightened his hold around her and pressed her against his mouth.

Then they forgot Jude and Jennie, and Ben lifted his head, and his eyes held all the messages she had ever wanted to see. "I need you," he told her hoarsely. "Oh, God, Sondra, I don't know how I let you go seven years ago, but I am not letting you go again. Do you understand what I'm saying? You can't walk out on me now. Whatever the problems are, we'll work them through together. But you won't get away from me again."

It might have frightened her, if her own answering need hadn't been there, waiting to hear it. If she had been in hiding still, she might have protested that she had to go her way alone.

But she loved him. Loved and needed him more deeply than she would ever be able to tell him.

Except, perhaps, through the medium of her body.

She put her hand on his hardened flesh, and her eyes half closed against the power of need, mental, emotional and physical, that tore through her. There had never been anything like it. Since the dawn of time there could never have been desire equal to this.

"I love you," she said hoarsely, for her throat seemed to have closed, and she could hardly speak. "Please love me now."

Jude and Jennie had grappled to completion on the floor, but Ben's urgency was more tender, and Sondra was a real live woman. He slipped his arm under her hips, guided her legs to the floor, and then stood up: and together they walked the long walk to the bedroom, and kissed and sank down onto the thick eiderdown.

And she did not claw, but whimpered gently as he entered her, for accepting him into her body was the most trusting thing she would ever do, and she was a woman, and knew it.

He knew it, too. He lifted his head and looked into her eyes as his body moved in her, giving both of them a nearly unbearable pleasure. And it was more than the pleasure of the flesh, for him and for her; it was the far deeper, immensely richer joy of union that they felt.

The union of male and female, of earth and sky, of spirit and flesh, trembled in their hearts and in their bodies, and became more and more urgent, and then its sudden heat flooded their one being. And they cried aloud as joy found them for one blinding, brilliant moment of time, and then lost them again.

Later, lying entwined in the dark, they heard the rain. It lashed the windows unmercifully now, the anger of winter not far away.

"The storm's building," she whispered, suddenly fearful, but not of the rain.

"Yes," he said. "But we can weather it, if we're together." His hand stroked her temple and then her cheek in the darkness, and she felt the lightest of kisses against the corner of her mouth. "Let's face it together, my love. It's so much easier together."

"Together," she said, "What a nice sound that has."

The second novel in an
original new paperback series
—Wagons West—
about the first
great wagon train westward.

NEBRASKA!

By the author of INDEPENDENCE!

WAGONS WEST

NEBRASKA!

STALWART MEN AND SPIRITED WOMEN BLAZING A TRAIL OF PASSION AND GLORY ACROSS THE PROUD AMERICAN NATION . . .

CATHY VAN AYL
Though a young widow, she is sexually innocent, and both drawn to and frightened by the manly ways of Whip Holt.

MICHAEL "WHIP" HOLT,
the lean, taciturn mountain man who is master of the frontier, yet a rank amateur when it comes to understanding women.

TONIE MELL
Hard-riding, fast-shooting, and beautiful, she may pay with her life for her Russian ancestry—and with the lives of the entire wagon train.

DR. ROBERT MARTIN,
the physician whose skills win even the respect of hostile Indians.

CINDY,
a former prostitute in search of a new life in the West. She once hated men—now one man could change her mind.

TED WOODS,
who would kill to protect the woman he loves.

MAJOR LAURENCE WOODLING,
a South Carolina aristocrat who lost his plantation but not his faith in the future.

CLAIBORNE WOODLING,
the Major's son. A demon rider, an expert swordsman, and a dangerous man.

EULALIA WOODLING,
the Major's daughter. A flirt, and a selfish beauty, until she suffers the ultimate degradation.

HOSEA,
an escaped slave who risks his life to save the wagon train.

STALKING HORSE,
Cherokee warrior, Whip's closest friend and blood brother.

PIERRE LE ROUGE
Tricked into an act of treachery, he redeems himself by a deed of daring heroism.

PRESIDENT VAN BUREN,
leader of the nation, who, in a desperate race against time, must save the wagon train from sabotage by foreign powers.

★★★★★★★★★★★★★★★★★★★★★★

Bantam Books by Dana Fuller Ross
Ask your bookseller for the books you have missed

INDEPENDENCE!—Volume I
NEBRASKA!—Volume II
WYOMING!—Volume III
OREGON!—Volume IV
TEXAS!—Volume V
CALIFORNIA!—Volume VI
COLORADO!—Volume VII
NEVADA!—Volume VIII
WASHINGTON!—Volume IX
MONTANA!—Volume X
DAKOTA!—Volume XI
UTAH!—Volume XII
IDAHO!—Volume XIII
MISSOURI!—Volume XIV
MISSISSIPPI!—Volume XV
LOUISIANA!—Volume XVI
TENNESSEE!—Volume XVII

WAGONS WEST * VOLUME 2

NEBRASKA!

DANA FULLER ROSS

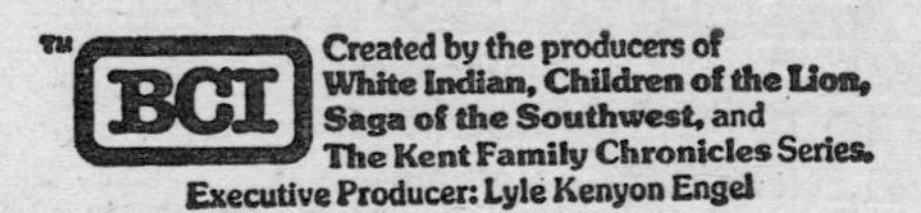

TM
BCI
Created by the producers of
White Indian, Children of the Lion,
Saga of the Southwest, and
The Kent Family Chronicles Series.
Executive Producer: Lyle Kenyon Engel

BANTAM BOOKS

NEW YORK • TORONTO • LONDON • SYDNEY • AUCKLAND

NEBRASKA!
A Bantam Book / July 1979

2nd printing ...... July 1979	*10th printing .... March 1980*
3rd printing ...... July 1979	*11th printing ..... April 1980*
4th printing .... August 1979	*12th printing . September 1980*
5th printing .. September 1979	*13th printing . November 1980*
6th printing ... October 1979	*14th printing .... March 1981*
7th printing .. December 1979	*15th printing ... October 1981*
8th printing ... February 1980	*16th printing .... March 1982*
9th printing ... February 1980	*17th printing . December 1982*

18th printing ... June 1984

Produced by Book Creations, Inc.
Chairman of the Board: Lyle Kenyon Engel

ISBN 0-553-24651-8

Published simultaneously in the United States and Canada

PRINTED IN THE UNITED STATES OF AMERICA

H 27 26 25 24 23 22

NEBRASKA!

THE DARING TRAIL
OF THE MEN AND WOMEN
OF WAGONS WEST AS
THEY CROSS THE GREAT
PLAINS TOWARD A NEW
ERA IN AMERICA

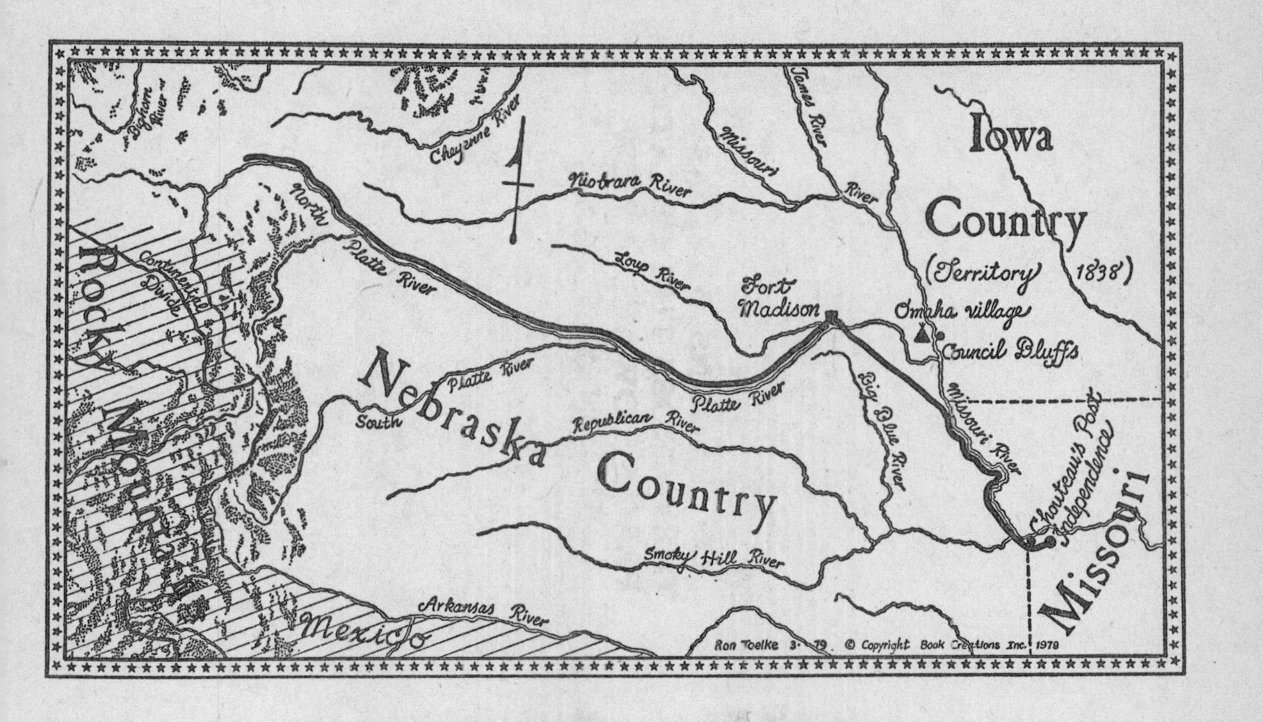
Iowa
Country
(Territory 1838)
Omaha village
Council Bluffs
Fort Madison
Missouri River
Chouteau's Post
Independence
Missouri
Big Blue River
James River
River
Missouri
Niobrara River
Loup River
Cheyenne River
Bighorn River
North
Platte River
Platte River
South
Platte River
Republican River
Nebraska
Country
Smoky Hill River
Arkansas River
Mexico
Continental Divide
Rocky Mountains
Ron Toelke 3-79 © Copyright Book Creations Inc. 1979

I

Heavy clouds, thick, black, and ominous, blew eastward from the Rocky Mountains across the Great Plains wilderness, obscuring the moon and stars. The ground was still warm from the early autumn sun that had shone down on Missouri the previous day, but the night air was cool. A white mist, as impenetrable as a bale of cotton, rose from the broad waters of the great Missouri River, bathing the area in a blanket of swirling mists.

High on the bluffs of the eastern bank of the river, a short distance from the frontier village of Independence, Missouri, stood the symbols of the future—covered wagons arranged in a circle. Within the scores of wagons, hundreds of men, women, and children were asleep. Some had begun their journey in the East and had been joined by others along the way in a daring and unique venture. They were the first pioneers who were blazing a path across the country to Oregon and to the Pacific Ocean.

Inside the circle, the horses and oxen were asleep, too, as were the dogs. There seemed to be nothing to fear. Independence was a sturdy little community of ranch owners and farmers—people who took the law into their own hands when necessary because no other law existed at this remote outpost. Bloodshed was not unknown, but violence occurred infrequently.

No one in the wagon train heard the two boats being rowed across the Missouri from the west bank; no one saw the little craft hauled ashore, beached and made secure; and certainly no one in the train knew that six armed men, frontier drifters who preyed on fur trappers or isolated farm owners, had found a tempting target.

The six men crept up the hill, pistols and knives in their hands. A shepherd dog stretched outside one of the wagons awakened and raised his pointed ears. Quietly the bandits crept closer, struggling as they made their way up the bluff.

Suddenly one member of the wagon train, a tall, lean man dressed in buckskins, awoke. Instantly alert, he threw off his blanket; he reached for his long rifle automatically and quickly rose to his feet from the grassy spot where he had been sleeping.

The mist was too thick for him to see through it, so he listened intently, his head cocked to one side. Then a faint, grim smile appeared on his face. Moving silently, with the experience of one who had spent years as a hunter, trapper, and guide in the Rockies, he went quickly to several key wagons.

In almost no time he was joined by three men, all of whom carried rifles. One was a burly blacksmith who had spent a decade in prison for murder. Another was a high-ranking Austrian nobleman who had joined the wagon train because he loved adventure. The third was a mild-mannered physician, a widower who sought a new life, far from the sorrows he had known.

The trio followed the man in buckskins to the lip of the bluff. No one could see more than a few feet ahead, nor could they hear a sound—they were reacting instinctively. Within a few seconds they were joined by an Indian brave, also clad in buckskins, a warrior who almost casually notched an arrow on the string of his bow. Like the man in buckskins, he had no need to see the approaching menace.

A broad smile appeared on the face of the man in buckskins. There was no doubt that he thoroughly enjoyed the challenge of danger. He didn't need to speak; his companions had traveled far with him and knew what was expected of them. They all waited.

By now the robbers were no more than five yards from the lip of the bluff, almost within reach of their goal. The man in buckskins nodded, almost casually, and four rifles spoke simultaneously, the weapons deliberately fired over the heads of the approaching men.

The startled bandits paused, then turned and fled down the steep slope, sliding and stumbling, falling and scrambling as they raced to the safety of their waiting boat.

Now it was the Indian's turn. He sent arrow after arrow toward the retreating men. The bandits saw the arrows dropping around them and increased their wild pace as they dragged their boat into the water and rowed off to safety.

The man in buckskins listened, heard the fading sound of oars, and nodded. His companions turned and strolled back to their wagons for another hour of sleep. He and the Indian wrapped themselves in their respective blankets. Within a few minutes they had drifted back to sleep.

The men, women, and children of the train were still asleep. Even those who had awakened briefly had mistaken the firearms volley for a crack of thunder.

The wagon train was secure.

As always, Cathy van Ayl looked lovely as she emerged from her wagon. Totally unaware of her beauty, she paused on the back step to tuck some stray strands of her long, blonde hair under her sunbonnet, then tightened the sash of her dimity dress. She looked like a young girl in her teens rather than a widow of twenty-three. That air of innocence wasn't accidental. She had never been intimate with her elderly husband, Otto, a miserly farmer from Long Island, who had died in a raid on the wagon train.

Cathy stepped down to the ground just as Whip Holt, the hired guide and wagonmaster of the Oregon-bound caravan, came into view. Tall and sinewy in his buckskins, he was armed, as usual, with a brace of pistols and a long bullwhip, wrapped around his middle, that gave him his name. His skin was leathery after years of exposure to the outdoors, and his eyes were hard. But when he saw Cathy he grinned at her, and suddenly he looked younger than twenty-nine.

She smiled at him in return, her heart skipping a beat. When Otto was alive, it had been necessary to conceal her interest in Whip, but all that had changed since the young mountain man rejoined the train, several weeks ago, as it moved westward across Missouri. Now she had no reason beyond her own sense of discretion to hide the way she felt.

Certainly Whip made no secret of his own feelings. "Morning, ma'am," he called, sauntering toward her.

"You're wearing a new buckskin shirt and trousers, I see," she said politely.

He was surprised that she had noticed what he was wearing. "Well, you know how it is. I get restless just sitting around Independence while we put in supplies and wait for the new folks joining us to show up. So one day I went hunting. He cleared his throat awkwardly. "You look mighty nice, all dressed up for a day in the city."

Cathy couldn't help laughing. Certainly no one else in 1837 would dream of referring to the frontier town of Independence, Missouri as a "city." One of the last outposts of civilization east of the Great Plains, it was visited by trappers, hunters, and traders bringing their furs from the Rocky Mountains to the East. Now, with other wagon trains scheduled to follow Whip's caravan across the wilderness to the fertile Oregon country, Independence promised to develop into a major supply center.

"I told my sister I'd buy some things in town for her and bring them along tonight."

Only a few days earlier, Cathy's older sister, Claudia, had been married to Sam Brentwood, the former leader of the wagon train. The couple would remain in Independence to establish a supply depot, sponsored by Sam's mentors, former President of the United States

Andrew Jackson and John Jacob Astor, a fur baron and the leader of a group of wealthy businessmen who were encouraging the settling of the Oregon country.

"Claudia and Sam asked me to supper tonight, too," Whip said, and shifted in embarrassment. "I—I wasn't so sure I wanted to go, seeing as how I don't sit down at a table indoors very often. But if you're going, ma'am, I'll be happy to escort you."

"I'd like that," Cathy said. She smiled again before turning away, then added, "I'm not really dressed up, you know. All I own are a few dresses like this, except for the old woolen things I wear on the trail."

"Could you use a doeskin dress, ma'am?"

"I'd love it, Whip." Cathy hesitated. "But I wouldn't want you to think I was hinting."

"No matter. Stalking Horse," he said, referring to his close friend, a Cherokee scout, "has been pestering me to go hunting again, so I reckon I'll have some skins for you by the time we push off."

Cathy thanked him, embarrassed by his generosity, then left the circle of wagons. Needing time to think, she stood, looking beyond the bend in the Missouri River, imagining the limitless wilderness and mountains that the wagon train would have to cross before reaching Oregon.

Otto van Ayl had been determined to go to Oregon and had given his wife no choice. But the widowed Cathy was free to make up her own mind. Claudia and Sam had offered her a home with them in Independence. And she wouldn't be dependent on their charity, either. Her wagon was as solid as any made in New England, where they had come from, and the four horses that pulled it were strong, surefooted and healthy. She could get a substantial sum for the wagon and team if she decided to stay behind when the train moved out. In addition, Otto had left her the fortune he had saved in a lifetime of miserly living, two thousand dollars in gold.

When they had started on the journey, Otto had concealed the money beneath a false floor in the wagon, but after his death, at Claudia and Sam's insistence, she had moved it for safekeeping to the enormous special wagon where the caravan's medicines, extra weapons, and emergency rations were stored.

So Cathy was wealthy, at least by the standards of the pioneers who were heading to Oregon. Certainly she could pay for her keep if she decided to stay with her sister and brother-in-law. Fortunately, she wouldn't have to make up her mind for a few days; she felt pulled in both directions.

Because of Whip and because of what she had heard about Oregon, she wanted to go on. But she was a grown woman, not a romantic adolescent, and she couldn't allow her interest in him to become too great a factor. On the other hand, she had begun the long trek, and she did believe in finishing what she started. Also, if any of the stories she had heard about Oregon were true, she knew it would be heaven on earth.

Tugging her in the opposite direction was the knowledge that powerful forces were at work trying to prevent the American settlers from reaching their destination. The ownership of the Oregon country was in dispute, with both the United States and Great Britain claiming it. A British agent, Henry St. Clair, who had joined the wagon train posing as a settler, had already made several violent attempts to halt the train. After he had been discovered and left the train, he had inspired a vicious attack on the caravan by army deserters.

The British attempt to sabotage the train wasn't the only one. Imperial Russia wanted to stop it from reaching Oregon, too. Russians had been the first to settle in Oregon. Although international pressures had forced the czar seemingly to abandon his claim, the government in St. Petersburg actually was doing no such thing. Cathy was one of the few members of the caravan who knew that attempts had been made by the czar's secret police to blackmail a lovely frontier girl named Tonie Mell into working for them. Tonie's parents, whom she hadn't seen since early childhood, were still in Russia. She had been forced to join the pioneers early in their journey and had been told that her parents wouldn't be allowed to come to America unless she committed acts of sabotage against the train. But, thanks to her own courage and the help of Sam and Whip, she had outsmarted them. Now she was continuing on to Oregon, this time in the company of her uncle, Arnold Mell, who had decided to sell his farm to Sam and Claudia and join his niece on her journey. But it was fair to assume that the Russians would try again.

In addition, there were terrifying rumors among the settlers about hostile Indian tribes in the wilderness ahead. Some pessimists predicted that every last man, woman, and child in the train would be murdered. But Cathy refused to believe these stories. No matter how great the menace of Indians might become, she had unbounded faith in Whip Holt's abilities. She had seen him in action, and she was confident he would lead the band of settlers, already four hundred strong and growing every day, safely to their Oregon destination. She was convinced that no Indians could prevent Whip from reaching his goal—for that matter, neither could the British and Russians.

Tonight, perhaps, she would discuss her situation with her sister—it might clarify her thinking.

Remembering her promise to buy some things for Claudia, Cathy headed toward the town of Independence. She passed log cabins and houses of whitewashed clapboard. Until the past year, Independence had been little more than a village. But now it boasted two general stores, a stable, and, on its main street, two brothels and at least a dozen taverns and saloons.

When Sam and Claudia finished making changes in the ranch, their property would become the principal supply depot for later wagon trains. The depot would sell both horses and oxen, as well as spare wheels, axles, and yokes. Claudia planned to put in a full supply of such provisions as bacon, flour, beans, and sugar—the staples that every family needed on the trek across the continent. Thanks to the generosity of Astor and his associates, as well as the official encouragement of the new President, Martin Van Buren, Sam would have enough funds to put in a stock of firearms, gunpowder, and ammunition, too.

As Cathy walked down the main street, the morning sun was warm, almost hot. The breeze was gentle and it seemed to her more like summer than the beginning of autumn. It was small wonder, she thought, that Whip was eager to start the march across the plains as soon as possible. Cathy knew from her own experience in the past six months that the caravan could travel ten to twelve miles per day in good weather, but that progress was slowed to a crawl when it rained. And when the rains were very heavy, it sometimes became necessary to call a complete halt.

Pondering her dilemma, paying scant attention to her immediate surroundings, Cathy was suddenly aroused from her reverie by the sound of a man's harsh, deep voice.

"That there one is the prettiest I've seen since we got to this town. I claim her!"

"Like hell you do," another man replied. "Maybe we'll draw lots for her, all of us, or maybe we'll leave the choice up to her. We got to be fair about this."

Startled, Cathy saw eight or nine men who had just emerged from a tavern directly ahead. In spite of the early hour, they had been drinking heavily. Some of them were dressed in shabby linsey-woolsey and others in worn, greasy buckskins. They had not shaved for days, and their hair was dirty and unkempt. All were armed with skinning knives, as well as either pistols or rifles.

These were the men Whip and Sam contemptuously referred to as "frontier scum," opportunists who earned a precarious living. Sometimes they bought furs from trappers down on their luck and sold them to traders. Sometimes they did odd jobs for local homesteaders. They were as unsavory as they were unreliable, and Cathy blamed herself for failing to see them in time to avoid them.

But she had little time for regrets. The group had spread across the road, blocking her path, and noting their leers, she was afraid that they would maul her if she tried to crowd past them. But she might be in even worse trouble if she turned and tried to flee; certainly that would encourage them in their game. There were no other pedestrians or riders in sight, so it would be useless to call for help.

The best way to handle the situation, she decided, would be to keep moving forward, remaining calm and ignoring the brutes. So, despite a strong urge to run, she continued to walk at the same even pace, her head high.

One of her tormentors muttered something, and the group quickly surrounded the girl. The man with the rasping voice, appointing himself the spokesman, grinned at her.

"You look like you need some lovin'," he said, "so take your pick."

"Let me pass, please." Cathy knew no escape was possible, but made an effort to speak calmly.

"Don't put on no airs with us, girlie," another declared. "You women up the road charge enough, so it's high time you give us somethin' free."

The stunned Cathy suddenly realized they had mistaken her for a girl from one of the brothels. Certainly they were in no mood—perhaps in no condition—to heed her denials. She was in real danger, and she didn't know how to escape.

Arnold Mell, leading two pack horses laden with the last of his belongings from the ranch, felt a sense of relief he wouldn't have admitted to anyone. The house was no longer what it had been prior to the recent death of his wife. It was crowded with too many memories, so he was glad to be rid of it, pleased that he was joining the wagon train.

Tonie had argued against the sale, thinking he was doing it just for her sake. She was partly right. He realized that in the time she had spent with the caravan before it reached Independence, she had fallen in love with the wagon train's personable and competent physician, a widower named Robert Martin. He wanted to give the romance every opportunity to develop. In fact, he was delighted. Never before had the tomboyish girl shown an interest in any man, and she deserved happiness. He and his wife had tried to substitute for his brother and sister-in-law, the parents she had left behind in St. Petersburg, but he had often felt she had missed her real mother and father. And she had been under a great strain ever since she had been blackmailed by the czar's secret police. Her courage in defying the might of a huge and powerful nation had been splendid, and she had earned the future she so badly wanted for herself.

But Arnold had his own reasons for joining the train, too. He had settled in Independence when it had been a wilderness, but life here was too tame now. At the age of sixty, he was in better physical condition than men half his age, and he looked forward to meeting the challenges of the Great Plains and the Rocky Mountains. What was more, his talents as a rider and marksman and his intimate knowledge of the Plains Indians would be a great help to Whip Holt, who would need all the assistance he could get in shepherding so large a company of men, women, and children all the way to Oregon.

Glancing at Tonie, who was riding demurely beside him, Arnold smiled to himself. A superb horsewoman and expert rifle shot who had spent most of her life in buckskins, she had chosen a different role for herself today. Her fiery red hair, which usually flew free, was piled high on her head, and she had used cosmetics subtly, to emphasize the depth of her green eyes and the fullness of her mouth. Instead of buckskins, she was wearing a snug-fitting dress of green linen with a low, scooped neckline—a gown that showed off her lithe, trim figure to its best advantage. And, thanks to the dress, she was actually riding sidesaddle.

Shaking his head, he started to laugh. The girl glanced at him archly, raising a slender eyebrow.

"I'll have to call you Antoinette instead of Tonie," he said.

She knew precisely what he meant, and she blushed. "I'll be wearing trousers most of the time crossing the Great Plains, Uncle Arnold," she said. "Whip Holt has already asked me to keep the job of monitor. So I'll be riding up and down the lines of march all day, making sure there are no problems or wagon breakdowns. The only chance I'll have to wear dresses and really look like a woman will be on Sundays when we rest."

"I'm not blaming you, Tonie, just teasing you a little," he said. "Your aunt would have been proud to see you looking like such a grand lady."

"Do you really think I do, Uncle Arnold?"

He nodded, chuckling again. "You bet, and I won't be the only one."

"Bob Martin doesn't know I'm alive," Tonie said flatly.

"Don't be so sure of that. And if he hasn't noticed you before now, he'll come to life in a hurry when he sees you today. I wondered what took you so long this morning. Now I know—and I must say the results are worth the time you spent."

"They'll be worth it," Tonie said as they reached the road that would take them into the heart of Independence on their way to the wagon train encampment, "if Dr. Martin really pays some attention to me and stops taking me for granted. What's that up ahead, Uncle Arnold?"

He looked, then shrugged. "Just some frontier men, seems like."

"They're up to something."

"That wouldn't surprise me."

As Tonie peered ahead, she became increasingly concerned. She caught a glimpse of a sunbonnet, blonde hair, and a flounced skirt in the middle of a circle of men. The men were taking turns tormenting the woman, trying to caress her breasts and reach up under her skirt. "I don't like this, Uncle Arnold!"

"Nobody thinks very much of men like that, and one of these days they'll have to be driven out of town. But they're not bothering us, Tonie, so I suggest we leave well enough alone." Arnold spoke mildly; a lifetime of fighting for the sake of principle had left him weary.

Suddenly Tonie saw the face of the trapped girl and was horrified. "It's Cathy!"

Before her uncle could stop her, Tonie spurred forward, her anger replacing her common sense. She was able to look after herself when she was armed, but she carried no weapons today and consequently was helpless. Arnold Mell followed close behind her, calling in vain for her to stop.

Tonie sent her mare charging into the circle, breaking the formation. "Clear the road and leave that lady alone!" she cried.

"Here's another!" one of the men shouted, then easily hauled Tonie from her horse.

She fought him, trying to kick him and rake his face with her nails, but her long-skirted, tight-fitting gown hindered her. "Take your hands off me, you filthy pig!" she screamed.

He subdued her easily, laughing as he pinned her arms to her sides. "I got to teach you to show a little respect."

"Ain't this nice?" the leader asked of no one in particular. "Now we got two."

"Let's see which is livelier, the blonde or the redhead," one of the men suggested.

Arnold Mell, still mounted, raised his rifle. "Take your hands off these ladies and go about your business," he said in a cold, quiet voice, "or somebody is going to get hurt pretty badly."

One of the men quickly stood behind Cathy and, using her as a shield, he twisted her arm behind her back. At the same moment, he held his skinning knife to her throat. "Grandpa," he said, "the first one to get hurt will be this woman. Pull that trigger just once, and I'll cut her from ear to ear, I swear it." Arnold knew he wasn't bluffing.

Cathy stood very still, scarcely daring to breathe. The long, slightly curved blade was only an inch or two from her throat. Tonie, too, stopped struggling in the grasp of her captor. Deadlocked, Arnold stared at the men and they returned his gaze.

Although those who were participating in the frozen tableau didn't yet realize it, the scene was being witnessed by three pedestrians who were approaching the site. They had been walking single file along the narrow part of the road when Dr. Robert Martin, who was in the lead, halted abruptly. "My God! Tonie and Cathy!"

Seeing the group, Stalking Horse, clad only in a loincloth, a bearskin cape, and moccasins, reached for his bow and an arrow from the quiver he always carried over one shoulder. "Me fix," he said.

Instantly Whip Holt assessed the situation. In sheer numbers the odds favored the gang, but he knew that he and Arnold Mell, even without Stalking Horse and Bob Martin, could overwhelm the gang. If a real fight developed, however, Cathy and Tonie might be hurt, or even killed. Their safety was his first concern.

"No, Stalking Horse," he said, taking charge. "Put down your bow. Bob, your belt is the right place for your pistol. Let it stay there." He sauntered forward casually, discreetly tugging at the handle of his whip to uncoil it.

"Mr. Mell, it would be a big help all around if you'd put down your rifle for a minute or two."

Arnold was surprised but instantly realized that Whip had a plan in mind. "You're the boss, Mr. Holt," he said, lowering his rifle.

Tonie displayed astonishing poise by grinning appreciatively at her uncle. She knew what the others did not—that he could fire with pinpoint accuracy even while holding the rifle in his lap. The muzzle, she noted, continued to point at the leader of the gang.

Whip strolled still closer to the men and their captives, his tone amiable. "I reckon we ought to have a little chat about this situation," he said. "Hanging may be too good for you boys, but we might let you go if you release these ladies. Right now—with no arguments."

"Don't come one step closer, I'm warning you!" the man who held his skinning knife at Cathy's throat shouted.

"Whatever you say," Whip replied, halting.

At the same instant his whip sang effortlessly through the air, and its leaded tip cut a deep furrow in the man's hand.

The man screamed in agony as the knife fell to the ground from his nerveless fingers.

The leader drew his pistol. "You were warned," he called.

Again the lash leaped toward its target, this time wrapping itself around the wrist of the gang's leader. Whip tugged gently, and the man's hand was forced up over his head. His pistol discharged harmlessly into the air. Whip tugged again, and the pistol dropped to the ground.

Not yet satisfied, Whip disengaged the lash, then let fly a third time, and the rawhide coiled around the leader's neck. A less than gentle tug brought him to his knees, and an instant later he pitched forward onto the ground, clawing in vain at the taut leather line.

"Mr. Mell," Whip said pleasantly, "I'd be obliged if you'd cover these bastards now. You, too, Stalking Horse. Shoot to kill if any one of them makes a single move." He continued to pull in the whip, dragging the leader toward him.

The Cherokee had already notched an arrow on his bowstring, and Arnold happily raised his rifle again.

Whip continued to pull in the rawhide line. Rather than be choked, the man was forced to wriggle forward on his stomach, unable to rise and unable to resist the steady pressure.

"Cathy," Whip said. "Come over here, please. Take your time and walk slowly."

Cathy felt like running but did as she had been directed.

"That's it," Whip said, still pulling on the lash and keeping a sharp watch on the rest of the gang. "Get behind Stalking Horse and the doctor."

As she did so, Whip said, "All right, Tonie, it's your turn."

"I'll be with you in a minute." Tonie turned to the man who had hauled her from her horse. Smiling slightly, she reached up and raked his face with her fingernails. Blood spurted from the scratches, and he groaned. But, keenly aware of the rifle and bow pointed at him, he did not dare even to raise a hand to protect himself, much less strike the girl.

Tonie spat in his face, then laughed. Turning away from him, she strolled toward her deliverers, the picture of elegance.

"Are you all right, Tonie?" Dr. Martin asked, his voice deep with concern.

"Never better, Bob," she replied lightly.

Arnold chuckled. His niece could look after herself, no question about that. And although she couldn't, and wouldn't, have planned the unsavory incident, she had certainly succeeded in calling herself to Robert Martin's attention. It was unlikely that he would ever forget the impression she had made.

"What about you, Cathy?"

"I—I'm all right now, Doctor. Thank you." Cathy was still shaken.

By now the leader of the gang was within arm's reach of Whip, who let the lash fall free. Then he coiled it around his waist with practiced ease.

As the burly man stumbled to his feet, Whip told him, "We don't like it when our ladies are molested." Quickly, before the man could move, Whip smashed his fist into the man's face.

The man tried to protect himself, but to no avail. Whip landed two hard rights to his face, followed by a solid blow to the pit of the stomach. The man doubled over. A hard, driving right straightened him for a moment, and then he toppled backward, sprawling on the dusty road.

"I'm giving you boys fifteen minutes to clear out of town," Whip said, nudging the body of the fallen man with his foot. "Take this one with you and don't come back, any of you. My Indian friend here hasn't taken any scalps lately, and he can have all of yours."

Several members of the gang came forward hesitantly to carry their fallen companion. Then the entire group, suddenly sober and badly frightened, left the scene as rapidly as they could, scattering as they ran.

Cathy was calmer now, and her eyes were grave as

she turned to Whip. "I'm very much obliged to you. More than I can ever say."

Although he was always self-confident in moments of crisis, he flushed beneath his heavy tan. "I just did what had to be done," he replied.

Gratefully he turned to Arnold Mell. "I'm glad you held off and didn't start blasting. The girls might have been hurt."

Arnold grinned. "Years ago when I was one of the first to settle in these parts," he said, speaking with no more than a trace of a Russian accent, "I learned two things. Always keep your gun loaded, but keep your finger off the trigger whenever shooting might cause more problems than it solves."

Whip nodded soberly, pleased with Arnold's answer. The old man was going to be a valuable member of the company. Anyone who understood the wilderness as he did was a valuable asset to the wagon train.

Dr. Martin's manner seemed professional as he looked at Tonie Mell. If his concern was personal, he succeeded in concealing it. "You look none the worse for wear after a nasty experience."

Tonie, outraged at his cool, professional tone and at his failure to compliment her on her appearance, said coldly, "Thanks to Whip and Stalking Horse, I've managed to survive rather nicely, thank you."

Then she turned to Cathy. "Cathy, were you heading into town?"

Cathy nodded.

"Good," Tonie said. "I have some errands to do, myself. Uncle Arnold, if you'll take my horse with you, I'll meet you at the wagon train later."

Bob Martin watched with consternation as the two girls walked off arm in arm, down the road. As a physician and as a widower, he thought he should have had a better understanding of women. But he could not figure out why Tonie had suddenly seemed so angry. What had he done to insult her?

A large, newly painted sign which had just been hung over the front door identified the ranch house and its outbuildings as Brentwood's Depot. It wouldn't be long, perhaps two or three months, before supplies and provisions would begin to arrive from the East and the depot would be busy. Today the air was festive as Sam and Claudia Brentwood gave their farewell party to the people he had escorted this far on their long, arduous journey to Oregon.

The lean and grizzled Sam, limping due to an arthritic hip, had butchered a steer and was roasting two sides of beef over a fire built in a trench behind the house. He had also slaughtered a hog for the occasion. Piled up in mounds were potatoes and fresh sweet corn, still in shucks, to be cooked in the coals.

Two enthusiastic young helpers were turning the spits for him. Danny was a former bound boy in his mid-teens, who, indentured to a cruel and violent man, had escaped and joined the wagon train. He had endeared himself to the whole company by his willingness to work hard. He worked in perfect harmony with Chet Harris, the eldest surviving son of the widowed Emily Harris, who was intent on making a new life for her family. The two boys were about the same age and had become such close friends that when one appeared the other was always close at hand.

The most intriguing member of the wagon train had insisted on taking charge of preparing the drinks. Baron Ernst von Thalman was a wealthy, middle-aged Austrian nobleman, formerly a cavalry officer in the Imperial Austrian Army. Lean and athletic, a deadly shot, he lived in a custom-built wagon that resembled an elegant home on wheels. He had jugs of hard cider for the men who wanted it, a less potent cider for the women, and a non-alcoholic cider for the children.

Cathy van Ayl and Tonie Mell helped Claudia Brentwood in the kitchen, as did Cindy, a former prostitute from Louisville who had reformed and was making a new life for herself. Working together, as they had learned to do on the road, the young women prepared salad greens and baked loaves of white bread, corn bread, and a variety of fruit pies.

Stoking the wood fire for them, carrying the baked

breads and pies to tables in the yard was Ted Woods, a blacksmith by trade. He was a swarthy, powerful giant, and it was no accident that he was always found in the vicinity of the slender, bubbling Cindy. It was obvious to her, as well as to her companions, that Ted had developed a deep interest in her, although he had said nothing about his feelings to anyone. Some thought he was shy, but Cathy knew better. Ted had spent ten years in an Indiana prison after killing his wife and his brother when he had discovered them in bed together. That experience had scarred him deeply, and Cathy, at least, wondered if he would ever dare to tell Cindy of his interest in her.

As they worked, Cathy and Tonie told the story of what had happened to them earlier in the day in Independence. Claudia Brentwood was concerned.

"Now I can understand why Sam taught me to shoot and makes sure that I keep a rifle close at hand whenever he's away from the house. This town isn't much better than the wilderness."

"Don't worry," Tonie told her. "Once word gets around the neighborhood that you know how to handle firearms, you won't be molested. In all the years I lived here, I never had any trouble until today. And it serves me right for getting dressed up. Bob Martin didn't even know I was alive."

Pushing a lock of hair out of her eyes, Cathy laughed. "You're fooling yourself, Tonie. I saw the doctor's expression when those troublemakers had us trapped. He may not even know it himself—yet. But he's sweet on you."

"Of course he is," Cindy declared. "I know men, and it's just a question of time before he proposes to you."

"By that time," Tonie said defiantly, "I may want to turn him down."

At that moment Ted Woods came into the kitchen carrying another huge load of firewood, so the girls quickly changed the subject.

"Was there no way you could protect yourselves this morning?" Claudia asked.

Tonie's smile was rueful. "It was the first time in longer

than I can remember that I wasn't carrying a rifle. If I'd been armed, I would have put a bullet between the eyes of the man who was encouraging the others, and that would have been the end of the matter."

"I think that learning to handle a rifle is the best thing that ever happened to me," Claudia said. "I can't tell you how grateful I am to Sam for teaching me."

"I've been wondering if I ought to learn to shoot," Cathy said.

"The same idea has been going through my mind," Cindy said as she put apples into a pie shell.

Ted, who was throwing short logs into the oven, made no comment, but his back stiffened.

"You don't approve, Ted?" Claudia asked.

He dusted his hands as he stood and turned. "No, ma'am. Tonie here grew up knowing how to shoot. You learned because it was something you really wanted to do. But Cindy here—and Cathy, too—they'd do themselves more harm than good. People shouldn't fool with guns."

Cindy couldn't resist the urge to tease him. "But we've got to be able to look after ourselves in country where there are Indians and renegades and goodness only knows what other dangers."

Ted stared at her for a moment. "The reason there's menfolks in this train is to look after ladies who can't take care of themselves." Then he turned and stamped out of the kitchen, heading in the direction of the wood shed.

The girls were silent for a time after he had left. Cathy was the first to speak. "Ted is sweet."

Tonie dared to ask what all of them were wondering. "What do *you* think of him, Cindy?"

Her strawberry blonde curls danced as Cindy shook her head. "As you know," she said, "I have my reasons for not thinking very highly of men. Oh, there are a few gentlemen in the world. Sam Brentwood is one, and Baron von Thalman is another. I don't yet know Whip Holt well enough to judge him, but Dr. Martin is a real love."

Tonie acted as though she had been physically struck.

Looking up from the dough she was mixing, she glared at the other girl.

Cindy, unaware of her reaction, continued to chatter. "I haven't made up my mind about Ted Woods," she said. "My first reaction to him was that he was a nuisance. But he's been so kind and helpful to me that I can't help feeling grateful to him. Beyond that—well, I don't yet know."

The kitchen door opened again, and Sam came in, followed by Arnold Mell and Whip Holt. "There are two hundred or more of the guests out there already," Sam told his bride, "and more are arriving every minute. A couple of the men are keeping an eye on the meat while we have a little private chat." He led the men into the parlor.

"Whip," Sam said as they settled into plain wooden armchairs, "I wanted a word with you, and I asked Arnold to join us because he's spent more time than either of us in this part of the world. You're aiming to push off pretty soon, I believe."

"We'll be ready in another couple of days," the new wagonmaster replied. "Nine more wagons joined us today —with about thirty-five people in them—and I want to give them time to pick up emergency provisions before we start."

"You'll be leading about four hundred and fifty people, then," Sam said.

"Closer to five hundred."

"That makes my worries all the more real. That's one hell of a lot of mouths to feed."

Arnold Mell absently rubbed the arm of his chair. "That shouldn't be a problem. There are enough herds of buffalo out yonder to keep us in meat."

"Until winter comes," Sam said. "Don't let this summer weather fool you. It's still the end of September. Arnold, how long do you estimate it will be before heavy snows start to hit the plains?"

The old frontiersman looked out of the windows at the sea of green grass that stretched toward the horizon. "Eight weeks, maybe, if the cold hits early. Ten or eleven weeks if the nasty weather holds off."

"That's pretty much the way I had it figured," Sam said. "Whip, I'm not interfering, and I'm sure as shooting not trying to tell you what to do. But I've been wondering about your plans for winter."

Whip Holt always found it difficult to think while he was sitting. He rose and began to pace up and down the length of the roughly furnished parlor. "The way I see it," he replied, "I've got two choices. Either I can play it safe and stay right here in Independence until spring, or I can get a good head start across the plains. Staying here has its advantages, but there are arguments on the other side. President Van Buren has made it plain he wants us to reach the Oregon country as soon as we can—before the British start establishing settlements on the Pacific coast south of Fort Vancouver or the Russians take heart and come back. Also, some of our people aren't the bravest in the world. They're making this trip because the U.S. Government will guarantee every householder a plot of six hundred acres —almost four times as much free land as they can get anywhere else. I'm afraid that many of them will lose what little courage they have and change their minds about going out to the Oregon country if they have to stay here in Independence until spring."

Sam nodded. "That makes sense."

"So I plan to push out across the plains and go as far as we can before the cold weather comes," Whip continued. "With luck we can travel as far as five hundred miles before we have to hunker down—provided the British and Russian agents leave us alone. Even if they stir up trouble, we should go quite a distance."

"Fair enough," Sam said. "I'm sure you realize as well as I do that the wagons are too flimsy for winter living and that buffalo will be harder to find once the snows come. So that brings up the question of finding a campsite near forests, where there will be enough wood for cabins and fires, and close enough to salt licks that buffalo use."

"You're right, Sam," Arnold said. "In all the trips I've made out into the plains, I've found very few patches of woods. I'm sure that Whip and I, between us, can pick a site in an area that buffalo frequent, even when the snow is thick. But finding forests is something else."

Whip continued to pace. "I'm going to trust my instinct. President Van Buren has been pestering us, and so has Sam's friend, Andrew Jackson. I want to put as many miles as I can between the wagon train and Independence. We'll keep our eyes and ears wide open. We know there are a few forests out in that Godforsaken wilderness, and somehow we'll find one of them before the snows come."

II

Members of the wagon train were frantically busy as they made their final preparations. The women emptied the few stores in Independence of their supplies of bacon, flour, beans, and other essential foodstuffs. Those who had traveled from the East Coast replaced the worn canvas covers of their wagons. Ted Woods worked from daybreak until night fitting new steel rims on wheels. The men bought lead, bullet presses, and gunpowder.

Everyone reacted to the approaching trek into the unknown in his own way. There was a good deal of tension between Lena and Terence Malcolm, one of the wagon train's most popular young couples. Lena had joined the caravan on her seventeenth birthday with her father and her illegitimate baby daughter, Lenore, in the hope of creating a new life. Terence Malcolm, nineteen, who had believed when he first joined the train that he was dying of consumption, had married her in order to give her baby a name. But the rugged life in the open air had cured him, and subsequently he and Lena had fallen in love.

The others believed that Lena and Terence had found happiness together, but no one seeing them as they sat on the rear stoop of their wagon would have thought so.

Terence stared off into the night, running a hand through his hair, while Lena glanced at him furtively. At moments like this he made her think of her father, now dead, who had become violent under the influence of alcohol.

"Terry," she said, speaking softly so they wouldn't awaken the baby who was asleep inside the wagon, "you pulled into a shell right after we got to Independence. Please—what's wrong?"

Her young husband continued to look at the few stars shining in a cloud-filled sky. She put a hand on his arm, and Terence felt her trembling. He could remain silent no longer. "I'm scared," he said.

Lena was shocked. "Of what?"

"Not for myself. For you and Lenore. You came on this expedition because your pa made you do it, not because you wanted to go to Oregon. I've been talking to some of the older men, and they say we face terrible risks. I have no right to subject you and Lenore to them. You might be killed by Indians or die of starvation. All kinds of awful things could happen to you."

"What are you trying to tell me, Terry?"

"I have to go to Oregon. I have you and the baby to support. At six dollars an acre, I can't afford to buy a farm anywhere in the East, or even in Illinois or Indiana. No matter how rough the travel may be, I'm obliged to go on to Oregon and stake my six-hundred-acre claim."

"You'd leave Lenore and me?" Lena was on the verge of tears.

"The way I see it, we have enough cash to pay for your room and board right here in Independence, where you'll be safe. Once I get to Oregon and build us a home, I'll send for you."

She was silent.

"All right?" he asked, sounding apprehensive.

Lena exploded. "If I didn't believe it's wrong for people to hit each other, I'd box your ears good, Terence Malcolm. Nobody made you marry me. You did it of your own free will, and I'm your wife!"

"Sure you are," he said, trying to soothe her. "That's the reason I suggested—"

"I don't want to hear one more word!" Lena cried. "I'd rather starve with you or have all three of us killed by Indians—together—than to be separated from you for even one single day. If you want us to drop out of the wagon trail, we'll do it, and maybe we can find jobs as a hired couple somewhere."

"That isn't practical. I want the best of everything for you and Lenore."

"Then we're coming with you, and that's the end of the discussion," she said. "Goodness mercy, I was afraid you didn't love me any more."

"There's no chance of that," he replied softly, his voice shaky.

Lena looked at him, her eyes shining. "We took a vow when we got married. We promised to stay with each other for better or worse. So far everything has been pretty wonderful, and that's the way it will always be."

The sound of her voice awakened the baby. "Mama! Papa!" she called.

"We're right here," Terence called. "Go back to sleep, Lenore." He looked at his wife, his expression sheepish. "You just don't know how worried I've been."

Lena pulled his head toward her, and they kissed. Terence's worries vanished, and he knew he was the most fortunate of men.

Whip Holt had no wagon, preferring to sleep in the open. Now, returning to the train late in the evening after a busy day that had started at daybreak, he intended to get his blanket and spread it on the ground just inside the circle of wagons. But he was delayed by the approach of a portly man in an expensively tailored suit, who was accompanied by two exceptionally handsome young people.

Whip had met them only two days earlier but knew them by sight immediately. They were not a family one could easily forget.

Major Laurence Woodling was a South Carolina aristocrat whose military title had been earned in his state's militia during the War of 1812. He had lost his plantation in the financial crisis that now gripped the United States, just as so many smaller farmers had gone bankrupt, and he was traveling to Oregon in the hope of starting life anew.

With him were his twenty-one-year-old son, Claiborne, whose arrogant strut indicated he knew he was good-looking, and his daughter of nineteen, Eulalia. As spoiled as her brother, Eulalia was a beauty, with a full, ripe mouth and seductive eyes. She wore a skin-tight dress with a daringly low-cut neckline that left little to the imagination.

Whip instantly sensed trouble.

"Mr. Holt," Major Woodling said in a deep, soft drawl, "we've been waiting for you all evening."

"What can I do for you, Major?" Whip was cordial but not effusive.

"We have two requests. We find one wagon very crowded for the three of us, and I wonder if we might be able to buy another."

Whip shook his head. "You'll have to travel a thousand miles or more toward the Atlantic to find a wagon and a team of horses or oxen that you could buy, Major."

"You see, Papa?" Eulalia was so annoyed she barely avoided stamping her foot. "I've been telling and telling you!"

Her father ignored the outburst. "What do you suggest we do, Mr. Holt?"

"You have two choices, Major. Either you make do with what you have, or you make other arrangements." He turned to the son. "You look as though you can ride and shoot."

"I was practically born in the saddle," Claiborne Woodling declared. "And if you'd care to make a wager on a shooting contest, you may pick your own type of firearms and the target."

"I don't shoot for pleasure," Whip was abrupt. "As it happens, I've been putting together a team of scouts, line monitors and the like. If you can shoot and ride as well as you seem to think, we'd gladly have you join us. Certainly I'm willing to give you a tryout.

We'll be sleeping in the open most of the time, so your wagon wouldn't be as crowded."

As he spoke, he realized that Eulalia Woodling was flirting with him. She was so open in her approach that she wasn't offensive. Unaccustomed to women flirting, he warned himself to be careful. But her violet eyes exerted such a magnetic power that he couldn't ignore her gaze, nor could he ignore the slight smile that parted her lips.

"I'm not that partial to the outdoors," Claiborne said. "What do you do when it rains?"

Whip grinned wryly. "We get wet."

"I see." The young man fingered his silk cravat. "I could use some spare money for entertainment on our journey," he said. "How much do these positions pay?"

"Pay?" Whip stared at him incredulously. "Boy, we're heading into country where the odds against survival are two or three to one. If you're a gambler, just think about that for a spell. Everybody in the train has chores to do. You'll be given your assignment tomorrow, Major, as will you, miss. You, too, boy, unless you try out for a monitor's job and are good enough to hold it. Folks in this company volunteer their services for the good of everybody, and they're happy to do it. We work together or we die!"

"You give me little choice, sir." Claiborne bowed stiffly. "I accept your offer. Just tell me what I'm to do."

"You'll work for Tonie Mell, who will give you your instructions in the morning." Whip turned to the Major. "I believe you said there were two matters you wanted to take up with me, Major."

"There are, Mr. Holt. I still have some funds, fortunately, and I'm willing to pay a reasonable sum for a slave who can attend to the chores of wagon-train living."

Whip didn't know whether to be annoyed or to laugh. "Major," he said, "you'll be driving your own wagon, hitching and unhitching your team, and looking after your horses all the way out to Oregon. Miss, you'll be washing clothes, keeping the inside of your wagon tidy, helping fix meals, and drawing water. From here to the

Pacific. The Oregon country is free soil. There are no slaves there. What's more, most members of this company come from the North and wouldn't tolerate slavery in the caravan."

Major Woodling's eyes burned, but he remained courteous. "I thank you for your information and interest, sir," he said, then turned and started off toward his own wagon. Claiborne clicked his heels, bowed, and walked off with his father.

Eulalia lingered for a moment. "Don't mind Papa and my brother, Mr. Holt," she said. "They've only known one way of life, and they haven't yet learned how to get along in the world." She turned away and, aware that he was watching her, allowed her hips to sway as she walked to her wagon.

She, too, had a great deal to learn, Whip reflected. If she flirted this brazenly with others on the journey, she would create an uproar. As he took his blanket from his saddlebag, he wished she were less attractive, and he warned himself to be wary of her.

Whip Holt had announced they would make an early start, so most members of the company had retired early. By ten in the evening, the campsite was quiet, and everyone seemed to be asleep.

Shortly before midnight, however, fifteen-year-old Chet Harris sneaked out of the wagon he occupied with his mother and two brothers and walked to Ted Woods's small, ramshackle wagon. Standing there, he coughed gently. Instantly Danny, who shared the wagon with Ted, crept silently into the open. The two boys hurried down to the bank of the broad Missouri River, following it to an area where the grass was waist high.

There they halted, and Danny called softly, "Hosea!"

Most members of the company would have thought they were dreaming if they had seen the man who emerged like a wraith from the thick, deep grass. Totally bald, with skin of shining ebony, he was attired only in a loincloth.

Much shorter than Danny and Chet, he was no more than five feet tall, but he was fully developed physically, with powerful shoulders, strong arms, well-muscled legs, and a thick torso. Around his middle, on a thong, he wore rows of what appeared to be decorations resembling small tenpins. Actually they were small weapons—wooden throwing clubs weighted with metal. Unknown in America, they were used in Africa by the Ashanti tribe to kill small game and, when necessary in battle, to stun an enemy whom the Ashanti wanted to capture rather than kill.

Over one bare shoulder, the black man also carried a leather container no more than six inches long. It appeared harmless, but he had already shown the two boys the contents—a blowgun and darts that he had dipped in the venom of snakes he had killed.

He grinned at the boys, waved, and then joined them, making no sound as he moved forward through the tall grass.

"Did you find the supper we left for you?" Chet asked. "We didn't dare call you because there were too many people around."

"Hosea find," the man said. "Good supper. Plenty much to eat." He patted his flat abdomen.

"We march in the morning," Danny said. "We'll take you to the special wagon and show it to you. Make sure you hide there before dawn and stay there until it's dark. We'll bring you food whenever we can."

"Hosea like food!"

"If you stay hidden until we put Independence far behind us, they won't send you back."

Danny felt a great sympathy for this African who had been captured by Arab traders and sent to the United States as a slave. Only recently had he removed his identification anklet, with a file the boys had brought him.

Danny had been a fugitive, too, and knew how difficult it was to live on the run. He was awed by Hosea's remarkable journey, all the way from the plantation in Georgia where he had been given his Biblical name, to Independence, Missouri. Anyone who could travel all that distance on foot, wearing only a loincloth, had to be an extraordinary person. No matter what Ted Woods might think, no matter how Whip Holt might react when he learned what the boys were doing, Danny intended to help the man he and Chet had befriended.

"The special wagon," he said, "is filled with all kinds of things. Barrels and sacks of emergency food supplies, medicines, spare wagon parts, and harnesses. Firearms and ammunition, too."

Hosea smiled slightly as he touched his blowgun container, then let his fingers slide over one of the tiny clubs hanging from his middle. He remained silent, but his reaction was plain: others could use firearms if they wished; he would place his faith in the ancient weapons of his people.

"There are lots of odd corners in the wagon, so it shouldn't be too hard for somebody of your size to hide there," Danny said.

"Easy," Hosea replied, then laughed.

"Just be careful, that's all," Chet said. "Somebody will be inspecting the wagon every day to make sure everything is in place. They won't go through it carefully, but they'll take a long look inside from the back flap. So stay up near the front, where nobody ever goes."

"Not worry," the escaped slave assured them. "Hosea be very safe in special wagon."

"Let's go, then." Danny was nervous, afraid that one of the adults, Whip in particular, might wake up and see them.

The boys walked together, assuming an air of nonchalance they were far from feeling, and Hosea followed them at a distance of a dozen paces. He managed to blend in with his surroundings in some mysterious way. The boys glanced repeatedly over their shoulders to make certain he was still behind them.

When they reached the special wagon, they halted behind it. Danny pointed to a burlap sack outside the circle of vehicles, which he and Chet had filled with a loaf of bread and dried buffalo meat.

Hosea's sense of smell, as highly developed as his other senses, immediately told him the contents of the sack. He scooped it up and slung it over his shoulder in a single, swift gesture. Opening the rear flap, he climbed inside the special wagon and closed the flap behind him.

It was astonishing to the boys that he could be so quiet; those who were asleep in the wagons to the front and rear were totally unaware that anything unusual had taken place. Danny and Chet stood outside for a moment, exchanged uncertain smiles, then went off to their own wagons.

Ted Woods opened one eye when Danny stealthily crept into their wagon. By Danny's movements, Ted knew that he had been up to something. Turning over on his pallet, Ted smiled as he went back to sleep. No secrets could be kept for long on the wagon train, and soon whatever it was would come out into the open.

St. Joseph, Missouri rivaled Independence as the principal frontier outpost in the United States, although it was gradually losing ground. The atmosphere was similar: fur buyers purchased the wares of trappers, traders, and hunters, and the saloons and brothels in the town quickly separated the mountain men from their hard-earned money.

There were very few respectable boarding houses in town, and Henry St. Clair lodged in one of them. A man in his thirties, dashing and trim, he wore expensive clothes and was sometimes mistaken for a sharp-witted representative of a fur company. Henry did nothing to discourage such ideas.

He had arrived in St. Joseph more dead than alive after being viciously beaten by the leader of a gang of army deserters who, at his instigation, had attacked the wagon train and, after suffering a catastrophic defeat, had taken out their anger on him. The one physician in town had been taking care of him. He was mending very well and considered himself fortunate—none of his bones had been broken and, although he was still somewhat battered, he could get around without too much difficulty.

Fortunately, the army deserters had not known about the money belt he carried around his waist. On the frontier, men would kill for much less. It was filled with gold and United States coins, more money by far than he would require to complete his mission. That task was a simple one, or so he had believed when his superiors in the British secret service had given him the assignment. He was under orders to slow the progress of the first major wagon train to cross the continent and, if possible, to prevent it from reaching Oregon. Obviously it would be far easier for Great Britain to claim all of the Oregon country, which it now held jointly with the United States, if Queen Victoria's subjects rather than American citizens were the first to settle there in large numbers.

The job was proving to be more difficult than Henry had imagined. When he had passed himself off as a settler, his sabotage attempts had been ineffective. He had suffered an even worse defeat after he had been discovered, fled, and enlisted the aid of the deserters.

Not that he himself cared whether the caravan reached the Pacific—he had no personal interest in the matter. But he was a professional agent, with a long history of achievements in Europe, Africa, and Asia. His reputation did not allow him to tolerate failure.

St. Clair also had high hopes for his future. He had been promised that he would be permitted to retire from the field once he ruined the plans of the United States. He would be given an office in London and a title, and he would remain in that city, spending the rest of his professional life as a supervisor.

London! Just the thought of returning there dazzled Henry St. Clair. It was his favorite place on earth, filled with inns that served the kind of food he most enjoyed and studded with taverns that employed amenable barmaids. After a long career devoted to hard work in unpleasant and uncomfortable surroundings, Henry was ready to retire to a desk and the joys of London.

Walking slowly up the dirt road that constituted St. Joseph's main street, he went to the office of the physician and, because he always paid his bills immediately, he was admitted without delay.

The doctor gave him no more than a cursory

examination. "You're healing," he said. "You were lucky you didn't do much worse to yourself falling down that cliff."

"How soon may I leave?" St. Clair demanded. He had to get on with his assignment.

The doctor tugged at his chin. "Well, if you could rest for another couple of weeks, it sure wouldn't do you any harm."

"But would it hurt me if I took off as soon as I get my gear together? I have urgent business elsewhere, sir."

The physician hesitated. "You seem to be in fairly good shape, I'll admit. I won't take responsibility if you suffer a relapse, but if you want to take that chance yourself, I'm not in a position to stop you."

That was all Henry wanted to know. He paid his bill and left the office. Wasting no time, he headed straight for the market district that faced the Missouri River. He approached a barn where a sign hung over the entrance: *For Sale or Rent—Horses and Carts.*

The proprietor smelled of the stables, and Henry wrinkled his nose in distaste. Americans were still a barbaric people. "I want to buy the largest wagon in your shop and a suitable team to pull it," the Englishman said.

The man gaped at him. "You ain't thinkin' o' gettin' a prairie schooner, Mister?"

"Whatever." Names meant nothing to Henry, and he shrugged, wanting only to complete the transaction as quickly as he could.

"Prairie schooners are as scarce as white buffalo, Mister. You got t' pick them up in New York or Hartford or Boston. Where are you aimin' t' travel?"

Perhaps the man thought he was being helpful, but in England no tradesman would dream of asking such a personal question. "I intend to do rather extensive traveling on behalf of my employers," Henry replied curtly.

The proprietor shook his head. "The best I got is a freight wagon I bought last month when the owner got himself killed in a bordello fight down the street. It'll carry merchandise, with room left over for people t' live in."

"I'd like to see it."

The man took him outside to the rear of the barn where several vehicles, most of them in bad condition, stood. "There you be," he said, pointing.

Henry stared at the largest wagon he had ever seen. It had twelve wheels and a yoke for six horses. This wagon was not only huge but cumbersome; on the other hand, it could easily accommodate all the goods he planned to purchase. And there would be more than enough room for him to sleep under the arched canvas roof.

The proprietor saw that he was impressed and began to push. "Do you want horses or oxen? We got both."

"If you have a strong team of horses, I'm interested. I know nothing about oxen."

The man frowned; never had he encountered anyone unfamiliar with oxen. But a major sale was pending, so he did not dwell on the matter. Instead he took the prospective client to a string of stables that stood at right angles to his other buildings.

There Henry found a team of six workhorses in prime condition, sturdy animals that appeared to be in robust health. His luck was better than he had dared to hope, and he exulted inwardly. "How much for the freighter and the team?" he demanded.

Judging by the stranger's clothes, the expensive dueling pistols he carried in his belt, and his superb, English-made rifle with a polished walnut butt, the proprietor knew Henry was a man of means. "Five hundred dollars," he said.

Henry grinned at him. "I'll give you two hundred."

The stranger wasn't a fool, after all, the proprietor thought, then sighed aloud. "Make it two hundred and fifty, and you've got a deal."

"That includes harnesses, of course," Henry said, driving a hard bargain.

The man hesitated. Then, unwilling to jeopardize a sale, he capitulated. "You got a deal, Mister," he said.

Giving him no opportunity to change his mind, Henry counted out the sum in American paper money. "Have the team hitched and ready to go by early this afternoon," he said, and gave the man an extra dollar.

Next he went to St. Joseph's largest general store and, in less than an hour of whirlwind buying, he had purchased everything he needed for his own use. He found two sets of buckskin shirts and pants that fitted him reasonably well, along with a buffalo-skin cloak to wear when the weather got colder. He could have planned to shoot his own on the Great Plains and cure the skins, but this would save him the trouble. He laid in a generous store of rations, including salted fish and smoked venison, as well as barrels of such staples as pickled beef, sacks of flour, beans, sugar, and salt, and sides of bacon and ham.

Even more important, he bought a mattress and several blankets, two pairs of oiled boots, and several rolls of canvas to replace the covering on his wagon. He found extra wheels, two axles, and a spare yoke for his team and, as a final precaution, he bought a hammer, a keg of nails, and two knives. Now he was almost ready.

Arranging to pick up most of his purchases later, he took one set of his new clothes with him and went to the better of St. Joseph's bordellos. It might be a long time before he would have another opportunity to bed a woman. He acquired the services of a blonde who satisfied him, even though she wasn't up to his London standards. Then he dressed in his new buckskins and boots.

Returning to his lodging house, he picked up his few belongings, paid his bill, then went to the stables for his waiting team and freight wagon. His next stop was the general store, where his morning's purchases were loaded into his wagon.

Finally, he went to a warehouse with a somewhat questionable reputation where he had engaged in intensive bargaining the previous day. A dozen unmarked, innocent-looking crates containing rifles were loaded onto the wagon, along with containers that were filled with gunpowder and heavy boxes loaded with lead bars from which bullets could be fashioned. Finally a large number of barrels of cheap whiskey were rolled onto the wagon. Ever since colonial days, it had been against the law in the New World to sell or give liquor to Indians, but Henry had paid more than the asking price for the whiskey, so the owner of the warehouse had conveniently forgotten to fill out the form required by the federal government when alcoholic beverages were sold in quantity.

Ready at last, Henry St. Clair drove his team to the bank of the Missouri River. There he paid the operator of a ferry fifty cents—double the usual price—to take him and his heavy load to the west bank.

"Where are you headed?" the operator asked.

Henry gave him the first answer that came to mind. "I'm starting a new kind of business. I'm taking supplies out to the Rockies to sell to mountain men."

The explanation made no real sense, but it satisfied the ferry operator.

Sitting on the front of the wagon and keeping his team under tight rein while the ferry traveled across the broad river, Henry St. Clair smiled to himself. He was truly pleased. Ahead lay the Great Plains, and he felt reasonably certain he would be moving into the area before the wagon train reached the region. He could travel far more rapidly than could a caravan of fifty or sixty wagons.

The unknown did not frighten him, the wilderness held no terrors for him. The liquor and weapons were virtual guarantees that he would be able to make a mutually satisfactory arrangement with one or more of the Indian tribes. The odds against him had been overwhelming, but he told himself he had every right to be proud of his accomplishments so far. The wagon train was doomed.

Sam and Claudia Brentwood intended to bid a last farewell to their friends on the wagon train, so they awakened two hours before dawn, dressed hastily, and hurried to the kitchen. There they found that Cathy, who had decided to spend the night with them, was not only fully dressed but had already made coffee.

Once on the road into Independence, Claudia exchanged a glance with Sam, and he raised the question that both had been reluctant to ask. "Cathy, you still haven't told us your plans, and you can't really hold off any longer. Are you staying with us and turning your wagon and team over to somebody, or are you going on to Oregon with the train?"

Cathy smiled faintly and sounded very sure of herself as she said, "I'm going to Oregon."

Claudia was surprised. "I thought that nasty experience you had in town a couple of days ago might have robbed you of any spirit of adventure you had left."

"I'm not interested in adventure," Cathy said. "What I enjoy is the freedom to live my own life in my own way. I went straight from papa's supervision to Otto's, and now, for the first time ever, I can do what I please."

Sam reflected that he would never understand any woman. "I know you and Otto worked a farm on Long Island," he said, "but I thought that life didn't appeal to you very much."

"It's the only life I know," Cathy replied.

"Then," he persisted, "you'll take six hundred acres from the government, build yourself a home, and start to farm the property?"

Claudia couldn't help smiling at the note of astonishment in his voice, and she couldn't blame him. A girl as pretty and petite as Cathy didn't look capable of cutting down huge trees, uprooting the stumps, and plowing the earth for planting, much less putting up her own house in the wilderness.

Cathy's smile indicated that she was fully aware of the difficulties that lay ahead of her. "I still have Otto's money, and if I can't work this out in some other way, I can always pay somebody to do the hard physical labor for me."

Sam wondered what she meant by "working this out in some other way," but Claudia knew instantly.

"I know you've entertained a rather high opinion of Whip Holt ever since you first met him," Claudia said directly, "and I suspect your opinion of him is even higher since he saved you from those roughnecks."

"Claudia!" Cathy grew scarlet, mortified because her sister had raised the matter openly in Sam's presence.

Claudia knew what was going through her sister's mind and was firm. "Sam is family now, so we'll keep no secrets from him. You can trust him to be discreet."

"Of course," the bewildered Sam said.

Cathy was badly flustered and peered off into the night. The stars had disappeared, and she could see only a short distance down the road. "It—it so happens I have a very high regard for Michael Holt."

At last Sam understood. He had never heard anyone else refer to Whip by anything other than his nickname.

"But I have no intention of throwing myself at him," Cathy went on. "I'm not a hussy. And I have no intention of marrying anyone so soon after Otto's death. What's more, I have no idea whether Michael Holt will ever want to settle down with any woman. I may be young, Claudia, but I'm not giddy, and I do try to be realistic."

"Are you sure there's nothing more to all this," Claudia asked, "than gratitude to Whip for rescuing you the other day?"

"I'm not sure of anything, but I plan to find out!" Cathy retorted.

Sam decided to intervene. "Cathy," he said, "watch your step. I've known Whip for a long time, and I've been as close to him as anybody can get, which isn't all that close. He's a good man, but he holds everybody at arm's length. And he values his freedom more than life itself. I don't think any girl, not even one as pretty as you, could ever lasso him and put a brand on him."

Cathy absorbed her brother-in-law's words in silence. Then suddenly the clouds parted, and the moon appeared, illuminating the wagons that stood in a circle high on a hill overlooking the Missouri River. Dark figures scurried around a roaring breakfast fire. She felt a lump in her throat, and for a few moments her heart raced faster. "No matter what," she said, "I'm going on to Oregon!"

The man who called himself André Sebastian arose early, as he always did. He ate a substantial breakfast in the dining room of the one respectable inn in St. Louis, then lingered at the table over coffee. He lit one of the expensive Latin American *segaros* that were his only weakness.

Perhaps he would leave today on the next stage of his journey, but he felt no need to rush. It wouldn't matter if he waited an extra day or an extra week. He could cover fifty miles in a day without exerting himself, while the most the American wagon train could manage was ten miles. There was no way the train could move fast enough to leave him far behind. And his own timing was of primary importance: he had no desire to make his approach in Independence. It would be far easier to strike after the wagons moved out into the lonely, unending reaches of the Great Plains.

That was something the *chargé d'affaires* of the Imperial Russian Legation in Washington failed to understand. But the *chargé*, like so many desk officers in the employ of the secret police, was an imbecile. In order to serve in a supervisory capacity, one had to have family connections in St. Petersburg, but common sense would indicate that men with field experience should be promoted to the higher posts.

Not that André Sebastian sought or would accept a desk job. He was too restless to shuffle papers, and his distinguished career, almost all of it served in the New World, proved that he was superbly efficient in the field.

It was difficult for anyone to tell whether he was twenty-five years old or forty, and that was one of his advantages. His hair was dark, his features were ordinary and his suit of broadcloth, although made for him by a tailor, was a dirty gray color. André Sebastian was not a man whom people remembered, which was precisely the appearance he had long cultivated.

Now that he was closing in on his quarry, he thought the time was appropriate for a review of this case. His one regret was that he hadn't been given the assignment to begin with. He had been on another job at the time, and Tonie Mell, who had been chosen for this one, had obviously failed to act.

This assignment required great finesse and stamina,

Sebastian reflected. Only a man who had crossed all of Siberia on horseback could be asked to follow the Yankee wagon train into the untamed vastness of the Great Plains.

At an appropriate moment, he would approach Antoinette Melichev, the girl who called herself Tonie Mell. St. Petersburg's terms had become harsher. He would notify her that if she failed to cooperate—perform acts of sabotage that would bring the wagon train to a halt—her mother and father not only would be required to remain in Russia, but might be imprisoned, sent in exile to Siberia or even executed.

André Sebastian hoped the threat would mean enough to the stubborn girl to convince her to act on behalf of the Russians. If not, he was authorized to take any steps necessary to force her compliance. Only if she continued to refuse did he have orders to intervene directly, to perform acts of sabotage that would disrupt and disorganize the train.

The reasons for this had been stressed to him repeatedly by the *chargé*, who had treated him like an idiot, but the purpose of the order was plain. Russia was posing as the one great power that was friendly to the United States; Martin Van Buren and his State Department were taken in by the ruse, just as Andrew Jackson, the previous President, had been. Great Britain, France, and even failing Spain might connive against the young, growing nation that was expanding so rapidly across the face of North America, but the government in St. Petersburg stated that it had no conflict with Washington.

The facts were far different. Imperial explorers and settlers had been the first to find and make their homes in the fertile lands of Alaska. The Oregon region then stretched from Alaska to California. Based on their explorations along the northern Pacific coast, Russia had laid claim to parts of the Oregon country.

The Americans and British, the United States and Canada, lying relatively close to the Oregon territory, also had laid claim to the area. Russia had faced a cruel choice: either withdraw or go to war. Granted that Oregon was a paradise, rich with timber and salmon, marvelously fertile soil, and precious minerals in her mountains. But she was not worth a war with Great Britain, at present the strongest nation on earth, or even with the Yankees, who had demonstrated in their War of Independence and War of 1812 that they continued to fight until they achieved victory. So Russia signed treaties with Great Britain and the United States, giving up its interests. Now Russia wanted the lands back and was taking a subtle approach to accomplish its goal.

André Sebastian knew he was the right person for the task that lay ahead. He was a crack shot, a deadly knife thrower, and capable of sustaining himself in the wilderness for long periods. Studying the glowing tip of his *segaro,* he calmly sipped his coffee. He felt confident that, one way or another, he would persuade or compel Antoinette Melichev to perform the deeds that the government of the czar demanded of her. And no one would ever learn of the Russian secret police's involvement.

Members of the wagon train ate a hearty breakfast of pancakes and bacon and, while the women washed the dishes and tidied the campsite, the men hitched their teams of horses and oxen. There were four barges used for river crossings in Independence, and Whip Holt hired all of them. The transfer of the animals and wagons took the better part of the morning, but at last the task was completed, and the company assembled on the west bank of the Missouri in a land occupied by the Kansa Indians and a few white men.

The route selected by Whip was simple. The company was so large—four hundred and seventy-six persons—that the need for water was constant. So he intended to travel almost due north along the Missouri until they came to one of its principal tributaries, the Platte, in the land of the Omaha nation. There they would turn west and would follow the Platte—and subsequently the North Platte—all the way to the Rockies.

The grass was high, but there were only a few, small, scattered trees dotting the landscape. The land that stretched out toward the horizon was flat. There were no hills here, no rises; it was evident that the Great Plains had been aptly named.

The absence of natural obstacles made it possible for Whip to arrange his caravan in three parallel columns of about fifty wagons each. The place of honor of the first wagon of the right column was held by Baron Ernst von Thalman. He had been elected president of the train by a unanimous vote—a rare sign of confidence in a foreigner. As the head of the community, he would act as judge in disputes between members of the company and would also act as spokesman for the travelers in dealings with the wagonmaster.

To lead the center column, to the surprise of many, Whip placed a couple who had been the butt of numerous jokes when they had joined the caravan months earlier. Nat Drummond, in his mid-forties, was short, slender, and balding, a quiet man who minded his own business and rarely raised his voice. His wife, Grace, towered above him by a head, outweighed him by fifty pounds, and subjected him to a constant barrage of criticism, which he ignored. Others had learned—and perhaps Grace was discovering, too—that little Nat was a solid man, a valuable member of the expedition. He never became flustered and never lost his head in a crisis.

The position of the first wagon of the left column was awarded to Cathy van Ayl. Some thought she had been given the place because of Whip's personal interest in her, but they were mistaken. She, her late husband and her sister had been the first members of the wagon train, so she held the coveted post by right of seniority.

Three scouts fanned out ahead of the wagons. After today they would depart every morning after an early breakfast and not rejoin the group until evening. Later, when the company traveled further and further from civilization, they might absent themselves for two or three days at a time, reporting back only when necessary. All three were the best men available. In the center was Stalking Horse, who had left his Cherokee Village in Tennessee as a boy and had spent much of his life in the West—which he knew intimately—and who had no ties to any of the Indian nations of the Plains. On the left was Arnold Mell, tireless in spite of his age, as experienced as Stalking Horse at smelling danger and reading signs that indicated bands of hostile Indians or other dangers.

On the right was a hunter whom Whip had known in the Rockies. Mack Dougall was almost fifty years old, stocky and with a potbelly. When he had joined the expedition at Independence, he had immediately made arrangements for Ted Woods to carry his supplies—which consisted mainly of two barrels of cheap whiskey. His thirst was insatiable, and his complaints about the aches in his bones were endless, but Whip knew from experience that Mack allowed nothing to interfere with his duty. When necessary, he could stay in the saddle day and night.

Danny was driving Tonie Mell's wagon. She had happily accepted when Whip promoted her to the post of chief monitor, and she and her assistants rode up and down the lines of wagons, making certain there were no breakdowns and that no animals became lame. If a serious emergency occurred, a halt would be called.

The buckskin-clad Tonie was introduced to one of her assistants, young Claiborne Woodling, at breakfast, and there was an immediate clash when he announced, "Taking orders from a woman will be something new for me. A man should be in charge of the monitors."

Tonie eyed him coldly. "I've been monitoring the line for months and I know what I'm doing. That's why Whip put me in charge. So you'll be working for me." Trying to be conciliatory, she added, "But I see no problems. The work is routine. As a matter of fact, sometimes it gets dull. You've got to resist the temptation to gallop as you go up and down the line."

"What's wrong with a gallop?"

"You tire your own horse unnecessarily," she replied, "and sometimes the workhorses and oxen get too excited. Just maintain a nice, steady pace and make sure you keep checking—wagon by wagon—as you ride. That's all there is to it."

Claiborne made no reply, but he had his own ideas.

When he felt like galloping, that was precisely what he intended to do.

Claiborne wasn't the only member of his family causing trouble. Eulalia was seething as she sat with her father on the board of their wagon.

"I just can't believe it," she said, shaking her hcad so her long black hair swayed. "That woman is impossible."

"What woman?" Major Woodling asked.

"That Van Ayl person. She actually had the nerve to ask me whether I wanted to join the dishwashing detail or the water-fetching group. When I told her that neither appealed to me, she said that was my choice. I refused, and she plain assigned me to washing dishes."

Her father sighed. "This is a new way of life for us, Eulalia. We've got to accept chores when they're given to us."

"Well, I went straight to Baron von Thalman during breakfast, and that's what he said to me, too. But I won't!"

"You will, Eulalia," the Major said firmly. "If we had any choice, we'd be back home, not riding in this convoy all the way across the continent. But we've got no alternative, so we have to accept their rules."

"I'll do it—for now," she replied grudgingly, "but I'll get even with that bossy Van Ayl woman. Just you wait and see."

A short distance from them, in the next line, Danny maneuvered the Mell team into place directly behind the special wagon. Waiting nervously for the march to begin, he hoped Hosea wouldn't get curious and peer out of the wagon. It would be all too easy for Whip and Baron von Thalman to send the escaped slave back across the river to Independence. And that would be the end of him. Many people there would be happy to pocket the reward given for any slave returned to his master.

At last all of the wagons reached their assigned places. The scouts had long since vanished, and Whip Holt took his place at the head of the column. "I reckon we'll be on our way," he said quietly to Tonie Mell. His horse started forward toward the northwest only a short distance from the banks of the Missouri.

Tonie, who had taken the center line for herself, started to ride toward the rear, giving the signal that the caravan was beginning to move. The moment was very special to her, but it was spoiled when she saw that Claiborne Woodling, on her right, was deliberately disobeying orders by galloping.

Soon the entire caravan was in motion. Between each wagon there was a comfortable gap so no one would breathe too much dust. The sun shone almost directly overhead in a hazy sky, and the gentle breeze from the west carried the faint but distinct scent of sweet prairie grass.

Now, after the long halt at Independence, the veterans in the caravan heard the familiar music made only by a wagon train. The newcomers, aware of it for the first time, soon would become accustomed to the harmonies. The hoofbeats of the horses set a steady, sharp rhythm on the hard ground, and the surprisingly softer, more delicate drumming of the hoofs of the oxen provided a counterpoint. The leather of harnesses creaked in time to the pounding, pulsing throb, and the squeaking wheels of the wagons provided the major theme. These pioneers to Oregon had no way of knowing that, until the coming of the railroads a half-century and more later, the music of their wagons and of all the wagons to come would echo and reecho across the continent.

The days of organizing, planning, and arranging were over. The long trek was under way.

III

By the third day of the journey into the wilderness, even the most inexperienced of the new arrivals had become accustomed to the routines. Each morning, the men of the fire-making detail were the first to arise, leaving their wagons as soon as the glow of the false dawn appeared in the sky. Since wood was scarce throughout many portions of the Great Plains, the men learned from Whip to make their fires of what were called "chips," dried buffalo dung, available in large quantities and sanitized by long exposure to the elements. A score of women volunteers led by Cathy van Ayl prepared breakfast each morning, and by dawn the entire company was assembled. All major chores, including the gathering of water and washing of dishes, were organized communally, but individual householders harnessed their own animals and moved into their assigned places in the three lines. The breakfast fires were extinguished, and the sun was rising by the time the caravan began to roll.

At midday the train always halted for an hour or more to rest the horses and oxen. This period was known as "nooning," and those who were hungry usually ate cold leftovers. Some people took naps, but the security-conscious Whip Holt assigned the men and older boys to sentry duty on a rotating schedule, and a watch was kept for bands of hostile Indians or stray, wild animals. Whip made it very plain that, in the event a buffalo herd was sighted, all male members of the company who could handle firearms should be summoned without delay.

The journey was rescued after the nooning, and the company rode on until about four in the afternoon. Whip knew where to call a halt for the night, the scouts having told him in detail what lay ahead. The first task was that of forming the wagons in a protective circle. The oxen and horses were set free inside the circle, to safely graze. Meanwhile water was carried from the Missouri, the older boys gathered buffalo chips and firewood when it was available, and the women went to work to prepare supper, the main meal of the day.

While the women cooked, foraging parties went out into the prairies to search for game. Deer were plentiful, as were rabbits, and there were wild geese and ducks to be found in ponds partially concealed by tall grass. Few fish were found in the Missouri River, but the smaller streams that fed into it were filled with them. The company tried to be self-sufficient. The provisions carried by every family were to be kept for emergency use only.

It was during this pre-supper time that Dr. Martin treated those who needed it; fortunately, most of the ailments were minor. On days when Ernie von Thalman didn't go hunting, he listened to complaints and tried to settle quarrels and disputes.

Supper was the highlight of the day. Newcomers tended to go off by themselves, but they swiftly learned that everyone mixed freely during the social hour. Many lasting friendships were formed. People who had been total strangers planned to become neighbors when they reached the Oregon country.

The scouts ordinarily arrived before the meal was served, and reported in detail to Whip concerning what lay ahead. It was during this hour, too, that the wagon-master's other lieutenants reported to him.

Tonie Mell waited for several days before going to Whip, but on the fourth night of the journey, she announced bluntly, "I may need a new monitor in place of Claiborne Woodling."

Whip pulled a blade of grass out of the ground, then nibbled on the white portion at the base. "What's wrong with him?"

"He'd be fine if he did what he's told. But he wears out his horse galloping up and down the line all day, and he's so busy showing off to the women that he doesn't really check to make sure there are no problems with any of the wagons."

Whip nodded, rose, and sauntered off toward the Woodling wagon, where Claiborne was chatting with his father and sister.

The wagonmaster stopped and beckoned to Claiborne. "You're a good rider," he said when the young man joined him.

Claiborne grinned, pleased that he was winning recognition.

"Your trouble," Whip continued, "is that you don't follow orders."

The younger man's smile faded. "I don't like working for women."

"That's what I figured. But nobody in this company is more competent than Tonie, and nobody has contributed more to our safety. You can go back to helping your father drive his wagon, and I'll find another monitor."

"Hold on." Claiborne enjoyed his assignment because he felt it set him apart from the other settlers. "It isn't fair to—"

"I'll give you one more chance," Whip said, interrupting. "In this train, folks work together and do what they're told. If Tonie comes to me again, you're finished."

Just then, Cathy van Ayl, standing near the fire, banged a cooking spoon on the bottom of a frying pan, the signal that supper was ready.

Whip did not look at the young man again. He turned and went off to eat with his scouts. Their good news caused him to forget Claiborne. Arnold had bagged a buck on the way back to the campsite, and Mack Dougall had shot a doe in the same vicinity.

"There wasn't time to cook 'em tonight," Mack said, reeking of whiskey as usual, but sober. "But Nat Drummond says he'll butcher 'em before he turns in, so we'll have plenty o' venison for tomorrow's supper—well, not quite enough for this many folks."

Stalking Horse was annoyed because, unlike the other scouts, he had not found any deer. "Where you catch?" he demanded.

"About five miles up the Missouri and three miles to the west," Arnold said. "There's a salt lick hidden behind some high brush near a little stream that flows into the river."

Stalking Horse said nothing, but his eyes indicated he had no intention of being outdone by his older, white colleagues. As soon as the meal was over, he slid a pair of knives into his belt, picked up his bow and his quiver of arrows, then went to fetch his gelding, a farewell gift from Sam Brentwood.

He led his mount beyond the circle of wagons and was about to vault onto the horse's back when he sensed that someone else was near. He stared, then reached for one of his knives just as a wraith-like, curious figure emerged from the special wagon and came toward him.

The man was blacker than the night, as short as a child, and almost totally bald. Hosea halted, then raised a hand in the Ashanti greeting.

The gesture was remarkably similar to the Indian sign of peace, and Stalking Horse loosened his grip on the hilt of the knife. He had never seen this little man before, and it was odd that he should have come out of the special wagon. But the Cherokee, unlike his white friends, had a live-and-let-live philosophy, and he felt a twinge of sympathy for this strange creature who was clad only in a loincloth.

Stalking Horse raised his own hand in reply to Hosea's gesture, then leaped onto the back of his horse and started off toward the north, quickly increasing the gelding's pace to a canter.

Hosea ran beside him, moving effortlessly. The Cherokee was startled—he had never encountered a man who could keep up with a cantering horse. But he admired the man's speed and stamina, so he allowed him to come along. Besides, he appeared harmless, carrying nothing other than a small container slung over one shoulder and some strange little objects tied to his middle.

Stalking Horse wondered how long the man could maintain the pace. Mile after mile the horse continued to canter, and mile after mile Hosea ran beside the horse, untiring, his breathing easy and unlabored, his gait steady.

Then, when they came to a place within a mile of the salt lick Arnold had described, Stalking Horse slowed to a halt, dismounted, and walked beside the horse. Hosea followed him. He must have overheard the conversation with Whip, Stalking Horse thought, and somehow figured out that he was going hunting.

They came to a small tree, and Stalking Horse tethered his gelding. Making no sound, he moved forward again. Hosea was equally silent.

The wind was blowing from the south into their faces, which was good since any deer in the vicinity of the lick wouldn't be able to get the scent of humans. The grass grew higher, and the pair snaked through it side by side, Stalking Horse telling himself that whoever this stranger might be, he was an accomplished hunter.

They circled the pond that Arnold had mentioned and saw the lick ahead. Peering through the thick grass, they saw a buck and a doe feeding.

Stalking Horse reached into his quiver and notched an arrow on his bowstring. As he did, his small companion removed one of the unusual objects hanging from his waist.

They struck simultaneously, Hosea hurling his miniature, weighted club at the same instant that Stalking Horse fired the arrow.

The Indian fully expected to kill his quarry and was in no way surprised when he put the arrow into the doe's heart. What amazed him was that the black man's club, aimed with unerring accuracy, had caught the buck on the head, and he toppled to the ground, too.

"Wait here," the impressed Stalking Horse commanded, then hurried off to fetch his horse.

Returning with the mount, he and Hosea loaded the deer onto the gelding's back. Because the horse was so weighted down, the walk back to the campsite took several hours.

Some members of the expedition had already retired, but the cooking fire was still burning. A number of people were sitting and standing around it, drinking coffee. Stalking Horse halted and removed the deer.

Hosea stopped outside the circle of the wagons.

"Use knife," Hosea said. "Need shirt and pants."

At last Stalking Horse understood. He handed him a knife, took his gelding and, entering the circle, immediately found Whip. He began to explain what had happened, deliberately speaking in his own language so that others wouldn't know what he was saying.

Whip immediately accompanied the Cherokee, who was still explaining when they approached the place where he had left Hosea. Working with great speed and dexterity, Hosea had already skinned the buck and was butchering the carcass. He looked up, the knife still in his hand, but he appeared resigned now to whatever fate might await him. He neither ran away nor tried to defend himself.

Whip had his hand on the butt of a pistol, but refrained from drawing it. "Who are you?"

The little man drew himself up proudly. "Hosea."

"Somebody had to hide you in the special wagon and bring you food. Who helped you?"

The black man hesitated, but knew that lies would only complicate his situation. "Boys."

"What boys?"

"Name of one Danny. Name of other Chet."

"Fetch them," Whip said, and Stalking Horse hurried back to the fire.

"Is it true," the wagonmaster demanded, his curiosity overcoming him, "that you actually killed that buck with one of those clubs?"

Hosea grinned and handed him one of the little clubs.

Whip held it in his hand, noted that it had a perfect

balance, and handed it back to him. At that moment Stalking Horse reappeared with the sheepish boys.

Danny was eager to explain before he received a tongue-lashing. "Hosea here is a wonderful fellow," he said. "He escaped from a plantation in Georgia and crossed the whole United States all the way to Independence without being caught."

"That's why we had to help him," Chet added. "Please, Whip, we don't care how you punish us, but don't send him back."

"Let him stay with us!" Danny begged.

Whip raised a hand for silence, then turned to the black man. "Anybody who can keep up with a cantering horse for miles and can kill a buck with a crazy weapon like this doesn't need to hide. Besides, all men have a right to be free." He grinned, then extended his hand. "Welcome to the wagon train."

Hosea shook his hand with great dignity.

The boys whooped with delight.

"Help him finish skinning and butchering these deer," Whip told them. "Hosea, tomorrow night you'll eat roast venison, and you'll eat with all the rest of us."

The little man bowed to express his appreciation, then suddenly waved the boys away from the deer. "No!" he told them. "Hosea take off skins. Best skinner in world. Then boys cut meat. Need skins for clothes."

Whip had skinned more wild animals than he could recall, and watching Hosea skin the doe, he had to concede that his boast was justified. He was remarkably nimble, his speed was dazzling, and at no time did he injure the skin. Had he chosen a career as a mountain man, he would have succeeded, and Whip could think of no higher praise.

"Sleep beside the fire, Hosea, until you can make yourself some buckskins. The nights are chilly." He turned and went back into the circle.

Stalking Horse continued to watch until Hosea was finished, and then, as the boys butchered the carcasses, Hosea allowed Stalking Horse to help prepare the skins. He and Hosea cut away the hair, scraped the insides clean of flesh, then rubbed the skins vigorously, using a mixture of salt, fat, and the brains of the deer, along with bunches of grass. It was late before they were done. Danny, returning after a final trip to the fire with the venison, which would be cooked lightly before being roasted the following night, brought word that Ernie von Thalman would allow the skins to be cured in the sunlight on the roof of his wagon. Finally, Hosea retired to the side of the fire.

In the morning, he created a sensation, and by the time the entire company assembled for breakfast, he was the center of attention. In spite of his scanty attire, he continued to conduct himself with grave dignity, bowing courteously to everyone who approached him and shaking hands with those who held out their hands to him. He answered all questions the members of the company asked, although some of his replies were vague.

Most of the travelers seemed to accept him, although some appeared uneasy when, in response to requests, he showed them his blowgun and miniature, weighted clubs. A few southern farmers and their families avoided him, but only the Woodlings were openly hostile. Eulalia solved the problem by pretending he didn't exist, but her father glared at the black man, and Claiborne went out of his way to be rude. "He should be sent back to Georgia in chains and whipped every day for a month," he announced to no one in particular.

Others more than compensated for this hostility, however. Ernie von Thalman and Dr. Martin offered him places in their wagons during the march, and Tonie said she would be pleased if he rode in her wagon with Danny. Cathy van Ayl and Cindy made certain he had enough food for breakfast.

Still courteous but offering no explanations, he refused all offers of places in various wagons. Then, when the workhorses and oxen were harnessed and the wagons broke up their night formation to start moving into line, he walked quietly to Whip, who was just mounting his stallion.

"Hosea go with chief," he announced.

Whip was puzzled. "That's fine with me, but I'm afraid I don't have a spare horse for you."

"No need horse. No want horse," Hosea replied. When the caravan began to move, he trotted amiably beside Whip's mount, never showing any sign of fatigue, never complaining.

During the next ten days, the weather gradually became cooler, and on two nights rain fell. On the second occasion, lightning filled the sky, thunder rumbled across the plains, and several wagon owners insisted that Hosea sleep under cover. He refused with the same gentle dignity he always displayed, but he did accept a blanket from Dr. Martin and consented to sleep under Ernie von Thalman's wagon.

Hosea was clever with his hands, but when the skins were finally cured, Cathy noticed that he appeared puzzled and sat for a long time after supper studying the shirts of several of the men. Realizing that he didn't know how to sew, she insisted on making his new wardrobe for him. She cut the skins for him, and for the next three days he drove her team while she sat on the board beside him and sewed his new shirt, pants, moccasins, and the short outer cloak he would wear when the weather turned still colder.

Her kindness won his loyalty. Thereafter, when she was preparing meals, he invariably appeared beside her and quietly performed tasks that required physical strength.

One evening, refusing food until Cathy was done with her work, Hosea finally accepted a dripping chunk of meat, which he placed on a slab of bread. The conversation near the fire was too noisy for him, so he retreated to the shadows near the special wagon. Sitting cross-legged on the ground, he began to eat. Suddenly he raised his head, listening intently.

Danny was coming toward him, but Hosea gestured for silence, then rose quietly and hurried to the far side of the fire, where he beckoned urgently to Stalking Horse, Arnold Mell, and Whip. They followed him without question.

Hosea halted near the spot where he had been eating his supper and stood still. Stalking Horse, too, heard the sound that had alarmed him. Then Whip and Arnold picked it up at the same instant and, exchanging glances, cocked their rifles. Although none of the others who were gathered around the campfire realized it, intruders had broken into the wagon directly behind the special wagon.

Whip took charge, indicating with gestures that he and Arnold would go into the open through the narrow space between the vehicles while Stalking Horse and Hosea crawled out under the special wagon.

Danny, curious and excited, wanted to accompany the men, but he was halted by a sharp, curt wave from Whip, who didn't want the burden of the boy's safety on his mind. Danny reluctantly stopped.

Rifles were less effective at short range than smaller firearms, so Whip and Arnold both carried their rifles in their left hands and drew pistols from their belts with their right.

As soon as they moved out into the open, they flattened themselves against the outside of the special wagon. They took in the situation at a glance. Six horses were tethered a short distance away, and a half-dozen Kansa warriors were systematically looting a settler's wagon.

The braves, their nationality identifiable by the bright red and deep purple stripes of paint on their cheeks and foreheads, had slashed the canvas at one side of the wagon. Making silent trips between the wagon and the spot where their horses were tethered, they were apparently stealing everything—sacks and barrels of emergency food supplies, bundles of clothing, and an old clock. They had piled more on the ground than they could comfortably carry, and were so intent on their thievery that they didn't realize they were being observed from the shadows a few yards away. Two of them, after jointly carrying a barrel of pickled beef, started back to the wagon.

Stalking Horse was the first to strike. Leaping to his feet and bounding forward, a knife held above his head, he gave his intended victim no opportunity to defend himself or even to shout a warning to his companions. Before the Kansa realized what was happening, the

Cherokee had slashed his throat, and he crumpled to the grass.

While Whip and Arnold watched, Hosea proceeded to dispose of the second Indian. Waiting only long enough to make certain that Stalking Horse was not in his line of fire, he sent a tiny dart from his blowgun at the warrior, who was reaching for the knife in his own belt. The needle-sharp point of the dart penetrated the Indian's face, and he grimaced, as though stung by a bee or wasp. He raised his free hand to his cheek to brush away the insect, but by that time the poison was taking effect. For a moment he stood erect, a bewildered expression on his face. Then the knife dropped from his nerveless fingers, and he collapsed in a heap, dying as he sprawled on the ground.

Whip and Arnold exchanged a quick glance. The same thought had occurred to both of them. The silent tactics instinctively employed by their companions were proving remarkably effective. The other Kansa who were rummaging inside the wagon didn't even know they were under attack. So Whip silently indicated to Stalking Horse and Hosea that they were to continue. Not only did Whip not want to warn the Indians, but he was afraid that any gunfire might attract members of the wagon train to the scene. The presence of hostile Indians could easily start a panic among the less experienced members of the wagon train, and it was possible that some of them might be injured.

Stalking Horse placed himself in the open space between the wagons, where it would be more difficult for him to be seen, and Hosea seemed to melt into the night as he dropped to one knee in the shadow of the special wagon. Soon two more of the Kansa emerged from the wagon, carrying a sack of grain. Stalking Horse literally flew as he hurtled toward the warrior closest to him and plunged his knife all the way to the hilt into the man's back. The brave had no chance to fight back, and, sprawling face forward onto the ground, he died without realizing what had happened to him.

Then there was a faint, popping sound as Hosea directed a strong puff of breath into the mouthpiece of his blowgun. The tiny dart was invisible as it flew toward its target. Again his aim was accurate—the dart penetrated the back of the other Kansa's neck.

He dropped the sack of grain, and began to reach up to swat what he thought was an insect. Then he staggered in a circle, agony reflected in his eyes. Dropping to his hands and knees, he crawled a few feet in the direction of the tethered horses and then silently collapsed.

Before Stalking Horse could remove his knife from the back of the warrior he had just killed, a fifth Kansa emerged from the wagon. The man carried a pile of clothes in his arms, but he immediately took in the situation. Quicker and more agile than his colleagues, he flung the stolen clothes aside, drew his own bone-handled knife, and leaped at Stalking Horse.

The Cherokee was still unarmed, and he rolled to one side to avert the full force of the impact, deflecting the Kansa's vicious attempt to knife him.

The Kansa landed on top of Stalking Horse. A deadly tug of war began for possession of the blade, with the Cherokee hanging on to his foe's wrist while the Kansa struggled ferociously to free himself. They rolled over and over in the grass, both men kicking, both hitting and punching with their free hands. Neither spoke, and only their deep grunts indicated the intensity of their combat.

Whip and Arnold were helpless. The two men writhing on the ground were twisting and turning so rapidly and convulsively that it was impossible to shoot at the Kansa without running the risk of killing Stalking Horse.

Hosea dropped his blowgun into its container and took one of his tiny clubs from the loop around his middle. Again and again he raised the club, but could not throw it for fear of striking his friend.

Whip had counted the intruders' horses and had realized that if each of them had ridden a separate animal and had brought no spare mounts, then one Kansa remained inside the wagon. So, even as he watched Stalking Horse, awaiting an opportunity to fire, he knew that at any second the last Kansa might appear and join in the fight.

Stalking Horse's opponent was taller and more powerful than he was, so the Cherokee had to rely on cunning as well as strength. Still unable to gain possession of the knife that meant life or death, he relaxed his grip for an instant. Then, as the Kansa gathered himself for the final blow, Stalking Horse drove a knee into his groin. The other Indian gasped and involuntarily doubled over.

The opportunity was momentary, but Stalking Horse took full advantage of it and punched his opponent in the solar plexus. The blow was sharp and deft, and the Kansa gagged.

Now the Cherokee had gained the upper hand. He seized the knife the Kansa had dropped, then stabbed the man repeatedly. Spurred by the violent intensity of the fight, he struck again and again, thrusting and stabbing, slashing and cutting in a frenzy until long after his foe was dead.

Arnold started forward, intending to stop him, but just then the last of the raiders emerged from the wagon.

Hosea immediately reached for his blowgun, and Arnold raised his pistol.

"No!" Whip ordered, his tone urgent.

Both stopped, without question.

The Kansa took in the scene of carnage, realized his companions were dead, and wanted only to save his own life. Dropping the hammer and saw he had been about to steal, he sprinted madly toward the little grove where the horses were tethered. Leaping onto the back of one of the mounts, he galloped off, not once looking back as he crouched low over his horse's neck.

Arnold knew why Whip had prevented the killing of the last Kansa, as did Stalking Horse. But Hosea was still confused. "Why Whip let Indian go?" he asked.

"Because I wanted him to go back to his own people and tell them what happened here. I want every warrior of the Kansa nation to know that any of them who try to steal from us will pay with his life."

Whip turned away, slipped through the opening between the wagons and called to everyone to join him outside. By the time the settlers assembled, Stalking Horse had scalped all five of the dead Kansa. Trying to be generous, he offered three of the scalps to Hosea, but they had no value to the black man, so he refused them. Stalking Horse promptly hung all five from his belt.

Some of the women became sick, and a number of the children wept when they saw the grotesque corpses illuminated by torchlight. Many of the men didn't seem too happy, either, but an angry Whip insisted that everyone look at the bodies.

Standing between two of the warriors' bodies in the dark field, he spoke. "Folks," he said, "if it wasn't for our friend Hosea being alert, we might not have learned we were being robbed. Thanks to him and Stalking Horse, all but one of the thieves were killed. I'm hoping the Kansa will take heed and keep their distance from us from now on. I know you don't enjoy looking at dead, mutilated bodies, but I wanted all of you to look—and look hard—at these warriors. I hope that this will help you remember we're a long way from civilization, and we're going a heap further. Those of you who carry firearms, keep them with you at all times. Don't wander away from camp without permission, or you may end up looking like these dead Indians. Keep your eyes and ears wide open, and don't take chances."

Somberly the families filed back into the circle. There was little conversation. A number of volunteers remained behind, some of the men removing and burying the braves' bodies while others gathered the scattered property of the family whose wagon had been ransacked. Several of the women, directed by Grace Drummond, got out needles and heavy thread and began to repair the slash in the side of the canvas. The woman to whom the wagon belonged sobbed silently with relief. Her husband put his arm around her and thanked God that their small children had not been in the wagon at the time. He tried not to think what the savages would have done to two pretty blonde girls.

These tasks were soon finished, and as the campfire burned lower, the company retired. But the circle of wagons no longer seemed as secure and safe as it had been, and many of the travelers lay awake listening to the strange and no longer friendly sounds of the night. The plains, which had seemed so similar to the prairies of civilized, settled Illinois, were desolate and wild. The Indians in these parts weren't dependable friends like Stalking Horse; they were savage creatures eager to rob and murder those who trespassed on their territory.

Somewhere in the distance a wild animal, probably a coyote, howled dismally.

Many of the travelers—burrowing beneath their blankets because the winds blowing across the Plains felt increasingly colder—wished they had never come on this lonely journey.

Mack Dougall was filled with a sense of excitement when he returned to the campsite from his scouting duties one evening. He indicated he wanted a conference with the company's leaders. Whip, Arnold Mell, and Ernie von Thalman sat down with him in the Baron's comfortable wagon, but Mack wasn't yet ready to talk.

Removing a bottle of whiskey from his hip pocket, he pulled out the cork with his teeth, wiped off the mouth with a grimy hand, and took a long swallow. "My joints are achin' somethin' fierce," he said, "and this here is the only medicine there is that saves me from bein' a complete cripple." Looking as though he felt sorry for himself, he offered the bottle to the other men, but they all declined.

Mack belched, drew the back of his hand across his mouth, and settled back in the Baron's only padded chair. "About twenty miles from here," he said, "I seen the biggest herd of buffalo I ever set eyes on. There had to be a thousand of them."

Whip whistled under his breath.

Arnold explained for Ernie's benefit. "Most herds run to two or three hundred buffalo. A really big herd may number as many as five hundred. I've only seen that many once or twice."

"I don't believe I ever have," Whip added.

"The way I figure it," Mack said, "two or three herds got together because they liked the taste o' the grass. They was nibblin' and munchin' away like crazy."

Whip nodded.

"It seems to me," Mack said, "that if we send out a big enough huntin' party—and can get anywheres near the combined herd—we can have enough meat to see us into the cold weather and enough hides to make winter cloaks for as many as wants 'em."

Arnold nodded but said nothing, lost in thought. Whip was silent, too, thinking.

Ernie became impatient. "Why do we wait? With the extra horses we got from the Kansa raiders, we must have enough mounts for at least twenty men. We can take the twenty best riflemen and go with Mack at once to find the herd."

Whip shook his head. "You don't understand, Ernie," he said. "It isn't that simple."

"Buffalo," Arnold added, "are strange, skittish critters. They're bound to hear twenty horsemen coming toward them, and they'll get so jittery they'll take off. And once they start to move, there's no telling which direction they'll go."

The Baron frowned. "Suppose we make a circle around to their rear—a few of us, that is—and drive the herd toward our main body of hunters, who will be waiting for them."

The others laughed. "Before we reached Independence, Ernie, you saw one small herd of buffalo stampede, and even that was a scary sight."

"I shall never forget it," Ernie replied.

"Just thinkin' about a stampede of a thousand buffalo freezes my innards," Mack said, reaching into his hip pocket for his whiskey.

"Mack is right," Arnold said. "Not only is it impossible to point them in the direction we want them to go, but there's no way to control even fifty buffalo. A thousand of them could tear a forest apart or destroy a town."

"There's something else to be considered. We can't make a detour to their grazing grounds with the whole wagon train." Whip was emphatic. "We'd need at least two days to get there, and then we'd have to spend two more days hauling ourselves back to the right trail."

"Why would we have to do that?" Again Ernie was confused.

"Consider this," Whip told him. "Suppose we take twenty hunters and kill as many as seventy-five buffalo."

"A reasonable assumption. Perhaps we could bring down even more," the Baron said enthusiastically.

Whip's smile was wry. "A bull may weigh a ton or more. A cow runs at least a thousand pounds. After we butcher the carcasses, we'll have to smoke the meat, which means building some mighty extensive trenches and fires. But that's just the beginning. Unless the entire wagon train is nearby, how can we transport thousands and thousands of pounds of smoked meat to the wagons? We'd need at least fifteen freighters—which we don't have."

At last Ernie von Thalman grasped the enormity of the problem. In the long silence that followed, Mack Dougall took another swig from his bottle.

"I see no way to solve this," Whip said at last. "I'd love to bring down enough buffalo to feed us for many weeks. But I see no practical way of doing it."

"Neither do I," Arnold agreed. "What's more, even if we go after them, they may have disappeared by the time we reach the grazing grounds. The worst thing about buffalo, Ernie, is that they're completely unpredictable. Nobody knows what sparks a stampede. Oh, it can be something obvious, like a rifle shot, or it can be nothing at all that any human being can figure out."

Mack chuckled. "I've seen it many times. One second the damn buffalo are just standin' around like cattle, chewin' away on grass as peaceful as you please. But the very next second, for no rhyme or reason, they're high-tailin' across the plains as though Beelzebub himself is chasin' 'em."

"They do have a marvelous instinct for avoiding large objects," Whip said. "Even when they stampede, they'll never run down a horse and rider, for instance, or a wagon. But they get so crazed that they probably wouldn't even notice a man just standing in the prairie."

"I believe they'd trample him to death," Arnold said. "Me, I don't intend to try the experiment. But that's not the point. There doesn't seem to be a way we can handle this oversized herd."

"There isn't," Whip said regretfully. "None of us has ever faced a situation that's involved so many people. It's too big a headache for us."

The next morning, however, there was an unexpected development. The scouts were served their breakfast early, and Whip was eating with them, as was his custom. Suddenly, Stalking Horse dropped to his hands and knees, placing an ear close to the ground.

Whip immediately followed his example. After a moment or two, he heard a faint, rumbling noise. Shaking his head in astonishment, he scrambled to his feet. "Until now I never believed in miracles, but that herd of buffalo seems to be heading this way. There's no telling whether they'll veer off, but we want to be ready. Mack, get Ernie for me, quick. Arnold, start rounding up the best riflemen in the train."

The group worked with frantic speed to prepare for the possibility that the giant herd might come close to the campsite.

While Ernie von Thalman sifted through the many volunteer hunters, selecting only those whom he knew were marksmen, Whip issued succinct orders to the entire company. All workhorses and oxen were to be kept penned inside the circle of wagons. Even if they became nervous and tried to bolt, they were not to be allowed out into the open, where they might be trampled by the stampeding herd. No women or children were allowed to go outside the circle, and every mother was to be held accountable for the whereabouts of her own family.

Tonie Mell protested. "Whip," she said, "you know I'm a better shot than most of the men. Why can't I join the hunt?"

"Because you're needed right here," he told her. "You've had more experience than anyone else in controlling the animals. You'll know how to calm them if they get panicky."

The girl sighed, but knew he was too busy for an argument.

"If I needed your rifle," Whip assured her, "I'd call on you, believe me."

Claiborne Woodling started to make a scene when he wasn't included in Ernie's band. "None of you has ever seen me shoot, so you don't know whether I'm good or bad. I have my own horse, and I demand—"

"All right," Whip told him, interrupting curtly. "Join us, then, provided you do what you're told—without argument."

Every few minutes Stalking Horse placed his ear to the ground and reported on the location of the herd. "Still coming this way," he said repeatedly. "Coming fast!"

Twenty-two horsemen followed Ernie into the open beyond the circle of wagons. Breakfast was forgotten by all but a few inside the compound.

Whip remained behind for the moment, giving final instructions. Realizing that Tonie couldn't handle such a large number of horses and oxen alone, he appointed Nat Drummond to help her. "Call on as many men as you need to keep the animals quiet," he said. "Panic is contagious, and we don't want them smashing into wagons and hurting people by trying to break loose."

Hosea was loitering nearby, looking anxious. Whip could read his mind. "You want to join us out yonder, I know, but you don't have a horse."

"Never need horse," Hosea replied.

"This is one time you'd need one." Whip was firm. "Stay here, and if any of our animals get too upset, put them to sleep for a while with those little clubs of yours. Gently."

Pleased because he had been given a major responsibility, Hosea bowed, then glided away.

As Whip headed toward his stallion, he found his path blocked by Danny, who held a gelding's rein in one hand and Tonie's rifle in the other. "Please, Whip," he said. "Let me join the fun."

Not only could Whip remember how he himself had felt when he had been in his teens, but he knew Danny deserved a reward. Hard-working and eager to help everyone, the boy with no family of his own had a harder lot than most. And Whip knew that a boy could grow to manhood only when he was given a man's duties to perform. "Come along," he said.

An ecstatic Danny followed him through the opening between two wagons into the high grass.

Ernie had arranged the riders in a single line, as though they were cavalrymen ready to charge an enemy. Whip held back the laughter that rose within him, not wanting to hurt his friend's feelings. He would have to reorganize the column, but first he needed more information.

Stalking Horse had already anticipated Whip's desire and was squatting, his ear close to the ground. "Buffalo come very fast," he said. "This way." He pointed off to the left, then mounted his own horse and started in that direction. Willing to let him take the lead, Whip rode behind him, beckoning to the others to follow.

No one spoke as they made their way in single file across the prairie, halting after they had ridden about three-quarters of a mile. The rumble of the approaching buffalo could now be heard by everyone, and the roar was quickly growing louder and louder.

Whip lost no time reorganizing the party into two columns. They formed in a V, and he placed himself at the critical point in the center, facing the direction the buffalo would approach. The next most important places were those on the flanks, at the outermost open ends of the V. Because of their experience, as well as their marksmanship, Arnold Mell and Mack Dougall were given those positions.

In the distance they could see a cloud of dust that grew thicker and rose higher as it came closer. The thunder of four thousand hoofs was so loud that Whip had to shout to make himself heard. "Hold your fire until I shoot," he told the party, "and make certain you hold your horses steady. That's as important as anything else you'll do. A horse gets skittish when he sees an army of buffalo charging toward him. All right?"

Everyone seemed to understand.

"Most important of all, there will be one bull in the lead. Leave him be."

"What would happen if we shot the lead bull?" Claiborne Woodling interrupted.

Whip curbed his irritation. "None of us would live long enough to find out. If he is brought down, the whole herd will lose its sense of direction. They would panic, and roll over us like a tidal wave."

The roar was so loud now that conversation was no longer possible, but Whip made a final adjustment. Pantomiming what he wanted, he moved Danny directly behind him to the left. The boy, excited and pleased, grinned at him, then kept checking his borrowed rifle.

The buffalo loomed on the horizon. They ran shoulder to shoulder in a solid mass nearly half a mile wide. Whip was awed. Mack was right; never had he seen a herd that spread out so far.

Glancing back over first one shoulder then the other, he saw that the hunters were holding their positions. None were openly panicked, and what was more important, all of them were in control of their horses. Rifles had been checked, and the hunters were ready for action. Whip looked at Danny and winked at him.

It was possible now to make out individual animals. The buffalo's eyesight was less acute than his other senses, and the leader, attracted by the blurred mass of the hunting party, galloped toward the men, unaware of the danger. The ground trembling beneath his churning hoofs, he ran recklessly, his head lowered.

The waiting men could see the buffalo clearly. The leader was a massive, mature beast, shaggy and unkempt, who weighed at least a ton and a half. Whip couldn't help admiring him, secretly glad that such a magnificent beast would be spared.

The organization of the herd was remarkable. Behind the lead bull were scores of other adult males, all of them in the prime of life, their horns fully grown. Others were stretched out on both flanks in single files, to keep strays in line. In the center, pounding forward, came the younger bulls, adolescents who had not yet reached maturity but had great strength and stamina. Behind them came the old bulls, whom seasoned hunters preferred to ignore because their meat was so tough. Their horns were gnarled, their fur was matted, and many of them found it difficult to maintain the pace. But still they ran, for their lives depended on their ability to keep up. Frequently an old bull's strength finally drained away, and he crumpled to the ground. The others then ran around him, never trampling him, and it was not uncommon to find the rotting carcasses of old bulls on the plains.

Next, although invisible in the surging mass of beasts, came the cows and their calves, the mothers nudging their young and driving close on their heels to force them to keep running. And at the very end of the formation were several more rows of strong, mature bulls who would not permit stragglers to drop out.

At the moment there was no way of determining the depth of the charging, seething mass of animal flesh. The herd charging toward the men reminded Whip of towering waves he had seen rolling toward the shore of the Pacific Coast wilderness.

Whip's stallion, ordinarily calm and responsive to his master, became skittish, pawing the ground and tossing his mane. His instincts urged him to throw his rider and flee, but Whip patted him, stroked him, and, hoping the animal could hear him above the roar, spoke to him soothingly. The stallion grew quiet.

The buffalo now stretched as far across the plains as the eye could see. Arnold and Mack, the only members of the party other than Whip who were experienced in dealing with buffalo, were even more awed by the size of the herd than the newcomers. The ground shook as though from an earthquake, and the thickening cloud of dust threatened to choke the riders and their horses.

But the hunters maintained their tight, V-shaped formation. The size of the group presented a large enough obstacle for the buffalo to notice it in the midst of their mindless charge, and so the men would be relatively safe—if the herd followed the usual patterns. But anyone who left the formation surely would be trampled.

The lead buffalo, in spite of his size, was remarkably swift and sure-footed. He actually seemed to pick up speed as he thundered across the prairie. The bulls in the rows directly behind him were being challenged and had to exert themselves to keep up the mad pace. As the females and older bulls tired and fell back, the size of the herd spread menacingly.

It seemed certain that the lead bull intended to smash through the barrier of men and horses. His momentum was so great that not even a hail of bullets would have prevented him from rocketing into the riders and their mounts. Whip's only protection was his knowledge of the buffalo's habits. If this leader and his followers were unpredictable, however, Whip would be the first to die, and it was doubtful if any of the others would be able to save themselves.

Whip could now see the red eyes of the lead buffalo. They were glazed, and there was no way of knowing what the maddened beast might do. He was almost close enough to touch when, suddenly, he veered to the right and swept past the point of the V-shaped formation.

The danger was far from over. Most of the bulls in the rows directly behind him followed his example, but others appeared leaderless; they could smash at any moment into the men and their mounts.

But the instinct for survival was as strong in the buffalo as it was in humans. A powerful, mature bull took it upon himself to become a sub-leader, and rather than crash through the barrier, he swerved to the left.

The hunters were like an immobile obstacle in a swift-flowing river, as the buffalo charged past them by the hundreds on both sides. Men and horses choked on the dust, their eyes stinging and watering: the stench of the herd was so unbearable that many of the new hunters retched.

Whip had won his gamble. He raised his rifle. It would have been difficult to avoid hitting a buffalo in that roaring, thundering mass, but he chose his target with care. He squeezed the trigger, and a bull in the prime of life staggered, lost momentum, and pitched forward onto the ground. Others in the herd instantly made detours around his body without slackening their pace.

The men had been waiting for Whip's signal. Arnold and Mack immediately opened fire, too. Stalking Horse let fly with an arrow, and Claiborne Woodling demonstrated that he was as good a marksman as he claimed, bringing down another bull with a single shot.

Rarely had hunters enjoyed such an opportunity, but suddenly a new crisis developed. Danny's gelding, already unnerved by the charging herd, was further upset by the sound of rifle fire. The boy could no longer handle him, and the horse reared, then plunged forward, throwing Danny to the ground.

Whip was powerless to save the horse. The frightened animal moved into the path of the onrushing buffalo, who knew only that he was not one of their number. The gelding was knocked off balance by the bulls and then disappeared from sight as he was trampled by the buffalo. For a moment or two, the horse's screams rose above the thunder, then faded away as he died.

Whip's only concern was Danny. The boy was dazed and stood indecisively, wavering on his feet. If he lost consciousness, he would fall directly into the path of the buffalo.

Whip quickly freed the rawhide lash from around his middle and took aim. The whip coiled around the boy's body. Meanwhile buffalo were charging so close to him that they missed him by inches. Little by little, Whip hauled him closer, finally bringing him to relative safety behind his own stallion.

Stalking Horse, who was next in line on that side, needed no instructions to close the gap; he moved his horse closer to Whip, and the two horses provided a wall for the boy, who now stood safely inside the point of the V.

The rawhide whip fell away, and Danny recovered his equilibrium. Gradually, as his fear and confusion subsided, he was filled with a sense of shame. He felt responsible for losing a horse, and he was afraid the men would regard him as a child who was unfit to become a member of their company.

He felt the urgent desire to redeem himself, and there

was only one way. Shielded by Whip and Stalking Horse, he could prove he was a man by bringing down buffalo, and that knowledge made him calmer. When he had been thrown, he had retained enough presence of mind to hold on to the borrowed rifle, and he still held it in his hands. He raised it and fired, and was pleased when a young bull stumbled and dropped.

Seeing this, Whip was relieved. He knew that Danny would do nothing foolish now.

As the cows and their calves were running past the V-shaped formation, Whip saw a young calf that was pure white. He was stunned—a white calf was very rare and extremely valuable.

Stalking Horse saw the calf, too, and caught his breath. Less superstitious than the Indians of the Plains nations after having spent long periods with civilized men, he nevertheless shared the deeply ingrained belief of the plains tribes that the rare white calf was a reincarnation of the moon god. The skin of such a calf brought its owner great good fortune and could not be sold or bartered. When presented by its owner as a gift, however, the fortunate recipient then became blessed by good health and prosperity.

Whip, knowing the value of the white calf, didn't want to mar the hide. Steadying himself, he took particularly careful aim and put a bullet between the eyes of the young buffalo.

Soon the bulls at the rear of the herd appeared. The hunters continued to shoot, firing and reloading as rapidly as they could, until the last of the column roared off across the prairie. Ernie took out his pocket watch and announced that almost forty minutes had passed since the buffalo had first started to move past the formation.

The ground was littered with the carcasses of bulls, cows, and calves, and Whip immediately sent a rider to fetch the wagon train. The detour would take the caravan out of its way, but that couldn't be helped. The entire company had to be put to work.

Whip himself first skinned the precious white calf, taking great care not to inflict any unnecessary cuts on the hide. That one skin could mean as much to the members of the caravan as the entire supply of carcasses.

As soon as he was done, he went to Danny and clapped the boy on the shoulder. "I'm proud of you," he said.

Danny looked up from the young bull he was skinning and flushed. "I feel terrible, Whip. I let everybody down."

"What happened to you could have happened to anybody. What I liked was the way you got hold of yourself and started shooting. You're doing fine."

Danny grinned, his self-confidence restored.

Without delay, the hunters went to work skinning the carcasses of the buffalo they had killed. Only Claiborne Woodling balked. "I'm a hunter, not a butcher," he declared.

Whip had no patience with him. "Winter is coming," he said, "so we'll need meat and hides. Anybody who won't work for the good of all can get out—and try surviving by himself."

A sullen Claiborne picked up his knife.

The caravan caught up with the hunters early in the afternoon, and everyone in the company was given a specific assignment. Mounted groups using wagons for hauling went off to the nearest woods and returned with piles of dead brush and logs. After the buffalo were skinned, some of the women began the tedious process of curing the hides. Meanwhile, the carcasses were butchered, long trenches were dug, and fires were lighted in them. The meat had to be smoked for seventy-two hours, and in all the journey was delayed by a week.

But no one minded. There were few who actually enjoyed the taste of smoked buffalo meat, but at least the travelers knew they wouldn't starve. And the cured hides would be used for coats, cloaks, and blankets.

Whip allowed no one to touch the skin of the white calf. After preparing it himself, he stretched it on the roof of Ernie von Thalman's wagon to dry.

At last the task of preserving the meat was done, and every family was given an appropriate share. Skins were spread on the canvas roofs of wagons by day, then removed at night when the air was damp. Cathy van

Ayl, who had already made herself a doeskin shirt and skirt, as well as Hosea's clothes, was besieged with requests for advice on the making of leather garments.

The younger children had a new game, buffalo hunt, and every evening they raced up and down inside the circle of wagons, screaming and shouting as they alternated playing the roles of hunter and buffalo.

The hunters in the company remained active, bringing venison and small game to the campsite at night. The smoked buffalo meat was intended strictly for winter use, when other meat would be unavailable.

Whip Holt breathed more easily after the encounter with the giant herd. He knew there were many dangers threatening the future of the wagon train, but the possibility that people would starve before spring was now remote.

IV

Hosea acquired the skin of a large bull buffalo, and after the westward journey was resumed, he spent most of his time in the evenings working on a special project of his own.

Danny and Chet, still fascinated by him, noted that one night he had cut several boughs of strong oak. Working with meticulous precision, he fashioned the wood into a double, diamond-shaped frame, binding the sections together with lengths of rawhide. Over the frame he stretched buffalo hide until it was taut. When he was satisfied that it was snug, he added a second layer of rawhide.

Not until Hosea placed a crossbar over the middle of his contraption, on the inner side, did the boys realize he had made a shield.

"Like Ashanti make in jungle," he said proudly.

Danny examined it and was dubious. "If anybody shoots at you with a rifle, Hosea, it won't stop bullets. It isn't that strong."

"No good for guns," the black man agreed. "But stop arrows, stop tomahawks, stop knives."

Two days later Hosea and Stalking Horse set off hunting. The Indian was mounted, as always, and carried his bow, arrows, and a spear. Hosea, trotting beside him, carried no weapons other than his clubs and deadly blowgun. There were those who claimed he was inadequately armed, but Whip did not agree.

"Hosea," he said, "will do as well as somebody carrying a whole arsenal."

There were many prairie dogs in the high grass of the plains—animals resembling woodchucks but smaller. Prairie chicken were everywhere, too. These were a variety of plump grouse that mountain men and others who traveled through the plains regarded as delicacies. The animals and birds were very shy, sensitive to the approach of humans, so they were difficult to catch.

The pair, far more silent than most white hunters, soon devised a system of their own. Hosea moved ahead, planted the base of his shield in the ground, then crouched behind it. There he stayed, making no sound and no movement, while Stalking Horse remained at a distance, ready to take part at an instant's notice.

Eventually a pack of prairie dogs or a flock of prairie chicken appeared, and curious about the immobile rawhide shield, they moved toward it. Once they came within range, Hosea threw his little clubs, always striking at least one or two. The others fled, and Stalking Horse was able to kill some of those with his arrows.

Hosea was a perfectionist, so he devised something new that aided him and his partner. Picking tufts of the long grass, he arranged them in his shirt and hair, making himself virtually invisible as he concealed himself behind his strange shield.

At noon the pair paused beside a small brook to drink, water Stalking Horse's mount, and eat some smoked buffalo meat. Hosea left his shield a short distance away in a field of tall grass.

Stalking Horse had begun to teach the escaped slave the language of the Kiowa nation, which virtually all the tribes of the plains used, and as the two men sat near the brook, relaxing, Stalking Horse took the opportunity to teach Hosea a few new words. But even when they were relaxing, the two men did not forget they were in the wilderness, and they remained alert.

At the same moment, both heard a faint but alien sound. Stalking Horse leaped to his feet, instinctively reaching for his bow and an arrow from his quiver.

Hosea dropped to his hands and knees and, virtually invisible thanks to his camouflage, snaked through the high grass until he reached his shield. Leaving it standing in the ground like a miniature fortress, he crouched behind it and peered out cautiously.

Five Indians, who had been hiding in the grass, approached on the far side of the brook. They were armed with bows and arrows, spears, and knives. Their scalp locks were stiffened with heavy grease, and their faces and torsos were smeared with streaks of white and yellow paint, identifying them as warriors of the small but warlike Topeka tribe. Silently one of them hurled a spear at Stalking Horse.

They had seen Hosea, too, although they didn't know what had become of him, but they weren't concerned with him, at least for the moment. They were concentrating on Stalking Horse.

The Indians moved closer. Perhaps they could capture their victim alive and take him back to their village as a slave.

But they had not reckoned on Hosea. While Stalking Horse held the Topeka at bay momentarily with his bow and arrow, Hosea fitted a dart into his blowgun. There was a scarcely audible popping sound, and one of the braves clapped a hand to his cheek. The man's scream of agony broke the silence, and he collapsed.

One of his companions threw a stone-tipped spear with all his might at Hosea, but it struck the rawhide shield, bounced off it, and fell harmlessly to the ground.

The Topeka were astonished, and a hail of arrows followed the spear. All but one fell into the grass after striking the shield, while one became embedded in the rawhide and remained there.

Hosea blew another dart from his blowgun. Again he found his target, the dart cutting into the lower lip of a warrior who stood for a moment, stunned, before he, too, dropped to the ground as the poison took effect.

Stalking Horse fired an arrow at the foe, but he was

too angry to concentrate, and for the first time in years, he missed his target.

A third Topeka boldly approached the shield. Neither he nor the other survivors had actually seen the tiny darts that had felled two of their number, and he was determined to destroy this strange and lethal contraption.

Hosea removed one of the little clubs he carried around his middle and hurled it. It struck the warrior in the temple, and he fell unconscious.

Only two of the braves were still in the fight, and Hosea, still protected by his shield, coolly killed one with another dart from his blowgun. He could have dispatched the last one, too. But, himself a warrior, he was conscious of the pride that Stalking Horse took in his own prowess. So he left the last of the warriors for his companion to kill.

This time Stalking Horse did not miss. His aim was true, and his arrow penetrated the brave's chest.

As he fell backward onto the ground, the Topeka struggled briefly and tried in vain to remove the arrow.

Now only the warrior who had been knocked unconscious by the club was still alive, and again Hosea left the honors to his friend. Stalking Horse went over to the man, stared at him coldly for a moment, then drew his knife, and cut the man's throat.

Emerging from the safety of his little fort, Hosea began to collect his spent darts and club.

While he was retrieving his weapons, Stalking Horse scalped all five of the Topeka and collected their weapons. In an attempt to be fair, he offered them to his companion, who had played the larger role in their victory.

Hosea regarded the spears as cumbersome, heavy weapons, so he had no use for them. He had never tried a bow and arrow, so he had no need for these weapons, but he finally selected a bone-handled knife that had belonged to one of the Topeka and slid it into his belt. Spoils meant nothing to him. He also declined an offer of the Topekas' scalps—wanting only what he might find useful.

Leaving the bodies where they had fallen, the pair resumed hunting.

"Not much time left," Stalking Horse said as he shaded his eyes and looked up at the sun. "Maybe we catch more chicken." The battle having ended, he saw no need to dwell on the matter.

But Hosea had something on his mind more important than prairie chicken. "Need more poison for darts," he said.

Stalking Horse recognized the urgency of the request, so they forgot the grouse and prairie dogs and searched instead for large rocks, which they cautiously overturned. They found no snakes, however, and they were about to give up their quest when Hosea stopped and pointed. Directly ahead the prairie grass was much thinner, and the area, stretching out for a distance of about two hundred yards, was strewn with a jumble of rocks. With unspoken accord they divided the field, taking care to leave Stalking Horse's mount safely behind. They hunted silently, swiftly—two wilderness men who knew precisely what they wanted.

At last Hosea's patience was rewarded. As he pulled apart a nest of rocks, a rattlesnake more than four feet long slithered into the open. Hosea's quiet grunt of satisfaction told his companion that he had found what he had been seeking.

The snake halted, saw the man, and instantly coiled itself, head swaying and fangs showing. Hosea remained calm. He had dealt with many kinds of snakes in his native Africa and with copperheads in the United States. If rattlers were new to him, that fact was irrelevant. He knew what he needed to do, and although he entertained a healthy respect for his deadly enemy, he felt no fear. Grasping his shield in one hand and the knife he had just acquired in the other, he took two steps backward, then waited.

Stalking Horse wanted to put an arrow into the snake. But the confidence of the little black man was so obvious that he decided it was wiser not to interfere and to let him handle the delicate situation as he saw fit.

Hosea could see that the snake, angry that its rest had been disturbed, was positioning itself to strike. He tightened his grasp on the handle of his shield, balancing his weight on the balls of his feet. He was reminded of an old Ashanti saying, that a battle with a serpent was a dance in which the loser died and the victor was rewarded with life.

The reptile stopped swaying, and the rattle in its tail sounded a warning that it was about to strike. A split second before the snake's head shot forward, aiming at its enemy's calves, Hosea lowered his shield to the ground. The snake struck viciously, its fangs making two tiny holes in the rawhide cover.

At that same instant Hosea retaliated, his own timing perfect. Leaning around the edge of the shield, he brought the knife down hard in a swift, slashing movement. His aim was as accurate as the rattler's, and before the snake could recover sufficiently to strike again, Hosea had severed its head from its body.

The head dropped to the ground, and Hosea picked it up. Placing it on a flat rock, he cut it open, his hand as steady as a surgeon's. At the back he found what he was seeking—the snake's twin sacs of venom. Taking all his darts, he inserted their needle-sharp points into the sacs. Poison oozed out onto the flat stone, and he took care not to touch it. Slowly, cautiously, he removed the darts from the venom sacs one by one, holding them by the blunt end, and placed them on another rock to dry.

Stalking Horse had joined him and stood a short distance away, watching.

Next Hosea picked up the body of the rattlesnake and deftly skinned it. Leaving the body for ants to devour, he placed the skin in his rope belt.

"Make new belt," he said, breaking the silence. Then he picked up the darts and dropped them into the container hanging from his shoulder.

It was dusk when the pair reached the campsite, and they went straight to Whip. For Hosea's sake Stalking

Horse spoke in English as he emptied the saddlebag of grouse. "Hunting not too bad today," he said.

Whip took note of the five scalps, not yet dry, which were hanging from the Cherokee's belt and saw the rattlesnake skin, yet to be cured, which dangled from Hosea's waist. These two could take care of themselves anywhere, any time, but apparently they did not consider their day's exploits worthy of mention. So Whip felt compelled to treat the matter lightly, too. "It seems to me," he replied, his voice dry, "that this was a pretty fair day for hunting."

The wilderness of the plains seemed desolate, devoid of all human life, but it was an illusion. Every evening, when the scouts returned to the campsite, they reported to Whip that they had seen Indians, some riding their ponies in pairs, some traveling alone and, occasionally groups of them. Arnold saw Kansa, Mack was certain he had spotted several Wichita, and Stalking Horse twice made out Topeka warriors in the distance.

The warnings to members of the wagon train were repeated. Men who owned firearms were once more reminded to carry them at all times. And under no circumstances were any members of the company to leave the circle of wagons after dark.

Cindy, who was now working on the cooking detail with Cathy van Ayl, found that order irksome. One night, their work done and their own supper eaten, they retired to the back stoop of Cathy's wagon for a chat.

They were a pretty pair. Cindy had given up the heavy makeup she had once worn, and both of them had given up trying to avoid the sun and were attractively tan. They wore shirts and skirts of doeskin.

Cathy was feeling depressed and, for reasons she couldn't quite understand, wanted to enjoy a few confidences with a friend. As nearly as she could figure, it was the vast emptiness stretching out endlessly in every direction that gave her a feeling of being lost, rudderless.

Recently she had found herself thinking more and

more of her earlier life, and she was able to see where she had gone wrong. It had started in New Haven, after Mama had died and her older sister, Claudia, had moved into the old house with her first husband. Richard had been so unsure of himself, so insecure that he had turned to the bottle in a vain attempt to bolster himself, and his drinking had not only made Claudia miserable, it had influenced her little sister, too.

Only now was Cathy beginning to perceive that her contempt for weak men had come from that period of her childhood. Then, the very night she had attended her first grown-up party, wearing a lovely pink silk dress that she and Claudia had made together, she had met Otto van Ayl, Papa's friend and a man old enough to be her father, who had been visiting the family. Shortly after that, he had asked Papa for her hand.

How eager she had been! She had mistaken Otto's rigid ways, his autocratic manner, and his insistence that he was right in all things, for strength of character. How stupid she had been. An innocent sixteen-year-old, an adolescent who had nurtured romantic dreams, she had been unprepared for the realities of life and marriage.

No, it wasn't the mistake of marrying Otto that was bothering her. She had slept with him only on their wedding night, and after that disastrous experience, he had treated her like a daughter rather than a wife. For all practical purposes, although she could not admit it to anyone except Cindy, she was still almost a virgin, even though she had been married to Otto for six years.

And now, whatever her married life had been, she was alone, left to fend for herself on this journey across the trackless plains.

"You know, Cindy," she said, "I think it's the emptiness out here that bothers me. Life wasn't easy on our farm—on Long Island. But the scenery was so varied—something different no matter which way you looked. We had a little brook out in back of the house that flowed into the Atlantic. And sand dunes! Sometimes I'd climb to the top of a dune and sit for hours, just watching the waves rolling in."

Cindy nodded. "From the window in my room at the —" she paused, "—house I could see the Ohio River. And watching the river is what saved my sanity in Louisville more times than I can remember. It was so dependable."

"We're very much alike."

"There's one way we aren't," Cindy said. "Now don't be offended, Cathy, but you're much more of a romantic soul than I—especially about Oregon."

"I'm looking forward to settling in the Oregon country," Cathy replied, "but I don't expect it to be the land of milk and honey that some people on this wagon train are so certain it will be. No land could be that perfect. But there will be mountains and forests and the sea. At least I hope we'll settle somewhere near the ocean. What I miss most is the sight of waves. Even that won't be enough, though." She became pensive.

"It sounds like you want a man." Cindy smiled.

"Not that I necessarily *want* one. I—I just have the feeling that I *need* one."

"Sex is overrated. Believe me, I know what I'm talking about, honey."

Color rose in Cathy's face. "I wasn't even thinking about that part of it!" she exclaimed. "I've come to know myself better in the months since this train left our farm. And I've pretty much come to the conclusion that I'm the sort of woman who needs a man to lean on."

"Don't you believe it, not for a minute!" Cindy was emphatic. "You're pretty, and I—well, I've got an air that makes me attractive to men, even though I couldn't compete with you in looks. So neither of us will ever have a lack of suitors, I can promise you. But we certainly don't need any of them."

Cathy became uncertain. "After being around people all day, dealing with all those women when we're fixing meals, talking to a couple of dozen men every time we stop, I'll admit I need privacy—"

"Of course you do. That's why we eat so quickly and leave the fire. I'd give anything if I could just wander out into the prairie by myself for an hour, but I know Ted Woods would follow me."

Cathy giggled. "He's terribly shy, but it's plain enough that he's sweet on you."

"I'm not ready for a romance with him—or with anybody else. I'm too busy getting men out of my system. The very idea of marrying anybody and settling down makes me a little bit ill."

"I can imagine how you feel," Cathy said, sobering, "but it isn't that way with me."

Cindy grinned at her. "From what you've told me about your life with Otto, you'll really be marrying for the first time when you do get married again."

"It scares me half to death, but it's what I want."

"Anybody special in mind?" Cindy raised an eyebrow.

Cathy shook her head. "Well, yes and no."

"You mean Whip, of course. Sometimes, when he looks at you, he just melts."

"And other times he doesn't seem to know I even exist. I tell myself it's because he has so many responsibilities for the whole train and has so much on his mind."

"You're the only one who can decide, but don't be in too big a rush."

"Oh, I won't."

Cindy's eyes became bright. "The way I look at it, a man is convenient to have around. On occasion. He can do all kinds of physical work that a woman doesn't have the strength to do. But I'll never let any man become my lord and master."

"I wouldn't want that, either."

"In the marriage service," Cindy said, "you're obliged to promise you'll obey your husband. That's not for me. There isn't a man in this world I could ever respect so much that I'd agree to take second place to him for the rest of my days."

"When you put it that way," Cathy said, sighing, "I can't possibly argue with you. It's just that I feel helpless when I don't have a man of my own to look after me and protect me."

"It strikes me you're taking care of yourself these days without a man."

Cathy paused, then laughed. "Why, so I am," she said. "I never thought of it that way."

"You see? You can do whatever you please, and you're not accountable to anyone but yourself."

"That's fine for now," Cathy said. "But I don't really think I'd like it this way forever."

Cindy sighed. Her friend's traditional background made it difficult for her to realize that marriage was not necessarily the right goal for every woman. Sometimes it was the beginning of a new way of life in which her freedom would be restricted. On the other hand, she wanted to be fair. "I'm not claiming that all marriages are bad. All I'm saying is that I don't know anybody I could love so much that I'd be willing to marry and make all the sacrifices and compromises that marriage demands from a woman."

"You'll agree, won't you, that frontier life isn't easy for either of us?"

"Easy?" Cindy looked out beyond the wagons at the endless prairie, as vast and uninhabited as the oceans that seemed to mean so much to her friend. "If I had known how hard it would be, I'm not sure I would have joined the train."

"A man," Cathy said, "could help make it more bearable. That's why I'd like a—well, a partnership."

Cindy's smile was cynical. "If there is such a thing as a partnership. Just remember this. A marriage to the wrong man is far worse than a marriage to no man!"

Suddenly Cathy sensed that they were not alone. She turned slightly, and a chill crept up her spine when she saw two tall, husky Indian warriors standing only a short distance from the opening between her wagon and the wagon behind it in the circle. They were so close they could almost reach out and touch her. Their scalp locks were greased stiff, and each sported a feather. They carried bows, with quivers of arrows slung over their shoulders, and the bone hilts of knives protruded above their belts.

They continued to stare, making no hostile moves, but Cathy found it difficult to catch her breath. Cindy was saying something she didn't hear, and Cathy managed to touch her on the arm and incline her head silently in the direction of the two braves.

Cindy saw their glittering eyes and the heavy streaks of dark brown and pale green paint on their faces. She screamed involuntarily at the top of her lungs.

In a moment Ted Woods appeared. Whip wasn't far behind him, and a score of others started toward the girls. The warriors held their ground, continuing to stare.

Immediately Whip took charge. "Folks," he called, "I'll handle this. Go back to the fire, drink your coffee, and tend to your own business." Reluctantly they obeyed.

Cathy noted, however, that Arnold Mell, Mack Dougall and Stalking Horse remained, and Ted Woods retreated only as far as the next wagon. Hosea came up beside him, a hand resting on one of his miniature clubs. Then Tonie Mell appeared, looking like a boy in her buckskin shirt and pants. She was also holding a rifle.

The support of so many armed friends was comforting, and Cathy felt somewhat relieved. But she was afraid a fight with the two Indians would erupt at any moment. Her experience with Indians was limited. She had no idea what the savages would do next.

Whip raised an arm, his hand held palm upward in a greeting that indicated friendship. The warriors returned the salute. Whip addressed them in Kiowan, his tone courteous, and they replied in the same tongue. Then they entered the circle, leading two Indian ponies.

As Whip conversed with the Indians, Cathy realized that social amenities were being observed. It bothered her, however, that the two braves continued to stare at her and at Cindy while they talked. She couldn't help fidgeting uncomfortably.

Then one of the warriors launched into a long, impassioned speech, occasionally flinging his arms wide. To Cathy's astonishment, Tonie Mell exploded in silent laughter. Afraid she would laugh aloud, which would have been discourteous, she hurried away and went back to the fire.

Arnold was grinning openly, as was Mack. But Stalking Horse remained wooden-faced, and Whip looked grave. After the warrior finished speaking, Whip replied at length. Ordinarily brusque in his speech, he now seemed to be indulging in flowery rhetoric. The two braves listened intently, but their eyes remained fixed on the two frightened girls huddling together on the stoop.

At last Whip offered a partial explanation in English. "Our visitors," he said, directing his gaze toward Cathy and Cindy, "are senior warriors of the mighty Omaha nation. They welcome us to the Great Plains and offer us peace. We haven't yet come to their land. They are on a scouting trip because their people are at war with the Kansa. They saw our fires, so they investigated, and they wish us no harm."

The two girls remained tense.

Whip sounded more casual. "Ted," he said to the blacksmith, "go to the special wagon. Bring me a little iron frying pan and a blanket. Don't appear to be in any hurry—I don't want our visitors to be alarmed."

Ted Woods was reluctant to leave while Cindy appeared to be in any danger, but he had received a direct order, and he obeyed it, sauntering off toward the special wagon. Again Whip and the two Omaha engaged in a spirited conversation.

Cathy became restless. "I'm cold," she said. "Let's go to the fire, Cindy."

Whip interrupted himself in the midst of a long statement to the Indians. "Stay right where you are," he said, his voice suddenly urgent. "Don't move!"

Cathy, who had started to rise, sank back onto the stoop and sighed. It was absurd that she and Cindy had to remain while Whip held his endless discussion with the Indians. She didn't want to argue in front of the others, however, so she obeyed his request, but she made her feelings clear by glaring at him.

After a short time, Ted returned with a small frying

pan and blanket. Whip took them from him and made another interminably long speech to the two warriors. At the end of his address, he handed the skillet to one and the blanket to the other.

The braves examined their gifts at length, then replied to Whip's address with even longer speeches. Then the warriors raised their arms in the peace gesture. Whip did the same, and the Omaha departed, leading their horses out of the circle.

Before they rode off, however, they turned for one long, final, lustful look at the two girls. Then they mounted their horses, and in the silence that followed, the retreating hoofbeats of their mounts sounded clearly.

Standing, Cathy asked with elaborate courtesy, "May we know what that was all about?"

The other men decided that discretion was advisable and retreated. Only Ted Woods remained.

Whip tried to keep a straight face. "The Omaha," he explained, "are one of the biggest and strongest of the Great Plains tribes, and these men were two of their senior warriors, which means they sit in the council of elders that decides questions of war and peace. The friendship of the Omaha will be very important to us when we move through their territory. They don't attack friends, so we'll be saved running battles and many casualties. That's why I treated the warriors so carefully and presented them with gifts."

Cathy nodded impatiently. "That's fair enough, I'm sure, but why did we have to stay?"

He hesitated for an instant, then said, "Because you two were the subject of our negotiations. They wanted to buy you and take you home to live with them as their squaws. In fact, their interest in you was so great they offered me their horses for you."

Cathy was outraged. "I don't take that as a compliment. You could have told them that in our world freeborn women aren't for sale!"

"But we're in their world now," Whip said quietly.

"All the same, you could have sent them on their way!" she retorted angrily.

"Not without offending them. I had to go through the

motions of considering their offer. I let them believe you were my squaws, and I finally told them I needed you more than I needed two new horses. But I gave them the gifts to show them I didn't resent their offer."

"*I* resent it very much," the furious Cathy said.

Cindy giggled. "No wonder Tonie was laughing so hard."

Cathy realized the situation had certain amusing aspects, but her sense of humor had deserted her. It didn't bother her that a barbaric Indian brave had wanted to trade her for a horse—the man simply didn't know any better. But it upset her that Whip had even pretended to negotiate, instead of putting the savage in his place. Suddenly, to her mortification, she burst into tears. Unable to stop crying, she raced into her wagon and pulled the flap down behind her.

Cindy could have explained her reaction to Whip, but she had no chance. Turning, he stalked off, angry that his efforts had not been appreciated.

Ted Woods vanished, as he always did when there was a chance to be alone with Cindy, so she walked back to her own wagon. She knew that Cathy would want to be alone.

Cindy envied Cathy who was a near virgin. She would marry again, be it to Whip or someone else. But no man, she thought, not even the lonely Ted Woods, would seek more than a temporary attachment to a woman who had been a whore. At moments such as this, Cindy wondered if she had been wise to stake her whole future on the Oregon-bound wagon train. Perhaps she should have saved more money, then gone to an Eastern city like New York or Philadelphia, where she could have kept her past secret.

As she drew near her own wagon, she saw a man standing in the shadows. Even before she could make out his face, she knew his identity by the cut of his expensive clothes and the sheen of his boots.

Claiborne Woodling came to her, smiling broadly. The expression in his eyes, which she had seen so often, told her what he wanted.

"I hear you had quite an experience tonight," he said. "Everybody is talking about it."

"Let them talk." Cindy tried to brush past him.

Claiborne grabbed her arm. "Don't be in such a hurry. I'm just trying to be friendly."

"Take your hands off me," Cindy told him, "and don't ever touch me again. I know your kind of friendship, and I want no part of it."

He tried to protest.

Suddenly she pulled out a knife, which she had bought in Independence, from the pocket of her dress. Ordinarily she would have tried to be civil to this arrogant young man. It didn't pay to make personal enemies on the long journey. But his appearance at that particular moment was unbearable, and her patience was exhausted.

"I'm not going to warn you again," Cindy said, brandishing the knife.

Claiborne was tempted to take the knife from her, but too many people were still awake, and he didn't want a scene. "You're a shrew," he told her in a low, menacing voice, "but one of these days I'm going to tame you." Then he turned and stalked off into the darkness.

Cold autumn rains fell steadily every day for a week, turning the vast prairie into a quagmire and forcing the wagon train to halt. Rivers overflowed, soaking the ground even more, and when the journey was resumed, it was difficult for Whip to pick a path wide and dry enough for the train to travel in three columns. The alternative was to place the wagons in single file, but he refused to consider the idea.

"If we move in one line," he told Von Thalman, "the train will stretch out for nearly three miles, and that's a risk we can't afford to take. We'd be too tempting a target for roving bands of Indians. Warriors could attack the rear of the train, kill the monitor, and those of us up front wouldn't even know what happened until hours later."

So the three-column formation was maintained, even though less ground was covered. The horses and oxen grew tired because the footing was uncertain, and several times a day the entire company had to halt because a wagon's wheels had become mired in deep mud. The train did well to cover eight miles in a single day.

By mid-November the sun rarely appeared, the sky overhead remained a dull, dark gray all day, and the winds that swept across the Great Plains grew steadily colder.

A number of people became ill, all suffering from sore throats, high fevers, and aches in their bodies that lasted for days. Dr. Martin made the rounds every morning, at the nooning hour, and again after the train halted each day. There was little he could do for his patients other than give them doses of an elixir of coal tar, along with oil of sassafras to rub on their chests. It was essential, he told them repeatedly, that they remain in bed. He would not allow anyone who was ill to drive a wagon, so the healthy pioneers from other wagons were pressed into service.

Available throughout the night to those who needed his services, Bob Martin refused to spare himself and began to look haggard. Tonie Mell worried that he would fall ill, insisted on helping him each day after she completed her own duties.

Then Mack Dougall became ill even though he tried to ward off the disease by fortifying himself with larger quantities of whiskey than usual. In spite of Mack's protests, Dr. Martin put him to bed in one of the wagons, thus leaving the wagon train with one scout less. No other member of the company was familiar with the Great Plains or the ways of the Indians. Tonie volunteered, but Whip rejected her offer.

"That would be tempting Providence," he told her. "If a band of warriors discovered that one of our scouts, operating alone, was a woman, they would haul you off to one of their villages and keep you there as a slave for the rest of your days."

"You forget that I'm a first-rate shot," she said.

"I'm well aware of it," he replied, "but don't you forget that you're a woman."

It was necessary to appoint a scout to act in Mack's place, and with great misgivings, Whip gave the position to the only other volunteer, Hosea, who refused the offer of a horse. Early each morning he went off at a run, carrying his rawhide shield, and every night he returned, still energetic. He learned his duties quickly and, somewhat to Whip's surprise, soon became expert in the difficult art of spotting the presence of Indians. Stalking Horse patiently coached him until he could easily distinguish one tribe from another. In an area where different tribes held different attitudes about white men, this identification was crucial.

One afternoon in late November, there were snow flurries in the air. That night Whip held a private conference with Ernie von Thalman.

"Once the snow really starts to fall, we'll have to call a halt," he said. "So from now on, we've got to search for a likely place to make a winter camp, and that won't be easy."

Ernie was well aware of the problems. "We'll need wood to build cabins because people can't spend the winter in their wagons. Buffalo chips are all right for cooking, but they don't give off much warmth, so we'll need wood for fires. And we've got to have shelter for the horses and oxen, too. Where can we find all that wood in a country where there's little but grass?"

"If many more people get sick, we'll have to stop out here in the middle of nowhere," Whip said, "and that means trouble. We're coming into the Nebraska country now, so we have two choices. There's a fine forest just south of the junction of the Platte and Missouri rivers, but I don't like it much."

"Why not?"

"Just a little ways to the north, on the Missouri, is one of the biggest towns of the Omaha, almost directly across the river from a trading post in the Iowa territory called Council Bluffs. By and large, the Omaha are a peaceful tribe, but they're strong, and there's no telling what they might do if a wagon train filled with horses and oxen, blankets and kettles and guns—not to mention good-looking womenfolk—made winter camp less than a day's ride away."

"I don't believe in putting my head into a noose and

handing someone the other end of the rope," Ernie said, frowning.

"Our alternative," Whip told him, "is to head west as well as north. About forty or fifty miles west of the Omaha town, right on the Platte River, there's another, even bigger forest. There's everything there—oak, maple, elm, pine, hickory, and juniper. It's a huge forest that spreads northward for many, many miles, so you can bet that plenty of deer and other game will be foraging there throughout the winter."

"That sounds better to me."

"I agree," Whip said, "although there's a possible problem. I'm told the U.S. Army has built an outpost at the edge of the forest, right on the river, called Fort Madison. The soldiers might not want us as near neighbors for the winter."

"But the government is sponsoring this expedition, and we have the personal approval of President Van Buren," Ernie said. "I don't see how the army could object to our making winter camp nearby."

"Not officially." Whip's smile was wry. "But, hellfire and damnation, Ernie, you were a colonel in the Imperial Austrian Army. Put yourself in the place of the commander of Fort Madison, which was just built and was put into operation only this spring. He's a king in his own realm, and he leads a pleasant life except when the Indians kick up a ruckus. All of a sudden he has to share his forest with a company of almost five hundred civilians. People will die; civilians will need help and protection; and his soldiers will start messing around with our young women. Van Buren or no Van Buren, he may tell us to take ourselves to the far end of the forest and not bother him."

"It's possible," Ernie said, "but there's only one way to find out."

Whip grinned broadly. "Ah, that's what I wanted to hear. As long as I have your support, we'll do it. And if the garrison commander doesn't like us, that's just too bad. He doesn't own either the forest or the Platte River."

The next morning Whip spoke briefly to the scouts, and that day the wagon train changed direction, moving more toward the west than the north.

Progress was still painfully slow. The caravan could travel no more than eight miles each day. The weather continued to grow colder, and frost killed much of the prairie grass. Mack Dougall, who had recovered and had resumed his scouting duties, was heard to remark that he couldn't remember a year when winter had threatened to come to the Great Plains this early. His dire comment spread through the camp, and some of the newcomers panicked.

But the veterans reassured them. "Trust Whip Holt," they said. "He knows what he's doing."

A week after changing direction, the wagon train approached the Platte River, one of the principal tributaries of the Missouri. The scouts returned during the nooning hour to report the news. In mid-afternoon the caravan came within sight of the river, which was swift flowing and more than a half-mile wide. On the far bank stood a large, solidly constructed log fort, with the flag of the United States flying from its highest ramparts, and behind the fort stretched what appeared to be an endless forest.

Many of the Oregon-bound settlers cheered when they saw the flag. However, there was one member of the company who was thinking seriously of returning to civilization. Arthur Elwood, who was approaching forty, had joined the expedition in the hope that he could buy some of the colonists' land-grant claims of six hundred acres per householder, and resell them, at a profit, to land speculators. He had offered cash for such tracts. But so far no one had responded to his offer, and he was tired of the inconveniences of wagon train living.

The wagons were moved into their customary circle for the night. Even before the task was completed, two officers in blue army uniforms trimmed in gold started across the river. To the surprise of many in the caravan, they rode rapidly across the Platte, which appeared to be very shallow.

Whip and Ernie walked to the river bank to meet them.

"Captain Haskell and Lieutenant Thompson," the senior officer said after they dismounted.

Whip introduced himself and the Baron.

"So you're Holt," the Captain said, smiling broadly. "The Colonel has been wondering whether we'd be seeing you."

"Then you've heard of our expedition," Whip said.

Both officers laughed heartily, and the Captain said, "We've heard of little else in the past two months. Two entire battalions of our regiment haven't shown up here yet, and it doesn't look as though we'll see them before spring. But the War Department has sent Colonel Jonathan at least three letters of inquiry about your wagon train, and even President Van Buren has written to him. The Colonel has been so nervous he's been on the verge of sending out patrols to search for you."

Whip and Ernie smiled at each other. The company would be welcomed at Fort Madison.

"We're relieved you decided not to make a crossing today, Mr. Holt," Lieutenant Thompson said. "There are only a couple of hours of daylight left, and you're going to need a full day for your crossing."

Ernie von Thalman was surprised. The water appeared shallow.

"The problem," Whip said succinctly, "is quicksand."

The two officers nodded.

Ernie was dismayed. "Obviously we'll have to move either upstream or downstream to an area where there is no quicksand."

Captain Haskell shook his head. "I'm afraid that isn't feasible, Baron. In those places the river is much narrower, and the water is deep, with the current so swift that no wagon could make the crossing."

"If the bed of the river here is similar to what I've seen elsewhere on the Platte," Whip said, "the quicksand acts fairly slowly. I watched you as you came across, and I saw you didn't give your horses much chance to tarry, so I figured there was quicksand here."

Whip turned to the Baron. "Ernie, we'll have no

trouble as long as each wagon stays in motion. The minute a team of horses or oxen stop, though, they'll be mired, and the only way to save them will be to cut them loose, drag them ashore on the far bank, and sacrifice the wagon—and its contents."

"A fair analysis, Mr. Holt," Captain Haskell said. "This Platte River quicksand is like glue. It may be slow acting, but once it catches hold, it sucks up anything and everything that gets stuck in it. Any team that tries to haul a trapped wagon will be mired, too, and the only thing left to do is shoot the poor beasts before they get sucked under."

"Our people," Whip said, "have been driving their wagons day after day for a long time. Those who came from the Eastern Seaboard have been traveling for more than a year. They're good at it. They know what they're doing, they don't get rattled, and they don't scare easy. I'm sure we'll make out just fine, provided we take a few precautions."

Ernie was dubious. "What sort of precautions?"

"Perhaps I can be of help to you, Mr. Holt," Captain Haskell said. "I have the honor of commanding what I believe to be the finest cavalry troop in the army—eighty men, all of them veterans. I suggest you send two wagons across at a time, about one hundred yards apart. I'll assign a full platoon to each passage, with Thompson here in command of one and my other lieutenants in charge of the second. I'll keep myself free to supervise the enterprise, and I'd be very pleased if you'd join me, Mr. Holt. Between us, I believe we can keep those wagons rolling."

They shook hands after agreeing to start early the next morning.

Whip and Ernie strolled together toward the wagon circle, where campfires had already been lighted. "As I see it," Whip said, "the problem is strictly one of confidence, especially for those who have to wait for hours on this side of the river for their turn to cross."

Ernie nodded thoughtfully. "I suggest that anybody who might get nervous be sent across fairly early. It won't bother the more experienced people to wait."

"Fair enough," Whip said, "and we'll start with women we know won't panic. Like Cathy van Ayl." Without realizing it, he was paying Cathy a compliment.

"I like that," Ernie said. "Any men who have doubts about their own abilities will feel much better after they've seen a couple of ladies negotiate the crossing. Do I gather you'll have no use for our own riders?"

"None," Whip replied flatly. "Our scouts do good work in their own operations, but they wouldn't know how to deal with quicksand, and neither would the monitors. Besides, young Woodling is so arrogant and unpleasant that somebody might get ornery just to spite him and stop dead in the middle of the river."

When they reached the fire, Whip summoned the entire company and told them in detail about the next day's operation. He didn't overemphasize the dangers of the quicksand, but at the same time he concealed nothing. "You'll have no trouble," he said, "as long as you keep moving. I've crossed the Platte dozens of times myself, and I know what I'm talking about."

The brief meeting came to an end, and Whip immediately sought out Cathy. "You'll go first in the column on the right," he told her, "so you'll have to be awake and ready extra early. You can turn over the cooking detail to somebody else for breakfast."

"Why me?" Cathy asked in surprise.

Why, he asked himself, did he always become tongue-tied in her presence? Unable to repeat what he had told Ernie, he replied curtly, "It makes sense, that's why." Then he walked away, leaving her staring angrily after him.

The fire-making detail started to work an hour before dawn the next morning, and Cathy organized the breakfast cooks before preparing for her departure. Whip joined her for a quick mug of coffee, but she was cool to him, and little conversation passed between them.

The stars vanished, and the sky was growing lighter as Whip rode his stallion into the chilly waters of the Platte, the scouts and male monitors strung out behind him, with each man carefully leaving a gap of about ten yards between him and the rider in front of him. Whip's stallion could feel the soft sand giving beneath his hoofs, and he responded instinctively. Lifting his legs high, almost as though he were prancing, he made the crossing without difficulty.

The others encountered no problems, either. But Claiborne Woodling, who brought up the rear, couldn't resist showing off. He walked his horse at a crawl most of the way across the Platte, then raced the final hundred feet, his horse splashing water madly.

The cavalry troop was already drawn up on the north bank, ready for action. Captain Haskell was standing near the water, holding the reins of his horse, and beside him was a handsome, white-haired officer with a small beard whose silver epaulets identified him as a full colonel.

"I'm Bert Jonathan," he said, extending his hand as Whip dismounted. "Welcome to Fort Madison. You can't imagine how pleased I am to see you, Mr. Holt. Now, perhaps, Washington City will stop pestering me."

"My people and I are grateful to you, Colonel," Whip replied. "We haven't enjoyed many luxuries on our trek."

Daylight had come, although the sky remained sullen and the river, ruffled by a cold, damp wind from the west, was leaden. Captain Haskell led his troop across the Platte, Whip riding with him at the head of the line, and the veterans proudly moved in formation.

Whip had decided that Tonie would lead the left-hand column, and the cavalrymen brightened when they saw her and Cathy van Ayl seated on the boards of the first wagons. Pretty girls were unknown at this remote wilderness outpost, and the men stared at them, grinned and saluted, then began to call greetings to them.

Whip felt an unexpected twinge of jealousy when he saw the attention Cathy was drawing. But there was no time now for personal reflection.

"Let's go!" Whip called sharply, and Cathy and Tonie drove their teams into the water, a soldier riding beside each wagon.

Whip and Haskell gave them a head start, then caught up with them, passed them, and led them to the far bank. The girls had become expert drivers. Their wagons moved at a slow but steady pace, and they came ashore safely.

The foot soldiers who would act as guides to the campsite were as delighted by the appearance of attractive young women as the cavalrymen had been, and even Colonel Jonathan and the three middle-aged officers who comprised his staff looked pleased. Again Whip felt a twinge of jealousy.

The second wagons in each column were arriving now, and the third wagons were beginning to cross. The operation was proceeding smoothly.

Extreme precautions were taken to get the special wagon with its irreplaceable supplies across. Twenty horsemen accompanied it, holding ropes that were tied to its wheels and axles. Trusting no one else to the delicate task, Whip drove.

The wagonmaster uncoiled his whip, and the twenty cavalrymen picked up their ropes. "All set, Mr. Holt?" Haskell called.

"Ready, Captain!"

The whip cracked over the heads of the eight oxen, who slowly moved into the chilly water. Two cavalrymen on each side accompanied them, and as the wagon inched forward, the other horsemen followed.

In spite of the cold, Whip discovered he was sweating. The regular driver who sat beside him shuddered slightly.

The oxen didn't like the feel of the soft sand under their small hoofs, and two of them hesitated. Before they could stop altogether, however, the wagonmaster's whip lightly touched one on the back, then the other. The blows were not hard enough to break the animals' skins, but stung them just enough to keep them in motion.

The cavalrymen strained at the ropes, forcing their mounts, unaccustomed to such degrading labor, to keep in motion. The wagon's progress was maddingly slow.

Having once established a rhythm for the oxen, Whip knew it had to be maintained. "Ee-yup-ho!" he shouted, standing on the platform so he could keep a sharp watch on the entire team. "Ee-yup-ho!"

The oxen responded to the cadenced call and continued to trudge forward through the chilly water, their pace unvarying.

Captain Haskell moved back and forth constantly behind the wagon, veering first to the left, then to the right. "Flint, hold your rope tighter!" he called. "Budman, don't slow your pace! Not too fast, Harrigan. Hold your place or you'll upset the balance."

"Ee-yup-ho!" The wagon had passed the center of the Platte and was crawling closer to the north bank, where soldiers and members of the train who had already made the crossing stood and watched anxiously.

The wind increased, and a wave struck one of the lead oxen, splashing the animal's face. Bewildered by the unexpected cold slap, the beast halted.

The whip sang out immediately, touching him lightly, then struck again with somewhat greater force. As everyone held their breaths, the animal began to move again, and the rhythm of the other oxen continued unbroken.

The special wagon inched nearer to the north shore. The worst was over now. If necessary, members of the cavalry troop waiting on the bank could ride into the water and assist their comrades with the ropes. But Whip kept up his cadenced call, and Captain Haskell called a steady stream of orders to his men.

At the bank, Arnold Mell plunged into the water, caught hold of the front end of the yoke, and guided the oxen ashore. The heavy wagon followed, its wheels cutting deep furrows in the bank, then rolling more smoothly on the hard ground.

Whip halted the team, turned the wagon over to the regular driver, and jumped to the ground.

Captain Haskell joined him, and they shook hands. "That was great!" the officer cried. "I owe you a drink!"

"I'll take it, tonight," Whip said, "when our day's work is done."

Meanwhile the crossings of the other wagons had been resumed, and in midstream Whip passed the wagon driven by Major Woodling, who was concentrating his full attention on his horses.

Eulalia, sitting on the boards beside him, looked as though she had just left her father's plantation for an afternoon's ride in the country. Her eyes were rimmed with kohl, her lips and cheeks were rouged, and she wore a fur-collared coat with a matching, frivolously feathered hat. Smiling broadly at Whip, she removed a hand from a fur muff to wave at him, and then, unable to resist the temptation, she smiled provocatively at Captain Haskell.

The officer made no comment, but Whip could see that the girl had sparked his interest, and Whip couldn't blame him. Eulalia might be somewhat irresponsible, but she was far friendlier than some members of the expedition —particularly Cathy van Ayl.

No serious accidents marred the crossing of the rest of the wagon train. Occasionally a horse balked or a frightened team of oxen faltered, but the drivers and the cavalry escorts kept the animals in motion.

The cavalrymen and their commander were tired after the long ordeal. Only Whip still had a spring in his step.

Members of the train had followed their usual practice of arranging the wagons in a circle, this time in the clearing behind the fort. The wood-gathering detail had done its work, and the women in charge of meal preparations were gathering. No soldiers intruded because, Whip was told, the area had been declared out of bounds.

He was just completing his own inspection of his charges when an officer approached him. "Mr. Holt," he said, "the Colonel would like to see you and the president of your train in his office as soon as you find it convenient."

V

Colonel Bert Jonathan leaned back in his leather-padded chair. Folding his hands on the plain pine table that served as his desk, he smiled at Whip and Ernie.

"I've had many weeks to think about the offer I'm going to make to you, gentlemen. I can get no information from Washington about why my men—two battalions—haven't arrived. That's typical of the War Department. In any event, I'm dead certain the rest of my regiment won't be here before spring. Now then, I assume you've been intending to build cabins for your winter quarters?"

"That's right, Colonel," Whip replied. "I've hunted in the forest behind your fort many times, so I know it well."

"There's no need for you to build anything," the Colonel replied. "You have about five hundred people in your train, so there's ample room for you here. The quarters my new battalions will occupy are empty. There are barracks, as well as private quarters for officers and noncommissioned personnel. The fort is solid, you'll have access to two large kitchens, and there are a number of fireplaces scattered throughout the quarters. You'll have to supply your own food and firewood, I'm afraid."

Whip was overwhelmed by the offer. "I don't know how to thank you, Colonel. Food will be no problem. There's plenty of game in the forest, and there are more fish in the Platte, winter or summer, than your troops and our people can eat."

The Colonel smiled. "I neglected to mention that we also have extensive stables to house your horses and oxen. You may need to send foragers out to find food for them before the heavy snows come, but they'll certainly be dry and warm."

"Your kindness is so great I can scarcely believe it," Ernie said, bowing slightly.

Bert Jonathan chuckled. "Not at all. I'm not charitably inclined, but I'll be obeying President Van Buren's request to extend every hospitality to you. And I have something else in mind, too. Some of the Indian tribes in my area are beginning to kick up their heels."

Whip nodded. "I've heard that the Kansa and Omaha may be going to war against each other."

"You're well informed," the Colonel said. "So I'm sure you can appreciate my dilemma. I don't have enough troops to police the region, and if trouble does break out, I have too few men to halt it."

"Perhaps," Ernie said politely, "we might be able to assist you."

"That's what I had in mind," Colonel Jonathan replied candidly. "How many effectives could you put into the field?"

Whip and Ernie pondered the question. "I'd guess about eighty," Whip said. "What do you think, Ernie?"

"As part of a larger force, not acting independently, I would place the total closer to ninety."

"I bow to greater knowledge." Whip turned to the American officer. "Baron von Thalman is too modest to tell you this himself, but he gave up command of a cavalry regiment in the Imperial Austrian Army when he came here and joined us on the march to Oregon."

"Splendid," Colonel Jonathan said. "I'm delighted to have a colleague on hand."

Ernie smiled. "You may be less happy if you call on us. Our scouts are the best anywhere, and if Whip

Holt goes scouting for you, there's no man in his class. But don't expect too much from the bulk of our people. They are American civilians, which means they are strong individualists who resist discipline. They work together best in a crisis. But some are able horsemen and expert shots, so I think we can give you solid support if you call on us."

"That's comforting to know," Colonel Jonathan said. "I just hope I won't need your help. Now, before you start moving your people indoors, there's only one more question to be resolved. I shall speak frankly. At a frontier outpost like Fort Madison, the men see no women for months at a time. There are a number of attractive—very attractive—young ladies in your train. I trust that my officers are gentlemen, and I'll place your quarters permanently off limits to the enlisted cadre. I trust you can exert some controls, too, in order to hold untoward incidents to a minimum."

Whip sighed, and Ernie said, "We cannot act as nursemaids, but I've observed that most of our younger women are sensible, and I'm certain they'll avoid problems. Our older women are a stabilizing influence, of course, so I think—at least I hope—you'll find that everyone will settle into routines here after the novelty wears off."

"Until then," Whip said, "It might create more problems to try to keep people apart. Colonel, we'll be pleased if you and your officers will join our company for supper tonight."

Colonel Jonathan accepted graciously, then sat back in his chair and smiled. "You may be having problems on your train, but your people are having smooth sailing compared to what they'd face back home."

"How so?" Whip demanded.

"I had some dispatches from Washington City and a couple of letters from New York when the mail pouch was delivered the other day. And frankly, gentlemen, between us, the United States is going through the worst period in her history." The Colonel became more serious. "The panic has been growing worse, and President Van Buren and his Treasury Department don't seem to be able to cope with it. There are thousands upon thousands of men out of work in New York, Boston, Philadelphia—and every smaller city and town. There were bread riots in New York, and troops had to be called out to restore order."

Ernie whistled under his breath.

"The banks," the Colonel said, "have had to crack down on people who can't pay their debts. Not only are factories going out of business, but farmers and city folks alike are losing their homes and property. And more than one hundred banks have failed. Think of it—more than a hundred!"

"That means Oregon will start looking better and better to the dispossessed," Whip said thoughtfully. "So will all the free land between Independence and the Pacific."

"That's why this fort has become so important," the commander explained. "We've got to keep order and stop Indian wars here for the sake of the settlers who are going to pour out here. Free land is the only salvation for people who would otherwise starve to death."

"We're lucky to be the first," Ernie said. "We'll have our choice of a place to settle when we reach the Oregon country. I hadn't realized that conditions in the East were so bad."

"They're bad," Colonel Jonathan said. "Henry Clay's giving Van Buren no peace. A friend of mine in the War Department says that Clay is making an average of three or four speeches a week, attacking the administration. All the newspapers that don't care much for Van Buren—and that includes most of them—reprint every last word that Clay and the other Whigs say. Van Buren was a first-rate diplomat, but I'm afraid that the present situation is more than he can handle."

"What we need," Whip said, "is Andy Jackson back in the White House."

The Colonel grinned. "I served with Jackson a great many years ago, in his Florida campaign. There's never been another like him, I can tell you. He had an instinct for knowing the precise moment to attack, but he also knew when to lie low. He's no financial genius, any more than Little Van is, though, and I'm afraid that even if he were still president, he'd have to lie low, too."

"What I don't understand," Ernie said, "is how a growing country like the United States could be in such great trouble."

"You've just explained it, Baron," the Colonel said. "We're suffering growing pains. We've been primarily an agricultural nation since our founding, but the industries of the East are growing as rapidly as the frontier is moving to the West. The whole nature of our society is changing."

Whip looked glum. "I reckon you're right, Colonel," he said. "I can see the changes coming out this way—and beyond."

Ernie was surprised. "Really?"

Whip nodded. "Before we took off from Independence, Sam Brentwood and I ran into a couple of mountain men we knew. They had just come from trapping on the Green River in the Wyoming country, and they said it was pretty damn sad. The old haunts are trapped out—you can't make a living at it these days. I guess the country isn't fit for anything but settlers. It won't be long before the whole region is civilized—people and more people every place you look."

"Yes, it's coming," the Colonel said. "The Indians sense it, too, you know. That's why so many of the tribes that have been living in peace for centuries are suddenly so touchy, ready to go to war with anyone who comes near their territory. They realize that things are changing."

"Forgive me," Ernie said, "but I come from the Old World, and I am not accustomed to seeing this huge amount of space. Both of you talk so blithely of settlers moving in. But how will they be supplied? How will they build their cities? How will they trade with other parts of the United States and the world?"

"I reckon they'll use wagon trains that carry only freight," Whip said.

"Not for long," Colonel Jonathan said. "Moving freight by wagon train is slow and cumbersome. I'm looking ahead twenty years now, but I believe—and a number of my War Department colleagues agree with me—that the day isn't too far distant when a network of railroads will extend to the Pacific in the West and as far as Texas in the South."

"Texas?" Whip was startled.

"In case you haven't heard," Colonel Jonathan said, "the Americans who have been settling down there won their war of independence with Mexico and have set up their own republic. It's only a matter of time before Texas is admitted to the Union. Sam Houston was the general who won the war, and now he's President of Texas."

Whip chuckled and shook his head. "I would have guessed if I'd known Houston was involved."

"Sam Houston was one of Andrew Jackson's protégés," the Colonel explained to Ernie, who looked puzzled. "He became Governor of Tennessee, and one day he quit. Nobody has ever found out why. He went to live with the Cherokee for three years—he had lived with them when he was in his teens—and he was known as the Big Drunk. Now he's the head of a new republic and certainly will be the first governor when Texas becomes a state. What's more, I'm told he doesn't touch liquor any more."

Ernie shook his head. "The more I find out about the United States, the more convinced I am that there's no other country on earth like it."

"That's the truth!" Whip said. "I remember an old bear out in the Rockies, mean and tough and ornery. He was wounded by an Indian arrow one autumn, and he went off to his lair. Everybody expected he'd die there. But he showed up the next spring, meaner and tougher and more ornery than ever. That's the United States. We may have unemployment, and banks may be failing, but don't think this country will shrivel up and die."

Afterwards the Colonel took them to inspect the quarters that members of the wagon train would occupy. When Whip and Ernie returned to the campsite, they called a meeting. When the settlers heard that they would be spending the winter indoors, they were elated.

Emily Harris suggested that sheets could be hung in the barracks to create separate areas where families would be able to enjoy a measure of privacy. The idea was enthusiastically received.

Ernie, who was acting as chairman of the meeting, announced that there were thirty private rooms, each large enough to hold two people. "So that everyone has a fair chance," he said, "I suggest we draw lots for these quarters."

Everyone agreed, but Emily Harris had a further idea. Still attractive and vigorous after losing not only her husband but also, in the earlier stages of the journey to Oregon, one of her four sons, she spoke in a loud, clear voice. "Mr. Holt and Baron von Thalman carry more responsibilities than the rest of us," she said. "So I propose that they be exempt from the lottery and that we simply give them one of the private rooms."

Whip intervened quickly. "I appreciate the thought," he said, "but I can't accept."

"Neither can I," Ernie added, "but I thank you, Emily. We'll take our chances with everybody else."

Straws were prepared, with sixty of them shorter than the others. They were placed in two bundles, and all who were eligible, including single people and the heads of households consisting of two persons, filed past the youngest of the Harris boys and a little girl who held the straws.

The first winners were Cathy van Ayl and Cindy, who promptly agreed to room together. Terence and Lena Malcolm, who were considered a family of two because their baby was so small, were elated when they drew a short straw. Arnold Mell was a winner, followed by Mack Dougall, and people roared with laughter when Arnold announced with mock ferocity that he didn't think he could survive a winter spent in close quarters with Mack.

A small barracks was assigned to the single women and another to the single men, with the four remaining rooms, all of them larger, turned over to families. Some people began to move bedding and other belongings indoors immediately. All property had to be taken into the barracks because the canvas covers would be removed from the wagons to prevent the canvas from rotting during the winter.

Eulalia Woodling was furious when she failed to win a place in one of the private rooms and complained to anyone willing to listen to her that the drawing had been unfair. But she quickly recovered her good humor when the officers arrived en masse for supper. Soon she was flirting outrageously and impartially with them; five of them were particularly attentive to her throughout the meal.

The other single women were far more reserved, and Cindy whispered to Cathy and Tonie, "Eulalia is really asking for trouble. God help her before we get out of here in the spring. She'll need all the help she can get."

The members of the expedition, some of whom had lived in their wagons for more than a year, could scarcely believe their good fortune. To them, Fort Madison seemed palatial. The outer walls were made of thick oak logs, filled in with clay, and the floors were fashioned of rough-hewn wood. Thick oilpaper covered the windows in the sleeping quarters. There were brick fire-places in the infirmary, the dining halls, assembly rooms, and the larger barracks. The wood-burning ranges in the two kitchens provided their own heat.

Work schedules were reassigned. The best marksmen were made permanent members of the hunting party. Others were given the duty of fishing in the Platte River and in a lake about a half-mile to the northwest, and still others became foragers who would collect grass and hay for the animals and find edible roots in the forest.

Cathy remained in charge of one kitchen, and Emily Harris took firm command of the other. When Eulalia Woodling tried to win release from the kitchen detail, Emily firmly put her in her place.

"I don't know who you think you are, young lady," the robust woman boomed in a voice that everyone could hear, "but if you want to eat, you'll work, just like the rest of us."

Hosea, who was given no immediate responsibilities, found what Colonel Jonathan later described as the "junk shack," located behind the main fort. In it were two defective three-inch cannon, the smallest size used by the army, each complete with its own carriage and firing platform; sheets of tin, the remains of the roofing used in the Colonel's office and the officers' mess hall; and a number of broken tools, bent nails, and used, discarded horseshoes.

Hosea went at once to Whip, who agreed to go with him to Colonel Jonathan, and the amused commander of the fort gave him permission to take whatever he wanted.

Ted Woods volunteered to provide new horseshoes for the cavalry mounts whenever it was necessary. He had already moved into the fully equipped blacksmith's shop adjoining the stables. These quarters were so large that he was happy to allow Hosea to use one corner of the shop.

Hosea promptly went to work on projects of his own, but offered no explanations to anyone.

A scant seventy-two hours after the wagon train had reached Fort Madison, Whip announced that he smelled snow in the air. All of the men and older boys, with the exception of a small hunting party, quickly went off into the forest to chop down dead trees and bring firewood back to the fort.

The men labored for two and a half days, cutting and chopping so much wood that they had to harness workhorses to three of the bare wagons in order to haul the wood back to the fort. They returned with enough wood for a month, but Nat Drummond, who had shown a remarkable aptitude for the task in spite of his small stature, argued that more should be cut as soon as possible, before the winter weather became too bad.

The next morning the snow began to fall, drifting down lightly at first, then becoming thicker. "This will be a heavy one," Whip predicted, and Stalking Horse agreed.

The snow fell for two days and nights. During that time, only the military sentries ventured outdoors.

When the snow finally let up, hunting, fishing, foraging and wood-gathering activities were renewed. The temperature continued to drop, and a thick layer of ice formed on the nearby lake. Stalking Horse showed the fishermen, including a fascinated Danny and Chet, how to cut a hole in the ice, drop a baited line into the water, and haul up fish, which responded to the lures more rapidly than they did in warmer weather.

The company's quarters were snug, and the settlers were grateful for their good fortune. Tonie, however, always restless unless she spent time in the open, persuaded Whip to allow her to accompany the hunters. She proved her worth by bagging more game than many of the men. Cathy and Cindy made a point of going out for a brisk walk each day, but took care to obey Colonel Jonathan's firm order that no individual—and no woman, in particular—wander more than a mile from the fort. Only armed groups of men were granted that right.

Some people rarely left the warmth of the fort, and one of them was Eulalia. Other than performing her kitchen duties, which she did with ill grace, she had little to occupy her time. She made it her business to learn the off-duty hours of the officers who were showing interest in her, and at those times she could invariably be found in one of the assembly halls, which members of the expedition were using as social gathering places.

Hosea continued to work long hours in private. Only Ted Woods knew what he was doing, and he kept it secret. It was two weeks before the Ashanti was ready to reveal the results of his activities, and then he invited Whip, Ernie, and Arnold to accompany him to the blacksmith's shop.

The astonished visitors could only stare at what he had accomplished. A grinning Ted Woods stood nearby, watching them.

Hosea had built a tiny forge, a replica of the ones he had used in Africa. It was only two feet long and eighteen inches wide and was made from scrap metal.

Near it stood a pot he also used, and Ted explained how it had been created. "Damnedest thing I ever saw," he said. "He made a little pot out of clay, and he fired it in a tiny mound filled with charcoal. You'll notice there's a hole in the pot. Well, damned if he didn't make himself more charcoal, smash it into hunks no bigger than my fingernail, and then he fired the pot still more. Show them the special tool you made for the pot and that you use on your forge, Hosea."

The Ashanti held up for inspection a miniature bellows, fashioned of wood, metal and discarded chunks of leather.

That was just the beginning. With little persuasion Hosea showed the men some of the objects he had been making with his tools. Among them were arrowheads of steel and strong, tiny fishhooks for Stalking Horse. He presented Whip and Arnold with tiny knives, their blades razor-sharp. And he gave the surprised Ernie a pipe reamer only two-and-a-half inches long.

Ted picked up some nails. "The army uses a finer grade of nail for horseshoes than I use," he said, "and there plain aren't any here right now. So Hosea made me these nails. They're an exact, perfect fit for the cavalry shoes."

Whip shook his head. "I reckon you can make just about anything," he said.

"Make anything," Hosea replied, then showed them several pairs of delicate earrings, no two pairs alike, which he had made for Cathy and some of the other ladies.

At supper that night Hosea's handiwork created a sensation. He basked in the admiration of the people who had become his friends.

Then Eulalia approached him. "There's a necklace I've been wanting for a long time," she said, "ever since I saw a friend of mine wearing the original. I'll describe it for you, and you can make it for me."

Hosea shook his head.

"But I want it!" the girl declared.

He met her gaze, but said nothing.

"If I must," Eulalia said, becoming angry, "I'll even pay you for it."

"No make," Hosea said, then turned away from her.

Angrily she stalked off, her heels clattering on the rough wooden floor.

Hosea would do anything in his power for those people he considered friends, but he would have nothing to do with anyone who looked down on him or treated him with contempt.

Two days later a sudden, critical need developed for Hosea's special skills. A breathless Danny brought the word to the blacksmith's shop. "Dr. Martin wants to see you, Hosea, in the infirmary. Right away."

The Ashanti sprinted to the fort so rapidly that he far outdistanced the boy.

He found Terence and Lena Malcolm standing in the examining room. They were obviously worried. Hosea heard Dr. Martin's voice on the far side of the operating chamber door and went inside without bothering to knock.

Tonie was holding the Malcolm baby in her arms, taking care to keep her upright, while Dr. Martin searched frantically through his instrument case.

"Lenore swallowed a thimble," Tonie said.

"I believe the thimble has lodged in her wind pipe," the doctor said, indicating that portion of the anatomy on his own body. "If she starts to cry or makes any sudden, jerking movement, she could dislodge the object —and choke to death. And because she's so small, I have no instrument I can use to fish up the thimble. If I draw you a picture of what I want, can you make an instrument for me?"

"Hosea can do," the little man replied without hesitation.

Bob Martin took a sheet of paper, dipped a quill pen into a bottle of ink that stood on a small corner table, and began to draw. "I'm no artist," he said, "but I'm making this picture as precise as I can. Here's the instrument and here's the handle. It must be as thin as a hair, as thin as you can make it. It will have to bend and conform to the shape of the baby's wind pipe as it goes down, but if it breaks, it will surely kill her."

Hosea watched carefully as the doctor drew.

"How long will it take you?" the physician asked. "I know you can't do the impossible, but every minute counts."

"Already working with forge today, so charcoal plenty hot. Will make in one hour. Maybe not so long." No one had ever heard Hosea deliver such a long speech. Snatching the sheet of paper, he bolted from the room.

When Hosea returned to the blacksmith's shop, Ted, who had just learned of the crisis, was at work, building up his own bed of coals, bringing them to a deep, intense red with a large bellows. "Anything I can do to help?"

"Make fire very hot," Hosea replied, and began a swift, systematic search through the objects he had taken from the junk room.

Soon he found what he wanted, the thin crossbar of a cavalryman's broken spur. He handed it to Ted, who immediately placed it directly over his roaring fire and used his great strength to coax still more heat from the coals with his bellows.

In a short time the steel strip was glowing, and Hosea went to work on his own forge. With two sets of pliers he made the bar thinner, then began to shape it with a little hammer and a curious, all-purpose tool that had a knife blade, a hook, and a sharp point.

Occasionally he glanced at Dr. Martin's drawing of the instrument, but he had the shape sufficiently clear in his mind to use the sketch only as a general guide. His fingers seemed to fly, and Ted marveled at his delicate, sure touch and complete concentration.

Hosea sighed gently. "Is done," he said, and holding the instrument with a pair of tongs, he plunged it into a bucket of cold water until it cooled. Then, still grasping it by the tongs, he raced back to the infirmary.

Lena Malcolm was cradling the baby in her arms, taking care to hold her upright while she and Terence tried to keep Lenore amused.

Bob Martin eagerly inspected the instrument. "Perfect," he said, and handed it to Tonie, who carefully dropped it into a bowl of brandywine to clean it.

"Lena," the physician said crisply, "give the baby to Tonie. You and Terence wait outside and please close the door behind you."

The young mother obeyed reluctantly.

After the door was closed, Dr. Martin said, "Tonie, place the baby's feet on the table. Stand behind her, hold her arms and body steady, and no matter what happens, don't let her move."

Tonie did as she was told, but Lenore, still too startled to cry, began to kick her feet.

Hosea stepped forward and standing beside Tonie, he gently but firmly grasped the baby's feet and held them still.

The physician worked swiftly, his touch sure and delicate. Taking the dripping instrument from the bowl with one hand and opening the baby's mouth with the other, he inserted the remarkably thin strand of steel down Lenore's throat.

Tonie spoke to the baby in a steady, calm voice, trying to soothe her.

Bob Martin seemed to know precisely what he was doing. He jiggled the handle slightly, for what felt like an eternity to Tonie but actually was only a few seconds. Then he grunted with satisfaction and slowly removed the instrument. Attached to the end was the thimble.

But there was still work to be done. As the angry, frightened baby opened her mouth to wail, the doctor snatched a glass containing a milky liquid and poured some of it down her throat.

Lenore almost gagged, swallowed a quantity of the liquid in spite of herself and then let loose with a scream of protest.

The smiling Bob Martin opened the door and beckoned. "She'll be fine now," he said as Tonie handed the shrieking baby to Lena.

Suddenly, abruptly, Lenore stopped wailing and dropped off to sleep.

"Here's your thimble," the physician said, handing it to Terence. "You may want to keep it as a souvenir."

The young couple stammered their thanks, but were

somewhat bewildered. "I'm worried," Lena said. "Why did she drop off to sleep the way she did?"

"Oh, that. I gave her a diluted dose of laudanum. It's an opiate, rather unpleasant to the taste, but very effective. She'll sleep for several hours, and when she wakes up she'll suffer no ill effects except a slight sore throat."

Lena managed to smile as she cradled the baby in her arms.

Bob Martin picked up the instrument, then silenced the couple as they tried to express their gratitude to him. "Don't thank me," he said. "Any experienced doctor could have done what I did. It was Hosea who performed the miracle, making this instrument to my exact specifications in less than half an hour. I'll never understand how he did it."

"Hosea," Terence said fervently, shaking his hand, "our whole family is in your debt as long as we live."

Hosea was embarrassed. He shuffled his feet, stared down at the floor, and suddenly bolted. His air of self-confidence had deserted him, and all he could murmur as he fled was, "Much work to do."

Snow continued to fall intermittently, and the weather turned bitterly cold. Whip said the winter promised to be the worst he had ever known in the ten years he had spent in the West. But the hunters and fishermen continued to enjoy good fortune. The foragers and woodcutters remained active, too, and the women busied themselves indoors making clothes of buffalo hides and preserving winter berries.

Fears of friction between the civilians and soldiers, spending the winter together in a place remote from civilization, gradually subsided. The troops discovered that the ladies were much like the mothers and sisters they had left at home. Occasionally there were disputes between individual soldiers and male members of the wagon train that developed into fist fights, but Colonel Jonathan and Ernie von Thalman wisely ignored these eruptions.

To be sure, the future settlers did not find living conditions at the fort easy. The men who went hunting or fishing, woodcutting or foraging, always in groups, considered themselves fortunate to get away; the others were forbidden to go beyond the palisades and soon became restless.

Although accustomed to communal living, here they were forced to remain in close quarters. The scene was unchanging, and they had to find ways to keep busy.

"I'm beginning to hate this place," Tonie said to Cathy one day. "Whip and Ernie make such a fuss about my going out with the hunters that I hang around here most of the time. I'm not used to being confined and having so little to do. Even if I do work at the dispensary, sometimes I have to keep myself from screaming from boredom."

"So do I," Cathy said. "Would you believe that I actually miss the farm? I hated living there mainly because of Otto, but it's the *place* I miss. My own snug bedroom. My own kitchen, where I could keep my pots and pans and knives exactly as I wanted them. And my own parlor, even though I didn't sit in it all that often."

"I know what you mean," Tonie replied. "When the wagon train was moving, we had a feeling of accomplishment. Now we're just twiddling our thumbs, so we think of home."

"Because we have no homes other than the wagons parked out yonder," Cathy said sadly.

"It must be harder for you than for me," Tonie said, "because you're basically such a homebody."

"I suppose I am. I never had much of a spirit of adventure, you know, and it was Otto who decided that we were going to Oregon. I had no say in the matter, and if he had given me my choice, we'd have stayed home. Home. How I like that word."

"For someone who didn't want to go west and who wanted to stay put," Tonie said dryly, "it seems to me you've performed miracles. You've adjusted better than most to wagon train life."

"That's sweet of you to say, but you'd change your

mind if you worked on one of my kitchen shifts. I scream and shout and carry on something awful when some of those women don't work as hard as they should. Really, Tonie, I'm becoming an awful shrew."

"You couldn't say an unkind word to anybody," her friend assured her.

"What really bothers me," Cathy went on, "is what we're going to do about celebrating Thanksgiving and Christmas. Not that I mind for myself. I honestly don't care. But some of the children were asking me the other day, and I didn't know what to tell them. There's no point in going to Ernie because he's not familiar with American customs. But I'm wondering if I ought to speak to Whip. And Colonel Jonathan. What do you think?"

Tonie laughed. "Don't speak to anyone," she said.

"But—"

"Uncle Arnold let something slip a couple of days ago, so don't dare repeat it—it's a big surprise. The hunters have found wild turkeys in the forest and have been shooting them, then freezing them in snow so they'll keep until Thanksgiving. Believe me, you'll have more birds to clean and stuff and roast than you'll ever want to see again."

Cathy was delighted. "How wonderful! Who thought of the surprise?"

"Whip, I believe. He's much more sensitive than some people realize, and he knows that with everyone just sitting around doing nothing for day after day, morale is low."

"He really *can* be sensitive," Cathy said. "I suppose that's why I become so furious with him when he behaves like—like such a lump of callous old mountain man."

What she was really saying, Tonie thought, was that she became angry when Whip, who found it difficult to overcome his shyness, could not express himself clearly in her presence. The way he looked at Cathy, however, particularly when she wasn't aware of his gaze, indicated his interest in her. But obviously Cathy hadn't made up her mind about Whip. His way of life was so alien to all she had ever known that she would need more time before she decided, as Tonie felt sure she ultimately would, that she wanted him.

"I have an idea," Cathy said, clapping her hands together in childlike enthusiasm. "Why don't we get some of the women together and make dolls and other toys we can give to the children at Christmas? Presents from all of us that they can open under the tree. We'll need a tree, of course."

Tonie laughed. "There are enough pines out beyond the palisades that the tree will be the least of our problems. As for the gifts, let's do it. That should help raise everybody's spirits."

They began work on the project that same day.

The first visitor to Fort Madison after the arrival of the wagon train was André Sebastian. He rode a handsome stallion and traveled with two heavily laden pack horses. Claiming to be a surveyor, he said he was on his way to the Rocky Mountains, and that he had been hired by a new fur company to determine approximately how many years beaver, lynx, and other animals whose pelts were in great demand would continue to abound in the Rockies.

Colonel Jonathan welcomed him, as did the people of the Oregon-bound caravan, and he accepted the invitation to stay for a few days. At mealtimes he always managed to find a place beside Tonie Mell at one of the long tables. A few people noticed and speculated that he was attracted to her.

Whip happened to be sitting on the far side of the table on the second night of André Sebastian's stay at the fort and engaged him in conversation. "It's none of my business, Sebastian," he said, "and I don't want to shove my nose into places where it doesn't belong, but I think you have more courage than good sense."

"How so?" Sebastian was smiling faintly.

"The worst of the winter is still ahead. Crossing the Great Plains at other seasons is no joke. And if you've spent any time in the Rockies, you know that mountain men hole up at this time of year. So do the Indians."

"True enough, and I certainly can't get much of my work done before the thaws come," Sebastian said, "but I want to be there when the weather turns nicer."

Whip made no further comment, but his shrug spoke for itself.

André Sebastian felt the need to offer some further explanation. "I have friends who have cabins in the mountains. I plan to stay with one of them."

Whip's interest was sparked. "Really? I've been spending about half of each year in the Rockies for a long time, so I know a good many of the hunters and trappers. Maybe I've run across your friends."

Sebastian's bland smile indicated that he had no intention of identifying his future hosts.

Whip immediately let the subject drop, but afterwards, he took Tonie aside. "There's something odd about that fellow," he said.

Tonie agreed.

"I can't figure him, Tonie, but it may not matter. He'll probably be leaving the fort soon, and it could be we'll never see him again. On the other hand, I had warnings from the government in Washington City and from Sam Brentwood—as you know better than most—that there are people who would do nearly anything to break up the wagon train. This André Sebastian seems kind of sweet on you, so maybe you could keep your ears open for as long as he's here, and you might just find out something."

She had tried hard to forget that she had ever been requested to commit acts of sabotage against the train, and she was happy that she was treated like other members of the company. But what Whip said made sense, and she agreed to do what she could.

The thought depressed her, however, making her restless, so at an early breakfast the next morning, she asked for permission to join her uncle, Whip, and Mack, who were going hunting in the forest.

Arnold Mell frowned. "There's snow in the air."

"If I get wet, I'll dry off when we come back here," Tonie replied. "I promise you I won't get lost in the forest."

The men had to laugh, and Arnold Mell raised both hands in a gesture of surrender. "You win," he said. "You always do."

They went off to their separate quarters for rifles, ammunition, and powder horns, and Tonie donned her new, hooded buffalo cloak.

When the little group reassembled at the back gate of the fort, they were surprised to see that André Sebastian was waiting for them. He, too, carried a rifle.

"I don't want to intrude," he said, "but I'm hoping you'll allow me to come with you. I'm leaving soon for the mountains, and I need to get in shape again after several days of soft living."

It would have been rude to reject his request, so the hunters nodded, and he fell in beside Tonie as they entered the forest and made their way through underbrush mixed with patches of snow.

"What game have you been bagging here?" Sebastian asked the girl.

Tonie didn't want to encourage conversation with him, but she remembered what Whip had said the previous evening. "The usual," she replied. "Plenty of deer and all kinds of small game. An occasional wild boar, although I haven't been lucky enough to spot one myself. And one day we came across a small herd of buffalo grazing on young evergreens. That was to the west of here, at the edge of the forest."

André Sebastian listened as though he cared. "Any bears?"

She shook her head. "Whip Holt has seen them here during the summer, but none of us has even caught a glimpse of bear tracks. Whip has a hunch they go up farther north to the Minnesota country to hibernate."

"Quite a fellow, this Whip Holt."

"That he is," Tonie said. "The best hunter and guide in the West, and a good, loyal friend. But I'd hate to cross him."

"I'll remember that," Sebastian said.

Tonie glanced at him obliquely, but his expression seemed innocent enough.

They trudged for the better part of an hour, covering

two to three miles, and then they scattered, agreeing to meet at noon at a place Arnold called "the red rock."

Sebastian looked blank.

"I assume you're planning to tag along with Tonie," Arnold said.

"Yes, if she doesn't mind," Sebastian declared. She felt compelled to agree to the man's company, and nodded.

The girl took the lead, heading eastward, with André Sebastian following several paces behind her, and she set a lively pace—too lively, she thought, for successful hunting. Wildlife would be sure to scatter when they heard the thumping of her boots on the frozen ground.

Sebastian must have known she was behaving like an amateur, but he made no protest and remained silent until she halted beside a patch of winter berries to search for deer tracks. "I've been waiting," he said quietly, "for an opportunity to have a truly private chat with you."

She looked at him, saying nothing, and waited.

"You are Antoinette Melichev," he said.

Tonie's heart pounded. Only the staff of the Imperial Russian Legation in Washington and agents in the employ of the czar's secret police knew her by the formal name under which she had come to the United States as a small child. "Who are you?" she demanded.

"My identity is unimportant."

"You're on the payroll of the Russian secret police."

"That is also unimportant. Miss Melichev, I bring you a message." His eyes seemed to bore into her.

"Don't bother repeating it," Tonie said wearily. "I'm sure I know the message."

"I think not." André Sebastian's voice became gentle, almost caressing. "Many months ago, in Washington, when you applied for a visa for your parents to come to America, you were asked to help your native country in a time of need. And in return, you were told the visa would be granted."

In spite of her attempt to remain calm, she could feel herself growing angry. "That isn't quite accurate. I was told that unless I cooperated, no visa would be granted. Well, I understand why the Russians don't want to sabotage the wagon train themselves. They don't want to become involved. It's so much better to have someone else do it. But I've made it clear I don't intend to be that person. I'm an American, not a Russian, and I'll do nothing to harm *this* country—even if it means that the mother and father I haven't seen since I was very little stay in St. Petersburg for the rest of their lives."

"The nature of the bargain has changed." His voice was barely audible now. "So I beg you to be sensible. The conditions here at Fort Madison are perfect for what has been asked of you. All you need to do is collect a number of pine branches. Surely you know how fiercely they burn. Place them on the flooring of the empty wagons that stand behind the fort, then take a tinderbox and flint to them. The winter wind will do the rest, and the wagons will burn to the ground. Your friends will be forced to return to their homes—traveling some distance on foot, to be sure—and it will take years for the Americans to organize another venture to the Oregon country."

"I think you're contemptible," Tonie said quietly. Suddenly she raised her rifle to her hip. "Come just one step nearer, and I'll kill you. I assure you I can fire from this position."

"I don't doubt your word," Sebastian said, seemingly calm, "but such heroics are unnecessary. I am merely a messenger."

She watched him narrowly.

"I mentioned a moment ago that the essence of the bargain that was offered to you has been altered. I have been asked to inform you that if you fail to accomplish what has been asked of you, Ivan and Olga Melichev will not spend their declining years in St. Petersburg. A formal charge of treason will be lodged against them. They will be found guilty and sent to a work camp in Siberia. They will remain there for the rest of their days—and the elderly do not survive long there."

"But they've committed no treason, and you know it. They've done no harm to anyone," Tonie protested, aghast.

"I form no personal opinion in these matters. They

are not my concern. I was sent into this wilderness to carry a message to you, and this I have done." He bowed mockingly and turned away, disappearing into the forest with surprising speed.

A blind rage enveloped Tonie; she wanted to follow him and shoot him down. But in spite of her fury, she could not do it. Besides, as he had said, he was only an agent, and his death would not remove the threat to her parents.

She could hear him running and knew she could not match his speed. Also, it would be dangerous for her to follow him alone. His one desire now had to be that of escaping before he could be captured, turned over to Colonel Jonathan, and taken to Washington City as a foreign agent. To avoid being captured, he would become the hunter rather than the hunted, and she was sure he would not hesitate to shoot her down.

Tonie cupped her hands at the sides of her mouth and gave the piercing cry of the owl—the prearranged emergency summons that indicated she was in distress. She waited a few minutes, then repeated the cry, again and again, to guide her companions to her. The wait was agonizing.

Mack Dougall was the first to arrive.

He knew nothing about Tonie's troubles with the Russians, and there was little he alone could do for her. Rather than give him a detailed explanation, she said, "There's a nasty problem. Wait until the others get here."

Mack shrugged, then helped himself to a generous swallow of whiskey from his flask.

Tonie repeated the owl cry, and this time it came back to her from a distance. But another quarter of an hour passed before Arnold and Whip arrived. By now over half an hour had elapsed since André Sebastian had left.

In spite of Tonie's attempt to speak dispassionately, her voice shook as she gave them a verbatim report of her conversation with the agent.

Arnold Mell cursed volubly in Russian.

"I made my decision months ago," Tonie said. "No matter what happens or becomes of anyone, I refuse to commit treason against the United States."

"You owe nothing to Ivan and Olga," Arnold said angrily. He paused before speaking the next words. "They were happy to get rid of you, Tonie, when Sophie and I offered to bring you to America. My brother's position as court jeweler to the czar gave him an inflated sense of self-importance, and they were having so much fun that they didn't want to be burdened with a daughter."

"Thank you for telling me, Uncle Arnold," she said softly. "This makes my decision easier to bear."

Until now Whip had said nothing. A white line had formed around his mouth, and when he spoke, there was a snap of authority in his voice. "I knew there was something strange about that bastard. You say he has at least a half-hour head start on us, Tonie?"

"By now it must be closer to an hour." It was difficult to tell the time, for the sun was hidden behind dark clouds.

"We've got to catch him if we can," Whip was grim.

"I want the pleasure of dealing with him," Arnold said.

They all started off, walking as quickly as they could, through the forest in the direction of Fort Madison.

Walking rapidly, Whip called over his shoulder, "We've got to turn him over to the government. Depending on what President Van Buren and the State Department want to do, this could mean breaking relations with St. Petersburg."

"First," Arnold replied, his voice harsh, "we must catch the man."

At last they saw the log palisades of the fort looming up through the snow that was now swirling about them. As they moved through the gate, Whip slowed his pace. Not knowing how André Sebastian might react, he didn't want to give the man warning.

Ernie von Thalman was just emerging from the blacksmith's shop, and when the group saw him, they came to an abrupt halt.

Tonie was sobbing for breath, on the verge of collapse, and her uncle placed an arm around her for support.

Ernie knew something was amiss, but before he could say anything, Whip asked him curtly, "Have you seen André Sebastian?"

"Yes," Ernie said. "As a matter of fact, he behaved very strangely. He came dashing in from the forest and went straight to the stables, where his horse was already saddled and his pack horses were ready to travel. He saw me—I was just going to have some words with Ted Woods—but Sebastian didn't even stop to say hello or goodbye. He just went riding out of the fort as though he were being chased by the devil!"

"How long ago was that, Ernie?"

The Baron removed a thick, gold watch from a waistcoat pocket and looked at it. "At least an hour."

Arnold cursed again in Russian.

Whip looked down at the ground. The snow was falling so rapidly and heavily that the footprints he and his companions had made only moments earlier were already obliterated. "There's nothing we can do," he said wearily. "We can ride much faster than a man on the move with two pack horses, but we don't know whether he's gone east, west, or south across the Platte."

"It doesn't really matter," Arnold said harshly as he squeezed his niece's shoulders reassuringly. "Our path and that of Mr. André Sebastian will cross again, and when that happens, we have a score to settle with him."

Tonie Mell sat alone before a roaring fire in what had been one of the small officers' parlors in the fort. Brooding and withdrawn, she stared into the flames, not noticing that Ernie had entered the room.

Ernie, aware of what Tonie was feeling and wanting to help her, had searched for her until he had found her. He knew that she had undergone a shattering experience and needed comfort and support. More objective than her uncle could be, he felt that his worldly background and his understanding of human nature on many levels would make it possible for this proud young woman to lean on him; yet he hoped he could help her without her quite knowing what he was doing.

He cleared his throat gently.

Startled, Tonie looked away from the fire, blinking at him.

"You needn't tell me," Ernie said. "You're still upset over your experience with André Sebastian."

"I'm angry," Tonie replied brusquely. "Furious, if you must know. If he came into this room right now, I could murder him with my bare hands."

The Austrian nobleman nodded calmly. "You wouldn't be human if you reacted in any other way."

"How dare he threaten me? And what makes the Russians think I'd harm my friends and be disloyal to my country? I'm an American, not a subject of the czar. Just because the parents I haven't seen since I was a baby happen to be living in Russia is no reason for me to become a hostage!"

"It makes no sense," he agreed. "But governments frequently are neither logical nor ethical. They do whatever they think is in their own best national interests, and they give no thought to individuals who may be made to suffer the consequences of their policies."

"It isn't fair!"

"Of course it isn't. But what you fail to take into account, my dear Tonie, is that life itself isn't fair. Animals kill in order to survive and so do humans. That's the basic law of nature, like it or not."

The girl stood, moved closer to the fire and, averting her face, looked into the flames again. "If you must know, I'm frightened. And until this experience, I was never in all my life afraid of anything."

Ernie smiled. "You sound as though you're ashamed of your fear."

"I am. I hate being weak!"

"Fear very often is a sign of strength, Tonie, not weakness. The hunter who knows no fear when he faces an angry mountain lion intent on destroying him is more than a dolt. He's an idiot. Fear sharpens one's reactions and enables us to be among the survivors."

"You really think so?"

"I know it," he replied quietly. "Before I came to

America, I took part in three major campaigns and fought in eight battles. Before and during those battles, I was badly frightened."

"But the Emperor of Austria personally decorated you several times."

"Only because I had the good sense to be afraid. Brother officers who knew no fear are in their graves today, but I'm here. There's a difference between recklessness and bravery, you know. The wise person knows when to lie low, when to protect himself or herself, when to fight back. There are moments when one should be bold, when one should press an attack. But there are times when one simply covers one's flanks."

Tonie slowly turned toward him. "Why are you telling me all this?"

"Because you're one of the few people I know who does this. There are women in this wagon train who would become hysterical if they had gone through your experience with André Sebastian. There are women who would give up the struggle, who would succumb to the pressure he was putting on you."

"I have no intention of doing that," she said, clenching her fists.

Ernie looked at her as she faced him defiantly, her eyes blazing, and he chuckled. "You prove what I've been saying about you. Of all the women I've ever known, you're better able than any to face whatever may lie ahead. Because you're self-reliant, my dear. You have faith in yourself."

"Well," she admitted, "I won't let the Russians or their agents stomp on me. I don't start fights, Ernie. But I fight back!"

"Every word you say proves my point," Ernie said. "As the Russians are learning to their sorrow, they chose the wrong person to intimidate."

For the first time since he had entered the room, she laughed. "You're giving me a swollen head, you know."

"Not at all. I'm merely being honest. And I'm enjoying this experience myself. It isn't often that I've seen a powerful nation being humbled. The inner strength you provide and the help that your loyal friends give you make a formidable combination, Tonie." He crossed the room and kissed her gently on the forehead. "This is one battle that Imperial Russia simply cannot win."

The girl was silent for a few moments, then nodded. "No, they won't win," she said softly. "I will, because I'm doing what I know is right."

VI

Roaring fires burned in the hearths of the adjoining dining halls providing warmth for members of the wagon train, who, grateful to be spending the bitterly cold winter indoors, sat at the long tables and ate their supper quietly. The lack of privacy was creating friction, but so far common sense had prevailed, and no serious quarrels had disturbed the peace of the community. Eulalia and Claiborne Woodling were being ignored by many people who regarded the brother and sister as obnoxious, but their far less abrasive father had won general acceptance.

In the midst of the meal, an aide to Colonel Jonathan came into the dining halls looking for Whip and Ernie, and when they went off with him, leaving their meal unfinished, people exchanged apprehensive glances. Obviously something was wrong.

The commander of Fort Madison was waiting for the men in his office, and when they entered, he wasted no time on preliminaries. "I need your help, and I need it fast. Holt, what do you know about the Ponca nation, whose territory is north of the Omaha's land?"

"I can't tell you much about them, Colonel, because I've always avoided them," Whip said. "You know where you stand with most tribes, but not with the Ponca. They're shifty, always trying to gain an advantage over everybody else. They break alliances as fast as they make them. A friend of mine—a chief of the Cheyenne—told me years ago to stay away from them, and I've always followed his advice."

"Is it true that they're good fighters?"

"From what I've heard, they're tricky," Whip said, "They wait for their enemies to make a mistake, and then they pounce. What's happening, Colonel?"

"Just a few minutes ago," Bert Jonathan replied, "one of my scouts arrived with word that the Ponca are on a rampage."

Whip whistled under his breath. "How many are there?"

"About fifteen hundred, all mounted," the Colonel said. "They're looking for loot—as well as women and children to take prisoner. I'm not worried about an attack on Fort Madison. They're too clever for that, and I'm almost certain they'll stay away from us. But they're bound to raid Omaha and Kansa villages and maybe attack other tribes."

"They'll stay out of Blackfoot country," Whip said. "No Plains nation would dare to raid a Blackfoot town."

"Attacks on the Omaha and Kansa would be bad enough, with those nations already sparring with each other. Before you know it, all of the minor tribes of the area will be joining in a free-for-all. And when Indians go to war with each other, the fighting can last for years. I've got to put a stop to it before it starts. My directive from the War Department is to keep the peace in this region."

"With your limited personnel," Ernie said bluntly, "I don't see how you can do it."

"I'm leading an expedition against the Ponca tomorrow morning, leaving here at daybreak," Colonel Jonathan declared. "I need your help, and I can supply you with as many as fifty horses if you don't have enough good mounts. How many men can you give me? I want only good riders—first-rate shots—men who are willing to obey orders."

Whip thought for a moment. "In warmer weather I might be able to scrape up ninety, but some of our people can't function too well in the snow and ice. Ernie and I will ask for volunteers, and then we'll screen those who respond. My offhand guess is that we can supply you with about seventy effectives."

The Colonel was pleased. "They'll be augmenting two of my cavalry troops, so that should be enough, and I'll leave fifty men behind to guard the fort."

Ernie was startled. "One moment, Colonel. You said the Ponca have fifteen hundred warriors in the field. Each of your cavalry troops numbers eighty men. So the addition of our seventy will give you fewer than two hundred and fifty. Surely you don't intend to send a force that small into battle against fifteen hundred mounted braves!"

Whip and Colonel Jonathan exchanged smiles. Frontier warfare in the New World in no way resembled the battles to which Europeans were accustomed.

"An attack on their whole body would be suicidal," the Colonel said. "Even if we won such a battle, we'd suffer a defeat. The Ponca would feel humiliated, and they'd come back at us again and again. They'd give us no peace for years."

"Ernie," Whip said, "our aim is to discourage them just enough so they'll come to their senses and go back to their own towns."

"I think I can explain," Colonel Jonathan interrupted. "A few years ago I was an instructor at the Military Academy at West Point. I taught our cadets the techniques used in the Imperial Austrian Army by your Hungarian cavalry regiments."

"Ah!" Ernie brightened. "Salami tactics!"

"Precisely," the officer replied. "We find ways to split the main body of the Ponca into segments, then inflict enough punishment on each portion to persuade them they ought to give up the whole idea of waging war. We don't follow the Hungarian salami tactics to their logical conclusion, however. At no time do we try to annihilate any segment. That would just be borrowing trouble for the future."

"We'll report back to you as soon as we have our

people set," Whip said. He and Ernie shook hands with Colonel Jonathan, then left his office and returned hurriedly to the dining halls.

There, they announced the Colonel's request for aid, and Whip made their own position clear. "When Colonel Jonathan took us in for the winter, we promised to help him in situations like this. But we want only men who can tolerate the hardships of a winter campaign. Anyone who might have to give up and return to the fort will be a burden."

He was not surprised when virtually every one of the men volunteered, and even the older boys begged for the right to go. A notable exception was Arthur Elwood, who had confided to various members of the company that he was thinking of leaving the wagon train.

Grace Drummond made a scene when her husband rose to volunteer. "I forbid you to go!" she cried in a loud voice. Nat ignored her protests.

Whip found it difficult but necessary to reject the services of Major Woodling. "Let your son represent your family," he said. "Your daughter needs protection. What would happen to her if both you and Claiborne were killed?"

The Major knew it was unlikely that both he and his son would suffer mortal wounds. "Mr. Holt," he said with a wan smile, "you've found a diplomatic way to tell me I'm too old for a venture like this."

Whip nodded.

"Thank you, sir, for being diplomatic." Woodling returned slowly to his place at the supper table. The others felt sorry for him.

Hosea was refused the right to accompany the party, too, and was distressed. "Hosea plenty good fighting man," he said with an injured air.

"There's none better," Whip agreed. "But no matter how long you can run without getting tired, the Colonel wouldn't approve of having one man on foot while almost two hundred and fifty others are mounted. Don't worry. You'll have plenty of other chances to show your skills as a warrior before we reach Oregon."

The following morning Cathy van Ayl and her helpers

went to the kitchens far earlier than usual to prepare breakfast for the departing men. Most members of the wagon train were on hand to see the group leave.

The cavalry troops were assembling on the snow-laden parade ground. Each volunteer was given a saddlebag containing enough dried beef and parched corn for a four-day journey, a blanket, and those whose supplies of ammunition were limited were given additional powder and bullets.

Colonel Jonathan had a brief talk with Whip. "I assume your scouts will join mine. Will you take charge of all scouting yourself, Mr. Holt, and coordinate your three men with my eight? Mine will be directly under your command."

"Sure. Glad to oblige."

The Colonel unfolded a map. "Here's where we'll camp tonight, on the western tip of this lake."

Whip borrowed the map, brought all the scouts together, and showed it to them, instructing them to rejoin the regiment whenever they could after sundown. All of them were veterans long familiar with the terrain. Whip then assigned each man a separate sector, reserving for himself the area in which he believed it most likely that the Ponca warriors could be found.

"It isn't enough just to locate the braves," he said. "Try to get a fairly accurate estimate of their numbers."

Whip said goodbye to Ernie, who was commanding the wagon train contingent and whom he would rejoin later, then bade farewell to the Colonel. After saluting Cathy, who had followed him out of the kitchen, he returned to the waiting scouts. "There's no need for us to wait for the main body," he said. "We'll be on our way."

Dawn had not yet broken as Whip led his scouts out of the rear gate of Fort Madison. They immediately scattered, each moving off in the direction of his assigned sector. The hoofs of the horses made a squeaking sound on the snow, and the cold was so intense that Whip gave his stallion his head.

The horse quickly began to canter to keep warm, as his master had known he would. When he tried to increase his pace to a full gallop, however, Whip had to give the reins a gentle tug. "No, boy, we'll do no galloping on this ground until we have to. Both of us will be in trouble if you take a tumble on the ice and break a leg."

The stallion settled back into a canter. Dawn came, and then the sky grew brighter, but the clouds overhead formed a thick, gray mass, and the sun did not appear. Whip was warmer now, but he kept his buffalo-skin cloak closed and his fox hat pulled low on his forehead. A man who grew careless in such weather could suffer frostbite long before he realized it.

Riding toward the northwest, with the edge of the forest off to his right, Whip saw the endless prairie stretching out ahead and to his left. This was his world, silent, forbidding, and alien to the outsider, but comforting to those who truly knew and loved the wilderness. The prairie looked deserted, but that was an illusion. There were herds of buffalo here if one knew where to find them. There were antelope and deer as well as small game, and somewhere in the vast space ahead there were fifteen hundred Ponca warriors intent on making war.

Whip was enjoying himself thoroughly. Although he liked leading the wagon train because the job was a challenge, this was infinitely better. On the other hand, he realized he couldn't spend the rest of his life as a scout and mountain man. Mack Dougall had lived such a life and was now forced to find his companionship in a bottle.

Some day, Whip reflected, he would settle down, establish a homestead claim, marry, and raise children. Until this moment the idea of staying in one place and putting down roots had not crossed his mind. He had taken it for granted that he would deliver the company to its destination and then return to his own way of life in the Rocky Mountains.

What, he wondered, had caused this sudden change? He suspected it was Cathy van Ayl. He couldn't put her out of his mind. Ridiculous—no woman was going to tie him down. The worst of it was that he could imagine himself married to her, living in a house he built himself near the great blue-green forests of the Oregon country. He tried to get rid of that mental picture, but it refused to disappear.

Whip sighed and reassured himself he wasn't being forced to make any drastic decision in the immediate future. Another year at least would pass before he guided his charges to Oregon, and many things could happen to change the situation. Cathy might fall in love with and marry someone else. She had the money she had inherited from Otto, in addition to her natural talents and beauty, so any bachelor in the wagon train who didn't court her was being shortsighted. Not that he himself gave a damn about her money, but it made her independent, and less likely to be interested in a mountain man like himself.

Cathy aside, Whip told himself, he had to think in terms of his future. But he found searching his own mind a painful process. He was a mountain man, no more and no less, and for years he had been content with his lot. He loved the thrill of pitting himself against the unknown, of using the forces of nature as his allies. He gloried in his ability to react instantly in an emergency, to act quickly and instinctively when danger threatened. But those abilities wouldn't be enough in the future. The world he had known and loved for so long was changing rapidly.

The five hundred men, women, and children in the wagon train represented the future. These pioneers soon would be followed by countless others, until the whole continent would become populated. The wilderness was vanishing, and the day was not far distant when the mountain man would become a figure of the past. In his place there would be the patient, steady farmer, the persevering rancher, the solid townsman who sought rather than shunned the company of others.

Where would he fit into this America of tomorrow? He doubted that he could ever be happy in a small town, much less a city. The regimen of a farmer, who performed the same chores again and again, did not appeal to him. He understood horses, though, and could handle cattle, so perhaps he could be happy as a rancher.

It shocked him when the thought occurred to him that he might be wise to claim a parcel of land for himself in the Oregon territory and settle there. He could, of course, lead other parties across the country to the

Pacific, and perhaps he could cling to his present way of life for as long as another decade. But in ten years he would be nearly forty, perhaps lacking the qualities needed to buckle down and start a new career. He knew mountain men who had turned into hopeless drunks when they had grown too old for the rugged out-of-doors life they had chosen, and he had no intention of becoming a member of that pathetic band.

Not that he had to make a decision today. The wagon train was still far from Oregon. Whip turned to the task immediately at hand.

At noon he paused beside a small lake, cutting a hole in the ice so he and his stallion could drink. He ate some smoked beef, along with a handful of parched corn, and was satisfied.

About an hour later he made out a smudge on the horizon that he first guessed might be buffalo. But the smear was spread out across the landscape, moving toward him, and he well knew that buffalo herds formed in depth as well as laterally.

It must be the Ponca. He needed to confirm the supposition, however. After making certain his rifle and pistols were ready he headed off in the direction of the blur on the horizon.

The next quarter of an hour passed slowly, Whip's suspense mounting. By the time he was sure that he was indeed approaching braves on horseback, the Ponca were well aware of his presence, and a group of twenty warriors separated from the main body and raced in his direction.

Thanks to his civilian attire, which they could distinguish at this distance, they had no idea that he was performing a task on behalf of the United States Army, so that much was to the good. It would not be difficult for them to tell immediately that he was a white man, however, as Indians of the Plains tribes rode far smaller horses. So those who had come in pursuit of him probably wanted to kill and scalp him, then take his stallion and his firearms.

He knew he could hold his own against a fairly large force, particularly when he was carrying a rifle and two pistols, and his foes were armed only with bows, arrows, and spears. But the odds of twenty to one were too great on the prairie, where there was no place to hide.

Whip's courage was unlimited, but he was practical, and he realized the time had come for him to retreat. The Ponca were reckless horsemen, indifferent to their own safety or that of their mounts, so he had no time to lose. He wheeled, then headed back in the direction from which he had come.

Glancing over his shoulder he saw that the braves were gaining on him. He would have to risk his stallion's neck and his own. He gave the horse his head, in spite of the ice and snow underfoot, and the stallion accepted the challenge, breaking into a full gallop. If he skidded or stumbled, he would fall, and that would be the end of him—and perhaps the end of his rider.

Again Whip looked over his shoulder and was relieved to see that the distance between him and his foes was increasing. Compelled to keep up his dangerous pace, however, he had to trust the stallion's instincts. In places the snow was at least a foot deep, and a hoof striking a hidden rock would mean sudden disaster, but he had no alternative.

He was outdistancing his pursuers, and a few minutes later the braves gave up the chase. The Indians were realists, too, and the prospect of the limited quantity of loot they could take from a lone traveler wasn't worth the effort they were making.

Whip immediately slowed his stallion to a safe canter. Only then did he realize that, in spite of the cold, he was covered with sweat. He shivered as he turned in the direction of the rendezvous point.

He rode for two more hours. The day was dying, and the regiment obviously had just arrived because only now were sentry outposts being established.

"Where's the Colonel?" Whip shouted, scarcely slowing his pace.

The sergeant of the guard pointed. Tents that would provide a minimal shelter were being removed from the backs of pack horses, and Bert Jonathan, who had himself dismounted, was watching the operation.

Whip jumped to the ground, noting that Ernie von Thalman, the commanders of the two cavalry troops, and members of the regimental staff, having seen his rapid approach, were hurrying to the Colonel's side.

"I've located the Ponca," he said, wasting no words, and gave a succinct but full account of what had happened to him.

Colonel Jonathan did not interrupt him, but waited until he had finished before questioning him. "How many were there?"

"I had no chance to make even a rough head count," Whip replied, "but there were so many that I know I saw their main body. On the other hand, I couldn't even guess whether there were five hundred or two thousand."

"At least we have an idea where to find them tomorrow," Captain Haskell said.

Ernie nodded in agreement.

"I hate to contradict you, gentlemen, but you're dead wrong," Whip said. "I know where they were a couple of hours ago, riding at a moderate pace, and I know the direction in which they were heading. But it doesn't necessarily follow that we can figure out where they'll be by morning. By then they could be blame near anywhere. Finding them again could be as hard as locating a kernel of corn you dropped in a field of tall grass."

Frowning, the Colonel asked, "Are you suggesting that we ought to make direct contact with the Ponca tonight?"

"That's right, Colonel. By this time they'll be stopping and making camp for the night. But they travel lighter than we do, and they don't have tents to pack. They'll be on their way again at dawn, and by the time we get organized and on the move, they can be far away. We might not locate them again for at least a week."

The Colonel glanced up at the darkening sky. The heavy, solid clouds would be certain to hide the moon and stars. "A night attack can be tricky. What do the unit commanders think? Captain Haskell?"

"My men are up to it, sir."

"Captain Smith?"

"So are mine, sir."

"Baron von Thalman?"

"I have no idea, Colonel Jonathan. Our people did defend their wagons admirably once when they were attacked by a band of army deserters, but they've never operated together as a formal cavalry troop, so I can't make predictions."

Whip felt compelled to interrupt. "Colonel," he said, "I suggest you hold the civilian troop in reserve. Once they see the way the army troops act, they'll have an example to follow, and I believe they can do it. But they're not up to initiating a complex maneuver."

"If our objective was to destroy the Ponca," Colonel Jonathan said, "I wouldn't even consider a night attack. Under those circumstances I'd prefer waiting until tomorrow, even if we lost them for days. However, since our aim is that of giving them a good case of cold feet that will send them back to their own towns for the rest of the winter, I'm willing to try. Gentlemen, reassemble your units and call in your outposts. We'll march again in ten minutes."

The officers hurried away.

"One more suggestion," Whip said. "The scouts are going to start trickling in soon and will be arriving here for the next hour or so. They won't know quite what to do if no one is here, so I suggest you leave a few men behind to direct them. I'm sure they'll catch up in time to join in the fight. And my own scouts can double as Baron von Thalman's lieutenants once we're all reunited."

"You think of everything, Mr. Holt." There was admiration in the Colonel's voice.

Less than a quarter of an hour later, the regiment was on the move again, with Captain Haskell's troop in the lead, Captain Smith's following, and the men of the wagon train bringing up the rear. Whip rode alone. There would be no opportunity to pause for supper later, so he ate some smoked beef and munched on parched corn in the saddle.

Within an hour he was joined by Arnold Mell and Mack Dougall, and ultimately Stalking Horse appeared. One by one the cavalry scouts also joined him.

"I'm worried about Stalking Horse," he confided to

Arnold. "The soldiers don't know him, and in the dark—with those feathers stuck in his scalp lock—he looks like any other Indian to them. So they might not be able to distinguish between him and the Ponca once the fighting starts."

They rode on for another hour, with Whip selecting the route by estimating how far the Ponca might have come if they had maintained their same pace and had not changed direction. He was guessing, he knew, but at last his gamble paid off—he and Arnold spotted several glowing clumps in the distance. Then the army scouts saw them, too, and tensed.

"Ponca campfires," Whip said, and called a halt. Summoning the commander of the vanguard, he said, "Send someone to the rear and ask the Colonel if he'll join us."

The request proved unnecessary. As soon as the column halted, Colonel Jonathan rode forward, followed by members of his staff.

The scouts counted eleven fires.

"There aren't as many Ponca in the main body as you were originally informed, Colonel," Whip said.

"That's right," Arnold declared. "Not that the difference is all that significant, but we've counted eleven fires, and I happen to know the Ponca traditionally assign one hundred to a fire. So we'll be facing about eleven hundred instead of fifteen hundred."

"It's still far too many for a full-scale attack," the Colonel said.

"I believe we can ride about a mile closer without being detected by their sentries," Whip told him.

"What would be the advantage, Mr. Holt?"

"I don't know—yet. But the closer we are the better we can make out their defense perimeter."

"Fair enough," Colonel Jonathan said.

"Just one thing, Colonel. We don't want to let the Indians know we're breathing down their necks. So I suggest you impose silence on the whole regiment. Don't allow anyone to light a pipe or *segaro*."

Whip waved the column forward again, and, with Arnold still beside him and the army scouts spread out in a line behind them, they rode on for another quarter of an hour. The eleven fires became more distinct, although it was too dark to make out anything else.

One fire, the fourth from the left, was bigger than the others, and attracted Whip's attention. Arnold reached out to tap him on the shoulder, and he nodded in agreement. They had advanced far enough. At this distance they could still consult, and the Colonel could issue orders without fear of being heard. Whip halted the regiment again and engaged in a low-pitched, earnest conversation with the army scouts and Arnold.

Again the Colonel moved forward to join them.

"We have noticed something we all find interesting. Look at the fourth fire from the left."

"Now that you mention it," the Colonel replied, "it looks twice the size of any other fire. What does it mean?"

"We think the sachem—the leader—of the Ponca is using that fire," Whip said.

Colonel Jonathan nodded. "I gather by your tone that you have a specific plan of action in mind."

"We've just been discussing it. I'll try it out on you. Just suppose," Whip said, "that you spread the regiment out in a semicircle—a thin line that starts parallel to the fire on the left and extends all the way to the fire on the right. At a given signal, the entire regiment—after first moving as close to the Ponca sentry outposts as we can—will open fire. Have the men reload and keep firing as rapidly as they can."

"But they can't possibly hit any target at that distance," the Colonel protested, "especially on a night as dark as this."

"I hope not," Whip replied. "The idea of the fireworks display is to confuse and frighten the Ponca and make them think they're being attacked by a force far superior to their own. Two hundred and thirty rifles can make a hell of a lot of noise."

"Aside from the fact that your wagon train civilians won't be making a direct attack, I don't see the advantage."

"While you're putting on your show, your scouts, Arnold and I will ride to the big fire. By now the Ponca are either sleeping or on their way to sleep. Tell him the rest, Arnold."

"It's this way, Colonel," Arnold Mell said. "A few years ago I visited a Ponca town and slept in the local chief's hut. The chief had a special blanket—beaded, with a lot of feathers stuck in it, so that even when he was asleep, people would know he was the chief."

"The principal sachem must be using a fancy blanket like that," Whip said. "He's our goal. We'll scoop him up and ride back to our lines with him. We'll arrange some signal with you so you'll know we're coming, and when we give the signal, the whole regiment pulls back, falls into formation, and rides back this way, fast. The sachem will be expecting us to kill him, and in the dark he'll have no idea how many of us are taking part in the overall attack. But you'll spare his life and send him back to his people unharmed—provided he gives you his word that he'll take his warriors home and stay there. When an Indian's honor is at stake, he'll keep his pledge."

"Astonishing," Colonel Jonathan said.

"We'll be holding casualties down to an absolute minimum," Whip explained. "We may have to put bullets in some of the senior warriors who are sharing the sachem's fire, but only if they get in our way. We may get out of this without any of my men or your troopers being killed or even hurt."

The Colonel shook his head, then stamped his booted feet to keep warm. "What about those of you who are taking part in this raid?" he demanded. "It strikes me you'd be taking a frightful risk."

"Not that bad." Whip shook his head. "Obviously the whole regiment will avoid shooting in the direction of the sachem's fire so we aren't hit by our own bullets."

"I'm thinking in terms of the Ponca capturing and murdering you!"

"If we do this right, we'll be in and out before they realize what's happening. And once we've captured the sachem, they won't dare to fire at us. They'll be afraid of hitting him."

The Colonel appreciated Whip's daring, but continued to disapprove. "I still think you're taking too great a risk. I hardly need remind you that your first obligation is to the people of your wagon train. If you should be killed, injured, or captured, they'd be forced to return to Independence and wait there until another wagonmaster competent to lead them could be found. The expedition to the Oregon country could be delayed for many months, and you know as well as I that the President is eager to settle that territory as soon as possible."

"I won't fail the wagon train company," Whip replied. "I've been in far more ticklish spots and have come through without a scratch. Believe me, Colonel, I've weighed the odds."

The expressions on the faces of the army scouts indicated they agreed with him. One of them, a grizzled trooper with leathery skin, spat into the snow. "I'm due to retire on a pension next year. I'm buying me a little farm near my brother's in Kentucky, and I aim to spend the rest of my days there, all peaceful and quiet. I'll be damned if any good-for-nothing, lazy Ponca warrior is going to deprive me of something I've been waiting for ever since I first volunteered for this army after the British burned Washington City more than twenty-three years ago."

"There can't be more than a hundred or so warriors at that fire," another scout, leaner and younger, said contemptuously. "In hand-to-hand combat or when they're making a raid of their own, they're dangerous. But with ten of us, all carrying rifles and pistols, I don't see how they can stop us."

"They can't," a third scout said flatly.

"We're not treating the Ponca lightly, Colonel," Whip said. "But conditions are perfect for an action that could solve all our problems. Sure, we'll be taking a measure of risk. But I didn't join you on this outing to sit back, twiddle my thumbs, and enjoy the winter air."

"I'm afraid I'll have to go along with you, Mr. Holt," Colonel Jonathan said, "but I'm doing it against my better judgment."

The Colonel summoned his unit commanders and gave the specific instructions. The two army troops moved to the flanks, leaving the weaker and less disciplined wagon train civilians to hold the center. Then all three units moved further apart until they formed a rough semicircle around the Indian encampment. There was a distance of ten to fifteen feet between each man, sufficient space to give the Ponca the impression that the attacking force was far larger than it actually was; yet the distance was not so great that the units would find it difficult to close ranks quickly in case a sudden, unexpected emergency developed.

When Whip told Stalking Horse that he did not want him to accompany him into the Ponca camp, he faced a personal problem. It was evident that Stalking Horse was hurt. "Whip no longer trusts his brother," he said in his own tongue.

"That is untrue," was the instant reply. "Whip has trust and faith in his brother as he has in no other man. It is because of his love for his brother that Stalking Horse must stay behind."

The Cherokee bristled. "Does some man question my courage?"

"I question the mind that was given to you by the great god of your nation," Whip said tartly. "You have a scalp lock with feathers in it. The Ponca have scalp locks with feathers in them. The animal skins you wear are like the animal skins they wear. You carry a bow and arrows, and so do the Ponca. It is very dark, and there will be great confusion when we ride into the camp of the enemy. I want no army scout to fire at you because he mistakenly thinks you are a Ponca warrior. I won't take that chance."

A reluctant Stalking Horse returned to his place in the wagon train line.

The scouts started forward again, moving cautiously as they advanced two hundred yards beyond the three units following them. They remained close enough to each other to see signals given by hand, and eventually a message was passed to Whip from the far left side of the formation: a Ponca sentry outpost was only a short distance ahead.

Whip permitted the main body to move forward another one hundred yards, and then they stopped. So far the conduct of the civilians was as professional as that of the cavalrymen.

With Arnold beside him, Whip motioned the scouts into a single line. Then Whip raised a hand, and when he let it drop, the scouts rushed forward, permitting their mounts to gallop. Not until they had raced far beyond the sentry line did the Ponca on guard duty realize their security had been breached. They raised a shrill, penetrating cry—a perfect imitation of a crow's call—to alert their companions.

By that time the scouting unit was rapidly approaching the large fire. One of the scouts recognized the ornate blanket in which the sleeping sachem of the tribe had wrapped himself. He rode straight toward the prone figure, the scouts on either side of him veering inward sharply.

Leaping to the ground, the scout struck the Indian leader sharply across the back of the head with a pistol butt, knocking him unconscious. He threw the leader across his horse. Then, mounting his horse again and holding the prone body of the Ponca in front of him, the scout began a wild dash back toward the regiment's lines, a scout on either side of him.

Whip, Arnold, and the five other scouts stayed behind for a few moments in order to give the others time to effect their escape. Ponca warriors were awakening now, leaping to their feet and reaching for their weapons. One, more agile than the others, managed to fit an arrow into his bow. Seeing him, Whip coolly shot him with a pistol, the bullet striking the unfortunate brave between the eyes.

The sound of the shot not only alerted the entire Ponca force, but was the ultimate signal that the regiment awaited. A volley of rifle fire erupted, the flashes briefly illuminating a vast semicircle.

Dazed, the Ponca believed that they had been surrounded by a superior force of white men with firesticks, and in their momentary confusion Whip and his companions began their own hasty retreat.

Crouching low in their saddles, they urged their horses

forward, and in a short time they overtook the other members of their party.

Meanwhile, the regiment directed a steady stream of rifle fire at all of the Ponca fires except the large one, leaving Whip, Arnold, and the scouts a narrow channel through which they could escape.

By now the Indians were sending shower after shower of arrows after the men who had abducted their sachem. But the warriors were afraid to pursue the fleeing scouts. The rifle fire held them at bay.

A whistle that Colonel Jonathan had given Whip dangled from his neck on a rawhide thong. He blew one high-pitched blast after another, indicating the successful return of the scouts with the still-unconscious chief of the Ponca nation.

Only now did it occur to Whip that he had neglected to make allowances for one vitally important detail. Instead of heading toward one of the cavalry troops, he and his companions were riding directly toward the men of his own wagon train, who might easily become rattled, think the riders bearing down on them were Ponca, and direct their fire on them. But Stalking Horse and Mack Dougall steadied them, and Whip was pleased to see a grinning Nat Drummond excitedly waving him closer.

Only one of the future Oregon settlers failed to obey orders. Claiborne Woodling suddenly moved forward out of the stationary line. Intoxicated by the success that had been enjoyed so far, he appeared determined to ride into the Ponca camp, which would have been a suicidal gesture. Mack raced after him, caught hold of his reins, and, blistering him with a string of oaths, forced him to return.

By now the scouts had reached relative safety behind their own lines, and a succession of whistle blasts conveyed this information to the regimental commander.

Colonel Jonathan promptly ordered his units to begin a withdrawal. His own troops obeyed quickly, still firing as they withdrew, but the maneuver was far more difficult for the civilians to accomplish. They managed to achieve it with some hesitation, however, and then the lines were contracted so all three units formed a solid phalanx.

Once the regiment halted, it was discovered that two of the scouts had suffered minor injuries. Dr. Martin, who had come to the center of the line with Colonel Jonathan and his staff, quickly took charge, cutting the arrows out of the flesh, pouring brandywine on the wounds, and then bandaging them.

The still-unconscious Ponca was removed from the scout's horse and laid on the ground. Two knives were removed from his belt. Then Dr. Martin revived him by placing a container of sharp, dried herbs under his nostrils.

The dazed Ponca sat up and saw that he was surrounded by white men, many on horses. Colonel Jonathan and Whip dismounted and were joined by Stalking Horse. All three of them faced the dazed sachem, who was just beginning to realize the seriousness of his predicament.

Colonel Jonathan, long accustomed to dealing with Indians, knew, as did Whip, that the chieftain had to be treated with the dignity his high office demanded if the ultimate goal of the maneuver was to be achieved. "Tell him, please, that we mean him no harm, Mr. Holt. Tell him we want no war with him and his people and that we seek only peace."

Whip translated his words, adding a few flourishes of his own.

The sachem drew himself to his full height, even though his head still ached, and gathered his beaded, feathered blanket around him. No matter where he looked, he could see white men with firesticks, many of them in uniform. The presence of Stalking Horse indicated there were Indians in this war party, too. "Why has White Eagle, the sachem of the Ponca, been taken from his sons? They will not rest until this insult has been avenged!"

Whip translated, then added, "Let me answer him, Colonel. I think I can handle this myself."

"The father of our warriors," Whip said to the Ponca as he inclined his head in the direction of the white-haired colonel, "means no disrespect to White Eagle. It is his wish that he and his sons become the friends of White Eagle and his people. White Eagle was brought to this place because there was no other way the father of our warriors could hold a powwow with him. He and his sons want to live in peace with the Ponca. They wish also to live in peace with the Omaha, the Kansa, and all of the other great nations of this land. Only those tribes that break the peace are our enemies."

Suddenly Stalking Horse intervened with a gesture that startled the Ponca chieftain. Holding White Eagle's knives on the palms of his hands, he gave them to him.

Only an Indian or someone who knew the tribes intimately could have understood this gesture. The sachem was being treated as a free man and an equal rather than as a hostage. Reacting slowly because undo haste would have appeared unseemly, he took the knives and slid them into his belt. His face remained stiff, expressionless, but his eyes betrayed his feelings and indicated that some measure of his pride had been restored.

Colonel Jonathan took advantage of this situation by making a gesture of his own. Slowly, elaborately, he withdrew his own army knife from its sheath and presented it to the sachem.

The blade was made of tempered steel, the handle was fashioned of metal and covered with leather. The weapon was far superior to the crude knives of the Ponca, and White Eagle was overwhelmed. It appeared that these men who used firesticks meant what they said and were not trying to trick him.

Aware of the impression that had been made, Whip made up his mind to bring the talk to its climax. The night was already well advanced, and if the negotiations continued until daybreak, the Ponca warriors would see how heavily they outnumbered their foes and might be tempted to launch a full-scale attack in the hope they could rescue their sachem.

"White Eagle," he said, "return with your warriors to the villages and towns of the Ponca. You will go with honor. You will take with you the friendship of our chief and his sons. Only if you make war against the other nations that occupy this land will you and your people be harmed."

Whip spoke quietly to one of the scouts. The man nodded, then left, and returned a few minutes later with a pack horse relieved of its burdens. Whip presented it to White Eagle. The sachem knew he was free to leave. The gifts he had been given had been presented to him unconditionally. If he violated the spirit in which they had had been given, he would be denying the ancient traditions of hospitality that the Ponca, like all other Plains tribes, regarded as sacred.

Whip glanced at Bert Jonathan, indicating that now was the time to strike a bargain.

The colonel extended a hand. "I pledge you peace," he said.

Whip translated, his voice sonorous.

White Eagle hesitated for an instant, and in that moment the question of war or peace hung in the balance. Then he held out his own arm, and he and the Colonel gripped each other's wrists. "White Eagle pledges peace," he declared.

The formalities were complete. Solemn promises had been exchanged, and the sachem would be dishonored if he violated them. He mounted the pack horse, which was far larger than any mounts the Ponca knew, and started toward his own lines.

Colonel Jonathan immediately gave the order for the regiment to withdraw an additional quarter of a mile. The crisis was not over yet—it wouldn't be completely resolved until the warriors accepted their chieftain's agreement.

Dawn broke as the dignified White Eagle rode slowly back to his own camp. He vanished from sight. His followers were undoubtedly astonished to see he was alive and well. There was a long wait, presumably while he conferred with his lieutenants. Then the Ponca campfires were extinguished, and the warriors began a quiet, orderly retreat toward the north.

Colonel Jonathan gave the order to return without delay to Fort Madison. Peace had been restored in the eastern Nebraska country at a cost of one dead Ponca warrior and two wounded scouts. What pleased Whip more than anything else was the knowledge that the men of the wagon train company had gained valuable military experience. They would need it when they resumed their own journey through hostile Indian territory.

The two mountain men who arrived at Fort Madison unexpectedly, on the way from the Rockies to Independence, were named Welden and Burke. One was tall and heavyset, the other shorter but equally brawny. Both were bearded, in their early thirties, raucously profane, and they were dressed alike in greasy buckskins.

"They're scum," Mack Dougall said in disgust. "The minute I saw them, I hid my cask of whiskey. They're the kind I'd send on their way if I saw them in the mountains."

"I know their type, too," Arnold Mell agreed. "When fellows like that showed up at my ranch in Independence, I'd meet them at the front door with my rifle in my hands and swear I'd shoot them if they didn't leave my property fast. I would have done it, too, but they always took me at my word. Colonel Jonathan should have sent them on their way."

"He couldn't," Whip explained. "They're U.S. citizens, and with a new blizzard threatening, he had to give them shelter. I know how you feel, but we've got to put up with them for as long as they hang around here. I reckon, though, that we ought to pass the word for folks to be on their guard."

There were no locks on the doors, so members of the wagon train company were warned to conceal their valuables and to keep watch over their other possessions. Most people tried to be courteous, however, and treated the mountain men politely. The pair were given bunks in the bachelors' sleeping quarters.

Tonie Mell was the first to have an unpleasant encounter with the two men. Since the storm made hunting expeditions impossible, she had spent the day working in the infirmary with Dr. Martin, and at sundown, as she left to return to her own quarters before supper, she was somewhat miffed. That day she had put on a dress, hoping to attract the doctor's attention. Bob Martin had appreciated her efforts on his behalf, as he always did, but he had made no comment on her appearance. If she didn't know better she would have sworn he was blind. Wiping her hands on the apron she still wore, she angrily made her way down the long hallways of the fort, her heels clicking on the rough-hewn floor.

Suddenly her path was blocked by two bulky figures. As they lurched toward her, she could smell the nauseating odor of cheap whiskey.

"Ain't she somethin'?" Welden demanded, leaning against the wall. "Sweetheart, you got no idea how long it's been since I've had a romp with somebody like you."

"Me first," Burke said. "I'm the one who saw her first!"

"We'll toss a coin for her," Welden declared, reaching for her.

Tonie, like her uncle, had dealt with men of their sort at home in Independence, and she reacted without hesitation. Reaching into her apron pocket, she withdrew the long, pointed pair of scissors she had been using in the infirmary to cut cloth for bandages. Holding the scissors like a dagger, she pointed them at the larger man.

"Touch me again, just once," she said, "and I'll carve out your gut."

Welden could only stare at her, speechless.

Burke laughed. "You goin' to let a woman talk t' you that way?"

"The same goes for you," Tonie told him. "But your stomach is smaller, so you'll get it in the groin."

The pair continued to gape at her, then looked at each other.

Tonie knew she was no match for them, but she was not intimidated. If they persisted, she would inflict as much serious damage on them as she could and would make enough noise to bring the entire wagon train company and a troop of cavalry to her assistance.

Welden was still sober enough to realize he had made the mistake of approaching a wildcat. He took a single step backward. His experience with respectable women was limited, but he could tell by her expression that she would not hesitate to use the scissors. He wanted a girl, but he did not want to be stabbed.

"Get out of my way," Tonie said, her green eyes

blazing. "I'm not going to tell you again." Her arm poised and her body tense, she was prepared to strike.

Welden wilted and stepped aside.

"You, too," she told the shorter man.

Burke flattened himself against the log wall.

Tonie swept past them, disdainfully, without a second glance.

"Holy Lord," Burke muttered. Taking a flask from his hip pocket, he drank so quickly that some of the whiskey dribbled down his unshaven chin.

Weldon took the flask from him and helped himself. "To hell with her," he said, wiping his mouth on his greasy sleeve. "She ain't the only doe in the forest."

Tonie didn't mention the incident to anyone. She knew what her uncle and Whip thought of the pair, and having defended herself successfully, she put the matter out of her mind.

An hour and a half passed before the members of the wagon train company were belatedly called to supper. As the men, women and children filed into the adjoining dining halls, a scowling Ted Woods, who stood near the entrance, tapped Whip on the shoulder and drew him aside.

"The reason supper is late," he said, obviously concerned, "is because Cindy and Cathy didn't show up to take charge."

"It could be they're resting," Whip replied. "They may have fallen asleep and not wakened."

"That isn't like either of them," Ted said stubbornly. "I don't like this one bit, and I aim to find out what's going on." He started off down the long corridor.

Sighing quietly, Whip decided to accompany him. He knew about Ted's volatile temper. If Cathy and Cindy were sleeping through the supper hour, a luxury they deserved, he didn't want Ted making an unwarranted scene.

They walked together in silence. Then, as they drew near the officers' room the two girls were sharing, they heard sounds of a scuffle and increased their pace. The door was closed, but they could hear a man's harsh laugh. "Hold still, sweetheart, you're goin' to like this!"

Whip quickly opened the door. Cathy and Cindy were lying on their beds, sprawled on their backs, their hands tied behind them and gags in their mouths. Looming over them were Burke and Welden, but the girls had not been completely subdued and were kicking violently, their skirts flying high, as they tried to ward off their attackers. Furniture had been upset, and clothing was scattered around the room. Cathy and Cindy had fought hard.

Just as the door opened, Cindy managed to free herself from her bonds and, reaching up, she clawed Welden's face.

He cursed her and cuffed her hard across the face.

Seeing this, Ted Woods gave a low, animal-like growl and hurled himself at Cindy's attacker.

Burke had been in the process of lowering himself onto Cathy's body when he heard Ted, and he looked across the room in surprise. At that moment Whip grasped him by the collar, hauled him to his feet, and drove a fist into his face.

Burke was drunk, but he had enough sense to realize he had to protect himself. He drew a knife.

Whip gave him no chance to use it. He put all of his weight behind a short punch to Burke's stomach and, as Burke doubled over, Whip took the knife from his hand and threw it under Cathy's bed.

"Fight like a man," Whip said, moving forward again.

Burke tried to protect himself from the hammer-like fists that battered his face and body, but even if he had been sober, he would have been no match for the thoroughly aroused Whip.

It was one of Whip's maxims that the man who wanted to win a battle had to keep his head. Now, even though he was angry, he was able to follow his own advice. His mind continued to function clearly as he gave Burke one strong blow after another.

One of Burke's eyes was closed, blood trickled from a corner of his mouth, and he retreated to a corner where he cowered, trying to escape the beating by covering his face with his arms. But his feeble attempts were useless.

Whip broke through his guard with a right to the face that straightened him. Then a well-placed left caught

Burke in the stomach, again doubling him over, and another right caught him full in the face again, slamming him against the wall. He crumpled to the floor and stayed there.

Cindy had removed her own gag and Cathy's, then untied the other girl's wrists. They huddled together, still dazed by the rape that had so narrowly been averted.

Whip had temporarily forgotten Ted and the other intruder. He turned to see the blacksmith sitting astride Welden's chest. Ted's powerful hands were clutching the man's neck, choking the life out of him, while at the same time he was raising the man's head and smashing it repeatedly on the floor.

"Enough, Ted! You've finished him, so leave him be!" Whip shouted.

Ted didn't hear him; he was conscious only of the man who had assaulted Cindy. There was a wild, maniacal expression in the blacksmith's eyes, and it was plain he was determined to kill the man. Welden tried in vain to remove the hands that were choking him. No man could long survive the punishment he was getting. Whip came up behind the blacksmith and tried to pull him away, but Ted's strength was too great.

All at once the room was filled with soldiers. Two of them joined Whip, and all three, straining together, finally managed to pry Ted away from Welden, who sucked in air painfully.

Colonel Jonathan was standing in the entrance to the room, and Whip quickly told him what had happened.

By the time he had finished, Ted Woods had regained his senses. He stood quietly, flexing his fingers and gazing at Cindy. "I—I hope you're all right, ma'am," he said diffidently.

Cindy could only nod. Not only was she shaken by her own experience, but Ted's violence had frightened her, too. She knew that if Whip and the officers had not intervened, Welden would be dead by now. She couldn't yet think straight, but it was frightening to know that a man with Ted's temper and bull-like strength had appointed himself as her protector.

"Haul those two into the corridor so the ladies can compose themselves," the Colonel directed.

Soldiers propelled the guilty pair into the hallway. Burke was still bleeding, trying to focus with one eye, and Welden, not yet breathing normally, grasped the back of his head, his gaze flicking apprehensively in the direction of Ted, who was following behind, along with Whip and Colonel Jonathan.

"What do you have to say for yourselves?" Colonel Jonathan asked, after closing the door to the girls' room.

There was a long silence before Burke mumbled, "We was just havin' an innocent little jamboree. Nobody got hurt until these two bulls came into the room."

"Are you suggesting that the ladies were accepting your advances willingly?" The Colonel spoke quietly.

Welden nodded as best he could.

"You lie!" Ted roared, and would have started forward again had Whip not laid a restraining hand on his arm.

"If that's the case," Whip said, "perhaps you'll be good enough to tell me why the ladies' hands were tied and gags were placed in their mouths."

The accused pair had no reply and remained silent.

Hearing what Whip had said, Colonel Jonathan said, "You're guilty." His voice was icy. "You were granted the privilege of a sanctuary here, and you abused our hospitality—mine, the army's, that of our civilian guests, and above all, that of the people of the United States, who own this property. Gather your belongings and leave. At once!"

The two men were shocked by the severity of the sentence. "We told you when we got here how we lost our horses," Burke said, speaking with difficulty. "Lord Almighty, Colonel! It's more'n forty miles from here to the tradin' post at Council Bluffs!"

Desperation made Welden eloquent. "Even in good weather, we'd have the devil's own time tryin' t' reach Council Bluffs, what with all them towns o' the Omaha b'tween here and there. But there ain't nobody can make it there in the kind o' weather there is out yonder right now."

Colonel Jonathan was unyielding. "Where you go or how you proceed there is none of my concern."

"But we'll die out there!" Burke was alarmed.

Colonel Jonathan ignored him. "Lieutenant Myers," he said to his aide-de-camp, "see to it that these men are escorted to the back gate. Make sure all of their belongings are delivered to them there, and have them escorted off government property. Notify the sentries that if they return or are caught loitering in the barns or elsewhere, they're to be shot on sight."

"Yes, sir," the aide said, and saluted.

"I deeply regret this incident, Mr. Holt," the Colonel said. "I'll be grateful if you'll tell the ladies I'll apologize to them in person tomorrow, when they'll be better able to receive me." He turned and went off to his own quarters.

Welden and Burke knew they could not disobey the order, so they allowed themselves to be led away.

Whip and Ted found themselves alone in the corridor.

The door opened, and the two girls emerged. They had changed into clean dresses and combed their hair.

"We heard Colonel Jonathan's verdict, but I can't say I feel sorry for those two," Cindy said.

Cathy went straight to Whip. "Thank you," she said simply. "It would have been ghastly for me if you hadn't arrived when you did—and taken care of that beast."

Whip was embarrassed and shrugged aside Cathy's thanks. "Are you all right?"

"Oh, yes. My wrists are raw, but they'll heal fast enough."

Still uneasy because of Cathy's obvious gratitude, Whip turned to the other girl. "What about you, Cindy?"

"Oh, one side of my face may be black and blue tomorrow, but I'll cover it with rice powder and nobody will know." She laughed, and there was an element of bravado in the sound. "I knew worse in the place where I worked in Louisville."

It was the first time Whip had heard her refer to her previous life as a prostitute, and he hastily changed the subject, pointing to Ted. "It was Ted who got me to come here with him to investigate. He's the one who figured there was something the matter when you didn't show up to fix supper."

Shuffling his feet, Ted stared down at the floor. This shy, tongue-tied giant bore scant resemblance to the wild-eyed demon who so easily would have killed a man only a short time earlier. For the moment his murderous impulses had been quieted. But his problem, as he knew better than anyone else, might flare up again without warning, and the consequences could be disastrous.

VII

Henry John Temple, Third Viscount Palmerston, was irascible, imperious, and endowed with unlimited energy, qualities that caused him to be feared by his subordinates, shunned by his peers, and disliked by his superiors, of whom he recognized only one, the young Queen Victoria. Palmerston held an Irish peerage, which made it possible under the rules of Parliament for him to hold a seat in the House of Commons. Passionately devoted to the protection and expansion of the world's greatest empire, he was, in his mid-fifties, universally recognized as perhaps the best Foreign Secretary in his nation's illustrious history.

One of the few men in England who was not afraid of him was the equally aristocratic Sir Edwin Knowlton, who had been his classmate at Harrow four decades earlier. Their goals were identical, but Knowlton elected to serve the Crown in the shadows. Not only had he created an espionage and counterespionage service of extraordinary efficiency—an organization that operated with precision around the globe—but his own desire for anonymity gave him a leverage in his dealings with the mighty, even the powerful Palmerston. Although such people knew him to be extraordinarily competent, they also knew he would never be a threat to their power or position.

Knowlton sat quietly in the enormous office overlooking Pall Mall, a faint smile on his face, making no comment as he listened to the Foreign Secretary speak.

"The Oregon country," Palmerston said in his booming voice as he paced the length of the Persian rug that covered the magnificent hardwood floor, "is ours. By right of discovery, by right of occupation, and by right of international law. The Americans go too far when they claim it, and I refuse to tolerate their impudence!"

"Do sit down, Temple," Sir Edwin said mildly. "Or you'll lose your voice before you make your policy speech in the Commons this afternoon."

"Quite so." Palmerston retreated to his desk, sat, and drummed his restless fingers on the polished surface. "Obviously the Americans want an outlet to the Pacific, and I say to them, take California from the Spaniards. Everything north of it belongs to us!"

"Temple, you're wasting your time and mine by telling me a policy we've been following for years."

"Edwin, you're being impertinent."

"Who has a better right? Get to the point."

"Very well,'" Palmerston said crisply. "American newspapers and magazines are filled with articles about the excitement being created by the first wagon train to cross North America. Congressmen make patriotic addresses on the subject, and a dozen new wagon trains are being organized. We must act—quickly—to prevent that first wagon train from reaching Oregon, or we'll be forced to compromise our own claims. Last year I made it clear to you that the train now in motion must be halted."

"So it shall." Knowlton spoke with confidence. "One of my very best agents is in the field attending to the matter."

"Who is he?"

"A chap named St. Clair. He has a distinguished record, and he's completely reliable."

"What is he doing?"

Knowlton was deflated. "To tell you the truth, Temple, he hasn't been in touch with my office in recent months. He's functioning somewhere in that Godforsaken American wilderness, and until he can get in touch with our garrison at Fort Vancouver, his means of communication with us are limited."

Palmerston's temper rose. "Then send out another agent, Edwin. Send a dozen! You know the stakes are high!"

As Sir Edwin Knowlton's subordinates knew, he, too, had a short temper. "Obviously you haven't considered the consequences. A mission of this sort is extremely delicate. If the American government should get wind of what we're doing, there will be hell to pay. The former President, Andrew Jackson, will demand that America go to war with us again, and he'll be supported by public opinion, even though President Van Buren is a civilized man who wants peace."

"I don't want war with the United States," Palmerston said slowly. "I'm not certain our own people would tolerate it. But the Oregon territory is a rich prize, Edwin, and we can't let it slip out of our hands. The American claim is as valid as our own, and if they settle there first, we'll have the devil's own time trying to squeeze them out."

"It will be the better part of a year before that train reaches Oregon. Long before then, I expect a report from St. Clair telling me he's succeeded. On the off-chance that something untoward should happen to him, of course, I have several competent agents I can send from Fort Vancouver to help him."

Again Palmerston drummed on his desk. "The situation does seem to require patience."

"I have faith in St. Clair," Knowlton said.

The Foreign Secretary stared at him. "For your sake, Edwin, for his and for the Empire's, I hope your confidence in him isn't misplaced."

Henry St. Clair was annoyed with himself. Driving his wagon across the Great Plains with his riding horse tethered to it, he bundled himself in his heavy cloak, pulled his hat lower onto his head, and reflected that he was stupid. A senior British agent, engaged in carrying out a delicate, vital mission had to think in terms of the present, and he had been remiss. He should have known he was leaving St. Joseph far sooner than necessary, since he could cover three or four times as much territory in a single day as the accursed wagon train could manage. St. Joseph wasn't London, not by a long way, but at least he had slept in a comfortable bed there, consumed edible meals, and had found a whore to his liking. Now he found himself in the middle of nowhere. Regardless of where the wagon train might have halted during the cold weather, he had to find adequate shelter for himself and his horses during the rough winter months that still stretched ahead.

Certainly he could take no action against the wagon train until spring, no matter what his superiors ordered. Men who spent their entire careers behind London desks had no real understanding of what went on in the field, so he usually ignored their specific directives. When he became an executive, he wouldn't demand miracles from his subordinates.

His problem, as he well knew, was that he had performed seemingly miraculous feats in India, North Africa and Siberia, so London was expecting him to produce again. Very well, he would, but he had no intention of moving alone against the wagon train. He had tried that approach and had almost been captured for his pains. His last venture had been ill-starred from the outset, but now he was confident he had a workable plan, both for surviving the winter and for sabotaging the wagon train.

Since leaving St. Joseph, he had encountered bands of Indians from several tribes, and thanks to his ability to speak Kiowan, which all of the Plains nations understood, he had avoided trouble. Now he was driving into territory controlled by the ferocious Cheyenne, who were alleged to be the equals of the dreaded Blackfoot. He hoped the Cheyenne would stop him, for they were part of his plans.

That morning he had been sighted from a distance by a lone warrior, riding bareback, who had watched him across the snow-laden prairie for a time and then had cantered away. The brave had been a Cheyenne, easily identified by his multi-feathered headdress, and Henry expected a return visit at any time. No tribe, the Cheyenne in particular, would be able to resist the temptation of killing a lone white traveler who owned several horses.

The day dragged on. Henry was chilled and wanted to halt to build a fire, but it was wiser not to change his plans at this point. At last his patience was rewarded. He saw four riders in the far distance, all of them moving rapidly toward him.

He halted his wagon team, mounted his riding horse, and waited confidently. Tactics he had used in dealing with other savages would be effective again.

The riders were coming toward him at a breakneck pace, obviously intending to overwhelm him. Holding his rifle across his knees, Henry St. Clair drew a pistol and fired it into the air, then took care to reload it with all possible speed.

As he had anticipated, the riders immediately slowed to a trot and became more cautious. Their headgear told him they were Cheyenne, so he was pleased.

The braves were carrying bows and arrows. They realized, however, that he was carrying a rifle, which had a far greater range, so they conferred on how to subdue this stranger without being hurt themselves.

Henry cut short their talk, astonishing them by raising his right hand in the universal Indian sign of friendship and greeting. "The son of the great sachem," he called at the top of his voice in Kiowan, "bids his brothers of the Cheyenne nation welcome."

His words and his fearless attitude bewildered the warriors, and they inched closer.

Henry had aroused their curiosity, which was precisely what he wanted. Now he had to dispel their suspicions. "The son of the great sachem brings gifts for all," he told them. Reaching into his saddlebag, he withdrew four old pistols, which dated back to the American Revolution. He held them over his head so the warriors could see them.

The Cheyenne, fascinated continued to draw nearer. The black and white streaks of paint smeared on their faces gave them a gruesome appearance.

They were close enough now for Henry to throw each of them a pistol, which he did. Then he repeated his initial gesture of firing one of his own pistols harmlessly into the air. While the warriors continued to observe him closely, he reloaded it. Now came the critical moment: he took a handful of bullets from a pouch and showed them to the Cheyenne.

His pantomime needed no explanation. The braves knew this white man was offering them the magic arrows he used in his firestick. They also knew that, although it would be easy enough to cut down this lone traveler with their spears, they didn't know how to use these powerful, alien weapons.

They had risen to the bait, and Henry became even more confident. "The son of the great sachem across the sea," he told them, "has many firesticks for other Cheyenne. And he will teach them how to shoot."

Greatly impressed, the Cheyenne communicated with each other with gestures.

Then Henry provided the final, clinching argument. He reached into his saddlebag again, and, drawing out a small flask of the cheap whiskey he had procured in St. Joseph, he tossed it to a brave whose intricately fashioned headdress indicated that he was the leader of the group.

The warrior examined the container, frowning in puzzlement as he turned it over in his hands. Then he saw the cork, pulled it out cautiously, and sniffed. Suddenly his stern expression vanished and, grinning broadly, he raised the flask to his mouth and drank. He shuddered in pleasure and passed the flask to the nearest of his companions.

Henry waited patiently until each of the Cheyenne had consumed a portion of the whiskey. There was no doubt in his mind that he would achieve his objective. "The son of the great sachem has drink for all of the braves of the Cheyenne."

The last resistance evaporated. The senior warrior raised his arm and gave the peace sign, and the others followed his example.

The rifle remained in place across Henry's knees as he calmly repeated the sign. He had dealt with too many savages in too many parts of the world to take unnecessary risks.

"Will the son of the great sachem ride to the town of the Cheyenne?" the senior warrior asked.

"It will be a great honor," Henry St. Clair replied gravely. He bent down and picked up the reins of the horses that pulled his wagon, then indicated he was ready to depart.

The Cheyenne formed a protective escort, two riding on the left and the other two on the right as Henry moved ahead, leading the wagon team. Even if they should encounter a war party of another tribe, none would dare attack a man who was enjoying Cheyenne hospitality.

The British agent rejoiced silently. He had found the perfect shelter for himself and his animals and would be safe through the rest of the winter, regardless of whether his hosts lived in huts or tents of skins. And, although the Cheyenne didn't yet know it, they would become his allies and would become the best of all instruments that would destroy the Oregon-bound wagon train.

The latest blizzard was the worst yet, and it raged for seventy-two hours. When the skies cleared, the reflection of the sun was dazzling, and the civilians and soldiers at Fort Madison saw that the snow covering the prairie was at least three feet high, while some drifts were mountainous. Whip predicted there would be a thaw soon, ultimately to be followed by another freeze, and that during the temporary warm spell the snow would melt appreciably. Arnold, Mack, and the army scouts agreed with him.

Until the temperature rose, however, it was impossible for anyone to leave the fort—even to hunt, fish, or gather wood. Now everyone understood why Whip had insisted that large stores of meat and fish be smoked and preserved and why he had demanded that high stacks of wood be cut and stored.

Many people had little to occupy their time. Small children became cranky, crying for no apparent reason, while older boys and girls were mischievous, playing tricks on their elders and trying to blame each other. Men became edgy, and women started to snipe at one another.

Ernie von Thalman, in his capacity as president of the train, was required to act as judge of countless petty disputes. He performed ably, doing what was required of him, but privately told Whip he was weary of senseless, infantile arguments.

No one was more bored than Eulalia Woodling. The young officers of the garrison had discovered, one by one, that she had no real interest in any of them and was flirting with them only for entertainment, so they now tended to avoid her. Members of the wagon train company, who resented her patronizing airs, were polite when necessary but paid her little attention.

The worst of her predicament, in her own eyes, was working as a kitchen assistant. On her father's plantation, all cooking had been done by slaves, and she hadn't even been responsible for planning meals or approving menus. Now, wearing an apron covering dresses that would have been more appropriate at a lawn party than in a frontier fort, she made pancakes by the hundreds, rolled dough for bread, butchered meat, and cleaned winter berries and root vegetables. Eulalia deeply resented the authority exercised by Cathy van Ayl. She was convinced that the other women working in the kitchens were united against her and forced her to perform the most menial tasks.

Her weary father was not sympathetic to what Eulalia regarded as her plight. "We aren't the first people to lose a fortune during hard times," Major Woodling said, "and we won't be the last. You and Claiborne should be glad for the opportunity to make new lives for yourselves. It's for your sakes that I joined this expedition to the Oregon country, and your lack of gratitude and understanding pains me. I know of no reason you should be spared when all the other women are doing their fair share. Besides, you spend only a few hours in the kitchen every day, and the rest of your time is your own, so I can't feel sorry for you."

Unwilling to accept advice that conflicted with her own desires, Eulalia devised a scheme that, she hoped, would win her release from the kitchen detail that she loathed. Perhaps, she thought, if she demonstrated her incompetence, she would be discharged.

She put her plan into operation that same afternoon. Sitting alone in a corner of the kitchen, she paid no attention to the chatter of the others as she peeled potatoes.

There an apron-clad Cathy van Ayl, holding a wooden spoon she used for tasting, came upon her. Stopping and watching her for a few moments, Cathy became irritated. "Really, Eulalia."

"Is something wrong?" Eulalia's wide eyes were innocent.

"Food is our most precious commodity, and we're lucky to have the luxury of enough potatoes for a meal. But look what you're doing to them!" She reached down and picked up a length of peel, to which almost a half-inch of potato still adhered. "This is wasteful. You're throwing away almost as much as you're using."

Eulalia became sullen. "If you don't like what I'm doing, give the work to someone else. You won't hurt my feelings."

Cathy kept a firm grip on her temper. "You've been assigned to the kitchen staff, so we're stuck with each other. I don't enjoy giving orders any more than you like taking them—"

"Oh yes, you do! You just love lording it over me!"

The other women stopped talking and listened to the confrontation.

"What I think or feel isn't important," Cathy said, still speaking quietly. "It's my duty to see that no food is wasted and that our meals are well prepared. I didn't ask for the job. I was given it, and I try to discharge my duties to the best of my ability. I suggest you do the same. Not for my sake but for your own and for the sake of everyone else in the company."

Several of the women nodded in sympathetic agreement.

Their opposition infuriated Eulalia. Not one of them had enjoyed the advantages she had known throughout her childhood. Not one of them had ever lived in a great mansion and had an army of servants to wait on her. Not one had ever owned a huge wardrobe of silk gowns or had been known throughout several counties as a belle. They were jealous of her, and the worst was this blonde who put on airs without cause.

"If I don't peel potatoes to your liking, Miss High and Mighty," she said, "get someone else to do it." She started to rise.

Cathy surprised herself by putting a hand on the girl's shoulder and pushing her back into the chair, then brandishing the wooden spoon only inches from Eulalia's face. "Anyone in this wagon train who wants to eat must do a fair share of the work, and that's final," she said. "If you don't know how to peel potatoes, I'll show you. Watch!" She dropped the spoon onto a counter, snatched the knife from Eulalia, and expertly, swiftly, peeled a potato. "There," she said, "Even a child can do it, and I'm sure you're not all that clumsy."

Reluctantly Eulalia returned to work. That was the end of the unpleasant incident, but the basic problem remained.

The next day Eulalia complained to Whip about her situation, but he firmly rebuffed her. Next she flirted with Dr. Martin, much to Tonie Mell's irritation, but stopped when she realized he was not in a position to help her.

Gradually it dawned on Eulalia that Ernie possessed considerable power and influence because of his position as president, and because he was an Austrian baron, she regarded him as a social equal who should understand her situation. So she went to him. He succeeded in curbing his annoyance at her requests, but nevertheless made it plain that no one was exempt from duties. Girls of thirteen and fourteen were required to perform chores, he told her, and suggested that if she disliked the kitchen so much, she might be able to trade responsibilities with one of the girls who curried and watered the horses. Suspecting that Ernie was laughing at her, Eulalia dropped the subject.

So she continued to work in the kitchen, and the rest

of the time she was restless and bored. She had no interest in sewing or preserving berries, and she shrank from such activities as smoking meat and fish or curing buffalo or deer hides.

Whip was unfailingly courteous to Eulalia because he was polite to all women. However, she was so eager to win approval from men that she misread his attitude and assumed he was interested in her. So she made up her mind to make another attempt to win his support, and this time she planned her campaign with care.

She made it her business to spend at least a few minutes each day chatting with him. Aware of his basic shyness with women, she adopted a subtle approach rather than flirting with him openly. She spoke to him only on matters that she knew were of concern to him, such as his hunting trips, and she made no mention of her own situation. She went out of her way to make certain he was served his favorite cuts of meat at meals.

Cathy knew that Eulalia was making a play for Whip, but she refused to compete. If Whip wanted to develop a closer relationship with her, Cathy told Tonie and Cindy, he would have to do it on his own initiative. Consequently she withdrew even further than she intended or realized: the result was unfortunate. It gave Eulalia an even better chance to strengthen her ties with Whip.

In the days that followed the big blizzard, Whip spent all of his time at the fort, so Eulalia was able to talk with him more frequently. Observing his routines, she discovered that he visited the kitchens late each afternoon, before the cooking staff reported for duty to prepare supper. So she made certain to be the first of the cooks to appear.

Eulalia learned that Whip checked the contents of the cold bins, shelters partly exposed to the winter air, where frozen and smoked meats and fish were stored. It was no accident that he usually arrived just in time to find her braving the elements in the open passageway outside the twin kitchens, taking meat or fish from one of the shelves.

These tactics failed to bring him any closer to her, however. Although he was still pleasant and polite to her, he remained somewhat remote. Eulalia made up her mind to step up the pace of her campaign.

One afternoon, after dressing in one of her prettier frocks and applying cosmetics, she made certain she arrived at the kitchens before he did. She listened for his approaching footsteps, which she recognized, then quickly went out into the freezing passageway and began to tug at a heavy, frozen section of buffalo meat.

The cold chilled her, the frozen meat stung her hands, and she dropped the heavy piece of meat onto the snow underfoot. As a child, she had learned to weep at will when she had wanted something that she could attain in no other way, so when Whip came out into the passageway, he found her shivering in the cold, her cheeks wet. "What's this?"

"I dropped this meat," she sobbed, pointing at it. "I can't leave it on the ground, but it's too heavy for me to carry."

"I see no problem, ma'am," he said, hoisting the section onto his shoulder and carrying it into the kitchen for her.

Eulalia's lashes were still attractively damp, but her smile was radiant as she followed him. "I'm so grateful to you, Mr. Holt," she said fervently.

"I didn't do much of anything," he protested.

"Oh, but you did. You don't understand. I don't know much about cooking, and the women are always teasing me. You've saved me from an unpleasant night. They would have spent our whole time here this evening finding ways to tell me how clumsy I am."

He was embarrassed by her frankness.

Seeing this, Eulalia instantly changed her approach. "If you have a moment to spare, Mr. Holt, perhaps you could help me."

"I'll be glad to try, ma'am."

"Until we came to Fort Madison and the weather turned so cold, I'd never even heard of frozen meat. In fact, I was afraid to eat any of it for days."

"No need to be," he said. "Throw a frozen buffalo steak or a leg of venison on a campfire, and it tastes as fresh as if it had been shot just an hour earlier. What most folks don't know is that frozen meat won't keep long after thaws come. Then, if the weather becomes very cold again, you have to throw it away. Meat that's been frozen twice makes people sick. I learned that from the Cheyenne tribe when I spent a winter with them."

"That's very good to know. I'll remember it." She actually didn't care in the least what they were discussing. "My problem is that I have a dreadful time cutting it. This section is too big to put on a kitchen fire, and it takes forever to thaw. So it has to be butchered now."

"Show me how you do it," Whip said.

Eulalia selected a long knife from a rack and began to saw the hard buffalo meat.

"No wonder it takes you so long. Here, I'll show you." Whip picked up a large cleaver and, wielding it deftly, cut about halfway through the entire section. "That's the first step. Now, try your knife again."

The girl made another attempt to saw. "You see? Nothing happens."

"Your knife is plenty sharp, and the point is just right, but you're using it the wrong way. I'll show you what I mean." Whip placed his hand over Eulalia's. "Push the point into the frozen meat this way, following the seams. As deep as you can. Then slowly push down on the handle so the metal blade digs into the rest of what you're trying to slice."

Eulalia paid scant attention to the instructions. At last she was making progress with this incredibly bashful man. They were standing so close together that their shoulders and hips touched. What's more, whether he knew it or not, he was actually holding her hand!

At that moment Cathy came into the kitchen, saw the couple in what looked like an intimate pose, and stopped short.

"Point and press, point and press," Whip said, unaware of Cathy's presence. "That's all there is to it."

Cathy inadvertently caught her breath. Eulalia turned

for an instant, saw the other girl, and couldn't resist smiling in triumph. Cathy picked up her skirts and swept out of the kitchen, her head high.

"Now you try it by yourself," Whip said, not aware that Cathy had entered and left the kitchen.

Trying to concentrate for his sake, Eulalia made an attempt to cut the meat alone.

"That's better. Keep practicing, and you'll soon get the hang of it."

"Thank you, Mr. Holt," she said. "You'll never know how much these few minutes have meant to me."

He thought her expression of appreciation was overdone, but decided that was just her way of talking. "Glad to oblige, ma'am," he said.

Going back out to the passageway, Whip checked the contents of the bins, then went back inside by way of the other, adjoining kitchen.

He went through to the corridor beyond it and there came face to face with Cathy. Why, he wondered, was her only greeting an icy glare?

The thaws came, as those experienced with plains winters had predicted, and vast quantities of snow melted. The weather gradually became colder again, but it was now possible for men to penetrate the forest, either on horseback or on foot. Early one morning several parties of hunters left the fort. Meat supplies were shrinking, Whip said, and needed to be replenished. Even Ted Woods was pressed into service because his great strength would speed the process of hoisting the carcasses of game onto the backs of pack horses. So Hosea was alone in the blacksmith's shop, where he busied himself at his miniature forge.

In late morning a visitor arrived, riding a gelding and leading two pack horses. His name, he told the officer of the guard, was Emmett Watson, and he had business with the wagon train company. He was admitted to the fort and taken to the section occupied by the future Oregon settlers.

Dr. Martin was busy in the infirmary, and both Whip and Ernie had gone hunting, so he was received by the two oldest men on hand, Nat Drummond and Major Woodling. Watson, who was husky, bearded and fair-haired, was disappointed when he learned that neither the wagonmaster nor the president of the company was on hand. He preferred, he said, not to discuss his business with anyone else.

The noon meal was about to be served, and since so many of the men were hunting, everyone who had stayed behind could be accommodated in one dining room. Watson was invited as a matter of course to stay for the meal, and he quickly accepted, going into the dining room with Major Woodling while Nat moved off to join his wife.

"You're a Southerner, judging by your accent," the Major said.

"I make my home in Georgia, sir. But I travel all over the United States. This trip, I must admit, is the longest I've made." Watson kept an eye on the door and stiffened when Hosea came into the dining room, but he made no comment.

The main course consisted of a thick soup, made of beans and buffalo meat flavored with wild onions, one of the company's favorites. Major Woodling, enjoying the dish, noticed that the visitor continued to watch Hosea, who sat on the far side of the dining hall.

"This isn't bad," Watson said. "But I'd give my soul for a bowl of real gumbo. Well, it won't be long before I'm eating it again."

The Major made a shrewd guess. Although they were sitting by themselves at one end of a long table, he lowered his voice. "You're a bounty hunter," he said.

The man made no attempt to deny it. "Does it show all that much?"

"Only to me, I imagine," the Major replied, smiling. "I lived my whole life in South Carolina before I came on this expedition. Whenever one of my slaves ran away, I hired somebody like you to find him and bring him back."

"I've spent a half-year on the trail of that one," Watson said, his voice quietly menacing as he nodded in the direction of Hosea. "He's led me one merry chase."

"Six months." The Major was musing. "He must be valuable."

"His master is paying me twenty-five hundred dollars, plus all my expenses, to return him alive."

"That's a small fortune."

"So it is, but this one is no ordinary slave. They claim he's very clever."

"Indeed he is," Woodling agreed.

"What's more, his master owns a very large plantation, and he's afraid he'll lose many more slaves unless this one is returned. So the bounty is cheap in the long run."

"You're not going to earn it," Major Woodling said.

Watson eyed him.

"Hosea is enormously popular with everybody on the expedition. He has more than made himself useful. He's made some valuable contributions to the company's welfare, and he's regarded as a free man."

"Is that the way you regard him, sir?"

Major Woodling was uncomfortable. "The way I feel doesn't matter. There are hundreds of people in this group, and if a vote were taken, I'm sure it would be unanimous in Hosea's favor."

"Nobody has asked for a vote," Watson said, and ate the rest of his meal in glum silence.

People began to file out of the dining hall, Hosea among them, but Major Woodling continued to sit with the visitor. "There's no chance that Whip Holt, who's the wagonmaster, or Baron von Thalman, our president, will agree to let you take that black man away with you."

"I don't plan to ask them," Watson said. "Where do you suppose he's going now?"

The Major hesitated, and there was a long silence.

"You claim you're a Southerner and that you owned a plantation," Emmett Watson said. "I don't want your active help. I wouldn't even think of asking for it. I know you've got to live with these people, that they're going to be your neighbors in Oregon. All I want from you is a simple answer to a simple question."

Woodling stared down at the table, looking ashamed. "He spends most of his time in the blacksmith's shop."

"Where's that?"

"In back of the main buildings, near the stables."

Watson stood and held out his hand. "I'm glad to have made your acquaintance, sir," he said. "If you ever come back and have a need for my services, my partners and I have our office in Savannah. Anybody there will tell you where to find me." He strolled away, looking unconcerned.

Major Woodling sat at the table for a long time, his face buried in his hands.

Eulalia saw him and came to him. "What's wrong, Papa?" she wanted to know.

"I have a touch of indigestion, that's all," he told her harshly. "I'm going to lie down for a spell."

She watched him as he left the dining hall, his face averted.

At least an hour later, Danny and Chet returned from the lake, where they had been fishing. Their catch filled a large basket, which was so heavy that both boys had to carry it to the kitchens.

"We lost a lot of our hooks today," Chet said.

"If Hosea isn't too busy, maybe he'll make some more for us. Come on." Danny led the way to the blacksmith's shop. There they found a small fire burning, but Hosea was nowhere to be seen.

"I'll wait here for him," Danny said. "Why don't you see if you can find him somewhere in the fort?"

Chet agreed and dashed away.

Danny wandered around the shop, looking at a set of horseshoes Ted had just made, and pausing to admire some metal arrowheads that Hosea had fashioned for Stalking Horse. Then something on the Ashanti's worktable caught his eye, and he picked it up.

It was a partly eaten chunk of a sugar confection known as a praline, and without thinking, he raised it to his mouth, then stopped himself. Holding it there, he reminded himself that the praline was Hosea's, not his. All at once he realized it had a disagreeable odor, and still holding it, he stared at it. It certainly didn't smell like sugar.

He was still holding it when Chet returned.

"I can't find him anywhere, Danny. There was a visitor

here earlier in the day, and the last anybody knows, he was on his way out here to see Hosea. My mother and one of my brothers saw the man."

"Smell this," Danny said, and handed him the praline. "I found it on Hosea's worktable."

Chet held it beneath his nose, inhaled deeply, and then sniffed more cautiously. "This is strange. It smells like the medicine we had to give Pa when he was so sick. He took it every single day before he died; it's a smell I'll never forget."

"What did the medicine do for him?"

"It was supposed to make him hurt less. I'm not sure it did him much good, but it sure did make him sleep." All at once Chet realized what he had said and stared at his friend.

"It's a drug!" Danny exclaimed.

"Do you reckon this stranger used it to put Hosea to sleep? Why would he do that?"

"He's gone, isn't he? We'd better see the officer of the watch!"

The boys sprinted to the front gate of the fort, paying no attention to the slush through which they had to wade. There the officer of the watch confirmed that the visitor who had arrived earlier in the day had already departed, his pack horses heavily laden.

"Which way did he go?" Chet demanded.

The young lieutenant shrugged, indicating that he hadn't noticed and didn't care.

Chet thrust the piece of praline into his shirt pocket and spoke frantically. "Danny, we got to find Whip—fast!"

They raced to the rear of the fort, ran into the open, toward the forest. Melting snow impeded their progress, and they stumbled and slipped frequently, sometimes falling. But they refused to slow their pace. Although they were breathless, once they were in the forest, they shouted Whip's name again and again. The forest remained silent.

The boys moved deeper and deeper into the woods, not knowing how much time was passing, and after an eternity, they heard an answering shout. Soon an angry

Stalking Horse came into view, leading his pony. "Why boys make noise?" he demanded. "Deer run away!"

In their excitement, they spoke simultaneously.

The Cherokee raised a hand to silence them, then pointed an accusing finger at Danny. The boy explained until his breath failed, and then Chet took up the narrative, concluding by taking the partly consumed praline from his pocket.

Stalking Horse's eyes narrowed, but his expression did not change. "Man put Hosea to sleep? Steal Hosea and go away?" he asked incredulously.

"That has to be what happened," Chet replied.

"Right," Danny added. "Hosea isn't in the fort. And the last anybody knows, the visitor was going out to the blacksmith's shop."

"My ma and brother saw them," Chet said. "We talked to the officer of the watch, and he told us the visitor is gone. He only stayed a few hours, and that's mighty peculiar all by itself."

"He was riding one horse, and he had two pack horses, piled up with bundles. You know how little Hosea is. He could have been inside one of the bundles." Danny was still in a frenzy.

The Cherokee's eyes glittered, and he took charge. "Boys go back to fort. Wait for Whip, then tell. Stalking Horse go now. Find Hosea. Bring back." He leaped onto the bare back of his small mount, and the animal started off through the melting snow and slush.

The Indian had no intention of returning to Fort Madison; he wanted to waste no time. Going around the fort rather than through it, he halted outside the main gate, facing the Platte River, and studied the ground, searching for prints in the rapidly melting snow.

Stalking Horse proceeded methodically. There was virtually no chance that the man who had abducted Hosea had crossed the river, which was overflowing its banks. The Platte was filled with rapidly moving ice floes, and no one trying to handle three horses would be able to cross it safely. No man in his right mind would try.

Logic dictated that the kidnapper was more likely to have taken his victim in the direction of the white man's civilization rather than out across the endless plains. So Stalking Horse first searched the ground that extended eastward. Crouching and moving slowly, he carefully studied the snow, ice, and slush. Nothing escaped his notice. He covered one hundred feet, then another hundred, but did not pause.

Something off to his right, a few yards from the waters of the swollen river caught his eye. He went to the spot at once, squatted, and looked more closely. There, in the melting ice, was a partly obliterated hoof print, a portion of the mark made by a metal horseshoe still visible. It was the only sign he needed.

Now he understood the kidnapper's tactics. The man was riding close to the water's edge deliberately, in the hope that the overflowing waters of the Platte would wash away his trail. Clever, but not quite clever enough.

Mounting his pony again, Stalking Horse rode eastward at a canter, staying close to the bank of the river. Unless the abductor knew the area intimately, he would use the river as his guide, at least for a time.

Dusk came, and Stalking Horse slowed his mount to a walk, waiting for night. The sky overhead was clear, he noted. That was all to the good. A three-quarter moon would be a great help.

Now that the sun had vanished, the weather was growing colder again, and the Cherokee grunted in quiet satisfaction. The slush and melting snow were starting to freeze. Within an hour it would be impossible to hide hoofprints. And the ice floes continued to move swiftly toward the junction of the Platte with the Missouri some fifty miles away, so there was virtually no possibility that the man would try to cross to the south bank.

Stalking Horse grunted again when the moon rose. The ice was becoming slippery, so he moved farther from the river bank, certain that his quarry would be obliged to do the same.

The moon rose higher, and suddenly the Cherokee dismounted. There was no need for him to bend low now as he studied the ground. He could make out the hoofprints of three horses, two of them the huge beasts that white men used to pull their wagons and freight carts.

He knew beyond all doubt now that he was on the trail of the right person.

He checked his bow, which he replaced over his shoulder, then touched the point of his knife with his fingertip. He was in no hurry now. A tracker traveling alone and unencumbered could move far more rapidly than a man burdened with a prisoner and two pack horses. The moonlight was sufficiently clear for Stalking Horse to easily follow the trail in the snow. He was relaxed but alert, conscious of the possibility that he could overtake the bounty hunter and his victim at any time.

Another hour passed, however, before the sound of a man's voice somewhere ahead told him that he had reached the end of the trail. Apparently the man had made camp for the night. The voice rolled on, but the Cherokee couldn't yet make out what was being said.

Now Stalking Horse saw three horses, tied to trees, and he made a wide detour around them, then dismounted, telling his superbly trained pony with a double pat on the neck not to wander away.

Now the man's voice was clearer. "Damn you," he said. "You've got to eat, or you won't live long enough to get back to Georgia. I tell you plain, I'm going to collect that bounty, so you'll eat if I have to cram the food into you."

The man was crouching with his back to the Indian, speaking to Hosea. The Ashanti was propped in a sitting position against a saddlebag, his hands and feet tightly bound.

The moonlight enabled Stalking Horse to see that his friend's expression was indifferent. Apparently he was still under the influence of the drug.

Nevertheless, Hosea was conscious. He heard the Indian, a sound his captor failed to discern, and for an instant, he raised his eyes. No recognition showed in them, but he lowered his gaze again so swiftly that Stalking Horse knew Hosea realized that help was at hand.

The distance between the Indian and his quarry was so short that it was impractical to fire an arrow. Stalking Horse silently laid his bow and quiver on a snowbank, then reached for his knife.

Watson was holding a chunk of dried beef in front of his prisoner's face, waving it angrily as he tried to force the captive to eat.

Hosea was sufficiently recovered from the effects of the sleeping potion to cooperate actively with Stalking Horse. He had been on the verge of giving in to the demands that he eat, but now he stubbornly closed his mouth and clenched his teeth.

The bounty hunter cursed him, then pressed the fingers of one hand against the sides of his captive's cheeks in an attempt to force his mouth open. At that instant Stalking Horse leaped across the intervening space, his upraised knife ready to strike.

Watson had not achieved success in his unpleasant trade by being unaware. Instinct told him he was being attacked from the rear, and he rolled to one side. Stalking Horse brushed against him, but the full impact of the collision was lost, and it was impossible for the Cherokee to wield his knife.

All he succeeded in doing was toppling the helpless Hosea onto his side. Because of his bonds, the Ashanti found it extremely difficult to struggle back to a sitting position.

Watson started to reach for the pistol he carried in his belt, but Stalking Horse knew, once his initial rush had failed, precisely how his foe would react. Unable to use his knife for the moment because he had thrown himself out of position, Stalking Horse reached out with his free hand, caught hold of the bounty hunter's nose and simultaneously tried to jam his fingers into the man's eyes.

Unaccustomed to this primitive but effective form of attack, Watson emitted a scream of pain and rage as he groped in vain for his pistol. Then the Cherokee's knee landed with full force in his groin. The bounty hunter doubled over.

He was immobilized for no more than a second or two, however, and Stalking Horse realized his first move must be to disarm the man. He took hold of the pistol and managed to yank it out of the man's broad belt. Having used firearms only infrequently, he threw it aside.

It landed on the ground only inches from Hosea. But Hosea, unable to free his wrists, was powerless.

Again Stalking Horse struck with his knife, but Watson caught hold of his attacker's wrist with one hand, and with the other he punched him in the face.

It had been a long time since Stalking Horse had utilized the techniques he had been taught as a boy by the senior warriors of his nation. Now he smashed a knee into the pit of his foe's stomach, then raised a foot and brought his heel down with hammerlike force. It caught Watson on the kneecap. The pain was excruciating, and the bounty hunter fell back onto the ice, releasing his grip.

Now Stalking Horse was free to use his knife, but to the surprise of the still helpless Hosea, he didn't drive it into the white man's body. The little Ashanti thought he was must be dreaming as he watched a scene that no man could have predicted.

Stalking Horse had chosen to fight in the style of the whites rather than his own people. Hauling the bounty hunter to his feet, the Cherokee battered him with punches, smashing his face and body with a succession of blinding lefts and rights.

The bounty hunter made an attempt to protect himself and fight back, but he was bloodied and groggy. The few punches that Watson managed to land were feeble and meaningless.

At last the punishment he received was more than he could tolerate, and he sank to the ground, unable to move. Stalking Horse quickly picked up his knife and severed Hosea's bonds. Then he took the same rawhide thongs and used them to secure Watson's ankles and tie his hands behind his back. In a final gesture of contempt, he propped the man in the same sitting position against the saddlebag lying on the ground that he had used as a cushion for Hosea.

Hosea managed to drag himself to his feet, but the effects of the drug had not yet worn off, and he wobbled in a precarious circle as he tried to walk. It was obvious to Stalking Horse that the Ashanti could not return to

Fort Madison on foot. He was still too weak. Picking up his friend, the Cherokee put him in the saddle on the back of the bounty hunter's gelding.

Then he mounted his own pony and picked up the gelding's reins. As a final gesture, he took up the reins of the two pack horses, too.

Watson realized he was being abandoned to his fate in the wilderness. He was being left with no mount, no supplies. Even if he managed to loosen his bonds, he would be forced to make his way back to civilization alone and on foot through hard-packed snow. And there was always the strong possibility that he would be attacked and killed by braves of the Omaha nation that patrolled the area.

"You can't leave me here to die!" he said in desperation, his speech thick because his lips were swollen and split.

Stalking Horse raised a hand in salute, then started off in the direction of Fort Madison. He had lived his whole life in a world where mercy to a defeated foe was unknown, and he felt only contempt for the man who had kidnapped his friend.

Hosea was too dizzy to look back; he clung to the saddle as his Indian friend led him back to safety and a future as a free man.

Watson heard the sound of hoofbeats growing fainter. He was alone in the snow and ice, struggling feebly to break his bonds, his own future sealed.

VIII

Spring came early and unexpectedly to the Great Plains. Little by little the weather became warmer during the last few days in March, and a week later the snow had virtually disappeared. Soon a pale green mantle of young grass began to spread across the vast prairie.

One of the first to be affected was Cathy van Ayl. After supervising the preparation of breakfast one morning in early April, she climbed the stairs to an empty watchtower and stepped into the open. She didn't quite know what had impelled her to come here, but the sun was gentle, its warmth covering and soothing her, and she sighed aloud.

The sight of the new grass extending as far as she could see was a startling sight. A wave of homesickness swept over her.

In her native Connecticut the oaks and maples would be budding now, bushes that had been brown and inert would be coming to life, and the apple trees in the orchard behind the house would be showing the first signs of green on their new branches. On Long Island, the earth would have a sweet smell and the new owners of her farm would be planting beans, squash, lettuce, cucumbers, and sweet corn. Flounder would be starting to appear in Long Island Sound, and within a few months great schools of bluefish would provide food for everyone. Even now there would be clams, oysters, and crabs waiting to be plucked from the sea. How she missed that world she had left behind.

And yet, in spite of her regrets and her desire to look back, she found herself staring hardest toward the West, thc land of her future. Oregon still lay half a continent away, but in her new mood she felt confident she could make the journey. Certainly after all these months at Fort Madison, the Great Plains were no longer alien and frightening to her. Their very size inspired awe, and now that the land was turning green, it reminded her of the ocean she loved.

Yes, she told herself, there is beauty here. Perhaps she had been clinging to her love of home because the future she faced was so uncertain. Now, with the sun smiling from a cloudless sky and with the earth itself coming to life, something within her stirred. Perhaps it was the spirit of spring, perhaps it was something more.

She thought for a time, enjoying the warmth of the sun's rays, and all at once she knew. The Great Plains, like the Connecticut and Long Island she had left behind, like Oregon that lay beyond the horizon, were part of America. All of it was her land, all of it was her home.

That knowledge strengthened her resolve.

"When are we leaving?" she asked Whip later that day.

"Spring is giving you itchy feet," he said, grinning broadly. "Me, too."

"I'm ready," Cathy said, and at that moment she left the last of her idealistic, romantic dreams behind her. She was a woman meeting the frontier on its own terms, realistically prepared for new hardships because the goal she and her companions sought was worth any struggle.

"If the weather stays like this," Whip told Colonel Jonathan, "we'll soon be on our way."

Preparations for the journey to the Pacific became more intense. Axles and wheel hubs were greased, the floors of wagons were checked carefully, and those planks that had rotted during the harsh winter were replaced. Women devoted themselves to repairing rips and holes in the canvas covers of their wagons. Ted Woods received so many requests for new metal wheel rims that he was swamped, and Hosea pitched in to help him fill the orders.

The hunters and fishermen stepped up the pace of their activities, too, and there was considerable excitement when Mack Dougall reported that he had sighted a herd of buffalo grazing on the new prairie grass just beyond the forest. Whip was eager to add to the store of smoked and dried meat before the trek was resumed. The army garrison was in need of more food, too, so a hunting party was formed, the regiment's scouts joining the civilians.

Thirty hunters were in the group that left Fort Madison early the next morning. They skirted the western edge of the forest and after about two hours they reached the prairie. Whip moved up to the head of the column to join Mack, who was acting as the guide. The sun was pleasantly warm, in spite of a cool breeze from the Rockies, and there seemed to be an elasticity to the drying ground. The men were in high spirits.

Late in the morning Mack sighted the buffalo herd not far from the place where he had seen them the previous afternoon. The beasts were still grazing peacefully, and Whip estimated that there were three to four hundred head in the herd. The buffalo were hungry so they continued to eat, and there was no indication they might stampede. Whip motioned for the group to move still closer. With luck they could bring down a good food supply before the beasts were aware of their danger and raced away.

Suddenly Stalking Horse pointed to the north. "Omaha," he said.

The men stared and could make out a party of at least fifty mounted warriors also riding toward the buffalo. It appeared that they, too, needed to replenish their meat supplies.

The Omaha edged slightly closer to the white men but continued to ride in the direction of the herd without slackening their pace.

Many of the men grew tense. They had heard that the Omaha were belligerent, refusing to acknowledge the peace offers that Colonel Jonathan had sent them, and some of the troops had told hair-raising stories about encounters with them. No one knew whether the stories were true that the Omaha tortured a white captive for days, scalping him before allowing him to die, and no one wanted to find out.

Whip remained complacent, however, and Stalking Horse, Arnold, and Mack were equally unperturbed, as were the army scouts. Like the band of Omaha, they continued to ride toward the buffalo.

"We're outnumbered!" an anxious Claiborne Woodling declared. "We've got to protect ourselves."

No one replied, but one of the army scouts snickered.

The young man moved up to the head of the column. "Whip," he said, "you're going to attack first, aren't you?"

"I don't aim to attack anybody," Whip replied calmly. "I came out looking for buffalo. I found them, and that's good enough for me."

"My God!" Claiborne's temper began to flare. "You heard Stalking Horse say those braves are Omaha. Sure, we have rifles and they don't, but if they're just half as mean as I've heard, they can kill and wound a lot of us before we drive them off."

"Sonny," Arnold said gently, "leave be."

Claiborne's anger increased. "Maybe all of you are afraid of the Omaha and don't think you can drive them off, but I'm not built that way!" He raised his rifle and began to take aim at the moving line of warriors.

Whip reacted instantly. Grasping his own rifle by the barrel and wielding it like a club, he struck the younger man's rifle so hard with the butt that the weapon fell to the ground, forcing the column to halt.

"Never open fire until you're given the order," Whip said in a mild tone of voice that belied his anger and the violence of his act.

A red-faced Claiborne dismounted, retrieved his rifle, and returned to the saddle.

"Those of you who are worried can just sit back in your saddles," Whip declared, raising his voice so everyone in the party could hear him. "The Omaha aren't on the warpath any more than we are. At this time of the year, after game has been scarce through the winter, they're more interested in hides than in scalps. Just pretend you don't even see them, and we'll have no problems."

Claiborne still was not satisfied. "Then why do they keep moving closer to us?"

"We're about to do the same," Whip said, and nodded to Arnold.

Arnold immediately rode off toward the south. The army scouts, Stalking Horse, and Mack followed him, and soon they moved into a formation parallel to each other.

"We're forming a single line now," Whip explained. "The Omaha are doing likewise. Between the two groups, we'll make a semicircle to prevent the buffalo from heading back this way when the shooting starts. If we don't bag enough game before they panic, it will be easier to follow them than to meet their charge."

It was inconceivable to Claiborne that the wagon train hunters and the Omaha warriors could be working together without either group acknowledging the other's presence. But that was precisely what was happening. Whip took the innermost position at the right end of the line. As he moved into place, the senior Omaha warrior shifted into the position adjoining his, less than a stone's throw away. The two leaders studiously ignored each other and both concentrated on the buffalo.

The attack on the herd was coordinated in the same uncanny manner. "Get ready," Whip called. "We're going to open fire soon."

As he spoke, the senior warrior raised an arm in a signal to his own party. Both groups simultaneously slowed their pace. Then Whip raised his rifle, and the senior warrior aimed an arrow. "Fire!" Whip called, and as the rifles discharged a volley, the Omaha sent a stream of arrows into the herd.

Both groups continued to advance, shooting as rapidly as they could.

A large number of buffalo, most of them bulls but a few of them cows and calves, fell to the groud before the herd quite knew what was happening. Then a mature bull took command and raced westward. In almost no time, the surviving members of the herd fell into place behind him. The stampede was under way.

But the men from the wagon train continued to press forward for a few more minutes, as did the Omaha. Whip was the first to call a halt, and shortly thereafter the Omaha pulled to a stop, too. Dead buffalo littered the ground.

Then the task of removing the skins and butchering the carcasses began. The men of both parties dismounted. There was enough game available so the two groups remained on either side of an invisible but definite line. The inexperienced members of the wagon train had the feeling that if just one man of either group stepped over that line, a wild battle would begin.

But no man stepped over the line, and no battle was even contemplated. Mack rode back to Fort Madison to summon several drivers and their wagons, and the warriors did not even glance in his direction as he galloped off.

The unrepentant Claiborne, forced to do his share of the dirty and unpleasant work of butchering, was the only man who seemed even remotely conscious of the presence of enemies on the prairie. The rest of the wagon train party followed Whip's example and concentrated on the task at hand.

Even when Mack returned, leading two wagons to the site, the Omaha stolidly continued to mind their own business. More experienced than the Oregon-bound settlers, they were finished first. Lacking the convenience of wagons, they hung their game on either side of their heavily burdened ponies and rode away toward the east, skirting the forest as they headed back to their own villages. After they had gone, some of the wagon train men mentioned that they felt as though they had been dreaming. The meeting still seemed unreal.

"From now on, we're going to see plenty of Indians," Whip said, "so let this be a lesson to all of you. When a brave minds his own business, do the same thing. Always wait until he proves to be unfriendly before you go after him. And when you do shoot, make sure your aim is accurate!"

For several days everyone at Fort Madison ate fresh buffalo meat. Meanwhile every available man and boy went to work smoking some of the meat and packing the rest in barrels filled with a mixture of salt and vinegar. The regiment took its fair share, and Whip was pleased to discover that the wagon train's portion was large enough for him to give each family a barrel of pickled meat as well as a smoked shoulder or hind quarter. What with more game moving into the prairie, where the grass steadily grew higher, it was certain that no one would starve during the spring, summer, and autumn to come.

Canvas roofing was taken out of storage, spread on the wagons, and then made secure. The people began their final task of moving their personal belongings from the fort back into the wagons where they would once again have to live.

On their last day at the fort, Whip wrote a letter to President Van Buren and one to former President Andrew Jackson, whose idea it had been to send the wagon train to the Oregon country hoping to strengthen the United States's claim. Whip also wrote to Sam Brentwood and considerately told Cathy that if she wanted to write to her sister, he would see to it that the letter was included in the packet that an army courier would carry.

In his letter to Sam Brentwood, Whip wrote with candor to his old friend and one-time fellow mountain man who was responsible for his role in the wagon train adventure.

> By now the tenderfeet are getting calluses on their hoofs. The wild stallions and a few stray mares who were trying to break out of the corral are broken to saddles. I'm not saying there won't be stampedes now and again, but I'm keeping the herd under control.
>
> I couldn't operate without Stalking Horse. And Ernie is the best president the company could have elected.

We're in for some rough times when we come across some of the mean Plains tribes, but I'm not alarming anybody just yet. We'll take our troubles one at a time.

Give my regards to your wife and tell her that her sister is surely a fine lady. She does her work, she never complains, and she inspires many of the other women. There are times I don't believe she likes me much, but I can't blame her. I never had much to do with ladies, and I can see in her face that sometimes I offend her without meaning to. Don't bet either way on whether she'll be speaking to me by the time we reach Oregon.

His letter to Martin Van Buren was formal.

I beg to report, Mr. President, that all goes well with us. As you've already heard from me, we now number almost five hundred persons, all in reasonably good health. Most are eager to go on with our journey. Like it or not, there's no turning back.

I reckon the War Department has shown you Colonel Jonathan's full report on our brush with an Imperial Russian agent. No harm was done, but we're keeping our powder dry. So far we have had no more trouble with the British, but we're alert to the danger and can deal with it.

God willing, we should reach Oregon next year. I hope we'll hit our goal of arriving at the mouth of the Columbia River by the early autumn of 1839 or thereabouts, if not sooner.

So far there's no need for military reinforcement, but I'll pass along the word in a hurry if a bad crisis develops.

In his communication to former President Andrew Jackson, Whip expressed the sentiments closest to his heart.

Not a day passes, General, but I wish you were making this trip with us. Every time I shoot a buffalo or meet up with ornery Indians or have a tangle with renegades, I think of you. I know how much you would enjoy this great trek.

It isn't all adventure and excitement, of course. I never let myself forget that we've got to beat the English and get to the Oregon country first. For all I know, they're sending a wagon train across Canada to get there first. If they are, put your bets on me, even though I don't know anything about diplomacy. I keep remembering what you said one time, that the best diplomacy comes out of the muzzle of a rifle.

What surprises me is that leading a wagon train can be such a heavy responsibility. I try to live up to it.

When we first talked about it, I didn't give much thought to the people. Now they are in my mind all the time. Most of them have strong guts and high spirits. They don't let bad happenings discourage them. All the same, they're civilians, not soldiers, and I know that often they're terrified, so scared they don't know what to do.

I can feel, in a very small way, how you must have felt when you were President. I not only have to look out for these folks and set an example for them, but I have to be father and mother to them, too. They depend on me for everything. A few natural leaders have been developing, but they don't know the country (except for a couple of old scouts, men you'd like to know).

Some days, and I'm sure you'll know what I mean, I feel like riding off by myself and never coming back to the train. I can't do that, of course, and I won't. Some nights I feel fifty years older, and for a man who has always been proud of his stamina, I get an ache in my legs I've never had before.

But what we're doing is worth all the effort and danger and hardship. The names of the folks in this train may not be written in the history books of the future, but they're going to make your dream come true. Thanks to them, America will stretch from the Atlantic to the Pacific. I'm proud to be one of them.

Cathy van Ayl's letter to her sister was personal.

Claudia dear, your baby sister is growing up. I have no choice, really, and I'm finding that being an adult has its advantages.

I've stopped being homesick for Connecticut and mooning over the Long Island farm. For some reason I don't understand, this wilderness no longer frightens me the way it did. Don't think I'm all that brave, of course. I am afraid, sometimes. But I see how good-humored all the people are (well, most of them, not including a newcomer who I think you met, that horrid Eulalia Woodling). They put up with so much; this journey would try the soul of a saint, but they're cheerful, and even the smallest children show great courage.

Cindy has become my good friend. Tonie is wonderful, as she has always been. I miss you badly, but they help cushion my loss.

I know that you and Sam have been hoping that Whip Holt and I would get together, but don't set your hearts on it, dear. You were none too subtle in hinting, and at the time I was inclined to agree with you, but now I'm not so sure.

Not that I dislike Whip in the least. On the contrary, I find him fascinating. I wouldn't have thought that someone who appears so simple on the surface could be so complex. He really cares about the people on this train, although he tries not to show it. I guess he's embarrassed by the idea of showing even a little of what he feels. At least that's the way I interpret him.

He's the most infuriating man I've ever known. One day he's kind and considerate, actually sweet. The very next day he becomes so remote that he doesn't know I exist. He's so frustrating.

I've met no one else who really interests me. Most of the new people (they aren't all that new any more) who joined us at Independence are married already.

All I know is that, although I'd prefer to be married than stay single, I have no intention of making the kind of mistake I made when I married Otto. As Cindy says, and she's right, no man is better than the wrong man. I've learned that lesson, and I intend to abide by it.

Civilians and soldiers mingled that night at a final celebration supper. The women who worked in the kitchen baked dozens of cakes in honor of the occasion. Drinking was strictly forbidden on government property, but glasses of dandelion wine appeared rather mysteriously, and Colonel Jonathan took care not to notice them.

A final breakfast was eaten before dawn the next morning. Then pots and pans, dishes and knives were packed, and bedding was carried out to the wagons.

"I wish I had a troop or two of cavalry to send with you as escorts, at least as far as the Rockies," Colonel Jonathan told Whip as they shook hands in the clearing behind the main buildings of the fort. "This was a rough winter, so the Indians are going to be rambunctious, and you'll need all the help you can get."

"We'll get along on our own," Whip replied, feeling as confident as he sounded.

"I hope so."

"We'll have to, Colonel. There's little choice."

Tonie Mell, wearing her buckskins for the first time in weeks, rode up to Whip, smiling broadly. "Everybody is set and raring to go," she said.

He quietly mounted his stallion and rode to the open rear gate of Fort Madison. "We're Oregon bound," he said, but his voice was so soft that only Cathy, who sat with Hosea on the boards of her lead wagon, was able to hear him.

No band played as the wagon train moved out and resumed the long trek along the north bank of the swiftly flowing Platte River, but the train made its own music. Harnesses creaked, and the hoofs of workhorses and oxen provided a background rhythm. Wheels squealed until the grease worked its way in, and occasionally objects that had been insecurely packed inside wagons clattered as they fell to the floor.

Tonie brought up the rear, waiting until the wagons moved into the three-column formation that had become so familiar to everyone the previous autumn. As she turned in her saddle to wave a final farewell to the officers and soldiers gathered in the clearing, two seven-inch cannon boomed, their roar echoing across the Great Plains, bidding farewell to the pioneers.

Progress that first day was slow, as Whip had anticipated. The work horses and oxen had received too little exercise through the winter, and consequently were out of practice; they had also eaten well and were fat and lazy. People took too long to unhitch their teams and then hitch them up again after the midday break. The scouts returned early to report that all was well, as they had known it would be so close to Fort Madison. When a halt was called that day and the wood- and water-gathering details went to work, Whip estimated they had covered only seven miles. But he wasn't worried. He knew that the wagons would increase their speed little by little as members of the company got back in stride.

Everyone had been in good health for at least a week, and that first evening only Eulalia Woodling excused herself from work as a cook and went to Dr. Martin's wagon.

"I'm feeling poorly," she told him.

Bob Martin thought she looked radiantly healthy, but nevertheless took her into the wagon, which was used as a traveling infirmary, and asked her to lie down on the cot.

Eulalia stretched sensually as she lowered herself on the cot.

"What seems to be the matter?" the physician asked, placing a hand on her forehead and assuring himself that she was not running a fever.

"I'm not sure."

"What are your symptoms?" he asked patiently.

"Well, I keep thinking I may faint," Eulalia told him, managing to flirt with him as he studied her.

He had a hunch she was malingering. "Sit up, please." He held out a hand to help her rise to a sitting position, and Eulalia clung to his hand while he examined the pupils of her violet eyes.

At that moment Tonie came in through the open flap, intending to resume her practice of helping the physician after her own day's work was done. Bob stood with his back to her, but she saw Eulalia grasping his hand and looking soulfully at him. Quickly and silently, she retreated.

There was one sure way of finding out whether his diagnosis was right, the doctor thought. He went to a chest at the far end of the wagon, unlocked it, searched through drawers filled with powders, elixirs, and other medicines until he found what he wanted. Fashioning a cone out of a small sheet of paper, he poured something into it, then closed and locked the chest.

"Take this in a cup of hot water," he said. "Make certain the water is boiling when you pour it into the cup and let this substance soak for about five minutes. Then drink all of the brew."

"What is it, Doctor?" She managed to look attractive even when she was apprehensive.

"An herb tea that should cure your condition. If you need more, don't hesitate to come back." As he escorted her firmly to the rear flap, he was willing to wager that she would enjoy a remarkably rapid recovery. She would indeed be drinking an herb tea, as he had told her, but he had deliberately refrained from mentioning that the brew was bitter, difficult to swallow, and left a thoroughly unpleasant aftertaste. It was a prescription frequently used to effect rapid cures in people suffering from imaginary ailments.

Eulalia thanked him profusely before making her way back to her own wagon, her hips swaying just enough to insure that he continued to watch her.

The doctor was watching her, all right, but she wouldn't have been flattered by his thoughts. Smiling slightly and shaking his head, he reflected that he had never known a more badly spoiled, self-centered young lady. Perhaps the right man could tame her and bring her to her senses, but he had no intention of becoming that man.

Meantime, a furious Tonie had stormed off to the cooking fire, and there she found Cathy. "A few weeks ago you wanted to kill that woman," she said, "and I wish you had!"

Cathy had rarely seen her friend so angry. "Eulalia?"

"Who else? Don't blame Whip for letting her confuse him. No man on this expedition is immune!" Still spluttering, Tonie related what she had just seen.

"Perhaps it didn't mean as much as you think," Cathy said.

"I reckon it means as much—or as little—as her flirtation with Whip in the kitchen. I keep trying and trying to get Bob to look at me, but nothing happens. I guess I'll have to develop a Southern drawl and some bold manners!"

Cindy, who was working on the other side of Cathy, had been listening quietly. Now she dried her hands on her apron, took Tonie firmly by the arm, and led her away from the fire. "I want you to listen to me," she said.

Tonie was in no mood for a lecture from anyone. "Why should I?"

Cindy's smile was wry. "Because I've forgotten more about men than you know."

Tonie felt chastised. "Sorry," she muttered.

"What will you do when you see Dr. Martin?"

"Either slap him across the face or pretend he doesn't exist."

"You'll do neither," Cindy said. "You'll forget what you just saw. You'll be as sweet as ever toward him. When I've been sick, I've had to lie down on that cot, too, but that doesn't make me Dr. Martin's mistress!"

Tonie was so startled by the other girl's frankness that she didn't know what to say.

Aware that she had made an impression, Cindy went a step further. "Was he stretched out with her, making love to her?"

"Hardly!"

"Then you're playing a childish game. You're as bad as Eulalia Woodling, and you're doing just what she'd do if your positions were reversed."

"That's unfair," Tonie protested.

"Unfortunately, it isn't," Cindy said. "Most men are polite—and embarrassed—when a woman flirts with them. Instead of telling her to go away and leave them alone, they tolerate her. But that doesn't mean they like her or admire her or want to have anything to do with her."

Tonie was incredulous. "You're sure?"

"Dead sure," Cindy said. "Cathy made a mistake when she started to snub Whip, although your experience may open her eyes and cause her to change her tactics. But you're making the same mistake. Few men are so stupid they can't see through somebody like Eulalia. She's all front, with no substance behind it. We had a saying about girls like her in Louisville. She promises, but she never delivers. And men know it."

Tonie was in no position to argue with her. "I guess I'll have to take your word for it."

"Please do. I'm sure Dr. Martin has put her out of his mind, so you'll be smart to forget her, too."

All at once Tonie's manner changed. Her anger faded, and she shrugged and smiled. "You know," she said, "I sound as though I desperately crave a man, which I don't. Not all that much. If Bob were foolish enough to fall for Eulalia's tactics, he'd be a simpleton I couldn't respect, and I'd want nothing more to do with him."

"Precisely!" Cindy declared.

"We're in the same boat," Cathy said, "all three of us."

Her friends looked at her.

"We're young and—without throwing bouquets—reasonably intelligent and more than reasonably attractive. All of us have been brought up to believe that marriage is the final goal in life—"

"Not I, thank you," Cindy interrupted, her voice dry. "My mother was a whore, and I never knew any other life, except that I learned to read and write—and think for myself."

"All the same," Cathy insisted, "you've been influenced by the society around you, just as Tonie and I have. But now we're in a completely different situation."

"I see what Cathy means," Tonie said. "This wagon train has changed us from ordinary stay-at-home women into pioneers, whether we like it or not."

"I didn't like it at first," Cathy said, "but now I'm becoming accustomed to living on my own, and I have to admit—just between us—that in many ways I enjoy it. Even though I'm still frightened at times."

"I wouldn't say frightened," Tonie said. "Occasionally I'm uneasy." She paused, then shook her head vigorously. "I'm a liar, or I'm fooling myself. Of course I get scared."

"Would the plains be any less strange or terrifying if you had husbands?" Cindy demanded.

They thought about the question.

"I guess not," Cathy said.

"Definitely not," Tonie declared. "The hardships and the hazards are real, very real, and no man could cushion us from them."

"The right man just might make me feel happier—if not more secure—because we'd be sharing the risks," Cathy admitted. "But the risks would be just as great."

"I find it challenging, not frightening, to face the hazards of the trail by myself," Cindy said. "Even to looking forward to a life alone in Oregon."

"Do you actually want to be alone?" Cathy asked.

"Yes and no," Cindy replied. "This winter at Fort Madison has been good for me. I've learned for the first time that men aren't necessarily lusting after me and that they—some of them, anyway—respect me as a human being. So the only way I can answer your question, Cathy, is to say that if I found the right partner, I'd be happy to live out my days with him. If not, I won't feel any great loss."

"I don't think I'd want to do without a man forever," Tonie said, "any more than most men would want to do without women for the rest of their lives. But I do see what you mean, Cindy, about our situation being a challenge. I think I'm in love with Bob. I'm not sure, really, because I've never felt like this before. But I'd want to be married to him only in a partnership, he'd have to respect me as much as I respect him. You'd never find me trailing four feet behind him the way Muslim women trail after their husbands on the Barbary Coast of North Africa, or so Ernie says."

Cathy laughed. "There was a time in my life when I

did trail around behind Otto. But I'm a big girl now, and I'll never do it again. That shouldn't be necessary in a happy marriage, and the women who behave that way are responsible for all the grief they create for themselves. Not for me!"

"Are you two telling me that you've come around to my way of thinking?" Cindy demanded. "That you're willing to cope alone–"

"I will if I must," Tonie said firmly. "My pride in myself must come first."

"I'm afraid there's no choice," Cathy said. "No matter what troubles lie ahead for us on the trail and in Oregon, if the choice is between staying single and making a bad marriage, I'll stay single, thank you. I've had the bad marriage, and nothing is worth that kind of life."

Routines were reestablished by the third day out of Fort Madison. The men, women, and older children knew what was expected of them and, for the most part, performed their tasks cheerfully. By now they realized they had entered a new phase of life; they had put the last outpost of civilization behind them, and they would see no towns, no villages, and no forts hereafter. The Great Plains and two chains of mountains, where potential enemies and other dangers lurked, stood between them and their longed-for destination.

On the fourth morning Grace Drummond made a discovery that she shared at breakfast with anyone who would listen to her. "You know something?" she asked in her booming voice. "We're pioneers!"

Most of the audience laughed heartily, but her words stuck in their minds. What she said was true: they *were* pioneers. Even though they had recognized their role, within themselves, the statement brought with it a stronger realization of that role, and gave them greater pride and dignity, as well as an increased sense of purpose.

Many people were still eating pancakes and drinking coffee, among them Lena Malcolm, who sat on the ground chatting with several other women while Lenore toddled off through the grass in the direction of a pile of rocks. Terence, who was now in charge of the water detail, had just gone off with members of his group to the river, where they would fill their pails so the cooking fires could be extinguished.

By now the travelers had regained their sense of timing. Those who were assigned the task of washing dishes were busy, but the others knew they could linger over their mugs of coffee for another quarter of an hour before the teams had to be hitched.

Lena kept her little daughter under observation as she talked with her friends, and suddenly she broke off in horror. Lenore had reached the pile of rocks and was bending down to examine something emerging from the pile.

Even at a distance, the young mother recognized it was a copperhead snake. About three feet long, it shimmered in the early morning sunlight. Lena could only scream in terror and point.

Most of the others were too petrified to move, but Whip went into action instantly and raced across the wagon circle. Lenore was unaware of her danger. Talking to the snake, the eighteen-month-old child extended her hand, hoping to pat the shiny creature.

Again Lena screamed.

Whip swiftly unwound the long lash that encircled his middle. At that moment the snake drew back its head to strike. Only inches separated its fangs from Lenore's chubby hand.

If the wagonmaster missed his target, he ran the risk of doing serious harm to Lenore. But he did not hesitate. He let fly with the whip, which made a hissing, singing sound as it cut through the air. Just at that moment the copperhead struck, but the rawhide severed its head, which seemed to disintegrate as the body writhed on the rocks.

Lena's fear propelled her across the grass, and she snatched up her baby. Lenore was not in the least frightened by the experience. On the contrary, she was amused by the sight of the harmless wriggling of the snake's body.

Lena was so relieved she began to weep and found it difficult to thank Whip. Then several members of the company who had hurried after her surrounded her and the child, all of them talking simultaneously.

Hosea approached Whip, who was winding his lash,

and the Ashanti's expression was doleful. "Bad to kill snake," he said. "Hosea could use."

Before Whip could reply, he became aware of further movement in the rocks. "Folks," he called, "move away, please, and give this pile a wide berth. It looks like there's a whole nest of copperheads in here."

The women needed no urging.

The news galvanized Hosea, who stared at the rocks for an instant, then sped off to Dr. Martin's wagon. Soon he returned with a glass container, and while others watched in fear and fascination, he removed the glass stopper, then moved close to the rocks.

Suddenly his hand darted into a crevice, and when he removed it, he was calmly holding a copperhead directly behind its head. The snake thrashed in his grasp, but he knew precisely how to render it harmless, and its fangs could not touch him.

Whip was on the verge of telling him to stop flirting with almost certain death, but changed his mind. It was plain that Hosea needed no advice and was well able to look after himself.

Some of the women were so sickened by the spectacle that they left the scene, but other members of the company gathered, watching from a safe distance. Soon the Ashanti had a silent, tense audience of more than fifty people.

Hosea was concentrating so completely on his task, however, that for all practical purposes he might have been alone. He placed the glass container on a flat rock, held the copperhead's head a fraction of an inch above it, and, with his free hand, began to stroke its lower jaw. The snake's fangs shot out, touched the inner rim of the container, and soon drops of a pale, somewhat milky fluid began to trickle from them down to the bottom of the glass.

Throwing the now harmless copperhead onto the far side of the rock pile, Hosea coolly reached into the crevice again and withdrew a second, even larger snake, which he proceeded to milk in the same manner. Totally fearless, his manner was brisk and businesslike.

Whip marveled, as did Ernie von Thalman, who joined

him. "If I weren't seeing this with my own eyes, I wouldn't believe it," the latter murmured.

The morning departure of the train was delayed while Hosea milked a third, then a fourth snake. By now the container was almost full, and Hosea sighed regretfully as he threw the fourth snake onto the rocks. "Two more in nest," he said, "but no more room in bottle."

Placing the stopper carefully into the container and making certain it was airtight, he dropped it into the pocket of his buckskin shirt and casually began to round up Cathy's workhorses.

Cathy moved her wagon into her regular place at the head of the line, and Hosea climbed up beside her. As they waited for other wagons to move into place, he removed the glass container and proudly showed it to her.

She had to use all of her willpower to force herself to look at the deadly fluid, for the sight of it made her ill. But she didn't want to hurt Hosea's feelings, and for his sake she feigned an interest. "That's—uh—wonderful, Hosea," she said.

He grinned and nodded complacently. Then, soon after they began their morning's ride, he reached into another pocket for some small, seasoned oak twigs. Removing a small knife from a hip pocket, he began the task of making darts, whittling and slicing, cutting notches and fashioning sharp points.

Absorbed and cheerful, he looked up only after he had finished making a half-dozen darts, a task that took him no more than an hour. Resting before he made still more darts, he took the glass container from his pocket and held it up to the light, somewhat disappointed because the sun had vanished and banks of dark clouds were rolling in rapidly from the western mountains, and he could not clearly see the fluid. "Kill many bad men now," he announced.

Cathy was relieved that he expected no reply.

Gradually the clouds overhead became thicker, the wind increased and the feeling of spring vanished as the air became raw and damp. In mid-morning, to the surprise of

Cathy and others who rode in the front portion of the train, Arnold Mell returned from his scouting duties and, riding beside Whip, conferred with him at some length. Those who realized he had come back to the train assumed that a problem with Indians might be developing, or perhaps another large herd of buffalo had been sighted.

Mack Dougall was the next of the scouts to arrive. Shoving his wad of chewing tobacco to the side of his mouth, he joined Arnold and Whip. Ordinarily undemonstrative, Mack gestured frequently, sometimes jabbing a finger skyward as though emphasizing a point.

Then Stalking Horse also returned to the train. Now Cathy was certain that something was happening. Never before had all three scouts rejoined the caravan so early in the day.

Whip raised two fingers to his mouth, and a sharp whistle summoned Tonie to the head of the line. He spoke to her briefly, she passed the word to her assistants, and then the entire company was notified that a halt was being called for the rest of the day.

Nearby was a wooded area where oak, elm, juniper, and pine grew. Nat Drummond was sent with his wood-gathering detail to bring back as much firewood as possible.

"Comb the woods for dead trees," Whip said. "I want enough to keep a roaring blaze going for at least twenty-four hours. If you must, chop down a few trees and cut them up, too. They'll take longer to burn, of course, but eventually they'll catch."

Although it wasn't yet noon, the wagons were placed in their overnight formation, the horses and oxen were set free to graze inside the circle, and Whip called a brief meeting of the entire company.

"Folks," he said, "some of you may find this hard to believe, but we're in for a day or two of unusual weather. Make sure your canvas wagon tops are secure. Keep the sides fastened, and stuff extra blankets along all the openings. I see that many of you are no longer wearing your greatcoats and cloaks. Get them out of your clothing boxes, along with your wool caps and mittens. The best we can do for the horses and oxen is to build a roaring fire and keep it going."

A stunned silence greeted his remarks. Some people stared at the carpet of green that stretched across the prairie to the horizon and found it impossible to believe that the problem was as grave as he made it out to be. Granted the weather had turned chilly, but the idea of donning heavy winter clothes seemed almost foolish.

"The change isn't all that unusual," Whip continued. "Take my word for it that many of the peaks in the Rockies are covered with snow all year, even during the height of summer. More years than not, there are severe storms in April, and when the winds are strong enough, the Great Plains get their share. Depending on how long the storm lasts, the grass may or may not be killed by frost and have to start again. But I'm worried about people and animals, not grass. So do as I say, and when the nasty weather strikes, stay in your wagons. All of you have ample supplies of emergency rations. Use them. We'll do no cooking during the storm. Right now I'd like everybody to give the water detail a helping hand. Fill your buckets and tubs and any other containers. You may have to thaw them at the fire, but at least you'll have drinking water for yourselves and your animals."

The wood-gatherers were the first to leave. Ted Woods and a number of other brawny men who weren't ordinarily part of the group accompanied them to saw logs, and soon a mound of firewood was piled in the center of the circle. Meanwhile, men walked to the Platte to fill water containers while women made sure the side flaps of canvas were secure and began to unpack the heavy winter clothing they had stored away.

The fire was lighted, and more logs were piled a safe distance from the flames. But the storm, if there was one, held off, and many people worked in a growing holiday atmosphere. In the past, Whip's advice had been sound, and he had never misled the company, but there were many who believed he was being too cautious this time or perhaps had misread the signs. Those who came from upper New York, Pennsylvania, Ohio, Illinois, and Indiana were familiar with late, freakish storms, but those who had spent their lives in the South found it difficult to believe that the flow of the seasons could be reversed.

The snow started to fall gently, shortly after noon, drifting down in tiny, lazy flakes that melted as they hit the ground. Gradually the snowfall increased, however, and by late afternoon a full-scale blizzard was raging. The ground turned white, and by nightfall the snow was several inches deep. The wind from the mountains became a gale and howled across the Great Plains; drifts piled up; the temperature dropped steadily.

Nat Drummond, Ted Woods, and a small group of volunteers tended the fire, which continued to burn, even though at times it seemed on the verge of being extinguished. Huddling together, horses and oxen edged closer and yet closer to the flames. Arnold, Mack, and Ernie supervised their feeding and watering, and although some animals were suffering extreme discomfort, none seemed to be in immediate danger. Thanks to the fire, they appeared able to survive.

The snow continued for more than fourteen hours, finally stopping in the early hours of the morning. Then the clouds dissipated, the stars appeared and a brilliant moon shone down on an endless sea of pure, silvery white. However, most people, burrowing under their blankets and wearing their heaviest clothing, remained inside their wagons and did not see the almost eerie beauty of the night. Only Whip and Stalking Horse had remained in the open, rolled in blankets near the fire. Thanks to their long experience in outdoor living, neither was the worse for wear.

Daylight came, and the flames of the fire still leaped high. People stayed in their wagons, however, and ate emergency rations of dried or pickled meat and parched corn for breakfast.

Only when the sun began to rise did the weather grow warmer. Then the temperature rose rapidly, and the thick snow began to melt. The older boys were the first to discover that the grass had not been destroyed, the thick layer of snow having protected it from the bitter cold.

Most of the animals were frisky, and only humans suffered real injury. A line formed outside Dr. Martin's wagon when many people found they were suffering from frostbite, and the physician, helped by the tireless, hard-working Tonie, treated more than fifty men, women, and children.

Members of the train congratulated themselves, believing they had escaped lightly, but their optimism proved premature. A woman's scream of anguish coming from one of the wagons indicated that one family, at least, had suffered.

People hurrying to the wagon found Ellie Fairbank, of Pennsylvania, hysterical. Her husband, Eb, was in agony, screaming deliriously that his left foot was on fire. In the other bed the two little Fairbank children, daughters of seven and five years, were dead, their tiny, pinched faces a pale blue color.

Women from neighboring wagons tried to comfort the distraught Ellie, while several men carried Eb to Dr. Martin's wagon. He fought them, cursing and shouting, flailing his arms and trying to escape from the "fire" that he screamed was consuming him.

Three men had to hold him down on the physician's operating table. A powerful man, he managed, nevertheless, to knock a glass of laudanum from Tonie's hand.

Without hesitation Dr. Martin amputated three of Eb Fairbank's toes. The task was grisly and difficult; Martin worked in grim silence, realizing the excruciating pain his patient was suffering. But he realized, too, that if he faltered or delayed, Fairbank well might lose his whole leg.

After the operation was completed, the doctor himself managed to pour a quantity of laudanum down the still-struggling patient's throat while the sweating volunteers continued to hold the man still. Gradually Fairbank calmed down, then fell into a deep sleep.

Ellie Fairbank no longer knew what was happening around her. Dr. Martin hurried to the Fairbank wagon and was able to persuade the hysterical woman to take a somewhat milder dose of the laudanum. Soon the sedative had the desired effect, and she, too, drifted off to sleep.

Meanwhile, another party of volunteers cleared away a patch of snow, and while Ted Woods and a carpenter from Kentucky hastily made two small coffins, another group of men quickly dug two graves in the soggy, drenched ground.

The two little Fairbank girls were buried there in a ceremony that was mercifully brief, and many of the women wept without shame, silently thanking God that their own children had been spared.

Ultimately the crippled Eb and his wife would have other children. But they would never recover completely from their tragic loss, and for the rest of their days, they would grieve for the daughters buried in shallow graves somewhere in the unmarked wilderness.

Everyone in the company realized anew that the price they were paying for their journey to Oregon was very high. Some even wondered as they stood by the two tiny graves whether the goal was worth it. But there was no turning back now.

There were some who were eager to leave the site without delay. But the snow was still too deep, and in many places the ground was too soggy for the journey to be resumed. Whip announced they would remain at their present campsite until further notice. Numerous volunteers accompanied the wood-gathering detail, and at Cathy's instigation, plans were made to prepare a hot meal at noon, the first since breakfast the previous day.

As the weather continued to improve, the owners of wagons came out into the open to feed and water their teams. Only then was it discovered that horses were missing. It seemed unlikely that the beasts could have wandered off during the blizzard, particularly as it would have been difficult for them to squeeze through the openings between the wagons.

A complete count was taken, with every wagon owner making a careful check. Nine horses were missing. The atmosphere became increasingly tense, and no one saw Whip and Stalking Horse quietly slip out and make a slow, thorough examination of the melting snow that surrounded the circle.

When they returned, Whip made an announcement. "I'm sorry to be telling you this," he said, "but it's plain that we were invaded during the storm. A party of Indians

—I can't tell you their tribe offhand—stole nine of our horses."

"How could they get around during a blizzard when I couldn't see more than a foot or two in front of my face?" a farmer from Tennessee demanded.

Whip's smile was thin. "The braves are accustomed to such weather. I reckon Stalking Horse and I could have done it, if need be. We've traveled in worse. But we're not accepting the theft as final. We've just found some prints out yonder, so I'm asking the scouts to follow them before the sun melts what's left of the snow."

Arnold and Mack immediately went off to saddle their horses, and Stalking Horse fetched his pony.

Hosea approached Whip. "Hosea go, too," he said, making a flat statement rather than a request.

Ordinarily Whip would have said no, but Hosea had amply demonstrated his ability to keep up with horsemen for long hours at a time. Whip also knew that Hosea felt he had been humiliated by his kidnapping and obviously wanted to restore his image as a warrior and scout in the eyes of the wagon train members. So Whip agreed.

Hosea carried his miniature clubs, blowgun, and poisoned darts with him at all times, but now he raced off to fetch his rawhide shield. He was ready to depart even before the three scouts gathered.

The hoofprints left by the raiders' mounts and the horses they had stolen were plain to see, and once assembled, all four members of the group moved off together, following the trail. The riders quickly increased their pace to a rapid canter, and Hosea ran beside them. When he went on a mission of this kind, he discarded his moccasins and preferred to be barefooted. Not until much later did he reveal privately to Stalking Horse that he had smeared his feet and calves with a coating of thick grease to protect them from the snow.

In places the drifts were still two and three feet high, but the group neither floundered nor paused. In a few hours, the snow would be reduced to puddles of water, and then the trail of the fleeing Indians would become more difficult to follow. Also, everyone in the party knew it was imperative to cut off the thieves before they reached a larger body of their own people. It was apparent from the prints that the raiding party had been fairly large. If reinforced by scores of other braves, it would be too strong to be attacked.

One factor favored the pursuers, as they well realized. Although their foes had a long head start, they could travel far more rapidly than men who were herding nine lumbering workhorses, incapable of attaining speeds faster than a riding horse's trot.

It seemed miraculous to Arnold and Mack that Hosea could keep up with them. Never faltering, never out of breath, the little man ran easily, his wiry frame relaxed, his heavy rawhide shield seemingly weightless as he held it several inches off the ground. He was extraordinary, and the day was not far distant when true stories told about him would become legends.

In late afternoon, when the pursuit had already lasted five hours, Stalking Horse finally raised a hand in warning. He was even more adept at reading signs than his companions, and now he saw something in the thin, remaining layer of snow that made him cautious.

"Indians and wagon train horses not far now," he said. "Maybe a mile. Maybe not that much."

Arnold peered hard at the signs and had to nod in agreement. The indentations in the snow and the soft earth beneath it were fresh. The old man immediately assumed command.

"I'll take the left flank, and Mack will take the right," he said. "Stalking Horse, you and Hosea keep moving forward right smack on the trail."

Mack spat a stream of tobacco juice at a diminishing snowbank. "Do we attack together after somebody gives a signal?"

Arnold shook his head. "That's not practical. You and I will be making detours, traveling greater distances, so Stalking Horse and Hosea will come upon the braves before we do. And once they're close enough for an assault, there's no way to hide. I recommend that they open fire as soon as they think it's practical. Then you and

I will pitch in as soon as we reach the scene. It shouldn't take either of us more than an extra minute or two to get there."

"Is good," Stalking Horse said, and Mack nodded in agreement.

Hosea made no comment. As always, he was indifferent to matters of strategy and tactics; it was enough for him that he would be engaged in a fight.

Arnold and Mack fanned out, one going to the left and the other swinging to the right. Stalking Horse continued to move forward at his same, steady pace, Hosea calmly running beside him.

Soon they caught a glimpse of four warriors bringing up the rear of the raiding party and keeping the stolen horses in line. At first it was difficult to determine their nationality, but then Stalking Horse managed to see one in profile. The man's face was smeared with streaks of bright blue paint that identified him as an Osage. Members of that tribe had a reputation as stubborn fighters, although not particularly imaginative ones.

Stalking Horse notched an arrow on the string of his bow and drew the arrow back. The braves did not yet realize that enemies were moving up behind them.

Hosea was at a distinct disadvantage. Neither his clubs nor darts could carry far enough.

Stalking Horse did not slow his pace as he sent an arrow flying in the direction of the rider on the left end of the irregular line. The shaft penetrated the left side of the brave's back, and a spreading patch of crimson stained his buckskin shirt. He slumped in his saddle, quietly pitching forward onto the neck of his pony. But the animal continued to move forward, carried by its own momentum, and the other members of the rear guard were still unaware of the assault.

Stalking Horse knew his good fortune could not last indefinitely, but he was determined to take full advantage of his opportunity while he could. He aimed at the back of the brave on the right side of the line.

This time he missed the center of his target by two or three inches, the arrow merely wounding the brave, who screamed in pain and anger. At the same moment the corpse of the man on the left tumbled to the ground.

The alarm was given. The other two members of the rear guard turned and saw the approaching pair, and their warning shouts alerted the entire raiding party. The Osage halted, ignoring the wounded brave. Most of the raiders wheeled and moved back to join their comrades at the rear, with only a few staying in place at the front and flanks to hold the riderless horses in line and prevent them from bolting.

Stalking Horse fired another arrow, and again he hit his target. But he realized that he and Hosea were now facing a group of at least twenty-five Osage; no matter how courageously they fought, the odds against them were overwhelming.

Hosea was enjoying himself. Sticking the sharpened center rod at the bottom of his rawhide shield into the ground to hold it in position, he was protected by his mobile, miniature fort. Now that the Osage were closer, he could use his darts, and he showed himself at the left side of his shield for an instant, then at the right, each time firing one of his poison-laden darts.

The Ashanti rather than Stalking Horse drew the bulk of the Osage return fire. A man on foot appeared more vulnerable, especially when he seemed to be armed with no weapons of consequence and depended on a curious leather shield for safety.

As Stalking Horse let yet another arrow fly, he noted that dusk had come, and he was relieved. Thanks to good fortune rather than planning, the timing of the attack was perfect. The Osage would find it difficult to count their enemies and discover how few there were in the attacking force.

An arrow grazed the Cherokee's shoulder, slicing through his shirt and breaking the skin, but he suffered no real harm. He could still fire his next arrow.

Spears were bouncing off the rawhide shield, and arrows were digging into the outer layer, but none could reach Hosea, who had killed several warriors.

Suddenly a rifle shot erupted on one side of the field,

and even as a brave dropped and sprawled on the ground, another rifle shot roared on the opposite flank. It, too, claimed a warrior.

By now at least six of the raiders were dead, and no fewer than three others wounded. The Indians seemed to be surrounded, and the firesticks of the white men filled them with terror. Convinced that they could not compete against such odds, they held their positions only until the senior warrior in command shouted at the top of his voice, urging every brave to save himself. That was the only signal the Osage needed. The healthy fled, leaving their dead and wounded—as well as the captured horses—behind them.

Pursuit would have been impossible, but there was no need for it—they had recovered the horses. The horses had become skittish and would have scattered, but Mack and Arnold gave them no chance. The experienced scouts herded them together, speaking to them soothingly until they became docile again.

Hosea appeared from behind his shield and, as the stars appeared and the moon rose, quietly retrieved his spent darts.

Meanwhile, Stalking Horse was performing a task of his own, systematically scalping the dead Osage. Each time he came across a brave who was still alive, he quickly plunged his knife into the warrior's body, then added another scalp to his booty.

Some of the Indians' ponies had bolted, following the retreating war party. But five were rounded up by Arnold and Mack. The battle was ended, and the victory was complete; not only had all nine of the stolen horses been recovered, but five enemy mounts had been captured, too.

"Take your pick, Hosea," Arnold said. "You can ride back to camp in style."

The Ashanti shook his head. "Hosea walk," he said.

The four men placed themselves at the points of an invisible square and started back in the direction of the wagon train, keeping the workhorses and Osage ponies inside the square. After they had traveled for more than an hour, they halted briefly to eat their only meal, dried buffalo meat and parched corn. Then they resumed their march.

Sentries had been posted around the circle of wagons, and their shouts of joy, mingled with disbelief, aroused most of the company. Only the youngest children and a few women slept through the commotion.

Whip seemed unruffled, having expected no less of the group he had dispatched on the difficult errand. The Osage ponies would be distributed the following day, he said, and as the better part of the night was already spent, the wagon train would stay at its present site for an additional twenty-four hours in order to give the scouts and Hosea the opportunity to rest.

As the members of the company headed back to their wagons, their joy over the outcome was tempered by a sobering thought. Nat Drummond expressed it best when he said, "I wouldn't have thought anybody could have been abroad during that blizzard. Well, the Indians not only did it, but they even sneaked into our camp without anybody knowing it. If they can perform that kind of magic, just imagine all the troubles we have waiting for us on the Great Plains."

IX

Real spring finally came to the Great Plains in the wake of the late blizzard. The ground dried in the balmy breezes so the thin metal rims of the wagon wheels no longer cut into the earth and became mired. People and animals seemed to have greater energy. Sometimes, as they rode, the pioneers sang songs about the good life that awaited them in Oregon, making up new words to the tunes of familiar favorites. The grass grew higher, and prairie flowers of scarlet and bright yellow, pink, white, and orange dotted the landscape.

Terry and Lena Malcolm held hands at every opportunity, Eulalia Woodling flirted with any man who would talk to her, and many of the unmarried people became restless. Tonie Mell confided to Cathy van Ayl that she dreamed of Bob Martin, and a red-faced Cathy told her in return that she found herself thinking of Whip Holt in unguarded moments.

For no apparent reason, Ted Woods began to keep an even closer watch on Cindy than he had in the past. He changed the position of his wagon so he now rode directly behind her in the center column; he kept her under observation when she worked at the cooking fire before breakfast and supper; and on evenings when he wasn't working, he loitered in her vicinity.

His surveillance was harmless, but it made Cindy nervous. Unlike the girls who had led far more sheltered, inhibited lives, she had long been accustomed to speaking her mind candidly to men. So she ignored the well-meant advice of Cathy and Tonie. One night after supper, when she felt Ted lurking in the shadows of the fire behind her, she turned suddenly and went straight to him.

"I'd like a word with you, Ted," she said.

The burly blacksmith became uncomfortable. "What about?"

"Let's go sit on the stoop of my wagon, shall we? There are too many people around here."

With great reluctance he accompanied her to the far side of the circle, where her wagon sat in the shadows.

Cindy sat on the top step, motioned Ted to a lower step, and instinctively fluffed her red hair. "Now, if you please," she said, "I want to know what all this is about."

"All what, Cindy?"

"I'm not angry with you, Ted, and I'm not upset. You've been grand to me, and I appreciate it. Particularly the night you saved me from that loathesome mountain man back at Fort Madison. But I can't help wondering why you're always following me."

Ted's shock was genuine. "I wouldn't do a thing like that!" he protested.

She had guessed that he wasn't actually aware of what he was doing. So she spoke even more gently as she said, "Every time I turn around, there you are, keeping an eye on me. Before and during breakfast, before and during supper—even during the nooning. You were doing it just now when I asked you to come with me."

For a long time Ted was silent, thinking. Then he nodded. "I mean you no harm," he said.

"Oh, I know you don't," Cindy assured him, impulsively touching his bare forearm for a moment. When she removed her fingers, he clapped his hand over the spot she had touched and unconsciously ran his fingers back and forth across it.

"I've got to be honest with you," she said, "and I hope you'll be the same way with me. All right?"

"I always tried to be honest." He spoke slowly and with dignity. "I ain't much for lyin'."

Subtlety was a waste of time in dealing with a man of his temperament. "I believe," Cindy said, "that you're sweet on me."

Ted was so surprised at Cindy's frankness that he lost his voice. His Adam's apple bobbed up and down, and when he opened his mouth, he could make no sound.

"I'm not asking you to confirm it," Cindy told him. "Both of us know what we know. I just think you're making a mistake, that's all, Ted."

He looked as though she had stabbed him with a knife. "If there's somebody else, somebody I don't know about, all you got to do is say the word, Cindy, and I'll leave you strictly alone."

"I give you my word there's nobody else," she said. "There's no man in my life."

He looked relieved.

"No man now," she repeated. "And no man in the future, as far ahead as I can see."

"Then it's all right," Ted said.

"No!" Cindy cried fiercely. "No man! That includes you!"

"You're tryin' to tell me you don't think very highly of me, is that it?" He looked crushed.

"What I think or don't think of you is beside the point, Ted. You seem to have forgotten something I can't allow myself to forget. I'm a whore."

Ted's eyes blazed. "Nobody can call you that, not even you. Maybe it's what you were, but you ain't one now."

"I'm not practicing the trade any more, if that's what you mean. And I'd rather die than go back to it. But that doesn't change what I am."

He refused to accept her logic. "All right. Here's somethin' I never told you. I killed my wife and my brother. I put a bullet into her and a knife in him when I caught them in bed together. That's why I spent ten years in prison. So I'm a murderer."

Cindy had already learned about his background, so his revelations neither surprised nor shocked her. "You paid for your mistakes in jail, so you wiped your slate clean. Nobody can call you a murderer any more, Ted."

"If you're a whore, then I'm a murderer. There's no two ways about it," he insisted.

"You don't understand. I just stopped what I was doing, but nobody sent me to jail for it. Society has not punished me."

"You're sayin' a body has to be punished before the slate is wiped clean, huh?"

She hadn't thought about it in those terms before. "Something like that."

"Then you're absolved the same as I am. Because you been punishin' yourself. It's my guess you been doin' it for a long, long time. Long before you ever left that whorehouse in Louisville, I'll bet."

"Maybe so." Cindy had no intention of discussing the inner agonies she had suffered. "But that isn't important. What matters is that I'm not for you, not for anyone."

"You aimin' to live your whole life alone? A lady as pretty and young as you?"

"I'm not all that young," she replied indignantly. "I'm almost twenty-two."

Ted chuckled, then sobered. "Cindy," he said, "I ain't forcin' myself on you. I respect the way you feel, even though I think you're wrong. All I'll say is I'll be around —providin' you're sure it really doesn't matter to you that I killed two people."

"I can understand your reasons, and I don't blame you."

"Then I'll be waitin'. I won't push, and I'll do my best not to make you uncomfortable by hangin' around you too much. But any time you need help—in anythin'—all you got to do is holler for me."

"You're very sweet, Ted," Cindy said. It was astonishing that someone who had such great strength could be so gentle.

"Don't talk like that," Ted said. "I'm tryin' to behave myself."

She held out her hand to him. "We can be real friends now. I like that."

He stared at her small hand for a moment, then, wiping his palm on his trousers, he enveloped her hand in his, treating it as though it were a live bird that might be crushed to death if he squeezed it. Abruptly, he released her hand, then stood.

She smiled up at him.

Unable to speak again, Ted suddenly bolted, hurrying to his own wagon, which stood directly behind Cindy's in the circle. He was too embarrassed to look around at her and quickly lowered the flap, even though Danny, who still shared the wagon with him, hadn't yet come to bed.

Cindy continued to sit on the top step of her own wagon. Perhaps she had been wrong to speak so frankly. It had been her intention to discourage Ted Woods, but instead she had caused him to show an even greater interest in her. Cindy sighed. It was infuriating that her past life as a prostitute in no way turned him against her. Well, she had tried, and she couldn't be responsible for him or his feelings. She didn't want to hurt him, but having warned him that she wanted no man, she couldn't do anything more.

On the other hand, she wondered what life would be like as Ted's wife. A man like Ted didn't give his love easily. Certainly she could persuade him to do anything she wanted. She also knew she would have to be careful not to make him lose his temper—she would not like his rage to be directed against her.

What rubbish she was thinking! She was sick of men, and no one, Ted included, interested her physically.

She supposed she was drawn to the blacksmith because of his desire to protect her. After all, every woman wanted to be cherished. But the mere thought of physical contact nauseated her.

Well, she couldn't marry Ted—or anyone else—while she felt that way. Too many of her Louisville customers had confided that they had come to her because they were married to women who didn't care for them physically. She had been good at pretending she cared. But when she joined the wagon train, she had sworn that she would never again allow herself to be placed in a position where pretense would be necessary. And that was one promise that she fully intended to keep.

So goodbye to Ted Woods and everyone else! In years to come she might change her mind, but she hadn't changed it yet—although she knew that to an extent, she was recovering from the injuries to her soul that she had suffered. She was able to see men like Whip, Ernie, and Dr. Martin in their true perspective now, and she had learned, however reluctantly, to admire them for being upright, gallant, and courageous. The mere fact that she did not hate them and could recognize their good qualities was an improvement. She recognized the change and was grateful for it.

She had her friends to thank, at least in part, for that improvement. Cathy van Ayl and Tonie Mell accepted her without reservation, even though they knew of her past. Cathy, at least, was a lady, and Tonie, although harder to define, nevertheless was someone who had great inner strength. The mere fact that they had extended their friendship to her, sharing with her their inner thoughts, was something of a miracle. Never before had Cindy enjoyed such relationships with anyone; at the Louisville bordello, the other girls had been selfish and suspicious, ready to fight for what they regarded as their rights.

She was prepared, in return, to do anything she could to help both Tonie and Cathy. They had won her total loyalty.

At the same time, however, Cindy had to admit to herself that she envied them. They were living straightforward, honest lives, uncluttered by shadows. Oh, it was true that Cathy had endured an unhappy marriage with a difficult, crabby miser, but she had done nothing of which to be ashamed, nothing that haunted her and kept her awake at night.

How wonderful it would be to clear the slate and start a fresh life, unsullied by the past! In a sense, of course, that was what she was trying to do by joining the wagon train and going off to Oregon. Ultimately she would put her past behind her, forget it, and emerge as a new woman. She was well on her way and would keep trying. Nobody, including the girl she herself had been, was going to stand in her way.

At length, Cindy became weary of her own thoughts.

Still too restless to go to bed, she rose from her seat on the wagon, walked slowly down the stairs, and then wandered around the inner edge of the circle. She was in no mood to make small talk with anyone, so she wandered aimlessly, then paused between two wagons to look out across the dark prairie. On a night like this the quiet of the wilderness was soothing.

Suddenly a hand touched her shoulder, causing her to jump, and a man's voice interrupted her thoughts. "You look lonely tonight."

Cindy brushed aside the hand as she whirled around, then grimaced when she saw Claiborne Woodling facing her. She still disliked the young man. The mere fact that he sought her company was irritating.

"I'm not in the least lonely, thank you," she said, and her tone was glacial.

Claiborne refused to recognize the rebuff. "Well, I am, and you're just the person to cure that feeling for me."

"I'm sorry," she said firmly, "but whether you're happy or sad—you or anyone else—is none of my concern."

"It was, not so long ago," he replied, moistening his lips.

Other members of the company were careful never to mention Cindy's past to her. Only this thoroughly unpleasant young man went out of his way to remind her of what she had been—as if she needed any reminders.

"I choose not to debate the point with you. Let me pass, please," she added when she saw he was blocking the opening between the wagons.

Claiborne did not move. Instead he folded his arms across his chest and grinned at her.

Cindy realized she had allowed herself to be placed in an uncomfortable position. The wagons on either side of her were dark; their owners were obviously still enjoying conversation over coffee at the fire. If she raised her voice, people would come running, but she dreaded creating an embarrassing personal situation. This was something she preferred to handle herself, if she could.

She was uncertain whether she was sorry or pleased that Ted Woods had given up watching her for the night. The proximity of the brooding giant might have deterred

Woodling. On the other hand, had Woodling persisted, Ted might have lost his temper—with consequences that even at this moment caused her to shiver.

"You're cold," Claiborne said, "but I can take good care of that."

"I don't care for your hints. If you really want to know, I don't like you."

"You'll change your mind when you come to know me better." His grin broadened.

"I don't intend to. Just because we happen to be traveling in the same wagon train doesn't mean we've got to be friends, you know." Cindy spoke stiffly, wondering whether to take the risk of pushing him aside and trying to squeeze past him. If she could time her move in a way that caught him off guard, she would be able to quietly rejoin those still lingering at the fire.

"What I've had in mind," Claiborne said, pulling her to him, "isn't exactly what I'd call friendship."

No escape was possible, but Cindy still wasn't ready to call for help. Virtually everyone in the train knew she had been a harlot. Some of the women still didn't like her, and she felt certain that many of them would believe that she had led Claiborne on.

Struggling, she pushed against his chest, but she was unable to break free of his viselike grip.

Claiborne laughed, his hold tightening. "I like it when a woman shows a little spirit—before I tame her."

"You'll never tame me," she gasped, fighting still harder to break loose.

He bent his head down to kiss her forcibly, but suddenly he released her and slumped to the ground. The astonished Cindy, breathing hard, saw that Claiborne was unconscious.

She turned around. There was no one there. Her deliverance seemed to be a miracle. Then she saw something lying on the ground; only a few inches from young Woodling's head. She bent down for it, then held it up to the dim light of the fire. Not until she saw it was a little wooden club did she realize what had happened.

Hosea materialized out of the dark and stood beside her. "Ted sleep," he said, "So Hosea keep watch." Calmly taking the club from her, he returned it to the loop around his middle.

Cindy thanked him profusely, feeling that anything she said would inadequately express her gratitude. At the same time she was worried. Claiborne had not moved, and she became increasingly fearful. "Did you—kill him?"

For an instant a faint smile hovered at the corners of Hosea's mouth. "Not kill," he said solemnly. "Whip and Ernie no like if kill. Get mad." He nudged Woodling with a foot, the gesture almost clinically impersonal. "Hosea make man sleep. Wake up in morning. Then head hurt all day."

A slight, barely perceptible shrug of disdain indicated his total lack of interest in any discomfort the young man might suffer the next day. Only one thing was important to him; again nudging the motionless figure at his foot, he said, "Not be bad with lady again."

Cindy's tension evaporated suddenly, and she hugged Hosea. In the future she felt certain Claiborne Woodling would take care to avoid her.

She knew, too, that there was no need for her to ask Hosea not to mention the incident to anyone. She trusted his discretion, and she realized, too, that he was wise enough to say nothing to Ted, who might be all too inclined to lose his temper.

Cindy, her spirits remarkably improved, decided to return to the fire for a last cup of coffee before turning in. Hosea walked beside her. He had developed an insatiable craving for the hot chocolate that the children drank instead of coffee, and Cindy decided that from now on, she would prepare a cup for him at every meal. That was the least she could do.

When they reached the fire she heard a man speaking in an angry, clear voice. Nat Drummond stood, feet spread apart and thumbs hooked in his belt, glaring at his wife. No one had ever heard Nat defy the overbearing Grace.

"Woman," he thundered, "I'm tired of being ordered around. Do this, Nat. Do that, Nat. I do my share and more. I supervise the wood-gathering detail, and I do it well. I hitch up our team twice a day, and I drive our wagon. I feed and water our team. I raise and lower the flaps on our wagon, and I repack the insides whenever anything is loose. That's all I aim to do!"

Grace glowered at him. "What about me? I work with the other women cooking meals—"

"Sure!" he interrupted, shouting. "But that's all you do!"

Some of those still gathered around the fire were embarrassed and turned away, talking to each other in low tones and pretending not to hear the surprising argument. But Cindy was fascinated, and she saw that Cathy van Ayl was listening, too, making no attempt to hide her broad smile. Obviously Cathy felt as she did, that Nat had been dominated for too long by a wife who treated him more like an indentured servant than a husband.

But that era appeared to have come to an abrupt end. Nat had gained a measure of self-respect on the long trek that he had never before known, and he was asserting himself with remarkable force. "It's too damn much when you order me to collect our dishes and take them back to the wagon. My sweat back home earned those dishes and mugs. Yes, and the knives we use when we eat. It's your place to wash them and keep an eye on them and take care of them. So you'll blame well do it from now on. Just as you're going to do a heap of other things!"

His rebellion was so strong and unexpected that Grace could only gape at him in stunned silence.

"I never believed in beating a woman," Nat said, "but I'm mighty tempted. Do what I tell you, Grace, and do it quick!" He clapped his hands together sharply.

All at once Grace sprang into action. Cindy thought she intended to pick up her husband and shake him. Instead she meekly went over to the fire, where piles of washed dishes were drying, picked up her crockery and a large kettle, then silently trudged off to her wagon.

Nat watched her for a moment or two, without any emotion. Then he quietly joined a group of people who were talking with Arnold Mell.

Cindy caught a glimpse of Grace Drummond's face as she turned away. The girl was surprised to note that Nat's tall, rawboned wife did not appear in the least upset. On the contrary, she was smiling and seemed to be at peace with herself. Some women were inexplicably contrary, and Cindy suspected that Grace would enjoy the new role she was being forced to play. When a woman truly loved a man, she didn't want to maintain the upper hand all the time.

Cindy thought it unlikely that she could ever love any man that much. Yet she knew she had been wrong, a short time earlier, about her ability to handle Ted Woods. Why was she even concerned about her relationship with Ted? She had promised herself that she would remain independent. Her freedom was too precious to her, and she fully intended to allow no one to interfere with it.

Chet Harris and Danny had developed into the most accomplished fishermen in the company. Armed with hooks made for them by Hosea, lines fashioned from remnants of cloth that Cathy van Ayl gave them, and poles cut under Ernie's quiet supervision, the pair organized all of the older boys in the caravan. Each night they returned to the circle with strings of fish. Trout were plentiful in the Platte River, but the boys preferred lake and pond fishing because they came away with larger, meatier catches. They were delighted when the train halted each night at one or another of a chain of lakes and ponds in the Nebraska country. These ran parallel to the route of march for more than sixty miles, so Danny was indulging in no idle boast when he said, "We'll be eating fresh fish for breakfast every day for at least a whole week."

On the third night of the journey past the chain of unnamed lakes, the older boys hurried away, as soon as camp was made, to start fishing in a small pond.

Mack had sighted a small herd of buffalo only a few miles from the campsite as he returned from his scouting duties, so a party had gone out hunting. Whip stayed behind deliberately—he didn't want the company to become too dependent on his efforts. Even those who had been new to this type of hunting were experienced by now.

Whip wandered through the woods that stood between

the campsite and the small pond, noting with approval that the wood-gatherers were concentrating their efforts on fallen and dead trees. The boys were hauling in a catch of fish and were completely absorbed in the task, while some of the older girls and women were busily gathering berries and edible roots nearby. The Oregon-bound settlers didn't yet realize it, but they were becoming increasingly efficient and more self-reliant in wilderness living. By the time these people reached Oregon they would be able to survive on their own.

Pleased with the progress they were making, Whip strolled back to the circle, where women were beginning to prepare supper. He stiffened slightly when he saw a strange gelding and a pack horse. Then he spotted a tall, broad-shouldered man wearing a shirt and trousers of heavy wool and store-bought boots. His rifle slung over his shoulder, he was engaged in conversation with several of the women.

The man introduced himself as Alvin Munson, but offered no other information.

The code of the wilderness was strict, and although Whip didn't much care for the man's looks, he had to extend the company's hospitality. "You'll stay for supper and the night?"

"Thanks," Munson replied. "I'm sure the ladies can cook better meals than I can prepare for myself, so I'll be glad to eat with you. Later, though, I believe I'll be on my way." He spoke with a faint accent that was impossible for Whip to identify.

Whip was surprised by the man's refusal to remain overnight. Only someone in a great hurry traveled through the Great Plains after dark. "Where are you headed, Mr. Munson?"

"Either Independence or St. Joseph, I don't much care which."

"You've spent the winter in the Rockies, then?"

The man nodded.

Again Whip felt a twinge. Munson's clothes didn't look like those of a mountain man, and he carried no furs—the only reason for anybody to endure the hardships of a winter in the Rockies. But common courtesy forbade Whip to question him too closely. Perhaps he was a fugitive on the run, or fleeing from personal enemies. A man was entitled to his privacy out here.

The hunters returned in time for supper, bringing with them the carcasses of three buffalo. One was lightly smoked so it would keep only until the following night, when both sides would be barbecued, and the others were cut up to be preserved in vinegar and salt, then added to the supply of emergency rations.

"This time of year," Whip said to Alvin Munson in an effort to make polite conversation, "nobody starves on the plains."

"So it seems," the visitor replied.

Very odd. The man spoke as though he were strange to the area. But that seemed impossible. In order to reach the Rockies and return from them, every mountain man had to cross the vast prairie twice, and anyone who managed that feat—and lived—became something of an authority on the prairie.

Various members of the company, happy to see a new face, sought out the visitor. But Munson, Whip observed, was uncommunicative with all of them. Perhaps he was naturally silent, as were many who spent a considerable length of time in the Rockies. Long months of solitude seemed to rob a man of his ability to converse with others. But this man seemed actively sullen.

Maybe it was wrong to judge the man, Whip thought. Although his appearance, attitude, and seeming lack of familiarity with the area belied his claims about himself, he was minding his own business and was harming no one. All the same, perhaps it was just as well that he had refused the invitation to stay overnight.

Only one member of the company seemed to attract his attention. When he heard someone speak Tonie Mell's name, he raised his head and peered at her intently for a few moments. Then he lost interest in her, too, and devoted himself to his dinner.

Night came long before the meal was finished. Whip again extended an invitation to remain overnight, but

Munson refused, although this time he was less curt. He expressed his thanks for supper, then mounted his gelding and, leading his pack horse, rode off into the darkness. Glad to be rid of him although he couldn't say why, Whip forgot about him.

The following morning the company stirred at daybreak. The fire, which had been allowed to die down but had not been extinguished, was rebuilt. As the flames rose again, the breakfast preparations began. Also more vinegar and salt were added to the new barrels of buffalo meat before they were closed and sealed.

The water-gathering detail went off to the little pond, armed with buckets, tubs, and other containers. As sometimes happened, they were accompanied by others who felt thirsty, among them Ernie von Thalman. Behind him sauntered Arnold Mell, who had already eaten breakfast and wanted a drink of fresh water before going off on his scouting duties.

Ernie dipped his silver mug embossed with his family crest into the pond, stood, and was raising the mug to his lips when Arnold suddenly knocked it from his hand. The startled Baron didn't know whether to protest the rude gesture or reply with a swift punch.

Arnold gave him no opportunity. He pointed to the pond. Dead fish were rising to the surface and floating there.

"Don't drink that water!" Arnold shouted to those who were filling their buckets. "Don't touch it!"

"Look at the dead fish!" Ernie called. "This pond is contaminated!"

"It was fine last night," someone said.

"Well, it isn't now," Ernie replied irritably.

They were interrupted by a woman's scream. Two men who had taken drinks of the water were writhing on the ground in agony. One was an earnest, bankrupt young farmer from Indiana, passionately devoted to the future he would enjoy in Oregon. The other man, easygoing and amiable, often entertained the company with his jokes and was liked by everyone.

A young boy raced back to the circle for Dr. Martin, who arrived, running, followed by Tonie. Whip came, too, and promptly sent everyone not directly concerned back to camp.

The physician couldn't prescribe an antidote. The best he could do was administer emetics, and by this time both of the sufferers were so far gone that Tonie had to open their mouths and hold their heads while Bob poured the medication into them.

Neither responded to the treatment. Both were bathed in cold perspiration, their skin a sickly, greenish-yellow, and both were struggling feebly.

Dr. Martin searched through his satchel for something to give them. "I can't imagine what's causing this," he muttered, "so I'm damned if I know what medication to use."

The victims were fading rapidly, their breathing now shallow.

Only the doctor remained calm. "Open their mouths again, Tonie," he directed. "This one first. Now the other. That's it." He poured quantities of a white powder onto the tongues of the men, both of whom had lost consciousness.

The patient stretched on the ground beside Tonie stopped struggling and lay still. "I—I'm afraid we've lost him," she said.

Bob examined him quickly, then turned to the other victim, who had also stopped moving. "They're both gone," he said. "I don't know what they drank, and I've never heard of any substance that would cause death that rapidly after ingestion."

Still squatting, resting his weight on his heels, he pondered for a time. "Tonie, did you notice anything unusual? Did you detect any strange odors?"

She nodded unhappily. "Now that you mention it, Bob, there was an awful smell on their breaths. Like rotten eggs."

"Sulfur of some kind, I believe. Whip, can you fetch one of those dead fish floating on the top of the water? Just handle it with care, please."

The wagonmaster returned with a fish. Bob sniffed it, his face contorting with disgust, then asked Tonie to do the same.

"That's the smell!" she exclaimed.

Bob Martin stood. "Whip," he said, "everybody drank water from the pond last night, and no one was hurt. All of us ate fish for breakfast that the boys caught, and there have been no adverse reactions."

Whip stared at the physician. "Are you telling me that somebody put poison into this lake between fishing and water-gathering time last night and this morning?"

"So it would seem." The doctor spoke reluctantly but firmly. "A poison, I'd say, with a sulfur base, one sufficiently strong to kill a man within a few minutes. I can't prove it, of course—but I'm willing to stake my professional reputation on it."

"Would you say it was deliberate poisoning?" Whip asked, speaking slowly.

"That I can't say," the physician replied. "All I can tell you for certain is that twelve hours ago fish were thriving in this pond. And right now there are hundreds of them dead out there. It's possible that an underground sulfur spring was diverted, causing the waters to become contaminated. It's also possible that someone poisoned the pond, although I find that difficult to believe."

"I aim to find out," Whip said grimly, then beckoned to Arnold and Ernie, who were standing nearby and had heard everything that had been said. "Get Stalking Horse to find the tracks of that fellow who was here for supper last night. Then take a small party, go after him, and find him. If he'll talk to you and his story makes sense, all well and good. If you have any reason to doubt him, bring him back to me."

"You'll stay in the camp right here, I assume," Ernie said.

Whip nodded, his expression somber. "We'll have to bury these poor devils and console their families as best we can. The whole company is bound to be upset."

Arnold had already moved off to find Stalking Horse, who could locate tracks more rapidly than any of their white scouts.

Tonie hurried after him. "Take me with you, Uncle Arnold," she said. "I haven't gone out on the trail in a long time, and you know I can be useful." She did not explain that she didn't want to spend the entire day with an indifferent Bob Martin. Arnold nodded, his mind already on the mission ahead.

Whip was preoccupied, too, or he would have forbidden Tonie to accompany the group. Certainly the search for Alvin Munson was no pleasure trip. A girl, no matter how expert at shooting, had no legitimate place in the party. Whip was, however, thinking of what consolation he could offer to the widows of the men who had died so suddenly and unexpectedly.

Stalking Horse needed only a short time to find Munson's tracks. It was significant that, although he had said he was traveling to Independence or St. Joseph, which lay to the east, he had ridden off to the west. Obviously he had a great deal to explain.

The search party consisted of the three regular scouts, as well as Ernie, Tonie, and the shield-bearing Hosea, who refused to be left behind. Stalking Horse had no difficulty in following the clear trail Munson's riding horse and pack horse had left in the grass, which was now calf high, and he led the party at a canter. Hosea ran directly behind him, tireless as always.

If it was true that the poisoning had been deliberate, a possibility so shocking it was difficult even to contemplate, the previous night's guest deserved to die, Tonie reflected. Ordinarily not vindictive, she couldn't help wishing that Hosea would kill him. It would be just retribution if someone who used poison was himself killed by a poison dart.

Crossing the prairie rapidly, the party headed inland a short distance from the Platte River. Arnold realized they were approaching a small pond, fed by natural springs, which he had selected as the next night's stopping place for the wagon train. A thick patch of birch trees and bramble-laden bushes stood near the pond in the damp, sandy soil, and there the trail came to an abrupt end. The party dismounted, waiting while Stalking Horse studied the ground more closely. The Cherokee stood, shaking his head, then bent down to the ground again.

The sound of a rifle shot emanating from the grove of

birch trees shattered the silence. A bullet passed so close to Tonie's ear that it sounded like the buzzing of an angry hornet.

Reacting instinctively, she threw herself to the ground. The others did the same. Armed with their rifles, they moved on their hands and knees toward the stand of birch, concealing themselves as best they could in the high grass.

Again a shot was fired, and again Tonie was the target, the bullet passing above her by inches.

Why should she be the object of the man's wrath, rather than one of the men, who presumably would be more dangerous? All at once the pieces of the puzzle fitted into place, and she knew. The man who had called himself Alvin Munson was a Russian agent. He had been dispatched by André Sebastian—or by someone like him—to interfere with the wagon train's progress. And finding the woman who had defied St. Petersburg in the party that had pursued him, he was trying to win extra credit for himself by killing her. The sun overhead was warm, but an icy chill crept slowly up Tonie's spine. She wished she had displayed the common sense to have remained behind at the camp.

Only Hosea was moving boldly now, advancing a few yards, his shield held before him, then halting for a few moments before starting again.

"Don't move for a spell, any of you," Arnold called softly. "He seems to be alone, so we'll wait until he fires again. This next time, keep watch for the flash of his rifle. Then we'll rush him before he can reload again." His companions agreed.

Tonie pressed herself against the earth, hoping she was invisible in the grass that stood almost a foot high. Only by arching her neck could she see the birch trees, and she discovered she was afraid to raise her head, afraid to move.

The heavy silence was almost unbearable. An ant started to crawl up the side of Tonie's face, and she felt a strong desire to brush it aside but managed to restrain herself. Then the insect began to move down the back of her neck, inside her open buckskin collar. She could hold off no longer. Reaching up impatiently, she brushed the ant away.

The enemy fired a third shot, again barely missing Tonie.

Her companions took careful note of the spot where the shot had originated. As Arnold, Ernie, and Mack leaped to their feet and charged toward the copse, Stalking Horse sent a single arrow through the brambles.

By the time the onrushing trio reached the spot, the man who had called himself Alvin Munson was dead, the Cherokee's arrow protruding from his heart.

It would be impossible to question him now. Arnold and Ernie were disappointed, but both refrained from lecturing Stalking Horse. In his world, a warrior had to kill or be killed.

However, they prevented him from scalping the man, and, as the others watched, they searched him. But he carried no documents, no identification of any kind. A manufacturer's stamp inside his boots indicated that they had been made in New York. His rifle had been made in New England, and the blade of his knife bore an insignia that Arnold recognized as the mark of a Pittsburgh metalsmith. Nothing on his person indicated anything about him.

They searched through his saddle bags, and finally, at the bottom of one of them, they found a cloth bag nestled inside a dirty shirt. When they opened it, they found an inner bag, made of thick paper. Opening it gingerly, they saw a handful of crystals, each the size of an almond. These crystals looked harmless, but they exuded the same pungent, nauseating odor that they had smelled at the pond.

At Arnold's suggestion a deep hole was dug, and the bag of crystals was buried in it. While the men were engaged in their task, Tonie walked to the bank of the spring-fed pond, with Hosea quietly keeping watch over her. Her knees felt weak. Fighting the desire to wretch, she inhaled deeply. Suddenly she recognized a faint but thoroughly unpleasant scent. Heavy clubs seemed to be beating at her temples.

"Uncle Arnold!" she called.

Within seconds she was surrounded by the anxious members of the party.

Tonic pointed toward the pond. "Smell that water!" she told them. "The stink of rotten eggs is there. It isn't strong, but it's the same."

Ernie dropped to his hands and knees, sniffing the pond cautiously. "Tonie is right," he said as he stood. "This pond wasn't rancid when you first saw it, Arnold?"

"It was pure and fresh and clean," the old man said quietly. "That means he must have come here after poisoning the first pond and poisoned this one, too, figuring the train would make its next stop here."

"We'll never know why he was so intent on killing innocent people who have done no harm to anyone," Ernie said, sighing. "At least we're rid of him, and that's all to the good."

Stalking Hórse carefully removed the dead man's boots, knife, and pistol, along with his ammunition and powder, before carrying the body away from the wagon train's path, where it would be allowed to rot.

"We will give the pack horse or the rifle to Tonie, whichever of the two she prefers," Ernie said gallantly as they started toward the wagon train camp.

"Thank you," she replied, "but I want neither."

Ernie assumed, as did Mack, that the girl was depressed because the man had been killed.

She did not disillusion them, but signaled discreetly to her uncle, who fell back to the rear of the line and rode beside her.

"I wonder if you noticed," Tonie said, "that all three of the man's shots were fired at me. As far as he knew, I was the least likely to hit him, the least dangerous to him, yet he concentrated his fire only on me."

"I know," he replied, speaking in Russian. "The secret police is like a snake with many heads. Remove one, and hundreds of others grow. That is an old proverb, Antoinette. From now on, we take no unnecessary risks with your safety."

Tonie shuddered, then felt ashamed of herself. "I was

scared when he was shooting at me, Uncle Arnold. I'm not a coward, I swear I'm not, but I was afraid."

"Of course you were," he told her. "You're not lacking in courage. But anyone who isn't afraid of a powerful, unseen enemy is a fool."

When they reached the wagon train, they found that funeral services had already been held for the two men who had died after drinking from the pond that morning.

Ernie made a brief announcement. "As we suspected, the man who poisoned the pond was the same man we entertained at supper last night. He has also poisoned the pond at which we would have stopped tomorrow. But he'll cause no more harm to anyone. Stalking Horse saw to that."

At Tonie's suggestion, the dead man's riding horse was given to one of the widows and the pack horse was presented to the other. Then her uncle took her arm and led her to Ernie's elegant wagon. There the Baron and Whip were sipping tiny glasses of colorless Austrian schnapps, and another glass was filled for Arnold.

"Not until we came back here did I realize you were personally involved, Tonie. I should have realized when Munson made you his only target that he was working for the Russians."

The girl nodded.

"The question now," Whip said, "is whether to tell everybody that the Russian secret police want to kill you because you defied them."

"Do what you please," Tonie said in a dull voice. "It doesn't matter."

A tap sounded at the door, and Dr. Martin entered. "May I intrude?" he asked, and assuming the reply would be positive, seated himself on the top of a mahogany chest of drawers. "Mack Dougall was just telling me the details of your encounter with Munson," he said. "I knew at once why he was firing at Tonie, and I figured that's what you'd be discussing."

Ernie nodded and poured him a glass of schnapps.

The physician handed the drink to the girl. "She needs this. I don't."

Tonie shook her head, but Bob gave her no chance to speak. "Drink it," he said. "Doctor's orders."

She managed to down the drink, and shuddered.

"We've just raised the question of whether to tell the whole company why the Russians want to kill Tonie," Whip said. "Myself, I'm torn. I can see arguments in favor of both sides. I think you have to make the choice yourself, Tonie."

"I just told you," she said. "It doesn't matter." The schnapps seemed to be burning a hole inside of her, but she had to admit that she no longer felt lethargic. Perhaps Bob's presence rather than the liquor was responsible.

"I want to be fair to everybody," Ernie said.

"My only concern is being fair to Tonie," her uncle declared.

"I see no useful cause being served by making this information public," Bob Martin said, his manner unexpectedly vehement. "We'd only be drawing attention to her, unnecessary attention. In this instance I say that what people don't know won't hurt them."

Tonie was surprised that he was taking such a strong interest in her personal situation.

"Arnold," Bob continued, "you understand the Russian mentality, and we don't. Are they likely to attempt another attack on Tonie?"

"Perhaps," the old man replied, frowning as he tried to solve the puzzle for himself. "I would say they are determined to damage the wagon train because it is in the czar's interest that we fail to reach Oregon. Certainly the Russians are vindictive, and they patently hate Tonie because she refused to obey their orders. So I would guess they well might make another attempt on her life."

"In that case we must change her routines," Bob Martin said briskly. "I see no reason she can't continue to serve as chief monitor. She spends her days riding between the center column and one of the wing columns, so it would be very difficult to isolate her there. But I think it would be wrong for her to go off again as she did with today's search party. And I believe it would be too dangerous to allow her to go out hunting again."

"That makes sense," Whip said.

"It does," Ernie replied.

Even Arnold slowly nodded.

Tonie didn't know whether to laugh or weep. They were restricting her future activities, and no one was even bothering to consult her. Life would be far more boring if she couldn't go hunting any more, but she could console herself with the thought that Bob wasn't as unconcerned about her as he appeared. Certainly his interest in her welfare was personal, his involvement greater than that of Whip and Ernie. Or was it? She had no way of knowing.

X

The long trek continued, the wagon train creeping slowly through the heartlands of the Great Plains. They still followed the Platte River, and some members of the expedition were surprised when the broad stream rose higher and flowed more swiftly.

"It always does that," Whip explained, "but this year there must have been more snow than usual in the Rockies. The thaws come later on the heights than they do down below, of course, so the melted snow is just now beginning to reach us from the North Platte, the South Platte, and some of the smaller streams that flow into the big river."

During one nooning, when the sun overhead was actually hot, Danny and Chet, along with some of the older boys, decided to get undressed and go for a swim, but the water was so unexpectedly icy they soon changed their minds. They were dressing, threatening to push the last one who finished into the chilly water, when their horseplay was interrupted by Whip, who ran toward them from the circle.

"I ought to skin you lads alive," he said. "I ought to hang you up by the heels, like we do with dead polecats. But even that would be too good for you."

Rarely did the wagonmaster become so angry, at least

in public, and the boys were shocked. Danny, who had frozen in the midst of pulling on a stocking, was the only one of the group who had the courage to raise his voice. "What—what did we do wrong, Whip?"

"What did you do? You still don't know?" Whip's fury increased. "You think of yourselves as men, or close to it. But it looks to me like you're babies. About the same age as the little Malcolm youngster."

They were still at a loss to understand what they had done to inspire his wrath.

"Finish dressing!" Whip commanded, glaring at them. The boys wasted no time.

"Chet Harris!" Whip barked. "See that stick in the grass? Pick it up."

Chet quickly picked up a portion of a broken tree branch. It was two feet long, about three inches in diameter, and it was surprisingly heavy.

"Pass it around!" Whip ordered.

The broken branch moved from hand to hand, and none of the boys knew what to do with it. Some weighed it, others turned it over and over in their hands, while a few got rid of it very quickly, as though afraid it would contaminate them. At last it was passed back to Chet.

"Bring it with you," Whip commanded, "and all of you come with me." He led them to the bank of the river, forcing them to stand with him on the wet, soggy ground. "Look at the river and tell me what you see."

Again Danny was the only one to speak. "One mighty lot of water," he muttered.

Several of the boys started to snicker.

"You, Chet! Throw that stick into the river. Heave it as far as you can toward midstream," Whip instructed.

Using all of his strength, Chet hurled the broken branch toward the center of the rapidly flowing river.

"Now keep your eyes on it," Whip said, "and tell me when it disappears."

The boys crowded close to the bank. They saw the branch bobbing up and down as it was carried eastward at a rapid speed.

"It's gone!" one of them shouted.

"No it isn't," Chet said, correcting him. "I can still see it. Well, maybe not. I reckon you're right. It's gone."

Whip remained firm. "Now," he said, "I want somebody to tell me what you've just learned."

There was a long, tense silence. Then Danny said, "That stick got carried away awful fast. The river looks pretty strong, but the current is even faster than we think it is—and stronger, too. So we might have been in trouble if we'd gone swimming."

"*Might* have been in trouble?" Whip raised an eyebrow. "Some of you—especially you, Chet—think you're pretty good swimmers. Well, I guarantee you that every last one of you would have been washed downstream and drowned in almost no time."

The chastened boys stared down at the river bank.

"After this," Whip said, "you check with Ernie or with me before you start doing things on your own. You're in the wilderness, not on somebody's farm property, and God help those of you who forget it! Remember—your life and everyone else's depends on your alertness. So keep your eyes open every minute of the day." He turned and walked back to the circle.

The boys straggled after him, their lesson learned. Anyone who toyed with the forces of nature in the vast expanses of the Great Plains was running a dangerous risk.

As the spring advanced, rain fell more frequently, and usually at night. The Platte continued to rise, sometimes overflowing its banks for a distance of ten or fifteen yards on both sides. Whip kept the river under close observation and took the precaution of establishing the campsite some distance from the flowing waters.

There seemed to be less need to exercise such extreme care during the nooning period, however. It was far easier and simpler to form the circle fairly close to the river so that the animals could be led to the bank for watering. At nooning the wagons moved into the circle, experience enabling the drivers to perform the task quickly. Teams were unhitched and taken to the river for watering, then allowed to graze inside the circle. Hungry children were given smoked buffalo meat or, in some families, leftovers from breakfast, and any adults who were hungry did likewise. However, most of them had gone on a schedule of eating only two meals a day and preferred to wait until evening.

No one ever knew who first became aware of the approach of catastrophe that day. All at once men began to shout, women screamed, and somebody called, "My God! The river!"

The fear in their voices was so intense that virtually everyone jumped up, and those who had been taking naps awakened. What met their eyes was so unbelievable that it paralyzed them.

As they looked upstream, they saw a towering wall of water bearing down on them. No longer just a swiftly moving river, the Platte had been transformed into a wildly raging torrent. The boiling, churning water, carrying entire trees and other debris, bore down on the wagon train in a mighty tidal wave.

The initial reaction of fright gave way to frenzied panic as people struggled for survival in the midst of the nightmare. Those whose wagons stood nearest to the river were in the greatest danger. They began to run across the circle to the far side, some carrying small children.

Only Whip's and Hosea's instant response prevented the damage from being even worse. Reacting independently, they began to drive the bewildered horses and oxen toward the far edge of the circle, away from the raging flood. Whip fired his pistols, then his rifle, while Hosea roared in a deep baritone, clapping his hands together repeatedly, trying to get the animals moving away from the danger.

The animals began to stampede, and even those that had remained calm joined in the race. In almost no time, most were pushing against the wagons at the outer side of the circle. The horses and oxen had no idea of what was happening, but their instinctive panic led them away from the flood.

The wave approached at blinding speed, the gray waters

spelling doom for everything in their path. The wagons that stood nearest the bank bore the brunt of the attack. Wood splintered, loose objects were picked up and swept away, and the roar of the water was so loud that the screams of the women and children could not be heard.

Then, as suddenly as it had come, the wave was gone, still churning furiously as it raced eastward. Gradually the waters subsided, and although the Platte had spread beyond its banks, it once again became relatively harmless.

A woman screamed. Her husband and small daughter, who had been napping in their wagon, had been swept away by the wave, and her teenaged son, who had been whittling as he had sat on the rear stoop of the wagon had also disappeared. Some of the men found his battered, lifeless body about half a mile downstream later in the day.

Only a head count ultimately revealed that another family, who had joined the caravan in Indiana, had been swallowed up by the great wave. The husband, the wife, and all three of their small children had simply vanished as though they had never existed.

A young bachelor, a former bookkeeper from Cincinnatti who yearned for a life on his own farm, had suffered a broken leg when heavy debris had smashed into him. "I—I'm lucky I'm still here, I guess," he muttered through his pain as Dr. Martin set his leg.

Emily Harris required stitches in her thigh, where she had been gashed by a tree uprooted by the raging river. Terence Malcolm had suffered a sprained ankle, but had no idea how it had happened.

Grace Drummond was also injured. The wave had picked her up, then slammed her against a wagon, knocking her unconscious. As nearly as Dr. Martin could diagnose, she was suffering from a brain concussion. For hours Nat Drummond stayed at his wife's side, applying cold compresses to her forehead. Late in the afternoon, she stirred and opened her eyes. Sitting upright, she began to berate her husband for his idleness.

The grinning Nat knew she had returned to normal. Walking away from her bed, he left her to her own devices. Not until Grace finally realized what had happened to her did her anger subside.

Three workhorses were missing, as were a pair of oxen. One of the riding horses had broken a leg when it had been rammed by floating debris, and it had to be shot.

Aside from the tragedy of the man and his daughter, one entire wagon and its contents had been picked up and carried away by the wave. No portion of the wagon itself, nor its contents, remained. The owners, a young couple who had come all the way from the mountains of Pennsylvania, were forced to move into another wagon with the girl's parents.

There was debris everywhere, scattered as if by a giant hand. Two uprooted trees, one of them a forty-foot oak, complete with a portion of its roots, lay in the muddy ooze near the bank of the now-normal river. Branches of all sizes, torn from trees along the river, were everywhere. Even rocks and boulders had been strewn about by the raging wave.

What shocked the pioneers most was the waterlogged corpse of a cow buffalo washed up by the torrent. They could scarcely believe their eyes. The beast was huge and must have weighed at least fifteen hundred pounds.

Smaller animals had fallen victim, too. Rabbits and gophers, chipmunks, a raccoon and an antelope doe had been smashed almost beyond recognition by the furious river.

Several of the wagons, at least a half-dozen by preliminary count, were severely damaged, while a large number of others had been badly battered. Canvas tops and sides had been ripped away, then carried downstream by the wave. Struts that had supported the canvas roofs were either gone or reduced to kindling. Axles had been twisted and bent and were now useless, and one wagon teetered precariously because its wheels on the water side had been torn off.

It would be a long time before the owners of the stricken wagons would be able to judge accurately how much of their property had been lost. All they knew was that the remaining contents of their wagons were a muddy, soggy mess. Emergency food supplies were ruined. Pots, pans, and broken crockery littered the area, as did odd items of clothing, including a child's shoe and a torn woman's shift, which was draped around a bush.

Those who ventured near the river bank sank almost to their knees, and several had to be hauled out of the gripping, sucking mud. Hours would pass before the ground there had drained and dried off sufficiently to support the weight of a person.

Everyone pitched in to help. The circle of wagons was moved even further away from the bank of the Platte, although it was unlikely that the extraordinary phenomenon would be repeated. Then the remaining contents of the stricken wagons were spread out to dry, and the women went to work scrubbing down the muddy interiors.

Men with experience as carpenters made new struts from supplies carried in the special wagon, which also provided new canvas and axles to replace those that had been damaged beyond repair. Whip promised the dazed owners of the wagons that the hunters and fishermen would give them enough meat and fish to replace what they had lost. Other wagon owners contributed jars of preserves and sacks of beans, coffee, flour, and sugar.

The lost clothing was yet another problem, but Arnold and Mack promised to provide enough buffalo and deer hides so that people could replace their wardrobes.

The task of repairing the damage cost the company two days on the trail. No one objected to the extra labor involved, to be sure, and the hunters kept their word, shooting enough game in the next forty-eight hours to provide the stricken with at least the beginnings of new emergency food supplies and new wardrobes.

Everyone was appalled by the shocking and unexpected experience, and the entire company suddenly realized that the forces of nature were capable of inflicting cruel punishment on the unwary. The very word "wilderness" was enough to inspire respect.

Fortunately game was marvelously plentiful in the late spring. Whip wanted to replace the losses as rapidly as possible, so he asked for volunteers to join the regular hunting parties. Tonie was the first to offer her services, but Whip politely declined.

She was furious, telling herself that Bob Martin was to blame for wrapping her in a thick, protective mantle. Although she continued to help him in the infirmary, she made it clear to him that she was annoyed.

Another volunteer, much to everyone's surprise, was Nat Drummond. The hunters were working in pairs now, and Arnold said he would make Nat his partner. The combination seemed incongruous, but Arnold withheld judgment. "I want to see how he makes out before I'll listen to any criticism," he said.

The new team went out late one afternoon, returning a scant two hours later with a buck. But the initial flurry of excitement subsided when it was learned that Arnold, not Nat, had shot the deer.

The next day Arnold returned to the campsite early, his scouting duties completed, and he and Nat went out again. They headed toward a wooded area that the scout had seen, earlier in the day, off to the northwest.

Nat looked clumsy in the saddle, but he had no difficulty in maintaining the pace set by his companion, and he appeared to be enjoying the outing thoroughly. In a talkative mood, he began to chat as they cantered. "Can I tell you somethin' private, Arnold? It's taken a lifetime for me to do what I've always wanted to do."

Arnold nodded encouragingly.

"I grew up near the Kentucky border, you see, and when I was a boy, I heard all kinds of stories about Dan'l Boone and the others who tamed the wilderness."

"Most of those stories are exaggerated, I'm sure," Arnold said. "I've heard some of them just as I heard many others about this part of the wilderness when I lived in Independence. Hunters and trappers and guides have done some wonderful things, but a lot of them are also good liars. When a couple of them would get together with my wife and me in our kitchen, they'd start bragging, and before long they'd be trying to tell bigger and bigger stories so they could outdo each other."

"I reckon you're right," Nat said. "But you still don't know what this means to me, ridin' across the wilderness in search of game. When I grew up, I had a lot of hopes and dreams, but then I got married. And you know Grace.

I had to buckle down and make a living on the farm, or she gave me no peace. But this is a grand life. I couldn't ask for anythin' better."

They rode on in companionable silence, and ultimately the woods came into view on the horizon. As the pair drew nearer, six Indians rapidly rode out of the woods toward them.

"Oh-oh," Arnold said softly. "Now we'll see how your daydreams have prepared you for a real crisis. They're warriors—I'm not sure of their tribe at this distance—and they're bent on making mischief. I wouldn't be surprised if they were heading for the wagon train when they spotted us. They'll pause long enough to knock us out of commission, if they can."

Nat displayed remarkable calm. "First they got to do it," he said, eyeing the onrushing braves. "Just tell me what to do, Arnold. You're the boss."

Shading his eyes as they continued to canter, Arnold grunted. "We're in for real trouble. They're Paiute. I'd rather walk barefoot into a nest of rattlesnakes. Paiute can't be bluffed. Either we kill them or they kill us. There's no halfway measures, no evasions. If we run, they'll chase us and catch us. If we stop and wait for them, we'll be sitting targets, and we'll never get off a shot."

"Are you tellin' me we keep ridin'?"

"Right! No matter what happens, don't slow your pace. You understand?"

"Sure."

"All right," Arnold said. "Get your rifle ready. After you fire, reload as fast as you can, then fire again. Keep doing it."

"All right." Nat still seemed calm.

"They'll spread out as they come closer. We may move through their formation—provided they don't hit us first. Then we'll turn and come at them again from the rear." Arnold turned for an instant to look at his companion, afraid that Drummond would begin to show signs of panic when he realized how badly the odds were against them.

But the stubby farmer grinned, showing two rows of crooked, yellowed teeth. "It seems t' me we got one big advantage, Arnold. These rifles have a much longer range than their arrows."

Arnold chuckled. Nat was going to weather the crisis in good shape.

"If we can reload quick enough, maybe we can get off two rounds before they start sendin' their arrows at us."

"Not maybe, Nat. Two rounds are a minimum. And we've got to make those bullets count. At close range they'll overwhelm us. They're deadly shots with their arrows, and they can handle spears expertly, too."

Nat checked his rifle, hunching forward in his saddle. "I'm ready any time you give the word."

Together as they rode, they kept a sharp watch on the oncoming Paiute. The braves held their bows and were reaching for their first arrows.

Arnold Mell calculated the distance coolly. He felt reasonably sure that at least one of his bullets would find its mark, and he could only hope that Drummond would hold up. If the Indians realized they were dealing with a novice, they would redouble their efforts.

The two groups drew nearer.

"Now!" Arnold called, raising his own rifle and firing.

A brave seemed to rise high in the air from the back of his pony, then toppled to the ground.

Nat took deliberate aim and squeezed the trigger. A second brave flung his hands over his head, tried to steady himself in vain and fell to the grass, where he lay motionless, face down.

Arnold was quietly elated. He hadn't expected his partner to be this effective. "Keep up the good work," he called.

Nat reloaded with the speed of a marksman.

Arnold had his rifle up to his shoulder, and again he fired, then cursed as he saw he had missed by inches.

Nat's every move was as deliberate as though he were firing at a stationary target. He squeezed the trigger again, and a third brave clutched his chest, then dropped to the turf.

By this time the remaining Paiute were close enough to

enter the fray actively, and they sent their arrows in the direction of the pair cantering toward them. But the warriors were rattled because of the losses they had already suffered, and their shots went wild.

Seeing their consternation, Arnold knew he and his companion had victory almost in hand. "Again!" he shouted.

Nat doggedly reloaded, but by this time the Paiute had had enough of combat for one day. Swinging their ponies in an arc, they fled toward the north, quickly increasing their speed to a full gallop.

Two of the riderless ponies followed, their panic so great that they eventually caught up with the retreating band. The remaining pony was bewildered, however, and stood uncertainly, near his fallen master.

Arnold slowed his own mount to a sedate walk. "No point in chasing them, Nat. They won't want any more fighting today. You did a great job."

Nat slowed, too, and chuckled. "We didn't do too bad," he admitted as he followed his partner's example and turned back.

"This takes care of our hunting for the day," Arnold said, "but we'll bring a few souvenirs back with us so our friends won't think we're making up frontier tales."

The chunky little farmer stared at him apprehensively. "You ain't plannin' to take scalps, Arnold?"

The old man laughed aloud. "That's one habit I've never bothered to take up." He dismounted, then walked quietly toward the riderless pony, moving slowly and gently so he wouldn't alarm the animal. Removing a lariat from a hook at his belt, he twirled it, then threw the loop over the pony's head.

The animal balked, but as it pulled back, the noose tightened around its neck, and it had the good sense not to fight the inevitable. It stood still again.

Arnold pointed toward the crumpled body of one of the braves. "Help yourself to his weapons," he called.

Only now did Nat Drummond become diffident. He paused for a long time before he summoned the courage to bend down for the dead warrior's bow and quiver of arrows.

Arnold had no such inhibitions. Working swiftly as he led the docile pony, he removed knives from the belts of the other two corpses, picked up a spear, and then bent low to take a necklace of elk's teeth from the body of one warrior. "You may want to give this to your wife," he said, handing Nat the necklace. "Here. And take the pony, too, along with the spear and this knife."

Nat was overwhelmed. "You caught the pony, I didn't. And you're keepin' nothin'."

"Not so. I'll keep this one knife. It so happens that I've got all sorts of souvenirs from fights in the past. Besides, you deserve the lion's share. After all, you took care of two warriors to my one."

Flushing with embarrassment, pride, and gratitude, the heavily laden Nat mounted his own horse and, leading the captured Paiute pony, rode beside the older man as they started back toward the wagon train campsite.

"For a fellow who spent his early years daydreaming, you're a mighty fine partner to have around in an emergency," Arnold said. "From now on, I'm going hunting with no one but you."

Supper was almost ready when they reached camp, and a ripple of excitement passed through the company when they saw the enemy weapons and the pony. Arnold was lavish in his praise of his companion and described his exploits at length while Nat looked down at the ground and shuffled his feet.

The older boys were awed as they examined the captured weapons, and people clamored for the privilege of offering Nat their congratulations. Whip and Mack pumped his hand, Ernie clapped him on the back, and Stalking Horse caught hold of his wrist in a gesture of brotherly affection. Ted Woods and Hosea made no comment, but their expressions indicated that they shared the general opinion that Nat was a hero.

The excitement began to ebb when Cathy beat the side of a kettle with a heavy spoon to indicate that supper was now prepared. People formed a line to help themselves to a stew of buffalo meat and root vegetables, including wild beets. Nat deposited his booty in his wagon, then joined his wife in the line.

Grace gave him no chance to speak. "You think highly of yourself, Mr. Drummond," she said.

"Now that you mention it, Mrs. Drummond, maybe I do." He took the bone-handled Paiute knife from his belt, turned it over in his hand as he studied it, and decided that from now on he would always carry it with him. "Behave yourself like a wife should, and maybe I'll teach you how to ride that pony. He's a quiet creature, which is what you ought to be, so by-and-by the two of you ought to get along just fine."

Grace drew in a breath, steadying herself for a retort. Those who stood near them in the line waited for the inevitable, loud outburst.

Nat gave her no opportunity to explode. "Before I forget it," he said, "I brought you a little present." He reached into the breast pocket of his linsey-woolsey shirt, then handed her the necklace of elk's teeth.

Grace looked at the highly polished teeth, and all at once tears came into her eyes. "How—how do I wear it?"

"See them rawhide thongs? They tie at the back of your neck."

"Will you tie it for me, Nat?"

He was startled by the unexpected humility in her usually strident voice. "Sure," he said, putting the necklace around her neck and tying it.

"How does it look, Nat?"

He glanced at the necklace but was even more conscious of the tears that were trickling silently down her weather-hardened cheeks. "Right pretty, Grace. That necklace suits you just fine."

Not caring who might be watching, Grace Drummond hugged her husband, squeezing him until he was breathless. "It was your pa and your brothers who used to tease you for wantin' to be like Dan'l Boone, wasn't it?"

Nat nodded. "Now and again they'd have their fun with me," he admitted.

"Well, I just wish they could see you now!" she exclaimed, speaking in her normal, booming voice. "Because you have the last laugh. Gracious, but I'm proud o' you, Nat Drummond!"

Arthur Elwood was fed up. The discomforts and hardships of wagon train living were almost unbearable, he found the food intolerable and the company dull beyond endurance. He was a city dweller, and he missed the luxuries of the East that he had known only in small quantities. He was dismayed by the prospect of settling in the Oregon country, and when others spoke of that supposed paradise as a land of milk and honey, he refused to listen.

He had joined the train only because he had hoped he could buy the land claims of the future settlers for a dollar or two per acre. He had expected to be able to purchase several thousand acres and then reap an enormous profit by selling them to speculators in the East for as much as ten dollars per acre. But not one member of the expedition had been willing to sell to him. These stubborn farmers had destroyed his chance to become wealthy.

He should have turned back at Fort Madison. Now each day's journey carried him farther from the civilization he craved. To hell with these crude people and their dreams of the future. He wanted his creature comforts now, while he was still young enough to enjoy them. A man in his forties had to think in immediate terms.

So, little by little, Arthur Elwood came to the conclusion that he should make a break and go back alone. He had never spent a single day in the wilderness by himself, but that didn't matter, he thought. All he had to do was follow the Platte until he came to the Missouri, and he didn't care whether his journey took him to Independence, St. Joseph, or Council Bluffs. Once he reached a real town, he had enough money in his belt to arrange for transportation to Chicago or Cincinnati.

How he would live once he returned to the East was a problem he would solve later. His immediate task was that of getting away. He could just take off on his own, he supposed, but it wasn't that easy. Stupidly, no doubt, he hadn't bothered to collect any emergency supplies, and he needed them badly. If he could sneak into the special wagon, he could fill his saddlebags with quantities of smoked buffalo meat or venison, along with parched corn, none of which he would ever touch again when he reached a world where people ate real food. He would be wise to take a spare rifle, too, along with plenty of lead, a bullet mold, and extra gunpowder.

In a sense, he told himself, he had earned whatever he chose to take with him. After all, he had worked as a member of the water-gathering detail, engaging in physical labor that he abhorred.

His greatest mistake, he knew, was that of having joined the wagon train in the first place. He had always had a desk job, working for various land speculation companies. He disliked the outdoors and loathed physical exertion.

Other men on the train had become hunters, fishermen and woodcutters. He was ashamed by the knowledge that he had been assigned to gather water because he had proved unfit for any other kind of service. Well, when he returned to the East, he would sit at a desk again and wouldn't ever leave it.

He simply had to get away from these people. The life they were leading and the future that beckoned to them kept them cheerful, even in the face of the same adversity and hardships that haunted him. He had no real friends in the company and had almost nothing in common with anyone. Claudia Brentwood had been kind to him, but she had remained in Independence. He had been attracted to Cindy, but she had rebuffed him. No one else interested him, and he spent the social hours alone each day, even eating by himself because there was so little he could discuss with the other travelers. He hated the wagon train and all it represented.

Elwood's desire to escape made him desperate. One warm evening in early summer, he found it impossible to sleep. After hesitating for a long time, he screwed up his courage and, sneaking out of his wagon, made his way to the special wagon. Just before reaching it, he stumbled, landing on the ground with a hard, noisy thud, but he ignored the pain and held his breath, hoping no one had heard him. There was no sound, and he was relieved.

It was easy enough to untie the back flaps and let himself into the wagon. First he dropped the flap behind him, but quickly realized his mistake. It was so dark inside that he could see nothing. So he raised the flap again and left it open.

After fumbling for a time, staring at boxes, crates, and barrels, he pried open a barrel with his knife. The strong odor of smoked buffalo meat almost gagged him, but he couldn't afford to take enough time to search for the milder-tasting venison. He crammed meat into his saddlebag, then carefully replaced the barrel cover. It took longer to locate a sack of parched corn, but now he acted quickly, making a small slit in one end with his knife and pouring enough of the contents into the saddlebag to fill it.

It took almost an hour to locate the spare arms and munitions. The rifle he selected was larger and heavier than his own weapon, but he was in no position to be particular, so he took it, along with a bar of lead and a horn filled with powder. Realizing it would be impossible to locate a bullet press in this gloom, he knew he had to alter his plans. He would hide his loot in his wagon. Then, when people were at breakfast, he would steal a press from a neighboring wagon that stood behind him. That meant he would have to wait until tomorrow night before he could leave. But no matter—he had attended to most of his needs, and after all these months, it wouldn't hurt him to wait an extra day.

The lead bar was heavy, but Elwood managed to squeeze it into his hip pocket before he climbed out of the wagon and lowered the flap behind him, carefully retying it. Then he hoisted the cumbersome saddlebag onto his shoulder, noting in surprise that day was breaking. He had finished his task none too soon. Staggering slightly under the weight of the bag and the lead, he turned away.

At that moment someone stepped out from between two wagons. Elwood saw Hosea, his blowgun in his hand, a dart already fitted into it.

Elwood panicked. "For God's sake, don't shoot that contraption at me! Look here, I—I have plenty of money, and I'll pay you well if you'll just forget that you've seen —"

"Whip decide what to do," Hosea said, gesturing in

the direction of the fire, which had burned low. "You come."

Fully aware that the blowgun could kill instantly, Arthur Elwood had no choice. His stomach, like his feet, felt leaden as he walked ahead of the grim Ashanti.

Whip was already awake, and he listened without comment to Hosea's explanation. Then he reached for the stolen rifle, examined the contents of the saddlebag, and asked, "What else did you take?"

It was useless to lie, so Elwood handed him the lead bar and powder horn.

"Don't say anything now," Whip told him. "I know what I'd do to you if it was up to me. But it isn't my place to decide." He led the way to Ernie von Thalman's wagon.

The Baron, who was just dressing, listened in stone-faced silence. "Hosea," he said, "keep Mr. Elwood under guard. Right here."

Soon the whole company was awake and stirring. Wood was gathered and the fire built up, water was carried from the Platte, and the women in charge of the cooking went to work.

Ernie waited until most members of the expedition had assembled, then made a short speech in which he explained what had happened. "I'm glad to say this is the first time we've faced such a situation, but now we've got to do something about it. As your president, I'm asking you—right now—to elect ten people as a jury. We don't want to delay our day's march too long, so I'll ask those who are elected to join me over yonder, in front of my wagon. Immediately."

Nat Drummond was the first to be elected. Whip declined the honor, as did the scouts, who departed on their regular missions as soon as they ate their usual early breakfast.

Before the meeting of the entire company broke up, Whip announced that he wanted to say a few words. "Folks," he began, "some of you may wonder why we're making so much of what's happened this morning."

"That's right," Cathy called out boldly, always willing to

champion an underdog. "It doesn't seem to me that Mr. Elwood committed any great crime. The food in the special wagon belongs to all of us. Every man here carries a rifle and ammunition, so I don't see what harm Mr. Elwood has done. Real harm, I mean. What he's taken is actually minor, so all this fuss strikes me as silly."

Whip had to respect her attitude. At the same time, he was glad she had spoken up because it would be easier now for him to emphasize the point he was trying to make.

"Mrs. van Ayl has a valid point," he said. "I think you folks know me well enough to realize I'm not vindictive, and I sure as shooting am not proposing that we boil Arthur Elwood in oil. But I'm afraid a lot of you may not realize the importance of the special wagon and what it means to all of us."

He paused, looked around at the people gathered in the circle, then spoke again very slowly. "That wagon is the key to our survival. It can mean the difference between life and death to every last one of us."

His words created a stir, and people muttered to each other.

"I mean what I say. Literally," Whip told them. "After the wave hit us, we'd have been in a pretty fix if we hadn't carried spare axles and canvas and wheels and such with us. We may have troubles with Indians before this trip ends, serious troubles, and I can see where one rifle and one lead bar that can be molded into bullets could make the difference between life and death."

The members of the company were beginning to understand, and Whip was rewarded by nods and other signs of recognition.

"On the day you joined the train, every last one of you was told that *nobody* is allowed to go into the special wagon, ever, without my own personal permission. I told you that included everybody—Ernie von Thalman, the scouts—I don't care who it is. Well, Mr. Elwood chose to disobey that order. I'll grant you that he didn't take much. But if fifty or a hundred others get the same idea and start taking things, what then? A rifle here, a barrel of pickled meat there, some gunpowder, an extra blanket or two. Pretty soon the special wagon will be plucked clean, and then—may God have mercy on all of us."

Cathy was forced to agree with him, her emphatic nod making the change in her attitude plain to everyone around her.

"There are no stores between here and Oregon. No stores once I get you there, either. The closest place you can buy a nail, a hammer, or a frying pan is way back in Independence. For at least two more years, until freight wagons start crossing the continent, you'll have to make do with what you already own or can make for yourselves. All that stands between you and sure disaster is that special wagon and the supplies it carries." He took a deep breath. "That's about all I have to say for now. I hope you'll remember it. For your own sakes, not mine, because I can get along on my own in the mountains." He stalked off, and the meeting broke up.

One by one the jurors gathered. Some of the older boys, who lingered, curious, in the vicinity, were sent on their way by a curt and unexpectedly stern Ernie. At last ten jurors stood in front of the wagon, and Ernie opened the wagon door. "You can come out now," he called.

A miserable Arthur Elwood appeared, closely followed by Hosea. Ernie thanked the Ashanti and dismissed him, sending him off for breakfast. Then he pointed to the saddlebag, rifle, lead bar, and powder horn. "These are the items Mr. Elwood stole from the special wagon. Do you admit it, Mr. Elwood?"

There was a moment's hesitation. "Not exactly. The saddlebag is my own."

Ernie was surprisingly patient. "Very well. But you took its contents. Meat and corn."

Elwood could only nod.

"Will you tell us your reasons?"

Suddenly the dam burst, and Arthur Elwood became eloquent, explaining in detail that he had long hated every aspect of wagon train living. "I took these things," he concluded passionately, "because I need them to get back to real civilization. I'm sick of this kind of living, and I just can't stand it any more. I'm not sorry I stole, and to hell with Oregon!"

His listeners were startled. It was unusual enough to hear someone refuse to express remorse for committing a crime. But people whose hearts and souls were devoted to the settlement of the Oregon country found it inconceivable that one of their number had lost the desire to make a new life in a land that was unique. What they failed to realize, of course, was that Elwood had had different desires from the very moment he had joined the company.

Ernie broke the heavy silence. "Let me see if I understand you correctly, Mr. Elwood. You want to detach your wagon from the expedition and go back East. Is that correct?"

"No!" Elwood had no idea that his voice was becoming strident. "I was planning to use one of my team as a pack horse and simply swap my other workhorse for a riding horse."

"Leaving your wagon behind?"

"I have no use for the damned thing." The man was bitter. "I couldn't tolerate the idea of creeping back across these infernal flatlands in it."

Ernie nodded, then turned to the jurors. "Gentlemen," he said, "I want to offer you a thought you can either accept or reject. The property Mr. Elwood stole from us has a strictly limited value. It's the theft itself, including that of the rifle, that's important. It seems to me that we can't compel a person to endure our company. All of us are voluntary members of this group, bound together by an unwritten compact and observing an unwritten code of conduct for the sake of our mutual good. Mr. Elwood chooses to break the contract, and in my opinion that's his privilege."

"We want no more to do with him than he wants with us," Nat said in a disgusted tone. "It ain't worth the fuss to turn his wagon into a jail and keep him in it. Let him go, that's what I say, and good riddance to him."

"You mean we ought to throw him out?" one of the other jurors asked.

Ernie shook his head. "We can't quite do that. These plains are inhospitable enough to men like Whip, who know the area well. I believe Mr. Elwood himself suggested the solution. We can trade one of the spare horses we've acquired for one of his workhorses. Let him take what he can carry of his belongings—food, clothes, cooking utensils and the like. Weapons, too, of course. Let him keep the food he's stolen, along with the rifle and ammunition. We'll take his wagon in return, along with any other belongings he chooses to leave behind. You needn't accept this idea, gentlemen. All I ask is that you consider it."

The jurors moved off down the line of wagons to confer privately. Some of the women brought them breakfast, then Ernie was given a plate, and Cathy insisted that Elwood be fed, too.

The jurors talked earnestly as they ate and needed no urging to reach a prompt decision, for they shared Whip's desire not to delay the start of the day's journey any longer than necessary.

Ernie ate in silence, refraining from conversing with Arthur Elwood.

Sipping their mugs of coffee, the jurors returned to the outside of the Baron's wagon. "Seein' it wouldn't be right to hang the bastard," Nat said, "we've decided your thinkin' is pretty good, Ernie. We'll make the trade, just like you said—on one condition. He's got to leave this mornin', right now. We don't want him hangin' around. And if you can spare the extra time, maybe you'll keep an eye on him while he packs to make sure he don't cheat us."

"You've heard the sentence pronounced by the jury, Mr. Elwood," Ernie said. "Do you have any comment?"

"It suits me just fine," Elwood replied angrily. "I'm happy to leave as fast as I can get myself organized."

The decision was communicated to Whip, and while the train made ready to leave on the day's march, Elwood returned to his wagon to pack another saddlebag and take his blankets, spare boots, and a frying pan. Ernie fetched one of the extra horses to give the man in exchange for his workhorse and brought it to his wagon, where Elwood was finishing his hurried task. Just then, a concerned Whip also appeared at the wagon. "I hope you know what you're doing, Mr. Elwood," he said. "Even men who have been hunters and trappers for years don't like traveling alone in these parts."

Arthur Elwood shrugged.

Whip looked at the saddlebags filled with food and made some mental calculations. "You're not carrying enough provisions to see you all the way to Council Bluffs or Independence. You'll need to shoot some game on the way."

"I see no problem, Mr. Holt. I'm not totally unfamiliar with the handling of firearms."

Whip had intended to enumerate the dangers of solitary travel in the Great Plains, but the man was being so hostile that he refrained. All the same, his conscience forced him to make one last remark. "In my opinion you're taking one hell of a big risk. I can't say I like or trust you after the way you broke into the special wagon, but we can't throw you out and let you flounder on your own."

"I'll make out fine," the tight-lipped Elwood replied.

Whip shook his head. "I know more about the Great Plains than you do, and I think you're wrong to leave our group at this time. I don't want to scare you, and I don't want to upset you, but I *am* suggesting you come all the way to Oregon with us. Other trains will be following us, and it won't be too long before there's a reasonable amount of traffic going back and forth between the Atlantic and the Pacific. Be patient, and eventually you can make the journey safely in a regular wagon train with an escort."

Elwood's laugh was unpleasant. "How long will it be before you reach the Oregon country, Mr. Holt?"

"I hope we'll get there a year from this October or thereabouts. If our luck holds, we'll be spending the coming winter in the mountains, and then it will take us another traveling season to reach our goal."

"And I suppose it will be another few years before trains will be moving back and forth regularly."

"Most likely." Whip spoke calmly.

"In other words, I might have to wait for as long as

three years before I could go back East with a convoy, Mr. Holt!"

Whip nodded. "It's better than starving on the prairie or being murdered or having a lot of disagreeable things happen, things I'd rather not even mention."

"You're very kind." Elwood was sarcastic. "I guess you mean well, but there's no way on earth that I could spend another three years with these people and retain my sanity!"

Whip made a final effort. "Don't give us your answer right away. I realize there's a lot of hard feeling against you right this minute, but if you keep your mouth shut, folks will forget what happened in a few weeks. Think, Mr. Elwood—and think hard—before you decide to work your way back to civilization alone. It's a long, tough, dangerous road."

"In another month, you'll be two to three hundred miles deeper into the wilderness, and it would be that much more difficult for me to go home. No, Mr. Holt, I'm leaving right now, as soon as I'm through organizing my belongings."

Whip looked at him sharply, recognizing a note of hysteria in his voice, and saw that his eyes were feverish. Until this moment he had thought that Arthur Elwood was rational, but now he knew better. Other men had reacted to prolonged stays in the wilderness in a similar way.

There had been a hunter who contracted what mountain men called "cabin fever" after being cooped up for too long in a remote hut in the far reaches of the Rockies one winter. His frozen body was found weeks later, after he had hanged himself.

Then there was the trapper who had run amok, murdering and scalping his partner.

Certainly Elwood had lost his balance, too, and although Whip knew it was a waste of breath to talk sense to him, at least he might be able to persuade the man to delay his departure until he recovered somewhat.

"Mr. Elwood," he said, "for your own good and well-being, I recommend that you stay with us for just a few more days."

"Ha! You're just trying to trick me, Holt. A few more

days in this wagon train, and I'll take leave of my wits!"

"I'm not asking you to take my word that you're doomed if you pull out. I only want you to give yourself a chance to reconsider, to weigh the odds more carefully than you've done."

"I'm going!" the man shouted, apparently unaware he was screaming. "And nobody in the world can stop me. You hear me, Holt? Nobody!"

"Well, sir," Whip said, speaking slowly, "we can use the wagon you'll be leaving behind. And we won't miss the rifle or the supplies you'll be taking with you. I wish you good luck."

"Thanks," Elwood said curtly, and swiftly turned to his blankets and frying pan so he wouldn't be required to shake hands.

Whip exchanged a long glance with Ernie, who had remained silent during the long exchange. Whip shrugged. He had done his best to dissuade the man from his venture and felt he could no longer be responsible for the consequences. He went off without another word to prepare for the day's journey.

"I'm compelled to agree with Whip," Ernie said. "You're being foolish. Just because you made one mistake doesn't mean you've got to compound it."

"I made no mistake," Elwood said. Leaving some of his belongings behind, he tied the saddlebags, slung them over the back of the pack horse, and then piled on the remaining property he was taking.

"Good luck," Ernie said, echoing Whip's farewell. Rarely at a loss for words, this was one occasion when he could think of nothing to say.

Elwood mounted his horse, picked up the reins of the pack horse and moved out of the circle, saying goodbye to no one. He ignored those who stared after him and did not bother to return the waves and calls of those who tried to bid him farewell. He set out toward the East along the Platte, riding at a trot.

Long before noon, Elwood had covered far more ground than the caravan had traveled in the opposite direction the previous day. When he finally stopped to water his horses and allow them to graze for a time as he ate a little of the despised buffalo meat and corn, he figured that he had already gone as far toward home as the train had achieved in two days. At this rate he would reach civilization easily by midsummer. The prospect made him lightheaded.

That afternoon Elwood again rode at a rapid clip, pleased because he was not pushing beyond his own endurance or that of his horses. Whip Holt, he decided, had deliberately exaggerated the hazards to be found in the wilderness in order to discourage him from leaving. The wagonmaster's reasons were not hard to guess. He would be discredited when it became known back home that the discomforts of wagon train existence were far greater than the proponents of the Oregon expedition had ever admitted.

Late in the afternoon Elwood came to a small patch of woods, and there he stopped. First gathering and cutting some dead birch and maple, he built a fire. Then, while his horses grazed peacefully, he fished in the Platte. Again he seemed to be enjoying the best of good fortune—within a remarkably short time he landed a fish considerably larger than a trout, big enough to provide him with supper as well as breakfast in the morning.

That night he cooked the fish, and for the first time since he had joined the train the previous year, he thoroughly enjoyed his meal. The day had been warm, but the night breeze carried with it a chill from the Rockies, so he built up his fire and, wrapping himself in a blanket, dropped into a deep sleep.

Arthur Elwood awakened at daybreak, but it wasn't the light that aroused him. Almost immediately he sensed an alien presence. When he opened his eyes, he saw three wiry Indian warriors, their faces hideously streaked with paint, staring down at him.

He tried to struggle to his feet, but a blow across the side of his head from the butt of one of his own rifles sent him sprawling. Too dazed to move, he lay crumpled helplessly on the ground while the braves tied his ankles and wrists with rawhide thongs that bit cruelly into his flesh.

As he regained his powers of speech, he protested, but the Indians paid no attention to him. It dawned on him that they spoke no English.

In any event, they were absorbed in searching through his belongings. Obviously they regarded his horses as valuable acquisitions. They admired his two rifles, passing them back and forth and commenting to each other in what sounded like grunts. The gunpowder meant nothing to them; one tasted it, made a wry face, and then shoved several pinches into the captive's mouth. They had no idea, either, that the lead bar was intended for the use of bullets. All they knew was that it was heavy metal, and one casually struck Elwood across the side of the face with it before dropping it onto the ground.

Elwood felt certain that his cheekbone had been broken, and his pain was so great that he whimpered. Now he realized what Whip Holt had meant about the hazards of wilderness traveling, but understanding did not help him. There was nothing he could do. He could only hope that the warriors would leave after taking what they wanted. Then he would find some way to cut his hands loose and proceed with his journey.

While Elwood watched in terror, two of the warriors produced knives, then slashed away his clothes and boots, unmindful of the fact that their blades sometimes cut into his skin. Meanwhile the third brave busied himself gathering long pine needles. The fire was built higher, then all three lighted needle after needle and applied them to their victim's body, first to the soles of his feet and gradually moving higher.

Elwood's screams echoed across the prairie as his flesh blistered and burned. Never had he known it was possible for any human being to suffer such torment, and his mind could no longer function clearly.

Arthur Elwood did not know that the warriors weren't being deliberately malicious. This was their customary way, their normal routine in dealing with a prisoner. He had no idea that they subjected their own young braves to similar torture before admitting them to full manhood and its rights.

The screams and sobs of the captive impelled the warriors to continue tormenting him. They applied burning needle after burning needle, until no part of his body was left untouched.

By now Arthur Elwood was delirious. No man could be subjected to such intense, constant torture and remain sane. He could no longer even hear the hoarse sound of his own voice as he brokenly begged his captors for mercy.

Then he felt a new pain, so intense and searing that he mercifully lost consciousness. One of the braves had scalped him while he still lived, and torrents of blood cascaded down his sagging, hideously distorted face.

There was no more the warriors could do. Taking the white man's horses and rifles, blankets and food, they mounted their ponies and rode away. Just as Elwood had not looked back when he had left the wagon train, the braves paid no further attention to the remains of the white man who would soon die.

The wilderness was quiet again, and there was no sound but the crackling of the fire. Elwood's agony was still so great that, even though unconscious, he sometimes groaned and stirred feebly.

After a time, several pairs of gleaming eyes peered out of the woods. Coyote, attracted by the smell of blood, stood, motionless. Patient as only wild beasts could be, they waited until the fire died down, waited until the wounded creature died before they devoured his body.

XI

Henry St. Clair had good cause to be pleased with himself and his accomplishments. His long winter with the Cheyenne had been completely satisfying. In return for several jugs of cheap liquor and a handful of rifles, along with instruction in their use, he had spent the worst season of the year in the tribe's main town, living in a hide tent that stood near a roaring fire that never burned low. He had eaten heartily of venison, fish, buffalo, and corn. He had been supplied with a squaw, too, and although he wouldn't have glanced twice at the girl under other circumstances, she had proved lively enough to satisfy him.

Most important of all, he had whetted the appetite of the Cheyenne for booty, and he knew for certain they would make small, repeated raids on the Oregon-bound wagon train. The promise of horses and rifles was sufficient to insure that such raids would be frequent.

It was unfortunate that he had been unable to persuade the leaders of the Cheyenne to conduct a major attack on the train with the hundreds of warriors at their disposal. Like so many of the Indian nations that lived north of the Platte, they were apprehensive about the intentions of their even more powerful and vigorous neighbors, the

Blackfoot, who badly outnumbered them. If the Cheyenne suffered appreciable losses in an assault on the wagon train, their weakened condition would almost certainly invite an invasion by the Blackfoot.

Henry St. Clair was content to leave well enough alone. The Cheyenne would create innumerable problems for the train, and that would be enough. Meanwhile, to lessen the chances of the wagon train ever getting to Oregon, he would go on to the land of the Blackfoot and try to persuade their sachem to wage all-out war on the large company of whites who, in the months ahead, would dare to pass through their sacred territory.

St. Clair was glad, too, that he had delayed well into the spring in the land of the Cheyenne. Their scouts had reported the approach of two white men, one coming from the southeast and the other from the northwest, both of them known to the tribe. In need of civilized reinforcements to help him deal with the Blackfoot, whom it would be dangerous for him to visit alone, St. Clair waited for the arrival of these unknowns, hoping they would be suitable aides and trusting in his own powers of persuasion if that proved to be the case.

The first to appear was André Sebastian, whom the elders of the Cheyenne greeted as an old and trusted friend. Somewhat surprised to see a member of his own race, Sebastian made no comment and instead presented the sachem, the principal medicine man, and the members of the council of elders with gold-handled knives. As nearly as St. Clair could determine, the gold looked real, at least from a distance of several feet, but for the moment, he said nothing. It was obvious to him that any man who gave the Cheyenne presents of such value was no ordinary visitor.

That night the two guests sat side by side at the cooking fire of the sachem. St. Clair was quick to note that Sebastian cut his meat with a knife similar to that which he had given to the Cheyenne. The pair were served by the young squaw who had been living with the Englishman.

Both men sparred cautiously.

"Where are you from?" St. Clair asked in his best American accent.

"St. Louis. How about you?" Sebastian could not hide the trace of a foreign accent.

"Oh, I hail from Pittsburgh."

"I see. Going to the mountains to make your fortune in furs?"

"Something like that." St. Clair's judgment of men told him the other man was lying, but he bided his time.

An opportunity presented itself when the squaw handed him a gourd filled with the herb-flavored water that the Cheyenne customarily drank with their meals. Pretending it had slipped from the girl's hand, St. Clair contrived to overturn it in the direction of the other visitor. Sebastian half-squirmed, half-jumped out of the water's path to avoid a drenching, and, precisely as St. Clair had anticipated, he dropped his gold-handled knife.

St. Clair snatched it from the ground. Turning it over in his hand as he tried to read the inscription on the blade by the light of the fire, he simulated rage at the girl to give himself more time. "You clumsy woman!" he roared in her own tongue. "I shall beat you for this!"

The girl shrank from him, mumbling apologies.

His mission accomplished, St. Clair handed the other man the knife and offered his apologies. Sebastian graciously accepted them, and the incident was forgotten.

After the meal, however, St. Clair leaned toward him. "It so happens that I'm carrying some genuine French brandywine in my wagon. Could I persuade you to share a glass with me?"

"I don't need much persuasion," the darker man said.

Henry waited until the Cheyenne went about their own business. Then, fetching two generous gourds of the potent brandywine, he returned with them to the fire.

In spite of the warming drink, Sebastian remained taciturn. St. Clair was quiet, also. Extremely aware of the value of perfect timing, St. Clair waited until they had consumed about half the contents of the gourds, and then he spoke quietly. "I see your knife was made in St. Petersburg. I assume the knives you gave the Cheyenne came from there, too."

Sebastian's black eyes narrowed. "Sometimes it doesn't pay to be too observant. Indeed, it can be dangerous."

That was all Henry St. Clair needed to know, and he smiled lazily. "It's a long way from St. Petersburg to this Godforsaken part of the world. Even farther than it is from London."

André Sebastian stared hard at him. "London?"

"Your servant, sir." Henry allowed his own English accent to emerge.

The other man continued to stare at him, then chuckled. "The only member of the secret police I know is Vladimir Raskovitch. We worked together in Constantinople some years ago when the Sultan and his Grand Vizier were thinking of expelling all foreigners from the Ottoman Empire. Together we managed to—ah—persuade them to change their minds."

"Vladimir sits at a desk now in St. Petersburg."

"Give him my fond regards when next you go there." It was Henry's turn to chuckle. "I was told before I left London that I might run across colleagues from another great power engaged in a mission similar to mine. I assume we have the same goal."

"I dare say we do." Sebastian sipped his brandywine with greater relish. "How odd it is that we should meet here, at the campfire of savages who have never heard of your great nation or mine. I assume you played a trick in order to read the printing on my knife blade."

Just because they were working on the same mission didn't mean St. Clair trusted his colleague, and his shrug was noncommittal. "I divined your identity," he said.

Sebastian let the question drop. The English were arrogant and opinionated. He had never liked them. But he, too, was prepared, for the sake of expediency, to work with someone who sought the same goal. "You are alone?"

"Always," Henry St. Clair replied proudly. "Most helpers are incompetent bunglers."

"How well I know it," Sebastian replied. "I gave my assistant the simple task of poisoning some of the wagon train's water holes, but he was so clumsy he allowed himself to be killed."

Reasonably assured the man was working without the assistance of subordinates, Henry felt more confident. He could handle the Russian, utilizing his services, telling him only what was necessary, and then dropping him when his presence became embarrassing. The interests of Great Britain and Imperial Russia coincided to an extent, but only to an extent. No English secret agent could allow himself to forget that Russia had once claimed the Oregon country. "Perhaps we could join forces," he said.

Sebastian had known the offer would be made and was ready for it. He would gladly give the Englishman his limited cooperation but would not go so far as to trust him. "Perhaps it would be to our best mutual advantage," he said, and the uneasy partnership was formed.

Martin Van Buren, the eighth President of the United States, had elected on the day of his inauguration to use the massive desk of his predecessor, Andrew Jackson. Old Hickory had been tall and slender, and the desk looked as though it had been made for him. "Little Van," as he had been nicknamed, was almost a foot shorter, so he gave visitors the impression of barely being able to peer over the rim of the desk. Consequently, many people came away from the President's office in the executive mansion with the unfortunate feeling that he was incompetent.

Nothing could have been farther from the truth. Martin Van Buren was a clear-thinking activist, and if he wasn't an innovator, he was nevertheless determined to carry out the policies established by Jackson.

No one knew his real nature better than the two men now seated in his orderly private office, John Jacob Astor and Major General Frederick Stovall.

Astor was often called the wealthiest man in the United States, and he, more than any other individual, had been responsible for striking the spark that was sending the wagon train to the Oregon country. His private funds had paid a substantial portion of the expense. He and Van Buren had worked together when the latter had been Secretary of State, and he had a high regard for the President's abilities.

Major General Stovall, Deputy Chief of Staff of the

United States Army and the nation's second highest ranking military officer, shared Astor's opinion of the President. It had been his privilege to act as Van Buren's aide-de-camp before being promoted to his present post, so he knew him well and was one of his strongest admirers and supporters.

Therefore, the atmosphere was friendly, but there was tension in the air. "Gentlemen," Van Buren said, "what passes between us this afternoon must remain within these walls. If any of the information should leak out or if the remedies we may devise to solve the problem should become known, the United States may be at war with Great Britain, Imperial Russia or both. Frankly, the economic health of the nation is insufficiently strong at the present time to permit us to become embroiled in a war with a major world power. Such a war would be disastrous."

His listeners nodded, neither of them surprised by his words.

Van Buren picked up a thin, leather-bound folder. "As General Stovall already knows and as you may have heard, Mr. Astor, American intelligence services have done inadequate work since the bulk of our information-gathering apparatus was dismantled by President Madison after the War of 1812. President Jackson intended to strengthen those services, but circumstances prevented it. I've shared his aim, but we've lacked the funds." He ran a hand across the top of his bald head. "Consequently, the information that has just come to my attention arrives here rather late in the day." He coughed behind his hand.

General Stovall knew that something of great significance had happened. Van Buren always paused before making an important statement.

"Our intelligence people," the President said, tapping the folder for emphasis, "have obtained incontrovertible proof that both Great Britain and Imperial Russia are taking active steps to prevent our wagon train from reaching Oregon."

"I'm not in the least surprised," John Jacob Astor said. "The stakes in Oregon are high."

"If the British and Russians succeed," Van Buren said, "the United States stands to lose hundreds of thousands of square miles west of the Rocky Mountains. We'll lose a lucrative fur trade, about which Mr. Astor knows more than I do. We'll lose salmon fisheries, lumber, and minerals. We'll lose the opportunity to expand our borders all the way across the continent from the Atlantic to the Pacific."

"The wagon train can't be allowed to fail, sir," General Stovall said.

"Obviously," Astor murmured.

"So far several attacks have been made on the train," the President declared. "According to information obtained from Sam Brentwood, who has taken charge of our new depot in Independence, the attack was launched by army deserters—which was repulsed—was British inspired. Several vicious but relatively minor assaults of one kind or another have also failed completely or have been averted. But the people in the wagon train are in trouble over their heads. Most of them are simple farmers. Even the few relatively sophisticated members find it difficult to deal with the problems that London and St. Petersburg can create. The man in charge at the present time—Mike Holt—is a competent guide and hunter, but he's never dealt with such matters, either."

General Stovall frowned and drummed on the desk, and John Jacob Astor tugged at the gold-link watch chain that stretched across his expansive waistcoat.

"Something must be done, gentlemen," Van Buren said. "The wagon train needs help that only the United States government can provide. I await your suggestions."

The General's reply was prompt. "Mr. President," he said, "we already have a regiment stationed at Fort Madison in the Nebraska country, and we can form another from smaller units in garrisons at other frontier posts. Let the army send two fully equipped cavalry regiments to help. They can escort the wagon train all the way to the Oregon territory, and may the Lord help anyone who gets in their way, tries any tricks, or interferes!"

Astor was dismayed. "With all due respect to General Stovall, Mr. President, there's nothing this country might do that could harm us more."

The General's temper flared, overcoming his sense of discretion. "I must disagree. If Mr. Astor is thinking in terms of making diplomatic protests—"

"I'm not. The British and Russians would turn us aside by insisting they're doing nothing to harm us. I've seen the game played too often."

President Van Buren listened but made no comment.

"All the same, Mr. Astor," General Stovall said, "I believe in the principle of fighting fire by building a bigger and stronger fire."

"And I believe in using a rapier instead of a bludgeon, sir," John Jacob Astor replied. "Mr. President, I don't pretend to know how London and St. Petersburg would react if we sent two regiments of cavalry to escort the wagon train. I assume they'd be annoyed, and I assume they'd let us know it. The one thing I can tell you flatly is that such a move would be catastrophic for the fur business—one of the few industries in the country that remains profitable in these hard times."

General Stovall was still belligerent. "Perhaps you'd explain why the fur industry would suffer if we provide the wagon train with the protection the people need and deserve!"

"Of course." Astor spoke with the self-confidence of a man who knew precisely what he was doing and why. "Dozens of hunters and trappers in Oregon are working for fur companies, which also buy pelts from the independents. The British do the same thing. On the surface they—and we—are friendly. There is no reason not to be —there are enough furs for everyone, at least for the present. But the British, as well as the United States companies, are looking toward the day when the supplies will begin to diminish. Still, at present the two countries cooperate. Keep in mind that the one military post in the area is Fort Vancouver, which flies the Union Jack, not the Stars and Stripes. The British garrison gives protection to American hunters and trappers, just as it does those from Canada. If they should withdraw their support from us—and become openly hostile—we'll have a great many new problems that will be almost impossible to solve."

"I see your point," Van Buren said.

"That's not all," the magnate continued vigorously. "Most fur company employees in Oregon are Russians, subjects of the czar, who stayed behind when their government gave up its official claim to the territory. They're highly temperamental people, and I know that almost all of them dream about the future when the czar will reassert his claims. If we send the wagon train with two cavalry regiments, we're serving notice that the United States is prepared to fight for its rights in Oregon. Every last Russian will walk out on us, and the American fur business in the Northwest—a business that brings this country more revenues than any other—will collapse overnight. That will make the present precarious financial situation even worse."

"I understand your reasoning, Mr. Astor," Stovall said. "But we simply can't leave almost five hundred American citizens unprotected when British and Russian agents are conniving against them."

"I wouldn't dream of leaving them to their own fate, General," Astor replied. "That would be stupid and shortsighted."

"Then what do you suggest?"

"The British and Russians are being subtle. Surely this government isn't so primitive that it can't find equally subtle means to counter the threat!"

President Van Buren stared out of the window of the executive mansion at the new gate, where military sentries were now posted for the first time. "American citizens have the right to expect their country to help them when they're threatened by foreign foes. I quite agree that a subtle weapon is preferable to an obvious one, but I insist on giving our people the protection they need."

General Stovall, deep in thought, absently fingered the hilt of his dress sword. All at once he laughed aloud and slapped his knee.

Astor looked at him in surprise.

"You've thought of something, Fred?" Van Buren asked.

"Lee Blake!"

The President smiled. "Perfect! This situation is made to order for him."

"Mr. Astor," the General said, "there's an officer currently on duty right here in Washington who is capable of dealing with the foreign agents who threaten the wagon train. Leland Blake is a lieutenant colonel, the youngest in the army. He fought Indians in Alabama, Florida, and Tennessee with Andrew Jackson. This job suits him especially well, since he spent three years as our military attaché in St. Petersburg and four more in London. At present he's the director of the counterintelligence section at army headquarters, which means he's in charge of ferreting out foreign spies. He's been so restless that he regularly requests transfer from a desk job to the field. So he'll welcome an opportunity such as this."

John Jacob Astor looked pleased. "Your Colonel Blake sounds almost too good to be true."

"He's very good," the President said. "He worked directly for me when I served as our Minister to Great Britain, and he performed admirably. Fred, offer him the assignment at once!"

"Yes, Mr. President."

"Give him the authority he needs, but tell him to handle relations with wagon train members carefully."

"I know what you mean, sir. I'll see to it!"

The President invited Astor to stay for supper, and General Stovall quickly walked the two blocks down Pennsylvania Avenue to the three-story frame building that served as headquarters for the United States Army and Navy.

A few minutes later, Lieutenant Colonel Leland Blake came into his office and saluted. Tall, slender, and dark haired, with a deceptively gentle manner, he was in his mid-thirties, so handsome that Washington hostesses pursued him relentlessly for their dinner parties. Their efforts were in vain, however. The social life of the nation's capital bored him. Duty was always paramount in his eyes, and his only shortcoming, in the eyes of his superiors, was his refusal to relax.

"Sit down, Lee," Stovall said, returning the younger officer's salute. "Read this."

Colonel Blake needed only a few minutes to peruse the report of the attacks made on the wagon train by British and Imperial Russian agents. "None of this is surprising, sir," he said. "You may recall I had a meeting with Sam Brentwood, at President Jackson's instigation, shortly before the wagon train was scheduled to set out from New York. At that time I warned him that these troubles were likely to develop."

"I do remember, Lee. And they've become so serious that President Van Buren wants a counterintelligence operative to join the train and travel with it, at least until the threats can be ended. If necessary, of course, he can see them all the way to the end of their journey."

"You'll want a competent officer, I imagine, sir. He'll need to wear civilian clothes so he'll be inconspicuous."

"Right."

"It seems to me," Lee Blake said, his mind working with its usual rapidity, "that no one other than the wagonmaster and the president of the train should know his real identity."

"A good safeguard," Stovall agreed, concealing a smile as he asked, "Whom do you recommend?"

"Let me go through my list of available officers, sir. It won't be an easy assignment to fill."

"I'm aware of it, so I already have an exceptionally competent officer in mind."

Blake hated top-level interference, but was in no position to protest, so he waited politely.

"The President," General Stovall said, "agrees with me that Lieutenant Colonel Leland Blake has all the necessary qualifications."

A broad grin spread slowly across the younger officer's face. "I can think of no one better."

"How soon can you leave?"

"Immediately, sir! I'll stop off in Independence, and perhaps I can persuade Sam Brentwood to guide me out to the train, since I'm not familiar with the Great Plains. What authority will I have to mobilize the members of the train?"

"As much as you may want and need. The present wagonmaster, a hunter and guide named Holt, is competent and had President Jackson's confidence. But you may find yourself in a ticklish situation if he resents your presence."

"That would create unfortunate complications, and I'll do my best to avoid them."

"I'm sure you will. Handle the problems of dealing with the British and Russians as you see fit, Lee. I have no idea what you might encounter out there in the wilderness, so it would be foolish to give you any specific instructions. Do as you see fit. Just make certain the wagon train reaches Oregon intact!"

"You can depend on me, General," Lee Blake said quietly. "And so can President Van Buren."

Horses and oxen were browsing indolently during the nooning, the sun was shining from a cloudless sky, and a pleasant breeze from the west dissipated the heat that soon would become a problem. Members of the wagon train rested; the children ate cold leftovers from breakfast. The day was like scores of others, and the mood of the travelers was relaxed and serene.

Suddenly the quiet was interrupted by a sentry's shout. "A party of three is approaching from the east on horseback!" he called. "A white man and two Indians."

The train's leaders gathered to greet the new arrivals, and soon a large crowd surrounded the strange trio. The two Indians, warriors in their early twenties, were tall and slender, their skins a darker copper than those of other tribes. Christian crosses were embroidered in beads on their buckskin shirts, which were dyed in brilliant reds and greens. They spoke no English, and both Whip and Stalking Horse were unable to converse with them in any of the Indian languages they knew.

The white man was dressed even more unusually. His moccasins and fringed buckskin trousers were those of a frontier dweller, but he wore the formal black shirt and white clerical collar of a missionary. A Bible protruded from the top of his saddlebag, but he carried a brace of pistols and a double-edged hunting knife in his belt. He introduced himself as the Reverend Jason Lee, and Cathy van Ayl instantly recognized his nasal drawl as that of her native New England.

"I've just come from Oregon, where I've established a little mission," he said, "and I'm on my way to Washington. I hope to persuade President Van Buren and Congress to recognize the area as a formal territory and to set up a provisional government there."

At the mention of Oregon, a surprised and pleased murmur spread through the throng.

"We're headed for the Oregon country ourselves," Whip told the man.

The clergyman was only mildly surprised. "I had a letter from one of my friends at the New England Methodist Seminary a few months ago telling me a wagon train was coming out our way," he said. "You'll be welcome, very welcome. I'm hoping to return to Oregon by ship and bring some more settlers with me. We'll sail around South America."

Soon Reverend Lee, who was a husky man, was besieged with questions from the eager pioneers. Here was someone with firsthand knowledge of the region to which they were traveling, the future home for which they were enduring so many hardships.

The clergyman first told them about his two young companions. They were members of the peace-loving Chinook nation, and he had converted them to Christianity. Now they lived in the tiny settlement he had established on the Willamette River, less than a day's journey from Fort Vancouver.

"What's the attitude of the English there toward American settlers?" Ernie asked.

Jason Lee's face clouded. "Dr. John McLoughlin, the chief factor of the Hudson's Bay Company, is a fine Christian gentleman," he said. "He doesn't much care whether the territory is under British or American jurisdiction, and he's told me himself that he's prepared to do business with us, no matter what flag flies over us. I'm sorry to say, though, that the officers of the British military command at Fort Vancouver are less generous. They make no bones about their aim. They're determined that people who move there will live under the Union Jack—just as I'm determined that the Stars and Stripes will fly there. That's the chief reason I'm going East. When the President and Congress realize the situation is critical, I'm quite certain they'll give us their full support."

"I reckon the arrival of this train will tip the scale in favor of American jurisdiction," Whip said.

"Oh, it will," Lee replied enthusiastically. "You say there are about five hundred of you. How wonderful that my prayers are already being answered by the Lord. It will be very difficult for the British to force a group this large to swear allegiance to Queen Victoria."

"There's no chance of that," Cathy van Ayl said firmly, then blushed because she had spoken out of turn.

But the emphatic nods and vocal support of dozens of future Oregon settlers made her feel less embarrassed. It was plain that the wagon train was united in its intention to make Oregon an American territory.

Further travel for the day was out of the question. An overnight camp was made, and scores of people spent the afternoon and evening bombarding the Reverend Lee with requests for specific information. His replies fascinated them.

"Oregon truly is God's country," he said. "The climate is superb, particularly in the valleys. The higher you go in the mountains, of course, the greater the probability you'll run into snow. But there's none in the valleys and on the Pacific coast."

He was partial, obviously, to the Willamette Valley.

Whip said, "That's good country, all right, but I'm aiming to take these folks farther north by about fifty or sixty miles."

"You prefer the vicinity of the lower Columbia River, I take it," Reverend Lee said.

"I do. It's strictly a personal feeling," Whip said. "The salmon are more accessible, and so is the Pacific for fishing."

"Well," the clergyman replied, smiling, "it is all the same country, and there's ample space for hundreds of settlements, even thousands. You good people have never seen so much fine land!"

Just about everything that man needed for survival could be grown in the territory, Reverend Lee said enthusiastically. At his own small mission he already had apples, pears, peaches, plums, and a variety of berries. "Wheat takes naturally to our soil. So do oats and barley, corn, rye, and buckwheat. You won't believe the way crops such as beans and peas grow, not to mention cucumbers and squash."

The farmers listened intently, their eyes bright.

"Oregon is perfect for grazing, too. So far the only cows in the area are to be found at Fort Vancouver, but I predict the day will come when the cattle being raised there will outnumber people by at least ten to one. And I certainly expect that hundreds of thousands of immigrants will come to Oregon!"

The mineral deposits of the area were unknown, he said, because no one had ever explored for them.

"What kind of trees are there?" someone asked.

The clergyman laughed. "No matter where you may be from, I promise you've never seen so many kinds of trees. Our forests are endless. Let me see. There are firs everywhere, and pines, both yellow and white. There are spruce, hemlock, larch, and cedar. Some of our Indians use the inner bark of cedar for food. Cook it the way they do, and you'll find it delicious."

Someone inquired about the availability of fish other than salmon.

Reverend Lee grinned. "Well, sir—offhand, I can think of sturgeon, halibut, cod, herring, carp, and smelt. There are oysters and crabs, and strange lobsters that have only one claw instead of two. There are so many fish in our rivers and in the Pacific that they could feed the entire United States, with ample left over. Oh, yes—there's something I neglected to mention earlier when we were talking about grazing. Our hills are perfect for sheep. I myself started with a tiny flock, and right now I have several hundred."

Far into the evening, the members of the train listened in wonder and delight. Here was a man who had no need to exaggerate, who by profession undoubtedly was truthful. The beacon light of Oregon burned brightly.

The heat of early summer was so intense that many members of the wagon train suffered from stomach disorders, and the medicines Dr. Martin had brought with him failed to cure them. Stalking Horse gave the physician a small quantity of a prairie herb that, he said, the Plains tribes used for the purpose. Bob Martin tried it, giving the herb to two patients, both of whom recovered overnight.

The next day was Sunday, when the company rested, so the doctor went out alone, on foot, to gather as many of the herbs as he could. He began to find the plants about a mile from the campsite, and he pulled them carefully, stuffing them into a burlap sack. To his surprise and pleasure, he also found another herb, broad leafed and bearing seed balls that would turn into flowers later in the summer. This herb, whose Latin name he had forgotten, was identical to one he had studied when he had attended medical school in Edinburgh, but he hadn't actually ever seen it or used it in practice.

As he remembered the information in his textbooks, these seeds, when removed from their pods, had strong antiseptic qualities and could be utilized to pack wounds in order to prevent infection. He seemed to recall a lecturer at the university saying that this herb grew only in one known place, the vast plains or *pampas* of the Argentine. It was exciting to find it on the prairies of the American West, and Bob Martin gathered as many as he could locate.

He would experiment with the seeds, naturally, and devoutly hoped they were indeed the same as those found in the Argentine. If that should be the case, he had made a discovery of importance to the American medical profession. Ultimately, when mail service was established between the Oregon country and the Eastern Seaboard, he would write to a classmate who was now serving on the staff of Harvard Medical School and would enclose some samples in his letter.

Then, hearing horses approaching, he looked up and was startled when he saw three Indians smeared with paint riding rapidly toward him. A glance over his shoulder told him he had wandered so far from the wagon train that it was no longer in sight, and he realized he was in serious trouble.

His rifle lay on the ground beside the half-filled burlap sack, but it was too late now to use it. One of the braves had a spear poised in his hand, ready to throw it, and the others had their bows and arrows ready.

All he could do was raise his right arm, palm upraised, in the Indian sign of peace. At least he was glad he had persuaded Stalking Horse to teach him enough of the language of the Kiowa to make himself understood.

The peace gesture startled the braves, and they hesitated before firing their weapons.

"I am a man of medicine," Bob called, using the only Kiowan phrase that identified his profession with any degree of accuracy.

The warriors remained suspicious, but it was contrary to custom to kill any medicine man in cold blood. Besides, this white stranger was speaking a familiar tongue.

One of the braves dismounted and, after picking up Bob's rifle, looked in the burlap sack. There he saw some of the herbs used for stomach disorders, which he recognized instantly. Snatching one of the plants, he showed it to his companions.

To Bob's infinite relief, the herb seemed to provide corroborating evidence for his claim.

"The medicine man," the eldest of the trio said, "will come to the town of the Wichita."

The physician had no choice and was forced to mount the oldest brave's horse, riding double in front of the Indian, while the warrior carried the rifle and the burlap sack. They rode off in the direction from which they had come.

Cursing silently, Bob realized that his own careless preoccupation was responsible for his grim predicament. The savages of the plains, Whip had stressed in their many talks on the subject, were friendly only with whites they knew and had reason to trust. Strangers who intruded on the hunting grounds, which they regarded as inviolate and sacred, were either killed by torture and scalped, or were compelled to live as slaves. Neither prospect was heartening.

A Whip Holt or an Arnold Mell might find some clever way to either overpower the warriors or fool them long enough to escape and return to the wagon train. Although certainly not lacking in courage, he was a doctor and a scientist, devoted to the art of healing rather than the performance of daring deeds. He was incapable of breaking away from his captors.

So far, at least, they hadn't mistreated him or bound his arms and legs. He couldn't help smiling wryly. Obviously a middle-aged man with a slight paunch and graying temples posed no physical threat to a trio of healthy, strapping warriors in the physical prime of life.

The braves rode in silence for about an hour, and then Bob heard the soft throbbing of a drum, a sound that was very faint at first but that grew louder and more intense. What he found odd was that the beat of the drum was slow, solemn, and unvarying.

At last the braves and their captive came to a group of buffalo-hide tents, erected on center poles. In spite of his dangerous situation, Bob noted that the tent walls were double skins, with the outer portion heavily greased to ward off the elements. He even caught a glimpse of buffalo skins on the ground inside some of the tents.

About two hundred men and women dressed in the skins of young buffalo were sitting solemnly in a circle, while a number of naked children and many dogs played on the fringes. A fire was burning in the center of the circle, and a naked boy of eight or nine was lying unconscious on a robe of buffalo hide near the flames. On the far side of the fire, the drum beater pounded methodically on an animal skin stretched tightly over a kettlelike container. Dancing frenziedly around the fire and pausing occasionally to hover over the boy was a masked man, naked except for a breechcloth of buffalo hide. Streaks of paint covered his body and limbs, and he carried a bone rattle so large he needed both hands to shake it, which he did incessantly as he pranced and leaped.

Bob's escort dismounted and led him to the circle. The squaws and younger girls were weeping openly, while the braves stared straight ahead, their faces expressionless and their arms folded across their broad, bare chests. The faces, arms, and shoulders of all were smeared with a heavy coating of what looked like ashes.

Behind the boy, sitting cross-legged, was a warrior wearing an elaborate headdress of eagle feathers that descended down his back to his waist. Apparently he was the chief of this Wichita community, and Bob guessed he well might be the child's father. Directly behind the man was a squaw, her hands covering her face, who rocked back and forth in silent hysteria.

But it was the boy himself who most interested the physician. His left leg and thigh were bloated, swollen to several times their normal size, and neither his knee nor his ankle bones were visible. In spite of his own danger, the doctor paused to look at the child, who appeared to be suffering from an infection.

A member of the escort addressed the chief at length in a language that Bob did not understand.

The leader was impatient. "The stranger is a medicine man?" he demanded, speaking in Kiowan.

"It is so," Bob acknowledged.

"The son of Golden Bear suffers a great sickness. The Wichita have prayed to the gods of the sun, the moon, and the wind, but the boy is still sick. Will the magic of the strange medicine man cure him?"

"I must examine the boy before I can answer the question of the sachem," Bob replied.

The man gave a curt nod.

Some of the women stopped weeping, and a number of braves stared at the outsider as he approached the stricken child and dropped to one knee beside him. The tribe's medicine man halted his gyrations. Only the steady, mournful beat of the drum continued unabated.

The physician placed a hand on the boy's forehead. As he had assumed, the youngster was suffering from a high fever. A swift but thorough examination of his swollen thigh and leg revealed that the focal point of the infection was located in the calf. This spot was so tender that the unconscious child stirred when probing fingers barely touched the spot.

Bob stood and faced the chief. He realized that his own

situation was hazardous, but it was obvious to him that he had to make an attempt to save the boy. If his efforts failed, he thought it likely that he would be tortured until he died. But a combination of instinct and the little he had gleaned about the ways of Indians told him to magnify the task that awaited him, to wrap it in an air of mystery.

"I will cure the son of Golden Bear," he declared solemnly.

The warriors continued to glare at him, and the tribe's medicine man pulled off his mask and stared jealously at the white intruder.

Bob pointed a finger at the hysterical woman. "Let the mother of the boy place water in a pot. Let her put the pot over the fire and keep it there until it makes many bubbles. Let no one else touch the pot or help her."

The sachem's squaw hauled herself to her feet and moved off through the crowd, returning shortly with a huge iron pot that had been obtained in a trade with a representative of one of the fur companies. At the least, Bob thought, the simple function she had been asked to perform would occupy her attention sufficiently to let her tears dry.

"Let Golden Bear give me the knife he is wearing," the physician said.

Reluctantly the chief took a knife from his belt and handed it to the stranger.

Bob was disappointed because the blade was dull and badly nicked. "There is no magic in this knife," he said. "Bring the hunting knife of Golden Bear!"

A young brave hurried off to the largest of the tents, returning with a long bone-handled knife that he handed to the chief.

After another long moment's hesitation, Golden Bear gave it to the white man.

"Evil spirits fill the son of Golden Bear," the doctor declared solemnly, after assuring himself that this blade was what he needed. Obviously it, too, had been obtained in a trade with whites: it was fashioned of tempered steel, and was razor-sharp. "All the people of the Wichita will see the evil spirits leave the body of the son of Golden

Bear." And if my diagnosis is wrong, or if I'm too late and the boy dies, he reflected, I'll pay with my own life.

"Now," he continued, "let two women bring another pot filled with cold water."

This, too, was done.

The physician needed cloth, but none was available as the Wichita's clothing was made of leather. Removing his own shirt, he took the sharp knife and cut the shirt into strips several inches wide.

By this time the water in the first pot was boiling. Bob gestured, and the drummer fell silent. There was no sound now, and everyone could hear the labored breathing of the patient.

Bob dropped a strip of cloth into the boiling pot, allowed it to remain there for a few moments, and then fished it out with the knife. After waiting for it to cool just enough so that it wouldn't burn the boy, he placed it, still steaming, on the calf of his patient's leg, where he doubled it, then doubled it again. While the heat drew out the infection, he held the knife blade in the boiling water to sterilize it.

"Let the sack of the medicine man be brought to him," he ordered.

The burlap bag that had been taken from him was placed at his side, and he could only pray that he had properly identified the herb that had antiseptic qualities.

Many of the seated braves and squaws could not see him. Overcome by curiosity, they rose to their feet. The Wichita medicine man hovered nearby, and all at once it occurred to Bob to involve him directly in the proceedings.

"Let the brother of the white medicine man put two more pieces of cloth in the water that bubbles," he said. "Let him be ready to remove them with a stick when they are needed."

Slightly mollified but still jealous, the Wichita medicine man obeyed.

Bob removed the steaming cloth from the patient's leg, dropping it back into the boiling water. Then, taking the knife from the pot, he lowered himself to one knee. The focal point of the infection had risen to a bump, so he made an incision almost a half-inch deep and an inch long. Then, still moving swiftly, he cut through the center crosswise.

Large quantities of pus spurted out of the patient's leg.

"The evil leaves the body of the son of Golden Bear," he announced loudly.

Then while the wound continued to drain, he cleaned the knife by plunging it into the boiling water. Motioning the Wichita medicine man, he watched closely as the savage, imitating what he himself had done previously, placed a steaming, folded section of cloth over the wound, which continued to draw and drain. As soon as the cloth stopped steaming, Bob ordered the process repeated. By now the swelling was somewhat reduced, although the child's leg was still puffed. When serum rather than pus began to drain from the cuts, Bob opened an herb pod. Using the sharp point of the knife, he pressed the seeds, one by one, into the wound. Then he took yet another strip of cloth from the boiling pot and allowing it to cool slightly, he made it into a bandage, placing it around the patient's calf and tying it securely, but not too tightly.

The boy opened his eyes, looking bewildered when he saw the stranger bending over him. Bob gestured to the chief and his squaw, who moved within their son's range of vision. The boy smiled and said something in the language of the Wichita. The chief replied, and his squaw dropped to both knees, then bent down to kiss her son on the forehead.

Bob's relief was so great he felt weak. The operation had been a success, so he had probably saved his own life. But his task was not yet done.

"Let no one lift the son of Golden Bear until the medicine man gives the word," he said. Later in the evening he would remove and replace the antiseptic seeds, and by morning the boy should be able to hobble around, with the help of a walking stick. The fever was already lower, and the thigh was less bloated.

The squaw sat on the ground and placed her son's head in her lap.

"Let the son of Golden Bear drink water," Bob said.

Someone handed him a gourd, and he dipped it into the

pot of cold water, then handed it to the squaw. Certainly the crisis was over, and he felt confident that the child's recovery would be complete.

Rising to his feet, he took the precaution of extending his thanks to the Wichita medicine man for the role he had played. The man's dignity had been restored, and he was so pleased that he exhibited no signs of jealousy. Another crisis had been averted.

Golden Bear enveloped the white man in a hug, then began to call orders to his people. A squaw appeared with a shirt of buffalo skin, which had been chipped so expertly that it was almost as thin as cloth. Two squaws pulled it over his head.

Then Golden Bear produced a square of buffalo bone about an inch and a half in diameter, on which a picture of the sun had been carved. It was attached to a loop of rawhide, and chanting an incantation, the sachem placed it around the doctor's neck. Not until it was in place did Bob Martin realize that Golden Bear himself wore an identical talisman.

"The new brother of Golden Bear is the greatest of medicine men," the sachem said in Kiowan. "Let all of the Wichita bend their knees to him and praise him!"

The entire assemblage began to chant, the drummer beat a lively rhythm, and, much to Bob's embarrassment, the people approached him one by one, prostrating themselves on the ground before him. Never, he thought, had any physician received such homage.

Eventually the men of the tribe feasted on antelope steak, the first that Bob had ever tasted, and with it they ate boiled ears of fresh corn, smeared with melted buffalo fat. The taste was unusual but surprisingly good.

After the meal, the physician removed the herb seeds from his patient's leg, and although the operation was painful, the child did not wince, a sure sign that he was improving rapidly. This time a poultice filled with seeds was placed on the outside of the wound, and at the doctor's orders, the child was moved into a tent.

"Now the son of Golden Bear will sleep," Bob said. "When the sun returns, he will be well again."

A special tent, complete with several rich buffalo robes

on the ground, was placed at the exhausted doctor's disposal. Before he dropped off to sleep, the squaw of the sachem came to him and offered herself to him, showing bewilderment when he declined the opportunity to spend the night with her. His willingness to abide by the customs of his hosts was limited.

Just before he fell asleep, he found himself thinking of Tonie Mell, and he wondered how she would react if he offered her his new shirt or buffalo bone talisman.

The entire wagon train was in an uproar when, at supper time, it was discovered that Dr. Martin had not yet returned. The night was cloudy, but the scouts and Hosea immediately went out beyond the circle of wagons to begin a search. It was the Ashanti who followed a trail of uprooted plants and who eventually found the place where the physician had been abducted.

Tonie Mell went wild when Hosea brought the word back to the camp. "We've got to organize a rescue expedition right now!" she said.

Whip disagreed. "On a night like this, it will be very difficult to follow signs across the prairie," he told her. "We'll do much better if we wait until morning."

"By then Bob could be dead!"

"Indians are never in that much of a hurry to kill their prisoners," he said.

"Then they could be torturing him," she insisted.

"Not at night," Whip replied. "They won't do him any serious harm before tomorrow."

Tonie refused to listen to him. "If you won't go tonight," she said, "I'll do it myself."

Only her uncle's persuasion and authority over her prevented her from dashing alone across the plains.

She was unable to sleep, and when a small rescue party was organized before dawn, she made such a fuss about accompanying the group that Whip decided to permit her to come along. Only he and the scouts would conduct the search, he said, refusing her request for a large party of armed men.

"If there are too many of us," he explained, "they'll kill Bob before we can get near him. You'll have to trust my judgment and let me handle this in my own way."

He refrained from telling her that he was taking the cured skin of the pure white buffalo calf with him. If necessary, he would offer it to Dr. Martin's captors in exchange for the physician's release, and he felt confident that no Indian would be able to resist such a bargain.

"We want to avoid open warfare with any nation," Whip said before they departed, and although his remarks presumably were intended for all his companions, he looked only at Tonie. "We can accomplish a great deal more through peaceful negotiations. I'll do the talking, and I want no one to fire a single shot without my express permission. Our aim is to save Bob, not punish a tribe for abducting him."

Giving the girl no chance to reply, he led his stallion out of the circle.

Arnold brought up the rear, Tonie riding directly in front of him, and Stalking Horse took the lead. It was a simple matter for the Cherokee to read and follow the tracks made the previous day by the band of warriors, and by the time the sun rose, the group had traveled a considerable distance from the campsite.

An hour later, as they still pushed forward, Stalking Horse suddenly raised a hand in warning. "Indians come," he called.

The group moved into a horizontal line, leaving ample space between their mounts. Rifles were checked, and Whip spoke casually to Tonie, who sat on his left. "Remember," he said, "keep your trigger finger quiet."

She nodded, but made no comment. If Bob Martin was in great danger, she reserved the right to act in any manner she saw fit, and to hell with the wagonmaster.

Stalking Horse recognized the distinctive warpaint worn by the approaching braves. "Wichita warriors come," he announced.

There were about twenty braves in the approaching party, so even Whip, Arnold, and Mack became tense, and Stalking Horse moved his quiver a few inches toward one side of his shoulder, where he could draw arrow after arrow quickly, should the need arise.

Tonie noticed that these Indians were riding horses as

large as those used by members of the expedition. "They're not mounted on ponies," she said.

"That's because we're in the real West now," Whip said. "These horses are the descendants of the herds originally brought to Mexico by the Spaniards. Wild herds were formed by runaway horses, and the Plains Indians who know about them go off into the mountain canyons, catch them, then tame them."

"The Wichita are good fighters," Mack said, "and they don't like strangers." He took a firmer grip on his rifle.

Whip waited until the approaching horsemen drew closer, then raised his arm in the sign of peace.

Two of the warriors responded with the same sign, much to the relief of the outnumbered little band.

Then one brave, wearing a beaded shirt and a headdress studded with eagle feathers, detached himself from the Wichita party and rode forward alone.

Even Whip was confused for a moment because he wore a white man's trousers and boots. The astonished Tonie was the first to recognize a broadly smiling Bob Martin.

"Put down your rifles," Bob called. "My brothers, the Wichita, are your friends forever."

Arnold chuckled quietly. "I might have guessed he'd do something like this!"

The two groups merged and dismounted. Golden Bear made a long, impassioned speech in which he praised his new brother, the great medicine man. Then, at his signal, his braves mounted their horses again, while Whip and his comrades followed their example.

Before turning back toward his village, Golden Bear looked at Tonie, then muttered something that caused every man present to laugh. The parties separated, and the wagon train group headed back toward their campsite.

Only Tonie was totally silent, and Bob fell into line beside her. "Thank you for coming after me," he said. "You had no idea what might be awaiting you, and I'm grateful you risked your life for me."

"Not really," she replied, shrugging. "I knew Whip and Uncle Arnold wouldn't let any harm come to me." Again she was silent for a time, but something continued to bother her, and at last she could not hold it in. "What made him think I'm your squaw?"

He shrugged, her belligerence making him defensive. "I don't know. The mere fact that you came after me with Whip and the scouts, I suppose."

"I'm no man's squaw," Tonie said firmly.

Bob had thought of offering her the buffalo bone amulet that was still hanging around his neck, but he decided it was best to take no chances when she was in an angry mood.

XII

Prince Nicholas Orlev, the personal representative of the czar and the most distinguished of his subjects ever to visit Washington, was weary after spending a day haggling with State Department officials in their current trade negotiations. But now, relaxing in the spacious Russian Legation office of the *chargé d'affairs* he brightened as he raised his glass of cooled Ukrainian wine. "To the czar," he said.

"The czar," Baron Alexis Tarnoff, the *chargé*, replied automatically.

"These Americans," Prince Orlev said, after swallowing half of his drink without stopping, "have the souls of merchants. All of them, including the President and Secretary of State. What boors they are."

"Greedy boors," Baron Tarnoff replied. "They are always hungry for trade advantages, for cash, for land—for anything and everything they can take."

"Ah, yes." The guest drained his glass and immediately refilled it, then belched. "That brings up a matter I find painful. These trade negotiations are not my only reason—or even my principal reason—for coming to America. Surely, my dear Tarnoff, you realize from the dispatches sent to you by the Ministry of External Affairs that the czar himself is deeply worried about the status of New

Russia—the land the Americans and the British call the Oregon country."

"It is always in my mind," the *chargé* said. "I become distressed when I read that the English are strengthening their garrison at Fort Vancouver. I become even more upset when I read that hundreds of Americans have joined the wagon train to Oregon and that other, similar expeditions are being planned. At the moment our own claims are distinctly small. We take third place."

The Prince struck the table before him with the flat of his hand, causing the glasses to jump. Then, rather clumsily, he rescued the wine bottle before it toppled. "If you know all this, my dear Baron, why do you procrastinate? Why hasn't the wagon train been destroyed? You had a perfect pawn in the young woman whose parents are still being held in St. Petersburg as hostages."

The Baron's face twisted. "You refer to the person who calls herself Tonie Mell. I interviewed her myself, you know, and offered to send her father and mother to America if she successfully sabotaged the train. But she has done nothing. No, that is not accurate. She has actually dared to defy Imperial Russia by remaining loyal to this upstart country."

"Then you are growing soft, my dear Baron." Orlev took a small knife from his pocket and began to dig at the grime that had accumulated beneath his overly long fingernails. "The woman should be killed as a lesson to all who defect. And others should be found who will attend to the sabotage of the train."

The *chargé* became bitter and spat in the general direction of a china bowl that sat on the floor beside him. "Do you suppose for one moment, my good Prince, that I am insensitive to the wishes of His Imperial Majesty? I have served him for almost thirty years, and I know what needs to be done!"

Orlev's smile was thin. "Why hasn't it been done, then?"

"Would you have me send a regiment of Cossacks chasing across the American wilderness? You forget, Prince Orlev, that the situation in which Imperial Russia finds herself is complicated by the bad advice given by your Ministry of External Affairs to His Majesty."

The Prince bristled. "That was done by my predecessors, not by me. They were stupid and shortsighted to abandon their claims to New Russia. But, now that the czar has changed his mind, we are required to do his bidding. First, the American wagon train must be crippled so badly it will either halt or turn back. Then we will notify the world that His Majesty is restoring his claim to Oregon. We will demand it for ourselves, and we are prepared to send a fleet from our colony of Alaska to take full possession of it!"

"Surely you have agents whose services you can command."

"Naturally. I have already called upon one such man. I'm sure you'll recall Daunevsky, who did such splendid work for us in the Balkans and who came to America under the name of André Sebastian. I sent him to force the Mell girl to commit sabotage, to kill her if she refused to halt the train herself."

"But of course. There is no agent in the entire network superior to Sebastian. His talents are unlimited."

"Indeed they are, and for that reason I sent him after the wagon train. I thought surely that between him and his assistant Munson the Americans would be stopped. Alas, I have heard nothing from either agent."

"It is impossible that Sebastian is dead. Munson—well, who knows? But Sebastian is indestructible!"

"That is my reasoning also," Baron Tarnoff declared. "I remain confident that Sebastian, at least, will do what is required of him."

"I hope so, but you cannot and must not place your sole reliance on one man. This Tonie Mell person represents a threat to the Imperial Crown, don't you understand? She was offered a generous bargain, and she rejected it. It is maddening to think that the demands of the czar himself are being frustrated by a stubborn, ignorant peasant girl."

"She deserves slow torture," the *chargé* said. "I would like nothing better, myself, than to spend a few hours with her alone—with a fire, a pair of tongs, a knife, and a hearth poker. Her screams would be music more joyous than the singing of the Imperial choir at the Church of St. Michael!"

"Then see to it!" the Prince rasped. "Send still more agents to catch up with the train, capture the woman, and bring her back to the legation. I don't care how you dispose of her, but in the name of the czar, I demand that the wagon train be halted or destroyed!"

A party of Cheyenne warriors rode out into the prairie wilderness at a gallop, and an hour later they returned in triumph, escorting a red-haired, heavily tanned white man in faded buckskins. The new arrival was a giant who stood at least six feet, six inches tall; he was lean and sinewy, which gave him the illusion of being even taller. He embraced the sachem, clasped forearms with the senior warriors, and even hugged a number of the squaws, a gesture in which no outsider would dare to indulge.

Pierre le Rouge was a native of the village of Montreal in French-speaking Canada. He had spent virtually all of his adult life in the Rocky Mountains, and his three pack horses, laden with bundles of furs, were proof of his skills. He hadn't seen another white man in almost three years, he told Henry St. Clair and André Sebastian, so he had interrupted his season's hunting, intending to take his furs to Independence and then return to the Rockies for the autumn season, when even more beaver and lynx would be available.

The Cheyenne declared a holiday in their visitor's honor. A bear, two deer, and an antelope were killed, with the best parts of the meat barbecued for the feast. Pierre seemed to know everyone in the Indian town by name and was on intimate terms with all of the Cheyenne, teasing them, joking with them, and playfully chiding them.

Henry St. Clair rejoiced quietly and bided his time. As he told Sebastian in confidence, the addition of such an experienced mountain man to their company would further guarantee their success. Late that night, after the Indians had retired, Henry offered the delighted Pierre a cup of his precious brandywine. "How do you happen to know these savages so well?" he asked.

"Pierre has made it his business to know all of the Indians—the Blackfoot and the Cheyenne in the plains, the Arapaho in the mountains—even the Comanche, who hate all foreigners and would rather take a white man's scalp than break bread with him. Most mountain men have partners, but Pierre works alone. He needs no partners." His words were boastful, but he spoke quietly, relating what he regarded as simple facts.

"You make a living that way, I presume?"

"Pierre is not rich, but he cannot complain."

"You're a subject of Queen Victoria, as I am," Henry St. Clair said.

"That is true." Pierre le Rouge inhaled the fragrance of the brandywine.

"How would you like to earn more in a few weeks than you could make in several years of hunting and trapping?"

Pierre's booming laugh echoed across the silent Cheyenne town. "Pierre always listens when men speak of money," he said.

Henry was encouraged. "You'd also be performing a service for the Queen," he said. "I'm sure you'd be awarded a medal."

"Pierre likes gold better than medals."

Henry offered him a simplified explanation of the situation. An American wagon train was traveling to the Oregon country, and it was in the best interests of Great Britain that it be halted and forced to turn back.

"There are farmers in this train?"

Henry admitted that most were farmers.

"They bring their families with them, their wives and children?"

"Yes, of course."

"Then they must not be harmed."

Henry was relieved that he had not admitted too much. "We don't want to harm them," he replied. "It will be enough if they become discouraged and return to their homes in other parts of the United States."

Pierre le Rouge stared at him for a long time, sizing him

up and making no comment. Then he spoke abruptly. "Pierre will think about this," he said. "In a day, maybe two days, he will give you his answer." He drained his cup, rose effortlessly to his feet, and went off to his own dwelling.

Henry felt uneasy. The stupid mountain man hadn't reacted as he had wished, but it would be unwise to press him for a positive reply, so there was nothing to be done except wait. Pouring himself more brandywine, he took it off to his own quarters.

Still restless, Henry remained half-awake until dawn. Only when day broke did he drop off into a deep sleep. It was almost noon when he awakened, and after he emerged into the open, he discovered that many of the braves had gone hunting, while most of the women and the older children were at work in the fields where they grew corn, beans, and sunflowers, whose seeds they prized as a delicacy. André Sebastian sat with the chief outside the latter's hut, lazing in the sun, but there was no sign of Pierre le Rouge anywhere. Neither his stallion nor his pack horses were grazing in the fenced compound beyond the dwellings.

"Where is Pierre?" Henry asked, interrupting the conversation.

The sachem displayed a double row of filed teeth when he grinned. "Pierre was gone before the sun came," he said. "That is his way."

Henry felt stricken.

Sebastian saw his expression and asked in English, "What's wrong?"

"I tried to recruit him last night. He was evasive and said he'd give me an answer in a day or two." Henry made no attempt to hide his anxiety. "If he locates the wagon train, he could warn them. I don't like this!"

"Neither do I!" Sebastian replied.

The sachem looked first at one, then at the other, puzzled by their use of the foreign language.

Henry quickly addressed him in Kiowan. "If the warriors of the Cheyenne will find Pierre le Rouge and bring him to me, they will be rewarded with two barrels of whiskey and many firesticks."

The sachem sat upright. This seemed serious. "What has Pierre done?"

"He has broken the trust of his brothers," Henry said. Virtually no Indian would blame a man for stealing the property of another, which they regarded as a legitimate activity, but the breaking of a brother's trust cast any warrior beyond the pale. The sachem was shocked.

"The Cheyenne have been told that much booty awaits them when they attack the wagon train that comes soon into their country," Henry said. "Pierre has gone to warn the white men that they will be attacked!"

The sachem was stunned by the revelation.

As a gesture of good will, Henry handed him a knife with a tempered steel blade. "We will leave this very day for the land of the Blackfoot so they will be ready when the wagon train enters their land," he said. "Thanks to the treachery of Pierre, we cannot stay here any longer. Send me the scalp of Pierre, and the warriors of the Cheyenne will be rewarded."

That, he reflected, was the best he could manage in a difficult situation. The Cheyenne were already primed to attack the train, and if they could apprehend Pierre le Rouge, he would pay them a bonus. He was relieved that he hadn't told the mountain man too much about his plans, but just the fact that the wagon train would be alerted would make attempts to sabotage it more difficult.

He had to rely on the Cheyenne now, and if his mood weren't so vindictive, he could almost feel sorry for the simple-minded Pierre.

Only a short time had passed since Claudia Brentwood had learned for certain that she was pregnant, but she couldn't yet afford the luxury of daydreaming about the day when she and Sam would be parents, for they were too busy establishing the depot. Day after day freight caravans arrived from the East, bringing supplies and provisions, wagon axles, wheels, and rifles for the depot. Sam had hired a number of men to help him load the various supplies in the outbuildings beyond the ranch house, so it was Claudia's place to prepare the meals for these hired hands, some of whom slept in the barns. Sam frequently needed her help and as frequently consulted with her, so there was little time she could call her own.

Today was Sunday, so there were only two extra mouths to feed. Most of the hired hands had gone into Independence to spend their week's pay on liquor and women, but the pair who remained behind would work until noon.

Jacob Levine sat at the breakfast table in the kitchen, silently devouring his fried fish and scrambled eggs. He was short and so slender that he looked as though a strong wind would break him in half, but Sam said that no hired hand worked harder. A former fur cutter from New York whose one ambition in life was to go to Oregon and settle there, Levine was hard-bitten and surprisingly resilient.

So, in his own way, was the Reverend Oscar Cavendish, who was tall, almost as slender as Levine, and very talkative. Freely admitting he had been discharged by his congregation and defrocked for deeds he refused to discuss, he shared Levine's appetite for work and food and had been infected with his partner's enthusiasm for life in the Oregon country.

As Claudia brought a second platter of eggs and fried fish to the plain wooden table, then joined the men for coffee, Cavendish launched into a discussion of his favorite subject.

"As we learn in Ezekiel," he said, "the flock of my pasture are men. Sam has said there are hundreds of souls in the wagon train that is traveling across the Great Plains at this very moment. Other people are beginning to gather in town for the next train, and still others will follow. It stands to reason there will soon be several thousand settlers in Oregon—men, women, and children who will need the counsel of a man of the cloth. They'll need someone to baptize them, to marry them, and to bury them. I feel I'm called by the Lord to help them."

Sam coughed behind his hand to hide his amusement. "I thought you were thrown out of your church, Reverend."

Cavendish was unabashed. "The Lord has forgiven the congregation's transgression, so I have done the same. A new pastorate awaits me."

"All I know," Levine said as he helped himself to more fish, "is that I won't be happy until I get to Oregon. This afternoon I'm going to spend a few hours at target practice on the range in back of the stables. You ought to come with me, Reverend. The Indians out yonder ain't going to leave you alone just because you put your collar on backwards."

Cavendish shook his head. "Beasts shall be at peace with me, just as the Lord promised Job they would be at peace with him. If I am unjustly attacked, I'll know what to do, but I cannot prepare for war."

Levine smiled faintly. "If you were pushed around the way I was, you'd have a good-sized chip on your shoulder, too."

"Just exactly how do you both intend to get out to Oregon?" Sam Brentwood asked them. "It's a long, long journey from here."

"The Lord will find a way," Cavendish replied.

"Maybe so, maybe not," Levine said. "Me, I'm saving my money. I've already bought a good horse and a rifle, and before I'm done, I'll have a team of mules and a snug wagon, so I'll be ready to join the next train. But sitting here ain't earning money. Thank you for breakfast, Mrs. Brentwood. Come along, Reverend. We got lots of work to do this morning."

The pair made their way to the barns, where sacks of gunpowder and piles of harness leather had to be unpacked and stored.

Sam lingered for another cup of coffee with his wife. "I'm sorry you have all this extra work to do, Claudia," he said. "It's something I didn't count on when we set up the depot."

"I don't mind, darling," she replied, brushing a lock of blonde hair away from her face. "If there's still so much cooking to be done after the baby comes—well, maybe we'll have to hire a woman to help. By that time I dare say we'll be able to afford it. But I refuse to worry about what will happen six months from now."

Before Sam could reply, there was a knock at the door.

Lieutenant Colonel Leland Blake stood in the frame,

his uniform and boots covered with dust. He shook hands with Sam, introduced himself to Claudia, and then added, "I've taken the liberty of feeding and watering my horse and turning him loose in your back pasture, Mr. Brentwood. We've been on the move all night, so he's as tired as I am."

Claudia offered the new arrival breakfast, which he gladly accepted, and Sam waited until he returned from the pump, where he went to wash away his grime, before questioning him.

"You're in a hurry to get some place, Colonel?" he asked.

"This is my first stop," Lee Blake said, handing him a sealed letter.

The wax imprint on the communication was that of the President of the United States, and Martin Van Buren's message was brief. "This letter will serve to inform you that Lieutenant Colonel Leland Blake, U.S.A., has my full confidence. I will appreciate your cooperation with him. Colonel Blake will discuss his mission with you, as the situation warrants."

As Claudia began preparing breakfast for the weary officer, Lee Blake seated himself at the kitchen table and glanced at his hostess, then his host. "Would you prefer that I wait until later to talk about business, Mr. Brentwood?"

Sam shook his head. "You can say anything in front of my wife that you can say to me."

"As a start, then, perhaps you can give me some information. I'd like to know everything you can tell me about the attempts made by British and Russian agents to sabotage the wagon train that's headed for the Oregon territory."

Sam spoke steadily and at length. Claudia chimed in too, having known Henry St. Clair fairly well after he had joined the train as a supposed Oregon-bound immigrant.

"He sounds like one of London's upper-echelon agents," Lee said thoughtfully. "All of them are dangerous, so I'm sure I have my work cut out for me." He went on to explain that he was being sent to join the wagon train in order to bring a halt to the incidents that were plaguing them.

"I can see why you've been riding hard, Colonel," Sam said.

"I can't afford to waste time, Mr. Brentwood. I'm hoping you will be able to provide me with a guide who can lead me to the expedition. Or, at the very least, perhaps you can give me a detailed map that will allow me to locate the train myself."

"I don't know of any reliable guides in Independence," Sam said. "Anybody who claims to be a mountain man and is hanging around these parts in summer can't be worth his salt."

Claudia, sensing what was coming, braced herself.

"Have you ever crossed the Great Plains, Colonel?"

"Never, Mr. Brentwood. I spent a long time in the Everglades, and I was part of a group that prevented the British from moving down into Minnesota from Canada, but the plains are new to me."

"Then I strongly urge you not to make the journey alone. Game is plentiful at this time of year, and so are berries and other edible plants, so food will be no problem. But many of the Indians between here and the mountains resent outsiders—especially the Blackfoot and the Cheyenne, along with any number of smaller tribes."

"Certainly no two Indian nations are alike," Lee replied, "and any man who values his scalp tries to minimize the risks he's required to take. But I don't see where I have much choice. I've been ordered to join that wagon train, and if there are no competent guides available, I'll have to travel alone."

"If my wife will give me her permission," Sam said, "I'll take you across the prairies myself."

Claudia swallowed hard, resisting the temptation to close her eyes for a moment. Her hunch had been right. She was certainly competent to take charge of the growing depot and supervise the laborers who were putting away the supplies. And even though she was afraid for Sam's safety, she could not and would not use her pregnancy as an excuse to keep him at her side.

"I won't pretend that I'll enjoy spending weeks—or

months—by myself," she said. "And of course I'll worry. But I have good friends on the wagon train, and my sister is a member of the company. So I can't be selfish and refuse you the right to do what you think is best, Sam. I couldn't live here, all safe and snug, knowing that the train is in constant danger."

Sam reached for her hand. He had known she would make the sacrifice without hesitation, and he was proud of her. "That's settled, then," he said. "Get all the rest you can today, Colonel, and we'll leave early tomorrow. How strong is your horse?"

"He's a big, tough stallion. I couldn't ask for better."

"Then I won't offer you one of mine. But I think we'll need to take a couple of spare mounts with us. We can make much better time if we alternate horses."

After Lee finished his breakfast, he was shown to one of the guest rooms in the ranch house, and Sam went out to the stables to check on the work being done by Jacob Levine and the Reverend Cavendish.

Both reacted instantly when he revealed that he was leaving the following day to guide a visitor, whom he carefully refrained from identifying as an army officer, to the wagon train.

"Take me with you," Levine said. "I already have one horse, and I have enough cash to buy another. I don't really need or want a wagon of my own."

"I want to go, too," the clergyman declared. "The Lord guided Moses through the desert of Sinai, and you shall be our guide, Sam. I believe I can scrape together enough cash to pay you for a couple of good horses."

Sam was impressed by their zeal, even though he remained dubious about their ability to make the journey. "I aim to set a fast pace," he warned them. "I'm not making this trip for pleasure or convenience. So, if you can't keep up, you'll be left behind, which could mean the end of you."

Jacob Levine's jaw jutted forward. "Nobody will leave me behind," he said. "I've spent my whole life waiting for the day when I can claim land of my own and farm it. Nobody's going to deprive me of that chance. Don't worry about me keeping up with you!"

Reverend Cavendish hesitated for a moment. "I've never fired a gun or used any other weapon. The Bible is my only protection, and the Almighty will give me the strength to maintain any pace that you choose to set. I refuse to be left behind!"

Sam shrugged. He had warned them, and he fully intended to keep his word. The safety and future of the wagon train members was of far greater importance than the fate of two adventurous strays.

When he returned to the house, he found Claudia preparing Sunday dinner, a rib roast of beef. She was concentrating on peeling potatoes and carrots, but Sam noticed that her eyes were red. Going to her, he put his arm around her shoulders.

"I wouldn't leave you alone if I thought you were unable to manage, honey," he said. "But you can handle a rifle as well as any man. You know what needs to be done here. In fact, you're better at it than I am."

"I have no worries about myself, only about you." She smiled up at him, unwilling to let him see the depth of her concern.

"Have you ever known me not to be able to look after myself?" he demanded.

She shook her head. It was true that his self-reliance was awesome. She put her arms around him, and she knew he would survive.

Pierre le Rouge knew he was being followed by a band of Cheyenne warriors, but the maneuver didn't surprise him, and he easily managed to outdistance his pursuers, simply by traveling each night for several hours after dark. Most Plains Indians halted their journeys at sundown.

So he reached the wagon train without further incident, arriving late one afternoon, after camp had been made and the hunters had gone out for fresh meat. He was in high spirits, pleased with himself after his efforts, and his mood improved still more when the first person he saw was Eulalia Woodling. She had become a member of the water-gathering detail and was filling two buckets in a small lake behind the circle of wagons.

The mountain man halted, removed his hat with a flourish, and bowed from the saddle. "Pierre le Rouge knows he has died and ascended to heaven," he declared, his English strongly accented. "Never on earth did I see such a lovely angel!"

Eulalia stared up at the bearded, red-haired giant. In spite of his rough attire, this stranger had the manners of a gentleman, and his gleaming eyes indicated that his compliment was sincere. All the same, she had spent enough time in the wilderness by now to recognize the dangers of engaging in conversation with strangers.

Smiling slightly to temper the severity of her attitude, she said, "Our wagonmaster has gone hunting, but you'll find people in the train who will look after you until he returns."

"Ah, but you will allow Pierre to carry those pails for you. Beautiful ladies should not be expected to perform such hard work."

"I do what I must," Eulalia replied, and insisted on carrying the pails herself. She tried to hide her reactions but was flattered by this man's attention. It had been a long time since she had been treated with the courtliness she felt she deserved.

Pierre bowed again, then rode on, turning once in his saddle and grinning broadly to indicate that she had not seen the last of him.

Ernie von Thalman was in camp and greeted the newcomer courteously but was unable to elicit much information from him. It was obvious to Pierre that Ernie was new to the plains, and he would tell his story only to the wagonmaster, who would be better able to make his own judgments.

Then Eulalia returned with her buckets of water, and Pierre instantly devoted his full attention to her. He hadn't known any ladies for more years than he could recall, having attended to his needs by visiting brothels in Independence and other towns on his infrequent journeys to civilized communities. This dignified young woman had the air of the great ladies he had seen from a distance coming in and out of the Citadel, the governor's palace-fort in Quebec, and perhaps for that reason she fascinated him.

Whatever the cause, Eulalia was delighted and flirted with him subtly. At the very least, she was showing other women in the company that, regardless of their opinion of her, men were still drawn to her.

A short time later the hunters returned. They had killed a bull buffalo, which they had already butchered. Whip dismounted and, seeing the new arrival from the rear, went to him. "What can we do for you?" he asked as the man continued to chat with Eulalia.

Pierre le Rouge turned, recognized him instantly, and pounded him on the back. "Whip Holt!"

"Pierre!" Whip was equally overjoyed.

"Not since we fought the Comanche together near the South Pass have I seen you! Are you the wagonmaster of this train?"

"Of course. What are you doing here?"

"Pierre must have words with you in private," the French-Canadian mountain man declared, his tone ominous.

They adjourned to Ernie's wagon, where the president of the company joined them, and there Pierre told them of the offer made to him by the British agent. "Never has Pierre le Rouge done harm to ladies and children," he concluded. "So I went away quickly. I was followed by a band of Cheyenne, but they couldn't catch me. Or, if they could, they had the good sense not to attack me."

"Tell us more about this British agent," Whip said, plainly concerned.

"His name, I believe, is St. Clair—"

"Say no more. That no-good bastard again. I was hoping we had seen the last of him, but we're in for more trouble. Real trouble."

Ernie nodded in sober agreement.

"You will need help?" Pierre wanted to know.

"We could sure use your rifle, if that's what you mean," Whip said. "But if you go along with us, you'll be heading in the wrong direction, if you aim to sell those furs your pack horses are carrying."

Pierre's roar of laughter shook the walls of the hard-roofed wagon. "Pierre was a little crazy for the company of people, that's all," he said. "The money I would earn from the furs I would spend in Independence on women and whiskey. The whiskey I do not need, and in this wagon train there are beautiful ladies. So I will be happy to travel with you."

"Just remember they're ladies," Ernie cautioned him, "not the kind you'd find in a town."

"Pierre knows when he must behave like a gentleman," was the indignant reply. Turning to Whip, he added, "How long Pierre will stay with you I do not know. Long enough to make certain that St. Clair is beaten."

At supper that evening, Whip announced to the company that his old friend was joining the train, at least for the time being, and would act as assistant wagonmaster. Now that they were entering the land of the Cheyenne—and the territory of the even more dreaded Blackfoot lay ahead—Pierre would be a valuable addition to the company.

As soon as the meal was finished, Pierre sought out Eulalia. Now that she had learned his identity, she was even more cordial to him, rightly suspecting that her presence was at least partly responsible for his decision to accompany the caravan for a time.

"There is a favor Pierre wishes to ask of you," he said.

"Tell me what it is," she replied coyly, "and then I'll decide whether to grant it."

He pointed to the bales of beaver and lynx skins that he had removed from the backs of his pack horses. "Do you have the space in your wagon to store my furs? I would like my pack animals to enjoy the rest they deserve."

"I'll make room for them," Eulalia replied quickly. It shouldn't be difficult to persuade this man, who so obviously liked her, to make her a gift of enough furs to fashion a lynx coat for the coming winter. Confident of her powers, she reflected that a few smiles and an occasional encouraging word should be enough to win her a prize that other women would envy.

Lieutenant Colonel Leland Blake looked like any other civilian frontier dweller in the old buckskin shirt and trousers he had borrowed from Sam Brentwood. Only his boots would have revealed to a sharp-eyed observer that he might be an army officer. Not even Jacob Levine and the Reverend Oscar Cavendish were told his true identity or the reason for his presence on the journey.

Sam took the lead, with Lee riding beside him, each of them leading a spare horse. Levine and Cavendish rode a short distance behind the pair, and they, too, had spare horses. After a few days in the wilderness, Sam's doubts about these volunteers began to disappear. Levine never complained, gathered firewood and water, and cheerfully accepted the chore of cooking breakfast and supper.

Cavendish proved to be even more surprising. In the saddle, he resembled a loose-jointed scarecrow. It seemed miraculous that he could keep his seat. Yet he managed to maintain the blistering pace that Sam set. He claimed to know nothing about the outdoors, but he caught several fish every evening, and he proved adept at lighting fires in the Indian manner, by rubbing sticks together. It was difficult to actually enjoy the company of a man who seemed incapable of speaking a complete sentence without referring to the Scriptures, but he was resilient and tireless.

By riding one horse mornings and another afternoons, it became possible to travel even more swiftly than Sam had dared to hope. They covered forty to fifty miles each day. If they could maintain the pace, they expected to catch up with the wagon train in two weeks or less.

No unexpected incidents occurred during the first days of their journey. On the fourth morning, however, the placid routine was broken when Sam suddenly pointed to some dark objects in the distance.

"There's a small herd of buffalo yonder," he said. "We'll shoot one—just one—to give us meat for the days ahead."

"I need the practice," Jacob Levine said. "I hope nobody will mind if I bring him down."

"All right," Sam told him, "but make a semicircle northward away from the Platte so you'll approach the herd downwind. And don't get too close before you shoot. Buffalo tend to avoid riders, but can be dangerous to men when they stampede."

Levine handed the reins of his spare horse to the clergyman, checked his rifle, and directed his mount on a wide swing so he wouldn't alert the herd. The others continued to follow the river, slowing their pace, and for a time Sam nodded approvingly. Then his attitude changed, and he spoke softly. "He's close enough now for a clean strike. He ought to stop and shoot."

Levine continued to move closer to the grazing buffalo. Lee Blake saw nothing wrong with what the former fur cutter was doing, but his knowledge of buffalo was limited. "What's wrong?"

"He isn't a good enough horseman to get out of the way in a hurry if the herd stampedes. It's an unnerving experience to have tons and tons of wild animals galloping toward you. I've known men to become so rattled they've been thrown and then trampled to death."

"Isn't there some way we can warn him?"

"Not without firing ourselves and maybe scaring off the whole herd." Sam increased his own pace, quietly checking his rifle to make certain he could fire it instantly.

"Ah," the relieved Lee said. "He's slowing down now."

"But not quite enough."

Reverend Cavendish started to pray softly, but they ignored him.

At last Levine halted, raised his rifle and, after what seemed like a very long time, squeezed the trigger. His shot struck a bull, which weighed at least two thousand pounds, but it only wounded the animal. Crazed by the pain, the beast lowered his head until it almost touched the ground, then charged his attacker, his hoofs pounding as he advanced.

"Get out of the way, Jacob!" Reverend Cavendish shouted. "Move, man!"

Levine was so startled by the unexpected assault that he continued to sit motionless. Finally, instead of urging his mount out of the path of the crazed bull, he began to reload his rifle, too confused by now to realize that he would have no opportunity to fire again before he and his horse were gored.

The others were two hundred yards away, but Sam Brentwood knew there was only one way to save the man's life. His rifle had a range of no more than two hundred yards, but he had no choice. He spurred his stallion, and as the great horse broke into a gallop, he raised his rifle, took careful aim, and fired.

His bullet entered the brain of the bull buffalo, who died instantly, plunging forward and collapsing almost at the feet of Levine's badly frightened gelding.

The other buffalo in the herd, unaware of the first shot, were at last alert to the danger. A wise, elderly bull was the first to bolt, and then the entire herd of about fifteen buffalo followed him as he raced off to the northwest, away from the scene.

Levine was still trembling when Sam led the others to him. "You don't have to lecture me," he said. "I know all the things I did wrong. Next time I won't make the same mistakes, and I thank God there will be a next time!"

He was the first to leap to the ground and begin butchering the bull, his experience as a fur cutter making him exceptionally adept at the task. Sam and Lee Blake exchanged glances. They both had to admire Levine's courage. Many men who had escaped death so narrowly would have been useless for the rest of the day. For the first time, it occurred to Sam that Levine might prove to be a welcome addition to the wagon train.

Pierre le Rouge quickly became accustomed to the routines of wagon train living. Sometimes he relieved Whip at the head of the column, he had to be dissuaded from going out with the scouts, and he was as skilled as Whip and Arnold at shooting game. Pierre and Hosea frequently went hunting together, each fascinated by the other's techniques. When they were joined by Stalking Horse, they made a formidable trio, and never failed to return with game.

Pierre delighted in teaching the older boys bawdy songs, which they sang at the top of their voices. As they sang in French, only Ernie von Thalman and Cathy van Ayl could understand the words; the former kept his own counsel so the fun wouldn't be spoiled, and Cathy resolutely ignored the lyrics.

The only objection anyone could find to Pierre was that he continued to devote too much attention to Eulalia Woodling. No one minded his open interest in the girl, but there were many—particularly the women—who resented the way Eulalia used him. She flirted with him when it pleased her and calmly accepted his help when he offered to do her chores for her.

On the night the wagon train reached the junction of the North and South Platte rivers, Whip announced to the company that they had reached a significant place in the Great Plains. Pioneers who chose to follow the South Platte would travel across Colorado, then head toward the southwest onto what was known as the Old Santa Fe Trail, eventually reaching Spanish California. Their wagon train, Whip said, would follow the North Platte to its headwaters in the mountains and would travel by way of the Wyoming country and the land of the Ute Indians, to the Great Divide, then cross yet another range of mountains that would bring them to Oregon.

They still had a vast distance to travel, but they had made good progress, and there was at least a chance they would be able to reach a sheltered, wooded canyon in the Rockies before they would have to establish a permanent winter camp.

"You've come a long way from Long Island," Whip told Cathy. "You have a right to be proud of yourself."

"I haven't done much of anything, except follow where you've led us," she replied honestly.

A scant twelve hours after starting to follow the North Platte as it meandered westward, its waters deeper and less sandy than those of the Platte itself, Stalking Horse returned early from his scouting duties. He reported without delay to Whip; then Pierre was summoned. The three conversed at length, speaking in an Indian tongue so no one would know what they were saying. As Whip pointed out, there was nothing to be gained by alarming the company prematurely.

At the insistence of Stalking Horse, they sent for Hosea, too, and Whip explained the situation to him succinctly. "We've come to the land of the Cheyenne now," he said. "Next to the Blackfoot and the Comanche, maybe, they're the meanest tribe there is. They hate foreigners as much as they hate other Indians, even more. They've had a quarrel with Pierre, who was their friend, because an enemy turned against him. Now Stalking Horse believes they've sent a large party of scouts to keep watch on us, and that means trouble. What we need to know, right off, is how many men there are in the Cheyenne scouting party. That will tell us something about their intentions. You understand me so far?"

The Ashanti, listening carefully, nodded but made no reply.

"Stalking Horse and Pierre are going out," Whip said. "They'll ride in the direction that Stalking Horse spotted the Cheyenne."

"The Cheyenne will recognize Pierre," the French Canadian mountain man interrupted. "That much will be good."

"They'll also see Stalking Horse," Whip went on. "Both of them will keep their distance. That should attract the attention of the Cheyenne—and, we hope, should keep that attention. Meantime, Hosea, maybe you could steal close enough to count their number and find out how heavily they're armed. That's information we badly need."

"Hosea do," the little man said, his manner confident and calm.

He immediately moved out into the prairie and began to pluck clumps of the knee-high grass. While members of the company watched, he covered his shield with grass, then hastily made and donned a plaited-grass shirt and cap. The members of the company were astonished at his ingenuity, and the results were almost magical. The camouflage was so effective that, at a distance of a scant one hundred and fifty yards, Hosea blended completely into the landscape of the prairie. One moment he could be seen, and the next he vanished.

Stalking Horse and Pierre left at once, riding at a canter through the tall grass toward the northwest. Hosea ran beside them, tireless as always. Even Whip could follow his progress only because the grass parted and waved slightly wherever he moved.

Voices carried across the open country, so there was no talk. After the trio had gone about three or four miles, Stalking Horse grunted quietly, and the two horsemen slowed their pace, moving apart until they were separated by several hundred feet.

Hosea moved off on his own, staying parallel with them but making his own way. Stalking Horse paid no attention to his friend, confident of his ability to take care of himself.

Although Pierre had gone hunting with the Ashanti every day for a week, he was seeing a new facet of Hosea's talents and was amazed.

All at once Stalking Horse raised a hand, pointed, and said in a clear voice, "Cheyenne!"

A cluster of horsemen could be seen in the distance, but it was impossible to make out their number. The two riders moved into single file, Stalking Horse in the lead, and rode parallel to the Indians, neither closing in nor allowing themselves to drift farther away.

The braves obviously were not intimidated by men who had no intention of challenging them. They respected Pierre, whom they were able to identify at a distance because of his height and beard. But the strange Indian who rode with him did not impress them, and they remained confidently on their own course.

Stalking Horse had learned patience in the long trials he had been forced to endure as a child and as an adolescent before he had been admitted to the councils of the Cherokee as a full-fledged warrior. He was able to play this seemingly simple game indefinitely, and he felt no stirring of impatience.

When Pierre le Rouge went hunting or was about to confront an enemy in combat, he, too, could be patient, but this situation annoyed him. He peered continually across the sea of grass that separated him from the Cheyenne scouts, but he could make out no sign of Hosea, even though he looked for a telltale parting and waving of grass. Perhaps, he thought, the little man had outsmarted himself. Certainly there seemed to be no way he could be moving through that grass.

The better part of an hour passed, and Pierre stared hard at Stalking Horse until the Cherokee looked at him. Then he shrugged to indicate his bewilderment. Stalking Horse merely grinned at him in return. Suddenly a voice was raised only a few feet from Pierre's mount, causing him to start violently.

"We go back to train now," Hosea said calmly, still hidden from view in the grass. "Hosea find out what Whip want to know."

Stalking Horse immediately turned back in the direction of the North Platte River, and Pierre moved up beside him. There was no sign of Hosea, however, until they left the Cheyenne patrol far behind. Then the Ashanti moved his shield slightly and could be seen running only a short distance from the two riders.

He was so eager to report his findings that he actually raced ahead of them and was the first to reach the spot where the wagon train had halted for the night. When the others arrived shortly thereafter, Pierre found it difficult to believe that the Ashanti was breathing normally, as though he had not exerted himself at all.

Whip was waiting.

"Count eighteen warriors in party," Hosea told him. "All carry bows and arrows. All carry big spears."

Whip sucked in his breath. "That's exactly what I needed to know," he said. Eighteen braves in a scouting party meant reconnaissance in force. The warriors obviously were ready for a serious engagement if they carried spears as well as bows and arrows.

That very night a new routine was established. Sentry posts were set up, and the men of the wagon train, particularly those who were able to make out potential enemy moves after dark, were on constant duty until daybreak.

[illegible] shrugged. He sort of continually [illegible] the [illegible] they were [illegible] on the [illegible] [illegible] and [illegible] make the [illegible] of Meaga [illegible] [illegible] the [illegible] and a [illegible] and [illegible] of [illegible]. Perhaps he [illegible] the [illegible] had [illegible] himself. Certainly there [illegible] for [illegible] happened [illegible] during [illegible].

The [illegible] part of [illegible] passed, and [illegible] [illegible] until the [illegible] at [illegible] [illegible] decided to [illegible] his [illegible]. Nothing [illegible] other [illegible] a [illegible] [illegible] quietly.

[illegible]

[illegible]

[illegible] and [illegible] and [illegible] the [illegible] was [illegible] of Hara. [illegible], until [illegible]. Then the [illegible] [illegible] and [illegible] [illegible] of [illegible].

[illegible]

[illegible]

[illegible] and [illegible] and [illegible].

Then they [illegible] a new [illegible] was established. [illegible] [illegible]

XIII

Lee Blake kept up the pace that Sam Brentwood set, but he had to admit to himself that at no time in his army career had he traveled at such a steady speed. Jacob Levine pushed hard, his determination making it possible for him to follow, and Reverend Cavendish, to the surprise of his companions, seemed untroubled. His resources were endless.

The quartet shot enough game to provide themselves with fresh meat each day, and the clergyman's fishing provided them with a measure of variety in their diet. On two different evenings, Levine found wild berries, which he presented to his companions. They slept in the open, rolled in their blankets, and at dawn each day, before they began their ride, they bathed in the always-cold waters of the Platte River.

Sam and Lee struck up a firm friendship on the trail and, after the manner of men who liked each other, began to exchange confidences.

"I'm more worried about my wife than I was willing to admit to her," Sam said. "But she's the most resourceful, courageous woman I know. If any man at the ranch steps out of line—well, I feel sorry for him. Only a mission like this would have taken me away from home when she's expecting a baby, though. All the same, I'll be back in Independence long before our son shows up."

"You know," Lee said, "I can't help envying the members of the wagon train. Oh, I'll grant you life can't be easy for them, crawling across the entire continent in all kinds of weather, facing hostile Indians and other hazards. But there's something solid waiting for them when they finally reach Oregon."

"You never married, Lee?"

"An officer in my kind of work never settles in any one place long enough to have a wife and a family. Every few years I've been moved to a new assignment, and I can't ask any woman to share that kind of a life."

"The right woman wouldn't mind."

"If there is such a woman, Sam, I haven't had time to find out. Between you and me, I had a private meeting with President Van Buren before I left Washington City. He told me there's a possibility, if I have to travel all the way to Oregon, that we'll establish an army post there to protect our citizens. I could have the command of that post if I wanted it, I'm sure. It's a temptation, but I'd be out of the mainstream, and it would take a very special girl to persuade me to spend the rest of my life on the Pacific."

Sam refrained from commenting that he had been a confirmed bachelor, too, until Claudia had come into his life.

Summer was the lush season on the Great Plains, so most of the nomadic Indian tribes stayed in one place, raising the crops they would store until the harsh winter arrived. Autumn was the season when they were on the move, hunting the vast herds of buffalo that had grown fat and sleek on the rich grass of the prairies.

Even in summer, however, Indian patrols were on the prowl, constantly watchful and alert, so their nations would not be subjected to surprise attacks launched by traditional enemies. On several occasions Sam and the members of his party saw mounted braves in the distance, but the warriors showed no interest in a group of only four white men.

One day, however, eight Kansa warriors emerged unexpectedly from a grove of trees.

"Hold your rifles ready, but don't shoot," Sam warned. "We may get out of this without any trouble, but the whole blamed tribe will be after us if we kill any of them."

Lee nodded and remained calm. Levine clutched his rifle, waiting for an order to fire. Reverend Cavendish raised his voice in a recitation from the Book of Psalms, but his companions paid no attention to him.

The Kansa came closer, and one of their number approached and raised a hand in greeting. Sam returned the salute. The Kansa addressed him in Kiowan, Sam responded in the same tongue, and then the braves rode off without further ado.

"What was that all about?" Lee wanted to know.

Sam was embarrassed. "Indians may steal," he said, "but they almost always speak the truth. They were planning to attack us, but they recognized me and changed their minds. I guess it occurred to them that they'd have a real battle on their hands if they insisted on a fight."

The army officer laughed appreciatively. "Now I can understand why you wanted to be my guide," he said. "I had no idea that even Indians were afraid of you."

"Not of me," Sam replied modestly. "Only of my rifle. They'd be leery of you, Lee, if they felt the sting of some of your bullets."

In the following days, they encountered more Indians on the prairies, including Wichita and Osage. A band of the latter appeared to be hostile, so Sam put a single bullet in the head of the leader's pony. The discouraged braves quickly disappeared.

At last the day came when the quartet caught up with the wagon train. They reached their destination during the nooning hour, and within moments, most of the company surrounded Sam, eager to shake his hand and inquire about Claudia. He spent a few moments alone with Cathy, managing to tell her that Claudia was expecting a baby, and he promised to spend the evening with her.

Then, while Levine and Reverend Cavendish began to acquaint themselves with the men and women they had joined, Sam and Lee Blake went off to confer privately with Whip. The wagonmaster read a letter that President Van Buren had sent him and seemed perturbed.

"It appears to me that you're replacing me, Colonel," he said.

"Not at all," Lee replied quickly. "I don't know the terrain—either here or what lies ahead. I'm totally unfamiliar with the operation of a wagon train, and I've never dealt with any of the Indian nations of the plains or Rocky Mountains. Even if I wanted to replace you—which I don't—I'm not qualified. I'm here because the War Department regards me as something of an expert in countering the work done by foreign agents. I'll step in only when I think it necessary, and I'll ask you for specific help only when I believe there's an opportunity to put British or Imperial Russian spies and saboteurs out of business."

"Fair enough," Whip said, but he still had reservations.

"Lee has become my friend," Sam Brentwood said. "He's our kind of man."

His friend's approval reassured Whip somewhat, and he brought the army officer up to date, telling him about the visit of André Sebastian to Fort Madison, the subsequent poisoning of the lake water, the death of the Russian agent and, finally, the current flurry being caused by the Cheyenne.

"I'm blame near positive the British are behind the Cheyenne," he said. "Pierre le Rouge saw St. Clair and another white man in a Cheyenne town to the northwest of us, and St. Clair tried to enlist his services. I reckon you'll want to talk with Pierre yourself."

"So I shall," Lee said. "But I don't want my real identity revealed to him or to anyone else. Let everyone think I'm just a new recruit, like Jake Levine and Reverend Cavendish. I don't want to restrict myself by starting to sleep in anybody's wagon, and I prefer not to join any of your hunting parties. I'll help out with various chores, but I don't want to be tied down to a regular job. From time to time, I may ask you and your assistants for specific help, but mainly I'll be working by myself."

"I reckon we're going to get along," Whip said, and

extended a hand. Lee's grip was equally firm, and Sam was relieved. A clash between these two could have had catastrophic results.

"After I've had a long chat with Pierre le Rouge," Lee said, "I plan to become acquainted with every adult in the wagon train. A good many of them won't require much of a check, but I want to make as certain as I can that there are no British or Russian agents currently in your company."

Whip was startled. "I think that's unlikely."

"I hope so, but it's my job to find out," Lee replied firmly. "Henry St. Clair once posed as an Oregon-bound immigrant, and from what Sam here reported to Washington, he almost wrecked the train. What one agent has done, another could do all too easily, so I intend to make good and sure that the inside of the house is clean before we start looking outside."

They separated, and that afternoon, while Sam rode in his familiar place at the head of the column beside Whip, Lee dropped back a few paces and fell into conversation with Pierre. Prodding gently, he managed to elicit the entire story of what had taken place in the town of the Cheyenne, but he did it so subtly that Pierre had no idea he was being interrogated.

When the caravan made camp for the night, Lee had a few additional words with Whip, in Sam's presence. "You probably realize this already," he said, "but I can almost guarantee that the Cheyenne will launch a serious attack on the train soon. An agent of St. Clair's caliber wouldn't rest until he managed to provide them with strong inducements. Apparently he was planning on pushing ahead into new territory, so his work with the Cheyenne seems to be finished. The only reason he'd move on would be that he's convinced the Cheyenne will follow through with his plan."

"My hunch," Sam said, "is that his next stop is the Blackfoot, and then the trouble will be even worse."

"I've been worried about the Blackfoot—and the Comanche in the mountains—ever since Andy Jackson asked me to join you in this whole enterprise, Sam," Whip said. "They're both strong and mean, and they hate everybody outside their own tribes. The best thing that could happen would be a war between them. If they bled each other enough, there would be peace in the wilderness for a few years. In the meantime, the Cheyenne are nasty enough."

"I think," Sam said, "that I'll spend a few days with you before I head back to Independence. My horses need resting, and I'd be perturbed if I left too soon to help you out."

"We sure can use you," Whip said.

"What precautions have you taken?" Lee wanted to know.

"I've posted sentries at night, and all our scouts are on the alert," Whip replied. "I'll double the sentry detail, just to make sure we aren't surprised in the middle of the night. And I'll tell our hunters not to roam too far from camp. I've already reminded the men to carry their firearms with them at all times, so there isn't much more that I'm able to do."

"How many men can the Cheyenne muster in an attack?" Lee asked.

Whip thought for a time. "They've never been a nation that uses mass assaults as a tactic, maybe because their towns and villages are so scattered. Myself, I've never heard of them sending more than a couple of hundred braves into battle at any one time."

"That's pretty much true," Sam added. "Of course, two hundred determined warriors can cause one hell of a lot of damage."

"And how many effectives can you use for defense purposes?"

"A dozen to eighteen marksmen, and another one hundred and fifty who range from fair shots to poor."

Lee Blake smiled and patted his own rifle. "It will be good exercise," he said. "After spending years sitting at one desk or another, all the way from St. Petersburg and London to Washington City, it will be interesting to do what any officer worth his salt enjoys most."

Supper was almost ready by the time they joined the rest of the company. Lee saw that Cathy was alone and decided to join her. For all practical purposes, he had already ruled her out as a possible enemy spy, but he told himself he had done enough work for one day. She was the most attractive girl in the wagon train, and he saw no reason he shouldn't indulge himself for a time.

"You and your sister don't look in the least alike, Mrs. Van Ayl," he said as he joined her.

"Oh, you've met Claudia?"

"I stayed with the Brentwoods for a day and a night before Sam brought me out here," he replied.

Cathy kept her suspicions to herself, but it was evident to her that Lee Blake was no ordinary immigrant. Joseph Levine and the Reverend Oscar Cavendish had tagged along on the journey, but she realized that Sam wouldn't have left Independence unless it had been important. She was in no hurry, however, to find out who this man was. It was enough for her that he was personable, handsome enough to arouse the attention of any romantically inclined woman, and well-mannered.

"Then you found Claudia well and happy?"

"Yes, and busy."

"That's an old family tradition," she said.

"I've noticed you preparing this meal. It can't be easy to direct the cooking for so many people."

"I do what I must."

Lee's curiosity about her was aroused. "Forgive me if I seem to be prying, but Mrs. Brentwood told me that she and Sam offered you the opportunity to stay with them in Independence. I find it surprising that an exceptionally pretty young lady should be going out to the Oregon country by herself."

"I don't like being beholden to anyone," Cathy told him. "That's an old family tradition, too."

"You intend to build your own house and farm your own property once you reach Oregon?" He was impressed by the task she was willing to undertake.

"Well, I lived on a farm with my late husband on Long Island, so farming isn't going to be a new experience for me," she said. "I realize I might be intending to try doing more than I can handle, but I won't really know until I make the effort, will I?"

"I salute you," Lee said, realizing it was the type of

spirit Cathy van Ayl exhibited that would establish a solid, viable American colony in the rich farm country in Oregon.

Their talk was interrupted by Whip, who was carrying his plate. "Cathy is spoiling fellows like me for wilderness living," he said. "I'm not sure I'll ever be satisfied to eat with my fingers again, even though it was the only way I took my meals for more than ten years."

Lee laughed.

Cathy smiled, too, hiding her surprise. This was the first time in days that Whip had actively sought her company, and for a few moments she didn't know what to make of his unexpected initiative. Lee was standing on her left, and when Whip deliberately moved to her other side and began to discuss ways to use leftover buffalo meat for breakfast, she realized he was deliberately trying to freeze the other man out of the conversation.

Then it dawned on her that Whip was jealous of the attention that Lee Blake was paying her. It was almost too good to be true. Whip Holt was actually jealous! So he wasn't indifferent to her, and he certainly wasn't taking her for granted.

Although Cathy showed no sign of the way she felt, she was elated. She had been so young when she had married that she had never had to deal with more than one suitor, but her instinct came to her aid. She managed to talk to both men, sometimes separately and sometimes together, taking care not to show a preference for either one.

She was very much aware that Whip bristled every time she addressed a remark to Lee Blake or smiled at him. Perhaps it was unfair to use this handsome stranger this way, but she told herself she was doing him no harm. Certainly the effect on Whip was almost magical.

Cindy, who saw the two men jockeying for position, looked at Cathy from a distance, then winked solemnly. It was all Cathy could do to keep from laughing aloud in triumph. At last she had proved to herself that Whip Holt was really interested in her.

Ultimately Sam appeared, put an arm around her shoulders, and started toward the stoop of her wagon with her.

"Sorry to break in," he said cheerfully, "but we're going to have us a little family chat."

As they made themselves comfortable on the wagon steps, he gave her a letter that her sister had written her, then answered her eager questions about Claudia.

"I think it's wonderful that you and Claudia are so right for each other," she said at last. "I find it hard to envision her being so domestic and so happy doing the things she always said she despised. What will the baby be named?"

"We've agreed to call him Andrew Jackson Brentwood. After all, it was Old Hickory who brought us together."

"What if Claudia has a girl?"

"She won't," he said firmly.

Cathy giggled.

Sam backtracked. "Well, Claudia says she'd name a daughter Martha, after your mother, and that's fine with me. But it won't happen."

She tried in vain to keep a straight face. "Of course not."

Sam was uncomfortable, and changed the subject. "You're not having any serious problems, I take it. You look just grand."

"To tell you the truth," Cathy replied, "I've never felt better in my life. Wagon train living agrees with me. I don't know how I'll act when we finally get to Oregon. It seems as though we've been traveling forever."

Sam leaned closer to her and lowered his voice, even though no one was within earshot. "Claudia and I have had many talks about you, Cathy. I wouldn't repeat this outside the family, but she's convinced you're in love with Whip."

Cathy hesitated for a long time before she spoke again. "One day I'm convinced I am, and the next—when he ignores me—I change my mind. You saw the way he was hanging around at supper tonight. That's because the new man, Lee Blake, was paying attention to me, and Whip was jealous. So that's a good sign, Sam."

"Maybe so." He drew his knife from his belt and absently slashed the tall blades of grass at his feet with it. "This isn't easy for me, so bear with me, Cathy. I've got to speak out because I promised Claudia I would. You know how firm she is when she makes up her mind to something." He paused, then took a deep breath. "Claudia and I hope you don't have your heart set on marrying Whip."

She wanted facts, not hints. "Why not?" she asked bluntly.

"Hellfire, girl, he's a mountain man. He's spent year after year by himself in the wilderness, never knowing a permanent home, cooking most of his own meals, going wherever he wants any time he's felt like going. Most of all, he's never been responsible for anybody but himself."

"But you were a mountain man, Sam. You spent longer in the Rockies than Whip has. Now you're happily married, settled in a permanent home, and about to become a father. So it does happen, even to the best of mountain men."

"For one thing," he replied, cutting the blades of grass more rapidly, "Claudia kind of crept into my bloodstream before I even realized what was happening. Every now and again a mountain man *does* find the right woman, and then they get married. But most fellows who have been hunters and trappers for any length of time just can't stand being tied down. When they see a woman—which doesn't happen very often—she's the wrong kind—not a lady, if you follow me. Look at Pierre le Rouge, who is almost my age and has been living in the Rockies ever since he was a youngster. A man like that will never marry."

Cathy thought of Pierre's obvious interest in the spoiled Eulalia Woodling. "Don't place any wagers on that."

He slid his knife back into his belt. "Claudia and I just don't want you to get hurt, that's all. I've known Whip ever since he first came out to the Rockies, when he was little more than a boy. He was a wild one, especially when he was younger, and he's always been the most independent cuss I've known. He doesn't get close to anyone, and he never lets on what he really thinks and feels."

"I'm convinced that's a front. People who are lonely often behave that way."

"Maybe so," Sam replied, sighing. "You'll do as you

please, of course, seeing you're a grown woman. And if you weren't headstrong, you wouldn't be Claudia's sister. Just remember that I warned you, Cathy."

The day began like any other. The sentries reported that nothing suspicious had happened during the last hours of the night. The campfire, which had burned low, was rebuilt. Small children emerged from their wagons to play, their shouts and laughter awakening many of the adults who otherwise would have slept later.

Members of the cooking contingent gathered at the fire, and under the direction of Cathy and Cindy began to prepare breakfast. Ted Woods, aided by Hosea, made emergency repairs on an axle that was sagging suspiciously. Some of the older boys would have gone fishing in the North Platte River but were stopped by Pierre, who told them to postpone their sport until that night's halt, when there would be more time for it.

Instead the boys were put to work cutting grass to be set aside as fodder for the horses and oxen. That noon they would be stopping in a sandy area where nothing grew, so the fodder had to be prepared in advance. Members of the water-gathering detail walked off through a patch of thick elm and pine to a clear, swift-flowing stream that flowed into the North Platte farther upstream.

Soon, Whip had announced the previous night, they would come to rolling countryside where they would catch their first glimpse of buttes—steep hills, each of which stood alone. Their appearance would mark the beginning of the Rocky Mountain foothills. Everyone was excited by the prospect and was filled with a sense of accomplishment.

As usual, Eulalia Woodling was the last member of the water-gathering detail to appear. The others had already returned to the camp after performing the chore, and she looked around for Pierre, hoping he would offer to take her buckets off to the stream and fill them for her. Unfortunately, he was supervising the grass-cutting efforts of Danny, Chet, and the other boys.

So Eulalia sighed petulantly and went off alone. All

through the long spring and summer, she had hated being obliged to perform such menial duties as cooking, washing dishes, and hauling buckets of water, but she had discovered that there was no escape from the chores. Whip and Ernie von Thalman showed her no sympathy, and even her father merely shrugged when she complained to him. Only Pierre showed her any kindness, but when he was otherwise engaged, she had to do the work herself.

Eulalia pouted as she left the circle. Instead of walking around the woods, as members of the detail had been instructed the previous evening, she elected to take a shorter route by going through them to the little river. Sometimes, she thought, Whip and Ernie deliberately made up rules for the perverse pleasure of forcing people to work harder.

Nothing stirred in the woods, and there was no sound. Eulalia dawdled, deliberately postponing her chore.

Then a brawny, brown-skinned arm caught her from behind, encircled her neck, and pulled her backward, knocking her off her feet. At the same instant, a soft gag of leather was shoved into her mouth, muffling her scream.

Eulalia looked up in terror as she fell, catching a glimpse of a husky Indian brave bending over her, his face and bare torso streaked with paint. In his scalp lock he wore several eagle feathers, and the stench of bear grease that was smeared over his whole body made her sick to her stomach.

She struggled, thrashing her arms and legs, but the man easily subdued her, binding her wrists behind her back with a strip of rawhide that he tied so tightly the leather cut into her flesh. He used another strip of rawhide to bind her ankles, then threw her over his shoulder, carrying her as though she were a sack of grain.

Eulalia realized he was taking her to a waiting horse, and again she tried to scream, but the gag muffled her voice. All at once she noticed that the woods and the open area to the north were alive with scores of other Indians, all mounted on large horses and armed with bows and arrows, spears, and long poles padded with dried grass.

The brave who had made her his prisoner threw her

over the folded buffalo robe that he used as a saddle, then mounted his horse and began to ride through the ranks of his comrades. The other warriors, intent on the grim business that awaited them, paid scant attention to the terror-stricken girl. Obviously her capture had been an unexpected bonus and had no bearing on what they were doing.

The brave continued to ride his horse slowly northward across the prairie. Not until he had gone several hundred yards did he strike the mount smartly on the flank. Then the horse bounded forward swiftly, and Eulalia was carried off.

Unaware that anything was wrong, Cathy beat on the bottom of an empty kettle with a large metal spoon to indicate that breakfast was ready. People began to line up for slices of buffalo fat cut from the center strip across the back of the huge beasts—a dish that, when fried, closely resembled bacon. With it the company was being served biscuits and a jam that some of the women had made from wild raspberries; pots of coffee were beginning to boil.

Suddenly one of the workhorses screamed and collapsed onto the ground, an arrow protruding from its head. Terence Malcolm staggered backward and sat down hard on the ground, staring foolishly at an arrow that was sticking out of his shoulder. And an indignant Grace Drummond plucked an arrow from her apron and brandished it over her head.

The mountain men were the first to react.

"Cheyenne!" Pierre le Rouge shouted as he recognized the short, thick arrows used by the warriors of the most dreaded Plains tribe.

"Cheyenne attack!" Sam Brentwood called in the same breath.

Whip instantly began to organize the defense of the circle. The entire company was caught by surprise, as Indian attacks almost always took place either at dawn or sundown. This assault, however, obviously had been planned for a time when it was least anticipated.

Most of the men moved to the openings between the

wagons, and the older boys, knowing from past experience what was expected of them, raced to the special wagon for spare ammunition, powder, and the extra rifles they would load while others were being fired.

The women, children, and animals were moved toward the river side of the circle, which was farthest from the area of active combat. Grace Drummond took charge of this maneuver, her booming voice rising above the shouts and the sound of rifle fire that was already starting to erupt. "Take your time!" she called. "Don't stampede like cattle or you'll trample your own little ones. Every mother is responsible for her own young. And look after your animals. Keep them away from the arrows as best you can. Don't let them stampede, either."

Whip was everywhere, organizing the resistance. Sam immediately slipped back into the role he had played for so long, mustering a number of the best marksmen into a special group. These included the scouts, Lee Blake, Pierre, and Ernie von Thalman, and they were joined voluntarily by Hosea and Claiborne Woodling, neither of whose talents Sam knew. Then Tonie Mell came to them, too, crawling close to the ground just inside the shelter of the wagons, and Sam didn't have the heart to turn her away.

Wiser and shrewder by far than other tribes, whose tactics usually consisted of a bold frontal attack, the Cheyenne remained in the woods, where they could see the defenders but could not be seen. From that shelter, they sent showers of arrows into the circle.

Cathy realized the cooking fire made an easily seen target. She began to extinguish it, indifferent to the arrows that fell around her. Cindy came to help her, and although terrified, the two girls tried to perform the task alone. Then Ted Woods saw them, and, his prowess with a rifle being limited, he came to join them. Wielding a heavy shovel, he piled dirt onto the flames, and as soon as they were extinguished, he shepherded the girls to relative safety on the river side of the circle, then devoted himself to calming the horses and oxen.

Meanwhile, the members of the elite unit huddled behind the special wagon, and there Whip conferred with them.

"There's no telling yet how many warriors are out yonder," he said. "We won't know until they show themselves."

"It looks to me like most of our shots are going wild," Sam said. "That's because too many of the men have never fought in a battle."

"I don't believe that matters," Lee Blake said.

Whip, aware of his high military rank, paid particular attention to this remark. "Why not?"

"Any kind of rifle fire is enough to hold savages at bay until we establish some kind of order here. And that's a job you seem to have done already. I'm not at all familiar with the Cheyenne, but if they're in any way like the tribes I know, they'll keep firing arrows until they think they've weakened us, and then they'll charge us on horseback and try to overwhelm us."

"I'm sure you're right," Whip said. "We've just got to be extra careful some of them don't sneak around to the river side."

"Some of us will see to that," Arnold Mell said. He worked his way around to the left, accompanied by Tonie, while Mack Dougall and Pierre le Rouge moved to the right. Any Cheyenne who tried to sneak down to the river side of the circle would be greeted by the accurate fire of sharpshooters who took pride in rarely missing their targets.

"Somebody is showing good sense," Lee said. "Instead of trying to pick targets in the woods, which is impossible, he's just sending a stream of fire into the trees to disrupt the enemy."

Whip grinned. "That's the new man, Levine," he said.

He beckoned to Chet and Danny, who were waiting nearby, hoping they would be chosen to reload the rifles of the marksmen. "Lads," he said, "make your way to every wagon opening that's being used for firing. Tell our men not to bother with individual targets. Tell them to just make certain their shots go into the woods. Easy now, boys. Take your time, don't expose yourselves in the open, and come back here as soon as you're done passing the message."

Soon all of the wagon train men understood what was

expected of them and concentrated on firing into the woods.

"There are fewer arrows coming this way now," Lee observed.

"A lot of the braves must be moving to the back side of the woods, where it's healthier for them," Whip said.

"But we mustn't be fooled by that maneuver." Sam was grave. "The Cheyenne don't scare easy. They won't give up—not with all the booty and scalps they could pick up here, not to mention firearms and horses."

Suddenly Arnold and Tonie opened fire, reloading and firing again as rapidly as they discharged their rifles.

"Ah," Lee said, "the enemy is growing impatient. Does that couple want any help?"

"Arnold will let us know if they do," Whip said.

The rapid fire continued. The army officer was impressed by Tonie's speed and dexterity as she reloaded again and again. Never had he dreamed any woman could handle firearms so well.

At last the firing stopped.

"We brought down three of them and got two of their horses as well," Arnold called. "I don't think they'll try sneaking around this flank again."

All at once the canvas of a wagon burst into flames. There was no way of extinguishing the fire, and not only was the canvas top eaten away but much of the contents were destroyed.

Now many more flaming spears soared over the roofs of wagons and landed inside the circle, making the animals restless and terrifying the women.

Whip made a quick decision. "Hosea," he said, "Get Ted Woods to help you and use as many of the men as you need. Smother those torches before they cause any more damage."

Hosea streaked away, organizing the task with astonishing rapidity. Apparently the Cheyenne were using something to launch the flaming spears, which continued to clear the tops of the wagons before they came to earth. But Hosea and Ted were equal to the task. A dozen men were helping them, but the pair managed to put out more of the fires than all of the others.

"If the savages had more sense," Lee Blake said, "they'd set fire to every last wagon we have. Then we'd be in real trouble."

"The Cheyenne are too greedy for that," Whip replied, smiling grimly. "They're already counting on all the food and blankets and other loot they're going to take home with them, and they don't want to destroy it."

Whip, Lee, and Sam continued to watch the woods for any sign of a decisive move on the part of the enemy. They were concentrating so hard that none of them saw Cathy van Ayl come up behind them. There was dirt on her hands, face, and clothes, and her hair was flying. She started to speak, panting from the exertion of running across the center of the circle.

Whip turned at the sound of her voice. "What the hell are you doing, going out in the open?" he demanded, his fear for her safety making him angry.

Cathy ignored his tone. "Dr. Martin needs help," she said, fighting to regain her breath. "Some of our people have been wounded by arrows—I can't tell you how many—and a little girl broke her leg getting away from one of the workhorses that almost crushed her."

"Well," Whip said, "Tonie can't be spared. We need her right where she is, doing what she's doing."

"Bob Martin knows that, and he isn't asking for her. Cindy and I would be glad to do what we can for him, but he needs somebody who knows what to do about the wounded without having to be told every step."

"Find that new man, Reverend Cavendish," Whip said. "A clergyman should be able to help a doctor in a situation like this. No, Cathy! Not you!" Whip shouted, as Cathy turned to go and look for Reverend Cavendish. "Go back to the other side, but work your way around, and stop taking needless risks with your life!"

Then he shouted, "Danny! You find Reverend Cavendish and take him to Dr. Martin's wagon. And let me know if he doesn't work out all right."

Whip turned back to observing the woods. Obviously he intended that his orders be obeyed, so Cathy meekly returned by a circuitous route to the far side of the circle. She knew that his anger had been sparked by his concern for her welfare, and that knowledge comforted her.

The shower of flaming spears continued, and Hosea and Ted gradually developed a new technique for disposing of these dangerous weapons. The blacksmith snatched them, sometimes catching them before they landed, his calloused hands not bothered by their heat. And Hosea calmly stamped out the flames with the hardened feet that had already carried him across so much of the continent.

The pair's courage and skill were remarkable, but they could not perform miracles. The roof and some of the contents of another wagon were destroyed. A farmer from Pennsylvania was struck by a burning spear; the man rolled on the ground to extinguish the flames, but he was burned seriously and had to be carried to the doctor's wagon.

The Reverend Cavendish, as calm as ever, understood exactly what was required of him. He worked in tandem with the frantically busy physician. None of the wounded laughed at the uninterrupted stream of Biblical quotations the clergyman uttered, and later many would express their gratitude for the comfort he had given them.

Then tragedy struck blindly. A flaming spear launched with greater force than those that preceded it reached the far side of the circle, where the women and children were gathered with the animals, and the point lodged in the ground, only inches from where Tommy Harris, the youngest of Emily Harris's surviving sons, was standing.

The nine-year-old boy, disappointed because he could take no active part in the battle, had been admiring the efforts of Hosea and Ted Woods. Now he had his chance to imitate them, and before anyone could stop him, he seized the flaming spear with both hands. His scream of agonizing pain and fright echoed across the circle.

Ernie von Thalman had been prowling the entire perimeter, doing his best to maintain order until such time as he was needed by the members of the group who were shooting into the woods. When he saw Tommy enveloped in flames, he dashed across the open to the child, ignoring his own safety.

The stunned Emily seemed paralyzed, unable to act, unable to move. Ernie threw the child to the ground, then fell on top of him, smothering the flames with his own body. After what seemed like an eternity, he put out the fire. Leaping to his feet and ignoring his own relatively minor burns, he picked up Tommy's limp body and raced with the boy to Dr. Martin's wagon. Cindy picked up his rifle, knowing he would soon need it, and followed behind, as did Cathy, who supported the staggering, weeping Emily.

Ernie knew even before he reached the physician's wagon that it was too late. Tommy was no longer breathing, and his sightless eyes stared vacantly from his small, scorched face. Gently he laid the body of the boy on a cot in Dr. Martin's wagon. Then, refusing treatment for himself, Ernie hurried to the command post behind the special wagon and related what had happened.

Whip was the first to break the long, tense silence. "We owe Tommy Harris a victory," he said. "Men who make war on little children deserve no quarter."

The Cheyenne gave the defenders no opportunity to alter their tactics or reverse the tide of battle. The attackers continued to remain hidden in the woods, and the flow of flaming spears into the compound seemed endless. Hosea and Ted worked doggedly, as did the men who were assisting them.

Sam Brentwood made a shrewd assessment of the situation. "I'm not making light of our casualties or property losses, which hurt," he said. "But we're not in too bad a shape. The women and youngsters are less panicky now, and the oxen and horses are quiet, except when a flaming torch lands near them. If we can just sit tight long enough, the Indians will have to try a more direct approach."

"When they attack another tribe's town," Whip declared, "their burning lances usually drive the defenders into the open. Then the Cheyenne divide and scatter them, which makes it easy for the major part of their force to capture the town, take the women and youngsters as prisoners, and go off with as much booty as they can carry. Right about now they must be getting a mite upset because we aren't reacting like their other enemies."

Pierre was aware of yet another significant development. "Their lances become fewer," he said. "They must be running out by now. Soon there will be a change."

"It seems to me," Whip said, "they've got to convince themselves we've been badly weakened. They can't move around our flanks, so they've just about exhausted their choices. Before long they'll have to make a big frontal attack, mustering their full strength and riding at us hard in the hope they can smash through the wagons and overwhelm us."

Such an assault sounded suicidal to Lee Blake, and he shook his head. "I think they'd be deterred by realizing they'd suffer one whale of a lot of casualties that way."

"The Plains nations aren't like others," Whip explained. "They believe that when a warrior is killed in battle, his spirit lives on forever in the land of their gods. That's what makes them fearless."

Gradually the stream of flaming lances thinned to a slow trickle.

"I reckon we'd best get ready for the main attack," Whip said. "I want our sharpshooters spread out—two to each wagon opening between us and the Mells on the left. Pierre, go back to your place with Mack, and we'll fill in the openings to the right, too."

The men began to move off.

"Danny, I want you to stay right here with Sam and me," Whip said. "Reload the spare rifles as fast as you can and keep feeding them to us. Chet, you do the same for Lee Blake and Ernie at the other end of the special wagon. We'll be the focal point of the attack, and we've got to hold them off here in the center."

The two boys obeyed eagerly.

"Where's Stalking Horse?" Whip demanded.

"Here," the Cherokee replied, materializing beside him.

"Get hold of Hosea. There's no need to tell either of you what to do. Station yourselves wherever you think you're most needed, and move around from one point to another any way you see fit to strengthen a position. And while you're at it, tell Ted and the men working with him to take complete charge of the animals as soon as the torches stop coming over. The riding horses are used to the noise and shouldn't be bothered by it, but the wagon horses and oxen will become excited when they hear sustained rifle fire. If they panic and start to stampede, they're likely to smash out of the circle and leave an opening big enough for the Cheyenne to pour through. We can't allow that to happen, no matter what, so tell Ted we're depending on him to keep the animals quiet!"

Stalking Horse glided away, returning a few minutes later, accompanied by Hosea. Whip and Sam had already stationed themselves on either side of the small opening between the special wagon and the smaller vehicle that stood adjacent to it, so there was little room there for Stalking Horse and the Ashanti.

Hosea solved that problem by stretching out in the tall grass in the open area between the two wagons, his shield on the ground in front of him, and Stalking Horse dropped on one knee beside him.

"We start here," the Cherokee said. "Move if get bad other places."

Whip and Sam agreed. The firepower massed at this one defense station would be so great that the attackers would quickly learn to avoid it. Both mountain men were relying on the knowledge they had acquired over the years about Indian behavior in battle. They knew that Pierre, Arnold, and Mack were equally well aware of the basic situation. No fighting men anywhere were more courageous and persistent than a body of Indian warriors, provided they were advancing. They would take risks that far more cautious white soldiers, even seasoned veterans, would not. However, once an Indian drive was blunted and the braves were thrown onto the defensive, they quickly collapsed, their bravado vanishing. When an attack failed, they were inclined to lose their zest for combat and frequently withdrew from the field.

"Here they come!" Ernie von Thalman shouted.

A long line of Cheyenne horsemen emerged from the woods and began to gallop toward the wagons, firing arrows as they rode. Behind them came a second wave, then a third, and a fourth. It appeared that, as usual, they were holding none of their band in reserve; any warriors who failed to take part in the initial assault would feel they had been slighted and would lose face.

Lieutenant Colonel Lee Blake, more experienced than his colleagues in judging the size of an enemy force, estimated there were approximately fifty warriors in each of the four lines, or about two hundred in all. Certainly the attackers outnumbered the defenders in what would long be remembered as the first major engagement fought by members of the wagon train.

Claiborne Woodling won the distinction of being the first to dispose of a foe. His rifle spoke a fraction of a second before any of the others, and he caught an oncoming brave between the eyes. The man was killed instantly.

Then Sam and Whip calmly opened fire. By unspoken agreement, they concentrated on the Cheyenne leaders, the warriors who wore the largest number of eagle feathers in their headdresses. Both knew that the braves were more likely to lose heart if they were deprived of their leadership.

Stalking Horse was taking his time, making each of his arrows count. Unflustered by the fury of the enemy drive, he fitted an arrow into his bowstring, let fly, and then reached for another.

Hosea was less fortunate. A number of Cheyenne arrows had already cut into his shield, but he himself was unharmed. The darts from his blowgun were effective only at short range, however, so he had to wait until the braves in the front row drew still closer before he could launch his own counterattack. He waited patiently, his dark eyes narrowed and gleaming with suppressed excitement. He knew that the battle presented him with an opportunity to repay the loyalty and trust the members of the wagon train had shown him, and his hand was steady.

After a wait of only a few seconds, which to him felt like a very long time, he had his chance. One of his darts caught an onrushing warrior in the throat, and a moment later the man slumped, then slid to the ground.

Lee and Ernie were methodically sending round after round of bullets at the foe, with deadly effect. Pierre and Mack more than held their own, and Tonie, keeping up the pace set by her uncle, brought down her share of attackers.

Arrows were sticking out of the ground, some were lodged in the canvas of wagon tops, and a number found their targets. Whip suffered a minor wound in his left arm but ignored it. Claiborne Woodling, who was proving his mettle as a man, discovered that an arrow had dug into his thigh. He pulled it out, paying no attention to the pain, and continued to fire, reload and fire again, despite the spreading bloodstain on his throbbing thigh.

Some of the less able defenders didn't fare as well. One member of the expedition who appeared in an opening between wagons was killed instantly by an arrow, and two others were wounded. Then Major Woodling, accustomed to the more formal type of battle fought by civilized armies, became careless. He allowed himself to be seen in the open for a brief moment. Those few seconds were enough to seal his doom. An arrow penetrated his body, killing him even as he fired his old-fashioned musket.

His body sagged, but remained upright, leaning against the wagon beside him. Frozen on his lips was the faint smile of pleasure that had mirrored his feelings when he had peered down the barrel of his musket and seen a brave.

The thrust of the first wave was broken, and a number of riderless horses milled around the area just beyond the wagons. Confused and frightened by the sound of gunfire, they panicked and took off across the prairie.

The second wave of Indians replaced the first, and the warriors in the front rank either turned aside in bewilderment or tried to join their comrades, who were now suffering the same fate that they themselves had endured.

"I need more gunpowder!" Tonie Mell called. "Gunpowder!"

She repeated the cry several times, but none of the

older boys who were helping the marksmen heard her above the roar of gunfire and the hoarse cries of the warriors who were trying to encourage each other. But Cindy, who was pressed against a wagon a short distance farther down the line, made out the voice of her friend, listened carefully, and knew something had to be done. She picked up a powder horn lying on the ground beside one of the farmers, and, not taking the time to find an appropriate messenger, she began to work her way toward Tonie, crouching low each time she came to an opening between wagons.

Terrified by the Indians' arrows, Cindy paid little heed to the ground underfoot. A harness was coiled there, and she caught her toe in a leather loop. Losing her balance, she pitched forward onto the ground. The powder horn she was carrying flew out of her grasp and landed on the ground just beyond her reach.

Although she didn't realize it, she was directly in the path of a Cheyenne warrior who had been thrown from his horse just beyond the outside of the circle. In the confusion, none of the defenders had realized that the brave was still alive and uninjured, determined to work his way inside the perimeter and kill enough of the riflemen to permit his comrades to make a breakthrough.

His presence unseen and unsuspected, the warrior was moving slowly on his stomach under a wagon, gradually making his way inside the circle. He had lost his quiver of arrows and broken his bow when he had been thrown, but he still had his knife. Carrying it in his hand, he had no concern for his own safety, but was intent on killing as many wielders of firesticks as he could.

All at once, as the breathless Cindy struggled to rise from the ground, she saw the face and painted body of this husky brave a scant yard from her. The warrior saw her at the same instant, and Cindy screamed in terror.

Claiborne Woodling stood at the next wagon opening, reloading his rifle after firing at another oncoming horseman. He heard the girl's cry above the din of battle, then took in the situation swiftly. The warrior, as startled as Cindy, took a firm grip on his knife and poised himself, raising the blade above his head in order to plunge it into the body of this squaw who was raising an alarm.

There was no time for Claiborne to reload and fire at the man. So he took the only course open to him. He raced down the length of the wagon. Grasping his rifle by its hot barrel, and wielding it like a club, he brought the oak butt down with all his might on the back of the warrior's head, just as the Indian was about to strike Cindy. The man died at once, his blood and brains oozing onto the ground.

Cindy felt ill, but she still had a duty to perform. The din of battle made it impossible for her to thank Claiborne, who seemed to want no thanks and had raced back to his post, resuming his fire. Cindy scooped up the warrior's knife, along with the powder horn she had dropped, then delivered the horn to the hard-pressed Tonie.

The battle raged furiously, both sides realizing that the climax had been reached. The defenders' burden fell on the marksmen. They were equal to their task, holding their places and firing again and again, until their arms grew weary.

The Cheyenne were growing increasingly frustrated by their inability to penetrate their foes' line. Some of the braves threw their spears in desperation, rather than waiting until they could fight at closer quarters, but the lances caused no substantial harm. Arrows were proving useless, too, and the attackers' casualties were mounting so rapidly that the surviving senior warriors finally realized they would be wise to withdraw while they could.

No formal order was given. One moment the braves were sending arrows at their enemies, trying their best to keep pushing forward in the face of murderous rifle fire, and the next moment their ranks broke, and they were in flight, some skirting the woods as they retreated, others plunging into the cover immediately.

Stalking Horse and Hosea wanted to pursue the warriors, but Whip objected. "Let them go," he said. "We've hit them so hard they won't come back."

The expedition's casualties were the worst the Oregon-bound settlers had ever suffered. Six members of the company were dead, including little Tommy Harris and Major Woodling, while a score of others, including three children, had suffered injuries. Dr. Martin was still at work, looking after the wounded. As soon as the warriors had vanished from sight, Tonie went to help him and Reverend Cavendish.

Fire had destroyed the contents of several wagons, but most of the losses could be replaced. There was spare canvas in the special wagon, and ample food supplies were on hand, thanks to the successes of the hunters and fishermen. Clothing of skins could be made to take the place of wool and cotton that had gone up in flames. At least the wagons themselves were intact, and miraculously, the horses and oxen had all survived.

Whip decided it was best, for the sake of the company's morale, not to delay the funeral services. Graves were prepared, and a number of the men helped Ted cut down trees and fashion coffins.

The hunger of the smaller children reminded their elders that no one had eaten anything that day. But the adults had little appetite, so no hot meals were prepared. People made do with strips of dried buffalo meat, parched corn, and preserved berries.

Cindy looked for Claiborne Woodling and found him near the bank of the North Platte, staring down at the clear, swift-running water. She found it strange to be in the debt of this brash young man who had caused her trouble in the past, but she forced herself to face him without flinching.

"I want to thank you," she said. "I was so scared I didn't know what to do when I saw that Indian. You saved my life."

"Anybody would have done what I did," he replied, showing none of the aggressiveness that had made him so unpopular in the past.

"Not anybody," the girl replied, correcting him. "Besides, you did it. I never saw anybody move so fast, and I'm grateful to you."

"I'm glad I could be of help," he muttered, and turned away to look down into the water again.

Cindy couldn't help feeling sorry for him and touched

his arm lightly. "I—I'm sorry about your father," she said.

Claiborne looked at her, his expression reflecting something unfathomable in addition to sadness. "It may be just as well," he said. "Papa joined the wagon train only because he could see no other future for himself or his children. But he never felt at home in the train, and I know he'd have hated setting up a homestead for himself in Oregon. He lived a different kind of life, and in a sense he died when we lost our plantation."

The girl took a deep breath. "I suppose—you'll be—going back East with Sam Brentwood when he leaves for Independence."

"Not I," Claiborne said, shaking his head. "There's nothing for me in South Carolina. I'm going all the way to Oregon with you people, and I'll make a life for myself there." He straightened his shoulders, but sounded forlorn as he said, "That's the least I can do in Papa's memory. If I don't justify the faith he showed in me when we joined this wagon train, I'll never be able to look at my face in a mirror again."

It occurred to Cindy, as she made her way back to the circle, that Claiborne had grown to manhood more in a few hours than he had in all his preceding years.

Not until the funeral procession to the open graves was about to start did anyone notice that Eulalia Woodling was missing. Her brother noticed her absence when he returned to the vicinity. A hasty search was conducted for her, and when she couldn't be located the search was temporarily called off. For the sake of the grieving members of other families, Whip didn't want to delay the funeral any longer. When Sam and Ernie agreed with him, the procession started slowly upstream, then turned northward away from the river, beyond the place where it might overflow in the autumn and spring. As they made their way to the waiting graves, they began to sing.

This was not a time for a hymn, even though they were mourning those who had been taken from them. Their hope for the future had to sustain them, no matter how much they missed the departed, and those who first raised their voices expressed the faith of the entire company in what lay ahead by singing "America." By the time they came to the last stanza, even the members of the families of those who had died joined in, tears streaming down their faces:

Our fathers' God, to thee,
Author of liberty,
To thee we sing;
Long may our land be bright
With freedom's holy light;
Protect us by thy might,
Great God, our King.

Reverend Cavendish conducted one service for all who had died, and there was no sound but the gentle whisper of the breeze through the tall grass of the Great Plains as he began to recite the familiar words: "I am the resurrection and the life, saith the Lord: he that believeth in me, though he were dead, yet shall he live: and whosoever liveth and believeth in me, shall never die. . . ."

Emily Harris stood with her surviving children, the younger in front of her and Chet on one side of her. Ernie von Thalman flanked her other side, as he had done on a similar, sad occasion in the past. He placed a comforting arm around her shoulders to sustain her and hold her upright.

Claiborne Woodling stood alone, his hands clasped behind his back, his feet apart, as though he were bracing himself in a strong wind. His eyes were fixed on his father's coffin. Although his expression was stiff, betraying no emotion, the arrogance that had been so much a part of his nature had been drained from him.

Cindy looked at him and had to restrain the impulse to move to a place beside him and take his hand. She knew he was suffering from loneliness, and she who had been alone so much of her life felt a deep pity for him. But she was afraid that others, including Claiborne himself, might misunderstand her gesture; besides, she was uncertain how Ted Woods might react. So she made no move and she, too, stared straight ahead, listening to Reverend Cavendish.

Before the service ended, many of the adults were thinking the same thought: the unknown perils that lay ahead were many, and before they reached Oregon, other graves would mark the long trail. But that knowledge could not deter them from reaching their goal. The promised land awaited the strong and the brave. They felt compelled to go on, so those who had lost their lives on the endless trek would not have died in vain.

At the end of the service, a group of volunteers filled in the graves with dirt and erected markers. Then a common grave was dug near the woods, and the bodies of the Cheyenne braves who had died were placed in it. Forty warriors had been killed in the abortive attack—a surprisingly large number. No one knew how many had been hurt because they had taken their wounded with them when they had withdrawn.

Claiborne Woodling stood alone outside the wagon he had shared with his father and sister, seeking solace from no one in his time of grief. Cindy found him there. Not speaking, she handed him the knife of the warrior he had killed when he had saved her life. For an instant her eyes met his, then she moved quickly away.

Whip quietly asked Stalking Horse and Hosea to search the entire area for any sign of the missing Eulalia. No warriors had entered the compound, except for the one brave Claiborne had killed, so it appeared impossible that the Cheyenne had captured the girl.

Late in the afternoon Hosea returned to the circle, caught Whip's eye, and beckoned. "Whip come," he said.

Together they went out into the woods. At the far side, near the bank of the little stream that flowed into the North Platte farther to the west, lay two of the expedition's wooden buckets. One of them had been crushed almost beyond recognition beneath the hoofs of a retreating warrior's horse.

Whip returned to the circle for a private talk with Sam, and then they went together to Claiborne, taking him with them into the woods.

"Look yonder," Whip said, pointing to the buckets. "I'm only guessing, but I think it's a pretty good guess, and so does Sam. We believe your sister was abducted by the Cheyenne while she was gathering water this morning. Before the attack even started."

The young man nodded. "I imagine you're right. What do we do now to get her back?"

"This isn't easy to say," Whip told him. "But—for the immediate future—we can do nothing."

Claiborne looked as though he had been struck; he started to protest. Sam raised a hand to silence him. "Hear us out," he said. "The Cheyenne's hunting grounds are extensive. It's impossible to know how many towns and villages they have in the area. At least twenty, I'd say, and maybe twice that number."

"In order to find Eulalia," Whip said, "we'd have to send out a search party—not just a few men, but a really strong party, in force—at least thirty well-armed men who know how to handle rifles. We've just beaten the tar out of the Cheyenne, and they won't forget that defeat in a hurry. It wouldn't surprise me any if Pierre le Rouge would like to hunt for your sister, and I'm sure you'd want to join him—"

"Of course!" Claiborne said.

Whip shook his head. "As Pierre would be the first to tell you, once he cooled down, such a mission would be suicidal. We can't afford to halt the entire train for weeks or even months while a big party of armed men travels from one Cheyenne town to the next. We can't afford to let our people run the risk of spending another winter on the prairie, this time in the open, without adequate shelter or firewood."

"Then you propose to abandon Eulalia?" Claiborne asked in a choked voice.

"Not at all," Whip said. "There's only one way to handle a situation like this. We keep on with our own journey, and that gives the dust time to settle. We haven't seen the last of the Cheyenne. They won't dare attack us again in force, but they'll undoubtedly send small groups of braves to make nuisance raids on us."

"That's their way," Sam added.

"When that happens," Whip said, "we'll find some way to detain one or two of them. They sure can't be holding any other white girl as a prisoner, and we'll be able to find out for sure where they're holding Eulalia. Then we'll go after her. Until then, we'll have to be patient."

"What's to stop them from killing her?" Claiborne asked, still visibly upset.

"Nothing," Whip said. "But it isn't their style to murder women." He refrained from mentioning how the Cheyenne *did* treat any unfortunate females held captive.

XIV

The buttes appeared suddenly in the midst of the flat prairie, their presence dramatic because it was so abrupt. The first buttes were small, standing only ten or fifteen feet high. Their sides were steep, sometimes almost perpendicular to the ground. Some were solid rock, like so many in the Dakota country that lay to the north, but many had soil on them and were covered with grass and weeds. Vegetation was not as lush as it was in the flatlands, however, and each butte stood alone in isolated splendor, rising by itself in the midst of the Great Plains.

André Sebastian was familiar with the area, but Henry St. Clair was seeing the region for the first time. Although he took pride in his ability never to show surprise, he realized this terrain was unique.

They rode side by side, leading the horses that pulled the Englishman's wagon, and Sebastian gestured toward the buttes. "We're in the land of the Blackfoot now, God help us."

"We'll get along with them." Henry showed his customary confidence.

"Don't try to trick them, that's all. Even the Cheyenne are afraid of them, you know. And only the Comanche of the mountains have an agreement of sorts with them, with neither invading the land of the other. It's the only way they both avoid total annihilation. Listen!"

Henry raised his head, strained, and heard the faint sound of drums in the distance.

"They know we've arrived on Blackfoot soil," Sebastian said. "Obviously we've been seen by their sentry outposts—who have made certain we haven't seen them. So we've got to watch our step now."

"In what way?"

"We do no hunting. It doesn't matter if a deer stops right in front of us. We ignore him. If we see a herd of buffalo, we ride around them. And if we should run across an elk or a bear, and there are both in the foothills, we close our eyes to them. Nobody hunts in Blackfoot country without the permission of their chiefs. If we brought down even small game, we'd be signing our own death warrants."

Henry was pleased rather than dismayed. "I believe I'm going to enjoy my visit with the Blackfoot. If they are as reliable as they are rugged, they're the very Indians I've been looking for, ever since I began my mission."

"Oh, they're reliable. They always keep their word—provided you do the same with them." Sebastian shaded his eyes with a hand and glanced up at the sun, which stood somewhat lower at this time of afternoon, now that autumn was at hand. "We'll arrive at one of their larger towns before dusk."

"Good."

"Most of their warriors will be off hunting buffalo, of course," Sebastian said. "This is the time of year when the animals weigh the most and have the best coats, so all the Plains tribes hunt them in force. But the Blackfoot are different. The sachems stay at home, and they keep enough warriors behind to protect their women and children. They're like Peter the Great, you know, always staying ahead of those who might become their enemies."

"They sound more like our Henry the Fifth." Henry allowed himself a slight smile.

Sebastian had no interest in a verbal duel with him. "Even their method of buffalo hunting is different. Closer to the mountains, where the hills become steeper, they send out parties of warriors who light firebrands, form a semicircle, and approach a herd of buffalo. The animals are afraid of the fire, so they take off in the opposite direction, and the Blackfoot drive them off the edge of a cliff. That kills the buffalo rather neatly, and the warriors simply go to the base of the cliff and collect the carcasses."

Henry stared at the Russian agent to see if he was joking but saw he was serious. Certainly he had made his point. Any Indians who managed to force buffalo to commit suicide by the hundreds while putting themselves in virtually no danger, deserved to be treated with both respect and great caution.

"The sachem we're going to see today is Gray Antelope. He claims he's fought more than a hundred battles and won them all. By the way, he'll expect us to prostrate ourselves on the ground when we first approach him."

"I must draw the line there. As a representative of Queen Victoria, I'm obliged to remember Her Majesty's dignity as well as my own."

"You won't look very dignified with your head stuck on the end of a spear," Sebastian said.

"On second thought," Henry declared, speaking emphatically, "I won't in the least mind abasing myself. In fact, I'll do anything the Blackfoot want if they'll cooperate with us and put an end, once and for all, to those people in the wagon train who have been leading such charmed lives!"

Eulalia Woodling labored on her hands and knees under a hot autumn sun, breathing in dust as she pulled weeds from the field of corn, soon to be harvested, in the land of the Cheyenne. She was barefooted and clad only in a skimpy breastband and short skirt of buffalo skin. Her hair was braided in two tight pigtails.

As she worked, she ignored the bugs and worms, paid no attention when she broke a fingernail, and barely paused to stifle a sneeze with one grubby hand. Certainly she didn't dare run the risk of looking up to see if the squaw who was in charge of the slaves was anywhere in the immediate vicinity. The woman, armed with a short, ugly whip made of several strands of rawhide, liked nothing better than to apply the whip to the back of any slave she caught malingering.

There were days when Eulalia no longer cared what became of her. Certainly she had abandoned hope that the wagon train leaders would send an expedition to rescue her from her miserable fate. The days ran together, and only the cold that settled over the Cheyenne town each night told her the season was changing and that autumn had arrived.

Nevertheless, today was different, perhaps because there had been enough buffalo stew left in the cooking pots at breakfast for the slaves to eat their fill after the Cheyenne had finished their meal. They had been able to eat before the slave mistress appeared with her whip and drove them like cattle into the fields, to work until sunset. A full stomach could make a great difference, even when the only food on hand was a greasy, somewhat rancid stew of tough buffalo meat.

There was another reason today was different, Eulalia realized. A large herd of buffalo had been seen only a few miles from the town, and almost all of the Cheyenne had gone off to hunt. That meant none of the older girls were on hand to torment the slaves when they had nothing better to do. The little boys had gone, too, so they couldn't prod the slaves with sharp sticks and then laugh when they squealed. And even the damned dogs that nipped at the heels of the slave women had departed. Her relief was infinite.

Tomorrow, to be sure, Eulalia knew that she and the others who shared her bleak existence would pay for the relative peace they were currently enjoying. Experience had taught her they would be sent to the scene of the hunt and required to perform the most loathesome of tasks—disemboweling the dead buffalo. But at least, if the hunt was successful, there would be enough to eat before the remains of the buffalo meat spoiled. She had learned to be grateful for the smallest favors.

Without warning the whip descended, wielded with such cunning that, although it caused welts, it did not break the skin. Startled, Eulalia straightened involuntarily, then wearily pulled herself to her feet, and fell into line behind the slave mistress. The work in the fields had come to an end.

One by one, other captives joined her. All were Indians, who concealed their feelings as only Indians could. Two were Wichita, Eulalia knew, another was an Omaha, and several came from small tribes whose names were new to her. One squaw was a Sioux whose nation lived in the Dakota country to the north. She was treated somewhat more leniently, perhaps because the Cheyenne and Sioux regularly exchanged prisoners.

There was one member of the shabby group whom Eulalia pitied more than herself. A Cheyenne, this miserable creature was actually a man who had shown cowardice in battle. He was condemned to spend the rest of his days as a slave—dressed as a woman. His hair was braided in long pigtails, and he was accorded the same treatment meted out to the others.

The captives were marched through the town and taken to a lake just beyond it. There they were required to strip and bathe in the chilly waters, itself an ordeal, but only a taste of what lay ahead. As they shivered, their bodies drying in the air, they were required to smear each other with pungent bear grease, which the Cheyenne regarded as attractive. Eulalia was convinced that, no matter how long she lived, the stench of that grease would remain in her nostrils.

Then the slaves were required to daub their lips and nipples with a red berry stain and smear the oil of a black plant root on their eyelids. The women were marched off to a row of small tents, set apart from the rest of the town. Each occupied her own tent, which had a buffalo rug on the floor.

Now the real ordeal began. Each slave was required to attend to the sexual desires of the Cheyenne warriors. A slave had no choice, accepting any brave who elected to appear at the entrance to her tent. The system was both simple and cunning. The unfortunate prisoners were given no food at night and were forced to rely on their clients for their evening meals. When a warrior was satisfied, he presented the woman with a portion of a buffalo tongue, regarded as the greatest of delicacies, part of an elk liver, or a chunk of grilled antelope heart.

Eulalia had been horrified and heartsick at first but had been driven by hunger to do what was expected of her. Some of the braves were stingy and she soon learned, through necessity, to dispose of them as quickly as possible. Others, who were more generous, she learned to treat to simulated pleasure.

The intimacies in which she was forced to participate no longer had any meaning to her. As best she could, she separated what was left of her spirit from her body and allowed the savages to use it as they pleased, all the while hating them and loathing herself.

To her astonishment, she was becoming expert in the tricks of the alien trade. She soon discovered that she and the former male warrior were the most popular of the prostitutes because they were different. When she was given more than she could eat, she shared the excess with the women the braves had ignored.

Her instinct for survival, she learned, was strong. Gradually, as she began to understand more and more of the language of the Cheyenne, she found out there was only one escape from her hard and degrading existence. A warrior, if he wished, could make a prostitute one of his squaws and take her off to his own quarters. There she would be subjected only to his authority and that of his senior wife. Such a position would mean no more beatings, a far less rigorous work schedule, and the need to take only one man to bed.

So Eulalia found herself exerting all of her charm on the senior warriors, the medicine man, and the son of the local sachem, who ultimately would succeed his father as the leader of the community. If she had to be an Indian whore, she told herself repeatedly, she would be a successful one.

Her endurance and attitudes were limited, however, and Eulalia found she could not allow herself to think of the life she had once led as a South Carolina belle. Even her wagon train existence, which she had despised, now seemed to her to have been such a paradise that she closed her memory to those months.

Sometimes she felt like giving in to hysteria, but the Indians had no patience with tears and tantrums. The slave mistress would punish her by administering a whipping that would leave her raw and bleeding, and she would still have to work the fields by day and service the braves at night.

She knew there was no way she could make her way back to civilization, no way she could rejoin the wagon train. If she was condemned to stay in the land of the Cheyenne until she died, she wanted greater comforts and a less exacting, grueling day-by-day existence. She had to earn them, so that was what she was doing. There was no way she could influence the harsh slave mistress who supervised her work in the fields and made her daylight hours such a hell on earth. But her smiles and pretended ecstacy well might persuade one of the more powerful men to ease her lot.

Fighting her way through the weariness that enveloped her, Eulalia willed herself to become more energetic. She ignored the vile stench of the bear grease that covered her and paid no attention to the sting of the berry stain or the smarting of her eyes as the plant root oil ran into them. She walked steadily to the entrance flap of her tent and forced herself to stand there naked, her pose provocative, a sultry smile on her lips, as she waited for the first of her evening's clients to appear. She was so ravenous that even the prospect of eating a piece of buffalo tongue appealed to her.

Everyone in the wagon train had heard by now that Eulalia Woodling probably had been captured by Indians, but nothing was being done to rescue the girl. The arrival of cooler weather, particularly at night, caused Cathy van Ayl to worry about Eulalia, and Cathy's own dislike for Eulalia increased her sense of guilt.

Ernie refused to discuss the problem with her, as did Arnold Mell. Claiborne, who had become friendlier with Cindy, kept his opinions to himself. She hesitated about going to Whip, not wanting to jeopardize the greater warmth he had been showing since Lee Blake had joined the train and had started paying attention to her.

The caravan came at last to the buttes. Soon, Cathy knew, the company would begin to search for an appropriate site, perhaps even in the mountains, to spend the coming winter. The realization that the Great Plains soon would be left behind had a sobering effect on Cathy, who was increasingly haunted by the fear that Eulalia would be forgotten. Sam, to whom she would have gone for advice, had returned to Independence some weeks before. So, one day during the nooning rest, she decided to confide in Lee.

He listened with the sympathetic understanding he consistently displayed toward her, then shook his head. "I've been concerned, too," he said, "but I'm sure Whip knows what he's doing. He's waiting until we can learn for certain whether the girl is being held by Cheyenne and, if she is, in which of their towns."

He did not tell her that he had a deep interest of his own in the developments. The Cheyenne also would know whether Henry St. Clair, having created a nasty problem for the wagon train during his visit with them, had moved on to the land of the Blackfoot or that of the Comanche in an effort to stir up even more serious trouble.

"Eulalia is no friend of mine," Cathy told him, "but the Cheyenne are vicious savages and might be torturing her or—worse. That's a horrible thought."

Lee had no voice in the matter and had to admit it. Unable to hold off any longer, Cathy went to Whip and told him her fears.

"I won't pretend to you that I think Eulalia Woodling is having an easy time of it as a captive," he said. "But I'm reasonably sure she's alive. It might take us months to search the whole Cheyenne country for her, so we've got to wait."

"Wait for what?" she demanded.

In recent days Whip had been developing a scheme of his own whereby it might be possible to obtain information, not only about the missing girl but about Henry St. Clair's intentions. But he wasn't ready yet to discuss his plan. Lacking the tact of more sophisticated men, he spoke abruptly, "You'll have to trust me to do what I'm able in my own way."

Cathy became angry. "If anything happens to her, that girl's blood will be on your hands."

"Have I ever shirked my responsibilities?" he demanded.

Although neither realized it, their near-romance had created its own tensions, which had been intensified by Whip's reluctance to tell Cathy of his growing interest in her. It seemed to her that his years on the frontier had made him insensitive to the feelings and sufferings of others, and her temper rose higher. "You wouldn't be so calm if you were the prisoner of the Indians!"

"I'd be dead," he said bluntly. "They wouldn't keep me alive very long."

"Well, I think—"

"Look here, Cathy. I don't tell you how to cook meals—"

"Now I'm not good for anything except cooking!" She knew she was being unreasonable and that the argument was no longer sensible, but she couldn't stop herself. "If you ask me, Michael Holt, you've lived around savages so long that you've become one yourself." Cathy turned and stormed off toward her wagon, but in spite of her rage she was ready to stop short and then forgive him if he offered her an apology.

Whip was in no mood to apologize, however. He couldn't remember when anyone had spoken to him so rudely, and he wanted to shake this headstrong girl until her teeth rattled—or kiss her until she melted in his arms. Or both.

His confusion was so great that, although he was almost always in command of his emotions, he now stood indecisively, clenching and opening his fists. The argument was absurd, and he tried to dismiss it from his mind.

What bothered him most was the suspicion that he was actually in love with Cathy van Ayl. That possibility horrified him. She had just now indicated that she thought of him as a rough mountain man, unmannered and crude. She was not only lovely, but a lady—and an heiress as well, having inherited two thousand dollars in gold from her late husband. Whip saw no chance that she would consider the suit of a man so far beneath her, a man who had nothing of substance to offer her.

Damnation! He *was* in love with her! But she had made it clear what she thought of him, and she would laugh if he declared himself to her. If he had any brains greater than those of a buffalo, he would keep his feelings to himself.

A young woman's scream of terror brought Whip back to the present. Turning in the direction of the sound, he saw that Tonie Mell, who had been climbing a butte, had fallen forward on the steep hillside. For some reason she was unable to move. He noticed she had dropped her rifle, which lay beyond her reach.

As he started toward the hill, he saw why she had screamed, and he broke into a run. A rattlesnake, the longest and thickest he had ever seen, was coiled on the side of the butte less than a yard from Tonie's face, its head moving back and forth as it prepared to strike. The girl might have escaped if she had rolled down the hill, although it was probably already too late. She seemed mesmerized, however, and remained motionless as she stared at the reptile.

Others were hurrying toward the hill, too, and Stalking Horse was already preparing to shoot.

"No!" Whip shouted at him, unwilling to let him take the chance of killing Tonie if his arrow missed.

By the time the wagonmaster arrived at the base of the hill, he had uncoiled his whip. He made a lightning calculation, hoped the whip was long enough to reach his target, and then lashed out with all of his skill and strength. The leather sang through the air, decapitating the snake before it could sink its fangs into its victim.

Still Tonie lay where she had fallen. Whip raced up the butte, shouting, "Get up, Tonie! Where there's one rattler, there's often another."

"I know," the girl replied through clenched teeth. "But I—I can't move. Something happened to my leg."

As Whip came closer, he saw that she had stepped into a gopher hole, which had caused her to lose her balance.

The lower part of her left leg stuck out at an angle; it was obvious her leg was broken.

"Here," he said, kneeling and gently rolling her over. "Put your arms around my neck, and I'll see if I can get both of us back down to the prairie without taking a tumble that will break our necks."

Obviously in pain, Tonie did as she was told. As Whip carried Tonie down the butte, Dr. Martin arrived. Hosea, who had witnessed the scene, had run to get him.

"Bring her to my wagon," Dr. Martin ordered. A white line showed around his compressed lips, but he made no comment until Whip had departed. Then, as he measured and cut straight oak branches that he kept on hand to use as splints, he addressed Tonie for the first time.

"May I ask what in the devil you were doing climbing that hill?"

"I wanted to see the real foothills of the Rockies up ahead of us." Tonie gritted her teeth, swallowed a gasp of pain, and continued. "Danny and Chet told me they saw the big hills, so I wanted to see them, too."

"You're somewhat older than Danny and Chet—or are you?" he demanded acidly as he tore a portion of an old sheet into narrow strips. "You not only broke your leg, but you almost got yourself bitten and killed by a snake. It's too bad you weren't born wealthy, Antoinette. You need a governess."

She knew he called her by her full Christian name only when he was exasperated with her. "Don't scold me, Bob. Please. I was so eager to see the hills—"

"Since you're not wealthy, what you need is a keeper," he declared. He fell silent as he removed her boot, then cut away her buckskin trousers and stockings above her knee.

The girl's pain made it difficult for her to speak. "You're ruining my buckskins," she said. "And I don't have all that many spare stockings."

"You have only one leg left," he said curtly. "Hold on to the sides of the table and save your breath. This won't be pleasant." Before she could reply, he began to scrub her leg with a cloth soaked in brandywine.

Her leg felt as though it were on fire. Ordinarily Tonie would have moaned, but under the circumstances her pride would not allow her to do so.

"Here," he said, handing her a block of hard wood about an inch deep, two inches wide and six inches long. "Bite down on this. It will help when you start to scream."

She had helped him so often that she knew what would happen next. "I won't chew wood," she said, "and I promise you that I won't scream."

"Woman, I wonder if you ever do what you're told. Even a keeper isn't enough for you. What you need is a jailer!" Bob studied her leg intently. "All right. I warned you. Now, whatever happens, don't twitch and don't thrash around. For once in your life listen—and follow orders!"

His hands firm, his touch deft, he set her leg swiftly and expertly. Tonie's agony was so great she thought she would faint, but through sheer willpower she managed to cling to consciousness. And, having given her word, she not only refrained from screaming but made no sound.

Bob put the splints in place, then bound them. Not until the operation was completed did he move to the head of the table.

Tears were streaming down Tonie's face, but she was still silent. Bob reached out behind him, his eyes filled with admiration for the rare, stubborn courage she had displayed, and then handed her a glass of milky liquid. "There will be no more pain, Tonie. Drink this."

"I don't want any laudanum," she declared. "I won't be put to sleep."

"Tonie," he told her, raising her head. "You're going to drink this, every drop of it, if I have to pry your mouth open and pour it down your throat!"

Tonie drank the laudanum.

Bob's manner changed abruptly, and his voice became tender. "I was wrong," he said. "You don't need a governess, a keeper, or a jailer. What you need is a husband. You're so obstinate and ornery that I can think of only one man stupid enough to marry you."

He bent down, then kissed her. As his lips met hers, Tonie reached up, her arms encircling him, and clung to him. Surely the laudanum had already taken effect and she was dreaming.

The flatlands of the Great Plains gradually gave way to more rugged terrain. By early October the wagon train was following the North Platte through the western reaches of the Nebraska country, where hills were high. The sense of elation that members of the company felt after crossing the prairie was tempered by the knowledge that another winter was on its way and the Rocky Mountains lay directly ahead.

The days were cool now, and frost was beginning to threaten at night. At least firewood was plentiful, the tall grass of the prairie being replaced in many areas by thick stands of pine and hickory, ash and juniper.

The buffalo hunting season was at its height, the cumbersome beasts having grown sleek and fat after feasting on grass for months. At Whip's instigation, large quantities of meat were smoked, and the basic Indian system of preservation was used, too. Meat was cut into long, thin strips, which were dried in the open air on crude frames, some of which were tied to the sides and tops of wagons. It was essential to put aside provisions for the winter that loomed ahead, and no one needed to be told the importance of hoarding. The travelers were veterans now, acclimated to the tribulations of the trail, and they were already making preparations for the hardships that awaited them.

The women put away their dresses of cotton and dimity, changing into wool, and the men rolled down their shirtsleeves. Those of both sexes who owned clothes of buffalo or deerskin changed into them and were so comfortable that others demanded similar garments. Cindy and several of the other women began to learn the difficult Indian art of chipping away layers from tough buffalo hide to make it thin enough for wear. These skins were rubbed with mixtures of salt and the brains of the animals to cure them, then lightly smoked to keep them flexible. By the time winter came, virtually every member of the company would own at least one leather outfit.

Frequently the hunters saw Indians in the distance, observing the size of buffalo herds and the direction in which they were moving. At Pierre's request, he was added temporarily to the roster of scouts, and Whip issued the group new instructions.

"One of these days soon," he said, "you're going to run across a party of Cheyenne keeping watch on a buffalo herd. Whenever that happens, don't wait until the end of the day to notify me. Let me know right off. It's high time we bear down and try to locate Eulalia Woodling."

Although the need to find a site for satisfactory winter quarters was on everyone's mind, a halt was called for twenty-four hours to celebrate the marriage of Tonie Mell and Dr. Robert Martin. Two antelope and a buck were shot for the feast, and Tonie herself was one of the hunters who brought down geese. The splints had been removed from her leg, and she walked with only a slight limp that, her future husband said, would soon disappear. Precious flour was used to make a wedding cake. Virtually every family contributed a jar of preserved fruit for the gala meal.

Tonie owned no white dress, so Cathy loaned her one, made of silk, and Cindy provided a delicate hat with a wide brim and a bunch of artificial flowers near the crown. The bridegroom wore his best suit, a high-collared white shirt, and a black stock, and Arnold Mell, who would give his niece away, was attired in linsey-woolsey—the first time on the journey that he had worn anything other than buckskins. Cathy was the matron of honor, and Bob asked Whip to serve as his best man.

The circle of wagons had been formed on a bluff overlooking the North Platte, and as safety precautions took precedence over the wedding, the horses and oxen grazed nearby as the company assembled for the ceremony.

A radiant Tonie emerged from the wagon she had shared with her uncle. She couldn't stop smiling as she took Arnold's arm and made her way slowly across the clearing to the spot where Bob and Whip stood, in front of Reverend Cavendish. Cindy was already weeping, and tears came to Grace Drummond's eyes, too.

Then a hush fell as the minister intoned the words of

the wedding ceremony. During the vows, even the nervous bridegroom couldn't help smiling broadly when Tonie promised to obey as well as love and honor her husband. Certainly he knew, as did everyone else, that marriage would not change Tonie's fierce sense of independence.

At the end of the ceremony the bride and groom kissed with tender enthusiasm, and some of the teenaged boys and girls began to cheer. In a moment or two everyone joined in.

As people formed a line to kiss Tonie and offer Bob their congratulations, several younger couples conferred with each other in whispers, then started to laugh. The usually sedate Terence Malcolm cupped his hands and called, "Now the best man has to kiss the matron of honor!" A dozen others took up the cry.

Whip's face became red, and he pretended not to hear. Cathy, unable to look at him, felt her own face turning scarlet. But there was no escape for them. Their obvious discomfort encouraged their tormentors, and it soon became evident that the chant would continue until they complied.

Whip took a deep breath, mumbled something unintelligible, and grasped Cathy by the shoulders. She began to tremble at his touch and hoped he wouldn't notice. Then he kissed her, lightly but firmly, and everything else faded from her consciousness. She didn't even hear the cheers of the company. When he released her, she refrained from looking at him. Flustered, she turned and hurried to the cooking fire to supervise the last phase of the preparations of the wedding feast.

An even more serious business occupied Whip. Mack, Pierre, and Stalking Horse had not been present for the ceremony, having gone out to scout the neighboring area, and now the Cherokee returned, his usually expressionless face grim.

Whip hastily left the wedding party, and, feigning unconcern so he would not put a damper on the festivities, he sauntered off with Stalking Horse toward the far side of the compound.

Stalking Horse spoke in his own tongue so possible eavesdroppers wouldn't understand. "About three miles from the camp, there are many buffalo. There the son of Roaring Thunder saw Cheyenne."

"How many?"

Stalking Horse held up five fingers, then added, "One was a senior warrior, maybe a sachem. There were seven feathers of the eagle in his bonnet."

"He must be captured and brought back here. Alive," Whip said emphatically.

The Cherokee nodded. "It will be done," he replied, a light of anticipatory pleasure appearing in his eyes. "Hosea will come with me, and we will return with the Cheyenne."

Whip frowned. "It will be best to send a strong war party to make him prisoner."

Stalking Horse shook his head. "No. Then many firesticks will be used to kill Cheyenne. Their sachems will thirst for vengeance, and a new battle will be fought. Hosea and the son of Roaring Thunder will need no help from their brothers."

Whip trusted him and was satisfied. "Do what you will," he said.

They returned to the company, and Stalking Horse next drew Hosea aside. No one noticed the Cherokee and Ashanti leave the circle together, on foot.

As soon as they left the wagon train behind, they began to jog, slowing to a walk only when they sighted the buffalo herd in the distance. They moved forward cautiously, and at last Stalking Horse grunted. "Cheyenne," he said.

Hosea smiled when he saw five horsemen, all of them loitering near the herd, facing in the opposite direction. He and his friend were about to engage in a game of wits, and he was already enjoying himself.

Stalking Horse dropped to his hands and knees in the tall grass, disappearing from sight. Hosea advanced very slowly now, seemingly alone. His companion, accompanying him, could no longer be seen.

At last, as the pair had hoped, the Cheyenne braves became aware of Hosea, who appeared unarmed except for his cumbersome shield. The warriors turned, their horses spreading out, and began to move toward him.

Ordinarily they would have killed a man alone, but they were unaccustomed to the sight of a man with black skin, and their curiosity brought them still closer.

Showing no fear, Hosea continued to advance. When he was no more than a hundred yards from the mounted braves, he halted, planted his shield in the ground, and waited.

One of the warriors began to circle toward the right as he continued to edge toward Hosea. Hosea made no move until the man came within his range. Then he removed one of his little clubs from a loop at his waist and threw it. The weapon caught the brave on the forehead, instantly knocking him unconscious, and he slumped on the back of his mount. The other Cheyenne were alarmed and immediately reached for their arrows.

Hosea had eyes only for the man who wore seven feathers in his headdress—he would leave the other three Indians to his friend. Stalking Horse was still unseen, his presence in the high grass unsuspected. Then he let loose an arrow and brought down a warrior, who fell from his horse without making a sound.

Several arrows landed almost simultaneously in Hosea's shield, penetrating the outer layer of leather. But the Ashanti remained unharmed behind the "wall" of his unique fort.

Again Stalking Horse fired an arrow, and again his aim was true. Now only two of the Cheyenne remained. One was the brave with the headdress. Hosea took careful aim with a club, then sent it spinning through the air with all of the strength he could command. It landed against the warrior's temple, and he tumbled backward onto the ground.

The remaining Cheyenne, having had enough of foes seen and unseen, galloped away, presumably to bring the unhappy news back to his town. Some of the horses followed.

Hosea and Stalking Horse raced forward together. They were elated when they saw that the Cheyenne with the fancy headdress had been knocked unconscious. They used strips of rawhide to bind him to the back of his bewildered horse, which had not left the scene, and were so anxious to take him back to the wagon train that Stalking Horse regretfully collected no scalps. Not only had their mission been successful, but neither the survivor who had fled nor the other, still unconscious, would be able to identify their foes as members of the wagon train.

Leading the Indian's horse, Stalking Horse and Hosea returned as quickly as they could to the campsite. Their captive was still unconscious when they arrived, so they took him to Ernie von Thalman's wagon, then quietly summoned Whip.

The wagonmaster tried to arouse the captive, but failed, although the brave's deep, regular breathing convinced him that the man was not seriously disabled.

The wedding feast had not yet been served, so Whip drew the bridegroom aside. "I hate to ask you to work today of all days, Bob," he said, explaining the situation. "But, as you can see yourself, it can't be helped."

The physician slipped away from the wedding party, went to his wagon to get his medical bag, then went to Ernie's wagon. Only Whip accompanied him. The doctor held a small vial of smelling crystals under the warrior's nose, and he stirred, groaned, and opened his eyes.

"Who are you?" Whip asked him, speaking the language of the Cheyenne.

When the brave saw that his interrogator was white, his eyes became sullen, even though he was still groggy. He made no reply.

"Do you want me for anything more?" Bob Martin asked as he packed away the vial in his black leather bag.

Before Whip could reply, the warrior caught sight of the Wichita buffalo-bone amulet hanging from the physician's neck. "You are a sachem," he said. "I am the son of a sachem!" With great pride he displayed the amulet that he was wearing.

Bob didn't understand a word, but Whip was quick to seize the opportunity. "Stay for a couple of minutes," he said, and translated the warrior's remarks.

Bob's smile was reassuring as he looked down at his patient on the cot.

"The son of the Cheyenne sachem will suffer no harm," Whip told the warrior. "We found you sleeping in the fields, and we will return you this day to your own town."

The confused Indian hauled himself to a sitting position, one hand clutching his aching temple. Uncertain as to whether or not he was being tricked, he waited warily.

"The Cheyenne will be our friends." Whip continued to speak soothingly. "We will prove our friendship by taking you to your own people. You can also prove you are our friend."

"How so?" the brave asked cautiously.

"Tell me if a young, white squaw is a prisoner in the land of the Cheyenne."

"It is so," the warrior replied at once, relieved because the request was so simple.

"Can you take us to her?"

The man nodded. "She is in the town of Rising Moon, next to the town of my father."

"Then we will take you to the town of Rising Moon, and you will be free to join your people there."

"It is agreed," the warrior said, and although he was not yet fully recovered, he folded his arms across his chest to indicate that a bargain had been struck.

Bob Martin returned to the wedding festivities, and Whip asked him to send Mack and Pierre, who had just returned from their scouting duties, to the wagon.

"You'll have to eat your wedding dinner later," the wagonmaster told them. "Our Cheyenne here—who doesn't realize we kidnapped him—has told me where we can find Eulalia Woodling and will lead us to her."

Mack looked incredulous. "Three of us will invade a Cheyenne town?"

Pierre was equally disturbed. "That is suicide! We will be scalped alive and tortured to death!"

"I don't aim to lose the top of my head," Whip said. "Just trust me."

Pierre and Mack were still dubious, but Whip gave them no choice. They got their horses, then rejoined him as he slung a saddlebag over his stallion's back. He even had the presence of mind to saddle a mare for Eulalia. The Cheyenne warrior was still weak, but his dignity compelled him to mount his own horse unassisted. The group sneaked away from the festivities, with no one but the bridegroom knowing they had gone. This was Tonie's great day, and Whip wanted to do nothing that would detract from it.

The four men rode at a rapid clip. It was evening by the time they reached their destination, a Cheyenne town rich in fields planted with corn and beans. A sentry halted them just outside the community, then admitted them when he recognized the warrior.

In almost no time the sachem of the town appeared, surrounded by fifty warriors armed with knives and spears, bows and arrows. Mack and Pierre exchanged glances as they clutched their rifles. If they were attacked, it would be difficult to save themselves, but they were prepared to make the savages pay dearly.

The warrior who had escorted the strangers explained that these men had saved his life after he had been attacked by a large, fierce band of Indians he had been unable to identify.

So far so good, Whip thought, and gave the gathered Cheyenne no time to think about possible flaws in the story. Addressing himself to the sachem alone, he said boldly, "We have come to bargain with Rising Moon. Give me the white squaw who is your captive, and I will give you a priceless gift in return."

Before the chief could reply, he dismounted, opened his saddlebag and, as the warriors crowded around him, removed the skin of the white buffalo calf. The braves fell back, muttering to each other in awe.

Mack and Pierre understood now what Whip was trying to do, but their apprehension grew. There was nothing to prevent the sachem from ordering the visitors murdered and calmly taking possession of the precious white hide.

But Whip promptly demonstrated that he knew even more about the ways of Indians than did these experienced mountain men. "There is magic in this skin," he said.

The Cheyenne nodded in assent, and Rising Moon's eyes gleamed with avarice.

"The skin keeps its magic when its owner presents it freely to a friend. It will bring good luck in the hunt to its new owner and his people if they keep faith with their friends."

"It is so," Rising Moon replied gravely.

At that moment Mack and Pierre knew that they were safe.

The sachem sent two senior warriors for the white captive. After what seemed an interminable time, they returned, leading Eulalia by a rawhide leash looped over her neck. She was barefooted, clad in the leather breast-band and short skirt that were her only attire. She had already prepared for her evening activities, so her skin was greased, her eyelids were smudged, and her lips were stained with berry juice.

"Don't say a word," Whip cautioned the startled girl as he took the loose end of the leash from the warrior, handed it to Pierre, and then helped Eulalia onto the back of the mare. "Mack, Pierre—get started back to the wagon train. I'll make a farewell speech to our new friends and catch up with you."

The trio promptly rode off, and it appeared to the Indians that the white squaw was being treated like a slave by her new owners.

Whip made a long, rambling speech—the kind the Indians enjoyed and expected—stressing his friendship and that of his people for the Cheyenne. The words did not come easily, but he persisted until he felt certain that Eulalia and her escorts had gone at least a mile.

At last he left the Cheyenne, letting his stallion gallop at full speed. Soon he caught up with the little party. Whip's first act was symbolic. He slashed the leash with his knife. "I know you've had a rough time," he said, "but you're safe now."

Eulalia nodded, but made no reply. Even though her unexpected rescue was a miracle that gave her infinite relief, she knew that her appearance told these men, experienced in the ways of Indians, that the Cheyenne had used her as a prostitute. She was so ashamed that she could look at none of them.

She tried to stammer her thanks for her deliverance. Then, after she fell silent, tears streamed down her face.

Pierre tried to comfort her by reaching out to pat her on the arm, but she shrank from his touch.

Guessing how she felt, Whip decided it would be wise to ease her gently back into the mainstream of wagon train life. So he waited until they were approaching the campsite before he said, "We'll take you straight to your wagon, and then we'll tell your brother you've come back." It would be best if Claiborne told her their father had been killed.

"Tonie Mell and Dr. Martin got married today, so I don't want to take away from the attention they're getting. You can get a decent night's sleep and change into your own clothes, and tomorrow morning will be time enough for folks to know you've returned."

Again Eulalia tried to express her thanks, but again words wouldn't come.

They approached the Woodling wagon from the outside of the circle. Not until Whip had seen the girl safely inside her wagon did he go in search of her brother. He found Claiborne eating wedding cake with Cindy, both of them chatting while a glowering Ted Woods stood nearby.

Whip quietly explained the situation.

"I'm coming with you," Cindy told Claiborne, and they walked together to the Woodling wagon.

They found Eulalia sitting cross-legged on the floor, still in her Indian attire. She looked dazed, and Cindy took charge. "Let me talk to her alone," she told Claiborne. "Wait until I come for you."

Claiborne had learned to trust Cindy's judgment and moved a short distance away. Cindy moved around the wagon, lighting lamps and, as she did, noting every detail of the other girl's appearance, including the welts on her back.

"I'll bring you some water so you can wash that grease away before you change into your own clothes," she said, then started to rummage in a leather clothing box. "Ah, here we are. A brush that will help you unsnarl those Indian braids."

Eulalia took the brush, then let it fall to the floor. "I wish I was dead," she said listlessly.

"I often felt like that in my day." Cindy remained calm.

"They shouldn't have brought me back here. It would have been better to leave me where I was."

Cindy went to the flap, beckoned to Claiborne, and sent him for two buckets of warm water.

"I'm useless here. Nobody will want anything to do with me," Eulalia said.

Cindy sat behind her on the clothing box, then began to unbraid and brush her hair. "Maybe it isn't as bad as you think."

"You don't understand. The Cheyenne made me be a whore. Man after man, night after night."

"Oh, that. I figured as much the second I saw you."

"It isn't just that they forced me to do it," Eulalia said. "I—I cooperated with them. I flirted with them. I pretended I loved every minute of it. Because they gave me food, and without it I would have starved."

"I would have starved, too, if I hadn't pretended to love entertaining my customers," Cindy said quietly. "You're no worse than the rest of us."

"Except that I had to sleep with savages."

Cindy was still unruffled. "Most men are savages in bed, especially with the women they pay." She went to the flap, took the buckets from Claiborne, and motioned him away again. "Here. Start to wash yourself. And scrub your face hard. You'll feel much better."

The lethargic Eulalia made no move.

"Here's one of your washcloths and a little jar of soft soap. Go to work, or I'll have to bathe you myself."

Eulalia heard the determination in her voice and, stripping herself, began to bathe.

"I'll grant you've had a nasty experience," Cindy said. "But those marks on your back will go away. And so will the marks inside you—if you let them."

"Everybody will know what happened to me."

"I very much doubt that they will—unless you tell them. But suppose they *do* find out. Just about everybody on this train knows I was a whore. But I have plenty of good friends, and I really wouldn't much want to know the others." She handed the other girl a towel, then took undergarments, stockings, a dress, and shoes from the clothing box.

Mechanically, Eulalia began to dress. "Civilized clothes. You can't imagine!"

"Yes, I can. You should have seen the flashy dresses I had to throw away." Cindy laughed, then sobered. "I'll tell you a secret. You can become twice the person you would have been without this experience."

"You're just trying to make me feel better. People will laugh at me—and shun me."

"A few will, I suppose," Cindy said candidly. "Let them. You don't need that kind. Start feeling proud of yourself. You had a hard time, but you lived through it, and you learned something. You'll be surprised, from now on, how easily you'll be able to distinguish between the men who just want your body and the men who like you for yourself."

Eulalia finished dressing, and a faint flicker of her old pride returned. Staring hard at the other girl in the flickering light of the oil lamps, she asked, "Why are you being so kind to me?"

"Because you'd do the same for me if our positions were reversed," Cindy replied promptly. "The person you used to be wouldn't have done it, but you're not that person any more. I can see the change reflected in your eyes, and I know a little something about what you've had to go through. Men are men, and it doesn't matter if they're Cheyenne warriors or the leading citizens of Louisville."

Eulalia took a deep, unsteady breath. "I think—I'd rather—let people know tonight that—I've come back. Instead of—waiting until tomorrow. If you'll come with me."

"Of course!" Cindy opened the flap, and for a moment they stood together on the top step. Then with one accord, they linked arms and started to walk toward the festive crowd.

Gray Antelope was the most powerful Indian leader in the West, perhaps in all of North America, and he knew it. All of the lower-ranking chiefs of the Blackfoot paid homage to him. For more than a decade he had ruled his nation as sachem of sachems. Although his face was becoming wrinkled, his hair was still a deep black, his build was still muscular, and, above all, he exuded an air of authority.

He sat cross-legged on the buffalo-hide rug in his tent of double skins, facing the fire outside, puffing slowly on his long pipe and studying the two white-skinned visitors who sat opposite him. After two long days of intensive discussions, it was plain to him that this pair were trying to use him. Fair enough—and he would use them. So he concealed the instinctive dislike he felt for any men who were not Blackfoot. Adjusting his cape of buffalo skin adorned with feathers, he spoke slowly so the darker of the pair could translate his words.

"Twice the sun has risen, and twice the sun has gone again while we have talked. Now Gray Antelope has made up his mind."

Henry St. Clair started to speak, thought better of it, and waited.

"You have told Gray Antelope of the riches in horses and slaves, firesticks and cooking pots, blankets and other good things that await the Blackfoot when they attack the carts of the white men and squaws who will soon come to this land. So be it. The Blackfoot can make good use of all those things. But you offer too little in return. You say you will give us one hundred firesticks. Not enough!"

"Your senior warriors have counted them in my cart. I offer you all I own." Henry sat back and waited for André Sebastian to translate.

Gray Antelope shook his head, and the many feathers in his ornate bonnet danced. "The Blackfoot can send more than one thousand warriors against their foes. The white men of the moving carts have more than one hundred firesticks. So the Blackfoot will need five hundred more before they will strike a bargain with you!"

Henry exchanged a quick glance with Sebastian. He had been afraid of this development, knowing of the greed for which Gray Antelope was noted. Fortunately he was prepared for it. "There are many soldiers of my country at Fort Vancouver, which stands beside the waters of the Great Sea," he said. "I will write to them. Let a swift messenger of the Blackfoot ride to them. They will send five hundred firesticks across the mountains at once!"

Gray Antelope felt a surge of elation, which he did not allow to show on his face. Armed with six hundred firesticks, his warriors could not only subdue the people of the moving carts, who were only a minor consideration, but they could use those firesticks to conquer the Arapaho, the Ute, and, above all, the hated Comanche. Those firesticks would make them the masters of all the flatlands and the mountains—of the entire world that was within reach.

"So be it," he said. "And while the messenger goes and the firesticks are sent, the visitors to the land of the Blackfoot will stay here. You will teach the warriors of the Blackfoot to use the one hundred firesticks you have already given us. You will teach my braves to shoot as well as you shoot."

The old man drove a hard bargain, Henry thought, but the price was worth paying. He felt certain the rifles would be sent from Fort Vancouver, along with ammunition and powder, no matter how much the brigadier in command disliked the idea of arming Indians with modern weapons. Even his own position as a semi-hostage while he acted as an instructor in marksmanship would be tolerable.

Now there would be no escape for the American wagon train. Attacked by one thousand Blackfoot, six hundred of them armed with rifles, they would perish. His own mission would be achieved without the government or people of the United States ever knowing that Great Britain had been involved.

"So be it," he replied solemnly.

The autumn wind that blew down from the nearby Rocky Mountains was chilly, and the sky overhead was leaden, as it had been for several days. But Cathy van Ayl was unconcerned about the approach of a new winter.

The wedding of Tonie and Bob Martin had made a marked change in her own life. When Whip had been teased into kissing her after the ceremony, the wall that had stood between them had crumbled and vanished. He was no longer as shy in her presence and sought her company whenever he wasn't busy. For the first time he spoke freely—not only about his past, but about his future.

The day before, he had told her in confidence that he was seriously thinking of settling in Oregon after he led the wagon train there. She had felt as though a bolt of lightning had struck her. She hadn't dared to hope that he might be willing to exchange his hard, nomadic existence for a settled future. Above all, the mere fact that he had taken her into his confidence was significant. Her instinct told her that he was thinking of establishing a homestead of his own because he wanted to share it with her.

So, at long last, she could admit to herself that she was seriously interested in him. Her sister had found happiness with one former mountain man, so it wasn't too much to hope that she could be equally successful as Mrs. Michael Holt.

Now, during the nooning halt, he came over to her again to talk. "This morning while we were riding," he said, "I got to thinking about a little valley I know in the Oregon country. There's no place in the whole world like it. The Pacific is on the western end, and on the other three sides it's surrounded by mountains. The forest is thick, so there's wood aplenty for building snug homes and for firewood. There are so many salmon in the river that flows along one side that nobody would ever go hungry. And the soil is as black and fertile as the soil you saw in Illinois."

"Is there enough room there for everybody in the wagon train?" Cathy asked.

"Enough and more," he assured her. "Even with the head of every family claiming six hundred acres, there's enough space for a couple of more wagon trains filled with people."

She was enjoying herself. "Surely there must be something wrong with it. I suppose we'll have to fight the Indians who live there."

Whip shook his head vehemently. "That's the beauty of my valley. Nobody lives there. There are Indians to the north and others directly to the east. But my valley isn't occupied. I've had a half-dozen sites in mind, but seeing as I may want to settle out yonder myself, my valley is going to be our goal."

Before Cathy could reply, someone shouted for Whip. He excused himself, and Cathy watched him as he hurried off to greet some unusual visitors—three mounted Indians, each of whom led a pack horse.

The trio dismounted, and it was plain that Whip knew them well. The two warriors exchanged greetings with him by raising their hands in the peace sign, and then, to Cathy's surprise, he embraced them each in turn.

But it was the third of the new arrivals, a young woman, who most attracted Cathy's attention. The girl appeared to be in her early twenties. Her chiseled features were flawless, making her a beauty by any standards. Her doeskin shirt and skirt fitted her closely, revealing a tall, perfectly proportioned body, and her hair, unlike the thick braids of the Plains squaw, cascaded down her back in a blue-black wave to her waist.

As Cathy stared at her, the girl prostrated herself on the ground before Whip. He quickly drew her to her feet, then embraced her, and a sense of jealousy surged up within Cathy as she saw the girl cling to him. At that moment, Stalking Horse came forward with great dignity and embraced the girl, who, Cathy later learned was his half-sister. He and his mother had traveled West many years before, where his mother had married her second husband, an Arapaho. Then the trio engaged in a spirited discussion with Whip.

Lee Blake was summoned, as was Ernie, and they joined in the talk, with Whip translating. The conversation went on for so long that, contrary to custom, the nooning was extended for a considerable period of time. The talk seemed endless.

At last Whip gave the order to resume the march. The three newcomers mounted their horses. Apparently they were attaching themselves to the wagon train. Lee Blake came to Cathy's assistance, helping her round up her horses and harness them. She knew better than to ask questions out of turn, but her memory of Whip's embrace with the lovely Indian girl still bothered her. "Who are these people?"

"Old friends and allies of Whip Holt's," Lee said.

He refrained from telling her the significance of their arrival, which she would learn soon enough. Mountain dwellers with whom Whip had spent several winters, they had brought word that the dreaded Blackfoot were being armed with rifles and were receiving instructions in their use from two white men. That portion of the news concerned Lee alone. It was his duty not only to learn more about the men but to counter their influence.

It was being rumored in the mountain tribes that the wagon train was coming into the Rockies and that the Blackfoot intended to annihilate the entire company. Lee realized he had his hands full, that he faced an unparalleled challenge. He would think in depth about the problem after he mounted his horse. Right now he was conscious of Cathy's steady gaze and knew he had to say something more to her. "They're members of the Arapaho tribe," he said.

Their nationality meant nothing to her. "The girl, too?"

"I believe so," Lee said. "She—ah—appears to be Whip's woman."

Cathy stiffened involuntarily.

Lee hoped that he hadn't said too much. He wondered if Cathy had more of a personal interest in Whip then he knew. Well, that couldn't be helped; by tonight the entire company would know of Whip's relationship with the young woman.

Mounting the board of her wagon, where Hosea was already sitting, Cathy saw the Indian girl look at Whip. The intimacy in her dark eyes required no further explanation. Too late Cathy realized she should have heeded Sam Brentwood's warning when he had told her not to become too involved with Whip. While she had indulged in foolish daydreams about a future in Oregon, Whip's common-law Indian wife had been traveling to him, and now she had joined him.

What had happened in the past didn't concern Cathy. In fact, she would have been surprised if Whip had remained celibate through the years. So the fact that he had chosen to live with a beautiful Arapaho girl was strictly his own business.

But that girl had joined him and was riding beside him at this very moment. Tonight they would sleep together. The realization was so crushing, so humiliating, that Cathy felt an almost overpowering urge to weep hysterically. How stupid she had been to pin her hopes for the future on such a man! Only the presence of Hosea on the seat beside her fueled her pride and kept her face immobile.

Cathy felt sure that, deep within, something precious and irreplaceable had been stolen from her.

Out of the corner of her eye, she caught a glimpse of Lee coming toward her again, his expression solicitous. Perhaps her preoccupation with Whip had blinded her to anyone else. How foolish she had been. Perhaps. Certainly Lee was good-looking and intelligent, sensitive and a man of integrity. And obviously, now that she thought about it, he was developing a deep and sincere interest in her.

But she couldn't think about him now, any more than she could allow herself to dwell on her disappointment in Whip. There was something far more important at stake.

Oregon still beckoned. The promise of the land that lay ahead was more vital than any personal relationship. She was more determined than ever to remain a member of the wagon train until it reached its goal.

MANDASUE HELLER

the club

Are you in?

HODDER

First published in Great Britain in 2006 by Hodder & Stoughton
A division of Hodder Headline

A Hodder paperback

1

All characters in this publication are fictitious and any resemblance to real persons, living or dead, is purely coincidental.

A CIP catalogue record for this title
is available from the British Library

ISBN 978 0 340 83831 0

Typeset in Plantin Light by Palimpsest Book Production Limited,
Grangemouth, Stirlingshire

Printed and bound by
Clays Ltd, St Ives plc

Hodder Headline's policy is to use papers that are natural, renewable and recyclable products and made from wood grown in sustainable forests. The logging and manufacturing processes are expected to conform to the environmental regulations of the country of origin.

Hodder & Stoughton Ltd
A division of Hodder Headline
338 Euston Road
London NW1 3BH

The Club is dedicated to my beautiful mum, Jean Heller – for everything you have been, and still are, in my life.

Acknowledgements

I would like to thank the following – as always:

My lovely partner, Wingrove Ward; my fantastic children, Michael, Andrew, Azzura, and my gorgeous new granddaughter, Marissa; my great sister, Ava, and her kids, Amber & Kyro, Martin, Jade, and Reece; Auntie Doreen; Pete & Ann; Lorna & Cliff, Chris and Glen; Natalie & Dan; and the rest of my family – love you all.

Many thanks to everyone at Hodder for being so supportive – again – especially, Carolyn Caughey, Isobel Akenhead, Emma Longhurst, and everybody in sales, marketing, art, etc . . . etc . . .

My agents, Cat Ledger and Faye Webber.

Norman Kaine Fairweather Brown; Betty Boo & Ronnie Schwartz; Wayne Brookes; Rosie Goodwin

– thanks to you all for your help, advice, friendship, and funny e-mails – it means the world.

A big Hi! to Martina. And all best wishes to Betty's Babes – keep up the good work, guys.

Nick Austin – with thanks, as ever.

Special mention to Sarj Duggal, with thanks for the financial advice.

And lastly, eternal gratitude to the buyers, sellers, readers, reviewers and the lovely ladies at the library.

PROLOGUE

'Damn it!' Jenna cursed, peering down at the ladder zigzagging its way over her knee. Less than an hour to go, her hair was still wet, she hadn't even started on her make-up, and now she had to find another pair of tights. But it was her own fault. She should never have chanced a bath when she was so tired. Not on an important night like tonight.

She'd stressed and fretted her way through every second of the last few months, petrified that she'd bitten off more than she could chew; terrified that it would all fall apart at the last minute. Now that everything that could be done *had* been done, she should have been able to relax. But she felt worse than ever, and wished that she could run away and hide until it was all over. Still, it was too late for that. She just had to lay the fears aside and get on with it.

Taking several deep breaths to calm herself, Jenna sat down on the dressing-table stool and dried her hair. That done, she carefully applied her make-up, then changed the laddered tights for a pair of sheer black lace-top stockings and slipped her shoes on.

Looking herself over when she'd finished, she smiled. Not bad, but she could do with spending a week or two in the gym to tone her stomach after all the fast food she'd been eating lately. And a few early nights wouldn't go amiss to lighten the shadows circling her eyes. But she'd do for now.

Her mobile rang just as she reached for her jacket. Seeing the name on the screen, Jenna smiled again.

Kalli was one of the young waitresses who had worked for her dad – and was the first to agree to come back when Fabian contacted the staff to let them know the score. A petite scrap-of-nothing Chinese girl, she was the prettiest little thing, with an elfin face and warm, almond-shaped eyes. She looked twelve, despite being almost twenty-one, but she had the air of a much older soul because she fussed over everyone like a mother hen. Particularly her flatmate, Austin, who was one of the waiters. And, as soon as she met her, Jenna.

Knowing that Kalli was probably checking up on her now to make sure that she hadn't run away, Jenna answered the call.

'Yes, I know I'm late, Kalli. I'm just leaving.'

'Just thought I'd best check in case you'd fallen asleep in the bath, or something,' Kalli said concernedly.

'Who's got time for a bath?' Jenna lied, reaching for her keys and heading for the door. 'Everything okay down there?'

'Fine – *now*,' Kalli told her. 'Maurice had a bit of a crisis earlier, but it was nothing I couldn't have sorted out in a nanosecond – if he'd bothered *asking*.'

'Oh?' Frowning, Jenna locked up and set off down the stairs. 'What happened?'

'He thought someone had stolen the champagne, and made all the boys leave what they were doing to search for it. I didn't know what they were looking for, or I could have told them it had been moved to the office for safe keeping. But you know Maurice. He'd rather *die* than ask a *girl* for help.'

Tutting softly, Jenna let herself into the residents' car park. Maurice was the head barman. He'd been with her dad right from the start, and still regarded him as the *proper* boss. He had a problem with females in general, but he particularly resented having one for a boss and had spent the last couple of days sulking and complaining while everyone else got on with the final preparations for the party.

'Fabian gave him a bit of a roasting,' Kalli went

on, chuckling softly now. 'That did *not* impress him, as you can imagine. But he wouldn't dare argue when Fabian's in that kind of mood.'

Sighing, Jenna climbed into her car. So, not only was Maurice still sulking, but Fabian was in a mood. Great! Just what she needed when teamwork was crucial to the success of the night.

Changing the subject before the nerves flared up again, she said, 'How's the queue?'

'Massive!' Kalli told her excitedly. 'And some have been waiting a good couple of hours already, so Fabian's got the security on alert in case anything kicks off when they don't all get in.'

'I'm sure we'll cope,' Jenna said, crossing her fingers. 'Anyway, I've got to get off the phone now, Kalli. See you in a bit.'

Disconnecting the call, she started the engine and eased the car out onto the road.

Turning onto Deansgate five minutes later, Jenna saw that Kalli had been right about the queue, which started at Zenith's brand new smoked-glass doors and snaked right down the block and out of sight around the corner.

It had been snowing all day, turning the roads to slush and the pavements to ice, and a fierce wind was punishing the skimpily dressed clubbers for their vanity.

The two doormen who were standing head and massive shoulders above the shivering crowd didn't seem fazed. But Jenna was sure they had to be freezing and, waving as she drove past, she made a mental note to see that they traded places with some of the other guys once everyone was inside.

Best leaving them out front for now, though, because they were easily the biggest of the security crew, and could most efficiently deal with trouble if Fabian was right and something *did* kick off.

Parking up behind the club, Jenna heard the staff talking among themselves in the main clubroom as she let herself in through the kitchen door. Taking her coat off, she hung it on a hook in the staff cloakroom, then slipped quietly in behind the bar.

Standing in the shadows, she took the opportunity to have a look around before anybody noticed her. She'd had so many wobbles since committing herself to this, convincing herself that they would never be ready on time. But not only had the building, painting, and refurbishing work been completed ahead of schedule, it looked way better than she had ever imagined it would.

The funky chrome bars that she'd had installed were gleaming; the plush new carpets were spotless; and the mega-expensive opaque-glass circular dance floor was alive with vibrant, colourful, built-in pulsar lights; while overhead, the new lighting rig rivalled that of any club Jenna had ever visited.

At Fabian's suggestion, they had turned the upper floor overlooking the dance floor into a VIP lounge, and a buffet of exotic foods had been laid out there earlier today for the invited guests, with a spectacular pyramid of sparkling glasses in the centre of it all for the champagne fountain. And little gift-packs containing expensive aftershaves and perfumes, and solid silver lighters engraved with the sword-slash 'Z' that Jenna had adopted as the new logo, had been placed on each table.

She'd been reluctant when Fabian had asked her to double the budget for the party, concerned that he was being unnecessarily extravagant on top of everything she'd already spent. But he'd persuaded her that they needed something special to impress the A-listers – in the hope that they would spread the word to their pals and really put Zenith on the celebrity map. And, all credit to him, she had to admit that he'd really pulled it off.

One of the waitresses spotted her just then and made her jump when she called, 'Wow, Miss Lorde! You look amazing!'

Embarrassed when the rest of the staff turned her way, Jenna fought the urge to turn and run. Most of them still secretly regarded her as the boss's daughter, she knew, and if she was ever going to fill his shoes this was the time to do it.

Watching as Jenna came out from behind the bar, her thigh-length chain-mail dress shimmering like liquid silver, her hair gleaming, her eyes huge, Kalli thought that she was just the most beautiful woman she had ever seen.

And she wasn't the only one.

Up in the DJ's booth, Vibes was holding one can of his headphones to his ear as he lined up his opening tracks. Glancing out of the window when he sensed the charge in the atmosphere below, he gave a low whistle when he saw Jenna. He'd thought she was pretty special from the first time he'd laid eyes on her, but, *man*, she looked hot tonight!

Flipping a button on the console, he pushed the faders up and flooded the air with the sweet sound of: '*Sexy . . . Everything about you, so sexy . . .*'

Blushing when the staff started laughing and clapping, Jenna held up her hands, saying, 'Okay, settle down . . . he's only testing the speakers.' Stepping back then, she said, 'Right, let's have a look at you all.'

Maurice was dapper in his self-chosen outfit of white shirt, black pants, and blue velvet waistcoat; the ten young waiters and waitresses looked gorgeous in their respective silver shorts and T-shirts and minidresses that Jenna had designed for them; and the six-strong security crew exuded class and professionalism in their bow ties and muscle-enhancing black suits.

'Perfect,' she said approvingly.

'Does that go for me, too?'

Coming down from the VIP area where he'd been doing last-minute checks, Fabian strolled towards her, handsome as a devil in a dark green suit, his hair falling lazily over his smoky eyes.

Glad to see that he was in a better mood than Kalli had reported, Jenna smiled. 'Of course it does.'

'Merci,' he drawled, letting his gaze slow-dance over her. 'And may I say that *you* look sensational.'

Flipping the mike on just then, Vibes's smooth sexy voice came over the PA speakers. 'Nearly time for the countdown, folks.'

'Ready when you are,' Jenna called, turning and waving at his silhouette in the booth. Crossing her fingers then, she turned back to the staff. 'What say we get this party started?'

Gritting his teeth when the grandfather clock chimed twelve, Leonard Drake cursed under his breath. Damn Avril! They were supposed to be at the club already, and he'd been ready and waiting for a good half-hour while the driver sat in the car outside clocking up a nice bit of overtime. But *she* was still at her vanity table, plastering yet more muck onto her jowls.

Well, he wasn't bloody well having it!

Pounding up the stairs, he burst into his wife's room and jabbed angrily at his watch.

'You *do* know what time it is, don't you? We're supposed to be there by now.'

Pausing with the lipstick halfway to her mouth, Avril flicked him a cool glance in the mirror. Then she slowly carried on with what she was doing.

'You are so infuriating sometimes,' Leonard complained. 'You know how much I've been looking forward to this. If you didn't want to come, you should have bloody well said so and I would have gone by myself!'

'No, you wouldn't,' Avril muttered, smacking her raspberry lips together. 'You never go *any*where new without me to hold your hand. I'm just a crutch, as far as you're concerned – an old pair of shoes that you slip on and walk all over.'

'Don't be ridiculous,' he retorted. 'James Lorde was a bloody good friend of mine, in case you'd forgotten, and I will *not* be late for his daughter's party!'

'You already are,' she reminded him flatly. 'And, for the record, dear, you and he were *not* good friends, you were acquaintances. There *is* a difference.'

'He was my *friend*,' Leonard asserted indignantly. 'My *father*'s friend, and then *my* friend. If he weren't, I wouldn't have received a VIP invitation, would I?'

'Temper, temper,' Avril clucked as purple blotches sprang up all over her husband's face. 'Mustn't get ourselves worked up. You know what it does to your complexion.'

Shaking his head with frustration, Leonard turned on his heel and marched out of the room.

Sighing when she heard the bathroom door slam shut down the landing a second later, Avril put the lipstick down and reached for her comb.

No doubt he'd gone to splash his face with cold water, but a blotchy complexion was the least of his worries. God only knew what he saw in the mirror these days, but he didn't seem to have realised that he was no longer the slim, handsome young man he had once been. His lovely thick hair had thinned considerably, and his once-sparkly eyes were just piggy little blobs in their puffy sockets now. But it was the belly bulging over the waistband of his suit trousers that betrayed just how far he'd let himself go. And the jacket sleeves were surely constricting the blood flow to his arms, but the vain bugger had squeezed himself into it nonetheless.

Coming back just then, Leonard tutted when

he found Avril exactly where he'd left her. But knowing they would never get out of the door if he started a row, he mustered every last ounce of self-control and calmly said, 'Will you *please* hurry up?'

Without answering, Avril took a few more moments to tease her newly combed hair into shape. Then she gave it a quick spritz of lacquer before standing up.

'Thank you,' he muttered, heading for the door. 'I'll be in the car.'

Avril hissed a breath out through her teeth. She knew that she was being a bitch, but she couldn't help it. Theirs had not been the easiest of marriages, what with the demands of Leonard's political career pulling them this way and that. But she had hoped that things would mellow between them when he retired last year.

And he *had* adjusted quite well, seeming content to potter about in the garden, or shoot some holes – or whatever he called it – at the golf club. It helped that they were still invited to his ex-colleagues' dinner parties, giving him the opportunity to meet up with his cronies and keep abreast of the latest gossip while Avril and the wives swapped recipes. But just when she'd finally begun to believe that their future was settled, that damned invitation for the nightclub reopening party had arrived, and he'd started acting like a kid who'd been handed the keys to the sweetshop.

'*AVRIIILLL!*' Leonard screeched up the stairs now. 'Bloody well come *on*, will you!'

Rolling her eyes, Avril checked herself one last time in the mirror. Then she switched the lamp off and settled her mouth into an unconcerned smile before heading down the stairs.

The sooner this was over, the sooner she could get back to her book.

Across town, in his plush third-floor hotel suite, Tony Allen stopped his impatient pacing and yanked the curtain aside. In the car park below, his right-hand man, Eddie, was leaning against the white stretch limo they'd hired, chatting to the driver. When a sleek black Mercedes pulled in behind it, Tony watched the long-haired guy who was staying in the penthouse suite swagger towards it. He was dressed in tight leather pants and a girly-pink silk shirt, and was flanked by an uptight-looking older man and three blonde bimbos in micro-miniskirts. He was supposed to be some sort of megastar singer, according to Melody, but Tony couldn't say that he'd ever heard of him.

Chase Mann . . . What kind of homo name was that, anyway?

Dropping the curtain when the group had

climbed into the Merc and taken off, Tony glanced at his watch. Twelve-fifteen. What the fuck was Melody playing at? She always liked to be late to be sure of making a big entrance, but this was the one night of the year when you had to be there on the fucking dot! How many times did she need to brush her hair or take her make-up off only to put it back on exactly the same, anyway?

Marching into the bedroom, he snatched the blusher brush from Melody's hand and hauled her up off the stool.

'What are you *doing*?' she squawked. 'I'm not ready.'

'Yeah, you are,' he grunted, marching her into the living room. 'Here, you can finish off on the way.' Snatching her handbag off the table he shoved it into her hands, then pushed her out the door and down the corridor to the elevator.

Melody complained all the way down to the foyer. But Tony ignored her, possessing that rare quality other men would pay to acquire: the ability to completely blank his women out.

Even those as gorgeous as Melody Fisher.

And she *was* gorgeous: angel face, devil of a sexy body, waist-length honey-blonde hair, and the most perfect tits he'd ever got his hands on – all bought and paid for by him. At thirty-two, and five-ten, she was a good deal younger than him and a little taller in her heels. But he was more than man enough to hold his own beside her, because he had that certain something about him: a menacing, brooding darkness, which, when added to his larger-than-life personality and the twinkle in his piercing eyes, created a powerful aura. *We'll have a laugh, but don't even think about fucking with me.*

'For Christ's sake, Tony!' Melody complained now, tottering helplessly on her stilettos as he pushed her out of the entrance doors. 'Do you have to act like such a fucking thug? You might get away with the He-Man shit in the fucking States, but we're in *England* now, remember?'

'Whatever,' Tony said dismissively, shoving her onto the limo's spacious back seat and climbing in beside her. Waiting until Eddie had got in up front, he tapped on the dividing window to tell the driver to get going.

Sighing loudly, Melody sat petulantly back, muttering, 'I can't be*lieve* you're stressing me out like this. Christ, I'm actually *trembling* – look . . .' Thrusting her hand out, she gave it an exaggerated shake. 'I need a cigarette,' she said then. Getting no response, she clicked her fingers sharply in front of Tony's face. 'A *smoke*, Tone, I need a smoke!'

'Not in the car,' he snapped, swatting her hand

aside. 'And don't call me that. You know I can't stand it.'

'*Sorry*, I'm sure!' Pulling her skirt down over her thighs with a huff, Melody folded her arms.

Reaching across, Tony pushed the skirt back up. 'Leave it there. I don't want people thinking I'm hanging out with a fucking nun.'

'No,' she sniped. 'You'd rather they thought I was a fucking *whore*.'

'Not just any whore,' he countered, giving her a sly grin. '*My* whore. And don't you forget it.'

Melody complained all the way to the club, only stopping when they pulled up outside and she saw all the heads in the queue turn their way as people tried to see who was behind the blacked-out windows. Getting her first real buzz of the night, she fixed her top for maximum cleavage and manoeuvred her skirt to pussy level, then waited for the driver to open the door, eager to get out and bask in the admiring glances.

Tony was having none of it. He'd just spotted the paparazzi hanging about on the other side of the road, and the last thing he wanted was to wake up and find his picture splashed across the papers. Taking a firm grip on Melody's wrist when they hit the pavement, he raised an arm to shield his face from the barrage of flashing lights and yanked her to the head of the queue.

'Tony!' she griped, twisting to free herself as he paused to show the doormen their invitation. 'You're hurting me.'

'So quit wriggling.'

'These people wanted to see me. I am *famous*, you know. It kind of comes with the territory.'

Giving a scornful snort, Tony said, 'Two films does *not* a superstar make.'

'*Hollywood* films,' she reminded him tartly.

'You still ain't no Jolie,' he flipped back. 'And I'd bet my life none of these idiots have got a fucking clue who you are.'

Not yet, maybe, Melody thought resentfully, folding her arms while they waited to be admitted. *But you just wait till my agent tells me I got that part I auditioned for. Angelina flaming Jolie won't know what's hit her when I get started!*

PART ONE

I

Jenna Lorde seemed to have it all. At twenty-six she could still pass for twenty-one, even on a bad day. Slim and curvaceous, with sleek shoulder-length black hair, a flawless complexion, and exotically slanted sea-green eyes, she had a good job at a major fashion house in the West End, a nice little flat in Maida Vale – and a shattered heart, having recently discovered that Jason, her charming, funny, passionate, unbearably handsome boyfriend of six years, was married.

Dumping him as soon as she found out, Jenna spent the next few months fielding the texts and phone calls claiming that his wife meant nothing to him, that it had all been a terrible mistake, and that Jenna was the only woman he'd ever loved. When that didn't work, he tried self-righteous anger, turning up at her flat, and – more embarrassingly – her workplace, accusing her of being selfish, and telling her to stop feeling sorry for herself and think what this was doing to *him*. And, finally, he tried reasoning that, as she'd already been sharing him with his wife all along, what was the difference if they carried on now as if nothing had ever happened?

And in one particularly weak, bleak moment, when she'd been missing him like crazy, and wishing that she'd stayed in blissful ignorance, Jenna had found herself actually considering it.

Which was when she came to the conclusion that she had to get as far away from him as possible if she was ever going to get her life back on track. But just as she was about to hand in her notice at work and give up the lease on her flat, fate stepped in. She got the call telling her that her dad had died.

Going home to Manchester to arrange the funeral and sort out her dad's affairs was a shock to Jenna's system. She'd been away for eight years, and in some ways it felt like she'd never been gone. But in others, it was truly weird to be back – especially knowing that her dad wouldn't be there when she reached the house.

Having kept in touch mainly by phone over the last few years, and only paying the occasional flying visit, Jenna hardly recognised the place when she stepped off the train. Piccadilly Station had had a major revamp since she'd last been there, and so had the rest of the city. But the people were exactly the same, she soon discovered – stoically determined to retain their northern-ness as the landscape mutated around them into a pastiche of the south. She didn't know if that was a good or a bad thing, but as she wasn't planning on sticking around after the funeral she didn't really care.

The funeral was a small affair, because Jenna didn't really know any of her dad's friends to invite them. In the end it was just her, a handful of their old neighbours, and Ruth Wolff – the widow of her dad's old solicitor, who had been the one who'd let her know that he'd died.

Jenna's older sister, Claudia, didn't come – but then, Jenna hadn't expected her to, considering that she hadn't bothered coming back for their mum's funeral either. Claudia had moved to Australia fifteen years earlier, and they hadn't clapped eyes on her since. Now she claimed that she couldn't afford the air fare – despite the fact that she and her husband ran their own business and owned a sprawling ranch-style house. But she'd always been selfish, which was why Jenna wasn't surprised when Claudia demanded that her share of the inheritance should be sent over as soon as possible.

Going back to Ruth's house after the service

for a small buffet, Jenna felt like an outsider as Ruth and the elderly neighbours swapped stories and reminisced about her dad. It was obvious that they had known James Lorde as a man in his own right, had chatted to him on an adult level and knew how he thought and felt about the world. Whereas Jenna had only ever known him as the dad who had been too busy running his precious nightclub, Zenith, to spend more than the occasional hour with his children every now and then. Who had nipped in and out of the house as if visiting an hotel, giving his wife perfunctory kisses on the cheek in passing and leaving the scent of Old Spice in his wake. But the man his friends talked of, who had, apparently, been the life and soul of every gathering and would give you the shirt off his back; the man who had kept the collection of porn magazines that Jenna had found hidden in his wardrobe when she was clearing the house out, who had left dirty clothes scattered around his bedroom floor, a stack of unpaid bills in the kitchen drawer, and a whole heap of empty whisky bottles beside his bed – she didn't know *that* man at all.

But, newly discovered secrets and childhood memories aside, Jenna still loved James Lorde as deeply as ever. She might not have seen him as often as her friends had seen their fathers while they were growing up, but he had always been a hero to her. A strapping man with a magical laugh, who would toss her into the air and then catch her and give her a big cuddle, who'd slip them money to buy their mum a birthday or Christmas present, who'd herd them all into the car on a Saturday afternoon and drop them off at the cinema. Even when she grew up and moved away from home, it was her dad that she still turned to for advice; him that she would phone whenever she needed a comforting voice in her ear.

Claudia had always been jealous of their relationship, calling Jenna a daddy's girl and accusing her of playing up to the fact that she was her father's favourite. But Jenna had never seen it like that – not until the will was read, and she learned that he'd left Zenith solely to her.

Wracked with guilt that Claudia might have been right all along, Jenna rang her sister, intending to tell her that she would sign half of the club over to her as soon as she could. But she immediately changed her mind when Claudia laid into her before she had a chance to say a word, calling her a gold-digging, grave-robbing tramp. Anyway, she figured that her dad must have done it this way on purpose: not because Jenna was his favourite, but because he'd known that Claudia would put the club on the market before the soil was settled on his coffin – which was exactly what she had insisted Jenna should do with the tiny semi in Rusholme where they had grown up and which he'd left to them both.

Not that Claudia would get much out of it when it went, because their dad had obviously done nothing to it after their mum had died and Jenna had left. The neglect showed in everything from the gate hanging off its hinges to the overgrown garden, from the rotting door and window frames to the stale odour of man-alone that tainted the air inside.

But, honoured as she was that her dad had trusted her enough to leave his club in her hands, there was just one major problem for Jenna: she didn't actually want it.

Taking it on would mean having to move back to Manchester, which she really didn't want to do. And she didn't even know if she was capable of running a nightclub, anyway. She'd never taken the slightest interest in the place when she'd lived here, and had resisted her dad's efforts to bring her in and show her the ropes, because she and her friends preferred the trendier student bars with their cut-price booze and cool live bands. And then she'd moved to London, which was worlds apart from Manchester when it came to club-life, so she was still none the wiser.

But then, her dad couldn't have known what *he* was doing when he started out, either, and he'd managed to keep it going for twenty years. And he'd done all the hard work, so all she'd have to do would be to walk in and pick up where he'd left off.

She just didn't *want* to.

But how could she walk away without even trying, when her dad had obviously wanted her to make a go of it?

Knowing that she owed it to him to at least consider it, Jenna decided to go down to the club and take a good look around. If her instincts told her to give it a shot, then fine, she would roll her sleeves up and throw her heart and soul into it, like her dad before her. But if they said no, she would put it up for sale. And she was sure that her dad would understand, as long as she'd given it real consideration first.

Jenna took a cab to the club and her heart sank before it had even pulled up to the kerb. Her dad had obviously missed the regeneration bandwagon when it had rolled into town after the bombings a few years back because, compared to all the bright new façades surrounding it, the club looked dated and scruffy. It had the same old scarred black doors as when he'd first bought it, and the wall was covered in messy posters, leaflets and graffiti.

It was so seedy and neglected that Jenna couldn't imagine anybody making an effort to come here for a night out. In fact, the only good thing about it was the location: smack in the middle of Deansgate, which had taken a massive upturn in recent years and was now chock-full of upmarket wine and coffee bars and swanky new apartment blocks. If she did end up selling – which was looking very, *very* likely – she'd get more for the postcode than for the actual building.

Using the keys that the solicitor had given her she unlocked the door and went inside. She'd only ever been here a couple of times, and that had been during opening hours when it was fully lit and crammed with people, with music pumping out at an incredible volume. Standing in the foyer now, it just felt cold, dark, and far too quiet.

Shivering, Jenna went through to the clubroom itself, which was pitch dark and really quite eerie. Propping the door open with a chair, she used the sparse light from the foyer to find her way to the lights control box which the solicitor had told her was behind the bar. Flicking switches at random, she had just found the one for the overhead lights when a door opened behind her and a man walked in.

Leaping back when he saw her, he cried, 'Holy *shit*! You scared the crap out of me!' Patting his chest then, he gave her a sheepish grin. 'Guess you're not an armed robber, huh?'

'Definitely not,' Jenna assured him, amused that he seemed even more alarmed than she was – he was lean and muscular and looked quite capable of taking care of himself. He was also very good-looking, she noticed. Mixed-race, clean-shaven, with ice-white teeth, unusual blue eyes and a soft American accent.

And a broad gold wedding band on the third finger of his left hand, which he wasn't trying to hide – unlike Jason, who had hidden his for six long years, the bastard!

Shaking the irritating thought of Jason out of her head, she asked the man if he worked here.

'Weekends,' he said, presuming her to be one of the waitresses who worked mid-week when DJs Fiddy or Marky Day had their slots. 'Shame we had to shut down, isn't it?' he murmured then, gazing around the room. 'It's a great place. And James was pretty cool for an old guy. But nothing lasts for ever, right?'

Jenna nodded her agreement, liking him because he'd obviously liked her dad.

'It's Vibes, by the way.' He held out his hand. 'One of the DJs – or, at least, I *was*.'

'Jenna,' she told him, shaking it. 'You say the club's been closed down?' she asked then, wondering why the solicitor hadn't told her about that.

'Yeah, the day James died,' Vibes said, frowning quizzically. 'Look, sorry, I don't mean to be rude, but shouldn't you already know that if you work here?'

'I'm the old guy's daughter,' Jenna told him, smiling when she saw the information sink in and show up in his eyes.

'For real?' Drawing his head back, he peered at her face, then nodded. 'Yeah, I guess I can see it. You've got the same nose.'

But not the same anything else, he thought, because she was absolutely stunning.

Snapping himself out of it, he said, 'So I take it you're the new owner, then, huh? And you're like – what? Just checking the place out?'

'Something like that,' Jenna replied. 'I wanted to see what my instincts told me before I made any decisions.'

'And what are they telling you?'

'Not sure yet.' She shrugged. 'It'll need major renovations if I do take it on.'

'Worth it, though,' Vibes said, adding quickly, 'not that I'm trying to sway you, or anything, but – well, you know. It's a great place.'

'So you said.'

'Bad habit, repeating myself.' Vibes flashed her a sheepish grin. Then, shrugging, he said, 'Suppose

I'd best let you get on with it, then. Don't mind if I just grab a bit of my gear, do you? Only Fabian's waiting out back to lock up and I don't want to keep him waiting, 'cos I don't think he was planning on sticking around.'

'No, go ahead.'

'Right, well, then.' Another smile. 'See you later, I guess.'

Watching as he strolled across the dance floor and tripped lightly up the stairs to the DJ's booth, Jenna bit her lip thoughtfully. She hadn't even considered what her decision would mean to the staff. If she sold Zenith they would all be out of a job. But even if she'd wanted to keep it open, she doubted that she'd be able to afford all the work that would be needed to bring the club into the twenty-first century. The decor was hideously old-fashioned, the seating worn and faded, the carpets so manky that she'd bet her feet would stick to them, and the bar was a huge wooden monstrosity with brass hand- and footrails that would have looked more at home in an old back-street pub – which was probably where her dad had picked it up from in the first place. It might look great in the alcohol-glazed atmosphere of night, but in this harsh overhead light it resembled a seedy old working men's club.

'Er . . . excuse me, but who are *you*, and how did you get in here?'

Jumping when she heard the accusing voice behind her, Jenna turned around and saw yet another good-looking man. This one was white, with expensively cut blond hair, slate-grey eyes, and a very good-quality suit.

Raising an eyebrow when he saw her face, Fabian King's gaze slid over the rest of her and a slow smile lifted the corner of his lip.

'You must be Fabian?' Jenna said, looking him in the eye, unamused by his leering.

His eyebrow went up another notch. 'How did you know that?'

'Vibes mentioned you.'

'I see.' Flipping into instant cold mode, Fabian frowned. Vibes had obviously tricked him into coming over, thinking he'd be stupid enough to let him in then get straight off and leave him to his little rendezvous. 'I suppose he let you in the front door, did he?' he demanded now, all set to tell her that she could damn well let herself back out the same way.

'No, I let myself in,' Jenna told him coolly, wondering what it had to do with him.

Eyes narrowing with suspicion, Fabian drew his head back and peered at her. 'How?'

'With these.' Jenna showed him the keys.

Scrutinising her face for a moment longer, Fabian clicked his fingers. 'You must be Jim's daughter?'

A flicker of a frown crossed Jenna's brow. She had never in her life heard anybody shorten her dad's name to Jim, and it didn't sound at all right. But then, maybe he'd liked it – who knew? There were plenty of things she hadn't known about him, it seemed.

'So, how are you?' Fabian asked, in a sympathetic *if you need to talk, I'm your man* tone. 'Funeral go all right?'

'I'm fine,' she told him guardedly, not liking the sudden switch from cold suspicion to warm familiarity. 'And it went as well as we could have hoped, thanks.'

'Sorry I couldn't make it,' he went on, as if he'd been invited – which he hadn't, because she didn't even know who he was. 'I would have loved to have been there, but there was too much to do over here, I'm afraid. And, knowing your dad, he'd have preferred me to get this place sorted than to waste time saying goodbye to a coffin.'

'Mmm,' Jenna murmured, thinking that his choice of words was a little insensitive, even if she did agree with what he'd said. Her dad *had* put the club first in life, so why wouldn't he in death?

Pity he hadn't thought to spend a little more money maintaining it, though. But judging by the state of this place *and* the house, he'd obviously let a lot of things slide lately.

'Care to join me for a drink?' Fabian was asking now. Adding, with a cheeky grin, 'Don't worry, I won't charge you.'

Jenna was starting to get irritated. First he'd called her dad 'Jim', which nobody had ever done – not even her mum. And now he was offering out drinks as if *he* owned the place.

Shaking her head, she folded her arms and said, 'No offence, but who exactly *are* you?'

'Fabian King,' he told her over his shoulder as he helped himself to a shot of brandy. 'The manager,' he added, turning back to her.

'*Really*?' She frowned. 'What happened to Frank?'

'Long story. Let's just say he and Jim stopped seeing eye to eye.'

'Dad never said,' Jenna murmured, wondering what could have possibly happened to make them fall out. Frank had been the manager here for over ten years, and her dad had considered him a friend as much as an employee. 'When was this?'

'Last year,' Fabian told her, leaning back against the counter. 'I came in to cover Frank's holiday time, originally. But your dad asked me to stay on, so obviously I said yes. Don't mean to blow my own trumpet,' he went on – doing exactly that, Jenna thought – 'but this place was going steadily downhill before I came on board. It's been a struggle, but we're on our way back up now. Well, we *were*,' he added, giving her a pointed look. 'Still could be, if we don't stay shut too long.'

Taking a sip of his drink now, he carried on looking at her, waiting for her to respond. When she didn't after a moment, he said, 'If you don't mind me asking, what *are* your plans?'

'I haven't made up my mind yet,' Jenna told him evasively. 'But don't worry, I'll let you know as soon as I do.'

Pursing his lips thoughtfully, Fabian nodded slowly. What he really wanted to know was, if she *did* keep the club on, would he still have a job? But she hadn't been very forthcoming, so far, and he sensed that it was probably best not to push her. Yet.

Vibes came back just then, several cases of CDs in his hands and a holdall of vinyl albums over one shoulder. Avoiding making eye contact with Jenna – because Fabian was already doing such a good job of leering at her and Vibes didn't want her to think she'd landed on Planet Lech – he said, 'I'll have to leave the rest for now – if that's okay?'

'It's fine,' Jenna assured him. 'If you want to give me your number, I'll give you a ring and let you know when I'm coming in again.'

'Cool,' Vibes said, putting his stuff down. 'Never remember it off the top of my head, though, so you'll have to give me a minute to find my phone.' Searching through his pockets then, he frowned. 'Damn! Don't tell me I lost it again.'

'Don't worry about it,' Fabian jumped in quickly. 'I'll have to take Jenna up to the office to show her the books anyway, so I'll give it to her from the file. You can get off now, if you're done,' he said then, giving Vibes a pointed look. 'I'll take it from here.'

Giving him a knowing half-smile, Vibes shared a brief conspiratorial look with Jenna which conveyed his question: *Are you all right with that?* and her answer: *Don't worry, I can handle him.*

'I'll leave you to it, then,' he said, picking up his things. 'Nice meeting you, Jenna.'

'You, too. I'll give you a ring within the week.'

'Much appreciated.' Nodding goodbye, Vibes opened the door and left.

Relaxing now that the competition for Jenna's attention was gone, Fabian downed what was left of his drink and put the glass in the small sink. Then, waving her through the opening in the counter, he said, 'Shall we?'

Jenna hadn't intended to stay long, but she decided that she might as well get this over with now rather than have to arrange to come back and meet Fabian at another time. He had the air of a man who was used to women falling all over themselves to get to him, and – handsome as he undoubtedly was – she found that kind of arrogant presumption incredibly off-putting.

Unlocking a door marked *Private*, which led to the upper floor where the offices, staff bathroom and boardroom were located, Fabian led her to an office part-way along the first-floor corridor.

'This was your dad's,' he told her, unlocking the door and reaching in to switch the light on. 'Sorry about the mess, but we thought we'd best leave it alone for the time being. He was in the middle of having an en-suite bathroom built into the cupboard space, you see, but they hadn't quite finished when he died.'

Stepping in, Jenna gazed around in dismay. Fabian was right about the mess, but it wasn't the builders' debris that bothered her, it was the personal stuff. Just like at the house, there were dirty clothes, newspapers, and empty whisky bottles all over the place.

'Was he sleeping here?' she asked, frowning when she noticed the sleeping bag and pillow spread out on the small leather couch.

'He'd started to over the last couple of months,' Fabian replied, shrugging as he added, 'I guess he just got too tired to bother going home towards the end. But he figured he had everything he needed close at hand, so he was fine with it.'

Jenna felt the guilt that was already eating away at her intensify. How could she have let her dad come to this? He must have been feeling really ill, but he'd never said a word. All those times she'd phoned him, crying over Jason and ranting about her petty little troubles, he'd never once told her to shut up, or pointed out that there were worse things that could happen – like losing the will to go home to your own bed at night.

Seeing the distress in her eyes, Fabian gave her a reassuring pat on the arm, telling her gently, 'If it's any consolation, I was keeping an eye on him. And I know it looks bad, but, honestly, he was doing okay, so don't upset yourself.'

Sighing, Jenna nodded. 'Thanks.'

'No problem.' Smiling, Fabian edged past her into the room and did a quick clean-up – tossing the guilt-inducing sleeping bag and pillow out of sight down the side of the couch and sweeping the mess of coffee cartons and sandwich wrappers off the coffee table into a plastic bag.

Walking behind the desk, Jenna sat down on her dad's battered old leather chair – where, the solicitor had told her, he'd been found the morning after he died. Running her hands over the scuffed arms, she gazed around the room, trying to envisage what he'd been looking at when it happened. The builders' mess to the left, or his own mess to the right, perhaps? Or maybe the framed black and white print on the opposite wall of an old tramp on a park bench, wearing a filthy old coat and a huge toothless smile as he waved his bottle of cider in the air. Had he been thinking about work, she wondered. Or reminiscing about his life, and the family he had all but lost. Or maybe he had simply fallen asleep and slipped away with his dreams.

Jerked back to the here and now when Fabian took several folders out of the filing cabinet and dropped them onto the desk, Jenna sat up straighter and tried to focus her attention as, for the next hour, he talked her through the paper life of the club. But the more she heard, the more concerned she became, because it seemed that her dad had died owing thousands.

'The drinks suppliers are by far the biggest creditors,' Fabian told her. 'But I've put them in the picture about the situation and they've agreed to hang fire until we know where we're at.'

'What about these?' Jenna asked, reaching for the letters that her father had obviously been ignoring because he hadn't even opened them. They were from the electricity company, the water board and BT, all threatening imminent disconnection and legal action to recover the debts.

'I have spoken to them, but you should probably think about sorting them out quickly to save having everything cut off and having to pay reconnection fees,' Fabian said. 'Everything else is in order, and the staff are paid to date,' he went on, adding, 'but we shouldn't leave them hanging too long, because some of them have already found new jobs, and it might not be so easy to tempt them to come back once they get settled.'

'Come back?' Jenna gazed at him, a deep frown creasing her brow. 'For what?'

'When we reopen,' Fabian said, jumping in at the deep end. However she responded, at least he'd know where he stood.

'I'm not sure it's even worth considering,' Jenna murmured, clasping her hands together. 'It would cost an absolute fortune to fix it up. And if most of the staff have already gone, what's the point?'

'I know it's a lot to take in, but it looks far worse than it actually is,' Fabian said. 'We went through a bit of a rough patch, but it's been getting better, and we've seen a massive upturn in customer numbers since we got the new DJs in. Particularly Vibes,' he added truthfully – much as it pained him to compliment the man. 'Fiddy and Marky Day are good, but Vibes is the best in Manchester, without a doubt. And that's half the battle won, because people don't go to clubs for the quality of the booze or the look of the place – they go to see their favourite DJs.'

'And he's that good?' Jenna asked doubtfully, sure that Fabian was just doing a hard sell because he wanted her to keep the club on.

'The best,' he affirmed. 'You'd have to see him in action to believe it. And it's not just women who love him, the other DJs pop in if they get a chance on their nights off to see what he's playing – and that doesn't happen unless they're really hot. Believe me, the guy is solid *gold*.'

Smiling at his description, Jenna said, 'Well, I'm sure you're right, but I can't see him being the answer to this mess.'

'He's a definite part of the solution,' Fabian countered bluntly. 'With a bit of effort, we could take this place to the top.'

'With respect,' Jenna said, 'I think it's going to take a damn sight more than that. *I* wouldn't go out of my way to come here – not when there are so many *decent* clubs in town to choose from. It looks disgusting from the outside, and it's absolutely horrible inside.'

'Your dad loved it,' Fabian persisted. 'And, all right, so, he let it slip a bit cosmetically, but there's a real soul to the place.'

'It's a dive,' Jenna cut in. 'My dad hasn't changed a single thing since he bought it.'

'Because he loved it exactly as it was,' Fabian pointed out. 'But it's yours now, so you can do whatever you like with it. Imagine it . . .' he went on, getting into his stride now. 'You get the builders and decorators in to revamp the interior, then you get the outside cleaned up, have a new door and sign fitted, and – *voilà*! It looks amazing, and everybody wants in.'

Sighing, because she was getting tired now, Jenna held up her hands to stop him. 'Look, I appreciate the advice, but I just can't see it, to be honest. I was considering selling up before I came here today, and now I've seen the state of it I really think that's the best bet.'

Peering at her across the desk, Fabian shrugged. 'It's your decision ultimately. But if you don't mind a bit more advice, I'd really think about it before you jump into putting it onto the market just yet, or you might end up losing out *big* time.'

'I've already thought about that,' Jenna told him. 'And I reckon I should get a fair price just for the location.'

Shaking his head slowly, Fabian said, 'I don't think you understand what I'm getting at. It's a given that the club's in dire need of modernisation, but you've got no idea what kind of shape it's in below the surface. A potential buyer would contract a surveyor to do a thorough inspection, and if they concluded that it's in as bad shape structurally as it is cosmetically, they'd have no option but to report it to the relevant authorities – and you might find yourself slapped with a condemnation order. If *that* happened, not only would you not be allowed to sell, you'd have to pay for the repairs – or, worse, demolition, which would be a *major* expense. Is that a risk you're willing to take?'

'Bloody hell!' Jenna gasped. 'Could that really happen?'

'I've seen it happen to places in better shape than this,' Fabian replied. Shrugging then, he said, 'Your choice, but I know what I'd do if it was me. I'd keep it on and bring it up to scratch, then open up and see how it went for a year or so. And if I still didn't want it at the end of that, *then* I'd think about selling, because it would be worth far more by then.'

Shaking her head, Jenna slumped despairingly down in her seat. There was an undeniable logic to what he'd said, but she just didn't want to move back to Manchester permanently. She'd only been toying with the idea because of the guilt factor, but if she did as Fabian was advising, she'd have no choice but to come back.

'Look, why don't you take some time to think it over?' Fabian suggested, seeing that she was becoming bogged down with it. 'It's still going to be here tomorrow, isn't it?'

'I suppose so,' Jenna agreed, sighing heavily.

Her dad had obviously thought he was doing

a wonderful thing by her but, by *God*, she wished he hadn't bothered!

'Out of interest,' she said, reaching for her bag, 'can I ask why you closed down before you knew what I was going to do? Surely the staff would have been better off if you'd stayed open until I'd got here, and there'd have still been money coming in to pay off those debts.'

'I couldn't,' Fabian told her. 'Your dad held the licence, so it would have been illegal to sell alcohol or provide entertainment. I could have applied for a temporary change of DPS, but the solicitor was away and his secretary wouldn't give me your number so I couldn't get hold of you to get your authorisation.'

'What's a DPS?'

'Designated Premises Supervisor,' Fabian explained. '*You* could apply for it now, if you wanted to. Or, if you didn't want the hassle, you could okay it for *me* to do it. It is a bit of a ball-ache, though,' he said then – seeming, Jenna thought, to be trying to persuade her to do the latter. 'The police do a thorough background check on you, for convictions and what-have-you. And then the licensing panel demand all sorts of references and credit checks and stuff. But I don't mind putting myself through it if you can't face it.'

'I have nothing to hide from the police,' Jenna

told him, smiling as she stood up. 'Anyway, thanks for your help, I really appreciate it.'

'Any time,' Fabian said. 'And if you need to talk before I see you again, feel free to give me a ring.' Reaching for a notepad, he jotted two numbers down and handed them to her. 'Home and mobile – you'll always catch me on one or the other. Day *or* night,' he added with a slow half-smile. 'I'm a very light sleeper.'

Thanking him, Jenna slipped the numbers into her bag. Then, remembering that she'd promised to ring Vibes, she located his number in the staff file and wrote it down.

'Right, then,' she said when she'd done. 'I'll get back to you as soon as I've made a decision. And in the meantime, I'll sort out those bills.'

'Good idea,' Fabian said, getting up to open the door.

Walking her down to the front door then, he let her out and waved her off, calling, 'See you soon – I hope.'

Arriving back at her dad's house a short time later, Jenna groaned when she saw the *For Sale* sign in the garden. The estate agent had been round earlier that morning to do a valuation, but she hadn't expected him to come back so soon. It felt like she was being rushed from all sides: Claudia rushing her to sell up; Fabian rushing her into making a decision on the club; and now the estate agent rushing her out of house and home.

Not that she *wanted* the house, because it held far too many painful memories for her to ever be truly comfortable there. But if she was going to be forced into staying around she'd need somewhere to sleep at night, and if the house went as quickly as the estate agent had predicted she'd find herself shelling out for hotels before she knew it – and that was an expense she definitely didn't need right now.

Making herself a coffee, she carried it through to the lounge and sat down. Kicking off her shoes, she reached for the phone and dialled the solicitor's number, hoping to sound him out about the stuff she'd discussed with Fabian. Getting no answer, she called Ruth Wolff instead.

Ruth was the only person she could think of who had known her dad for longer than she herself had. Almost seventy years old, she was still as sharp as a butcher's knife. She was also one of the most honest, no-nonsense people Jenna had ever met and, having been married to a solicitor for so long, she would have much more of an idea about the legal aspects of this situation than Jenna.

'Hate to say it,' Ruth said when Jenna had explained everything. 'But it looks like this manager chappie might be right about it being more trouble than it's worth trying to sell. A surveyor *would* be duty-bound to report a dangerous structure to the local authorities. And, let's face it, my love, your father was a one for cutting corners – bless him – so you could be opening a very large can of worms if you proceed with the idea of selling.'

'Great,' Jenna muttered. 'So I'm stuck with it.'

'Is that really such a bad thing?' Ruth asked quietly. 'Your dad wanted you to have it more than anything in the world. We were discussing it after his first heart attack, a couple of months ago, and he told me—'

'*Sorry*?' Jenna interrupted. 'Did you just say his *first* heart attack?'

'Ah . . .' Ruth murmured guiltily. 'Sorry, my love. You weren't supposed to hear that.'

Jenna felt as if she'd been punched in the stomach. 'Why didn't anybody tell me?'

'Because he didn't want to worry you,' Ruth told her gently. 'You'd had a hellish few months, but you seemed to be on the up and he didn't want to drag you back down.'

'Did he think I was so wrapped up in my own problems that I wouldn't want to know something like *that*?' Jenna gasped incredulously. 'Christ, Ruth, I wouldn't have given any of that a second thought if I'd known that my dad needed me. I'd have come straight home to look after him.'

'Which was precisely what he didn't want,' Ruth chipped in firmly. 'He couldn't bear the thought of forcing you to play nursemaid to a dying man. You've been doing so well since you left home, and he knew how happy you were – apart from the boyfriend situation, of course. He desperately didn't want you to lose all that.'

'But I've lost it anyway,' Jenna told her. 'I'd already decided to move on and start again.'

'So, why not here?' Ruth suggested smoothly. 'All he ever wanted was for you to be secure, and leaving you the club was his way of guaranteeing that. Claudia's husband runs his own business, so he didn't want *her* to have it. And, anyway, he knew that if you went for it, you'd be as passionate about it as he was.'

'Doesn't look like I've got much choice, does it?' Jenna murmured resignedly. 'But how am I supposed to pay for it?'

'Oh, that's the easy bit,' Ruth told her breezily, sounding pleased that Jenna was coming around to the idea. 'You honour the debts before anybody takes legal action. Then, once you've got a clean credit rating, you use the club as collateral and secure a bank loan to finance the work that needs doing. Simple.'

*

Jenna's head was spinning by the time she came off the phone. But now that she'd told Ruth she was willing to give it a go there was no turning back. She just hoped it was going to be as simple as Ruth had insisted it would be.

Phoning the bank, she made an appointment for the following morning. Then she called Fabian and told him what she'd decided, and asked him to meet her at the club at noon tomorrow. Then, lastly, she took a deep breath and rang Vibes.

'Oh, right,' he murmured disappointedly when she told him that he should come for the rest of his things tomorrow if he liked. 'I take it you've decided to sell, then?'

Smiling, Jenna said, 'No, I've decided to *keep* it. If all goes well with the bank, I'll be getting the builders in as soon as possible. I just thought I'd better warn you, because I didn't think you'd want your stuff in there while they're ripping the place to pieces.'

'For real?' Vibes sounded delighted. 'Oh, man, that's so cool! Anything I can do to help?'

'Well, there *is* something, actually,' Jenna said, nervous now, because it was a big favour she was about to ask of him. 'Fabian reckons it could take about four months to get everything done if we started now, so I know I'll probably lose most of the staff because they won't be able to hold out for that long. But I really, really don't want to lose *you*, so I was wondering if you'd consider keeping your diary clear for when we reopen? Only thing is . . . I, er, don't think I'd be able to pay you a full wage while the work's being done.'

'Hey, don't even worry about that,' Vibes told her without hesitation. 'Money ain't an issue for any of the DJs, 'cos we all do other residencies on our free nights. You just do what you got to do, and let me know when you're ready for me. To come back, that is,' he added quickly, kicking himself for sounding like he was hitting on her. 'Anyway, four months is perfect timing for the party.'

'Sorry?' Jenna said, not understanding what he was getting at, because she hadn't mentioned a party.

'It's September now,' Vibes explained. 'So four months would take us to the beginning of January – and what better night than New Year's Eve for a reopening party? You'd have plenty of time to plan it, and you could invite all the local celebrities. It'd be fantastic publicity.'

'I don't know any celebrities,' Jenna admitted, disappointed because it really had sounded like a great idea.

'Leave that to Fabian,' Vibes told her knowingly. 'I guarantee he'll come up trumps. But do yourself a favour, and tell him it was your idea.'

'What's wrong with telling him the truth?'

'Let's just say I know enough about him to know he'd be more receptive if it came from you.'

Shrugging, Jenna said, 'Okay, whatever you think best.' Then, 'Right, well, I guess I'll see you tomorrow, then.'

'Looking forward to it,' Vibes said softly. 'Later, Princess.'

Smiling, Jenna said goodbye and hung up. What a lovely man. And what a lucky lady his wife was, because she obviously had nothing to worry about, judging by the way he'd corrected himself just now to make sure that Jenna didn't think he was flirting with her. She really respected him for that.

And resented Jason all the more.

But she wasn't going to think about him any more. From now on, she was going to put all her time and effort into the club.

Her club.

2

Jenna was standing with Fabian inside the club-room door, greeting people as they arrived. She'd been convinced that none of the celebrities he'd invited would turn up, sure that they'd have far better things to do than try out what was in effect a brand new club, on the biggest night of the year. Amazingly, most had decided to chance it – which was a huge relief. And somebody had obviously tipped the press off, because several photographers had set up camp across the road and were busy snapping everyone who came in – which would be fantastic publicity when the papers hit the stands in the morning, just as Vibes had predicted.

All in all, everything seemed to be going really well so far. But Jenna was particularly impressed with Fabian now that she'd seen him in action. He'd been indefatigable in the gruelling months leading up to this, taking on every challenge with gusto. Jenna had done her bit, but Fabian had far surpassed her in energy and imagination. And he was totally on the ball tonight – which was a minor miracle, Jenna thought, considering he'd been at the club from early this morning, making sure that everything and everyone was ready.

His customer-service skills were exceptional. He'd known every one of the guests' names without once referring to the list and had treated them all like old friends, subtly adjusting his manner to suit their individual status: respectful to the older, more established stars, like Glenda Jackson and John Savident; suave and sophisticated for Victoria Beckham's group; cool and flirtatious with Charlotte Church and her gal-pals, the pretty girls from *Coronation Street*, and the three blondes who arrived with Chase Mann – but not too much so with the latter, in case they came back at a later date celeb-less and expected preferential treatment; then matey with Chase himself, having met him a few times previously.

'You really enjoy this, don't you?' Jenna said when they'd wished Chase and his entourage a Happy New Year and had one of the waiters escort them to the VIP lounge.

'Usually,' he replied, adding quietly, 'but not always. Hope you've got a tissue handy.'

'Sorry?'

'The Honourable Drakes.' He nodded towards the main doors, where an older couple were just entering. 'He's got the sweatiest hands I've ever come across – and it's not pleasant, be warned.'

He wasn't wrong, as Jenna soon discovered when Leonard Drake made a beeline for her and grasped one of her hands between both of his. They were fat, wet, and very hot – it felt like being swallowed by an enormous slug.

'You must be Jenny,' he gushed. 'I can't tell you how pleased I am to meet you.' Sighing loudly then, he shook his head sadly. 'Terrible business, your father going like that. He was a good friend, and I shall miss him terribly.'

'Me too,' Jenna said, not bothering to correct his mispronunciation of her name as she slid her hand free. 'I must apologise for not inviting you to the funeral,' she said then, 'but I hadn't had a chance to go through my dad's papers at that point, and I wasn't sure who his friends were – other than those I knew personally, of course. I hope you weren't too offended?'

'Not at all,' Leonard assured her, beaming widely. *So much for Avril's snipe about James Lorde not regarding him as a friend!* 'I'm just delighted to be here now. And very honoured that you thought to invite me.'

Holding her hand away from her dress in case the sweat stained it, Jenna smiled. 'My dad wouldn't have been happy if I'd neglected his friends.'

'Especially not such an eminent one as Mr Drake,' Fabian chipped in, his eyes twinkling as he noticed what Jenna was doing with her hand. 'He was an MP for many years,' he went on – seemingly full of admiration, although Jenna was sure she caught a hint of a mocking tone as he added, 'and quite the local celebrity, too. There was a time when he was never out of the papers or off the TV.'

'That was some time ago now, I'm afraid,' Leonard murmured wistfully. 'Seems they only want young, pretty faces on screen and page these days.'

'Probably a blessing that you retired when you did, then,' Fabian said soothingly. 'Give you a chance to relax and get your privacy back. And I'm sure *you*'re happier to see more of your husband, Mrs Drake?'

'Absolutely,' Avril lied. Turning to Jenna then, she said, 'I'm Avril. Very nice to meet you, dear.'

'You, too. And I hope you have a lovely time with us tonight.'

'Oh, I'm sure we will.' Avril smiled, but the dullness in her eyes didn't escape Jenna. 'I think we've taken up enough of your time,' she said then, linking her arm through her husband's. 'Shall we, Leonard?'

Calling one of the waiters over to escort them

to their table, Jenna watched as they walked away, wondering how an overweight, overly sweaty, rather unattractive man like Leonard had ever managed to net himself such a refined, lovely-looking wife.

'How well did he and my dad actually know each other?' she asked Fabian when they'd gone. 'I invited him because his name was in Dad's address book, but I don't actually remember Dad mentioning him.'

'They were friends,' Fabian said. 'But I think it was more of a business-contact kind of thing. Drake's the son of one of your dad's old college mates.'

'My dad went to college?' Jenna glanced up at him with genuine surprise in her eyes. She hadn't known that. But then, she had discovered a lot of things that she hadn't known since coming back, and this was just the latest in a long line of revelations.

'He was very intelligent,' Fabian told her. 'But he liked people to think he was a simple man, because then they wouldn't have too many expectations and he'd be free to get on with what he loved.'

'The club?' Jenna said, knowing that was what her dad had loved above everything.

'Among other things,' Fabian said, with no

intention of elaborating, because he doubted that Jenna wanted to hear about her dad's extra-curricular activities at the lap-dancing clubs he frequented outside of Zenith.

'So, he met Leonard through *his* dad?' Jenna asked now.

'Yeah, Drake senior introduced them when your dad bought the place, because Leonard was working in the town hall at the time and your dad needed help getting the liquor licence pushed through.' Lowering his voice now, Fabian added, 'Don't quote me, but I got the impression it might not have been entirely above board.'

'Don't be ridiculous,' Jenna snorted, sure that her dad would never have been involved in anything less than legal. If there was one thing she *did* know about him, it was that he respected the police and the law above all else.

'Just the impression I got.' Fabian shrugged. 'Could be wrong.'

'I'm sure you are,' Jenna said with certainty. 'So, what about Mrs Drake?'

'Typical celebrity wife,' Fabian said, scathingly. 'Got used to hubby being the Tory poster boy, and wasn't too happy when his looks went and his career hit the skids and they were pushed out of the limelight. I met them last year when we hosted some old judge's retirement party in the boardroom, and she was miserable as sin that night, too.'

Pursing her lips thoughtfully, Jenna said, 'I thought she seemed more sad than miserable.'

'Same thing, isn't it?' Fabian gave her a sly grin. 'Anyway, wipe your hands. You're about to meet a real live movie star.'

'Oh?' Raising an eyebrow, Jenna looked around. 'Who?'

'Melody Fisher.' Fabian nodded in the direction of the group who were just entering the foyer.

Jenna watched as the woman strolled in, pausing – seemingly innocently, although it just *had* to be deliberate, Jenna thought – directly beneath one of the overhead spots to light the cigarette that one of the men had just given her. Seeming not to notice that every male tongue was hanging out, she arched her lovely neck and blew her smoke elegantly into the air.

'Stunning, isn't she?' Fabian whispered, folding his arms to watch the show.

'Gorgeous,' Jenna agreed. The woman had the most incredible figure she'd ever seen: tiny waist, endless legs, and amazing breasts. 'I don't think I know her, though.'

'You will,' Fabian assured her. 'She was in a Sandra Bullock movie last year, and another with George Clooney after that. She's being tipped for the big time, by all accounts. Definitely had surgery, though,' he added conspiratorially. 'But she's been living in the States, and it's practically compulsory over there, isn't it?'

Smiling, because that was exactly the kind of thing a woman would have said, Jenna asked who the men were.

'Little one's her boyfriend, Tony Allen,' Fabian said, lowering his voice. 'Don't know too much about him except that he's American. Big one's rumoured to be a minder.'

'Rumoured?' Jenna glanced up at him amusedly. 'By who?'

'My sources.' Tapping a finger to his nose, Fabian gave her a secretive smile. 'Pays to keep your ear to the ground in this game, you know. How else do you think I found out they were here, and where they were staying so that I could send them an invitation?'

Shushing her then, he stepped forward to greet the trio as they approached.

'So glad you could make it, Ms Fisher,' he cooed, reaching for Melody's hand and lightly touching his lips to it. 'And good evening to you, too, Mr Allen. Welcome to Zenith, and may I—'

'Do I know you?' Tony cut him off rudely, sizing him up and deciding that he was a creep.

'Fabian King – manager of Zenith,' he said,

holding the smile in place despite taking an instant dislike to the other man. 'And this,' he gestured towards Jenna, 'is the owner, Jenna Lorde.'

'Owner?' Drawing his head back, Tony gave Jenna a disbelieving look. 'At your age? What are you – like, nineteen, twenty?'

'I'm older than I look,' Jenna assured him, amused by his straightforward manner.

Melody had been busy ogling Fabian, who was the exact opposite of Tony. Fair, fantastic-looking, fit body. Catching the interest in Tony's eyes as he looked at Jenna, however, she snapped her attention back to them, her rival-antennae twitching. Giving Jenna the once-over, she decided there was nothing to worry about. Tony liked blondes, not brunettes, and the tits were natural – and nowhere near big enough.

Giving Jenna a wide smile, Melody stepped forward to make her presence felt, saying, 'Yeah, me too. No one ever believes I'm not twenty-one any more.'

'I can see why,' Jenna lied, certain that Melody had to be at least thirty now that she could see her up close. And Fabian could be right about the surgery. But she was very attractive, even so. 'You have beautiful skin. You'll have to tell me your secret.'

'Do you think so?' Melody raised a hand to her cheek. 'I thought I'd gained a few lines recently.'

'Well, if you have, I can't see them. And *please* tell me you have to suffer to keep your body in that kind of shape?'

'Oh, you're a doll,' Melody purred, her face lighting up. 'You and me are going to get along fine.'

Baffled as to how a couple of words about nothing could bring Melody out of a mood so fast, Tony shook his head.

'I don't know what you just did, but thanks for doing it, 'cos I thought she was going to have a face on her all night. Pleased to meet you, Jenna.'

Surprised by the contrast of soft skin and powerful grip when she shook Tony's hand, Jenna said, 'You, too, Mr Allen.'

'Hey, it's Tony to you,' he scolded. Then, jerking his head, 'And this here's Eddie.'

Glancing up at the man, Jenna said hello, then smiled nervously when he just stared unblinkingly back down at her. She didn't know about Melody being a film star, but *he* looked like he'd just stepped off the set of *The Sopranos*. Tall, and quite muscular, he had an almost feral face, and the darkest eyes she'd ever seen.

'Best get moving before this shower of free-loaders necks all the booze,' Tony said then, casting a scathing glance around the already crowded club-room. 'And what's the chance of getting this racket turned down, 'cos I'm going to get a fuck of a headache if I have to listen to this shit all night.'

'You're so loud, you won't even notice it once you get talking,' Melody contradicted him, rolling her eyes at Jenna. 'Nice meeting you, Jen,' she said then. 'But I'd best get him moving before he bores you to death. We'll catch up later, yeah?' Letting her gaze slide slowly over Fabian then, she said, 'Later, Babe.'

'Who you calling Babe?' Tony demanded as she took his arm and tugged him through the room.

'It's a girl thing,' she assured him breezily. 'We all do it.'

'Well, I don't like it, so quit it.'

'Okay, Babe.'

'Don't fucking push it, Mel!'

Laughing as their voices faded into the crowd, Jenna shook her head. 'They were sweet, weren't they?'

'Oh, you're good,' Fabian drawled, folding his arms and giving her a wry smile. 'I saw the way you stroked her little ego.'

'I don't know what you're talking about. Women like being complimented, that's all.'

'Yeah, I know. But other women don't normally pull it off that good. They usually make it sound sarcastic, but even *I'd* have believed that you really thought she was that young.'

'Well, if it makes her happy . . . ?' Shrugging, Jenna glanced at her watch. 'Right, I'll leave you to it, if you don't mind. I want to have a word with Jacko about replacing the doormen before it gets too late. Will you be all right by yourself?'

'I'll be fine,' Fabian assured her. 'Most of the guests are here now, anyway, so I think I'll give the go-ahead to let the motleys in.'

'*Paying customers*,' Jenna corrected him, giving him a mock-stern look before walking away.

Narrowing his eyes, Fabian gazed after her. That was the longest he'd spent with her on a one-to-one basis since she'd taken over, and she'd surprised him. In the months following her dad's funeral, she'd been so stressed that she hadn't bothered with make-up, and had practically lived in her jeans. Even in that raw state she'd been a looker, but what an absolute *babe* she was when she made the effort. And now that she'd chilled out, she was way more approachable than he'd initially thought. And if this was the real her, he reckoned that things were definitely going to pick up around here – just so long as she didn't start interfering. She might own the place, but *he* called the shots – and that was exactly how he intended to keep it.

Jacko, the head of security, was checking the fire doors on the lower floor when Jenna found him.

Asking him to send some of his boys out to replace Bobby and Flex, she went to the bar and called Maurice over to ask if he'd remembered to send a drink up to Vibes.

Giving her a defiant *why-are-you-bothering-me-with-this-nonsense* look, Maurice said, 'Who?'

'The DJ,' Jenna reminded him, knowing full well that he knew exactly who she was talking about.

'Oh, *him*,' Maurice replied dismissively, already turning away. 'No. I forgot.'

Biting down on her irritation, Jenna called out firmly, 'Two glasses of champagne, please, Maurice.'

She saw the slight tensing of his shoulders, and guessed – rightly – that he was dying to tell her to piss off and get it herself. But if he thought she was going to roll over and let him disrespect her, he had another think coming.

Thanking him when he placed the drinks on the counter, Jenna nodded towards a small pile of broken glass in the corner beside the fridge.

'Clean that up before somebody slips on it, would you?'

Nostrils twitching, Maurice pursed his lips and glared at her.

Raising an eyebrow when several seconds had passed and he still hadn't moved, Jenna said, 'You *do* know where the dustpan is, don't you? Only

I'd like you to do it *now*, before somebody cuts themselves and sues me for negligence.'

Giving a triumphant small smile when Maurice reached under the counter for the hand-brush, she picked up the glasses and walked away. She didn't want to add insult to injury by standing over him while he did it, but he'd needed to be put in his place – even if it *had* made her legs feel like jelly.

God, it was hard running your own business. But kind of fun once you got into the swing of it.

Carrying the champagne carefully up the narrow stairs to the DJ's booth, Jenna tapped on the door and let herself in. Vibes was leaning over the console, bobbing his head to the beat in his headphones. He smiled when he saw her, his teeth dazzling in the fluorescent lights pulsing through the window.

'Hope I'm not disturbing you,' she whispered, conscious of the microphone. 'But I thought you must need a drink by now?'

Taking the headphones off, Vibes nodded towards a case of bottled water on the ledge behind her.

'I tend to stick to that when I'm working. But I'll make an exception, seeing as it's New Year.' Taking one of the glasses, he raised it. 'Hope it's a good one, Princess.'

'Me, too.' Clinking her glass against his, Jenna

took a sip. The heat in the small room enveloped her like a damp blanket. 'God, it's boiling in here,' she said, fanning a hand in front of her face. 'How do you stand it?'

'It's the equipment,' Vibes told her, wiping his brow on the fluffy white towel looped around his neck. 'There's nothing you can do about it, so you just get used to it.'

Shivering as a bead of sweat trickled down her back, Jenna said, 'Do you want me to get you a fan?'

'Nah.' Vibes shook his head. 'They just stir it up and make you feel sick. And they're noisy as all hell, which don't sound too good over the mike. But thanks for the thought.'

'Let me know if you change your mind,' Jenna said, taking another sip of her drink. Gazing out at the rapturous faces on the dance floor below, she said, 'I don't think I've ever been to a club before where everyone's dancing before they're even half drunk. I guess you *must* be as good as they say, huh?'

'Why, thank you, kind lady.' Vibes gave her a playful grin. 'Does that mean I get a raise?'

'Please say you're joking,' she groaned, gripping her glass a little tighter.

Jenna wasn't even paying *herself* yet – and probably wouldn't be able to for some time to come, because she was up to her neck with bank-loan repayments and the rent on her apartment. But she couldn't afford to lose Vibes. Fabian had told her that great DJs were stars in their own right, and that their fans followed them to whichever club they were playing at. She was lucky that Vibes had agreed to come back after she'd effectively laid him off for the four months it had taken to refurbish Zenith, but if she lost him now she'd probably lose most of her customers, too.

Seeing the fear in her eyes, Vibes quickly assured her that he *was* joking – and wondered, not for the first time, if her skin was as soft to the touch as it looked.

Shaking the thought away, he reminded himself that there was no point thinking like that. Jenna was sweet, gorgeous, and intelligent – and not in the least bit flirtatious, unlike most of the British women he'd met so far. He didn't know if it was the American accent that they got off on, or just that they had never seen a black guy with blue eyes before, but he'd been inundated with phone numbers and blatant propositions since coming over here. And while he would have lapped the attention up a few years back, now it just turned him off.

Taking the hint when he finished his drink and reached for his headphones, Jenna picked up his glass and said, 'I suppose I should get back out there and mingle. Can't hide away up here all night, can I? See you later.'

'Later, Princess,' Vibes said, pulling the headphones down over his ears and flipping the mike on to introduce the next track.

Jenna was smiling as she went back down the stairs. She liked Vibes. He was polite, gentlemanly, and really easy to be around – and to look at, of course. The perfect man, in fact. Now if only she could find one like him for herself, she'd be laughing.

But decent *single* men were as hard to find as great DJs, in her experience. And you couldn't just take their word for it when you *did* find one – as she had learned to her cost with Jason.

But there was no point raking over *those* old coals. What was done was done, and she just had to make sure that she never made the same mistake again.

3

The party was in full swing by two; everybody buzzing as they soaked up the booze and lost their inhibitions.

Great for the club, but not so good for Fabian, who had managed to get himself hijacked by a group of frisky older women. He'd tried to get away, but they seemed intent on holding him hostage on the dance floor, and every time one let go of his hand another one snatched it up.

The one he was with now was actually making him feel ill, rubbing her saggy breasts against him and winking at him seductively. Convinced that she was just waiting for the chance to go in for a full-on snog, he broke free after their third dance and lied that he'd just been summoned by his boss from across the room.

Escorting the woman back to her table, it was all Fabian could do not to scream when one of the friends grabbed him and said, 'Me next. Don't you go and forget about me, now.'

Promising to come right back as soon as he could, he rushed to the safety of his office, wondering what the hell the old witches were doing here, anyway. They weren't on the guest list, so they must have paid to get in. But surely they should be tucked up in bed with their cocoas by now, not out on the town flirting with men young enough to be their great-grandsons!

Locking the door in case anybody walked in on him, he opened his wall safe and took out a small bag of coke. Chopping a thin line on the mirror, he snorted it quickly and leaned his head back to savour the instant tension-easing buzz.

Sorted, Fabian put everything away and headed back down to the club floor with a fresh swagger in his step. Pretending that he hadn't seen the old biddies when they started waving their bingo wings at him, he headed on up to the VIP lounge to give his celebrity friends a dose of the King treatment.

Sitting at her table, surrounded by some of the brightest stars of British stage and screen, Melody should have been in her element. She wasn't happy though – as they would have known if they'd bothered to look at her. But none of them *had* bothered, which was precisely why she was so pissed off. It wasn't like she expected to be the centre of attention or anything, but there was no excuse for people being so rude as to totally ignore her.

She blamed Tony.

Ever since they'd landed two weeks ago, they couldn't go anywhere without people falling all over themselves to talk to him. And once they did, they were hooked. He'd had so many invitations to parties since they'd got here, it wasn't even funny. Everyone in Manchester seemed to think he was some kind of big shot and wanted to be his new best friend, and that really peeved Melody, because he was nothing but a big-talking hood who liked to splash the cash. Whereas *she* had two hit movies on her CV – and many more to come, if the critics who had been calling her *America's Next Big Thing* were right.

Melody had been so pleased when the invitation for tonight's party had arrived at the hotel in *her* name; thrilled that at *last* somebody had realised she was alive and kicking in Tony's shadow. But the thrill hadn't lasted long once they'd got here, because Tony only had to open that big mouth of his for the spotlight to turn firmly his way.

Brenda Thompson had been the first to invite herself to join them. She'd sailed up to their table, almost knocking Melody clean off her chair in her effort to squeeze herself in beside Tony.

'Don't mind if I join you, do you?' she'd asked,

in the breathy rasp that Melody had spent hours copying as a teenager. 'But I simply *had* to meet the man behind that wonderfully evocative accent. New York – am I right?'

For a very brief moment, Melody had been thrilled to be in the presence of her long-time acting idol. But that had soon changed when she'd tried to join in the conversation and received the frosty raising of a pencil-thin eyebrow and a turned back in return. She was so offended that she nearly lamped the old cow!

And her mood hadn't improved when two bitches from a top soap came along and proceeded to air-kiss their 'good pal' Brenda and suck up to Tony, while looking down their noses at Melody. Followed by some ugly old Lovie-Dahling actor who was more plastic than Cher, and his *personal assistant*, Clive. Like Clive wasn't his boyfriend – *much*!

Chase Mann was the last straw. Despite slagging him off when they'd seen him at the hotel a couple of days back, Tony had greeted him like a long-lost mate tonight. Melody hadn't minded at first, because she'd thought that Chase would at least talk to her, given that they were closer in age and attractiveness than the rest of these idiots. But he was so stoned that he'd barely even glanced at her. And the tarty little slappers who were sticking to him like gold-digging leeches wound her up by giggling and whispering behind their hands whenever they looked at her.

Shifting irritably in her chair now, Melody glared at Tony, but he was too busy telling jokes to notice. So she gazed down at the crowded dance floor instead, toying with the idea of grabbing a good-looking man and dragging him off to the toilets for a revenge fuck. Tony would notice *that*, she was sure.

Yeah, and then he'd kill me – stone, no messing dead! These people might think he was a charming teddy bear of a man, but Melody knew *exactly* what he was capable of.

Sighing loudly, she snatched up one of the champagne bottles that were cluttering the table and poured herself a large glassful. She might as well get hammered if she had to sit here listening to Tony's boring stories all night, and watching these shitty never-really-weres laughing their facelifts off. Boring, boring, boring!

Fabian arrived at that exact moment.

'How's everyone doing?' he asked loudly, a big smile on his handsome face.

'Having a blast,' Tony grunted, giving him the cold eye. Glancing past him then, he frowned. 'Where's the boss lady?'

'She'll come and say hello as soon as she gets a chance,' Fabian assured him. 'Anything I can do in the meantime?'

'Nah, don't trouble yourself.'

Narrowing his eyes slightly, Fabian said, 'Right, well, I'll leave you to it, then.' *And I hope you choke on your free champagne, you dismissive cunt!*

'Just a minute,' Brenda Thompson called out huskily as he started to back away. Picking up her gift pack, she dangled it off the tip of her finger. 'Are you responsible for this?'

'Er, yes,' Fabian admitted. 'Is there a problem?'

'Oh, no, it's delightful,' she purred, reaching for his hand and pulling him towards her. 'I just *adore* the lighter,' she said then, gazing seductively into his eyes. 'And the perfume smells divine. But I was wondering . . .'

Peering at Fabian when he dipped his head to listen to whatever Brenda was saying, Melody felt a sickening tug in her gut when she noticed the fine white traces under his nose. Coke! Oh, God, what she wouldn't give to get her hands on some of *that* right now. But there was no chance of that with Tony keeping tabs on her. According to Mr Big Shot, '*Ladies don't touch that shit*.'

'What's up with your mush?' Tony asked out of the corner of his mouth, making her jump.

'Nothing,' Melody snapped, pushing her chair back with a dull scrape. 'I'm just fed up of all this yakking, that's all. I'm off for a dance.'

'Not on your own, you're not,' he hissed, gripping her wrist.

'Come with me, then,' she hissed back, knowing full well that he wouldn't.

Flashing her a warning glare, he said, 'You know I don't go for all that jiggy-jiggy shit. But I ain't letting you loose with all them chancers down there, so forget it.'

'What . . . so, now you don't trust me?'

'Sure I do. But you've had too much to drink, and I don't trust *them*. Eddie'll go with you.'

'Oh, come *on*,' Melody moaned, glancing at Eddie who had been leaning against the wall behind Tony all night. 'He'll scare everyone off the dance floor. Have you seen the way he's looking at people – like he wants to skin them and *eat* them.'

'Well, you ain't going alone,' Tony said flatly. 'Take it or leave it.'

'What about him?' She nodded in Fabian's direction.

'You putting me on?' Tony frowned darkly.

'Oh, for God's sake!' Melody tutted softly. 'He's *gay*, you big idiot. Can't you tell? Look at his *hair*. And the way he talks.'

Tony peered at Fabian for a moment and decided that he *did* look kind of effeminate.

'Yeah, you could be right,' he conceded. 'Okay, you can go with him – but no funny business.'

'What, like getting him to give me make-up tips?' Melody sneered.

'You know what I mean.' Giving her a hooded look, Tony turned to Fabian and clicked his fingers. 'Yo! A word.'

Extracting himself from Brenda's clutches, Fabian said, 'What can I do for you, Mr Allen?'

'She wants to dance.' Tony jerked his head at Melody. 'But she's loaded, so I want you to go with her and make sure she don't get mauled by none of them cunts down there.' Pausing, he sent a clear message with his eyes as he added, 'Wouldn't wanna spoil the night having to warn anyone off – you get me?'

'Got you.' Fabian agreed, feeling the coke buzz turn into a sharp stab of paranoia. 'I'll see she gets back in one piece.'

'You do that.' Grinning darkly, Tony reached up and patted his cheek none too gently.

'Come on, then,' Melody snapped, looking at Fabian as if she'd rather be swimming with sharks than about to dance with him.

Following her down the stairs, Fabian was conscious that his legs were shaking. He hadn't liked Tony Allen from the off, but he'd sensed something dangerous about him just now, and he was sure the threat had been aimed at him. But whether or not it had been, there was no mistaking what it had meant: if any man – Fabian included – stepped out of line with his woman, Tony Allen would take it very, very personally.

Melody's mood changed as soon as she and Fabian hit the dance floor. Smiling now, she thrust her breasts at him and yelled, 'That was fun, wasn't it?'

'What was?' Fabian yelled back, glancing around self-consciously.

'Getting you alone without raising suspicion,' Melody told him, raising her arms above her head and throwing her hair back sexily as she twirled around to a remix of Chic's 'Freak Out'. 'Course, he only let you come with me because you're gay.'

'Ex*cuse* me?' Fabian gasped, not sure he'd heard right.

'Why else would he trust me with such a good-looking guy?' she teased, bumping him with her shapely hip. 'Unless he thinks you'd be more interested in *his* bits than mine. You're not gay, though, are you, Babe?'

'Absolutely not!'

'Didn't think so.' Looking up at him through her lashes, Melody bit her lip seductively. 'You really are gorgeous, though. Bet you're hot as hell in the sack.'

Jerking back when she moved even closer and pressed herself against him, Fabian shot a nervous glance up to the VIP lounge, where, he was glad to see, Tony had his back to them.

'Jeezus!' he squawked when Melody suddenly slid her hands over his buttocks. 'Are you trying to get me shot?'

'Aw, now that's not nice,' she scolded when he pushed her away. 'I thought Tony told you to look after me.'

'I doubt he meant like *that*,' Fabian protested. 'Look, why don't I go and get you a nice cup of coffee?'

'Rather have something stronger.' Melody gave him a knowing look.

'I don't know what you mean.'

'Sure you do.' Raising a finger to her nose, she said, 'You really should check yourself in the mirror when you're finished.'

Realising what she was getting at, Fabian quickly wiped the coke traces away. Christ! If *she*'d noticed, who else had? *Jenna*? Oh, God! He'd lose his job. Then he'd lose his apartment, because he wouldn't be able to afford it. And his car. And—

Interrupting his racing thoughts, Melody said, 'Chill, Babe. I won't tell if you don't.'

Exhaling nervously, Fabian ran his hands through his hair and gave her a sheepish smile. 'Pretty careless, huh? But thanks for the warning. I would have been in real shit if anyone else had seen it.'

'No problem,' Melody drawled, a glint of something steely sparking in her eyes. 'All you have to do is give me some, and I'll never mention it again.'

'Yeah, right!' Fabian grinned, sure that she was joking.

'I'm serious,' she retorted icily. 'Give me some, or I'll tell Tony you were trying it on with me. And you *know* he'd believe me.'

'Ah, but he thinks I'm gay,' Fabian reminded her, still grinning – still sure it was a joke.

'Only because I *told* him you were so he'd let me dance with you,' Melody countered smoothly. 'But I could have made a mistake, couldn't I? It's easily done. So, how about it, Mr Manager? You going to make your new favourite customer happy. *Or . . .*'

Gazing down into her lovely face, Fabian realised that it wasn't a joke. The bitch was actually trying to blackmail him. And what the hell was he supposed to do about it? If he didn't do what she wanted, she'd drop him in it with her bad-ass boyfriend. But if he did, and got caught, he'd lose his job.

'Well?' Melody said, still managing to dance – although Fabian didn't know how, because *his* limbs felt like lead weights.

'Look, I only had a bit,' he lied, hoping that she would back off. 'If I'd known you were into it, I'd have saved you some, but I didn't.'

Narrowing her eyes, Melody pursed her lips petulantly. He was lying, she could tell, and she hated being lied to.

'Aw, now, you wouldn't be fibbing, would you?' she drawled with a mean edge to her voice. 'That's not very nice when I'm trying to be friendly.'

As friendly as a rattlesnake! Fabian thought incredulously, wondering how he'd managed to get himself caught up in this.

Softening her tone suddenly, Melody moved closer, whispering, 'I'll make it worth your while. Babe. I know you want me – I can see it in your eyes.'

Fabian glanced at the people surrounding them, terrified that someone might have heard. Under normal circumstances, if a gorgeous woman came on strong like this he'd go for it good style. But these were not normal circumstances, and he had too much to lose if anybody got hold of the wrong end of the stick. Tony Allen, for example.

'Look, I *swear* I haven't got any left,' he whispered back, praying that she believed him. 'If I did, I'd give it to you.'

'Fine,' Melody snapped, losing patience. 'I'll just have to go and tell Tony what you've been doing, then, won't I? And he hates it when anybody upsets me.' Blinking rapidly now, making her huge eyes swim with tears, she quivered her bottom lip and whimpered – loudly, 'No . . . please don't . . . I don't want to.'

Fabian's heart sank. If he hadn't seen and heard it for himself, he'd never have believed that anybody could switch it on so fast – and so convincingly. Glancing around for witnesses to verify that he hadn't touched Melody should he need to prove it, he was dismayed to see that none of the sweaty, drunken dancers were paying him the slightest attention. It would be his word against hers.

'All right,' he hissed when she started to back away with a terrified expression on her face. 'Over here.'

Motioning with his head for her to follow, he walked off the dance floor and found a quiet corner in the shade of a potted palm tree.

'I'll see what I can do,' he said when she joined him seconds later. 'There's a guy I know who might have something, but you'll have to give me time to find him. See that door?' he said then, nodding at the door to the offices. 'I'll leave it on the latch. My room's on the first floor, halfway down the corridor.'

Smiling slyly, Melody reached up and stroked his cheek. Laughing softly when he jerked back, she waggled her fingers at him. 'See you in ten, then. And make sure you've got it, or I won't be a happy bunny.'

Rushing to his office when she'd gone, Fabian took out his stash and chopped two thick lines on the mirror. Snorting one quickly, he cursed her under his breath. He hadn't intended to do any more tonight, but his nerves were shot to pieces thanks to her.

Tapping on the door a few minutes later, Melody let herself in without waiting for an answer. Seeing the line he'd left for her on the mirror, she gave a triumphant smile.

'I see you managed to find your friend, then?'

'Yeah, but I nearly got caught,' Fabian lied, giving her a resentful look. 'Do you know how much trouble I could get into for this?'

Sighing remorsefully now, Melody flopped down on the visitor's chair and crossed her legs, giving Fabian a flash of sheer black panties.

'Sorry, Babe, I didn't mean to heavy you like that, but I was desperate. I'm having the shittiest night *ever*. When Tony gets on a roll, he just goes on and on, and I might as well be invisible for all the attention he gives me. We've been here two weeks now, and all he's done is . . .'

Listening as she poured out her woes, Fabian felt the anger that had been holding him rigid melt away. It sounded like she'd been having a rough time of it, and she was only kicking out at him because she couldn't kick out at her boyfriend. She looked so vulnerable – he felt a wave of protective indignation wash over him. Tony Allen must be some kind of idiot if he couldn't see that bagging himself a prize like Melody Fisher came at a price. Stars needed more attention than normal people – and there were thousands of men out there who would gladly give Melody Fisher the attention she was craving. If Tony Allen wasn't careful, it would be nobody's fault but his own when Melody found what she was looking for in somebody else's arms.

Fabian's, maybe.

Well, why not? What man in his right mind would refuse if she was offering it on a plate?

'Am I forgiven?' Melody peered up at him with little-girl-lost eyes.

'Yeah, sure, forget it.' Smiling, he handed her the rolled-up twenty note he'd been using as a straw.

Snorting her line, Melody leaned her head back and inhaled deeply as Fabian's gaze slid over her body. He'd had more women than the average teenage boy had had hot wanks, and most had been way up there in the looks department, but this one was something else. With the added bonus that she was almost really famous. How cool was that?

Smiling as if she could read his mind, Melody passed the note back to him and stood up. Putting a hand on his cheek, she kissed him softly on the lips.

'Thanks, Babe, I really needed that. You're a star.'

Reaching for her, Fabian's hands hit empty air when she backed towards the door, biting her lip and waving her fingers at him. He had a hard-on to die for – and another attack of paranoia coming on. Now that she'd had what she wanted, she'd have nothing to lose by dropping him in it. It might be her idea of fun.

'Hey, you're not going to do anything stupid, are you?' he asked, panic rich in his voice.

'*Would* I?' Melody teased. Then, shaking her head, she said, 'Course not, Babe. He'd kill you. And where would that leave me? I could be stuck in this stinking place for months the way he's going on, and I'm going to need you to keep me sane.' Blowing him a kiss then, she opened the door and slipped out, whispering, 'Don't worry, it'll be our little secret.'

Locking the door behind her, Fabian leaned back against it. She'd said that Tony would kill him if he found out – and he had no doubt that the man was more than capable of it.

But, no, come on. This was *England*. That kind

of thing might happen every day in America, but Allen couldn't be crazy enough to think he'd get away with it over here – *could he*?

Whether or not he could, one thing was sure: Fabian would have to tread very carefully until he knew that Melody could be trusted.

Looking down when his dick gave a plaintive throb, he shook his head disbelievingly. Scary as it was to think of the trouble she could cause him, he had to admit that the hard-to-get act was a turn-on. But it was a very rare woman who could resist him for too long once he'd set his sights on her, so he wasn't worried about that. And, who knew – if their little secret *stayed* secret, Fabian might get to see a fair bit more of her than Allen had bargained for when he'd told him to keep an eye on her.

Avril Drake was bored, and becoming increasingly irritated. So much for Leonard's belief that he was as well known and popular as ever: nobody had so much as said hello to them since they'd arrived, apart from the gushing manager and the pretty young owner. And Leonard had a face like a wet weekend in Wigan. But at least it should make him think twice about dragging her back here in a hurry.

Sighing heavily, she stared wistfully down at the

smiling dancers below. It wasn't that she didn't enjoy music and parties, because she did. In fact, she'd been quite the life and soul – once upon a very long time ago. But Leonard had soon stopped that, because he didn't *do* dancing and partying, claiming that it didn't suit his image. So, apart from the occasional waltz at some stuffy political do or other, she hadn't had the pleasure in a good long time.

She resented Leonard for robbing her of her best years, but there wasn't a damn thing she could do about it now because she was far too old to start again. Too settled with her life – such as it was – to face the upheaval.

Glaring at her when she released yet another heavy sigh, Leonard hissed through clenched teeth, 'Are you just going to sit there pulling that miserable bloody face all night?'

'Why?' she retorted sarcastically. 'Are you worried it'll outdo yours?'

Tutting loudly, he shook his head.

'Careful,' Avril muttered. 'You'll have people thinking that we're not quite as *together* as you'd have them believe.'

'I don't care what anybody thinks,' he grunted – blatantly lying, because that was all he'd *ever* cared about.

'If you're not enjoying yourself, why don't we

just go home?' Avril suggested hopefully, feeling a sudden longing for the warm, cosy solitude of her bed.

'And make myself look a complete idiot?' Leonard snapped. 'I'm not going anywhere, so give me a break and make like you're having fun, for God's sake.'

'Fine,' she replied, a hint of hurt in her eyes. 'If you're sure that's what you want?'

'I wouldn't have said it if it wasn't,' he said, folding his arms over his belly.

'Right!' Pushing her chair back, Avril stood up. 'I'm going to dance.'

'On your *own*?' Leonard looked at her as if she'd gone mad. 'Don't be ridiculous!'

'You told me to have fun.'

'With *me*.'

'Is that possible?' Avril replied coldly.

But who was she kidding? She'd no more dance alone than Leonard would walk into a room full of strangers without her, and they both knew it.

Shoulders slumping, she pushed her chair under the table, saying resignedly, 'I'm going to the toilet – *if* that's all right with you?'

'Fine,' Leonard grunted with satisfaction. Then, looking around for a waiter, he said, 'I shall have to have words with that Jenny girl. Let her know that her staff have been neglecting her guests.'

'Don't make waves,' Avril cautioned wearily. 'And while I'm gone, could you please think about going home, because neither of us is enjoying this.'

Flicking her a dismissive glance, Leonard turned his head, his face all false smiles now as he nodded to the music and gazed around the room. He had no intention of slinking away like an unloved dog before the party was over.

Shaking her head, Avril walked calmly away. She didn't really need the toilet, she just needed a break from her husband's miserable company. Tapping a waiter on the shoulder en route to the stairs, she pointed out their table and asked him to take a very large Scotch rocks over to Leonard, in the hope that he would get drunk and cheer up.

Self-conscious by himself, Leonard agitatedly tapped his fingers on the table. He would never admit it to Avril, but she was right about him not enjoying himself. He didn't know what he'd expected when he came here tonight, but it certainly hadn't been to sit in virtual isolation. And while he knew a lot of the faces around him, having seen them on TV or in the papers, he found it quite wounding that they obviously didn't recognise him.

But, then, maybe they did, he told himself

consolingly. Maybe they knew exactly who he was, but were put off approaching him because of Avril's uninviting face.

'Your drink, sir.'

Glancing up in surprise when the young waiter placed a large Scotch on the table, Leonard said, 'Oh, right . . . thank you. Just a moment.' Pulling a ten-pound note out of his wallet, he placed it on the tray.

'You don't have to pay,' the waiter told him, holding it out. 'Everything's complimentary for invited guests tonight.'

'Yes, I know that,' Leonard blustered, having completely forgotten. 'It's a tip.'

'Oh, no, sir, I couldn't.'

'I insist.' Leonard was smiling now. 'I *want* you to have it.'

'Okay, thanks.' Returning the smile, the waiter pocketed the note. 'I'll be around if you want anything else. Just give me a wave.'

Watching as the boy walked away, Leonard shook his head, wondering how on Earth these kids managed to squeeze themselves into such tight clothing. Oh, to be young and fit again. He'd have given these boys a run for their money in his prime – before Avril got her claws into him and sucked all the joy out of his bones.

Sighing wistfully for his lost youth, he sipped

at his drink and let his gaze wander. The room was packed out, but there was a particularly large gathering at a table across the room where a loud American was holding court, making everybody laugh with stories that Leonard couldn't hear.

Pursing his lips thoughtfully, he peered at the man's face. He must be very famous, judging by the way the other stars were hanging on to his every word, but Leonard couldn't quite put his finger on where he'd seen him before.

Clicking his fingers when it suddenly came to him, he thought, *Of course!* Lord Kimberley's charity auction-cum-dinner at The Lowry last week. Tony Allen – that was his name.

Feeling a small thrill of excitement when it occurred to him that it might break the ice with some of the other guests if he were to go and say hello to Allen, Leonard eased himself out of his seat and strolled over.

Edging casually in among the people who were hanging about on the edge of the circle, he manoeuvred himself in until he was close to Allen – who was too busy telling a joke to notice him. Coughing to attract his attention, the blood rushed to Leonard's cheeks when everybody turned and looked at him.

Irritated by the interruption, Tony frowned up at him. 'Yeah?'

'Oh, sorry . . . didn't mean to disturb you,'

Leonard said, suddenly nervous because Allen obviously didn't recognise him. 'I, er, just saw you and thought I'd best come and say hello.' Grinning then, he added, 'Wouldn't want you thinking I was ignoring you, or anything.'

'Do I know you?' The frown deepened.

'We met last week,' Leonard reminded him. 'Lord Kimberley's do.'

'Kimberley?' Tony repeated slowly, narrowing his eyes.

'At The Lowry,' Leonard prompted, embarrassed now because people were beginning to smirk. 'Auction and dinner in aid of the dialysis unit? Lord Kimberley introduced us.'

'That the old dude with the horse-face wife?'

'Maureen,' Leonard affirmed, smiling again. 'Yes, that's them. I was sitting across from you on the long table at dinner. We discussed some of the lots.'

'Can't say I remember too much about it.' Tony shrugged. 'It must have been boring.'

'Those things often are,' Leonard agreed disloyally. 'So, I, um, guess you won't be going to his *Poloquet* party next week?'

Repulsed by the smarmy conspiratorial grin, Tony said, 'Whatever the fuck that means – *no*, I won't be going.'

Excusing herself just then, Brenda Thompson

got up and squeezed her way out from behind the table.

'Do you mind?' Leonard indicated her vacated seat.

'Free country, last I heard,' Tony grunted. 'Wouldn't be here otherwise.'

Leonard laughed, but quickly stopped when Tony flicked him an irritated glance. *Okay, keep it cool,* he told himself, squeezing onto the chair. *Don't get carried away and make a fool of yourself when everything's going so well.*

Over at the bar, Kalli was casting disapproving glances in Leonard's direction as she washed a pile of glasses. She'd seen the leering way he'd followed Austin with his eyes when Austin had taken him a drink a short while ago, and she hadn't liked it one little bit.

Austin would say she'd imagined it, but she hadn't – and she knew better than most about men and their disgusting ways, having been forced to cater to all manner of filthy pigs when her father had sold her to the brothel owner in Hong Kong. Just like that fat man, *those* men had smiled like angels while making their deals with the Devil. And Austin, with his cute dimples, bleached-blond hair and baby-blue eyes, was prime meat for that kind of man.

Austin bounded over just then with a fresh order. Waving a hand in front of her face, he said, 'Oi, quit staring at the stars and get on with your job.'

Snatching the order slip from him, Kalli gave it to the other waitress and grabbed his hand.

'*Ooer*, get off!' he protested, jerking back and looking at the soapsuds in disgust. 'Now look what you've done. I'm all wet.'

'Never mind that,' Kalli said impatiently. 'What were you and that man talking about?'

'*Man*?' Austin repeated bemusedly. 'Honey, in case it's slipped your distracted attention, there's about a *zillion* men in here tonight, and I've been talking to them all, like the good little waiter I am.'

'*Him*.' Kalli jabbed a finger in Leonard's direction.

'I wasn't talking to him about anything,' Austin told her innocently. 'Oh, except to tell him that he didn't have to pay for his drinks.'

'So, what did he give you?' Kalli persisted. 'And don't lie, because I saw you put something in your pocket.'

'Check *you*, Miss Marple!' Austin teased. 'But for your nosy information, it wasn't his number, so you can drop the slapped-bum mush.' Pulling the ten-pound note from his pocket, he dangled it in front of her face for a second, then stashed it away again before the other waitress saw it and expected him to put it in the tips jar. 'Keep quiet, and I'll split it with you later.'

Sighing, Kalli shook her head. 'No, it's yours. Just be careful, yeah?'

'Okay, *Mum*.' Grinning cheekily, Austin took his newly loaded tray off the other waitress and winked at Kalli. 'See ya later, Dominator.'

Kalli pursed her pretty lips as she watched him skip away through the crowd. He was very perky tonight. *Too* perky, and she suspected that it had something to do with his boyfriend Xavier's visit to their flat earlier this afternoon. If she found out he'd been taking Es again, she'd be having very strong words with him. And Xavier would get a good telling-off next time she saw him, too.

It was almost four in the morning when Jenna dragged herself back up to the VIP lounge. She was exhausted, and her feet were screaming for release from her high, strappy shoes. But they would just have to wait, because nobody looked in any hurry to leave any time soon. *God*, how she wished she'd settled for a three o'clock licence instead of an all-nighter.

Making her way to a quiet corner of the bar, she smiled when Kalli came over. 'Hi, sweetheart. How's it going?'

'Fine.' Kalli peered at Jenna with concern. 'But you look tired.'

'I am. But don't tell anyone. It's not the best impression to give the customers, is it? The hostess who can't stick the pace.'

'Don't worry, nobody will notice.'

'*You* did.'

'Yes, but I see more than most.'

'I'm sure you do.' Jenna laughed softly. 'Could you get me a cranberry juice, please?' Yawning when Kalli went to get her drink, she jumped when Tony Allen suddenly appeared at her side. Throwing a hand over her mouth, she rolled her eyes apologetically. 'Sorry about that. I guess I'm not used to such late nights.'

'Not so hot on staying up all night myself, these days,' Tony drawled, giving her a lopsided grin. 'Mind if I sit down?' He patted the stool beside hers.

'Not at all.' She moved her knees to give him room. 'I'm just getting a drink. Can I get you anything?'

Settling on the stool, he said, 'Yeah, that'd be good. JD on ice. Ed?'

Sitting on the other side of him, Eddie nodded.

When Kalli had brought their drinks, Tony took a sip of his and exhaled loudly.

'Hope you don't mind me invading your space

like this, but I needed to escape before I lost my mind.' He jerked his head in the direction of his table, where Leonard was sitting alone now, everyone else having drifted away. 'Kind of boring, having people agree with every word you say – especially when you know you're talking shit. But one man's idiot is another man's pain in the ass – and all that.' Reaching into his pocket, he took out a pack of cigars. 'Mind?'

'Not at all,' Jenna told him. 'Go ahead.'

Lighting up, Tony exhaled a thick plume of noxious smoke, then swivelled in his seat to gaze around.

'You know, this is quite some place you got here. I wasn't too sure at first, but it's pretty cool once you get used to it.'

'Glad you like it.' Jenna smiled, resisting the urge to waft the smoke away. She despised the smell of cigar smoke, but he *was* a guest.

'Oh, I like it.' He nodded slowly. 'A lot, as it goes.'

Jenna raised an eyebrow when he gave her a disarming smile. For a squat man who wasn't overly blessed in the looks department, he was almost handsome when he wasn't scowling.

'So, you inherited this place off of your old man?' Tony asked suddenly, catching her off guard.

Wondering how he knew, she said, 'Yes. He died a few months ago.'

'So I hear. How you coping?'

'Okay, I suppose. You just have to get on with it, don't you?'

'Guess so,' Tony agreed, leaning an elbow on the bar now and crossing his legs, as if settling in for the night. 'Mom doing all right?'

'She died a while back,' Jenna told him. 'Not long after . . .' Pausing, she flapped her hand in a subconscious *brush the pain aside* gesture. 'My younger brother was killed, you see, and I don't think she ever really got over it.'

'Jeez, that's rough.' Tony squinted at her through the smoke. 'Died of a broken heart, did she?'

'No, Alzheimer's. It was a mixed blessing, though, because it affects the memory, so she seemed to forget all about Damian once it kicked in. She didn't recognise *any* of us by the end.'

'Man, you've had it bad,' Tony commented sympathetically. 'So, now you got no one?'

'A sister,' Jenna told him. 'But I don't really see too much of her, because she married when I was quite young and moved to Australia.' Frowning now, she reached for her drink, wondering why she was revealing so much personal stuff to this stranger.

'You're doing good, considering you've had to go it alone,' Tony said admiringly. 'You can't knock yourself for that.'

'I'm managing,' she murmured.

'Better than managing,' Tony persisted. 'Like I said, this is a great place – and I should know, I've had one of my own.'

'*Really*?' Jenna was surprised. She hadn't actually considered what he might do for a living, but running a nightclub wouldn't have been her first guess.

'Yeah, but it wasn't really my bag, so I sold up and shipped out to "good old Blighty".'

Groaning at his affected English accent, Jenna shook her head. 'That was terrible.'

'Sounded better than half the clowns I've been listening to tonight,' he chuckled. 'Some of 'em sound like they're munching on their own bazoomas.'

'Ah, the *actors*.' Jenna gave him a conspiratorial smile. 'Don't let them hear you saying that. They spend good money learning how to speak like that.'

'Yeah? Well, maybe they should put their dough in the bank and save us the pain of having to listen to it.' Blowing out yet more smoke, Tony brought the subject back to her. 'So, what's your plans for this place? You got partners . . . shareholders?'

'No, it's just me,' Jenna said, irritated that she couldn't bring herself to tell him to mind his own business. None of the other guests had gone beyond congratulating her and wishing her luck for the future, but Tony Allen seemed to be probing, and she wasn't sure that she liked it.

Gazing around thoughtfully, Tony said, 'You know, anybody else messing with this much chrome would have had it looking like a slot machine, or something. But you've got it real classy. And I like the way you've got the kids dressed to match. That's a nice touch.'

Accepting the compliment with a modest smile, Jenna said, 'You've quite an eye for detail, Mr Allen.'

'Hey, come *on* . . .' Drawing his head back, he frowned at her. 'I thought I told you to call me Tony? Only ass-lickers and dick-wipes have to call me Mister – like that fat fuck back there. No offence,' he added quickly. 'I know he's your guest, an' all, but there's something not right about him. He gives me the creeps – know what I mean?'

'Mmmm.' Jenna struggled to keep from laughing out loud at the look of revulsion on his face. Leonard Drake had obviously made quite an impression, and she wondered if he and Tony had shaken hands.

'Who is he, anyway?'

'A politician,' Jenna said, jumping when Tony slapped his hand down hard on the bar.

'Ha! Shoulda known! *That*'s why he's so fucking creepy. Always on the make, those guys. Goddamn liars, too, promising shit they ain't got no intention of delivering. And *greedy* – don't even get me started. Ain't one of 'em not on *some*one's payroll!'

'It's the same for every political system the world over, isn't it?' Jenna commented bemusedly. 'Greed and deception are just part of the job description.'

'Hey, whaddya know . . .' Sitting back, Tony gazed at her with open admiration. 'A broad with a brain – never thought I'd see the day. Most of the women I know can't talk about nothing but clothes and make-up. And those that *do* have more interesting things to say generally turn you off when they start combing their crew-cuts.'

Smiling, Jenna said, 'I'm sure I'm not the only heterosexual woman you've ever met who's got a mind of her own.'

'Maybe not,' he conceded. 'But you're sure as hell the prettiest.'

Jenna's smile faltered. Oh, God! She hoped he wasn't hitting on her. Apart from the fact that she wasn't attracted to him in the slightest, he was Melody Fisher's boyfriend.

Fortunately, an actress friend of Brenda Thompson decided to come and introduce herself to Tony just then, so Jenna was spared having to find out if he was trying his hand. Promising that they'd talk again soon, she made her escape.

Avril had been back from the toilet a long time when Leonard finally gave up on Tony Allen and slithered back to their table. Seeing the look of dejection on his face, she smiled tightly.

'What's the matter, dear? Did your new friend chase you away?'

'No, he did *not*,' Leonard grunted. 'For your information, it was *me* who left *him*.'

'Of course it was,' Avril murmured, fanning her face with her hand as a hot flush came over her.

'You're sweating like a pig,' Leonard muttered nastily. 'Haven't you any powder in your bag of tricks to soak it up?'

'Didn't think I'd need any.'

'Well, you do. It's very unflattering.'

'Don't take it out on *me* because *you*'ve been rejected,' Avril snarled.

'If you were watching, you know that he didn't just leave *me*, he left everybody,' Leonard informed her, feeling a little better as he said it, because he realised that it was actually true. 'He needed to discuss something with Jenny in private. But, as you're so interested,' he added, blatantly lying now, 'he asked if I'd be here again tomorrow, because he'd rather like to talk some more.'

'Oh, would he now?'

'*Yes*. And I said I'd be delighted, so there we go.'

'I see. Well, perhaps you'd better go back and tell him that you won't be able to make it because we'll be at the Buckleys' – or had you forgotten?'

'No, of course I hadn't,' Leonard blustered. 'I just thought we could come straight from there.'

'It's too far. We'd be too late to get in by the time we got here.'

'Not if we left early.'

'What, earlier than everyone else?' Avril gave her husband a disbelieving look. 'You who *always* stay till the bitter end in case they talk about you when you're gone?'

'I'm sure they'll manage without us,' Leonard muttered, wishing that she'd shut her sarcastic mouth. 'Anyway, you're always complaining that you don't get out enough, so you ought to be grateful.'

Raising an eyebrow, Avril peered at him incredulously. *Grateful?* Did he think she was a dog desperate to be walked, or something?

'It's late. Let's go,' Leonard said suddenly, snatching up his glass and downing what was left of his drink. 'I just want to have a quick word with Jenny first.'

'Why?'

'To thank her for inviting us tonight, of course.' Getting up, Leonard peered down at his wife. 'You really should lay off the drink if it makes you forget your manners.'

'Don't concern yourself with *my* manners,' Avril retorted indignantly. 'And I've only had three drinks all night, as you well know, so don't insinuate that

I'm some kind of alcoholic. I might just have another, in fact,' she added defiantly.

'I've a busy day tomorrow,' Leonard informed her, as if that were the end of the matter. 'And *you*'re going to need all the beauty sleep you can get.'

Glaring after him when he walked away in search of Jenna, Avril snatched up her handbag. She didn't want to stay, but it galled her that he just assumed command as and when it suited him. She'd been asking to leave for hours and he hadn't budged, but they could go now that *he* was ready.

And she had no choice but to comply, because he'd think nothing of leaving her to make her own way home if she didn't. And he'd probably lock the gates, too, forcing her to ring through to the house to get him to open them.

Jenna was nowhere to be seen when Leonard reached the bar. Looking around, he spotted Fabian hovering in the shadows and made a beeline for him instead.

'Ah, hello there . . . I was looking for Jenny. You wouldn't happen to know where she is, would you?'

'Jenn*a*'s busy at the moment,' Fabian told him, emphasising the pronunciation of her name. 'Will I do?'

'Well, I suppose you'll have to,' Leonard grumbled disappointedly. He had really wanted to talk to the girl in person – to let her know that, as a trusted friend of her late father, he was always available should she ever need any advice or guidance, or even just a fatherly chat. But it would have to wait, he supposed. Remembering his manners now, he said, 'I wanted to thank her – and yourself, of course – for inviting my wife and me tonight. We've had a lovely time.'

'Glad you enjoyed it.'

'Oh, we did. Everything was wonderful. The food, the drinks, the service – couldn't fault a thing.'

'Very pleased to hear it,' Fabian murmured distractedly, his gaze fixed firmly over Leonard's shoulder on the Allen table, where he could see Melody being touchy-feely with Tony. She'd obviously forgiven the ugly lout for neglecting her, but Fabian hoped she didn't get *too* relaxed and let anything slip.

'Are you open tomorrow?'

'Sorry?' Snapping his attention back to Leonard, Fabian frowned. 'Tomorrow? Oh, right – yes. And every night thereafter. Shall we expect to see you?'

'Absolutely!' Leonard beamed, taking it as an actual invitation.

It was six before the club was totally cleared of guests, and by half past most of the staff had gone, too.

Bumping into Fabian on her way to the lower bar, Jenna gave him a tired smile. 'Good night, wasn't it?'

'Fantastic,' he agreed. 'Bet you're wondering what you were so worried about?'

'I wasn't worried,' she lied, her eyes twinkling because they both knew how panicked she'd been. 'You were great, by the way. I was watching you with Melody Fisher.'

Fabian blanched. *Oh, shit! What had she seen?*

'It was really nice of you to dance with her,' Jenna went on, oblivious to the wariness in his eyes. 'Not that it could have been all that hard, considering how lovely she is, but I know you only did it to help Tony out. So, well done.'

'Thanks,' Fabian muttered, more relieved than she could ever know. 'All in a day's work.'

'A very *good* one, in your case,' Jenna said. 'Staying for a drink?'

Fabian was tempted, but when he saw Vibes, Kalli and Austin loitering by the bar he decided against it. Much as he'd have liked another one-to-one with Jenna, there was no way he was wasting his time on the hired help. Anyway, he was still on edge about the whole Melody situation and needed to get home to relax.

'Actually, I'm a bit knackered,' he said, yawning to emphasise the point. 'And I've got to come in first thing to wait for the delivery, so I'll give it a miss, if you don't mind?'

'Course not. And don't worry about that delivery. I'll come in early and help you with it.'

'No need, I've got it covered. You just stay in bed till you're good and ready.' Leaning towards her, Fabian kissed her on the cheek. 'Happy New Year.'

'You, too,' Jenna said, sitting down wearily on one of the tall bar stools.

Stepping out of the way to let Fabian past, Kalli put her hands on her non-existent hips and gazed around at the mess of glasses, plates and overflowing ashtrays littering the bar. Pushing up her sleeves, she set about clearing up.

'Leave that,' Jenna told her. 'The cleaners will do it in the morning. Come and have a drink – I think we all deserve one.' Looking around at them all now, she said, 'Thanks so much for everything you've done, guys. You've really helped make it go well tonight.'

'We *were* pretty damn good, weren't we?' Austin crowed, going behind the bar to pour the drinks.

Straddling the stool beside hers, Vibes said, 'I hope you're including yourself in that, Princess, because *you* were fantastic.'

'Hear, hear,' Kalli agreed, sitting on the other side of Vibes. 'You were brilliant, Jenna. Nobody would ever guess it was your first time.'

'*Like a virgin*,' Austin sang camply, popping the cork out of a half-full bottle of champagne that Maurice had left under the counter.

'Shut up, you idiot,' Kalli scolded. 'Jenna's trying to relax.'

'It's okay,' Jenna assured her. 'I don't mind a bit of music. Subject of,' she said then, turning to Vibes. 'You were *amazing*.'

Dipping his head, Vibes gave a modest shrug. 'I was okay, I guess.'

'Oh, come on, you were *way* hot!' Austin chipped in enthusiastically, laying four glasses out on the counter. 'When the doors opened and you hit it with the Big Ben chimes, I thought I was gonna *die*, it was that spine-tingly. And the way you came out of that gospel version of "Auld Lang Syne" and blasted straight into that Kylie remix . . . Oh, my *life*!' Closing his eyes, he hugged the champagne bottle to his chest. 'It was like getting into an ice-cold shower after a sizzling sauna!'

'I think we get the picture.' Jenna laughed. 'Now, do you think we could get the drinks?'

But it was true what he'd said. Vibes had turned the room on its head tonight, drawing people onto the dance floor and holding them there, never giving them a chance to think about sitting down as each track raised the pace of the last. But his real brilliance had shown itself in the final hour, when he'd started to mellow the mood, subtly slowing the pace down to the final laid-back bluesy smooch.

'Fantastic,' Jenna murmured, sighing happily.

'Isn't he?' Kalli agreed, resting her chin on her hand. Blushing then, she added, 'I meant as a DJ.'

'Me, too,' Jenna said quickly.

'What-*ever*!' Austin murmured amusedly.

Smiling, Vibes looped his arms around their shoulders and hugged them to him. 'You are one pair of terrific ladies – you know that?'

'What about me?' Hand on hip now, Austin tilted his head and pouted flirtatiously. 'Don't you get hugs round here if you haven't got boobs?'

'You, my friend, get a high five!' Vibes laughed, slapping palms with him across the bar. 'I'd like to propose a toast,' he said then, picking up his glass. 'To friends . . . and to Jenna's success.'

'That's two toasts,' Kalli said, smiling slyly as she noticed that Jenna and Vibes couldn't seem to look each other in the eye for more than a few seconds at a time.

'Oh, who cares, Little Miss Perfect?' Austin tutted. 'Button up, and *bottoms* up!'

Reaching for her glass, Kalli said, 'You'd better take it easy, 'cos you're not having another one after that. And I am *not* cleaning the taxi if you throw up in the back again.'

★

Letting Kalli and Austin out a short time later, Jenna set the alarms and locked up, then stood with Vibes outside the front door to wait for his cab. He'd booked it from the same firm as the rest of the staff, but everyone else's had been and gone a long time ago and there was still no sign of his.

It was pitch dark outside, and absolutely freezing. Jenna was shivering, and her nose felt like an icicle, but there was no way she was leaving Vibes by himself. There had been too many reports of gangs attacking lone men in the city lately, and she'd never live with herself if that were to happen to him.

'You should go,' Vibes told her. 'It's too cold to be hanging around out here.'

'I'm fine,' she lied, smiling to disguise the fact that her teeth were chattering. 'What time did they say they'd be here?'

'Twenty minutes ago.'

'Bloody hell. I didn't realise they were that late. They've probably forgotten.'

'No worries.' Shrugging deeper into his jacket, Vibes stepped forward to look down the deserted road. 'I'll give it another five and start walking.'

'Don't be daft,' Jenna said, glancing up at him. 'My car's out back. I'll take you.'

'Nah, it's cool.' He shook his head. 'I don't want to put you out.'

'You won't be,' Jenna said firmly. 'But if you stay out here for much longer you'll be too ill to come to work tomorrow – and that's no use to me, is it?'

'If you're sure?' Vibes peered into her eyes – then glanced quickly away when it suddenly struck him where he'd seen that shade of green before.

The sea in Tahiti, when I took a honeymoon stroll on the beach with Aliya, just a few short hours after we later figured that Tashei must have been conceived . . .

Shaking the memory away before it took hold and burned, Vibes said, 'Second thoughts, I think I'd best just wait. That cab's probably gonna come racing round the corner any minute, and I wouldn't want to miss it and waste the guy's time on a day like this.'

Jenna knew better. Turning, she walked away, calling back over her shoulder: 'Come on.'

Catching up with her when he realised that she wasn't taking no for an answer, Vibes adjusted his stride to match hers. He'd never noticed quite how petite she actually was, and the glow from the street lamps gave her hair a beautiful blue sheen.

'You'll have to direct me, because I don't know my way around Withington,' Jenna said when they were in the car.

Rubbing his hands together as the heater blasted

delicious hot air at him, Vibes said, 'Left at the corner and keep going straight.' Falling silent then as Jenna reversed out of the yard into the narrow alleyway, he leaned his head back against the rest and thought about how well the night had gone.

Fabian had done himself proud with the guest list, and the rest of the staff had really pulled their weight to make sure everything went smoothly. Particularly Kalli, from what he'd heard. But then, he wouldn't have expected any less of her. She might be the smallest and youngest of the waitresses, but it was to her that they all turned when they needed help or advice.

'She's a good kid,' he said out loud. Adding, '*Kalli*,' when he realised that Jenna wouldn't know what he was talking about.

'She is, isn't she?' Jenna smiled fondly. 'I haven't known her as long as you have, but you just get the feeling you can really rely on her, don't you?'

'That's because you can,' Vibes murmured. 'And that's good, 'cos we all need someone to rely on.'

'Very true,' Jenna agreed. 'Bit of a rare luxury for me, these days, though, because I lost touch with most of my friends when I left Manchester. I've met lots of new people since I came back, but it's not the same, is it?'

'I hear that,' Vibes said softly. 'Many faces in the picture – few close to the heart.'

'Very poetic.'

'Very *safe*,' Vibes said, glancing at her out of the corner of his eye. Dawn was only just beginning to break, and the dull street lamps were casting long shadows across Jenna's tired face, but she was still one of the most beautiful women he'd ever seen. There was a proud tilt to her chin, and a dignity in the way she held herself which told him that she would be a faithful lover, or a lifelong trusted friend.

Or both, if a man were lucky enough.

Shaking the thought away, he sat up straighter and concentrated on staying awake as they travelled out of town and into Withington.

'It's the next turning on the left, then second right,' he said when they reached the village centre. 'First house on the left.'

Pulling up at the kerb outside the corner house a minute later, Jenna smiled when she saw three grown men chasing each other around the garden with water guns. 'They look like they're having fun.'

'Oh, man, I thought the party would have been over by now,' Vibes groaned. 'Gina must be having a fit. It would have been murder getting the baby to sleep with these fools making so much noise.' Sighing now, he unclipped his seat belt. 'Best go see if I can get them to cool it.'

Reaching for the door handle now, he hesitated, unsure how to say goodbye. It was New Year's Day, but should he kiss Jenna on the cheek and wish her a good one like he would have any other female friend? Or would she think that completely inappropriate because she was his boss?

Opting for the cautious approach, he nodded at her. 'Right, well, thanks for the lift. And I'll, er, see you tomorrow, I guess.' Smiling shyly, he added, 'Don't go falling asleep at the wheel on your way home.'

'I won't,' Jenna assured him. 'See you tomorrow.'

Hopping out, Vibes stepped back to the gate to wave her off.

'Who's that?' Kenneth asked, coming up behind him with a sly grin on his face.

'My boss,' Vibes said, pushing the gate open.

'Hot *momma*.'

'Wouldn't let Gina hear you saying that.' Strolling up the path, Vibes nodded at Kenneth's friends, who were sitting on the doorstep now, skinning up. 'Happy New Year, guys.'

'Certainly is,' one of them called back in a loud whisper. 'I'm happy as fuck, me. Fancy a puff to see it in, mate?'

Shaking his head, Vibes said, 'Thanks, but I'm gonna hit the sack.' Touching fists with Kenneth then, he said, 'See you in the morning, man.'

'Sweet dreams,' Kenneth called after him as he made his way inside.

Knowing exactly what he was getting at, Vibes flipped him the finger.

4

Fabian had barely slept, but nobody would have guessed it to look at him when he was getting the club ready for opening that night. His hair was perfect, his nails buffed, and his skin glowing, thanks to a visit to Toni & Guy in between overseeing the cleaners and sorting the delivery earlier that day. It was an expensive indulgence but, in his experience, women appreciated a well-groomed man – especially a well-groomed man in a suit. And his midnight-blue Armani and silver-grey shirt couldn't have looked better if it were being strutted down a catwalk in Milan.

But he didn't just *look* good. He felt good, too.

Coming down off the coke in the restless early-morning hours had mellowed him enough to think the Melody Fisher situation through more rationally, and he'd come to the conclusion that she wouldn't dare tell her boyfriend what had happened. If everything was honest and open between her and Tony Allen she wouldn't have had to engineer getting Fabian alone like that – she'd have come right out and asked him for the coke in front of Tony. But she obviously hadn't wanted Tony to know, and that gave Fabian something to hold over her if she got out of line.

With the weight of that gone from his shoulders, he was on top form when Jenna arrived. Greeting her with a kiss on the cheek, he told her about the dozens of calls they'd received from last night's guests and customers, saying how much they'd enjoyed themselves and asking if they'd be open tonight.

'Is that good?' Jenna asked, shrugging out of her jacket and blowing on her icy fingers.

'It's *great*,' he assured her. 'Believe me, people don't usually bother giving feedback. But the machine was chocker when I got here, and the phone hasn't stopped all day.'

'Wow,' she murmured, impressed by his enthusiasm. 'Hope it lasts.'

'Oh, it will,' he told her confidently. 'I've got a feeling we're going to be right up there with the best before too long. You watch.'

'Fingers crossed.' Jenna gave him a nervous smile. Glancing at her watch then, she said, 'Best go drop my stuff in the office while I've got time.' Walking away, she turned back to call, 'You're looking good, by the way.'

Smiling, Fabian called, 'You, too.' And he meant it, because she looked sensational again, in a figure-hugging black halter-dress, and emerald necklace and earrings that perfectly matched her eyes.

The front door opened just then, letting a blast of icy air in. Turning to see who was using the out-of-bounds customer entrance, Fabian frowned when he saw that it was two of the waitresses, JoJo and Vanessa.

'It's fucking freezing!' JoJo yelped, stamping the slush off her shoes and shaking the snow out of her hair onto the polished floor.

Smile gone, Fabian marched towards them, barking, 'How many times have I told you to come round the back? Let me catch you using the front doors again and you're out! Now get that mess cleared up before someone slips on it and breaks their neck. And hurry up – or I'll dock your wages.'

The queue was even longer tonight, the crowd just as skimpily dressed despite the heavy snow-fall and icy temperatures. After just half an hour, Fabian went out front and told the doormen to stop letting people in – which didn't impress those at the back of the queue who had been waiting for hours. But no amount of flirting from the girls in their best *fuck-me* outfits worked, because Fabian was determined not to reach their full quota with

Joe Public punters if it meant having to turn celebrities away.

Inside, Jenna was doing the rounds: chatting to the customers who'd been lucky enough to get in, and making sure that everybody was happy. A fair few regulars from her dad's day were here, but there were many more new faces – which was a great sign, as long as they didn't drift straight back to their usual clubs as soon as the novelty wore off. James Lorde had never succeeded in luring the hard-core clubbers and A-list celebrities in, but Jenna was hoping that the funky decor would change all that. And, if last night was any indication, they were definitely on the right track.

Finished with the lower floor, she made her way up to the VIP lounge and looked around, happy to see that several of last night's celebrity guests had come back. And there were lots of soap and sports stars who hadn't made the party but had come to check the place out on the recommendation of those who had.

Spotting her just then, Tony Allen strolled over to say hello. The picture of elegance in a charcoal-grey suit, his jet hair slicked smoothly back from his brow, he said, 'Hey, look at you. You look beautiful.'

Jenna was a little surprised when he pulled her to him and kissed her on both cheeks. It was a bit familiar, given that this was only their second meeting, but she supposed it must just be the American way. Fighting the urge to fold her arms when he let her go, she said, 'Nice to see you again. How are you?'

'Cool,' Tony said, putting his hands in his pockets and gazing around. 'Had a bit of free time, so I thought I'd come and check the place out again.'

Edging in beside him just then, Melody linked an arm through his and gave Jenna the once-over. Satisfied that she looked way hotter than her, she gave her a glowing smile. 'You're looking lovely, Jen.'

Rolling his eyes ceilingward, Tony muttered, 'Christ! Why does she always have to clip the end off of everyone's goddamned name? See, if she calls me *Tone* one more time, I swear to God I'll rip her fucking tongue out.'

'Aw, shut up,' Melody scolded, playfully pinching his cheek. 'You're such a grouch sometimes.'

Shaking his head wearily, Tony said, 'Be a good girl and go amuse yourself somewhere else for a bit, will you? I wanna talk to Jenna.'

Melody would have been furious if he'd dismissed her like that a couple of seconds earlier, but she'd just seen Fabian making his way to the bar. Glad of the excuse to escape, she gave Tony a kiss and told Jenna that she'd see her later. Then she tripped away through the crowd, her hips swaying sexily.

'Cent short of a dollar,' Tony murmured, watching her go. 'But you gotta love that ass.'

Jenna smiled. They were such an odd couple: Melody a blonde bombshell; Tony short, dark and squat, and almost handsome in an ugly sort of way. If you took them at face value, you'd wonder what Melody saw in him. But there was obviously far more to Tony Allen than met the eye, and Jenna sensed that he would be deeply loyal to few – and deeply dangerous to many.

'Have you got a minute?' he asked her now.

Jenna was faintly amused when he immediately placed a hand on the small of her back and guided her to an empty table, pulling a chair out for her when they got there and waiting until she sat down before taking his own seat. Strange manners, considering she hadn't actually agreed to talk to him – arrogant presumption mixed with olde-worlde charm.

Silent as ever, Eddie sat down and folded his arms, watching the room with unreadable eyes.

'How's about a drink before we get started?' Tony said, looking around for a waiter. Spotting one, he clicked his fingers in the air. 'Yo! Three large JDs – and don't take all night about it.'

'House white for me,' Jenna chipped in quickly, a little less amused that he was presuming to order for her now.

Shrugging, Tony said, 'And a house white.' Clicking his fingers again when the boy turned to go, he pointed towards Melody, who was standing at the bar with Fabian now. 'Give her whatever she wants, and tell her not to rush back, yeah?'

Leaning towards Jenna when the waiter had gone, he nodded in Melody's direction. 'What's with that guy?'

Following his gaze, Jenna said, 'Fabian?'

'Yeah, him. D'yuh trust him?'

'Of course. He's a very good manager.'

'If you say so,' Tony muttered, not sounding too convinced. 'He's a bit of a smooth bastard, if you ask me.'

'That's just his way,' Jenna said, not wanting to sound disloyal. 'The customers seem to like it.'

'Yeah, well, I don't buy all that polite namby-pamby shit,' Tony sneered. 'He needs to get his finger out of his ass and start acting like a real fuckin' man.'

Wondering where this was coming from, Jenna frowned. Fabian hadn't done or said anything offensive, as far as she was aware, but Tony obviously disliked him for some reason.

Thrusting a twenty at the waiter when he brought

their drinks over, Tony handed Jenna and Eddie theirs, then took a swig of his own, still eyeballing Fabian.

'So, what did you want to talk about?' Jenna asked, hoping to draw his attention back to her before Fabian got scorch marks on his back.

Turning to face her, Tony shrugged and took another drink. 'You, as it happens. I've been thinking about what we was talking about last night, and I've got to admit I'm intrigued.'

Unnerved by the intensity of his gaze, Jenna said, 'There's really nothing to be intrigued about. I pretty much told you everything last night.'

Guessing what she was thinking, Tony chuckled softly. 'Relax, Angel-face, it's your mind I'm interested in, not your body – hot though it is.'

Jenna felt the blush flare across her cheeks.

'I ain't hitting on you,' Tony assured her with a chuckle. 'Melody's always saying I give off the wrong signals, and it don't usually bother me, but I wouldn't want you thinking I don't respect you, 'cos I do. That's why I want to get to know you better.' Giving her a sincere look then, he said, 'You all right with that?'

Nodding, Jenna said, 'Okay, but let's not talk about me again. I'd rather hear about you and your club. I imagine you do things very differently in the States?'

'Oh, it's different, all right,' Tony said, thinking that, for starters, a little girl like her would never get to play in a big man's game like this without a whole heap of trouble.

Blissfully unaware that he had just been the focus of Tony Allen's scorn, Fabian was enjoying making Melody grovel. She'd apologised for last night and promised that she would never try to force his hand again, but he wasn't as fooled as his easy smile would have her believe. He knew that she'd get around to asking for coke sooner or later, but he wasn't about to offer it on a plate. Far better to let her make the running so he could retain some control over the situation.

Right now, though, he was just enjoying the foreplay.

Sexy as hell in a red satin dress that clung to her hips and moulded itself to her breasts, with her hair swept up, leaving just a few long strands to frame her gorgeous face, and some serious bling sparkling at her ears, throat, wrists and fingers, Melody way out-glammed every other woman in the club – and, *boy*, didn't she know it. Fabian's dick was straining to get at her as she flirted with him, brushing up against him so that her breasts grazed his arm, fluttering her long eyelashes, and pouting her glossy red lips.

Determined to play it cool, he put a hand in his pocket to disguise the bulge and leaned casually back against the bar, gazing nonchalantly around the room.

Sensing that she was losing his attention, Melody eased her knee between his. 'Where's your head at?'

'Just wondering what your boyfriend would say if he knew what you were doing.'

'Oh, let's think . . .' Melody tapped a long red nail against her lip. 'Well, first he'd boil you in oil, then he'd hang you out to dry with a pig's head sticking out of your ass.' Looking him in the eye now, she said, 'Worried?'

'Not at all,' Fabian drawled unconcernedly. 'I'd be more worried about you, to tell the truth.'

'Tony would never hurt me.'

'You trust him that much, do you?'

'Of course.'

'Even if he found out what we're doing?'

'But he's not *going* to find out, is he? Anyway, stop depressing me. I've been dying to see you, and all you've done is talk about Tony.' Leaning closer, Melody raked her nails up his thigh, whispering huskily, 'You heard what that waiter said – he wants me to take my time. So, how about we nip to your office while no one's looking?'

'Love to,' Fabian said, glancing pointedly at his

watch. 'But I can't right now. We've not been open long enough for me to pull a disappearing act.'

'Just long enough to get me wet, huh?'

'Oh, yeah?'

'Yeah,' Melody purred, gazing promisingly into his eyes. 'So don't keep me waiting *too* long, or I might have to go and find someone else to play with.' Winking sexily now, she picked up her glass and began to move away.

Lust winning out over his determination to play hard to get, Fabian reached out. 'Wait.'

Turning back, Melody looked down at his hand on her arm. 'Changed your mind, Lover?'

'Five minutes,' he told her quietly.

Tipping her head to one side, she let her gaze slide down to his groin. 'Sure you can wait that long?'

Grinning, he shook his head. 'You're going to get me into trouble, Miss Fisher.'

'We'll see,' she murmured. 'Just give me a minute to have a word with Tony, and I'll follow you down.'

Fabian exhaled slowly when Melody sashayed towards the table where Tony and Jenna were sitting chatting. He must be crazy, he reckoned, getting deeper into this after the worry of last night, but she was too sexy to resist. And where was the harm – as long as they didn't get caught?

Apologising to Jenna for interrupting, Melody

cupped her hand around Tony's ear and whispered, 'Gay-Boy's offered to dance with me again. You okay with that?'

'Yeah, whatever,' he said, eager to get on with his conversation. 'But no funny business.'

Flicking her tongue into his ear, Melody giggled when he squirmed. 'That's the only funny business I'll be getting up to tonight, Tiger.' Waggling her fingers at Jenna then, she headed for the stairs, fully aware that every man in the room was following with his eyes.

Seeing Fabian going down to the lower floor, Kalli waited a couple of minutes, then poured a glass of chilled orange juice and slipped out from behind the bar. Telling Vanessa that she wouldn't be long, she nipped down the stairs and made a dash for the DJ's booth, keeping her eyes peeled for Fabian.

Smiling at Vibes who was lining up his next track, she edged in behind him and checked out the view through the three-sided window. It was the first time she'd been up there, and she was surprised how much of both the lower and upper floors you could see.

Slipping his headphones down around his neck after a moment, Vibes reached for the juice and took a long drink, then wiped his mouth on the back of his hand. 'Thanks, you're an angel.'

'You're welcome,' Kalli murmured, still looking out. 'Doesn't she look gorgeous?' she said then, sighing softly.

Following her gaze, Vibes felt something catch in his chest when he saw Jenna. She looked so beautiful, and classy with it – and *so* out of his league.

'She sure does,' he murmured resignedly. Then, 'Who are those guys?'

'One of them is Melody Fisher's boyfriend,' Kalli told him, flicking a glance at the swarthy man sitting across from Jenna. 'He's American, like you.'

'Uh huh,' Vibes said thoughtfully.

'Something wrong?' Kalli asked, gazing up at him.

'Nah, nothing,' Vibes said, shrugging off the dark sense of foreboding that had come over him when he'd looked at the man. 'So, who's Melody Fisher?'

'I'd have thought *you*'d know that, her being a big Hollywood star.'

'Can't say I've heard of her,' Vibes said, shrugging.

'She's down there dancing with Fabian somewhere,' Kalli told him, gazing out at the dance floor. 'You couldn't miss her, she's absolutely gorgeous.'

'Ah,' Vibes said, a light switching on in his head. 'Blonde?'

'Yeah. Have you seen her.'

'Oh, yeah, I've seen her,' Vibes murmured. 'So, if she's the mystery man's girlfriend, what do you reckon's going on with her and Fabian? Only they were acting real shady last night, taking off right in the middle of the party.'

'Taking off?' Kalli's eyes widened with curiosity. 'You mean they went out?'

'Got down, more like!' Vibes gave her a knowing grin. 'I saw them having a cosy chat in the corner, then he went up to the office, and she followed a few minutes later. Then *she* came out, and *he* followed *her* a few minutes later. What do you make of that?'

'Nothing good, knowing him,' Kalli snorted.

'Don't think too much of him, huh?'

'Not much,' Kalli admitted.

'Well, well,' Vibes said, chuckling softly. 'Speak of the Devil.' He nodded down to the dance floor, where Fabian and Melody were casually dancing their way towards the edge. 'If I'm not very much mistaken, they're going for a rerun.'

Glancing down at them, Kalli frowned disapprovingly. 'Dirty pig! Do you think I should tell Jenna?'

Shaking his head, Vibes said, 'Nah, you don't

need to be getting involved, and neither does she. If Fabian wants to get his fingers burned, he ain't taking my two favourite ladies down with him.'

'You think so?' Kalli gazed up at him trustingly.

'I *know* so,' he said. 'Anyway, you'd best get out of here before he comes back. Wouldn't want him taking his guilt out on you.'

Nodding, Kalli said goodbye and hurried back up to her bar. Fabian was a dog, but Vibes was right to tell her to stay out of it. It would end in tears without her intervention. These things always did.

Locking the door when Melody came into the office behind him, Fabian pushed her up against the wall and pressed himself against her, his lips covering hers, his hands sliding over her buttocks.

'Not yet,' she gasped, holding him at bay.

'I thought you said you were wet.'

'Soaking, Babe, but I need something to *really* get me going.'

'I'll do that,' Fabian assured her breathily, reaching for her breasts and circling her erect nipples through the satin with his thumbs. 'Oh, Christ, they're incredible.'

'Yeah, I know.' Melody impatiently slapped his hands away. 'But I really, really need a line. You *have* got it, haven't you?'

'Yeah, I've got it.'

Backing off with reluctance, Fabian took the coke out of the safe and laid out two thick lines. Snorting his, he handed the straw to Melody. Moving behind her then when she leaned over, he rubbed up against her. Encouraged when she let out a tiny gasp, he eased up her skirt, groaning lustfully when he saw her diamante thong.

'Oh, that's good,' she moaned, rocking back against him when he slipped his hand between her thighs. 'Oh, yeah . . . keep doing that.'

Unzipping his fly, Fabian freed his hard-on and slid into her. Keeping still then, afraid that he would come if he moved, he held on tight to her hips.

Melody couldn't wait. Arching her back as the coke rushed to her head, she put her hands flat on the table and bucked against him, crying, 'Oh, God, *now*!'

Pounding into her until he felt the first searing rush of ecstasy, Fabian pulled out and swept everything off the desk. Flipping her onto her back, he tore off her panties and tossed them aside, then pushed her dress up over her breasts and bit down on her nipples. Wrapping her legs around his waist, Melody sank her nails into his back, holding on tight as waves of pleasure tore through them both.

Easing herself up when her breathing had

slowed, Melody shoved Fabian off and stood up. 'Oh, shit!' she moaned, looking down at the creases in her dress. 'Look at the *state* of it.'

'Don't panic,' Fabian said calmly, running his hands firmly down the material to smooth it. 'It'll be fine.'

'Best had be,' Melody grumbled. 'Tony will flip if he sees me like this. Christ, my *hair*!' she gasped then, reaching up to find the diamante clips that had been holding it in place. 'I've got to get cleaned up or we're both dead. Where's the bathroom?'

'You'll have to use the staff toilets,' Fabian told her, cursing Jenna for not getting him an en-suite when she'd had the one that her dad had started completed. 'Just let me make sure no one's out there first.'

Going to the door, he frowned when he noticed the tiny red light glowing in the corner. He was sure he'd switched the CCTV off when he came in this morning, but he must have forgotten. It would have caught the whole thing, and how damning would that be if it got into the wrong hands? But he didn't have time to erase it now, because he had to get Melody out of here before anybody caught them.

Sticking his head out, he peered both ways along the corridor, then waved her out when he saw that it was clear. Waiting for her outside the toilets, he hopped nervously from foot to foot, wondering what excuse to give if anybody came along just now.

Or, worse, what if her boyfriend had seen them coming in here?

But if Tony Allen *had* seen them, Fabian had no doubt he'd have followed them or sent his goon to see what was going on – and Fabian would be picking up his teeth right about now.

So, no, they were probably safe this time. But it had been a stupid risk to take, all the same, and he wouldn't be doing it again any time soon – even if it *had* been one of the best fucks of his life.

'How do I look?' Melody asked, coming out just then.

'Great,' he grunted, just wanting to get her out of here.

'My pants,' she squealed as he grabbed her arm and rushed her down the corridor.

'I'll get them later,' he promised, pulling her on down the stairs.

Easing the lower door open, Fabian was relieved to find a group of drunks weaving about in front of it, blocking them from view. Slipping out after Melody, he headed for the downstairs bar while she made her way across the room.

*

Two burly doormen were standing guard at the door to the VIP stairs, and they were refusing to let Leonard and Avril go through. When they stepped aside to let a blonde tart in a red satin dress in, Leonard almost blew a fuse. Already furious because the Buckleys' party hadn't finished as early as he'd expected, this sleight was just adding insult to injury.

It was Avril's fault for making them get here so late. If she'd bothered to tell him that the Buckleys were celebrating their silver-wedding anniversary, he'd have guessed how thoroughly tedious the party was going to be and would have invented a life-threatening illness to get out of going. At the very least, he'd have found a way of getting out of there before the toasts. But, thanks to Avril, he'd had to endure a five-course meal – very little of which he could actually stomach – followed by a two-hour session of whining neoclassical tripe from a string quartet. Then there'd been an hour of congratulatory speeches from the couple's family, friends, and associates.

Flooring his precious Jag when they had finally escaped, Leonard reached the club in record time, only to be told that he'd have to pay twenty pounds – *each*. And, if *that* weren't insult enough, these imbecilic thugs were now refusing to let them go upstairs. It just wasn't on!

'If you don't have a VIP pass, we can't let you in, sir,' one of the doormen was telling him for the fourth time.

'But I'm a friend of the owner,' Leonard told him – again. 'And I spoke to the manager just last night, and he personally invited me back tonight.'

'Sorry, sir, but we need to see your pass.'

'No, you *don't*!' Beads of sweat burst out on Leonard's brow and upper lip now. 'I don't *need* one, because I'm a *friend* of the *owner*. Go and get her. She'll tell you.'

'Sorry, but we can't just go walkabout, sir. If you haven't got a pass, you—'

'Oh, for Christ's sake!' Leonard barked, spraying Avril with sweat as he shook his head angrily. 'This is outrageous. I will *not* be treated like this.'

'Leonard, leave it,' Avril cautioned when one of the burly doormen took a step forward. 'There's a perfectly good table over there.'

Turning on her, Leonard yelled, 'You can sit down here if you want to, but I'm not going anywhere until I get the respect I bloody well deserve.'

Hearing the commotion, Fabian made his way over to see what was going on. Reaching them just as the doormen were about to escort Leonard out, he said, 'What's the problem?'

'These *people* are refusing to allow my wife and

me upstairs,' Leonard told him indignantly. 'I've told them that *you* invited me, but they're being deliberately obstructive. And they wouldn't go and get Jenny to verify that I'm a personal friend. They just keep going on about bloody VIP passes.'

'I'm sure they didn't mean any offence,' Fabian told him, his tone placatory. 'It's my mistake. I must have overlooked you when I was allocating passes. Why don't you let me get you a drink by way of apology?'

'Very kind,' Leonard grunted, casting a last glance of displeasure at the doormen as Fabian waved him up the stairs. 'You really ought to have strong words with these chaps about their treatment of your personal guests, you know.'

'Oh, I will,' Fabian assured him, sharing a conspiratorial glance with the grinning doormen – who resumed their places as if nothing had happened.

Following Leonard and Avril up, he escorted them to the bar and told Vanessa to give them whatever they wanted. Then, apologising again, he promised to sort out the VIP pass as soon as he had a minute.

'That was so humiliating,' Avril hissed when he'd gone. 'Why do you always have to throw your weight around?'

'I wouldn't need to if people knew their places,'

Leonard retorted self-righteously. 'And if it wasn't a problem for the manager, I don't see why *you*'ve got to make an issue of it.'

'Because I'm the one you made a bloody fool of.'

Bored now, Leonard flapped his hand dismissively. 'There's an empty table. Go and sit down. I'll be over in a minute.'

'Why, what are you doing?' Avril asked, unwilling to sit by herself when she didn't even want to be here in the first place.

'Getting another drink,' Leonard informed her frostily.

'We've only just got these.'

'Yes, and at the rate you were putting them back last night you'll need another before your backside hits the seat.'

'Oh, don't start that again,' she moaned.

But Leonard wasn't listening. He'd just spotted Tony Allen and Jenna sitting together across the room.

Turning to see who he was staring at, Avril's lips puckered with irritation. 'Go on, then. Go and see your new friend, why don't you?'

'I'll go when I'm good and ready,' he muttered, sticking his hand into his pocket in an attempt to look casual.

'You're so full of crap!' Avril spat, turning on

her heel and marching away. She knew full well that he wouldn't go over to the man while she was watching, because he didn't want her to see him being shooed away again. He must think that she was a complete fool.

Stepping aside to let Brenda Thompson and her obscenely young male escort pass, Leonard downed his drink and turned back to the bar. 'Scotch rocks,' he said, keeping half an eye on Tony. 'And a G-and-T, please.'

'Anything else?'

Shaking his head, Leonard said, 'No, thanks.' Then, on impulse: 'Actually, yes . . . I was here last night, and, um, a young man served me. Blond, about so tall.' He held a hand up to his nose. 'He was wearing a gold stud in his ear, and I think he might have had a pierced eyebrow.'

'That'll be Austin,' Vanessa said, dipping her voice to ask, 'he didn't do anything to upset you, did he?'

'Course not.' Smiling, Leonard reached into his pocket for his cigarettes. 'He was very helpful, as it happens.' Lighting up, he rested an elbow on the bar. 'Is he, um, working tonight?'

'Yeah, he should be around somewhere.' Gazing out over his shoulder, Vanessa scanned the room, then shrugged. 'Can't see him. Would you like me to tell him you're looking for him?'

'Erm, no, it's okay,' Leonard said quickly. 'I'm sure I'll bump into him before the night's out.'

'Yeah, probably.' Smiling, Vanessa placed his drinks on the counter and held out her hand. 'Nine-eighty, please.'

Leonard blanched. Almost ten pounds for two drinks? Outrageous! He'd have to make sure that Avril didn't go overboard tonight, or he'd be bankrupt come the morning. Tugging his wallet from his pocket, he peeled off a ten-pound note and thrust it at her, telling her to keep the change as he snatched up his drinks and walked away.

'How generous,' Vanessa muttered.

Spotting Austin a few minutes later, she waved him over. 'That fat guy over there's looking for you. But don't expect a tip, 'cos I only got twenty pee.'

'You should learn to be nicer to the customers,' Austin told her, with a cheeky grin.

Making his way over to Leonard's table, he gave Avril a polite nod. Then he turned to Leonard, saying, 'I was told you were looking for me, sir?'

Eyes narrowed to slits, Avril gave a scornful snort. 'Oh, I'm sure he was, dear, but I doubt you'd be so eager to—'

'Shut up!' Leonard hissed, giving her a warning glare. Blushing now, he said, 'Please excuse my wife. We came straight from a dinner party, and

I'm afraid she may have had one too many.'

'Nonsense!' Avril snarled. 'I'm just telling the boy that he might expect to be run off his feet catering to you.'

'Shall I come back later?' Austin suggested, taking a step back.

'Preferably when I'm not here,' Avril snapped. Then, tutting, she shook her head, reminding herself that it wasn't the boy's fault her husband was such a shit. Downing the drink that Leonard had just brought her, she held the glass out. 'A large G-and-T, please.'

Doing the same, Leonard said, 'And I'll have a—'

'Scotch rocks,' Austin finished for him. Then, feeling Avril's glare boring into him, he said to her, 'That *was* what you told me to get for him last night, wasn't it?'

Smiling tightly, she said, 'Excellent memory, dear. Shows you have the makings of a good barman.'

'Thanks,' Austin said, sure that she'd meant it as an insult. 'And yours is a large G-and-T. I won't forget. Can I get you anything else?'

Oh, I'm sure Leonard could think of something, Avril thought bitterly.

'No, thanks,' she said. 'That will do for now.'

Turning on her when Austin made his escape,

Leonard said, 'What the hell was *that* all about? You bloody well embarrassed me.'

'Not half as much as you *constantly* embarrass me,' Avril shot back, looking at him with disgust. 'Or yourself, for that matter.'

'I don't know what you're talking about,' he retorted indignantly. 'You're only being like this because the boy remembered me.'

'No, I'm being like this because *you* went out of your way to look for him.'

'I did not!' Leonard lied. 'The girl on the bar must have got the wrong end of the stick. She asked if we'd been happy with the service so far, and I mentioned that the boy had been very helpful last night, that's all.'

'And she just happened to know *which* boy you were talking about? How very convenient.' Shaking her head disbelievingly, Avril folded her arms.

'You're just miffed because nobody's paying *you* any attention.'

'Oh, bugger off!'

'Where are you going?' Leonard demanded when she pushed her chair back and stood up.

Leaning towards him, Avril patted his hand. 'Don't worry, dear, the little boy will be back soon to keep you company. Anyway, I thought you were supposed to be meeting that awful man again?' Casting a glance in Tony Allen's direction, she sneered. 'Doesn't look much like he's waiting for you, though.'

On his way back with the drinks just then, Austin waited until Avril had gone, then approached Leonard with a smile. 'There you go, sir. One G-and-T, and one *very* large Scotch rocks.'

'Thanks.' Sighing wearily, Leonard reached for his wallet and handed him a twenty. 'Keep the change,' he said, running a hand through his hair. Wiping it on his trousers when it came back wet, he slumped down in his seat, looking thoroughly dejected.

Gazing down at him, Austin shook his head sympathetically. The poor sod's wife was a grade-A bitch to talk to him like that in public. Christ, *gays* were supposed to be bitchy, but they weren't a *patch* on so-called loving wives when it came to verbal emasculation. Thank God *he*'d never have to put up with some razor-tongued harridan ripping *his* balls to shreds.

'Look, I hope you don't think I'm being nosy,' he said when Leonard glanced up at him questioningly. 'But is everything all right? Only your wife seemed a bit upset.'

'My wife is perpetually upset about something or other,' Leonard muttered, his belly rising and falling as he gave another deep sigh.

'My mum's the same,' Austin confided quietly.

'Her mate reckons it's the menopause, but nobody dares mention it, 'cos she, like, *totally* flips.'

Looking into the boy's bluer-than-blue eyes, Leonard felt a mirthless chuckle bubble up in his throat. Oh, if only it were as simple as the menopause. At least there was medication for that.

'Anyway.' Austin flapped his hands. 'I just wanted you to know that I understand. And if you ever need to talk . . . well, – you know.'

Leonard's eyes misted a little as it struck him that the boy was being sincere. It was so unexpected that he didn't know quite how to react. It had been so very long since anybody had shown him any compassion or understanding.

'You're very kind,' he murmured gratefully.

'No problem.' Austin gave him a pitying smile. He couldn't bear to see people upset – unless he'd caused it, in which case they deserved it, so it didn't count.

'Do you, um, have a girlfriend?' Leonard asked suddenly.

'God, no!' Austin yelped. Then, glancing quickly around, he whispered, 'I'm not that way inclined.'

'Ah, I see.' Nodding thoughtfully, Leonard drummed his fingers on the table for a moment, then said, 'Are there many – you know – *places* for you young people to meet?'

'Oh, yeah!' Austin subconsciously adopted a

girlish hand-on-hip stance. 'The Village is *fabulous*.'

'Really.' Leonard nodded again. 'Well, that's good, isn't it? I mean, it would be terrible if you had to hide away.'

'There's none of that, these days,' Austin told him breezily. 'We're out and about all over the place. In fact, you'd be surprised how many of us there are.' Pausing then, when it occurred to him that this man was of an age that he might not actually approve, he shrugged. 'We tend to stick to our own places, though, so it's not like we're shoving it in anyone's face.'

'Probably just as well.' Leonard sighed again. 'There are a lot of ignorant people in this world.'

'Tell me about it,' Austin muttered, thinking of some of the scrapes he'd found himself in before now. It was his own fault, because he got a perverse kick out of flirting with straight men, but you never knew which way they would take it. Nine times out of ten they laughed it off – and some even played along. But the odd one would turn nasty and batter you senseless. Much as he liked to pooh-pooh Kalli's concerns, he *did* know that he should be more careful.

Like now, for example, chatting away to this man like they were mates when the man was probably only being friendly because his wife was such a bitch and he was grateful to have somebody on his side – *not* because he was interested.

Not that *Austin* would be interested even if *he* was, because he preferred the classic tall, dark and handsome type – like Vibes. Now *there* was a man he'd be only too happy to . . .

Stopping the thought dead before it showed up in his shorts, Austin said, 'Right, well, I'd best go back to work. Shout if you need me.'

'I will,' Leonard said quietly. 'Thanks again.'

'I was watching that,' Kalli hissed when Austin came back to the bar. 'What's going on with you two?'

Raising a prim eyebrow, Austin said, 'Er, he's *married*.'

'That doesn't usually stop you.'

'No, but I'm behaving myself – Guide's honour. I *do* listen to you sometimes, you know.'

'Glad to hear it,' Kalli murmured, not sure that she totally believed him.

'I don't half feel sorry for him, though.' Austin glanced back at Leonard, who looked thoroughly miserable again. 'His wife treats him like a *dog*. You should have heard her tearing strips off him just now. It was brutal. And she didn't even care that *I* was standing there.'

'Keep out of it,' Kalli told him firmly, sure that the fat man probably deserved whatever his wife threw at him. 'And promise you'll stay away from him.'

'Okay, I promise,' Austin agreed wearily, crossing his fingers behind his back.

'Without the crossed fingers.' Folding her arms, Kalli raised an eyebrow and gave him a stern look.

Grinning, Austin brought his hands up and waggled his fingers. 'Is that better?'

'Much,' she said, giving him a satisfied smile and walking away.

'Yeah, but I didn't promise that time,' Austin whispered to her retreating back. If she thought he was letting one of the other waiters nab his big tipper, she had another think coming.

Still buzzing more than an hour after her visit to Fabian's office, Melody was amusing herself by winding up Tony's celebrity friends.

Calling, 'Cheers' to nobody in particular, she slurped her drink and smacked her lips loudly – to the obvious disgust of those close enough to hear. Then, slamming the glass down, she lit one cigarette after another, blowing her smoke into other people's faces, and rudely jumping in and out of their conversations.

Tony was watching Melody with suspicion. She couldn't seem to sit still, and she was being way louder than usual, pushing herself into conversations that didn't concern her and tossing out insults disguised as compliments. If he didn't know better, he'd swear she was on something. He was sure she wasn't, though, because she didn't know anyone to score off. But, high or not, she was definitely acting up – and he wasn't impressed.

Excusing himself after a while, he got up and jerked his head at her. 'Yo. Over here a minute.'

'What's up?' Melody asked, jiggling to the music as she followed him to the bar, her eyes darting every which way.

'That's what I want to know.' Tony gave her a piercing look. 'You're acting weird. Are you on something?'

'Oh, give me a break,' she snorted, putting her hands on her hips. 'I decide to get into the swing of things, and you have to go and ruin it by accusing me of all sorts. I don't *have* to talk to your boring friends, you know. I was only making an effort for *you*. But if that's all the thanks I'm gonna get . . .'

'That'd better be all it is,' Tony said in a low voice. 'If I find out you've been doing something—'

'You'll what?' Melody interrupted cockily. 'You can't tell me what to do, Tony. I'm your girlfriend, not your daughter. Though, Christ knows, you're *old* enough to be my fucking dad.'

'That's right,' Tony warned her quietly. 'You just keep flapping that mouth and see what it gets you.'

Catching the glint in his blacker-than-black eyes, Melody struggled to bring herself under control. It was mega-difficult with the coke still coursing through her veins, but her deeper instincts screamed at her to behave before he flipped out and she managed to latch on to a sliver of common sense and quieten down.

Pouting now, she looped her arms around his thick neck and dipped her head to drop little kisses on his face.

'Sorry, Sugar-Wugar. I'm trying to be nice, but the nasty people don't like me – and that upsets me, 'cos I haven't done nothing wrong.'

Gazing down into her cleavage, Tony felt his anger evaporate. Man, she was one horny bitch.

'Nah, they're just jealous 'cos you're such a doll,' he told her, giving her nipples a tweak. 'But if that's your idea of being *nice*, quit it, for fuck's sake. It sounds more like insults to me.' Chuckling now, he said, 'And don't think I didn't hear you telling that broad she's lucky she's going bald.'

'Yeah, well she is,' Melody said playfully. 'All she has to do is open the window and her little nest's dry. Me, I gotta spend two hours drying this little lot.' Reaching up, she ran her hands through her own lusciously thick hair.

'Smart-mouthed bitch.' Tony laughed, copping a handful of ass. 'Just pack it in, yeah?'

'If you say so,' Melody agreed, slipping her arm through his. 'But you'd best start paying me some attention, or I might get bored and start amusing myself again.'

Catching Fabian's eye when they passed him on their way back to the table, Melody gave him a little wink and let her gaze slide to his groin. Smiling when he blanched, she cupped her hand around Tony's ear and whispered, 'How's about we cut out early and go fuck our brains out?'

Sure that Melody had been whispering about him, Fabian beat a hasty retreat to the safety of the lower floor. Yet again, the buzz was well and truly shattered, and the stabbing paranoia was back with a vengeance. He needed a hit of vitamin C to bring him down.

Going to the bar, he snapped his fingers at JoJo and demanded a fresh orange juice.

'Yes, *sir*!' she muttered, her slim nostrils flaring with irritation as she flipped her platinum hair back over her shoulder and marched to the fridge. Pouring his drink, she slammed the glass down on the counter in front of him. 'Anything else?'

Fabian narrowed his eyes meanly. 'Who am I?'

A confused frown flickered across JoJo's brow.

What kind of whacked-out question was *that*?

'Who *am* I?' he repeated slowly.

'Fabian,' she replied. Adding, 'Mr King,' when he carried on staring at her. Then, 'The manager.'

'At last she gets it,' Fabian snarled. 'Me manager – *you* waitress. And if you ever dare speak to me like that again, you'll find yourself out on the street where you belong. Got me?'

'Got you.' Lifting her chin proudly, JoJo bit her tongue to prevent herself from telling him to go fuck himself. She needed this job too much to give him an excuse to sack her.

'Good!' Fabian snatched up his glass. 'And don't forget it.'

Sticking two fingers up at his back when he walked away, JoJo snarled, 'Yes, Mr King . . . no, Mr King . . . and would you like me to suck your tiny little dick while I'm at it, Mr King?'

'Ex*cuse* me?' Austin gasped, coming up behind her in time to catch this last bit. 'Don't tell me you've got the hots for Fabulous Fabian? Oh, my fucking *life*, girl. Just wait till I tell the others.'

'Fuck off,' JoJo snapped. 'He's a jumped-up little twat.'

'That's more like it,' Austin chuckled. 'Anyway, forget him. Have you got my thingy?'

'Shut *up*!' Glancing quickly around, JoJo grabbed his arm and dragged him into a corner.

'Fucking hell, man, you're going to get me shot with that big mouth of yours.'

'Sorry. I wasn't thinking.'

'You never do.' Scowling, JoJo reached down her top and pulled out a small plastic bag of tablets. Taking one out, she shoved it into his hand. 'There. And don't ask me for any more tonight, 'cos you're acting too hyper.'

'Can't help it.' Austin grinned. 'I'm buzzing off this place. Don't you think it's *fab* since old man Lordey kicked it?'

'Would be if we had a different manager,' JoJo agreed, smiling now because Austin's glee was infectious. 'Glad *you*'re here, though.'

'And Kalli.'

'Yeah, *right*,' JoJo muttered, wondering what everyone saw in the miserable little Chinky. Always telling people what to do, and giving it with the inscrutable-eyes business. JoJo couldn't stand her.

'See you later, Terminator,' Austin said, already dancing away.

'Oi, money,' JoJo called after him. 'You still owe me for the last one as well, and I've got to buy a leccy card on my way home or I won't be able to have a bath.'

'Stop whinging,' Austin said, whipping a tenner out of his shorts and shoving it in her hand.

'Oh, that's gross,' she complained, holding it

away from herself. 'It's still warm. And I bet it *stinks* of bummy cock.'

'Oi, you cheeky whore. I'll have you know I spray my willy with Lynx every ten minutes.'

'Yeah, and I have to cut *mine* off every night 'cos it keeps growing back.'

'I always knew you were a man,' Austin snorted.

'With tits like these?' JoJo retorted sarcastically. 'Yeah, right.'

'Call *them* tits?' Austin shot back. 'I've seen better on the trannies down the Brittania.'

'Fuck off!'

'Love you too.' Blowing her a kiss, Austin danced away with his E clutched in his hand. Waving as he passed Leonard and Avril on their way out, he called, 'See you later, Mr and Mrs D.'

'Did you *hear* that?' Avril snapped, glaring after him. 'Mr and Mrs D, indeed! Who the bloody hell does he think he's talking to?'

Ignoring her, Leonard struggled to hide his smile as he continued on out of the door. The boy had not only shown him a kindness tonight, for which he would be eternally grateful, but he'd obviously gone to the trouble of finding out their names, too – which quite took the sting out of what had otherwise been another thoroughly miserable night.

He still hadn't managed to speak to Jenny alone

yet. And he'd missed the opportunity to chat with Tony Allen, too, because the man had left early – with the same sluttish blonde whose easy passage into the VIP lounge had so enraged Leonard earlier.

Still, it was nobody's business but Allen's if he chose to pick up prostitutes. It wouldn't make Leonard think any less of him. All Leonard had ever wanted was to be a part of the celebrity circles he'd spent so many years on the edges of; to have people acknowledge that he was still a force to be reckoned with. And what better way of gaining the recognition he craved, than by being associated with Tony Allen, who obviously had the power to draw influential people to him.

At closing time, Jenna eased herself onto a stool at the lower bar while Fabian saw everybody out. Apart from the twenty minutes or so that she'd spent chatting to Tony Allen earlier, she hadn't sat down all night and, once again, she was exhausted.

Smiling when Vibes joined her, she said, 'You look as wiped as I feel.'

'I am,' he admitted, covering a yawn with his hand.

Popping her head out of the kitchen door just then, Kalli said, 'I'm making coffee if anybody wants one?'

'Oh, yes, please,' Jenna said.

Telling her that he'd love one, Vibes picked up a beer mat and turned it over and over on the bar, wondering how to ask Jenna the questions that had been on his mind all night. Deciding that the direct approach was best, he said, 'You know that man you were talking to earlier – Melody Fisher's boyfriend. He's American, right?'

'Yeah.' Jenna nodded. 'Not that you'd ever guess that you two came from the same place,' she added, smiling as she thought how different Tony's loud, aggressive accent was compared to Vibes's altogether softer, more laid-back drawl.

'What's his name?'

'Tony Allen. Why? Do you know him?'

Narrowing his eyes, Vibes pursed his lips as he rolled the name over in his mind. 'Don't think so,' he said after a moment. 'I just thought he looked kind of familiar. What do you know about him?'

'Not a lot,' Jenna admitted, thanking Kalli when she put their coffees and a small sugar bowl on the counter. 'I met him for the first time last night. He's only been in England for two weeks, apparently – brought his girlfriend over for a break, because she's been working so hard. Isn't that sweet?'

'Mmmm,' Vibes murmured, stirring sugar into his cup.

'Something wrong?' Jenna asked, curious about his response.

'Not sure,' he replied quietly. Then, shrugging, he said, 'Nah. I'm probably way off track. Don't worry about it.'

'Worry?' Jenna repeated, frowning now. 'Well, if there's one thing guaranteed to *make* me worry, it's being told not to.'

Sighing, Vibes ran a hand over his face. He should have kept his mouth shut, but it was too late now. Jenna was waiting for an explanation.

'Look, don't quote me, because I could be totally off the mark,' he said. 'But he's got a look about him, that's kind of like . . .' Pausing, he shrugged. 'Let's just say he looks connected.'

Gazing blankly back at him, Jenna shook her head.

'To the mob,' Vibes said quietly.

Laughing incredulously when she realised what he meant, Jenna said, '*Tony*? Don't be daft! He's far too charming to be involved in something like that.'

'Hey, don't be fooled by the friendly face,' Vibes warned her. 'Some of the most charming guys in the States are connected. Sophistication and charisma are tools of the trade for those guys.'

Smiling now, sure that he was wrong, Jenna said, 'Oh, come on. I'm sure you'd be able to tell if someone was into something like that.'

'You're too trusting,' Vibes told her quietly. 'Look, tell me to mind my own business by all means, but can I ask what you were talking about?'

'Nothing really.' Jenna shrugged. 'We were just comparing notes, because he had a club of his own. I think it amuses him that a woman can run an empire without a man to guide her. Apparently, it wouldn't be so easy for me in the States.'

'True,' Vibes admitted, peering shamefacedly down into his coffee. 'It's still a bit of a man's world over there, I'm afraid.'

'I suppose I should be grateful that *you* don't think like that, then?' Jenna teased. 'Or you'd never have stayed on to work for me after my dad died.'

'Sure I would,' Vibes murmured, smiling shyly as he added, 'women are *way* more appreciative.' Forcing himself to look at her then, he said, 'But, seriously . . . about that guy. Like I said, I could be wrong, but just in case I'm not, do yourself a favour and don't get too involved with him.'

Seeing the concern in his lovely blue eyes, Jenna nodded her agreement. She knew that he wouldn't make something like that up for the sake of it, but even if he *was* right, Tony was just a friendly customer as far as she was concerned – nothing more, nothing less. And whatever he did or didn't do when he was at home was none of her business.

Finishing her coffee now, she changed the subject, asking Vibes if he had anything planned for tomorrow.

'Nah, I'm just gonna laze around,' he told her. 'Gina's taking the baby to her mom's, so I'm planning on catching up on my sleep while it's nice and quiet. She's a cute little thing, but, *man*, does she make noise now she's teething.'

'Painful.' Jenna gave him a sympathetic smile. 'So, Gina's English, is she?' she asked then, not wanting to seem like she was being nosy, but curious to know about Vibes's wife.

'Yeah, she's from Yorkshire,' he said. 'Took a bit of getting used to the accent, but she's a great girl. And lord only knows how she copes, what with the baby crying all night, and Kenneth making an unholy mess wherever he goes. The guy can't put *nothing* back where he found it.'

'That drives me crazy,' Jenna said, laughing softly. 'I like everything to be in its place, but Jason just thinks I'm a neat freak.' Clamping her mouth shut as soon as the words slipped out, she gritted her teeth angrily. Why the hell was she still talking about that bastard in the present tense? Would she *never* be free of him?

Vibes sighed softly. So, there was a Jason, was there? Well, at least he knew for sure now, so he could stop wondering. Shame, though, because he had a feeling that he and Jenna could have had something. But, hey, who was he kidding? She was his boss – end of.

5

Before Jenna knew it, Zenith had been open for a full month and was doing better than she'd ever dreamed possible. The publicity that they'd received after the opening party had certainly helped, especially the picture of Chase Mann on the front of the *Evening News*, with the club's smoked-glass doors with the etched gold 'Z' clearly visible behind him. That had proved to be a huge draw for young girls from all over the country, who turned up in their droves, desperate to get near the sexy rock star – and, hopefully, be the one he chose to take back to his hotel at the end of the night. But he was usually so out of it by the time he left that his manager would literally have to carry him out.

Shots of various stars coming and going had begun to feature regularly in some of the nationals' gossip pages since then and Jenna kept a close eye on them, making sure that the publicity stayed positive. So far, it had all been good, and she couldn't have been happier as her profits climbed steadily. She was actually contemplating paying herself a wage instead of just covering her living expenses if things carried on as they were, and she might even think about taking a day off, too. A whole day to just lounge around in her night-clothes and watch TV, read, or listen to music. Or maybe she'd take a drive out to the country and lie on a nice secluded river bank somewhere, watching the swans float serenely by. Or she could visit the cemetery and put flowers on her parents' and Damian's graves. *Anything* that didn't involve the club, because she'd been living and breathing it for five solid months now.

As had Fabian.

In her office with him at the end of the month, counting the takings ready for banking in the morning, Jenna noticed the dark hollows under his eyes, and the yawns that he kept covering with his hand, and realised that, like her, he hadn't had a single day off since this had started. But while it was one thing for *her* to give up her life for the sake of the club, it was quite another to expect him to sacrifice his.

Pouring two glasses of wine when they had finished, she joined him on the couch and told him it was time that he took a break.

'I don't need one,' Fabian replied without hesitation. 'I'm fine.'

'No, you're not,' Jenna laughed. 'You're shattered.'

'I am *fine*,' he repeated firmly.

It was a lie, but he wasn't about to admit that Melody Fisher was the real cause of his exhaustion. He'd never met a woman who could outfuck him before – and that was saying something. But it was no longer the thrill that it had been at the start. Quick dash to the office whenever she clicked her fingers. Quick snort. Quick shag. No talking. No affection. No satisfaction. Fabian was beginning to understand what his past conquests had meant when they'd complained that he only wanted them for their bodies. Not that he wanted a relationship, or anything, but it was *so* cold that he was finding it increasingly difficult to get aroused. Although it didn't seem to have affected Melody's ability to orgasm. The woman was insatiable.

But it wasn't just the sex that was wearing him out. The coke situation was doing his head in, too.

Melody had been in every single night since the reopening party, and she expected Fabian to have her supplies ready and waiting. But it didn't seem to have occurred to her that he actually had to *pay* for it. And it was more expensive than ever right now, because there was a shortage and the dealers were milking it. And there was all the other stuff to take into consideration, too – like all the running around he was having to do to get hold of it, and his increasing paranoia at the thought of being caught in possession of it and losing everything he'd worked so hard for.

If Fabian could've turned back the clock he'd have wiped his damn nose before setting foot out of his office that first night, because if Melody hadn't caught him she'd have had nothing to hold over him. He would probably still have shagged her, but it would have been on *his* terms. Now she had him over a barrel and it could only get worse, because the more frustrated she got about Tony's seeming reluctance to take her home, the more coke she demanded. And the more she took, the more she craved it. It was a vicious circle, and Fabian was terrified that she would get careless one of these days and drop a bomb that would explode in his face.

He was so worried, in fact, that he had kept the CCTV tape that he'd accidentally recorded of them that first time. Initially, he had intended to destroy it in case it got into the wrong hands. But then he'd decided that it would be better to keep it as insurance – proof that she'd been a willing participant, should she ever cry rape or anything stupid like that. It would be an absolute last resort, though, not something he would bring out unless she gave him no choice. And then he would have to run, because Tony Allen would probably try to kill him.

Right now, though, Fabian was stuck between the rock of meeting Melody's demands and the very high ledge of not doing so. And there wasn't a thing he could do about it, except sit it out and pray that Tony would agree to take her home soon.

Watching Fabian as he wallowed in his thoughts, Jenna shook her head. If he was as fine as he made out, how come he was struggling to keep his eyes open? And why was his chin getting closer and closer to his chest? Tapping his leg, she smiled amusedly when his head jerked up.

'Not tired, huh?'

'I'm fit as a fiddle,' he grunted, sitting up straighter and widening his eyes. 'There. Do I *look* tired?'

'You were practically asleep,' Jenna pointed out. 'Anyway, I'm not asking you, I'm *telling* you to take a break. I'm sure we'll manage without you for a week or two.'

'I don't *want* you to manage without me,' Fabian countered, frowning now. 'You might decide that you don't want me back.'

Before Jenna had a chance to deny this, there was a knock at the door.

'Guess what I've just heard . . . ?' Kalli burst in

without waiting for an answer, her pretty face glowing with excitement. Stopping in her tracks when she saw Fabian, she said, 'Oh, sorry. I thought you were alone.'

Assuring her that she wasn't interrupting anything, Jenna said, 'What have you heard?'

Flicking a nervous glance at Fabian, who was giving her the cold eye, Kalli said, 'Austin's friend works at Morgan's, and he reckons their door takings are right down. And The Nest is supposed to be even worse. They've started a happy hour to try and bring the customers back, but it isn't working.'

'Wow!' Smiling, Jenna turned to Fabian. 'That's great, isn't it?'

'Yeah, great,' he murmured. 'Is that it, Kalli?'

'Er, yes.' Kalli backed towards the door. 'I just thought Jenna would want to know. Anyway, I'd best get going. Austin's waiting for me.'

Turning to Jenna when they were alone again, Fabian said, 'I don't want to burst your bubble, but that might not be as good as you think. It's one thing losing a few customers, but nobody can afford to lose too many. If the other clubs realise we're the cause, they're going to get pissed off.'

'But that's just part and parcel of business, isn't it? Nobody's got the monopoly on customers.'

'No, but businessmen aren't the most magnanimous of people when their profits are under threat.'

'Well, that's not very fair,' Jenna said, frowning now. 'It's not my fault if my club's more popular than theirs. They should make more of an effort to keep people interested.'

'True, but that won't stop them blaming you. Just don't be surprised if they start playing dirty, that's all I'm saying.'

'Dirty? How?'

Shrugging, Fabian said, 'Slashing their door prices. Going all out on drinks promotions so that we can't compete. There's all kinds of ways they could get at us. And if it costs them more in the short term, they might figure it's worth it to put you in the red.'

'That's outrageous,' Jenna gasped. 'We're only charging the going rate on the door, and the drinks aren't cheap, so it's not like we're undercutting anyone. What am I supposed to do? Sack all the DJs so nobody wants to come?'

Peering into her angry eyes, Fabian smiled to himself. She was clueless about the cut-throat nature of this highly competitive business, but she looked so damn raunchy when she was pissed off, if she wasn't his boss he'd be tempted to . . .

Whoa, there! He pulled himself up short. He might go there one day – when Melody had gone and his dick had recovered. But not now. He was too knackered to even *think* about getting it up.

Sighing resignedly beside him, Jenna finished her drink and shrugged. 'Oh, well. If anything happens, I'll just have to deal with it, won't I? But I'm proud of what we've achieved, and I've got no intention of lowering my standards to satisfy whoever can't match them.'

'Fair enough,' Fabian said approvingly. She had balls, you had to give her that. Finishing his own drink then, he put his glass down and got up. 'Think I'll make a move,' he said, stretching languidly. 'Anything you want me to do before I go?'

Smiling up at him, Jenna said, 'Yeah, book yourself a holiday. Just let me know when you're going and I'll have the agency send a temp in to cover for you.'

Sensing that she wouldn't stop going on about it if he didn't seem to make an effort, Fabian agreed to think about it, but he had no intention of doing it. This was *his* club, and there was no way he was leaving the way clear for some chancer to come in and take over – like he had with his predecessor.

Anyway, there was no way he was risking going off the scene while Melody was still in town. If she started suffering coke withdrawal symptoms and he wasn't there to make her feel better, there was no telling what she'd do. And he didn't fancy coming back to find Tony Allen and the goon waiting for him.

Across town just then, dropping Fabian in it was the last thing on Melody's mind. Not long back from the club, she'd been banished to the bedroom of the hotel suite that was fast becoming home – to Tony, at least – while he and Eddie got on with some 'private' business in the lounge.

Melody was sick to death of Tony and his secrets. Every night for weeks he'd been dropping her off here after the club and pissing off out to God only knew where with Eddie. And on the rare occasions that he actually stayed in, he spent all his time with Eddie, having conversations that she wasn't allowed to join in with. She'd given up trying to listen through a glass, because the walls were too damn thick and she could never make anything out, so she invariably went to bed to catch up on her beauty sleep. But she was way too wired to sleep tonight, so she decided to call her agent, Scotty Nash, on the off chance that she might actually reach him this time.

Melody had been here for six weeks now, and to start with Scotty had called daily to tell her what was happening back home, and to ask when she was coming back, because he had big things planned for his 'favourite girl'. But two weeks ago he'd suddenly stopped calling, and she had found it impossible to get through to him since. If she called his office, his secretary said he was in a meeting; and whenever she tried his mobile it was either switched off or he just wasn't answering – and she suspected the latter to be the case.

Realising that her mistake was to always call him from her mobile, the number of which he obviously knew and could therefore ignore, she decided to trick him by using the hotel line. Asking the operator for an international line, she tapped Scotty's number into the bedside phone and settled back against the pillows.

'Ah ha!' she crowed when he answered on the second ring. 'So glad I caught you when you weren't busy – *for once*!'

'Melody,' Scotty said, his voice betraying that she had been dead right about him avoiding her. 'Hi, Sweets. How are you? I've been meaning to call, but you know how it is this end. Work, work, work!'

'Yeah, and I'm supposed to be your most important client,' Melody reminded him icily. 'So, what's happening, Scotty? What have you got lined up for me?'

'It's been a bit hectic lately,' Scotty said evasively.

'What with the Oscars coming up, and the preparations for Cannes, and everything.'

'What about my audition?' Melody cut in impatiently. 'Have you been in touch with the producers?'

'Sure, I've been in touch. But you know how it is with those guys – too many dinners to eat, too much booze to drink.'

'Never mind that, what are they saying about *me*?'

'Ah, well, that's the thing, see . . .' Scotty sounded like he was sweating now. 'They, um, kinda passed.'

'Passed?' Melody repeated croakily, feeling like a bucket of ice water had just been tipped over her head. 'What do you mean, *passed*? They didn't want me?'

'Something like that, I guess. But, hey, you know . . . there'll be other parts.'

'I don't want *other* parts,' Melody whined. 'I want *that* part. Why didn't you get it for me, Scotty? You're supposed to have stayed on it. That's what I pay you for, you dumb shit!'

'Hey, don't be ragging on me,' Scotty shot back at her. 'It ain't my fault you took yourself out of the picture for so fucking long and let them producers forget you exist. I did warn you. You know how competitive this market is.'

'It's only a *holiday*,' she gasped. 'It's not like I'm never coming back.'

'Try telling them that,' Scotty countered. 'These guys got better things to do than sit around waiting on someone who ain't even in the news no more.'

'I'm not?' Melody murmured, feeling sick now because she'd been a regular column-filler before leaving – if not quite the headliner she'd planned on becoming once the Julia Roberts film was in the bag.

'Nope. Not a thing in weeks,' Scotty told her – sounding remarkably unconcerned, she thought, considering that he should have been tearing his hair out thinking up ways of keeping her name in print while she was away: feeding gossip to the press, leaking rumours – *any*thing to keep her out there.

'So, have they cast the part yet?' she forced herself to ask – not wanting to hear an affirmative, but needing to know if there was still time to get home and rectify things. If they hadn't chosen anyone else yet, she might still be able to persuade the producers that she was their girl. Or maybe she could go directly to Julia. She'd read through the scene with Melody at the audition and had said she was fantastic. If Melody could get to her—

'Remember that girl, Deanna Shelby?' Scotty cut into her thoughts.

'*No*,' Melody muttered, feeling sicker than ever. 'Please don't tell me *she* got it?'

'Yup. *Wowed* 'em, by all accounts – really blew them away.'

'How?' Melody gasped. 'She might as well *be* me – but without the talent. She's a fucking freak! Copying my style, and turning up at all the same auditions.'

'Well, it's obviously working for her,' Scotty commented snidely. 'Word is, it was actually a toss-up between you and her for a while. But she's been getting herself out and about since the audition, and you've disappeared off the face of the earth, so it wasn't that tough a decision in the end.'

'But that's not fair!' Melody whined. 'I'm the real deal, she's just a fucking clone! And the critics—'

'Are raving about Deanna now,' Scotty jumped in. '*She*'s their *Next Big Thing* now. And you should see the headlines she's been getting. *Boy*, that girl knows how to get herself column inches!'

Hearing him chuckle at his end, a light switched on in Melody's head.

'You're representing her, aren't you?' she demanded icily.

'Well, *hell*, yeah,' Scotty admitted. 'I'd have been a fool *not* to when she was practically begging me, don't you think? I mean, now she's in there with Julia, it's gonna be mucho buckolas all the way.'

Melody slammed the phone down.

Scotty had told her everything she needed to know. She was on her way out; the door was already closing behind her. The fickle producers who had so recently wined and dined her had already forgotten her; and Scotty scumbag Nash was effectively dumping her, because he'd be too busy pouring all of his time and energy into his new money-cow from here on in.

And Deanna Shelby was the biggest cow going!

The ugly witch had crawled out of the woodwork last year and come trailing after Melody like the annoying slug that she was, copying Melody's clothes, getting the same hair colour and extensions, and the same porcelain veneers. She'd even gone to the trouble of finding out which tuck-and-suck man Melody had used, and got herself the same boobs, nose and lips. She'd been so desperate to *be* Melody, and it looked like she'd finally achieved her aim. In six short weeks she had stepped neatly and completely into Melody's shoes – and there wasn't a goddamned thing Melody could do about it, because she was wasting away over here, in the no man's land they called Manchester, England; while Deanna was stealing her thunder back home.

And it was all Tony's fault for bringing her here in the first place, on this holiday that he'd booked behind her back as a 'reward' for all the hard work she'd been doing lately. The holiday she'd never even wanted, and hadn't enjoyed one fucking bit!

Screaming with frustration now, Melody snatched her glass of brandy off the bedside table and hurled it at the wall.

In the lounge, Tony heard the sound of shattering glass and, fearing that Melody had had an accident, rushed in to see if she was all right.

Stepping back when a piece of glass crunched under his shoe, he looked down at the shards embedded in the thick carpet, then up at the wet patch staining the expensive flock wallpaper as the brandy dripped slowly down.

'What the fuck are you doing?' he demanded, glaring at Melody, who looked like a madwoman, sitting in the middle of the bed with her face a mess of tears and her hair all over the place. 'Have you lost your fucking mind? I'll have to *pay* for this.'

'*Good!*' she screamed, balling her hands into fists and slamming them down on her thighs. 'You *should* pay for what you've done to me, you bastard!'

'Keep it down,' he barked, closing the door. 'You want the whole fucking place to hear you?'

'I don't *care*!' Melody wailed, snatching up a

book and throwing it at him. 'You've ruined my *life*!'

Narrowing his eyes, Tony frowned deeply. She was acting crazy, and he didn't have the first clue what was eating her.

'I just spoke to Scotty,' she yelled at him accusingly. 'And guess fucking *what*, Tony? I didn't get that part I was after!'

'Is that it?' he sneered. 'You just cost me thousands, all because you didn't get one fucking part?'

'Is that *it*?' she screeched, really blazing now. 'Don't you get it, Tony? I'm *finished*! They picked some big-titted long-legged *freak* who thinks she's *me* – and it's all *your* fault, because *you* kept me *here* when I should have been *there*!'

'Aw, quit freaking out,' Tony grunted, laughing at her now. 'I told you you was no good from the start, but would you listen? No. So now you're gonna have to feel what it's like to hear it from the rest of the world.'

'No good?' Melody repeated incredulously. 'What kind of crap is *that*? I'm great – everyone's been saying it. I knocked them dead in that Clooney film!'

'Aw, get over yourself,' Tony shot back at her. 'You're an average actress, and it was an average film. Yeah, they was hyping you for a while, but only 'cos they had nothing better to do. Do you think they'd have forgot you so fast if you was great? Jolie could take *ten* years off, and they'd be lining up with their tongues hanging out if she said she wanted to come back. You're away six weeks and they can't even remember your name. Think about it.'

'You got the hots for her, or something?' Melody demanded jealously. ''Cos you sure sound like it – always comparing me to her. If she'd kept her fucking clothes on she wouldn't be *half* as famous as she is, but I don't suppose you care about that, do you?'

'Clothes on, clothes off – who gives a shit?' Tony replied scathingly. 'Fact is, *she*'s got it, and *you* ain't – not for the kind of acting you want to do, anyway. I always said you should stick to doing what you do best.'

'Oh, yeah, you'd like that, wouldn't you?' Melody hissed. 'And there was me thinking you actually *loved* me. Well, I guess I know the truth now, don't I? You don't love no one but *you*. Well, that's it, Tony. I've had it with you and your shit. First thing tomorrow, I'm going home – without *you*!'

'No, you ain't.'

'Oh, right, so you're allowed to do whatever *you* want but *I*'ve got to do what *you* tell me?' Melody demanded. 'That the way it works in your thick head?'

Tony didn't answer. He just stared at her with rapidly darkening eyes. A sure-fire warning that Melody was too fired-up to heed.

'Well?' she continued, thrusting her chin out at him, her eyes sparking with pure hatred. 'That how you think it is with us, Tone? You do whatever the fuck you want, and I just go along with it – like all them fucking *whores* you used to be hooked up with?'

'You remember what you was doing when I picked you up?' Tony cut in quietly.

'What's *that* got to do with it?' she spluttered. 'Christ, Tony, have you any idea how *sick* I am of listening to your macho crap? I've been *begging* you to go home, but you've been so busy making friends with these up-your-ass morons round here, you don't give a toss what you're doing to my career. Well, you can go screw yourself if you think I'm staying now, 'cos I'm going home, and I'm gonna get my life back on track without *you* hanging round my neck like a flaming millstone.'

'That right?' Tony snarled, losing patience now. 'Let's see how far you get without *this*, then, eh?'

Marching to the dresser, he wrenched open the drawer and took out her passport. Slipping it into his back pocket, he looked around for her handbag.

Guessing what he was thinking, Melody lunged across the bed, but Tony beat her to it. Shoving her roughly aside, he snatched the bag up off the floor and rifled through it until he found her credit-card wallet.

'Give that back!' Melody screamed, throwing herself at him and beating him with her fists. 'That's mine! You've got no right!'

The punch sent her sprawling across the bed. Winded, she lay on her back, blood from her cut lip trickling down her cheek. Staring up at him with huge, terror-filled eyes when Tony came and stood over her, she held her breath.

'Look what you done now,' he said, his voice deceptively soft as he unzipped his fly. 'Gone and got me all worked up.'

'You can't be serious?' she gasped when he flopped his dick out and started rubbing it. 'You can't expect me to *sleep* with you after what you just did?'

'What makes you think I'm asking?'

'You can't *force* me. Eddie's out there.'

'And what's *he* gonna do?' Tony gave a nasty laugh. 'He don't give a flying fuck about you. Anyway, you think he's never heard me putting a smart-mouthed bitch back in her place before?'

'But I'm not like the others,' Melody cried. 'You said I was special.'

'You was till a minute ago,' Tony said, shoving her legs apart.

'No!' Melody yelled, struggling with him as he climbed on top of her. 'Pack it in, you twisted bastard! I don't want you to touch me. I hate you! You make me *sick*!'

Grabbing her hair with one hand, Tony forced her head down into the mattress and gave her a couple of hard slaps. Bringing his face down then, until their noses were touching, he hissed through clenched teeth, 'Make you sick, do I? Well, what do you think your moaning and whining does to me? You think you're so fucking special, but you're a demanding, talentless, money-grabbing, pig-thick *whore*, who's only ever been good for one thing – and you ain't even so good at *that* no more!'

Realising that she'd pushed him way too far, Melody stopped struggling and gazed tearfully up into his eyes. 'I'm sorry, Tony,' she murmured in a tiny remorseful voice. 'I didn't mean it. It just slipped out because I was mad at you about that film. It's my fault.'

'Yeah, I know,' he snarled. 'And so's *this*, 'cos you should learn to zip it when you're told to. You was nothing but a whore when I found you – a filthy little tramp who spread her legs for any cunt who had the price of a wrap of smack. I took you away from all that and turned you into something decent, and you repay me by telling me I make you *sick*?'

Crying for real now, Melody held on to Tony's wrists to ease the pressure of his grip on her hair.

'Please, Babe, I don't want to fight. I swear I didn't mean it. You've been good to me, and I don't deserve you, but you know I love you, don't you? You're the only one I've *ever* loved. And I haven't looked at anyone else in the whole time I've been with you, so that's got to tell you something.'

'You couldn't be stupid enough to look at no one else while you're with me.'

'And I haven't.' Reaching out, Melody stroked his cheek. 'You're everything I've ever needed or wanted. Please, hon . . . let's just forget this ever happened and get back to how we were before.'

Breathing hard, Tony peered dark and deep into her eyes. 'Yeah, all right, I'll forget it, but I'd best not hear any more shit about going home, 'cos it ain't happening – not till *I* say so. And before you get any smart ideas about running away,' he said then, his voice so low that she could barely hear him, 'just remember that I bought and paid for every inch of this body. *And* this . . .' He gripped her face and squeezed it hard. 'All mine. And nothing that's mine gets away from me till I'm good and ready for it to be gone. You got that?'

Wincing with pain, Melody nodded.

'Good girl.' Smiling nastily, Tony let go of her

face and patted her cheek hard. Pushing himself up then, he got off her and zipped himself up.

Sitting up gingerly, Melody watched as he walked to the dressing table and straightened his clothes. Then, opening a tub of wet-look gel, he slicked his hair back.

'Are you going out?' she asked, sure that this would all be over if she could just get him to come to bed.

'Yep.' Splashing on aftershave now.

'Do you have to?'

'Don't know how long I'll be gone,' Tony said, as if she hadn't even spoken. 'Don't wait up.'

Lying down when she'd heard him and Eddie leave, Melody let the tears of self-pity slide down her cheeks. She'd always prided herself on succeeding in taming him where his other women had failed, but she'd been stupid to confront him like that – and really, *really* stupid to tell him that she was leaving, because that was a red rag to a bull with a control freak like Tony. If only she'd kept her mouth shut, she could have waited for the right opportunity and sneaked away. But he would never let her have her cards and passport back now that the battle lines had been drawn.

And there was nothing she could do about it, because nobody could help her. Not Eddie. Definitely not Fabian. And it was more than her life was worth to even *think* about involving the police. All she could do was carry on acting the loving, doting girlfriend until Tony trusted her again – however long that took. And she might as well forget getting her career back on track, because if it wasn't already over it sure as hell would be by the time she escaped – if she ever did.

'She all right?' Eddie asked as he and Tony headed down to the car park where the taxi they had ordered was waiting.

'She's fucking lucky, is what she is,' Tony grunted. 'But I got more important things to think about right now. That call I got just before she kicked off? That was Ronson saying the Feds have just pulled Zorba in, and they got the Johnson brothers as prosecution witnesses.'

'Might be a good time to make the money disappear,' Eddie muttered, holding the door open for him. 'While the heat's on and no one's looking too hard.'

'Could be right,' Tony agreed, pursing his lips thoughtfully as they climbed into the cab.

He was quiet on the ride to the casino, thinking everything over. He'd given Melody a hard time just now, but better that than have her run back to the States to a certain death. If she did but know it, he'd saved her life by dragging her over here when he had, because she'd be in a concrete box at the bottom of the Hudson by now – and, to teach Tony a lesson, Zorba would have taken great delight in fucking her front, back, and inside out, before personally pouring the liquid cement over her screaming head.

But she didn't know that – and she wasn't *going* to, because Tony didn't trust her. He didn't trust *any*body all the way, except maybe Eddie. But he definitely didn't trust *her*, not while she was so mad at him for fucking up her career.

It couldn't have come at a better time, as far as he was concerned, because, brilliant as *she* thought she was, she hadn't reached the point of being unforgettable to the public yet, so it wouldn't be too long before she was plain old Fiona Dawn again. And when she was, Tony would marry her, ensuring himself a permanent ticket to stay in England. Nobody would give a toss *who* she married by then, so there would be no publicity. No publicity – no way of Zorba reading about it and knowing where to look for him.

In the meantime, he had to find a way of investing the money he'd stolen while Zorba's men were concentrating their efforts on getting to the Johnson brothers. And they *would* get to them, because in all the attempts the Feds had ever made there had never been a witness *yet* who'd made it into court to testify against Zorba. Tony had until then to get something sorted, but the way things were going it wasn't looking too good.

Ripping the money off had been too good an opportunity to miss, and Tony had whacked it into his bank back home before anyone realised, withdrawing the bulk in a draft and the rest in cash a couple of days later. Then he'd grabbed Melody and Eddie and jumped on the first plane to England, thinking it would be a doddle to set himself up in business and make himself untraceable once he got here. But it was proving to be much harder than he'd anticipated because the British banks were tougher than Fort Knox to get into. With no paper proof as to how he'd come by such a large amount of money, they wouldn't touch him.

Stuck with almost one hundred gees in US bills that needed changing over, he'd been going into the local bureau de change every few days, changing a couple of hundred at a time. And, by night, he'd been rotating around the few casinos that Manchester boasted, playing the tables like a butt-lucky novice. But you could only win so many times without raising eyebrows, so he was having to lose as well – which was time-consuming, and more than a little frustrating, because he could have wiped them all out in a single night if he'd been free to play his usual game.

But while that might be tedious, it was at least doable. But the million-dollar bank draft wasn't. With no account to deposit it in, he was stuck with it. And, in his pocket, as it had been the whole six weeks he'd been here, it wasn't worth the paper it was printed on.

But something would come up, Tony was sure, because he was nothing if not determined. Sooner or later, he would find a way around the mess. But until then he would have to carry on doing what he was doing – and keep a very close eye on Melody to make sure she didn't do anything stupid and blow him sky-high.

Still awake when Tony came back a few hours later, Melody kept her eyes firmly closed and pretended to be sleeping when he came into the bedroom and stood over her. Wincing when he traced a finger over her bruised lip, she held her breath, praying that he didn't try and wake her.

Leaving her be, Tony slipped his jacket off and hung it over the back of the bedside chair. Then he went into the bathroom, closing the door behind him.

Peeping out through half-closed eyes to be sure he'd really gone, Melody eased the quilt back and tiptoed across to his jacket. Stare riveted on the door in case he came back and caught her, she slipped her hand into his pockets, hoping to find her passport and cards. They weren't there, but there was a thick wad of cash in the inside pocket. Taking it out, her eyes widened when she saw that they were all twenties and fifties.

There must be thousands of pounds there – but what could Tony possibly have been doing to make this kind of money in just a few hours? And, more to the point, *who* had he done it with, because he didn't know the city well enough to have made the kind of contacts he'd need for this.

Or did he?

Tony *had* been putting himself about quite a bit since they'd got here, and who knew what he'd been organising? He could have recruited himself a gang and had them out robbing banks, for all she knew. She wouldn't put it past him. And it wouldn't matter that he'd had more than enough to start with, because men like Tony could never get enough.

But wherever this money had come from, it might be Melody's only opportunity to get her hands on any cash for months, and she'd need it if she was ever going to escape. It was a huge risk, because Tony might have counted it, but he wouldn't necessarily think that *she*'d taken it. He might think he'd lost it, or that whoever he'd done his 'business' with had ripped him off.

Deciding it was worth the risk, Melody slid a small bundle of the notes out and put the rest back where she'd found it. Looking around then for somewhere to hide it, she remembered the jumbo pack of sanitary towels in her toiletry bag. Tony would never think of looking there – he hated anything to do with *that* side of women.

Taking one of the individual packets out, she carefully unwrapped it and took the towel out. Putting the folded notes in its place, she rewrapped it and slotted it back in between the others. Perfect.

So perfect, in fact, that she could probably get away with replacing every towel like that over time. If she took just a little whenever she found money in Tony's pockets, she'd soon have enough for a plane ticket. All she'd have to do then would be find her passport and she'd be free.

Hearing the toilet flush, Melody rushed back to the bed and pulled the quilt over herself, just as Tony came back.

Glancing at her, he quietly picked up his jacket and went into the lounge. Taking the money out, he stashed it right down inside the couch with the rest – US currency to the left, British banknotes to the right. Hardly the ideal hiding place – but it would have to do for now because he certainly couldn't be carrying it around in his pocket.

And Tony couldn't afford to make too many

more mistakes like the one he'd just made, either. Fortunately, Melody had been asleep, but he might not be so lucky next time, and if she got her hands on that kind of money and did a runner, he was fucked.

He had to get this moving. Now.

6

Jenna had just had her morning shower and was sitting on the bed brushing her hair when her mobile rang. Reaching for it, she smiled when she saw Vibes's name on the screen.

'Good morning. How are you?'

'Not too good, actually,' he said, sounding uncharacteristically glum. 'There's something I need to talk to you about. Have you got a minute?'

'Course I have,' she assured him. 'Fire away.'

'I suppose I could have waited till I saw you tonight,' he said. 'But I thought you'd appreciate having as much warning as possible.'

'Warning?' she repeated questioningly. 'Is something wrong?'

'Nothing for you to worry about,' he told her quickly. 'It's just that I had a call a couple of hours ago – from back home. And, well . . .' Pausing, he inhaled deeply. 'Thing is, I've got to go back.'

'Oh, right,' Jenna said, her heart sinking. 'When?'

'Flight's booked for Monday.'

'*This* Monday?'

'Uh huh.'

'Wow. That soon?'

Sounding as sick as he felt, Vibes said, 'I'm real sorry, Jenna. If there was anything I could do to change it, I would. But something's come up and I've got no choice. It's, um, family stuff, you see.'

'You don't have to explain,' Jenna told him quickly, sensing from his tone that he didn't really want to discuss it. 'Just tell me how long you'll be gone so that I can arrange someone to cover for you.'

'That's the thing,' Vibes said quietly. 'I don't know how long this thing is gonna take, or even if I'll be *able* to come back when it's over. It all depends what happens when I get there. Not that I don't want to,' he added quickly. 'But there's no point making promises I can't be sure of keeping, is there?'

'I suppose not,' Jenna murmured. Then, pulling herself together because Vibes was obviously feeling bad enough about this without her making him feel worse, she said, 'Well, I can't say I won't miss you, because I will – we *all* will. But there will always be a place for you at the club if you do make it back.'

'That's real nice of you.'

'Rubbish!' Jenna laughed to ease the tension. 'I'm not being nice, I'm being selfish. You're the best DJ in town. I'd be a fool to close the door on you. Subject of,' she said then, crossing her fingers tightly, 'are you going to be able to make it in tonight, or were you planning to finish as of now?'

'God, no!' Vibes said quickly. 'I wouldn't dream of dropping you in it like that. Anyway, I've got to do my last weekend. It wouldn't feel right to go without saying goodbye to everyone.'

Sighing with relief, Jenna said, 'Okay, great. Well, I guess I'll see you tonight, then.'

Hanging up, Vibes dropped his head into his hands. That had been one of the hardest calls he'd ever had to make, and he felt terrible for leaving Jenna in the lurch like this. But he'd meant what he'd said: there was no way he could have contemplated leaving without saying goodbye to everyone at the club – customers included.

It was Friday now, which left just three short days to get the most out of everything he was about to lose, because he would probably never see the place again once he had gone. Or Jenna, or any of the others at the club. He'd stay in touch with them all, of course, but it wouldn't be the same as seeing their faces every day, hearing their voices, sharing their laughter and tears.

But, while he would miss them, it was Kenneth he would miss the most. Kenneth, his homeboy, who had moved to England and had invited Vibes to come and stay for a few weeks – never once so much as hinting that he'd outstayed his welcome as those weeks rolled into almost two years. He owed Kenneth big for that. He owed him his *sanity*. And Gina, too, because between them they had dragged Vibes out of the pits of hell and helped him back on his feet. And for that, he would be eternally grateful to them both.

Tapping on the door just then, Kenneth popped his head around. 'Everything all right?'

'Cool,' Vibes lied, forcing himself to smile. They didn't need to be worrying about him any more than they already were. 'I've just told my boss I'm leaving.'

'How'd she take it?'

'Fine, I guess.' Shrugging, Vibes stood up. 'I said I'd work out the weekend – give her time to get a replacement.'

'You sure that's wise?' Kenneth asked, concerned that it would all be too much for him. 'You're leaving Monday, and you're not gonna have much time to settle in when you get there before everything gets rolling. Don't you think you'd be better taking this time out to really get your head around it?'

'I hear what you're saying,' Vibes replied softly. 'But I think it's better if I keep myself occupied right up till I get on the plane, 'cos then I'll have nothing to do *but* get my head around it.'

'Still planning on staying at Tyler's?'

'Couldn't say no after Delores was so good to me, could I?' Sighing deeply, Vibes shook his head. 'Gonna be tough, though, 'cos you can see my house from his front yard.'

'Don't go if it's gonna be too much for you,' Kenneth said quietly. 'I'm sure Ty's mom will understand.'

'Nah. I've got to face it some time. Can't keep running for ever.'

'True, but you don't have to torture yourself by staying that close. You could find a motel near the courthouse. And if money's an issue, I can always—'

'Thanks, bro, I appreciate the offer, but I'm fine for cash,' Vibes assured him. 'And I've made up my mind to do it this way for my own sake. The deeper the wound, the faster it heals. Right?'

Chuckling softly, Kenneth said, 'I don't know where you heard that, but if you come down to A and E when I'm working a Saturday shift, you'd know what a crock it is. The deeper the wound, the louder the screams and the more blood to mop up, in my experience.' Shrugging then, he said, 'But you know your own mind, so I ain't gonna preach. And you know I'm at the end of the phone if you need me – any time.'

'I know.' Vibes nodded. Then, glancing down at his watch to hide the tears in his eyes, he said, 'Man! Is that the time? I can't be chatting to you all day. I got things to do.'

'Well, don't let me keep you,' Kenneth said, stepping aside. 'Just don't go *over*doing it, yeah?'

Jenna's mood sank like a stone after the call. She'd always known that Vibes would have to leave one day, but now that it was imminent she was absolutely dreading it. Not only because she might never see *him* again, but because she was bound to lose customers, too – and that would be a massive blow when everything had been going so well. But she wouldn't try to persuade him to stay. He had his own life to live, and she just had to get over it – and hope to God that she found a decent replacement.

But she would deal with that later. Right now, she had a leaving gift to buy.

Heading into town, Jenna spent hours searching for the perfect 'something' to thank Vibes for all his hard work. She wanted it to be personal, but not *too* personal; expensive, but not over the top. But that proved much harder than she'd anticipated, because nothing seemed quite right.

Forced to make a snap decision when the shops

began to close around her, she rushed back to the first jeweller's she'd visited on King Street and bought the chunky matt-silver watch that had caught her eye in the window. It cost way more than was probably decent for a boss to spend on an employee, but she was beyond caring by then. And she didn't have to justify herself to anybody, so what was the harm?

Jenna had to pause for thought when the jeweller asked if she'd like to have it engraved, though. 'To . . . with love from Jenna' would have been perfectly acceptable for anybody else but, given the illicit feelings she'd been harbouring towards Vibes lately, she was paranoid about giving the wrong impression – to him *or* to his wife.

Sticking to safe ground, she plumped for the sword-slash Z logo – to remind him of his time at the club, but not necessarily of her.

Dropping into the club now on her way home, she'd just popped the watch into the wall safe when her desk-phone rang. Reaching for it, she said, 'Hello?'

'That you, Jenna?' It was Tony Allen. 'Sorry for disturbing you outside of work hours, but I needed a favour.'

Frowning, Jenna glanced at her watch, hoping this wasn't going to take too long. She'd been in town much longer than she'd intended already, and she needed to go home and eat, then get ready for tonight.

'Actually, it's more advice than a favour,' Tony went on. 'You got time to talk?'

'Well, I *am* in a bit of a rush,' Jenna said, trying not to sound like she was fobbing him off. 'But if you want to give me the gist of what it's about, we could discuss it in more detail tonight.'

'I was thinking more along the lines of calling in on you now, so we could have a proper chat without distractions,' Tony said. 'But I guess if you're busy, you're busy.'

'Sorry.'

'No problem. I could probably do with a shower, anyway, so I guess I'll catch up with you tonight. It's only a bit of business advice, so it shouldn't take too long. Just need some facts about British business – laws and regulations, that kind of stuff.'

'Ah, well, I might not actually be the best person to talk to,' Jenna admitted. 'I'm a bit of a novice, as you know, and I haven't had to deal with too much of that side of things yet.'

'Oh, right,' Tony murmured. 'Oh, well, not to worry. I'll just have to think of someone else.'

'You could always try Leonard Drake,' Jenna suggested, remembering what Fabian had said about Drake having helped her dad.

'Who?'

'The politician.'

'That fat creepy guy?'

'Mmm.' Jenna bit her lip to stop herself from laughing. 'I believe he used to have something to do with the liquor licensing board, so he ought to know something about business law.'

'Worth a try,' Tony said thoughtfully. Then, 'Yeah, why not? Go on, then, give me his number. I'll give him a ring.'

'I don't actually have it on me,' Jenna lied. 'Maybe it would be better if you waited to see him at the club.'

'He might not come in tonight, and I don't really have time to waste,' Tony said. 'Just see what you can do for me, will you? I'll leave you my room number so you can call me back when you get it.'

Jotting the number down, Jenna promised to get back to him. Putting the phone down then, she chewed on her thumbnail, wondering how best to deal with this. It wouldn't be right to give the Drakes' number out without their consent, but would it really hurt if *she* rang and passed the message on? Tony would only keep ringing if she didn't, and she would feel awkward if she had to keep lying.

Opening the desk drawer, she reached to the back for her dad's old address book and looked up Leonard's number.

'Oh, hello, Mrs Drake?' she said when Avril answered. 'Sorry to disturb you, but this is Jenna Lorde.'

'Sorry, *who*?'

'Jenna Lorde – from Zenith, on Deansgate. I was wondering if I could have a quick word with your husband?'

'Oh?' Avril's voice was filled with suspicion. 'Leonard's not here at the moment. May I take a message?'

'It's just about somebody who's trying to contact him,' Jenna explained. 'They asked me for his number, but I didn't think it my place to give it out, so I thought I'd best pass the message on and let Mr Drake deal with it himself.'

'And who would this person be?'

'One of my customers – Tony Allen.'

'I see. And I don't suppose you'd have any idea *why* he'd like to speak with Leonard?'

'None whatsoever,' Jenna admitted. Then, 'Look, I'm really sorry. I probably shouldn't have bothered you, but he did say it was important. So, if you'd like his number . . . ?'

'I suppose so.' Avril sighed audibly. 'Just give me a moment to find a pen.'

Apologising again when she'd passed the number on, Jenna put the phone down and shook her head. Avril Drake had sounded so unfriendly, but Jenna could hardly blame her. Your home was the one place where you should be able to relax without people you barely knew disturbing you.

Groaning when the phone began to ring again, she closed her eyes, praying that it wasn't Tony Allen calling back already. What was she supposed to say? That she didn't want to give him the Drakes' number, but had passed *his* number on to them? It seemed quite insulting put like that.

Reaching for the receiver, she was about to say hello when a deep male voice hissed, 'I've been watching you, and I hope you're ready to die, cunt, 'cos I'm gonna slice your fucking throa—'

Slamming the phone down as if it had burned her, Jenna stared at it when it immediately began to ring again, at exactly the same time as somebody knocked on the door.

Vibes was smiling when he popped his head in, but soon stopped when he saw the expression on her face. Coming in, he closed the door.

'Hey, what's up?'

Jenna shook her head. 'Nothing. It's all right.'

Frowning, Vibes looked at the still-ringing phone. 'Aren't you going to answer it?'

'No.' She shook her head again, and folded her hands together in her lap.

'Want me to get it?' he offered, wondering even as he said it if he ought to be interfering. What if it was her boyfriend, and they'd had an argument?

'Would you mind?' Jenna gazed up at him, her cheeks flushed now, sure that he must think she was acting like a silly little girl.

'Course not.' Still frowning, Vibes snatched up the receiver and barked, '*YEAH?*' There was a moment of silence at the other end, then the dial tone. Shrugging, he hung up. 'No one there.'

'Good.' Releasing a jagged breath, Jenna stood up and came around the desk.

Reaching out when she tripped on the waste-paper basket, Vibes peered down at her. 'Hey, you're shaking. What's going on, Princess?'

Conscious of the musky scent of his aftershave and the warm strength of his solid arms as he held her, Jenna gave a nervous laugh. 'Nothing. I'm just being stupid. It's not the first time I've had a malicious call, and I doubt it'll be the last.'

'Malicious?' A spark of anger flared in Vibes's eyes. 'Who was it? What did they say?'

'No idea who, but he didn't say anything I haven't heard before.' Embarrassed for making so much out of nothing, Jenna sighed. 'It took me by surprise, that's all. But I'm fine now. Honestly.'

'Sit down,' Vibes said, pushing her gently but firmly towards the couch. Perching beside her then, he nodded towards the now-silent phone. 'Looks like my voice did the trick, anyway.'

'Thanks. Saves me having to waste the police's time – like they haven't got enough to do without chasing round after silly women who get freaked by stupid phone calls. Anyway, forget about it.' Flapping her hand now, Jenna sat back. 'What brings you in at this time of day?'

'I came in to pick something up and saw your car out back,' Vibes said. 'And I had a favour to ask, so I thought I'd best see you now before we get too busy.' Giving her a sheepish smile, he said, 'I know it's a liberty, but is there any way I could leave some of my gear here when I go? Only, there's no room back at the house, and I don't want to leave it in storage 'cos it'll get wrecked. I'll find somewhere else if you haven't got the space, but—'

'It's fine,' Jenna assured him. 'You can leave it in here.'

'You sure?' Vibes asked. 'There's a couple of decks, and a whole heap of CDs. And you don't even want to *know* how many albums.'

'Will it fit back there?' Jenna indicated the space between the back of the couch and the wall.

Glancing over, Vibes shrugged. 'I guess so. But it shouldn't be in your way too long. I'll send over for it as soon as I know what's happening.'

'It won't be in my way. Take as long as you need.'

'Thanks. You're an angel.'

Their gazes met, and Jenna was conscious of her heart thudding noisily in her chest. She knew it was so very, very wrong, but she just couldn't help herself wondering what if . . .

The phone began to ring again.

Spell broken, Vibes jumped up and rushed to it. Snatching it up, he yelled, '*WHO IS THAT?*' Then: 'Oh, sorry, sweetheart, didn't mean to shout. Just a minute.' Turning to Jenna, he grimaced guiltily. 'It's Kalli.'

Passing the phone to her when she came over, he glanced at the clock on the wall behind her. It was almost six-thirty, and he still had tons to do back at the house. Mouthing for her to call him if she needed him, he backed out of the door.

Waving, Jenna sat down, aware that she was shaking again.

'Is everything all right?' Kalli asked, concerned because it was so unusual for anybody else to answer Jenna's phone – and even more unusual for Vibcs to shout.

Exhaling slowly to calm herself, Jenna said, 'Everything's fine. What can I do for you?'

Not sure whether she believed her, but aware that it was none of her business, Kalli decided to let it go. If Jenna wanted her to know, she'd have told her.

'Can Vibes hear me?' she asked now.

'No, he's just gone,' Jenna said. 'Why? What's up?'

'Nothing, really. Well, apart from him *leaving* – which is just the worst thing ever.'

'He told you?'

'Yeah, he rang this afternoon.'

'I see,' Jenna murmured, biting down on a sudden twinge of jealousy. Why *wouldn't* he call Kalli? she asked herself sharply. They got on really well, and Vibes had actually known her for longer than he'd known Jenna, so of course he'd want to tell her something like that.

'I wanted to get him a going-away present,' Kalli was saying now. 'But I've been looking for ages, and I still haven't found anything. I wondered if you might have some ideas?'

'I'm sure he'd love anything you chose to give him,' Jenna assured her. 'But don't spend too much, because I've already got him something – from all of us,' she added, deciding that it was probably best to keep it impersonal. Especially so, after that little fit of green-eye. 'But please don't tell anyone, because I want it to be a surprise.'

'I won't tell a soul,' Kalli promised. 'But can I ask what it is, only I'll be dying of curiosity if I have to wait to see it.'

'It's a watch,' Jenna told her. 'And I've had the club logo engraved on the back.'

'Oh, he'll absolutely love that,' Kalli said approvingly. 'It'll remind him of us every time he looks at it.'

'That's what I thought. Anyway, I was thinking we should present it at closing time on Sunday.'

'I can't wait to see his face,' Kalli said softly. 'He'll be so p-*pleased*.' Giving a tiny sob then, she said, 'Oh, I'm sorry, but I'm going to miss him so much.'

'We all will,' Jenna murmured, biting her lip as tears flooded her own eyes. Blinking them back, she pinched herself hard to snap herself out of it, then said, 'Right, well, I'd best get on.'

'Me, too.' Kalli sniffed softly. 'Any idea what I can get him?'

Thinking about it for a moment, Jenna said, 'The other DJs have been putting together CDs of their nights, and I know Vibes likes Marky Day, so why don't you see if you can get something of his?'

'He won't be in till Wednesday,' Kalli pointed out disappointedly. 'That's too late.'

'You should be able to pick one up at that white-label place at the back of the Corn Exchange,' Jenna told her. 'I'm sure someone said they'd been selling them from there.'

'That would be brilliant,' Kalli said, sounding a lot happier now. 'I'm still in town, so I'll nip over there now. See you later.'

Hanging up, Jenna dropped her face into her hands and rubbed at her eyes. She would hold it together if it killed her, but it was going to be harder than she thought to say goodbye to Vibes. And she'd have to deal with it alone, because she couldn't let *anyone* know that she'd allowed herself to like him as much as she did.

Snatching her jacket off the back of the chair, Jenna slipped it on and picked up her bag – just as the phone started to ring. Sure that it was the malicious caller again, she rushed out, slamming the door much harder than she'd meant to behind her.

In his own office along the corridor, Fabian had just laid out a thin line of coke on the mirror. Thinking that someone was kicking one of the doors in when he heard the bang, he swept the incriminating evidence into his drawer and grabbed the little rubber cosh he kept under the desk.

Easing the door open, he peeped out into the corridor, dreading coming face to face with Tony Allen and the goon; terrified that they had found out about him and Melody and were hunting him down. Shaking with relief when he saw Jenna outside her door, struggling with her handbag, the strap of which seemed to be caught, he hurried towards her.

'Need a hand there?'

'*Shit!*' she squawked, spinning around with a hand on her heart. 'Do you *have* to sneak about like that?'

'Sorry.' Frowning, Fabian ran a trembling hand through his hair. 'You looked like you were having problems, and I thought you might need—'

'I'm fine,' she cut him off testily, wrenching the strap free. 'I just need to get out of here.'

'Your phone's ringing,' he called after her as she abruptly turned and walked away.

'Thank you, Fabian,' she snapped without looking back. 'But I *have* got ears!'

Staring after her, a glint of anger sparked in Fabian's eyes. What the hell was *that* all about? He'd only been trying to help, but the moody bitch had practically bitten his head off. And if there was one thing he hated, it was women treating him like a prick!

Going back to his office, Fabian kicked the door shut and took his stuff out of the drawer to finish what he'd started.

Hissing, 'Fuck!' when his own phone started to ring, making him spill the powder onto the desktop, he snatched up the receiver. Hearing Melody's voice, he narrowed his eyes nastily.

'I can't hear a word you're saying,' he told her, dabbing at the coke with a wet fingertip. 'You'll have to speak up.'

'I *can't*,' she whispered urgently. 'Tony's in the shower, and he could come out any minute. I just wanted to see if you can get me something extra for tonight – only I want some to bring back here with me, because I'm stressed to the max.'

'My guy's out of town,' Fabian replied coolly, taking it out on Melody because Jenna had pissed him off.

'Can't you get it off anyone else?'

'Depends.'

'Oh, come on, Fabian, don't mess me about. Can you get it or not?'

Saying nothing, Fabian retrieved what he could of the coke and rubbed it over his gums. Sliding down in his seat then, he swung his feet casually up onto the desk.

'All right, how much?' Melody hissed. 'If that's what this is about, name your price.'

'Did I mention money?' he drawled, beginning to enjoy himself. She'd never offered to pay before; she *must* be desperate. 'I just don't know if I can get hold of anything right now, that's all.'

'*Please*,' she begged, a note of hysteria creeping into her voice. 'I *need* it, Fabian . . . Are you still there?'

Sighing wearily, he said, 'Yeah, I'm here. All right, I'll try and sort something out. But I'm not making any promises. And, seeing as you brought it up, I *will* need you to pay for it.'

'Fine.' She gave a relieved sigh. 'How much?'

'We'll talk about it later.'

'It had better be good,' Melody said, hanging up.

'Who was that?' Tony asked, coming out of the bathroom with a towel slung loosely around his spreading gut.

'Room service,' Melody lied, the colour draining from her face.

'Did you tell them the bar needs restocking?' he asked, whipping the towel off and rubbing his hair with it.

Averting her eyes from his hairy nakedness, Melody shook her head. 'No, I forgot.'

'So what *did* you tell them?'

'That I wanted a sandwich,' Melody said, her eyebrows puckering together as she turned to look at him now – exactly as she would have done if she'd been innocent. 'Christ, Tony, what's with all the questions? Don't you trust me, or something?'

Grunting, 'I don't trust no one,' he strolled into the bedroom, dropping the towel en route. 'I need a rub-down,' he called back to her, the mattress springs complaining loudly as he threw himself down on the bed.

'I'm busy,' Melody muttered, reaching for a

bottle of bright red nail-polish to paint her toenails. It was obvious what he wanted, and she *so* wasn't in the mood.

She'd accepted that she would never escape alive unless Tony chose to let her go, or – God willing – died. And she was willing to play the game as usual, but no *way* could she bear the thought of him touching her right now. Her stomach was so tight, she might just throw up in his face.

'Yo!' Tony barked from the doorway just then, making her jump because she hadn't heard him get up off the bed. 'Am I talking to myself here, or what? I said, what's taking so long?'

Biting down on her anger and resentment, Melody took a deep breath and said, 'Sorry. I'm just getting ready for tonight.'

'You got plenty of time for that. But this can't wait. Look.'

Turning her head, Melody gave a silent groan when she saw that Tony was waggling his hard-on at her.

'Aw, not now, hon,' she murmured. 'My nails are all wet.'

Tony's eyes narrowed. *Not now, hon . . .* ? What kind of shit was that?

'You forgetting that little chat we had last night?' he snapped, marching over to her.

Shaking her head, Melody shrank back, pressing

her head deeper into the cushion to escape the bitter stench emanating from his groin.

'I just don't feel so good, that's all.'

Peering at her face, Tony noticed the lack of colour in her cheeks and the dark rings under her eyes. And the deep purple bruise around her lip.

'Yeah, maybe you don't look so hot,' he relented. 'Maybe *I* should be giving *you* a rub-down, huh?'

Tensing when he reached for her, Melody shook her head. 'It's all right, Babe. A shower should do it.'

'Aw, come on,' he insisted, his tone cajoling now as he went behind the couch and started roughly kneading her shoulders. 'It won't take a minute, and you know I'm good.'

The damp heat of Tony's palms on her bare shoulders made Melody's stomach churn. But she steeled herself and let him carry on, scared of him sensing her revulsion and kicking off again.

'How's that?' he asked after a while.

'Great,' she lied, her knuckles white from clenching her fists so hard. 'You're the best, Babe.'

'You'd better believe it.' Tony slipped his hands down to her breasts and tweaked the rigid nipples – the result of tension, not desire. 'Methinks the lady's looking for a fucking,' he said, chuckling huskily.

'Please, Tony . . . I can't. I—'

'Sure you can.' Coming back around the couch, Tony aimed his resurrected erection at her mouth.

Knowing there was nothing for it but to get it over with, Melody closed her eyes and opened her mouth. The right flick of her tongue would bring him off in two seconds flat – as long as she didn't puke first.

Just as she'd predicted, it was no time at all before Tony was done. Leaving a slimy trail on her chin, he swaggered towards the bedroom, whistling to himself as he scooped up the towel he'd discarded earlier to wipe himself.

Melody waited a couple of seconds, then strolled calmly into the bathroom. Locking the door, she made a dash for the toilet and puked all the frothy semen down it.

Trembling when the retching finally stopped, she stepped under the shower and leaned back against the cold tiles as the steaming water lashed down on her. She felt like shit. And, yes, she knew it was her own fault for starting on the coke again, but she needed *some*thing to get her through. And at least it wasn't smack. Coke she could handle, but smack was a complete bastard to get off once you were hooked.

It was nice when you were doing it, though, wasn't it? The voice she hadn't heard in a long time whispered into her ear. *Made you feel wonderful, didn't it – warm, and safe, and insulated.*

Snarling 'Fuck off!' under her breath, she turned the shower to cold to blast the monkey off her back.

She hadn't touched smack in five years, and had thought that she was well and truly clear of it. But it was true what they said: once a junkie, always a junkie. There was something about it that you just couldn't forget. Like your first true love: fantastic when you were in each other's arms, but so murderously bad when you were apart that all you wanted to do was get back together again.

It was an endless cycle of pleasure and pain. And a damn sight cheaper than coke, which just made it all the more attractive. But the real price came later – as Melody knew only too well. And there was no way she was going down that route again.

Fabian had better come through for her tonight, or she didn't know what she would do. But what a fucking little weasel, asking her to *pay* for it! She'd like to see what he'd do if she made him pay for all the good sex he'd had off her. He wouldn't be able to afford to *look* at her tits, never mind touch them.

Tony was still undressed when she went into the bedroom, standing in front of the mirror in all his glory, spraying Lynx all over his furry body.

Almost choking on the toxic fumes, Melody sat down on the bed to dry her hair.

'Room service never showed,' Tony said, glancing at her in the mirror.

Smiling nervously at his reflection, she shrugged. 'Oh, well.'

'Oh, well, nothing,' he snorted, turning suddenly and sauntering into the lounge. 'I'm gonna bell the lazy bastards – see what's taking 'em so long.'

Squeezing her eyes shut when she heard him yelling down the phone, Melody prayed he wouldn't mention the sandwich she'd never ordered.

Coming back a few seconds later with the phone still clutched in his hand, Tony jerked his head towards the door.

'They're sending someone up to restock the booze. Get something on and let them in, will you? And don't come back till I give you the all-clear,' he said then, sitting down heavily on the bed. 'I got a couple of calls to make.'

Pulling her dressing gown on, Melody did as she was told, pulling the door firmly shut behind her.

When the room-service boy had been and gone, she poured herself a neat vodka and switched the TV on. Sitting down on the couch then, she leaned her head back against the cushions and gazed unseeingly at the screen.

All day she'd been trying to hold it together and act like everything was normal. But Tony was getting on her nerves big time, and Fabian had really pissed her off. She didn't know how much more she could take before she snapped and did something stupid.

Like drug Tony, take her credit cards and passport and book herself onto the first flight home.

And, as a parting shot, she might just let Tony in on her and Fabian's little secret while she was at it. From the plane, of course. She wasn't stupid enough to imagine she'd be able to tell him *that* little snippet face to face and survive.

But it was never going to happen, because she'd have to incapacitate Eddie as well – and there weren't enough drugs in the *world* to knock out that big idiot.

'You've had a call,' Avril said when Leonard came in from the golf club that evening.

Folding her arms, she watched from the living-room doorway as he heaved his clubs into the cupboard beneath the stairs. Straightening up, he rubbed at the small of his back.

'From?'

'That girl, Jenna, from that nightclub you keep dragging me to,' Avril told him, her tone conveying her disapproval. 'Apparently, your *friend* Tony Allen is trying to contact you.'

'Oh?' Leonard's eyebrows shot up.

'Mmm. He called her for your number. Which I found a little surprising, actually, because I'd have thought he'd already have it if you're the good friends you claim to be.'

'Would you please stop saying *friends* as if it's an insult,' Leonard snapped. 'And tell me exactly what she said.'

'*Exactly* what I've told you. Tony Allen called her for your number, but she felt it inappropriate to give it to him without okaying it with you first, so she left *his* number instead.'

'You've got Tony Allen's number?'

'Isn't that what I just said?' Sighing irritably, Avril shook her head. 'Really, Leonard, these golfing sessions seem to be affecting your memory.'

'Don't be ridiculous,' Leonard muttered, walking past her into the lounge and looking around. 'I trust you wrote it down?'

'Of course.'

'Well, do you think you could tell me *where*?'

Avril's nostrils flared as she inhaled deeply and pursed her lips. She had been in two minds about telling her husband about that call, and had only done so in the end because he'd have been sure to find out as soon as they next went to the club. It was annoying, though, for this to happen now, when she'd been so sure that Leonard was on the verge of giving up his new-found zest for the nightlife.

They had gone to that club every single night without fail for the first two weeks. But that had tapered off to just a couple of nights a week recently, and Avril had sensed that Leonard was becoming disheartened with the whole experience. And like any canny mother having to deal with a wilful child, she had therefore decided to stop complaining about it, knowing that if she allowed it to run its course Leonard would quit going of his own accord. Whereas if she were to try to *make* him stop, it was guaranteed to have the opposite effect. And it seemed to have been working. Until now.

'Do you think I should call him?' Leonard murmured, peering nervously at the number on the pad.

'Well, that's the only way you're going to find out what he wants, isn't it?'

'I suppose so. Yes, you're right.' Nodding decisively, Leonard flopped down onto the couch and reached for the phone. 'I'll do it now.'

Going back to her chair, Avril picked up her knitting and feigned a lack of interest as he made his call.

'Oh, hello, is that Mr Allen?' Leonard said, sitting up straighter all of a sudden – as if, Avril thought, he were talking to a superior. 'This is Leonard Drake. We, um, met at the *club*?'

Avril shook her head ever so slightly, wondering why on earth he was introducing himself as if it were *he* who had precipitated the contact.

'Oh, no, it's not a problem at all,' Leonard said now, making Avril's eyebrows pucker with irritation because he sounded so toadying. 'Yes, I could be there. Absolutely. What time? Ten? Yes, that's perfectly acceptable. Right, well, ten it is, then. I shall look forward to it.'

'What did he want?' Avril asked when he'd hung up.

'To meet at the club tonight,' Leonard told her, getting up and heading for the drinks cabinet.

Watching him out of the corner of her eye, Avril noticed that his hands were shaking.

'I thought it was supposed to be urgent?' she said quietly. 'That was the impression the girl gave when she rang.'

'Yes, well, he's too busy to talk right now,' Leonard said, pouring himself a Scotch. 'Apparently, he would have liked to have spoken to me earlier, but nobody thought to let me know at the time.'

'And how was anybody supposed to do that?' Avril asked, knowing full well that he meant that *she* should have done it. 'You left your mobile here.'

'You could have reached me at the clubhouse. They would have called me in.'

'Yes, well, I didn't.' Sighing, Avril laid the knitting aside again. 'Still, I'm sure you're quite satisfied with the outcome. I'll just go and see what I've got in the wardrobe, shall I? Wouldn't want to embarrass you by wearing something I've been seen in a thousand times already.'

'Don't put yourself to any trouble,' Leonard said, smiling suddenly – which immediately roused Avril's suspicions. 'I know you don't really like the place, so there's no need for you to tag along if you'd rather stay at home tonight.' Another smile. And a bead of sweat on the brow. 'We'll only be talking business, and it's hardly fair to make you sit alone.'

Avril returned his smile, her teeth firmly clenched beneath her tight lips.

'Not at all, dear. I shall be there for you, as always.'

Relaxed after a shower and a rest, Jenna went back to the club with her tail between her legs. Finding Fabian doing a stock check in the storeroom, she gave him a sheepish smile.

'I just wanted to apologise for talking to you like that earlier. I was completely out of order, and it should never have happened.'

Getting a waft of Chanel No. 5, which evoked immediate memories of a particularly horny several-night stand with a foxy pole-dancer in Ibiza a few years back, Fabian's handsome lips arced in a secret smile.

'Don't worry about it,' he said, flicking his gaze over her body. She looked great, as usual, and the sincerity in her gorgeous eyes made them an even richer shade of green. 'Feeling better now?'

'Much, thanks.' Jenna smiled, reluctant to explain what had made her so jumpy earlier. He'd only think she was stupid for letting an idiot on the other end of the phone get to her like that – and he'd be right. 'I just had a bit of a headache, but it's gone now. Anyway, I wanted to set things straight with you before we open. And I promise it'll never happen again.'

Knowing the power of magnanimity, Fabian gave her a reassuring smile. 'It's cool, Jenna. You've been working too hard, that's the problem. Any time you want a break, just say the word. I'm more than happy to look after things.'

'Isn't that what *I've* been trying to tell *you*?' Jenna raised an eyebrow. 'I seem to remember that you were supposed to be booking yourself a holiday.'

'Is that the time?' Fabian said, grinning as he pantomimed looking at his watch. 'Best get out of here before we get locked in. And who's going to look after the place without us?'

'Okay, I get the point. You don't want time off. Well, fine. You just keep working till you can't stand up for exhaustion.'

'You and me both,' Fabian quipped, waving her out and locking the door. Strolling up the stairs beside her then, he said, 'So, it's Vibes's last night on Sunday?'

'Mmmm,' Jenna murmured, wishing that he hadn't reminded her.

'Thought of anyone to take his place yet?'

'Don't ask,' she groaned. 'I've been ringing everyone, and no one can step in at short notice. Marky Day's going to call me later to let me know if his friend can do it, but I don't know what we're going to do if he says no.'

'Glad you said that,' Fabian said, grinning. ''Cos I know the perfect guy. Fresh in this morning from a winter season in Tenerife and looking for a residency, at least until summer.'

'Can't be too well known if he's been out of the country,' Jenna commented worriedly. 'Won't that be a bit of a risk for the weekend slot?'

'Do you know how many Brits spend their summers partying in places like that?' Fabian said. 'And then they have to come back to this damp, dark dump, with nothing but memories to carry them through to the next year. Imagine how chuffed they'd be if they found out we'd got one of the guys who was spinning the tunes when they were having the best time of their lives. They'll *kill* to get in. You watch. He'll wipe Vibes off the map in no time.'

Still smiling, Jenna kept her mouth firmly shut. Fabian could think what he liked, but in her opinion Vibes was going to be a hard act to follow.

Still, she didn't have an awful lot of options right now and something was better than nothing. And if this guy didn't work out she didn't have to keep him.

'I'll leave it with you,' she said. 'But I hope you're right about him being good, or we're in trouble.'

'Oh, he's good, don't worry about that,' Fabian assured her. 'I'll go and give him a ring – and hope I catch him before someone else snaps him up.'

7

Tony was dressed and ready to go when he came out of the bedroom. Frowning when he saw Melody dozing on the couch with the TV blaring, still in her dressing gown, her unstyled hair as dry as a scarecrow's, he reached down and gave her a rough shake.

'Yo! It's time you was getting ready. Eddie'll be here in a minute.'

'Uh . . . ?' Waking in confusion, Melody struggled to open her eyes. 'What time is it?'

'Eleven.' Lighting two cigarettes, he passed one to her.

Dragging deeply on it, she shivered. 'Christ, it's cold in here. Have you got the air-con on?'

'Jeez, you *must* be ill. It's hotter than a goddamn furnace.'

'I'm freezing,' she moaned, wrapping the gown tighter around herself.

'Go to bed if you're not feeling right. Sleep it off.'

'No! I'll be fine. Just give me a minute.' Jumping up, Melody stumbled into the bedroom.

Coming out of his own small room two floors up a short while later, Eddie trotted down the stairs and tapped on the door.

'Ready?' he asked when Tony let him in.

'Near as dammit,' Tony affirmed, pouring them both a drink and handing Eddie's to him. 'Just waiting on Mel.'

'You get through to that guy yet?' Eddie asked, going to the window to check if the taxi had arrived.

'Yeah, he rang earlier. I said we'd meet him at the club.'

'Reckon he'll know anything useful?'

'He's got to know more than us,' Tony said. Then, with a shrug, he added, 'Whether or not it's useful is anyone's guess.'

Walking in just then, Melody peered at them suspiciously. 'What you talking about, Tone?'

'Nothing for you to worry about,' he told her dismissively.

Casting a resentful glance at Eddie who was standing by the window, his face as impassive as ever, Melody folded her arms. These two were so far up each other's backsides, it wasn't even funny.

'What you stewing about now?' Tony demanded, giving her a dark look.

'I suppose *he* knows?' she muttered accusingly.

'Pack it in!' Tony barked, downing his drink and slamming the glass down on the table. 'He's family, so don't fucking push it.' Stalking to the door then, he jerked his head for them to follow.

Leonard and Avril arrived at the club at five to ten. Slapping his money down on the pay-desk, Leonard propelled Avril into the clubroom with a hand on her elbow.

Jerking her arm out of his grip, she said, 'Don't push, Leonard.'

'"*Don't push*",' he mimicked under his breath as she strode on ahead with her nose in the air. He'd push her, all right – right out of the bloody door with her suitcases if she carried on like this.

Following Avril up to the VIP lounge, Leonard headed for the bar while she went and found them a table. Glancing around while he waited for the waitress to fill his order, he spotted Tony Allen in a corner booth. The blonde hooker was with him again, and the weird tall man. But, thankfully, none of the sycophantic fan club was around for a change.

Scolding himself for feeling so nervous about this meeting, he reminded himself that once upon a time – many years ago, admittedly – he had prided himself on being able to tackle any situation head-on. He'd stood tall in his years as party news-spokesman, and had given confident, informative after-dinner speeches since retiring. So why on earth he was so nervous about approaching one man for a civilised chat, he didn't know. Especially when the man had requested the meeting in the first place.

Telling himself to get a grip, Leonard downed both his *and* Avril's drinks when they came, then tossed a ten-pound note to the waitress and marched across to Tony.

'Hello, there. I hope I'm not late?'

'Bang on time,' Tony said, peering up at him with a hint of amusement in his penetrating eyes.

Christ, the guy was ugly. And fat. And where the fuck all that *sweat* came from was anybody's guess, but it sure wasn't normal.

'Take a seat,' he said after a moment. 'Drink?'

Squeezing himself onto the bench seat, Leonard said, 'Yes, thank you, that's very kind. Scotch rocks, please.'

Ordering their drinks, Tony sat back and peered at him. Intimidated by the scrutiny, Leonard slipped a finger into his collar to loosen it as a trail of perspiration snaked down the side of his face.

The sight of it, coupled with the pungent stench of fear and excitement coming from his sodden armpits, made Melody's already sensitive stomach flip.

''Scuse me,' she muttered, lurching to her feet and scrambling to get out from behind the table without touching Leonard.

'Where you going?' Tony asked her sharply.

'To the toilet,' she said. Then, to Leonard, who still hadn't moved: 'Will you *please* let me out!'

'Yo!' Tony barked. 'Don't be rude to our guest.'

Melody opened her mouth to retort that Leonard was no guest of hers. But the look on Tony's face stopped her.

'Sorry,' she mumbled instead, giving Leonard a tiny sick smile. 'Could you please let me out? I really don't feel too good.'

'Thought you said you was better?' Tony frowned.

'I thought I was,' she lied. 'Must be a bug.'

'Best go back to the hotel, then.' Turning to Eddie, he clicked his fingers. 'Take her back, will you?'

'No!' Melody yelped. 'I'll be all right in a minute, hon – honest. I just need to go to the ladies' and splash some cold water on my face. Really, I'll be fine.'

Watching as she made a dash for the toilets, Tony jerked his head at Eddie. 'Go see if they got any antacids in the first-aid kit, or something.'

'Actually, I've always found that peppermint cordial works rather well,' Leonard volunteered.

'That's what my, um, wife usually takes when she feels under the weather.'

Nodding at Eddie, Tony waited until he'd gone, then took out a pack of cigars and lit one. 'So, you're married?' he said, offering one to Leonard.

'Oh, yes.' Leaning towards him for a light, Leonard sat back and pointed Avril out. 'That's my good lady wife over there.'

Glancing at her, Tony saw the crossed arms and furious scowl. 'She don't look too happy.'

'She's fine,' Leonard assured him breezily. 'She's just got a few things on her mind, that's all.'

'What, like wondering where her drink is?' Tony chuckled, noticing the lack of glasses on her table. 'Think we ought to send her one over?'

'Well, I, um, *yes*, I suppose we should,' Leonard spluttered guiltily. 'I was actually in the process of ordering when I spotted you.'

'What'll she have?' Tony clicked his fingers at yet another waiter.

'G-and-T.'

Ordering a double and asking for it to be taken to her, Tony sat back and gave Leonard an amused smile. 'Well, well . . . who'd have thought you was married? Tell the truth, I had you down as a queer.'

The blush covered Leonard's face like wildfire. 'God, no! We've been married for twenty-eight years.'

Nodding slowly, Tony surmised that his first impression was spot on. The man could have been married for ever, but he was definitely gay. And that he was so keen to hide it could prove very useful in the future.

Letting the squirming worm off the hook – for now – he said, 'So, you're a politician?'

'Er, yes,' Leonard said, recovering his composure with difficulty. 'How did you know?'

'I make it my business to know these things. So, tell me Lenny – don't mind if I call you Lenny, do you?'

Thrilled by the familiarity, Leonard shook his head. 'Not at all.'

'Lenny it is, then.' Tony smiled. 'So, tell me, Lenny – what exactly is it that you do?'

'Well, to be absolutely truthful, I'm retired,' Leonard told him. 'But I still have quite a lot of clout.'

'How so?' Tony squinted at him through the smoke.

'Oh, you know . . .' Leonard gave a modest shrug. 'I still have irons in various fires. Most decisions that are made in local government fall to a panel of my closest friends, you see, so it's inevitable that my advice should be sought from time to time. I'm *very* well respected.'

'I imagine so,' Tony lied, paying the waiter when

he brought the drinks over and ordering the same again.

'Oh, yes,' Leonard went on, gaining in confidence as the drinks he'd already had began to loosen his tongue. 'I was quite the high-flyer in my time, so people tend to take my opinions seriously.'

Reaching for his drink, Tony took a long sip and peered at him over the rim of the glass. Was this guy for fucking real? One minute, sweaty little mouse; the next, raving egomaniac.

'So, that other shit you mentioned,' he said. 'The local-government stuff. What kind of influence would you say you've got with that?'

'Oh, plenty,' Leonard told him conceitedly. 'I've been at it for a long time, you see – know all the ins and outs.'

'That's good to know,' Tony murmured. ''Cos that's kind of what I wanted to talk to you about. See, I've been thinking about investing in something over here, but I don't know too much about your laws, and I don't want to get started on something only to hit a brick wall.'

'Confidentially,' Leonard said, leaning toward him and lowering his voice, 'every law can be, if not broken, then certainly *manipulated.* If you know the right people, of course.'

'That right?'

'Oh, yes. Because everything comes down to a human decision in the end, and every man can be swayed.'

'You mean bought?'

'In some cases,' Leonard conceded. 'But it's not always necessary for actual cash to change hands. Quite often it's a simple case of favour for favour. You rub my back, I'll rub yours – so to speak.'

'So, say someone was thinking about setting up a casino over here,' Tony said smoothly. 'Who would he have to know to get a smooth ride?'

'Oh, it would be terribly difficult,' Leonard said knowledgeably. 'They'd have to have a considerable amount in the bank to begin with.'

'Say that wasn't a problem?'

'Well, then an application would have to be made to the Gaming Commission – which is top-level security stuff.'

'Not like the "old friends" stuff *you*'ve got going, then?'

'Oh, no, I'm afraid casinos are way out of my league,' Leonard admitted. 'It involves all sorts of legal bodies, you see. Police, Customs and Excise, Inland Revenue.'

'I see,' Tony murmured. 'So, they'd want to know all sorts of stuff about you.'

'*Every*thing,' Leonard affirmed. 'And, believe me, there is *nothing* they can't uncover once they start delving. The gambling industry is notorious for its connections to organised crime, and this government has to be seen to be taking a stand. If the individual concerned were foreign,' he went on, guessing that Tony wasn't asking hypothetically, 'they would have to provide records from the police in whichever country they had come from, too.'

Taking all this in, Tony nodded slowly. The casino idea was an obvious non-starter: there was no way he could allow anyone to delve so deeply into his affairs, because there were far too many things in his past that needed to stay buried. But just because *that* was out of the question, it didn't mean that he couldn't get involved in something else.

'What about a gig like this?' he asked, flicking his cigar ash casually onto the floor. 'How easy would it be for a foreigner to set up a nightclub?'

'Somewhat easier than a casino,' Leonard told him. 'But you'd still have to undergo the security checks, I'm afraid, because you're still talking alcohol and entertainment licences. If that were going to prove *problematic*,' he said then, 'my advice would be to consider investing in a going concern, which would allow you to build a credit history on the back of somebody who had already been passed by the relevant boards.'

Nodding thoughtfully, Tony mulled this over. There was no way he could put himself under any kind of scrutiny, and he knew enough about Melody's background to know that she had several convictions on her record from when she'd lived here before, so it might not be so easy to open something in *her* name, either. What he needed, it seemed, was to find somebody squeaky-clean to hook up with. Somebody who would be the public face of respectability while Tony sat back and watched his dirty money get clean.

Reaching for his glass, he raised it. 'Cheers, Lenny. You've given me food for thought there.'

'Well, I really haven't done much of anything,' Leonard said. 'But anything I can do in the future, you need only ask.'

'Much obliged.' Taking another puff on his cigar, Tony said, 'So, tell me about yourself. Got kids?'

Flattered that Tony seemed so interested in him, Leonard said, 'Yes, two. Boy and girl. They're both grown now, of course, with families of their own. But they're doing well for themselves. Son in banking, daughter married to a stockbroker.'

'That right?' Tony remarked, clocking up more potentially useful future contacts. 'You must be very proud.'

'Oh, I am.' Smiling, Leonard laced his fingers

together over his gut. 'We Drakes have a prestigious financial history, as it happens. My grandfather was a name in the Bank of England, and amassed himself a fortune from share-trading, which my father inherited and quadrupled before he was thirty. Made quite a name for himself in politics, too.'

'That why you went into it?'

'For my sins.' Leonard grinned. 'We're a very traditional family, so the sons tend to follow the fathers. Not that my son followed *me*,' he added – with a hint of bitterness, Tony thought. 'You'll have to meet him sometime,' he said then, imagining the look on Rupert's face when he saw the connections his stuffy old father had been making since he and his wife Barbara had last deigned to visit. 'Perhaps we could arrange a dinner party? I'm sure Avril would be delighted to have you. She's a wonderful hostess.'

Flicking a surreptitious glance at Eddie who had just come back with a glass of peppermint cordial in his hand, Tony said, 'That'd be great. And I'm sure Melody would enjoy getting to know her. Give me a call sometime – we'll work something out.'

'Oh, I will,' Leonard said eagerly. 'I'll have Avril get on to it as soon as we get home.'

'You do that,' Tony said. Then, nodding in Avril's direction, he said, 'She's looking kinda lonely.'

Glancing at his wife, Leonard was about to say that she was fine but quickly decided against it. He didn't want to give the impression that he didn't care about her – not when he'd just been gushing about his marvellous family. And not when Tony had admitted that he'd thought Leonard was gay, because that was absolutely the last label a man in his position needed. The general public might be heading in a more accepting direction, but politicians were lagging sadly behind, and Leonard had seen for himself how cruelly and absolutely some of his former peers had been excommunicated when news of that nature leaked out.

'I guess I should go and pay her some attention,' he agreed, casting a fond smile in her direction. 'She's such a trooper. And my pals adore her.' Grinning conspiratorially now, he added, 'Quite jealous, most of them. Wishing they could have a little bit of what *I* get at night – if you know what I mean?'

'Mmm,' Tony murmured, wishing the guy would quit the blokey guff and piss off.

'Lovely-looking woman,' Leonard went on, still gazing in Avril's direction as he struggled to get his gut out from behind the table.

'Sure is,' Tony agreed, easing his cuff back and glancing pointedly at his watch. 'Man, look how late it is. Wonder where Melody's got to.'

'Right, well, it was good to talk to you,' Leonard said, loudly enough for the nearby celebrities to hear – making sure they knew that he and Tony were friends. 'Call you soon about dinner.'

After a quick visit to the toilets to throw up, Melody had gone looking for Fabian. Finding him chatting up two tarty-looking women on the edge of the dance floor, she waved to catch his eye, then slipped back into the shadows to wait for him.

'Did you get it?' she demanded when he reached her.

Drawing his head back, Fabian frowned. 'Is that it? No, "Hello, nice to see you"?'

'Please don't play games,' she hissed. 'I can't deal with it right now. I feel like shit.'

'Yeah, you don't look so good,' he agreed, the frown deepening when he noticed her bruised lip. 'What's happened to your mouth?'

'I walked into a door,' Melody told him evasively.

'You sure Tony didn't do it?' Fabian persisted, worried about her now. And about himself.

'Course not,' she snapped. 'I told you he'd never hurt me. Now, have you got it or not?'

'Yeah, I've got it.' Glancing nervously around, Fabian pulled the wrap out of his pocket.

Snatching it from his hand, she said, 'How much?'

'Later. Go and sort yourself out, then come and find me when you get a minute.'

'Fabian . . .' Reaching out as he began to move away, Melody gave an apologetic shrug. 'Sorry, Babe. I know I'm being a complete shit, but I'm just—'

'Don't worry about it,' Fabian cut her off, giving her an understanding smile. 'We'll talk later, yeah?'

Squeezing the wrap tightly in her hand when he walked away, Melody slipped back into the ladies' and locked herself in a cubicle. Laying out a line on the toilet cistern, she leaned down and snorted it straight. To hell with hygiene – she needed this.

'Are we celebrating something?' Avril asked, glancing up at Leonard suspiciously when he returned to their table with a bottle of champagne and two glasses.

'We most certainly are,' he beamed, seeming to have totally forgotten that they had barely been speaking when they'd arrived. 'I've just had a most interesting chat with Tony Allen.'

'Oh yes?'

'Yes, indeed. And I've invited him and his lady friend to dinner, so we'll have to get our heads together and come up with something wonderful. Oh, and I was thinking, maybe we should invite the children. It's been a while since we all got together, and it would be nice to see the little ones.'

Drawing her head back, Avril peered at him incredulously. He detested having the grandchildren in the house, almost as much as they detested coming.

'To my beautiful wife,' Leonard said suddenly, handing a glass to her and raising his own. 'And good times ahead.'

If Avril hadn't already had the large gin-and-tonic that Tony had sent over, and the two she had ordered for herself in Leonard's absence, she'd have been highly suspicious of this sudden lift in his mood. But she was feeling quite mellow at the moment – enough to be grateful that her usually dour husband seemed happy for a change. So, touching her glass to his, she smiled.

'To good times.'

And she damn well hoped he meant it, because she'd had more than her share of bad times recently, enough to last her a lifetime.

Melody felt and looked much better when she came back from the toilets. She'd regained some of her colour, and her eyes were sparkling again.

'I was just about to come looking for you,' Tony told her. 'I had some broad check out the bathroom, but you weren't there.'

'The upstairs ones were full, so I had to use the downstairs ones,' Melody told him, sitting down.

'Feeling better now?'

'Yeah, loads. Must have been that chicken I had for lunch. I thought it tasted a bit funky.'

'Better tell the Drakes not to put chicken on the menu when we go for dinner, then, eh?' Tony said, handing the peppermint cordial to her. 'Wouldn't want you hurling all over their table, would we?'

'Dinner?' Melody repeated with a grimace. 'Aw, not tonight, Tone? There's no way I can eat tonight.'

'Nothing's been arranged yet,' he assured her. 'I'll let you know when, and Eddie can take you shopping for some new clothes.'

'What do I need new clothes for?' she asked, not relishing the thought of being babysat by Eddie. Shopping was supposed to be fun, not torture. And how was she supposed to ask him if something suited her when he'd barely said two words to her in three years?

'These people have got money,' Tony said, relighting his cigar. 'We don't wanna turn up looking like trash, do we?'

'Tony, honey,' Melody purred, leaning towards him and flicking her tongue into his ear. 'I *never* look like trash.'

Tony's eyes narrowed as the saliva from her tongue left a ghost of a tingle in his ear. If he wasn't very much mistaken . . .

But, no, she couldn't have. She didn't have a single cent in her purse – he'd made sure of that. And nobody was idiot enough to give coke away for free. Anyway, she'd only been to the bathroom, so unless some broad had set up shop in there – which he very much doubted – she couldn't have got her hands on anything.

Taking a sip of the cordial just then, Melody grimaced. 'Ugh! What the hell's *that*?'

'Peppermint, to stop you feeling sick.'

'Guaranteed to *make* me sick, more like,' she complained. 'I can't drink that, hon. Get me a proper drink, will you?'

'You feeling all right?' Tony asked, his eyes giving nothing away as he watched her wriggle about in her seat.

'Yeah, I feel great,' Melody said. 'Always do after a good vomit. And I love this song. *I don't see nothing wrong . . .*' she sang, squeezing his thigh under the table, '*with a little bump and gri-ind.*' Pouting prettily now, she slipped a finger in through the button of his shirt and played with the hair on his chest. 'Mind if I go dance while I'm in the mood?'

'Yeah, why not?' Tony agreed, moving her hand.

'Find Gay Boy and have a couple of spins with him while I finish my drink.'

'Thanks, Babe,' Melody chirped, jumping up without hesitation. 'See you in a bit.'

Turning to Eddie when she'd gone, Tony said, 'Go keep an eye on her. She goes near anyone other than the queer, come get me.'

Fabian was having a drink at the downstairs bar when he saw Melody come down the VIP stairs and make her way to the dance floor, where she stood on her tiptoes and looked around. Putting his glass down, he set off towards her, to see if she was okay. He was a bit worried about that bruise on her mouth. There was no way she'd done it walking into a door – but if Tony had done it, what else was he doing to her? She definitely wasn't her usual self at the moment.

Halfway there, Fabian spotted Eddie in the crowd behind her and stopped in his tracks, half expecting to see Tony as well. Frowning when he realised that Eddie was alone, and that he seemed to be trying to mingle casually while keeping a close eye on Melody, his heart thudded painfully in his chest. Eddie was following her. And it had to be on Tony's orders. But why? What did he suspect? The drugs – or that she'd been shagging Fabian's brains out for a solid month?

Shaking wildly now, fearing for his life, Fabian edged back towards the bar, planning to slip quietly away before anybody noticed he'd gone. He would give Jenna a ring on her mobile as soon as he was out, tell her he'd had to rush off to visit his sick mother, or something.

'Oi, watch it, you wanker!'

Spinning around, Fabian found himself faced by three unfriendly-looking men. The one in the middle was glaring at him, his hand dripping with drink that had spilled out of his glass.

'Sorry,' he apologised. 'I didn't see you there.'

'No fucking kidding.'

Sensing that the man was spoiling for a fight, Fabian glanced around for the security guys, but there were none in sight. Needing to stub this out before it escalated and led Eddie straight to him, he switched on his smooth manager smile and offered the man a fresh drink – on the house.

'On the house?' The man looked him up and down. 'You the boss, then, are you?'

'Manager,' Fabian told him, waving him towards the bar. 'Just tell the barman what you want, and I'll sort it out.'

'What about me mates?' The man jerked his head at the others who were smirking over his shoulder. 'You ain't just ruined my night, you've ruined theirs an' all.'

Fabian's nostrils twitched with irritation. The cheeky bastard was pushing it now, but there were still no security guys around so there wasn't a lot he could do about it. And – worse – Melody had just spotted him and was heading his way, with Eddie in slow pursuit.

Trapped, Fabian smiled his best matey smile at the man who was posing the more immediate threat and said, 'All right, just this once. But don't tell anyone, or they'll all be banging into me for free drinks, eh?' Going behind the bar then, he clicked his fingers at Maurice en route to the kitchen door. 'Give them whatever they want, but don't charge them.'

'As long as you don't blame *me* when the receipts don't tally,' Maurice muttered to his back. Then, smiling tightly at the three louts, hc said, 'What'll it be, gents?'

'Three cognacs' the man told him, finishing what was left of his original drink and sliding his glass across the bar. '*Triples*.'

Reaching the bar just then, Melody eased her way in between the men to ask Maurice where Fabian had gone.

'Who knows, who cares,' he muttered, shrugging unconcernedly as he went to get the men their drinks.

Leaning an elbow on the bar, the man Fabian

had bumped into gave Melody a lingering once-over. 'All right, darlin'? Haven't I seen you somewhere before?'

'Very likely,' Melody said, flicking him a mildly dismissive glance. She usually enjoyed being recognised, but she wasn't in the mood right now.

'Yeah, I know who you are. You're that bird out of *Baywatch*.'

Gritting her teeth, she said, 'No, I'm not.'

'Yeah, you are,' the man persisted. 'I never forget a good pair of tits, me.' Laughing he held his hands to his own chest. 'Red swimsuit, running down the beach. Phwoar!' Clicking his fingers now, he said, 'Pamela Anderson!'

'You need glasses,' Melody told him sharply. Why did people always think it was a compliment to mistake her for that vacuous tart? She was Melody Fisher. Her name spoke for itself. At least, it had started to in the States, but these ignorant thugs obviously hadn't caught up yet.

'Gonna let me buy you a drink, then, Pammy?'

'For Christ's sake, I am *not* Pamela fucking Anderson. Just back off and go find someone else to wank over, will you!'

'She likes me,' the man said, grinning at his mates.

'In your dreams,' she muttered, tapping her long fingernails on the bar. God only knew why he thought he stood a chance. He was nowhere near good-looking enough, and he had the worst case of cheap-gold-overload she'd seen since that awful gangsta-rap crew's album launch in LA last summer.

'In *my* dreams,' the man drawled, still grinning. 'I'll give you the best fucking dreams you've ever had, darlin'.'

'Will you just piss off!' she hissed, giving him a dirty look. 'I'm not interested – all right?'

Coming up behind her now, sandwiching her in between his mates and the bar, one of the men ran a hand over her backside, whispering, 'Nice arse, love. Be even nicer with my dick in it.'

'Get your fucking hands off me!' Melody yelped, jerking her arm back to elbow him in the stomach.

Laughing, the first man grabbed her wrist and held on to it. 'Now, now, no need for violence, Pammy. We'll play fair, won't we, lads?'

'Yeah, we'll pay,' the second onc said. 'I'vc got a tenner to spare. What'll you do for a tenner, love?'

'All three of us, by the look of her,' the third one quipped, sliding a hand up her thigh. 'Get that bruised gob sucking cock, did you?'

'Back the fuck *off*!' Melody shouted, twisting angrily around so that her back was against the bar. 'If my boyfriend sees what you're doing, he'll *kill* you!'

'Oh yeah?' the first man laughed. 'And who's your boyfriend, then? David fucking Has-a-toss?'

Feeling a tap on the shoulder, he was still laughing when he turned around. The head-butt came from nowhere, splitting the bridge of his nose and knocking him spark out.

'Fuck are you playing at, y' cunt!' one of his mates snarled, launching himself at Eddie as the other one snatched a bottle out of a girl's hand and smashed it on the bar.

'*FABIAN!*' Maurice yelled at the top of his voice, pushing the kitchen door open. 'Get in here quick! Those blokes are attacking that big ugly American!'

Halfway out of the back door, Fabian groaned. He didn't want to get involved, but he could hardly justify running out in the middle of a situation now that he'd been told about it.

'Get security,' he told Maurice, coming back in.

Back out in the bar, bar stools were going down and people were leaping out of the way as feet and fists started flying. The man with the bottle was dancing around his mate and Eddie, trying to get a clear shot with the jagged edge.

Hand over her mouth, Melody pressed herself back against the bar as Eddie sidestepped one of the men and brought his elbow down hard on the back of his neck, sending him sprawling on the floor. Then, grabbing the other one's arm, he twisted it around and pulled it high up his back, making him drop the bottle and fall to his knees in agony. But just as he was about to snap the arm, three of the doormen waded in and pulled them apart.

'Right, you, *out*!' Jacko barked, gripping the lapel of Eddie's jacket. 'You're barred.'

'*Don't!*' Melody yelled fearfully, seeing the smile on Eddie's lips.

Thinking she was talking to him, Jacko said, 'Sorry, love, but he's out. Can't have shit like that going on in here.'

'It wasn't him,' Fabian said, coming around the bar just then. 'It was them.' He nodded at the other three who were being held by Bobby and Flex now. 'They were harassing the lady, and he was just helping her out.'

Nodding, Jacko let go of Eddie. 'Sorry, sir.' Then, jerking his head at his guys, he said, 'Get 'em out.'

Holding on to his bleeding nose, the first man gave Eddie the evil eye as Bobby dragged him past. 'Big mistake, pal. We'll be seeing you again.'

Staring intensely back at him, Eddie's smile deepened.

Shuddering, Melody folded her arms. It wasn't

the first time she'd seen Eddie fight, but it never ceased to shock her when he did because he was like a robot: no noise, no emotion, just vicious, economical action. And that smile was seriously creepy.

'What's going on?' Tony asked, reaching them just then. 'You all right, Melody?'

Nodding, she said, 'Those blokes were harassing me. But Eddie sorted them out.'

'I thought *you* were supposed to be looking after her?' Tony turned on Fabian angrily.

'He wasn't here.' Melody jumped in quickly. 'He was out back, and I was waiting for him when those guys started feeling me up.'

'Feeling you up?' Eyes murderously dark, Tony glared at Fabian. 'What the fuck are you running here? Some kind of whorehouse, that the men think they can come in and have any woman they lay fucking eyes on?'

'I really had no idea what was happening,' Fabian replied honestly. 'If I had, I'd have dealt with it.'

'Oh yeah? *How?*' Tony sneered. 'Hit 'em with your fucking *purse*?'

'Leave it, Tone,' Melody said, looping an arm around his waist and resting her head on his shoulder. 'It wasn't his fault. Anyway, I told them to get the fuck away from me or you'd kill them.'

Giggling now, she added, 'Then Eddie came and nearly did it for you. Should have seen him, hon – he was a *monster*.'

'Yeah, well, they'd better not come back,' Tony growled, still eyeballing Fabian. 'I see them in here again, your guys best stay clear, 'cos they're mine. Got that?'

Fabian was relieved that Eddie obviously hadn't been watching Melody because of him, but this was something he couldn't afford to agree to. There were procedures, and they had to be followed to the letter.

'Much as I'd love to okay that, Mr Allen, I'm afraid I can't,' he said, flapping his hands in a nothing-I-can-do-about-it gesture. 'My guys are highly trained, fully licensed doormen, but our insurance doesn't provide for unauthorised persons interfering with troublemakers. I'm sure you understand?'

'All I understand is that you ain't got a fucking clue about *real* security,' Tony retorted sharply. 'Eddie had it in hand way before your lot got involved – but what would have happened to Melody if he hadn't got to her in time?'

'I can only apologise for that.'

'Yeah, well, apologies don't mean *shit* when you got blood on your hands.'

Melody's beautifully lifted brow puckered into

a ghost of a frown as it suddenly occurred to her to wonder how come Eddie *had* managed to get to her so quickly. Her confrontation with those men couldn't have lasted more than a minute, but even if he'd seen it start he'd never have made it down the stairs and through the crowd in that time. He'd have had to have jumped over the balcony and run like mad, in which case there would have been a pile of bodies in the wake of his enormous frame. But there weren't, so he must have already been down here – close enough to reach her in time to rescue her, but not so close that she had noticed him.

He'd been following her!

Shocked by the realisation, Melody cast a nervous glance at Tony, thinking exactly what Fabian had thought: that it had to have been on Tony's orders. But why? What did he suspect?

Turning up just then, having been told about a disturbance at the lower bar, Jenna caught the antagonism in Tony's eyes as he glared at Fabian.

'Everything all right?' she asked.

'Fine – *now*,' Tony spat, shooting a poisonous look at Fabian as he added, 'No thanks to *him*. He was nowhere to be fucking seen while she was out here being molested by some dirty bastards.'

'Molested?' Jenna gasped, turning to Melody. 'Are you okay? What happened?' Spotting the bruise on her lip, she said, 'Oh, please don't tell me they did that to you? Let me go and call the police. They need to be caught and punished.'

'No!' Self-consciously raising a hand to her mouth, Melody shook her head. 'I did this on a door. Those guys were just trying it on, but Eddie sorted it out, so there's nothing to worry about.'

'Well, as long as you're sure?' Jenna said. Then, turning to Fabian, she said, 'Where are those men now?'

'Jacko and some of the boys are throwing them out,' he told her, folding his arms.

'Good. And make sure they don't get back in again, because I don't want that kind of customer.'

'Now, *that*'s the response I expected,' Tony said, sneering at Fabian. 'That's all you'd have had to do to show me you was taking this seriously. None of this shit about insurance and "unauthorised interfering".'

Coming to Fabian's defence, Jenna said, 'To be fair, Tony, there *are* strict guidelines when it comes to security.'

Looking at her for a moment, Tony sighed and ran a hand through his hair. 'Sure there are. Sorry. I just get kinda heated when anyone disrespects Melody like that.'

Fabian raised an eyebrow but kept his mouth shut. The bastard could apologise to Jenna, but not to the person he'd been yelling at. But that was fine. Fabian didn't need an insincere apology, anyway. And at least he didn't have to leave the country just yet. But if this had taught him anything it was that this thing with Melody had to stop – now. And he would tell her so the first chance he got. Once she realised that it was for her own good as well as his, he was sure that she'd back off.

'Can I get you a drink?' Jenna was asking Tony now.

Glancing at Melody, pale and shaking beside him, Tony shook his head. 'I think I'd best just get her back to the hotel.'

'Of course,' Jenna said, peering at Melody with concern. 'I'm so sorry your night ended like this. But I hope it won't put you off coming back?'

'The hell it will!' Tony snorted. 'Take more than a couple of idiots to run *us* out of town. See you tomorrow.' Putting an arm around Melody's shoulder, he walked her out, with Eddie following on behind.

'That man is so bloody ignorant,' Fabian complained under his breath.

'Don't take it personally,' Jenna said, smiling at his outraged expression. 'He was only angry because somebody disrespected Melody. I'm sure you'd be the same if it was your girlfriend.'

'Mmmm,' Fabian murmured, thinking that she couldn't be more wrong. There were too many maniacs in this world to risk getting beaten, stabbed – or worse – over a woman. And in a city like this, where everybody seemed to think that fear represented respect, 'worse' was the more likely outcome of any confrontation these days.

Which reminded him . . .

'I'd better have a word with Jacko and make sure they keep the front doors locked.' Fabian glanced at his watch. 'There's still a couple of hours to go, and those guys might come back mob-handed.'

'Just because they got kicked out?' Jenna asked. 'Surely not.'

'No, because they got a good *kicking,*' Fabian said, pointing to the floor behind her. 'One of them left that – and I don't think he's going to just crawl away and forget about it.'

Glancing to where he was pointing, Jenna grimaced when she saw the pool of blood. 'My God. What happened?'

'Eddie knocked seven shades out of them.'

'*All* of them?'

'Yep.' Fabian nodded slowly.

Exhaling loudly, Jenna said, 'Bloody hell. I guess your sources were right about him being a minder. And a bloody good one, too, by the look of it.'

Fabian stared at her, amazed that she was treating it as a joke. Tony Allen and his goon were serious trouble waiting to happen, but she didn't seem to have a bad word to say about them.

'You're probably right about locking the doors,' Jenna said now. 'But if anything happens, we'll call the police and let them deal with it.'

'Yeah, whatever,' Fabian said distractedly. 'See you in a bit.'

Watching as he walked away, Jenna frowned. Had she just imagined it, or had he been a bit off with her just now? She couldn't see why, though, so maybe he was just upset about Melody and those guys.

Shrugging it off, she turned back to the bar and called, 'Maurice – could you get someone to come and mop this mess up, please?'

8

The men didn't come back that night, or the next, and Jenna forgot all about them as, all too soon, Sunday came around.

Determined not to disgrace herself and reveal her true feelings about Vibes leaving, Jenna forced herself to smile and chat to the customers as usual as the night wore on. She noticed that the rest of the staff were a little subdued, but that was only to be expected, she supposed, because none of them were looking forward to saying goodbye to him.

At the end of the night, when the music stopped, the house lights came up, and the last of the customers had finally left, she locked the doors. Then she called the staff together on the dance floor.

Going up to the DJ's booth, where Vibes was quietly gathering his stuff together, Jenna asked him for his radio mike. Then she went out onto the top step and jerked her head for him to follow.

Frowning questioningly, he came out and looked

down at everyone standing below. 'What's going on?'

'You'll see,' Jenna told him quietly. Switching the mike on then, she said, 'Thanks for staying behind, everyone. Now, as you know, Vibes is leaving us tonight . . .'

Down below, Kalli shushed Austin when he let out a loud sob.

Smiling sadly because she knew exactly how he was feeling, Jenna took a deep breath.

'Anyway,' she continued, 'I'm sure you'd all like to join me in wishing him the best for the future – wherever and whatever that may be.' Pausing as a cheer went up, she took the gift-wrapped box out of her pocket. Waiting until she had quiet again, she said, 'As a mark of our appreciation, I'd like to present this to Vibes.'

'What's she doing?' Fabian muttered, folding his arms. 'She didn't tell me about this.'

'I think she wanted it to be a surprise,' Kalli said, glancing innocently up at him. Smiling then, she went back to watching the presentation, aware that Fabian was fuming beside her because she had obviously been in on the secret and he hadn't.

'So, Vibes . . .' Jenna turned to him now. 'This is for you – from all of us.'

Taking the box, Vibes shook his head. 'I don't know what to say.'

'Don't say anything – just open it!' one of the waitresses yelled.

'Okay, okay!' Laughing, Vibes tore the paper off and opened the box. Seeing the watch, his mouth dropped open and, wide-eyed, he turned to Jenna. 'You shouldn't have done this,' he whispered. 'It's *way* too much.'

'You deserve it,' she whispered back.

Taking the watch out of the box, Vibes turned it over in his hand. Seeing the engraved logo, he shook his head and traced his finger over it.

'To remind you of us,' Jenna said, getting a little choked as she saw the tears in his eyes.

'I could never forget you,' he murmured, looking into her eyes and then glancing quickly away. Then, pulling himself together with an effort, he looked down at the people below and smiled. 'Thanks, y'all. This means the world.'

'For he's a jolly good fellow . . .' Austin start singing in a choked voice, urging the others to join in. 'For he's a jolly good fellow . . .'

A short time later, when he'd said his goodbyes and most of the staff had gone, Vibes brought the last box of albums up to Jenna's office and put it behind the couch with the others.

'All done,' he said, rubbing the dust off his hands. 'Sure it won't be in your way?'

'It's fine,' Jenna assured him. 'Join me for a last drink?' she asked then, holding up a bottle of brandy.

'Love to.' Sitting down on the couch, Vibes leaned his head back and exhaled wearily. 'Man, I'm gonna miss this place.'

'Aw, you'll forget all about us once you're back home with your friends, seeing all the old sights,' Jenna said over her shoulder.

'No, I won't,' Vibes murmured truthfully. 'How could I, with *this* to remind me?' Flipping the box open for the umpteenth time, he gazed at the watch and shook his head. 'You really, really shouldn't have done this. These things cost the earth.'

'Everybody chipped in,' Jenna lied, bringing their drinks back and sitting down. 'And if it's any consolation, I think it's a fake.'

'Hope so,' Vibes chuckled, knowing full well that she was joking. 'I can just see them letting a black guy through Customs with a genuine Rolex without tossing his ass in jail.'

'You're not serious?'

'Nah, just fooling,' Vibes said, grinning as he added, 'You *do* have the receipt, though, right?' Laughing at the look of horror on her face, he said, 'Relax, Princess. It was a joke.'

'Thank God for that,' Jenna said, laughing softly. 'If I'd had to give you the receipt, you'd have known that it only cost two quid.'

'You're crazy, you know that?' Shaking his head, Vibes sipped at his drink. Leaning forward then, he put the glass down on the table and took something out of his pocket. 'Since we're giving gifts,' he said, suddenly nervous, 'I, er, got *you* something, too. It's sort of like a thank-you, 'cos you've been real good to me since you took over.' Handing her a small black velvet box, he said, 'Hope you like it.'

'You didn't have to,' Jenna murmured, gazing down at it with genuine surprise.

'Yeah, well, I wanted to.' Vibes shrugged, hardly daring to look at her.

Opening it, she gasped when she saw the delicate gold necklace with its semiquaver charm made up of tiny diamonds.

'For the lady who always strikes the right note,' Vibes said, his voice low and husky.

'Thank you *so* much,' Jenna murmured tearfully. 'It's beautiful.'

'Let me fasten it for you,' he offered, taking the chain from her trembling hands and looping it around her neck.

Just inches away from each other, their gazes met and, before either of them could stop themselves their lips were locked in a kiss so sweet and tender that Jenna felt as though she were drifting away.

Coming to her senses suddenly, she pulled back and covered her burning cheeks with her hands.

'Oh, God, I'm so sorry. I shouldn't have done that. It was completely out of order.'

'No, it was my fault,' Vibes said, disgusted with himself for taking advantage when he knew that she had a boyfriend. She must think he was a complete slime-ball. 'I'm really sorry.' Then, getting up he said, 'I guess I should go.' Shrugging, he added, 'It's late, and I've got that early start tomorrow.'

Mad at herself, and convinced that Vibes must be, too, Jenna nodded. 'Yeah. You're going to need all the sleep you can get. I know what it's like flying long-haul when you're strung out. It's not good.'

'Tell me about it,' Vibes said, trying desperately to lighten the atmosphere – he couldn't bear to leave her like this.

Taking a deep breath to bring herself under control, Jenna stood up and linked her hands together. 'Right, well . . . I guess this is it, then.'

'Guess so,' Vibes murmured. 'I'll, er, be in touch – about the gear, yeah?'

'Don't worry about it,' Jenna told him, smiling now. 'It's not a problem. Anyway, I hope you'll let us know how you're getting on from time to time? Everybody's going to be asking after you.'

'Course.' Vibes nodded, admiring the way that

she'd put them back onto a professional footing. Reaching out on impulse then, he gave her a quick hug and turned abruptly away. 'See you, Princess.'

Sitting down when he'd gone, Jenna closed her eyes and traced a finger over her lips, where she could still feel the softness of his; still taste the sweetness. But, she kept on telling herself, she should never have done it. He belonged to another woman, and this time she didn't even have the excuse that she didn't know: he had never once tried to hide his wedding ring.

Jumping when somebody tapped on the door, she sat up, hoping wildly that it was Vibes, even though she knew how very, very wrong that would be.

It was Kalli.

Her pretty eyes red and swollen, the girl came in and sat down next to Jenna. She gave her a tentative smile. 'Are you all right?'

Exhaling slowly, Jenna nodded. 'Yeah, I'm fine. You?'

'Oh, you know.' Kalli shrugged.

'Drink?'

'Best not,' Kalli murmured. 'Austin's already drunk enough for both of us. I just wanted to make sure you were okay before I took him home.'

Reaching out, Jenna squeezed Kalli's hand. 'Thanks, sweetheart. But really, I'm fine.'

Nodding, Kalli took a tissue out of her pocket and dabbed at her eyes. 'I know we'll all miss him – but you'll miss him the most, won't you?' Looking up then, her gaze was filled with such understanding and compassion that it pierced the wall that Jenna had been building ever since she'd heard that Vibes was leaving.

Jenna lowered her head. 'I won't deny that I like him. But it's wrong, and I've just got to get over it.'

'Why, if he feels the same about you?' Kalli asked softly.

'Oh, don't!' Jenna groaned, swiping at the tears she'd been holding at bay for so long. 'I know you mean well, but I shouldn't be thinking things like this about a married man. It's just not right. And if you knew what I'd . . .' Stopping herself, she shook her head. 'I should know better, that's all.'

Looking at her, Kalli nodded. 'You've got to do what's right for you.'

'Thanks,' Jenna said, taking a deep breath. 'Phew,' she said then, giving a sheepish little laugh. 'It's been quite a night, hasn't it?'

'And then some,' Kalli agreed. 'It was nice, though, wasn't it? I'll never forget the look on his face.'

Touching the necklace, Jenna smiled wistfully. 'Me neither. Anyway, you'd better go,' she said then. 'Austin will be waiting.'

Tutting softly, Kalli rolled her eyes. 'I suppose I'd better get him out before he drinks his way through all the leftovers. You sure you're okay?'

'Absolutely fine. See you tomorrow.'

Glancing at her watch when Kalli had gone, Jenna groaned when she saw that it was almost four a.m. She was so tired, she felt that she could just lie down right here and go to sleep.

Leaping to her feet as soon as she'd thought that, she snatched up her jacket and bag and headed for the door. Her dad had spent every last minute of his life at this place – eating, drinking, sleeping and, eventually, *dying* here. No way was she going down that same road.

Letting herself out, Jenna drove home and went to bed – then lay staring sleeplessly up at the ceiling as the dawn crept slowly in.

Another time, another universe, things might have been different. But, here and now, it was never going to happen, so she had to let go of the longing and concentrate on the real things in her life. And, right now, the club was the only real thing she had.

9

Melody was still in bed when Tony and Eddie went out the next morning. Pretending to be asleep when Tony popped his head round the door to check on her, she waited until she'd heard them leave, then went to the window and eased the edge of the curtain back to make sure that they really were going and not just tricking her. Seeing them climb into a cab down below a couple of minutes later, she watched until it had driven out of the parking lot. Then, taking the last of the coke Fabian had given her, she got dressed and set about searching for her passport and cards.

They hadn't been in his pockets when she'd searched them after he finally fell asleep last night, so Melody figured he must have hidden them somewhere in the suite. Turning the place upside down now, she spent the next few hours searching every drawer, cupboard, corner and shelf. She had even been prepared to risk her expensive acrylic nails by sticking her hand down the back of the couch. But she had been so disgusted when she took the cushions off and saw the caked-in dust and bits of disgusting shrivelled-up foodstuffs edging the gap that she couldn't bring herself to do it. There was no way Tony would have put his hands down there if she couldn't. He hated dirt even more than she did.

Gazing around the room when she'd searched every nook and cranny, she groaned with despair. She had to put it right before Tony got back or he'd know what she'd been doing, but she loathed cleaning almost as much as she loathed him right now. But it had to be done.

Standing by the door, Melody waited until she heard the maid's trolley rattling along the corridor. Nipping out when she heard the maid going into the room next door, she nicked an armful of cleaning sprays and cloths, and a pair of rubber gloves.

Putting the TV on, she flipped it onto Sky's MTV Base channel, and danced her way around the room, singing along to the American R&B songs she'd been missing so badly. Tony liked Sinatra and all that boring old shit, so that was all she ever got to hear these days.

Quite enjoying herself once she got started, she'd worked up a fair sweat by the time Tony and Eddie came back later that evening.

'Fuck's got into you?' Tony asked, gazing around the spotless lounge in amazement.

'I was bored off my skull,' Melody lied, gathering the cleaning equipment together.

'Where did you get that?' Tony asked, suspicious about how she'd managed to buy anything with no money.

'The maid left the trolley outside the door, so I helped myself,' Melody told him, putting it all out of sight in the bathroom. Coming back, she peeled her rubber gloves off and pushed her damp hair away from her flushed face with the back of her hand.

'Shoulda gone down to the gym and built up a sweat down there while you had the chance,' Tony grunted, taking his jacket off and slinging it over the back of the chair. 'You've put on a bit around the middle lately.'

'Thanks a fucking bunch!' she snapped. 'I can't help it if I'm bleeding.'

'Aw, for Christ's sake, do you *have* to?' he groaned, snatching up a bottle of vodka and two glasses and flopping down on the couch. 'It's bad enough I have to know about it at all without you shoving it down my throat.'

'Sorry for being a *woman*, I'm sure,' Melody sniped. Then folding her arms, she raised an accusing eyebrow when he poured two shots and handed one to Eddie. 'Don't I get one?'

'No,' Tony said, grinning at her look of outrage. 'You're taking a shower and getting dressed, 'cos we're taking you for a spin in the new car.'

'You've got a car?' Melody frowned. 'Why?'

''Cos I'm sick of paying fucking cab fares.'

'But you're not legal to drive it,' she reminded him. 'You haven't got a licence.'

'You'd be surprised what you can get your hands on if you know the right people to ask,' Tony told her, smiling mysteriously. 'Anyway, never mind that. Go get cleaned up, and be quick about it, 'cos we're going out to eat. Then we're going to the club.'

'It's a bit old, isn't it?' Melody complained when they set off in the ancient bronze BMW a short time later. 'Couldn't you have got something a bit sportier?'

'We ain't in the States now,' Tony reminded her. 'Anyway, sporty's out, executive's in. And this baby is a classic.'

'Classic what?' she muttered, folding her arms and glaring out of the window. 'Banger?'

'Quit griping, or I'll kick you out and you can make your own way back,' Tony warned her.

Snorting softly, Melody thought, *Chance would be a fine thing*. But there was no point saying anything, because he didn't mean it. Anyway, it *was* pretty comfortable, she supposed. And it beat the constant cabs, because at least now he might take her somewhere other than the club without moaning about the expense.

London, maybe, so she could see something she recognised. Some*body* she recognised, even. Somebody who might be able to bung her a bit of cash and help her to get out of this hell-hole.

But she'd still need her passport – damn him!

'By the way,' Tony said, twisting around in his seat to look back at her. 'Me and Eddie might take off for a couple of days.'

'Oh?' Melody sat up a little straighter. 'Where?'

'Not sure yet,' he told her evasively. 'But don't worry,' he added, giving her a pointed look. 'I'll be close enough to keep an eye on you – make sure nothing bad happens.'

Sinking back down, Melody sighed. So, he'd be spying on her. Great!

'What am I supposed to do with myself?' she asked sulkily. 'It won't be much fun stuck in the room all day, and you know I don't like going into clubs on my own.'

'You ain't going to the club without me,' he told her, setting her straight from the off. 'Not after them guys hassled you like that.'

'Aw, Tone, that's not fair,' she complained. 'They

wouldn't dare go back there – not after what Eddie did to them. Anyway, Gay-Boy will look after me.'

'He didn't do such a great job of it the other night, did he?' Tony reminded her flatly. 'You ain't going – period. Anyway, you'll have to stay put to make sure no one gets at our stuff. And there's plenty to occupy you at the hotel till we get back.'

'What, like, facials and flaming massages?' Melody muttered. 'Yippee!'

Still sulking when they reached the club that night, Melody ignored Tony's friends when they swarmed around him as usual. She hated them all. Especially those who were doing well in the soaps, because every last one of them was shit, and she didn't see why they should be allowed to get on with their stupid little careers when her much bigger, brighter one was in tatters.

Grunting a reluctant hello when Leonard Drake brought his wife over to introduce her, Melody folded her arms and glared at the floor when Avril took the chair beside hers. All she wanted was to get to Fabian, but there was a fat chance of that with Tony watching her. And now she was stuck with Granny Grump.

Greeting Leonard warmly, because he'd decided he could potentially be of use to him, Tony said, 'Hey, everyone, meet my friend, Lenny. Some of y'all probably know him already. He's one of your big-shot politicians.'

Leonard felt like a king when everyone turned to look at him. And no humiliating smirks this time, just interested smiles.

'I know you,' Brenda Thompson said, peering up at him. 'Where from . . . where from . . . ?' She clicked her fingers suddenly. 'That time in Brighton with Tony and Cherie. We all went on to the hotel afterwards and got blitzed on champagne, and everybody ended up in the swimming pool.'

Leonard was about to tell her that she'd attached him to the wrong party, but decided against it. Why burst the first little bubble of recognition he'd had in years?

'Wonderful night,' he lied, taking her hand and kissing it. 'And you're looking just as lovely now as you did then.'

'Oh, you old flatterer.' Brenda laughed huskily.

'And so it begins,' Avril muttered, rolling her eyes and sighing heavily.

'*What*?' Melody said irritably.

'Oh, nothing, dear. Just talking to myself.'

'What's everyone drinking?' Tony asked, looking around for a waiter.

'Champagne,' Brenda said, putting her arms in the air and swaying to the beat of the music. 'More champagne for everybody!'

'I think she's had more than enough already,' Avril murmured under her breath.

Ordering several bottles of champagne, Tony said, 'So, how's it going Lenny?'

'Pretty good,' Leonard said, squeezing past Brenda to sit beside him. 'I'm glad you're here, actually,' he said then, lowering his voice to add, 'I've been thinking about our little discussion last night, and I've got a couple of suggestions.'

'That right?'

Back on their side of the table, Avril said, 'Leonard tells me you're coming for dinner?'

'Mmmm,' Melody murmured, not wanting to get into a conversation.

'I'm looking forward to having you,' Avril went on. 'It'll be such a relief to have some good female company while thcy *man* talk.' Sighing now, she shook her head. 'You know, I spent *years* listening to Leonard prattle on about politics and high finance, and when he retired I actually thought I'd heard the last of it. Then he met *your* chap, and now he's back on the business buzz like he's never been off it.'

'I know what you mean,' Melody muttered. 'Tony's always yapping on about it.'

Leaning a little closer, Avril whispered, 'You wouldn't mind, but they're so *boring*, don't you think?'

Casting a resentful glance at Tony, Melody thought, *Too right he's boring.*

But Tony hadn't always been like that. In fact, he'd been a lot of fun to start with, always dragging her out to the casinos and nightclubs, and showering her with flowers and gifts. And he'd been proud to show her off to his high-rolling friends back then, too, relishing the look of envy in their eyes as he paraded her around with the fantastic new face and body he'd paid for. But there had been none of that over here. And after that fight, she doubted she'd ever see the fun times again, because he'd made it quite clear that he had no intention of going home any time soon. And there was nothing she could do about it, unless she fancied more of what he'd given her the other night. And she knew enough about him to know that he could do far, far worse than give her a cut lip.

'Is everything all right, dear?' Avril asked her quietly.

Sighing heavily, Melody shrugged. 'Yeah, I'm fine. Time of the month, that's all.'

'Oh, I don't envy you,' Avril murmured. 'Mine have finished now, thank the Lord. Not that *Leonard*'s noticed. But that's okay, because I can still use the old PMT as an excuse for biting his head off if he annoys me. If only more of us knew how to use it to its best advantage, we'd have these buggers whipped in no time, eh?'

Smiling now, Melody actually looked at Avril for the first time. Whether it was the fickleness of Hollywood rubbing off on her, or just her own innate vanity, but women who fell on either side of the sixteen-to-thirty-five threat range were usually invisible to her. But Avril was quite nice-looking for her age – which Melody guessed to be around fifty. Her skin was reasonably smooth, except for a few crow's-feet around the eyes, and a slight sagging of the jawline; her eyes were a lovely purply-grey shade; and her hair was a nice rich auburn, which looked almost natural, Melody thought.

And she was actually talking *to* Melody, not at her or about her, like the rest of the snotty bitches around the table. Jenna was all right, but apart from her, and now Avril, not one woman had actually given Melody the time of day since she'd got here.

Sensing that the girl was scrutinising her, Avril smiled. They were of a different generation – although maybe not as far removed as their appearances might have anybody believe, because Melody was obviously older than she looked once you saw her up close. But Avril recognised the look of frustration and boredom in the younger woman's eyes, and guessed that she, like Avril, had secret depths of which few were probably aware – least of all the men they had chosen to saddle themselves with.

Leonard was a blustering, self-important man, with not the least understanding of the female psyche. To his mind, women should be exact replicas of his late mother, Ethel, who had been the epitome of the good Conservative wife: never less than perfect in appearance; her food never less than Michelin standard; her home never less than immaculate; her husband never less than the most important man in the world to her. How she had managed to maintain those standards into her eighties and still manage to walk, talk, and breathe fire, Avril did not know, but she was the reason that Avril would be forever lacking as a wife in Leonard's eyes.

And this poor girl's partner was no better, Avril thought, looking at Tony Allen now. He might have a different approach than Leonard, in that he was obviously a lot livelier and far more self-confident, but the controlling edge was undoubtedly there. She could see it in his eyes when he looked at Melody: a dark, watchful sharpness that betrayed his need to know that she was doing only that of which he approved. And Melody's obvious depression, combined with the tarty clothes and make-up, told Avril that she had probably succumbed to his demands. She was the classic fantasy whore: there to satisfy her man's sexual desires, but not expected – or allowed – to have an opinion of her own.

'You girls ready for another drink?' Tony called over just then, breaking into their thoughts.

Smiling politely, Avril said, 'That would be lovely.' Turning back to Melody then, she muttered, '*Girls*, indeed! My dear, if that man's penis is even *half* the size of his ego, you must surely be the luckiest woman alive.'

Laughing, because it had been so unexpected, Melody said, 'I can't believe you just said that!'

'I haven't always been an old trout,' Avril told her amusedly.

Nudging Leonard as he watched their women chatting, Tony said, 'They seem to have hit it off, huh?'

'They certainly do,' Leonard said quietly, his eyebrows raised with amazement. Avril usually took time to warm to new people, but he would never in his wildest *dreams* have imagined her giving Tony's sluttish girlfriend the time of day. But then, she knew how important his friendship with Tony was to him, so she was probably pushing her distaste aside for his sake.

To be fair, he had to admit that she'd been quite pleasant today. She'd discussed his plans for the dinner party with more enthusiasm that he'd anticipated, and had even suggested that he buy himself a new suit for the occasion, pointing out that his wardrobe needs might have *changed* a little over recent months. Which was rather diplomatic of her, he thought, given that she *could* have just said that he'd let himself get fat, as he knew to his shame that he had. But he was pleased that *she* had suggested it, because he'd been wanting to update his wardrobe since they'd started coming to the club but had resisted for fear of raising her suspicions about his motives.

All in all, Leonard was quite pleased with *every*-thing just now. He was beginning to feel like his old self again and, with Tony Allen as a friend, he had no doubt that he would soon be right up at the top of the social tree.

Avril was having a hot flush. 'Phew!' she said, fanning a hand in front of her face. 'That wine is rather strong. I think I'd better go and powder my nose.'

Seeing a chance to escape from Tony's watchful gaze, Melody reached for her handbag. 'I'll come with you.'

'Just going to the little *girls'* room,' Avril told the men as they passed. 'Won't be long.'

Strolling off to the VIP toilets together, Melody's mind went into overdrive, wondering how she could get away from Avril for long enough to find Fabian.

As luck would have it, there was only one free cubicle. Telling Avril to go ahead and take it, Melody waited a second, then tapped on the door.

'The sanitary-towel machine isn't working,' she called through. 'I'm just nipping down to the other toilets. Won't be a minute.'

'I'll wait here for you,' Avril called back. 'I need to touch up my make-up, anyway.'

Hissing a jubilant 'Yes!' under her breath, Melody cracked the main door open and peeped out to make sure that Tony wasn't watching. Slipping out then, she darted down the stairs.

Fabian jumped when Melody ran up behind him and grabbed his arm.

'What are you doing?' he hissed, glancing nervously around for Eddie.

'I haven't got time to chat,' she hissed back, tugging him towards the office door. 'I just need you to give me something.'

'*I* haven't got time, full stop,' he retorted, prising her hand off his arm. 'We're busy, and I need to be on the floor.'

'It'll only take a minute,' Melody persisted. '*Please*, Fabian. I'm desperate.'

'I'm not in the mood for sex,' he told her bluntly. 'Anyway, I've been meaning to talk to you about that, because I think we should quit while we're ahead. It's been great, but it's getting too dangerous. You *do* know you were being followed, don't you?'

'Yes, I know,' she said, frowning now. 'But Tony's busy right now, so stop messing about. Anyway, I don't want sex, I just need some coke.'

'Keep your voice down!' Fabian muttered, taking his keys out. 'Okay, I'll give you some, but this is the last time, Melody – and I mean it. I thought I was going to get my legs broken the other night.'

Peering up at him, Melody's frown deepened. 'Hang on . . . how did *you* know I was being followed?'

'I saw Eddie watching you.'

'Is that why you took off?'

'What did you expect me to do? Wait for you to start mauling me, so Tony would know for sure there was something going on?'

'I do *not* maul you!' Melody retorted indignantly.

'Yeah, whatever.' Unlocking the door, Fabian ushered her quickly through.

Taking his stash out of the safe when they reached his office, he ripped a square of paper off a letter-headed sheet and tipped a little of the coke onto it.

'I need more than that,' Melody told him, taking one of the fifty notes she'd stolen from Tony out of her bra and thrusting it into his hand. 'Just give me the bag.'

Looking from the money to the bag, Fabian frowned. If he gave all the coke he had to her he'd have to go out and score again when they'd closed – which was a ball-ache, *and* dangerous at that time of night. But fifty quid was fifty quid.

'All right,' he agreed, tipping the wrap back into the bag and handing it to her. Taking the money, he slipped it into his pocket and waved her to the door. 'Let's go.'

'Do you have to be so cold?' she asked, giving him a reproachful look. 'I thought we were friends. And I won't see you for a couple of days, so the least you can do is be civil.'

Sighing, wondering why she was determined to make this difficult, Fabian said, 'Look, I'm not being funny, Melody, but I can't take this. It won't be long before your boyfriend puts two and two together – if he hasn't already.'

'He doesn't know about us,' Melody assured him. 'But, yeah, you're right, he *is* watching me. I think he thinks I'm doing drugs, or something.'

'Oh, great!'

'Don't worry, he doesn't know it's coming from *you*,' she said, slipping the bag into her bra before he got any ideas about taking it back.

'Oh, come on, Melody, you're not exactly discreet, are you?' Fabian retorted. 'You'll probably neck most of that before you go back up to him and make it really bloody obvious that you're off your head. How long before he links it back to me?'

'Will you quit freaking out,' she snapped, annoyed that he was more concerned about saving his own skin than the shit *she* was going through. 'He doesn't suspect you of anything. And, for your information, *no*, I *won't* neck half of this now, because it's got to last until Tony comes back.'

'From where?'

'How the hell should *I* know? You don't seriously think he tells *me* anything, do you? He's the most secretive bastard I've ever met. All I know is, him and Eddie are pissing off for a couple of days and I've got to stay at the hotel like a good little girl. And this –' Melody patted her breast '– is the only thing that's going to keep me sane. So, *sorry* for being such a pain, Fabian, but it's not exactly a barrel of laughs for *me* right now, either.'

'Yeah, I know,' he murmured, running a hand over his face. 'Sorry, but I'm just really wound up about your boyfriend's goon following you. I was about to leave the country.'

'Leaving me to get mauled by those losers,' Melody reminded him sourly. 'Yeah, well, thanks for that, Fabian, 'cos I was this close to getting raped.' Raising her hand, she pinched her fingertips together. 'They wouldn't have stopped if Eddie hadn't made them. They'd have probably dragged me into the toilets, or waited for me outside, or something.'

'You can't blame me for that,' Fabian said indignantly. 'I had no idea what was going on.'

'Oh, forget it.' She sighed. 'But next time you see me getting followed, do me a favour and tell me, yeah?'

'Sure,' he agreed. Then, '*Now* can we go?'

Nodding, her eyes clouded with disappointment that he could be so dismissive, Melody walked out with her head held high.

Strolling to the downstairs bar as she dashed back up to the VIP toilets, Fabian told Maurice to get him a large brandy. He felt guilty now. The look on Melody's face had got to him. She'd looked so defeated and let down, and he supposed he *had* let her down, because this wasn't all her fault. Under different circumstances, he'd have been delighted to be involved with her, because she was gorgeous, and sexy, and really quite nice once you scraped the Hollywood gloss off. But she was just too dangerous to be around. And *he* was too damn handsome to risk having his face scarred for life over her.

Tony looked at Leonard with a wry smile on his face. Maybe the guy wasn't quite as stupid as he looked, after all. He'd just made a suggestion that was so obvious, Tony didn't know why he hadn't thought of it himself.

'You know what?' he said approvingly. 'That's not such a bad idea.'

'Well, I did a lot of thinking after we spoke last night,' Leonard said, feeling more than a little pleased with himself. 'I was trying to think of anybody I know who might be looking for investors, and Jenna came to my mind. I'm not sure what her status is regarding finances, but it occurred to me that she must have spent rather a lot to overhaul this place, because her father certainly didn't leave it like this. It was a bit of a mess when he had it, actually. But that's by the by. I just thought it might be worth asking her.'

'Well, there's only one way to find out,' Tony said, pushing his chair back when he spotted Jenna making her way to the bar just then. 'Let's go ask her.'

'You want me to come with you?' Leonard said, a little surprised because he'd thought that Tony would want to keep this between himself and Jenna.

'It was your suggestion, so why not?' Tony shrugged. 'Anyway, she doesn't really know me, so she might get a bit nervous about me launching something like this on her. But you're an old friend of her dad, so she's bound to feel safer with you there. Don't mind, do you?'

'I'd be delighted,' Leonard agreed proudly.

Jenna was in no mood for talking. She'd spent the whole day moping about, first at her apartment, where she'd wandered restlessly from room to room, and now here at the club, where she just couldn't seem to escape Vibes's presence.

She'd been thinking about him all day, wondering if he'd got any sleep; if he'd made his flight on time; if he'd got through Customs without being hassled about the watch.

If he felt as guilty as she did about that kiss.

Desperate for the night to finish so that she could go home and escape in her dreams, she'd come up to the bar now to have a quiet drink to see her through the next two torturous hours. But no sooner had she got her glass of wine in her hand than Tony, Leonard, and Eddie came over.

Going with them to an empty booth when they said they had something to discuss with her, Jenna frowned when Tony sat on one side of her and Leonard on the other. And Eddie dragging a chair up to the table so that he was facing her just completed the claustrophobic circle.

Forcing herself to smile politely, she looked

from one to the other of them, saying, 'What can I do for you?'

'Remember when I called you?' Tony said, taking the lead. 'Said I needed advice about some business ideas I had going?'

'Friday,' Jenna murmured, remembering it clearly, because that was the same day that Vibes had told her he was leaving.

'Yeah, Friday,' Tony said, frowning because her eyes had clouded over. 'You all right, Jen?'

'Uh?' Snapping her gaze back to him, she nodded. 'Sorry . . . yes, I'm fine. What were you saying?'

'Well, you suggested I talk to Lenny,' Tony continued, watching her carefully. 'And we did have a chat that night, which kind of put me right about a couple of things.'

Cutting in here, oblivious to Jenna's distracted state, Leonard said, 'You see, Tony was having a little difficulty knowing what to do with his money.'

'I want to set something up over here,' Tony jumped back in. 'And I was thinking along the lines of a casino, to start with, but Lenny pointed out that I'd be wasting my time pursuing that, because—'

'Oh, it's an incredibly tough procedure,' Leonard chipped in. 'Terribly difficult.'

'So, *any*way . . .' Tony said, frowning at Leonard

to shut him up. 'Then I was thinking along the lines of opening up something like *this* place. As you know, I've had one of my own already back home, so it seems kinda logical to stick to what I know best.'

'Yes, I remember you saying,' Jenna muttered, feeling a little sick from having to twist her head from side to side to look at each of them as they spoke.

'Well, Lenny kind of scotched that for me, as well,' Tony said.

'Because that's equally hard for a man in his position,' Leonard interrupted. '*Sorry*,' he said then, holding up an apologetic hand.

'Anyway, like he said, it seems *that* might be a bit of a problem, too,' Tony went on. 'Me being foreign, and all. But then he suggested I should think about investing in a going concern, instead of trying to set something up from scratch. And I've been mulling it over all night, but I couldn't think where to start, 'cos I don't really know anyone well enough yet to approach them. But then he suggested I talk to you.'

'I don't think there's anything I can tell you that Leonard probably hasn't already,' Jenna said. 'I've already told you that I don't really know very much about the business side of things yet.'

'No, you don't get me,' Tony said, smiling now.

'He meant talk to you *about* you. Well, not *you* personally,' he added quickly, 'but this place.'

'Oh, you mean as in talk to me about investing in the club?'

'Exactly.'

'Well, I'm flattered that you thought of me,' Jenna said, smiling apologetically. 'but I'm not really looking for a partner right now.'

'I'm not suggesting leaping headlong into a fifty-fifty deal, or anything like that,' Tony assured her, sensing that she needed convincing. 'It's just that *I* need something to put my money into, and I'm pretty sure *you* could do with an injection of ready cash. I know you inherited the place, and Lenny's told me how much work you've done to get it like this, so I figure you must be up to your neck in it with the bank.'

Choosing her words carefully, because she didn't want to offend him, Jenna said, 'That's not something I feel entirely comfortable discussing, actually, Tony. With respect, I like to keep my business private.'

Looking at her, Tony said, 'I understand that, and I wouldn't want you to think I was trying to pressurise you. But will you at least think about it?'

Sighing, Jenna shrugged. 'There doesn't seem much point when I already know the answer.'

Looking at her for a moment, Tony nodded respectfully. 'I appreciate the honesty, but don't rule it out altogether, yeah? If you ever think about taking a partner in the future, you know where I am.'

'Of course,' Jenna said, relieved that he wasn't going to push it. 'I doubt it'll happen, though,' she added, just to be sure that he wouldn't go away thinking it was a done deal. 'And you might not even be here by then, anyway. But if you are, you'll be the first to know.'

'That's good enough for me,' Tony said, smiling again. 'Me and Lenny will put our heads together and come up with something else in the meantime. Right, Len?'

'Absolutely,' Leonard agreed, feeling as if he'd let Tony down somehow. 'Anything I can do – you know that.'

'Well, good luck with that,' Jenna said, standing up. 'And I'm always willing to talk if you ever want to discuss anything – not that I'll be much use to you. But, if you'll excuse me, I think I'd better get back to work.'

'Take it easy,' Tony said.

Having got up to let Jenna out, Leonard sat back down and sighed heavily. 'Sorry about that. It probably wasn't one of my better suggestions.'

'Hey, don't knock yourself,' Tony told him. 'It

was a good idea. Anyway, who knows . . . she might still go for it at some point.'

'Yes, but what are you going to do now?'

Winking at him, Tony said, 'Don't you worry about me, Lenny. Something will come up. And you've been a great help already.'

'I tried,' Leonard murmured dejectedly, wishing there was something more that he could do.

Sitting back, Tony sipped at his drink, narrow-eyed as his mind ticked over new possibilities. He liked the idea of hooking up with Jenna, but that wasn't going to happen for a while, if at all. But Leonard was a different matter. Tony had a feeling he'd be a pushover if he was handled right, and he sure had the necessary qualities to make him useful: came from a moneyed background; owned a mansion; had been something of a name in politics. But, best of all, Leonard was so desperate to *be* somebody that he'd probably agree to just about anything Tony asked now if it meant being allowed to bask in his limelight.

'You know, you've surprised me,' he said, switching the charm on and looking at Leonard with respect. 'First time I met you, I thought you were a bit flaky.'

'Flaky?' Leonard repeated, wondering if that were good or bad.

'Yeah, you know, sort of out there,' Tony elaborated, leaving Leonard none the wiser. 'But you're a pretty astute guy when you get right down to it, aren't you? Real keen business sense.'

Flattered, Leonard gave a modest shrug. 'Well, I do all right, I suppose.'

'Better than all right from what I've heard,' Tony said. 'I mean, politics is a tough business, what with all the corruption you hear about. But to come out the other end as straight as you, that takes something extra. I really admire you for that.'

'Well, it's not easy,' Leonard admitted. 'I've already told you how much – shall we say – *underhanded* stuff goes on in government. So, yes, it is rare to come out untarnished.'

'Takes special smarts, if you ask me,' Tony said, tapping a finger on his temple. Taking his cigars out then, he offered one to Leonard. 'Which kinda makes me wonder,' he went on, lighting his own and holding the flame out to Leonard, 'why you retired so young. I mean, look at all that experience, all that nous, *wasted*. And you're only, what – forty-four, forty-five?'

'Well, actually, I'm a little closer to fifty,' Leonard admitted, puffing the cigar to life.

'Sure don't look it,' Tony told him. 'But, whatever, I'd still say you was too young to be putting yourself out to graze like that. Don't you reckon, Ed?'

Nodding, Eddie smiled. 'I reckon.'

Taken aback as much by the smile as by the fact that it was the first time he'd ever heard Eddie speak, Leonard blinked rapidly.

'Know what I think your problem is?' Tony gazed at him thoughtfully. 'I don't think you've ever let yourself be who you really are. Am I right?'

Dropping his gaze, Leonard reached for his glass as the heat rose to his cheeks. 'I, um, don't really know what you mean.'

'Sure you do,' Tony said, his voice soft and low. 'See, I knew what you was from the off.'

Leonard's hand was trembling now. *Please, God, no . . .*

'But I think other people misunderstand you,' Tony went on, in full schmooze mode now. 'They see the politician, and assume you're the same as all the rest. But you're not the same, are you, Lenny? You're decent, and honest, and generous enough to spare a stranger like me the benefit of your knowledge.'

Still shaking, Leonard glanced up. He'd been so sure that Tony was going to mention the 'Q' word again, and he didn't think he could have coped with an outright confrontation.

'Hey, see what a good guy this is?' Tony said, turning to Eddie and shaking his head incredulously. 'Give him a fucking compliment, and he gets all choked. Now, that's a *real* man.'

'Sure is,' Eddie agreed, playing along. He didn't know quite where this was headed yet, but if he knew Tony – and he did, better than anyone – he was setting the guy up for some kind of sting.

'Yep,' Tony murmured, sighing now. 'Just a shame you're retired, 'cos I reckon we could kick some serious ass if we put our heads together. But you've still done something good for me tonight, Lenny.'

'I have?'

'Oh, yeah.' Reaching for his drink, Tony nodded. 'See, I've been walking around with this million-dollar bank draft in my pocket, thinking I was never gonna find a genuinely honest person to entrust it to. But you've shown me that the good guys do exist, so now I just gotta relax and wait for the right one to come along.'

Peering at him, Leonard frowned. 'You've got a *million-dollar* banker's draft?'

'That what you guys call it, huh?' Reaching into his pocket, Tony showed it to him. Shrugging, he put it back. 'Not that it's any use at the moment, mind.'

'With respect,' Leonard said worriedly, 'I really don't think you should be carrying it around like that.'

'Sure as hell can't leave it at the hotel.'

'Wouldn't it be safer in the bank?'

'How?' Tony looked him in the eye. 'Do you know how much shit someone like me has to go through to open an account over here? I tried, but they want all kinds of paperwork that I haven't got. And I can't even use my old US one no more, 'cos I emptied it out to get this draft, thinking I'd easy find something to invest it in over here.'

'There must be something you can do,' Leonard murmured. 'I had no idea you were talking about that kind of money. Why don't I speak to my son?'

'No point,' Tony said, finishing his drink. 'Without the paperwork to prove that these are legitimate funds from selling my club, no one will touch it.'

'Can't you contact whoever bought your club and get duplicates of the contracts?' Leonard suggested helpfully.

Laughing softly, Tony shook his head. 'That ain't the way things work in my neck of the woods, Lenny. See, it turns out the guy I sold it to wasn't quite as honest as you and me, and he only wanted it to pull some kind of insurance scam. Couple of weeks after he takes it off my hands, *poof*! Biggest fire *I* ever seen.' Sighing now, he flapped his hands in a what-can-you-do gesture. 'No contracts, no records, no nothing left to prove it was ever even there – or that *I* ever had anything to do with it when it was.'

'My God,' Leonard muttered. 'How awful.'

'So you can see my predicament,' Tony said. 'Not one of your fine banks will touch me – and I can't say I blame 'em.'

'There's got to be a way around this.' Leonard frowned. 'A banker's draft isn't like a cheque. It's as good as having the physical money in your hand.'

'Yeah, well, soon as I find someone to invest it with who's willing to put it in their account till I'm sorted, I'll be rolling,' Tony said. 'Till then, it's just gonna have to stay right where it is.'

'That might not be so easy,' Leonard pointed out. 'You see, whoever takes it off your hands is going to have to prove where *they* got it from to be able to deposit it, and if no physical asset to that value had changed hands, or service been done to justify it, the bank would likely query it, which would lead them straight back to you.'

Looking at him, Tony's eyebrows knitted together. 'You got to be kidding me?'

'I'm afraid not,' Leonard said sympathetically. 'You see, there would still be the burden of proof, and I can't imagine any legitimate businessman being willing to risk his own finances being investigated. A corrupt one might, but you don't want to be involved with that kind of person, do you?'

'No, I don't,' Tony muttered running a hand through his hair. 'Oh, man, that's a downer. What the hell am I supposed to do now?'

'I really don't know,' Leonard said, feeling guilty for having burst Tony's bubble. 'But let me have a think about it, because I've plenty of colleagues with experience of this kind of thing. *Some*body ought to have a suggestion.'

'Hey, no offence, but I don't want no one knowing my business,' Tony said quickly, his voice ringing with disappointment. '*You* I trust, but I wouldn't trust no one else with that kind of information.'

'Oh, God, no, I wouldn't dream of telling anybody,' Leonard assured him. 'But leave it with me. I'll do whatever I can.'

Glancing at Eddie, Tony gave him a sly half-smile. The big fat worm was wriggling nicely onto the hook. Now all they had to do was wait for him to bite himself in the ass, and they would be part-way to a solution.

In his lounge later that night, when they had got home from the club and Avril had gone to her bed, Leonard sat on the couch with a glass of Scotch in his hand, his mind working overtime. He really wanted to help Tony out; not only because they were friends, but because Tony had done something for him tonight that money couldn't buy: he'd given him back his self-respect.

Leonard had never admitted his real reasons for taking early retirement. But it hadn't been for the sake of enjoying his last years without the pressures of politics, nor to spend more time with the family, to potter about in the garden, nor play golf, nor any of the other recreational excuses that many of the older guard had used upon standing down. It had been to escape the indignity of being shuffled further back into the political wastelands and the humiliation of knowing that the youngsters who were infiltrating the party had no clue who he was. He had not wanted to suffer the injustice of having to kowtow to the snot-nosed bastards as they rose through the ranks, nor had he looked forward to the indignity of having to ignore the condescending smirks and disrespectful remarks they made behind his back.

He hadn't *wanted* to retire: he'd been forced to. And, in taking that step, he thought that he had killed off every last shred of hope of ever regaining his place in the public eye. But then he'd met Tony Allen, a man who had everything that Leonard craved: power, presence, and a firm foothold with the rich and famous.

With Tony's help, Leonard had tonight found himself welcomed into the celebrity circle that he'd spent years trying to break into. His early moments in the press and on TV as a political poster boy and spokesman had given him a taste for it, but he'd only ever managed to achieve local renown –

and that hadn't been nearly enough. He'd wanted the general public to recognise him, and for the stars to think of his name when they organised their parties. And now that he'd finally got a foot in the door he was determined to stay there. But, for now, he was just visiting that world as Tony's guest, and if Tony tired of him before he'd made his own mark there he had no doubt that he'd find himself cast out again in a heartbeat. So he needed to do something to guarantee that Tony would continue to want him around, and helping him out with his problem seemed the best bet. But how?

A light switched on in his head when his gaze came to rest on the Matisse hanging over the fire-place: the huge ugly old oil painting that his father had bought as an investment, and which his mother had liked so much that she'd made Leonard promise to let it hang there for all time – despite knowing how much he hated it.

My God, that's it! he thought, sitting bolt upright in his seat.

Getting up far more quickly than a man of his size should have been able to, Leonard went to the door and checked that Avril wasn't moving about. Closing it quietly when he heard nothing, he rushed back to the couch and reached for the phone. He knew it was late but he was sure Tony wouldn't mind.

'I think I've got the answer,' he said when Tony answered. 'Remember we were talking about you finding somebody to deposit your money for you? Well, how about me?'

'You?' Tony replied cautiously. 'I don't know, Lenny. I thought you said it'd be too difficult – that the bank would still come back to me.'

'Not necessarily,' Leonard went on excitedly. 'You see, it occurred to me that *I* could *earn* that money – if, for example, I decided to sell one of my assets.'

'What, so you want me to buy something off of you?'

'No, no. I wouldn't actually have to sell anything, I could just *say* I had. You see, I have a number of rather valuable paintings in my possession, which the bank knows about because of the insurance. Now, if I were to produce a sales receipt for some of these, the bank would have no reason to doubt its legitimacy, because it's an entirely feasible transaction. Then I could deposit your banker's draft as "payment", and when you've managed to open your own account I can simply transfer it.'

'But wouldn't they want to know why you were giving me the money back if I'd bought the paintings?'

'Yes, but I would claim that I had received the payment in advance, and that the overseas buyer

– *yourself* – had asked me to hold on to them until they were able to collect, which would explain my need to retain the insurance cover. Then I would simply claim to have changed my mind before the handover, and transfer the money as a refund.'

'But I'm not really buying them?' Tony asked.

'No, but the bank would *think* you were,' Leonard said patiently. 'So when I transfer the money all they'll need to know is that I'm repaying the person who paid me in the first place. Which would work out perfectly for you,' he added, 'because *you* would have the original receipt to show to *your* bank, proving that you had legitimately owned the asset that you were now, in effect, selling. Do you see?'

'I think I do,' Tony said, chuckling softly. 'Man, I gotta say that's some kind of genius. You got it all covered, don't you?'

'It just seemed so logical,' Leonard replied modestly. 'My father was always buying and selling, so there's a family history of major financial transactions such as this. And no earthly reason, therefore, why it should raise any eyebrows if *I* were to take up the tradition.'

'Well, I'm choked that you'd offer to do that for me,' Tony said sincerely. 'And it *would* solve my problem.' Pausing then, as if something were troubling him, he said, 'But, you know what, Lenny?

I'm gonna suggest we sit on it for now, 'cos it's a huge risk.'

'It's no risk to me,' Leonard assured him, touched that Tony was being so considerate in light of how difficult his own situation was. 'I'd still have my paintings, so I've nothing to lose. You're the one who'd be taking a leap of faith by handing your money over.'

'Hey, if there's one thing that ain't in question, it's your honesty,' Tony said without hesitation. 'But I still want you to have a good think about it, 'cos I don't want you committing yourself and then regretting it. If you want to go ahead after that, great. But if not, I'd totally understand.'

Leonard knew that he *would* go ahead, because there was simply no reason not to. But Tony was right to insist on him making an informed decision. Who in their right mind would want to hand over a million dollars to a foolhardy idiot who jumped headlong into things without thought?

'Okay,' Leonard said. 'I'll talk to you again when I've thought it through some more. But could I ask you to keep this quiet?' he asked then, almost whispering now. 'You see, I don't want Avril to get wind of it. I, um, have a separate account, you see, which she knows nothing about.'

Smiling slyly at his end, Tony said, 'She'll never

hear a thing from me, Lenny, you got my word on that. And if it makes you feel any better, I won't even tell Melody. It'll be just you, me, and Eddie. Agreed?'

'Agreed,' Leonard said, sighing with relief. The last thing he wanted was for Avril to find out. Not that it should, but if, God forbid, anything *were* to happen between depositing the money and repaying it, she would not only strip the flesh from his body as far as his house and assets were concerned, she would suck the marrow right out of his bones, too. And Tony's money would be bound to get caught in the crossfire.

Back at the hotel, Tony put the phone down and relayed the conversation to Eddie with a grin on his face.

'Sure we can trust him?' Eddie asked, reaching for the vodka bottle to refill their glasses. 'It's a lot of dough to risk on a stranger.'

'Yeah, well, we can't do nothing with it if we don't,' Tony pointed out. 'Anyway, he ain't gonna fuck us about. He's got too much to lose. He messes up, we take him and his lovely wife to pieces. Then we'll go and take what's ours, 'cos there's gonna be a set of million-pound paintings sitting there with my name on 'em.'

'Yeah, but he wants to transfer the money to

your account after it's sorted, and you can't get one,' Eddie reminded him.

'Not yet,' Tony conceded. 'But I'm sure the fat boy will be happy to hold on to it until we can.'

'You reckon?' Eddie asked doubtfully. 'Sounds to me like he's only willing to do it because he thinks it's a short-term deal. Can't see him wanting to drag it out too long, or he's gonna start getting jumpy about his paintings.'

'Leave him to me,' Tony said, chuckling softly. 'I'm gonna have him licking the shit off of my shoes before too long – you watch.' Raising his glass now, he said, 'Nearly there, Ed.'

Raising his own glass, Eddie sipped at his drink, frowning thoughtfully. Leonard Drake might well be sincere, but there were too many potential holes in the plan for it to run as smoothly as he and Tony seemed to think it would.

Leonard's wife, for starters.

Eddie was a people-watcher, and Avril Drake had something about her that told him she wasn't the dumb little wife she made herself out to be. There was a keenness in her eyes that a lot of broads didn't have and, like Eddie himself, she listened – hard – and was smart enough to keep her own mouth shut while she was taking everything in. And that was a rare and dangerous quality in a woman, because ladies like that were so unobtrusive it was easy to forget they were there, and before you knew it they had a shit-load of information on you that you didn't even realise you'd given away – and they had sussed out exactly how to use it against you.

Tony would be wise to keep Melody well away from her, in Eddie's opinion. Melody wasn't stupid by any means, but she was a damn sight more stupid than Avril Drake, and if Avril wanted to get something out of her, Eddie had no doubt that she'd soon know everything that Melody knew. And, unlike Melody, who had swallowed Tony's story without question, Avril would probably rip it to pieces and then spend as long as it took putting it all back together until she had the complete picture.

Still, Leonard must know what she was like or he wouldn't have asked Tony to keep her in the dark about their plan to deposit the money in his account. So as long as Melody never got to know the real facts about their situation, they shouldn't be in too much danger. But Eddie would be watching them both closely, nonetheless.

10

Tony was still sleeping when Melody woke up the next morning. Easing the quilt back, she got up and pulled her dressing gown on, then tiptoed into the bathroom to take a shower. She felt quite light-hearted for a change. She'd accepted that she couldn't escape – yet – but she was looking forward to having a bit of time to herself while Tony was away. Two whole nights of not having to wait in dread anticipation of him returning from whcr-ever he and Eddie kept disappearing to, a brief respite from the nightmare prospect of him coming back into the room and climbing on top of her. Bliss!

She'd taken to pretending to be asleep when he came in. Sometimes she actually *was,* but that didn't stop him. Asleep, awake, unconscious – he didn't care. She could be *dead,* and he'd probably still go for it if he was horny enough.

Coming back to the bedroom with a towel wrapped around her hair a short time later, Melody quietly opened the dresser drawers and lifted her clothes out onto the floor.

'What you doing?' Tony asked, waking up just then and eyeing her with suspicion as she rooted through the pile. 'I thought I said you wasn't coming with us.'

'Don't panic, I'm only looking for this,' Melody said, finding the Lycra exercise suit she wanted and pulling it out. 'Think it'll still fit?' she asked, holding it up against herself.

'Not with the weight you've been putting on,' he grunted, reaching for a cigarette.

'Which is exactly why I'm going down to the gym,' she retorted, wishing he'd drop dead. Snatching up the other clothes, she stuffed them back into the drawer. 'Got to do *some*thing to amuse myself while I'm under house arrest.'

'Don't get smart,' Tony warned her, pushing the quilt back.

Pulling a face at his hairy back when he strolled naked into the bathroom, Melody stuck two fingers up when he kicked the door shut. He said *she*'d put on weight, but he should take a look in the mirror sometime, because those bulges were more like industrial cargo carriers than love handles. No wonder her bones were aching, having to bear *that* pounding her into the mattress night after night.

Three long years she'd been tolerating it, telling

herself that it was worth it for the money, the presents, and the surgery he'd paid for to help her achieve her acting aims. But it was getting harder and harder to stomach now that she'd tasted Fabian's forbidden fruits. Not that she *loved* Fabian, or anything ridiculous like that, but he was a hell of a good-looking man, with such a different approach to fucking than Tony's rodeo saddle-up-and-ride-'em-hard style. Tony seemed to think that orgasms were a man's right, and women should be grateful if they chanced upon one along the way. But Fabian was the exact opposite, priding himself on his abilities to bring pleasure.

And boy, *had* he!

Melody had fucked a lot of men in her time, but none had ever come close to hitting the spot as often as Fabian did. They'd only had snatched moments together since their fling had started, but he had never failed to satisfy her, and she would miss that now that he'd called it off.

Not quite as much as she would miss the coke, though. But that was just tough, because she was in no position to start heavying him about it. Not now that Tony was on her case – and definitely not now she knew that Eddie had been following her. If Tony suspected her of something, it really wouldn't be wise to stir him up about another man. Better to say and do nothing, and let whatever was going on in his head die down – and use the time between to think up ways to escape.

Coming out of the bathroom in his dressing gown just then, Tony picked up the phone and called room service to order breakfast for three. Then he called Eddie's room and told him to come down.

'Your mobile's ringing,' Melody told him, reaching for it. Looking at the screen she frowned. 'How come you never have no names come up like normal people?'

Snatching it off her, Tony said, 'And how come you never mind your own business, like normal people?'

Walking into the lounge, he pulled the door firmly shut behind him and answered the call.

'Yo?'

'I was about to give up on you,' Ronson said.

'Yeah. Well, I'm here now,' Tony grunted. 'What's up?'

'I'm just watching the news. One of the brothers is out.'

'Out?' Tony repeated, lighting another cigarette and sucking on it hard.

'Of the picture,' Ronson elaborated darkly. 'Seems they got to him in the armoured truck on the way to some military base where they were going to hold him till the trial. Guard's a straight-A medal plate for thirty-odd years, then he goes and switches sides. Takes out Johnson and the other guards, then gets himself snipered getting out of the truck, so he don't even get to pick up his dough. Go figure, huh?'

'But they still got the others?' Tony asked. 'They could still make it to court?'

'What's the chance of that?' Ronson snorted. 'Word is, they've changed the plan and decided to chopper the others to some other high-tech nuclear bunker now. But for Zorba's guys that just narrows down where to start looking, don't it? Anyway, I'm keeping the news on 24-7, so I'll keep you updated.'

'Thanks,' Tony muttered.

'No problem,' Ronson said. Then, 'So, how's it going in sunny Rio? Carnival started yet?'

'Nah, not yet, but I'll send you a ticket as soon as, so you can come over and join in.'

'They still got the bare-ass parades?'

'Sure have,' Tony lied. 'I can see the main street from the hotel, so I'm getting a bird's-eye of the *un*dress rehearsals when the floats go past.'

'Lucky bastard,' Ronson chuckled. 'I've all but forgot what a pussy looks like since that bitch dropped the fucking syph bomb on me.'

'Didn't think a little thing like that would stop you fucking your way round the world?'

'It wouldn't have. But I only went and passed

it on to a freaking *cop*, didn't I? Bitch threatened to bust my ass for attempted fucking murder if I "knowingly" gave it to anyone else before I got myself clean. Only reason she didn't report me straight out is 'cos she'd have had to admit she spends her free time trawling the bars picking up lowlifes.'

'Like you, huh?' Tony chuckled.

'Hey, I'm no lowlife, I'm just smart enough to choose the bars where easy pickings like her hang out,' Ronson countered. 'I mean, come on, man, what's the point in going upmarket when them bitches expect you to take 'em out to a fucking fancy restaurant before they'll open their legs. I ain't paying for no bitch to get fat.'

'Better than paying for syph shots,' Tony pointed out.

'True,' Ronson said, sighing. Then, 'Anyway, subject of whores, any sign of Melody yet?'

'No, there ain't,' Tony snarled. 'But don't worry. I ever get to Australia, I'm gonna track the bitch down and take her out.'

'You do that,' Ronson said nastily. 'And make sure you give it to the pilot she took off with, an' all.'

'Don't worry,' Tony grunted. 'I ever see him again, he's a dead man.'

'Too right,' Ronson agreed. 'And you want to

get yourself checked out for the clap while you're at it. You never know what the cunt was up to before she shafted you like that. Don't be leaving it too late like me.'

'I hear you,' Tony said, glancing at his watch now. He needed to cut the call. If Zorba had already got to a top-notch guard, he could certainly find out where Tony's phone signal was coming from. 'Anyway, look, man, I gotta hit it. Let me know as and when anything happens, yeah?'

'Will do. Keep it cool, Tee.'

'You, too.'

Disconnecting, Tony smoked the rest of his cigarette and mulled over this new information.

Zorba's people were obviously pulling out all the stops to get his case dusted. Tony had to get his shit sorted, because they would come after him with everything they had soon as Zorba was free. He was all right for now, because Ronson was the only person he had any contact with back home – and *he* thought they were in Brazil, so that was all he'd ever be able to tell anyone, even if they tortured him. And he thought Melody had left him and taken off with a pilot to Australia, so nobody would put him together with her now.

Still, now that Leonard was hooked the bank draft wouldn't be a problem; and he and Eddie had the car, so it wouldn't take long to change the rest of the money over. It would just be a matter of utilising it after that without Tony's name being attached to it. And he knew exactly how to do that.

Stubbing the cigarette butt out, Tony got up and went to get dressed.

Kissing Tony goodbye when he and Eddie left a short time after breakfast, Melody made her way down to the hotel's state-of-the-art gym with a spring in her step. Despite his snipes about her weight, she knew how hot she looked in her Lycra get-up, and was quite looking forward to the envious glances of the women who congregated there in the mornings to gossip as they wobbled their bingo wings and created earthquakes with their thighs on the treadmills and exercise bikes.

Strolling in with her shoulders back and her chest out now, she smiled to herself when the pudding club's chatter turned to an immediate low hum as they turned their surreptitious attentions to her. Putting her bag down beside a free treadmill, she tied her hair up, aware that the bitches were eyeing her every move. Doing some sexy warm-up stretches then, as if she hadn't noticed them, she got onto the treadmill and programmed herself a two-mile jog. She'd just set off when the door opened and Chase Mann walked in.

The low hum turned to an excited buzz as the

women recognised him. Walking past them as if they weren't even there, Chase came to a stop at the weights machine next to Melody. Noticing her, he gave her one of his famously sexy smiles and put his bag down. Then, taking off his jogging pants and leaving just a pair of shorts to show-case his great thighs, he put a foot up on a chair to tie his trainer laces. Frowning questioningly, he glanced back up at Melody.

'Hi,' she said coolly, breathing easy as she got into her stride. She still hadn't forgiven him for ignoring her at the club.

'Hi,' he said, still frowning. 'Sorry, but don't I know you?'

'I don't know,' she replied, not bothering to look at him. 'Do you?'

Unused to women being anything less than on the point of fainting if he spoke to them these days, Chase was intrigued. Either she was using the old I'm-not-interested trick to try and hook him and drag him in, or she genuinely didn't recog-nise him – and how likely was *that*? Every bird in the UK, Europe, the States and Japan recognised him by now.

Putting him out of his misery – because he was obviously having a hard time coming to terms with not being instantly adored – Melody said, 'We met at Zenith.'

'Zenith?' Chase frowned again.

'Nightclub, New Year's Eve,' Melody helped him out. 'I was with my boyfriend, you had three tarts hanging off your wallet.'

'Ah,' Chase murmured sheepishly. 'The blonde bombshells.'

'More like bomb*sites*,' Melody muttered scathingly.

'Probably right,' Chase agreed, with another sheepish smile. 'I think I was a bit the worse for wear that night.'

'And the next,' Melody reminded him. '*And* the next, come to that.'

'Yeah, well, I was getting myself geared up for the German tour,' he said, quite enjoying the novelty of not being fawned over for a change.

'Is that where you've been?' she said, starting to glow now with the running. 'Thought I hadn't seen you around for a while.'

'Oh, so you noticed, did you?' Chase asked, grinning now.

'Yeah, but only 'cos me and my boyfriend used to put bets on how many women we'd see getting out of the penthouse lift in the mornings. I think your record was five.'

'Not all mine,' Chase told her quickly. 'That was a party.'

'Weren't they all?'

'So, this fella of yours,' Chase said, sitting down on the weights bench now and reaching for the bars. 'Have I met him?'

'Everyone in Manchester has probably met him by now,' Melody replied, with just a hint of sarcasm in her voice. 'His name's Tony Allen.'

'Ah.' Chase remembered. 'American. Big minder.'

'That's the one.'

'Right, yeah.' Glancing around now, mock-scared, he said, 'Hey, he's not watching us now, is he? Only I don't want him thinking I'm chatting you up or anything.'

'If he was here, you'd be talking to him, not to me,' Melody said, coming to the end of her jog and punching an extra mile onto the clock at speed-walking pace. 'You were certainly more interested in him last time we met.'

'Can't remember, I'm afraid,' Chase admitted. 'But if I was rude, I'm sorry. I was a bit wasted. That's why I'm here now, actually. Under orders to get my shit together.'

'Orders from who?'

'Record company.' Chase rolled his eyes. 'They're on my case. Reckon I single-handedly fucked up the tour.'

'And did you?' Melody asked, watching his muscles tighten with his exertions.

'Nah, I just got bored,' he said. 'Sick of doing the same old songs over and over, hearing the same old shit guitar riffs, and them drums pounding in my head. So I left the band to it a couple of times and got off for a spliff. But they reckoned I should have waited till the set was finished and not walked off stage halfway through a song.'

'Yeah, but that's your job,' she pointed out logically. 'If you stop putting your heart into it, your fans will find someone else to spend their money on, won't they?'

'Oasis have been getting away with it for years,' he countered. 'And I sell as many records as them, easy.'

'If you say so,' Melody said, switching the machine off and reaching for her towel.

'Don't you believe me?' Chase asked, letting the weights go and standing up, reluctant to end the conversation. 'I've got platinum discs all the place. My last album went triple, here *and* in the States.'

'Oh, I know you're big,' Melody said, her eyes sliding surreptitiously to his shorts as she patted the sweat from her neck. 'But you know what they say: the higher you are, the further you fall. Why risk everything you've worked for for a spliff? If I was you, I'd be working my backside off to stay up there.'

'I suppose,' he murmured glumly. 'It's just really hard to keep at it when you've got no choice.'

'Take it from me, it's a damn sight better than not being able to do it at all.'

'That the voice of experience?'

'Mmm,' Melody murmured, not really wanting to talk about it, because it was still too raw and she just might end up screaming.

'So, you're a singer, too, are you?' Chase persisted.

'Actress,' she told him, putting her towel back into the bag. 'Hollywood stuff. You probably won't have seen them if you've been working.'

'I watch shed-loads of DVDs on the tour bus,' Chase said, realising that she was about to leave and wanting to delay her. 'Tell me what you've been in – I might have seen it.'

'Okay,' Melody said, smiling now, because she always got a buzz talking about her films. 'I did *Help Wanted* with Sandra Bullock last year, and *Gentle Rain* with George Clooney a few months ago.'

'Seen the first one,' Chase told her. Then, smiling sheepishly, 'Don't remember seeing you in it, though. Which part did you play?'

'Sandra's room-mate.'

'No way!' Drawing his head back, Chase looked at her hard. 'She was really plain.'

'Er, that's why they call it *acting*,' Melody said,

delighted that he'd obviously been telling the truth and had seen it.

'Christ, you were good,' he said admiringly. 'I mean, *I* thought you were, anyway, the way you and Sandra bounced off each other. And when you had to team up and go undercover as hookers to get in with the bad guys, you were so kind of . . .' Pausing, he shrugged. 'Realistic, I suppose. But now I'm seeing you in the flesh, I'm realising how good you *really* were. To make anyone believe you're that plain and frumpy when you're actually . . . well, pretty hot, I guess.'

'Yeah, well, I thought I was pretty good,' Melody said, sighing now because it was bringing up memories that she didn't want to be thinking about right now.

'So, what's next?'

Shaking her head, Melody said, 'Nothing. I'm taking a break at the moment.' Shrugging then, she added, 'Knowing my luck, nobody will want me by the time I get back, anyway.'

'You've got to be kidding,' Chase said sincerely. 'I mean, I know I didn't recognise you, and probably still wouldn't if you hadn't told me who you were in the film. But you've got talent. Why wouldn't they want to use you again?'

Oh, let's see, Melody thought bitterly. *Maybe because they've got a clone going by the name of*

Deanna Shelby to keep them occupied. And she hasn't got a control-freak man forcing her out of the limelight.

Anyway, nobody ever *did* recognise her, so she might as well stop kidding herself. The Sandra Bullock film had come up before her biggest bout of surgery, so it hadn't been as hard as Chase imagined for her to act the part of a plain girl. And she'd been in a black wig for the whole of the Clooney film, so even though she'd had the tits and lips by then, still nobody would know it was her unless she darkened her hair. In taking on character roles, she'd missed her chance to be known as herself. The Julia Roberts film would have given her that, and she'd have been right up there with the best after it hit the screens. But that was gone now, so she might as well give up dreaming about it.

'I, um, don't suppose you'd fancy having lunch with me, would you?' Chase asked her suddenly. 'Only I haven't had a decent chat in weeks. Not one that doesn't include the words "fuck-up" and "or else", anyway.'

Looking at him, Melody thought, *Why not?* Tony wasn't here to stop her, and nobody at the hotel could think enough of it to go running to him with stories when he got back. They'd be just two guests having a chat over lunch. And it would be nice to talk to someone who appreciated her for her abilities, instead of putting her down or mocking her.

'Yeah, okay,' she said, picking up her things. 'Just let me go take a shower and get dressed.'

'Meet you in the lobby. Half an hour all right?'

'That's fine.' Smiling, Melody left, blatantly ignoring the envious gazes of the fat women.

Lunch gave Chase and Melody a chance to air their grievances against the people who they saw as screwing up their lives. Melody stopped short of telling him the whole truth of her situation, just in case it ever got back to Tony, but she felt better for having a good old general moan. And Chase felt better that somebody had actually listened to his gripes about touring without telling him to pull himself together. Although Melody did manage to persuade him that he must still have a love for his music buried inside him somewhere, and that he should stop seeing it as something he was doing for everyone else and start doing it for himself again.

Taking their conversation up to the penthouse suite, they wasted the afternoon lying on the huge circular bed, getting stoned and giggling at their reflections in the overhead mirror as Chase's albums played on a loop over the built-in speakers.

'I think I'm a convert,' Melody told him when

the first album came around again. 'I'm an R'n'B girl usually, but I could really go for some of this stuff. Not the really rocky ones, 'cos they're just noise, but definitely the ballads. You've got a lovely voice.'

Thanking her, Chase leaned up on his elbow and peered down into her eyes, which were sexily half-closed. 'You've got a lovely voice, too,' he said. 'And a lovely face.' He stroked a finger down her cheek. 'And a lovely body.' He let the finger continue on down to her breasts.

'And you've got a lovely dick,' Melody giggled, not trying to stop him.

'How do you know?' he asked.

'I was looking at it when you were doing the weights. You really should wear underpants if you're going to sit with your legs apart, you know.'

'Yeah, and you should wear a bra when you're running on the treadmill,' Chase said, smiling seductively. 'Those nipples send out "come and get mc" signals.'

'So what are you waiting for?' Melody murmured, peering up at him with a challenge in her eyes.

'The right time,' Chase said softly. 'I've had too many meaningless fucks in this bed. I want this time to be different.' Pausing now, he bit his lip. 'How do you feel about coke?'

'With my brandy?' Melody asked, knowing exactly what he was getting at. 'Yeah, great.'

'No, with a *straw*,' he said, rolling across to the bedside table and reaching into the drawer for his stash.

Looking at the glistening white heap he tipped onto the mirror, and at the gold purpose-made snorting straw, Melody licked her lips. 'My, my, you *do* know how to keep a lady happy, don't you, Mr Mann?'

11

Jenna was not in a good mood when Friday came around. Ever since she'd taken over the club, this had been the start of Vibes's weekend slot, and she'd looked forward to it more than any other night because, even without the attraction, she'd liked him more than the other DJs, and preferred his style of music. But he wouldn't be here tonight – or ever again.

Spending the day in the office, doing the books and getting all of the mundane paperwork out of the way to keep herself occupied, she locked up when she'd finished in the afternoon. She intended to go into town and do some shopping, then head home and get ready for tonight. Her dark mood deepened when she got down to the club floor and saw Fabian showing his friend up the stairs to the DJ's booth. Watching from the doorway as the man strutted into the small room and stood silhouetted in the window, his head bobbing to an imaginary beat as he got a feel for the place, Jenna decided there and then that she didn't like him.

In her – admittedly limited – experience, DJs fell into one of three categories: the gift-of-the-gab tossers who thought themselves *hilarious* and super-cool, and who interrupted every track to make supposedly witty comments; the flashy, smooth-talking lover-boys who dressed better than the punters and spent the whole night focusing on one "special lady" on the dance floor, with the aim of taking her home at the end of the night – and her mate the next; and, lastly, the genuine talents – like Vibes – who weren't looking for the sex, and who didn't have to impress with gimmicks or catchphrases or fancy clothes, because their pure love of music shone through without effort.

And *this* one, Jenna surmised when Fabian led him back down the stairs to the dance floor, and she took in the sunglasses perched on top of the scruffy bleached-blond head and the junkie-surfer-boy clothes complete with patterned knee-length shorts and flip-flops, was a definite gift-of-the-gab merchant. She didn't care *how* good Fabian reckoned he was, she just *knew* he was going to be terrible.

Bringing him over to meet her, Fabian said, 'This is the guy I was telling you about, Jenna. Bubba Zee – Jenna Lorde.'

'Enchanted,' Bubba drawled, giving her a cheeky

grin as he added, 'Don't worry, Fabes has filled us in on what a slave-driver you are, so I'll stay out of your way as much as. Just chuck a wet bone in the cage every so-so, and I'll be sorted.'

'Ex*cuse* me?'

'He means he'd like a drink taken up to the booth for him now and then,' Fabian explained.

'I see,' Jenna replied coolly. 'Well, I'm sure *you* can arrange that, Fabian.'

'Hey, Babes, don't stress,' Bubba said. 'I was only joking.'

'I'm not stressing,' she snapped. 'And don't call me *Babes*.' Turning to Fabian, she said, 'I've got some things to do in town, then I'm going home. I'll be back by ten. Call me if you need me before that.'

'Do I get the job?' Bubba called after her as she walked away.

'Depends if you're any good,' she called back without looking at him.

Watching her, Bubba whistled softly. 'Man, she is *fit*. Just like Liz Taylor at her wank-inducing best.'

'Told you.' Fabian gave him a sly grin. 'Don't think she likes *you* much, though.'

'She will.' Bubba gave an unconcerned shrug. 'I just take a bit of getting used to.' Looking slowly around then, he pursed his lips. 'Kinda *Hit Man*

& Her meets *Come Dancing* on the Starship Enterprise, innit?'

'Wouldn't let Jenna hear you describing it like that,' Fabian chuckled. 'It's her pride and joy, this place. She spent an absolute fortune getting it like this.'

'Nowt wrong with it that can't be fixed,' Bubba said. 'Just needs something – I dunno – a bit *sexier*, maybe.' Giving Fabian a nudge then, he said, 'Remember that gig I had in Crete, where they wouldn't let the girls in till they took their tops off and rode the pole? *That*'s what this gaff needs. Bit of sleaze and grit, and we'd have 'em piling in from all over.'

Snorting softly, Fabian shook his head. 'Don't really think that's the kind of place Jenna's looking to run here.'

'And there was me thinking *you* was the decisions man,' Bubba teased.

'Cat – skin – plenty of ways,' Fabian replied enigmatically. 'Right – so have you got everything you need?'

'Just about,' Bubba said. 'But I wouldn't mind a shufti through that stuff you said the last guy left. Sounds like he had some good imports.'

'I don't know,' Fabian said uncertainly. 'I really don't think Jenna would like it.'

'Aw, man, you've lost your balls but *good*!' Bubba

laughed. 'And if that's what working for a woman does to you, I don't think I'll be sticking around too long.'

'I didn't say no,' Fabian retorted, annoyed that Bubba was taking the piss. 'It's just that it's all locked in her office.'

'Haven't you got a key?'

Pursing his lips, Fabian thought about it. He *did* still have the key, although Jenna didn't know that. And would it really hurt if he let Bubba take a couple of bits? Vibes would probably never come back for it, anyway, so nobody would be any the wiser. And the customers had loved his music, so it would benefit the club.

'Okay,' he said. 'But don't mess anything up in there, and don't take too much. And don't tell a soul, or it'll be my arse on the line.'

'My lips are sealed,' Bubba assured him, grinning slyly.

Jenna was even more irritated by the time she'd finished her shopping and gone home. There must have been an idiot convention in town, because people were running around like fools. She couldn't count how many times she'd been barged into on Market Street, and she'd come very close to punching the woman who had deliberately run over her foot with that shopping-laden pram in the Arndale. Her toes were still hurting.

Tutting when her mobile began to ring just as she was struggling to get her bags through the door, she dropped everything in the hall and kicked the door shut. Then she dragged the phone out of her pocket, answering it without even looking at the screen because she was too busy kicking her shoes off.

There was a moment of static, then, 'Hello, Jenna . . . you there?'

Her heart lurched at the sound of his voice. 'Vibes? Is that *you*?'

'Yeah, it's me. How you doing, Princess?'

'Fine,' she told him, hopping through to the lounge and sitting down on the couch, her bad mood evaporating in an instant. 'It's really good to hear from you. Everybody's been asking about you all week.'

'How are they all?' Vibes asked, thinking that nothing had ever sounded sweeter than Jenna's voice.

'They're good,' Jenna said, laughing softly as she added, 'Austin's been moping about all over the place, but we knew that was going to happen, didn't we?'

'He's a good kid,' Vibes said. 'Never met anyone quite like him before, but he's cool. And how's Kalli?' he asked then.

'Being an absolute sweetheart, as usual,' Jenna told him. 'Missing you like crazy – but then, who isn't?'

There was a slight pause as Vibes wondered if he ought to ask after Jason. He hadn't met the guy, but he *was* Jenna's boyfriend, so it would be only polite. Deciding against it, he asked about the club instead.

'Pretty normal, so far,' Jenna told him. 'But tonight's going to be the tester. Fabian's hired a guy who's just come in from Tenerife, and he reckons he's really good. But *I* think he's going to be terrible.'

'Oh?' Vibes murmured, feeling a little envious because he wished he was still there, getting ready for *his* show tonight.

'He just *looks* wrong,' Jenna explained, not wanting to say what she really meant: that nobody would suit her, because they weren't him. 'Anyway, I don't want to talk about that. Tell me what you've been doing? Have you seen lots of your old friends?'

'Yeah, a few,' Vibes said quietly.

'You must be having a great time?' Jenna said, her voice a little wistful now as she stroked the necklace around her throat.

'I guess,' Vibes said evasively. 'Anyway, I'd best let you get back to what you were doing. I just thought I'd let you know I got here okay, and make sure everything was cool back there.'

'Everything's fine,' Jenna said, wishing she could keep him talking but knowing she had to let him go because his wife was probably waiting for him to go off and do something more exciting. 'Well, thanks for calling. I'll let everyone know you're all right.'

'Take it easy, Princess.'

'You too. Bye.'

Disappointed that it had been such a short call, Jenna hung up and thought about the little that they had actually said to each other. It was so obvious that he had only called out of courtesy and hadn't wanted to get into anything deep. But she supposed that he was still feeling bad about that kiss and had decided it was best not to give her the wrong idea – in case she misinterpreted it again and got false hopes that he would ever feel the same about her as she did about him.

Still, at least she knew he was all right.

Sighing, Jenna got up and went to retrieve her shopping. Vibes wasn't coming back, so she might as well let go of the past and start looking to the future.

Lying back on the bed when he'd disconnected, Vibes gazed around the room. It was his best friend

Tyler's kid brother's room, and even though Nate was eighteen and in college now, rooming with a bunch of his music-class buddies over in Harlem, all his stuff was still here. Every shelf was crammed with books, CDs, and Little League trophies, every corner stacked with magazines, while the closet was packed with clothes and sneakers. But Vibes didn't mind the lack of space; it just felt good to be surrounded by reminders of his old life.

The life he'd lived and loved before it was all snatched away from him.

Almost three years had passed since that awful night, and now he was having to face the bastards who had stolen his family from him. Sitting across from them in the courthouse, watching them smirk and pass secret hand-signal messages to each other as if they werc in school detention while the prosecution outlined its case against them.

His beautiful wife Aliya, their gorgeous three-year-old daughter Tashei, his precious mom, and his own kid brother Dylan – all gone. Shot to pieces in their beds by the gang who had broken into their home in the middle of the night, mistaking it for the crack-house next door.

And, like the prosecutor had said yesterday, they must have known as soon as they got in there that it wasn't no crack-house. Apart from the fact that there was actual furniture in there, rugs on the polished floors, and pictures on the clean walls, no crack-house had ever smelled that good. They *must* have known. And, knowing, they could have walked straight back out and gone after the piece of shit they were really looking for. But they had chosen to take a look around instead, to see what they could steal before they went on their way. But Dylan must have woken up and, being the brave kid that he was, gone into the hall to confront them and protect his mom. And they'd shot him dead, just like that, then gone from room to room taking out the rest of them as they slept in their beds, just so they could still go after the bastard next door without fear of being identified.

And Vibes hadn't known a thing about it until he got home and saw the police crawling all over the place, because he'd been too busy at his gig downtown – the gig he'd taken on at the last minute, despite Aliya asking him not to.

She'd been getting on his case a lot back then, worrying that she was losing him because he was spending more time behind his decks than he did in her bed and concerned that Tashei would grow up hardly knowing what her daddy looked like. But he'd carried on regardless, taking every gig that came his way and justifying it by telling Aliya that he was doing it for them, to get the money to move them to a nicer place – away from the drugs that had been slowly creeping into their neighbourhood, and the gangs that had started to form on the street corners.

Vibes had been so wrapped up in his future plans that he'd been blind to the present dangers. And by the time he'd opened his eyes, it was too late, because all he could see then was his family lying side by side on the slabs in the morgue.

The gang had escaped, but Vibes hadn't. The pain had torn him to pieces, and the guilt that he hadn't been there to protect them had eaten him up so bad that he'd started acting crazy, sleeping in the yard all day, and sitting up all night with a gun in his hand.

Tyler's mom had made Ty go drag him back to her house in the end, where she'd watched over him like a baby for the next few months, forcing him to eat and drink and remember that he hadn't died with his family.

Vibes had been slowly recovering when Kenneth got in touch and invited him to go stay with him and his new wife, Gina, over in England. And getting on that plane had completed the process, making him strong enough to come back here now and do what had to be done. At least now he could look out at his house across the road without thinking that he was going to die from the pain. And one day he might even be able to face going over there to sort through the things he'd left behind. But not yet, because he needed all his strength to get him through the next few months.

When this case was done, and those boys were behind bars where they belonged, *then* he would tackle the rest. And then he would sit down and make plans to start his life over.

Maybe back in England.

And, maybe, depending what happened between now and then, he might tell Jenna how he felt about her when he got there – if her damn fool of a boyfriend still hadn't gotten around to putting a ring on that bare third finger of hers.

Until then, he wouldn't call her again, because it was just too hard to hear her voice and then have to say goodbye. And he didn't need to be going into that courtroom and facing those bastards with that kind of pain in his eyes. When they looked at him, Vibes wanted them to see nothing but contempt.

12

Some of the regulars did drift away after Vibes left, but more decided to stay and check out his replacement. And Fabian's posters advertising Bubba's arrival in town drew a fresh crowd of *his* fans, so the club was as busy as ever, which pleased Jenna. Despite her initial determination to find fault with him, she had to admit, once she'd seen him in action, that Bubba was good. Not as good as Vibes, of course, but better than a lot of the other DJs she'd heard. And his music wasn't too far removed from Vibes's style, so at least it wasn't a major change for the regulars.

While having a drink at the VIP bar one Friday night a few weeks on, Jenna frowned when the music suddenly stopped and she heard screaming and shouting from the public area. Rushing to the balcony, where a lot of the celebrities were already gathered, she gasped when she saw a mass brawl going on all over the lower floor. Rushing down the stairs, she'd just reached the bottom when Fabian came through the door.

'What the hell's going on?' she asked.

'Nothing to worry about,' he said, relieved to see her. 'Just go back upstairs and stay there. I'm going to lock this to make sure nobody gets at the celebs. I've already called the police.'

'I'm coming with you,' Jenna said when he started backing out of the door.

'I'd rather you didn't,' he said. 'Someone's supposed to have seen a knife.'

'Oh, my God,' she gasped. 'Nobody's been—'

'Not as far as I know, but I don't want to take any chances. Please, Jenna. Just go back upstairs and let me deal with this.'

Just then, Tony and Eddie came thundering down behind her.

'Need a hand?' Tony asked, cracking his knuckles.

'No!' Fabian told him quickly, sensing that things would get far worse if these two got involved. 'I've got it in hand. The police are on their way.'

Shrugging, Tony said, 'Okay, well, I guess they can handle it, huh?' Looking at Jenna then, he frowned. 'You ain't going out there, are you?'

'No, she's going back up where it's safe,' Fabian said before she could answer.

'Good.' Tony gave him a nod of approval. Looking at Jenna then, he said, 'Come on, I'll get you a drink – we can watch what's going on from the balcony.'

Feeling a little railroaded, Jenna reluctantly agreed.

The fight had turned into a full-scale battle now; feet and fists flying every which way, and chairs and tables being used as both weapons and shields. Thankfully, it was reasonably short-lived, because as soon as the police sirens cut through the screams and grunts the perpetrators booted the emergency doors open and took off into the night.

It took a while for the rest to realise that they were fighting fellow victims and quit, and then they stood around in panting, confused groups, trying to figure out how it had started in the first place. But nobody had seen it coming, so it was impossible to make any sense of it.

Several of the customers were taken by ambulance to the local hospital to be checked over, but, fortunately, there were no serious casualties. And with all the guilty parties gone already, the police couldn't make any arrests. So, after advising Jenna to put her doormen on alert to stop it happening again, they left her to clear up the mess.

And what a mess it was. Furniture overturned, the floor littered with shattered glass, blood everywhere. But at least it was all cosmetic, so Jenna supposed it wasn't too bad. At least she wasn't facing a huge bill to replace fixtures and fittings.

Piecing it together from what had reportedly been seen and heard, they knew that at least four fights had broken out simultaneously around the room, each started by groups of at least four men who had, their victims claimed, been drinking and chatting quietly together before it kicked off. But at exactly midnight, each of these groups had suddenly jumped up and started laying into anyone and everyone. And because nobody was sure who they were defending themselves against, they inevitably ended up fighting whoever was closest to them.

Sitting with Fabian at the bar when the last of the customers had gone, Jenna shook her head. 'I've never seen anything like that.'

'Me neither,' he admitted. 'I didn't have a clue what was happening. One minute everyone was dancing, the next they were screaming and fists were flying. I was waiting to see if Jacko and the guys could handle it, but when I heard someone say they'd seen a knife, I was straight on the phone.'

'Good job you did call the police,' Jenna said. 'I dread to think what might have happened if it had gone on any longer.' Taking a sip of the coffee that Kalli had just made her, she sighed. 'Remind me to call the hospital tomorrow to make sure that pregnant girl was all right.'

'She should be,' Fabian said, covering a yawn with

his hand. 'Probably more shocked than anything. I don't think anybody actually touched her.'

'I hope not,' Jenna murmured. 'Do you think this had anything to do with those guys who were hassling Melody that time?' she asked then. 'You did say you thought they'd come back after Eddie beat them all up like that.'

'Could be, I suppose.' Fabian shrugged. 'No way of knowing for sure, though.'

'Hi, guys,' Bubba said, coming over just then. 'Good night, huh?'

'I hope that was a joke?' Jenna frowned up at him. Not that she thought he meant it nastily. He was actually quite nice when you looked beyond the garish clothes and in-your-face banter.

'Would I joke about a thing like that?' he teased, flipping her a wink. 'You look tired, Babes.'

'I am. And I thought I told you not to call me that.' Giving him a mock-stern look, she finished her coffee and stood up.

'Not going, are you?' Bubba asked, squeezing onto her stool before she'd even moved away from it.

'Want me to reserve you a place in my grave?' she quipped, stepping back so that he could get his legs straight.

'Only if we both drink the elixir of everlasting life, so we get to make love for all eternity,' Bubba said, grinning.

'What, and have nothing to look at for all eternity but your disgusting hair?' Jenna shot back playfully. 'I don't think so.'

Frowning, Fabian pursed his lips. Jenna had hated Bubba to start with, and it really bugged him that they had such an easy relationship now. Bubba talked to her as if they were flirty mates, and she didn't seem to mind – which really pissed Fabian off, because he could never imagine himself talking to her like that and getting away with it.

'Right, I'm going,' she said, sighing now as she looked around the room. 'It's going to be a hell of a morning clearing this lot up.'

'Leave it to the cleaners,' Fabian told her, reasserting his own place in her life as the caring, take control, relieve-her-of-her-burdens manager that she could trust above all others. 'I'll be here early, so I'll make sure it gets done properly. You just have a lie-in.' Kissing her on the cheek then, he said, 'Don't worry about tonight. Fights are inevitable when you've got so many people drinking in one place. But we don't tend to get more than the odd scuffle, so this was probably a one-off.'

'Thanks,' Jenna said, smiling gratefully for the reassurance. 'Night, Bubba,' she said then.

Saluting her, Bubba said, 'Night, boss.' Turning

to Fabian when she walked away to get her coat and bag from her office, he grinned. 'When's the wedding?'

'What are you talking about?' Fabian asked, going behind the bar and tipping his coffee down the sink.

'You *lurve* her,' Bubba teased. 'I know you, my friend, and them hots have turned into a burning flame of red-hot lust.'

'Don't talk shit,' Fabian snorted, pouring two doubles and handing one to Bubba. 'I like her, but there's no way I fancy her. She's way too cold. I prefer them hot and heavy.'

'Not if you're talking about that tart with the huge tits I saw you sloping off with the other night,' Bubba said, chuckling softly. 'A pure case of *who let the dogs out*. Where did you take her for the big bang, anyway. Up to your office?'

'I wasn't talking about *her*,' Fabian said dismissively. 'But how did you know about that, anyway?'

'You'd be surprised how much I can see from the pod,' Bubba told him, smirking now. 'I've counted seven different tarts in the last two weeks getting your dubious pleasures. You must have a kennel club up there by now. What do you do, lure them up with your big meaty chews?'

'Fuck off. They're not all ugly.'

'Most of 'em are. Man, you've got to start looking at their faces instead of their tits, 'cos you're in serious danger of losing your babe-magnet rep if you keep going for any old barker.'

'Yeah, well, you wouldn't say that if you knew who else I've shagged,' Fabian said, adding smugly, 'and dumped.'

'Go on,' Bubba said, sighing exaggeratedly. 'I know you're dying to spill.'

'Melody Fisher,' Fabian told him, watching his face carefully.

Shrugging, Bubba said, 'Am I supposed to know her?'

'You know her,' Fabian insisted. 'Blonde, absolute stunner, best tits in England. Sits in the corner of the VIP lounge, surrounded by the stars.'

'The Mafia moll?' Bubba laughed. 'Fuck off! There's no way you've had that.'

'She's not a Mafia moll,' Fabian said, frowning again. 'She's an actress.'

'She might well be, but them blokes she hangs with are *pure* Mafia,' Bubba declared. 'Haven't you seen *The Sopranos*, man? He's Tony Wotsisname through and through.'

'His name *is* Tony, as it happens,' Fabian said. 'But he's not Mafia. He's just a thug.'

'You think what you like,' Bubba snorted. 'But I knows what I sees.' Shaking his head now, he grinned at Fabian. 'So, you reckon you've shagged her, do you? And when was that, then? In your wildest wet dreams?'

Before Fabian could answer, Jenna came back. Calling, 'See you tomorrow, guys,' she waved and made her way behind the bar to leave. Popping her head back in after going into the kitchen, she said, 'Everybody's gone from back here, Fabian, so can you just check the toilets again before you lock up? I don't want to come in tomorrow and find some injured person got locked in and died.'

Assuring her that he would check, Fabian waited until he'd heard the back door close, then went and got himself and Bubba another drink. 'Want to see something?' he asked, handing Bubba's glass across the bar.

'Only if it comes with something white and buzzing,' Bubba said, pulling three twenty-notes out of his pocket and slapping them down on the bar.

Picking them up, Fabian slipped them into his pocket and, grinning, gave a mock bow. 'Care to accompany me to my office, sir?'

'Not if you think you're gonna shag me when we get there,' Bubba laughed. 'I'm not one of those easy girls, you know,' he said then in a feminine voice, getting off the stool and putting a hand to his breast. 'I am a laydee. And it takes more than a couple of drinks to get *my* bloomers orf.'

Up in the office a few minutes later, Fabian took his stash out of the safe. Then he reached for the DVD of him and Melody that he kept there for safe keeping.

He hadn't needed to play the insurance card yet – and probably never would, because Melody seemed to have lost all interest in him lately. But he still couldn't bring himself to destroy it, and he sometimes took a look at it just to remind himself of those fantastic tits and that beautiful pussy. Maybe one day he'd get rid of it. But not just yet.

'What's it about?' Bubba asked, picking it up and turning it over in his hand as Fabian sorted him a wrap from the stash bag. 'It's got no title.'

'Let's just call it *Bubba eats shit*,' Fabian said smugly, handing the wrap to him. Laying out two lines from his own stash then, he snorted one and pushed the mirror across the desk.

'Better be good,' Bubba said, watching as Fabian went and unlocked the cupboard housing his DVD player and small monitor screen. 'I'm not getting all hyped up on this to watch Mary fucking Poppins. I want action, man.'

'Thought you'd have given the dolls up a long

time ago,' Fabian quipped, slotting the disc into the machine.

'Eh?' Holding his breath, Bubba squinted at him.

'Action Man,' Fabian repeated. Shaking his head when Bubba just shrugged, he said, 'Never mind.' Going to his chair then, he sat down and pressed play on the remote.

The screen lit up and Bubba frowned when a shot of the office came up. 'What's this, dude?'

'Watch,' Fabian said, licking his lips, his eyes taking on a beady coke glow.

Exhaling impatiently, Bubba licked his fingertip and dabbed at the traces on the mirror. He'd got it halfway to his mouth when Fabian walked into shot on the screen, quickly followed by Melody Fisher, looking hot as hell in a red satin dress, cut up to here and down to there, her long legs amazing in glossy flesh-coloured stockings.

'Oh, man,' he said huskily, leaning forward for a closer look. 'I've only seen her from the distance before, but she is *fit*.'

On screen, Fabian laid out two lines of coke and snorted one. Handing the straw to Melody then, he came up behind her as she leaned down to snort hers and ran his hands over her body.

'Jeezus!' Bubba drooled. 'Look at the arse on that.'

Back on screen, Fabian was rubbing up against her.

'Oh, that's good,' screen-Melody moaned, rocking back against him when he slipped his hand between her thighs. 'Oh, yeah . . . keep doing that.'

'You dirty fucking dog!' Bubba chuckled as he watched screen-Fabian free his hard-on and slide into her, holding on tight to her hips, his face a mask of restraint. 'Yeah, that musta took some doing, guy. I'd've been ramming it home by now. I'm hard enough just fucking *watching* it.'

On the screen, Melody arched her back and put her hands flat on the table, bucking against Fabian, crying, 'Oh, God, *now*!'

And Fabian obliged, pounding into her for a while, then pulling out and sweeping everything off the desk with the back of his hand. Flipping Melody onto her back, he tore off her panties and tossed them aside, then pushed her dress up over her breasts and bit down on her nipples as Melody wrapped her legs around his waist and sank her nails into his back.

Looking at Fabian with admiration in his coke-glazed eyes when the screen went blank, Bubba grinned. 'You're hung like a fucking *elephant*, man! How come you never let on about *that* when we was doing the summer gigs? I could've earned a sweet little backhander selling your services to the ladies.' Laughing now, he added, 'And I bet a good few of the lads would've paid for a bit of you, an' all. We could have been minted.'

'All right,' Fabian said, smiling. 'You were supposed to be watching her, not me. So, now do you believe me?'

'Oh, yeah, I believe you,' Bubba said, reaching out across the desk to stroke Fabian's thigh. 'But I think I love *you*. Oh, take me now, hot boy! I need you. Oh . . . Oh!'

'Pack it in,' Fabian laughed. 'Or I might just sell this tape to the Sunday papers.'

'You what?' Bubba squawked. 'Don't tell me you're taping us now?'

'You'll find out if you keep messing about,' Fabian warned, getting up and taking the DVD out of the machine. Locking it back in the safe, he said, 'Fancy going on to somewhere else? I'm too wired to go home, and there's a new all-night pussy club just opened in Salford.'

'Bring your dick and I'll think about it,' Bubba said, grinning for the camera in the corner as he added, 'We always had such good sex when we were a couple, didn't we? Shouldn't be so different now we're just friends.'

'We were never a couple,' Fabian said to the camera, playing along.

'Oh, how could you deny me like that?' Bubba wailed, pretending to cry now. 'I thought I was the one.'

'Get out,' Fabian laughed, shoving him towards the door.

The rest of the week passed without incident after the fight, and everybody had forgotten about it by the time Friday came around again. But in an almost exact replica of the previous week, midnight hit and suddenly there was mayhem on the lower floor.

'I don't believe this!' Jenna gasped as, yet again, Fabian told her to stay in the VIP lounge with the stars, and locked the door to keep them safe.

And yet again, Tony and Eddie offered to help, only to be told that the police were on their way.

'You think you've got a problem?' Tony asked Jenna, sipping his drink beside her as they watched the fight from the balcony.

'Well, *obviously*,' she snapped. Throwing a hand over her mouth then, when she saw three men kicking another in the head as he lay on the floor, she said, 'Oh, my God! They're going to kill him!' Spotting her head of security wading through the crowd below, she waved her arms and pointed the victim out, yelling, '*JACKO* . . . Help him!'

Shaking all over when Jacko and Flex yanked the men off the victim, Jenna backed away from the balcony and sat down heavily on a chair.

Coming and squatting down beside her, Tony took her hand in his. 'You okay?'

'I think I'm going to be sick,' she muttered.

'It's gonna be all right,' he assured her, his voice quietly confident. 'Soon as the police come, the bastards who started it will take off like last time.'

'Do you think it's the same people?' Jenna asked.

'Could be.' He shrugged. 'Anyone been putting the screws on you lately?'

'What do you mean?' Frowning, Jenna gazed at him.

'Seems a pretty typical trick to me,' Tony said. 'Had it happen once in my place back home. Some guys came in and started a ruck. Did it again the next week. Then the next, some dude comes in and tells me he can sort it all out for me – for a price.'

'You mean like a protection racket?' Jenna asked.

Chuckling softly, Tony said, 'Yeah, I guess that was the intention. But they didn't figure on *me* being the owner.'

'What happened?'

'Enough that they never bothered me again,' Tony said, his eyes dark as he peered into hers. 'But I'm a man.'

Frown deepening, Jenna said, 'What difference does that make.'

'Unfortunately for you, quite a lot,' Tony told her quietly. 'I mean, face facts, Jen. What are you gonna do if some guy comes threatening to break your legs unless you pay up?'

'Call the police,' she replied indignantly.

'Oh, yeah, sure,' Tony laughed. 'Is that after the nasty man's *gone*, or when he comes back, pissed off 'cos you didn't do as you were told?'

'Christ, do you have to make it sound so awful?' Jenna muttered sickly. 'I'm sure people probably get away with that stuff in the States, but it can't happen here.'

Shrugging again, Tony gestured dismissively with his hands. 'Hope for your sake you're right.'

Interrupting them just then, Fabian said, 'Sorry, Jenna, but the officer wants a word.'

Looking over at the police sergeant who had come upstairs with Fabian and was standing by the toilet door now, conspicuous in his yellow coat, his flat hat in his hand, she nodded.

'All right, bring him over.' Turning back to Tony then, she said, 'You'll have to excuse me for a minute.'

'No worries,' he said, patting her hand again and standing up. 'I want to get Melody back to the hotel, anyway. You got my number if you want to talk.'

Thanking him, Jenna said goodnight, then stood up to greet the police officer when Fabian brought him over. Taking him to a quiet corner table, she waved for him to sit down.

Sergeant Dave Poole was a little overawed, not

only because he was surrounded by so many famous faces but because Jenna was one of the most beautiful women he'd ever seen – and being around the same age, he might well have chatted her up if they'd met here when he was in his civvies.

Sitting awkwardly on the edge of his seat now, he said, 'I thought we'd best have a chat, because I'm a bit concerned about what's going on here.'

'You and me both,' Jenna murmured.

'It's just that there seems to be a bit of a pattern developing.' Pausing, Poole shifted self-consciously in his seat when two girls from *Hollyoaks* stopped by to say goodnight to Jenna on their way out. Clearing his throat when they'd gone, he said, 'I'm concerned that you weren't better prepared after last week.'

'How?' Jenna peered at him incredulously. 'My doormen have been really vigilant all week, but everything's been as quiet as usual. There were no signs that anything was going to start again tonight.'

'So, they didn't see any of the same men from last week coming in tonight?'

'Nobody knows who they were,' Jenna reminded him. 'Hundreds of men come in every night. It could have been any of them.'

'What about gangs?'

'We don't let *gangs* in,' Jenna told him, a frosty edge creeping into her voice. 'In fact, we've got a strict policy not to allow groups of more than four men *or* women in at a time. And since last week, the doormen have been watching the queue like hawks, making sure that there were no groups that seemed even to know each other.'

Jotting something in his notepad, Poole said, 'What about stag parties?'

'They have to book in advance, and they're shown in independently of the queue,' Jenna told him. 'But we haven't had any parties in during the last two weeks, so that's not an issue.' Sighing heavily then, she said, 'Look, I know it must be a pain for you to have to come out again for nothing, but we've done everything we could to prevent this, and I don't know what else we *can* do, short of banning men altogether. And I don't think *that* would be very good for business, somehow.'

'No, of course not,' Poole agreed, closing his pad and putting it back in his pocket. 'All I'm saying is, you're going to need to tighten your security, because . . .' Pausing, he shrugged. 'Well, you're probably aware that there's been a lot of unrest about the levels of drink-related violence in the city recently, and certain bodies are demanding action.'

'So they should,' Jenna said, fully agreeing. 'I think it's disgusting.'

'They're going for a zero-tolerance approach,' Poole went on, not sure that she was getting the picture. 'The aim being to make club owners more responsible. If they push it through, you might find that you get billed for the police time.'

'You mean I'd have to *pay* for calling you out?' Jenna gasped.

'Obviously, we'll always respond to any emergency,' Poole assured her. 'But there could well be financial consequences in the future, depending on what we find when we get there.'

'I see,' Jenna murmured, pursing her lips angrily. 'So, if something like this happens again, I won't only have to pay to clean it up and replace anything that's broken, I'll have to pay your wages as well – even though I pay my taxes and do my damnedest to run a respectable club?'

Shrugging, Poole stood up. 'I'm not saying it's going to happen, just warning you that it might. All I can suggest for now is that you make sure your security are on the ball, 'cos my super might get a bit touchy if we're called out for the same thing again next week. And, between you and me, he's been known to petition to have licences revoked.'

'That's outrageous,' Jenna said, standing up herself now. 'There are fights going on all over the place, all the time, but just because I call for help when it happens to me, I'm in danger of getting my licence revoked?'

'I wouldn't *not* call us,' Poole warned her. 'Not

if there's a chance somebody could get seriously hurt as a consequence.'

'This is the second time anything like this has happened,' Jenna reminded him indignantly. 'It's not exactly a notorious trouble hot spot, is it?'

'None of the bad ones start off bad,' Poole pointed out quietly. Nodding then, he gave her an apologetic smile. 'Hope we don't meet under these circumstances again, miss.'

'Me, too,' she retorted icily.

Fabian caught up with Jenna at the foot of the VIP stairs after he'd shown the police out and locked the doors.

'Everything all right?'

'Not really. Christ, look at the state of it again. The cleaners will have a fit.'

'Never mind them. If they don't like it, there's plenty more who'll gladly take their places. What did the sergeant want?'

Relaying the conversation that she'd had with Poole, Jenna shook her head angrily. 'I just don't see what else we can do.'

'Well, you can stop worrying about the licence, for starters,' Fabian told her firmly. 'They would never revoke it over a couple of little incidents like this. There would have to be serious problems on a regular basis, and you'd have to be seen to be doing nothing about it.'

'Yeah, well, I don't want to risk it,' Jenna muttered, folding her arms. 'Can you get Jacko to arrange for the guys to come in tomorrow? I think we need a meeting to review security.'

'They're doing everything by the book,' Fabian reminded her, not wanting her to blame them. 'But I'll see what I can do.'

'Thanks. And I think we should take a look at the CCTV tapes from this week and last week – see if we can spot any of the same people in the thick of it when it kicked off.'

'I've already checked last week's, and you can't see anything specific,' Fabian told her. 'They're not very good angles on the interior cameras, unfortunately. They mainly cover the doors, and the fights have started well out of range. All you can see is a lot of men running out of the fire door – from behind, so you can't see their faces.'

'Great.' Jenna tutted. 'So, we need some of those cameras that scan the room?'

'Have you any idea how much it would cost to install enough of them to cover the whole place?' Fabian asked her.

'More than my licence is worth?' Jenna asked, raising an eyebrow.

'Well, no, obviously that's worth more,' Fabian conceded. 'But I think we need to calm down and think this through before we go jumping in at the deep end. I genuinely don't think we've got as much of a problem as you think. This looks bad, but it could be a lot worse.'

'That's what I told myself last week,' Jenna said. 'But I'm starting to wonder.'

'Let's just hang fire and see what happens,' Fabian urged. 'We'll have a talk with the lads, if that makes you feel better. But I really think this is a one – well, a *two*-off.'

'I hope so,' Jenna murmured.

Just as Fabian had predicted, the fights *were* a two-off. But the next week brought a completely different problem.

An anonymous caller had apparently tipped the police off about somebody selling drugs in the men's toilets, and Jenna could do nothing but stand by and watch as the police swarmed all over the club, stopping people from leaving, searching them, and taking their details. She felt terrible when the dogs were brought in and sniffed out several of her customers, who were immediately arrested for possession of cannabis and cocaine – a couple of possessors of the latter substance being celebrities.

The VIPs were not amused to be made to come down to the lower floor to give their details in earshot of the 'everyday people'. Some even threatened to sue if anything untoward happened as a result of their addresses being overheard, and Jenna wasn't sure if the threats were aimed at her or the police. What she *did* know was that she would probably never see some of her star guests again, because they wouldn't want to risk their reputations being tainted by being associated with a club that was getting a bad reputation. And that they would most probably spread the word among their friends, too.

It was all so dispiriting after everything had been going so well. But if Jenna had thought the drug bust was bad, worse soon followed. This time it happened on the Saturday, taking them all by surprise, because they had expected it to be the Friday again, as per the developing pattern that Poole had spotted.

Armed police burst in this time, weapons drawn as they ordered the terrified clubbers to hit the floor. They were responding to reports of a gang of men seen entering the club with a sub-machine gun. But eventually they left when they had searched the entire place and everybody in it, and had found no guns of any description.

No arrests were made, but it was enough to put a huge black mark against the club. Jenna just knew that things were going to start going to hell on a bobsleigh if she didn't put a stop to the nonsense soon.

She'd already figured out that it was personal before Fabian reminded her about the conversation they'd had that time, when he'd warned her that the other club owners might start playing dirty if she became too successful and stole too many customers. Fearing that he could be right, she took the Sunday off and spent the whole day calling into every other club in town to speak to the owners, managers or whoever was available to beg them – if they were behind it – to stop.

Jenna was worn out by the time she'd finished, and her instincts told her that the other club people had all been telling the truth when they'd said that they weren't involved. But she didn't know if her instincts could be trusted any more, so she was still none the wiser.

Tony Allen had been lucky enough to be out of town on the two occasions when the club was raided, sparing him the indignity of being searched and questioned. Coming in on the Sunday night, he came straight over to where Jenna was sitting at the VIP bar, having a miserable, solitary drink.

'Hey, beautiful,' he said softly, giving her a hug. 'I hear you've been having some more trouble while I've been away?'

'You could say that,' she murmured, her eyes telling a clear story of her inner despair.

'Bad, huh?' Tony said, peering at her with sympathy.

Snorting softly, Jenna waved her hand. 'Take a look around and tell me what you see.'

Glancing around the lounge, Tony shrugged. 'All right, so it's not as busy as usual. But it ain't the end of the world. It'll get back to normal once you find out what's going on and who's behind it.'

'And how am I supposed to do that?' Jenna asked hopelessly. 'I've tried everything. The security crew have been on full alert, but they haven't seen any of this coming. And some of the staff have already walked because they're so freaked out. And you don't even want to *know* how many customers I've lost.' Sighing now, she took another sip of her drink and shrugged. 'But it's not your problem, so I guess I shouldn't be moaning to you about it.'

'Hey, that's what friends are for,' Tony said quietly, his voice so kind and sincere that Jenna felt like crying.

Biting down on it, Jenna said, 'Thanks, that means a lot right now. But forget about me. You've got your own worries, haven't you? Any luck finding something to invest in yet?'

Shrugging, he slipped a hand into his pocket, reaching for his cigars. 'Not yet, but me and Lenny have teamed up now, so it shouldn't be too long.'

Lighting up, he squinted at her through the smoke. 'He's a pretty savvy guy when you get to know him. And straight as a die, so it can't hurt, can it?'

'I suppose not,' Jenna agreed.

'We've had meetings with a few companies,' Tony went on. 'But it's got to be exactly right before we commit to anything, 'cos we're talking a lot of money, the two of us combined.' Chuckling softly now, he said, 'Mind you, he makes *my* contribution seem like diddly-squat, what with his millions and his mansion in Alderley Edge. You ever been there?'

'No.' Jenna shook her head. 'I don't really know him all that well. He was my dad's friend.'

'So he tells me,' Tony said, taking another drag on his cigar. 'Had a lot of time for him, by all accounts.'

'I would hope so.' Jenna smiled fondly, ignoring the smoke swirling around her face. 'My dad was a lovely man. Bit unorthodox in some respects, but his heart was always in the right place.'

'He'd be real proud of you, I imagine. The way you've handled all this shit that's been happening.'

'I don't know about that.' Sighing deeply, Jenna blinked back the tears and gazed around. 'He really loved this place, you know. He bought it for next to nothing and kept it going for twenty years. Me, I come in and strip it bare, because I think I can do it better. But I've not even been open six months, and I've almost lost it.'

'Hey, quit being so hard on yourself,' Tony told her firmly. 'This is a glitch, that's all. Someone's fucking with you, but you'll ride it out and come back stronger than ever.'

'We'll see,' Jenna said, her tone clearly conveying how much she doubted it.

'Yeah, well, you know where I am if you need me,' Tony said, patting her hand reassuringly.

'How's she doing?' Eddie asked when Tony came back to their table a short time later.

'Pretty much as you'd expect,' Tony told him quietly. 'Cracking under the pressure.'

'Offer any solutions?'

'Not yet,' Tony said, a flicker of a smile lifting his lip. 'But it won't be long.'

13

The next month was agonising for Jenna, who could only watch helplessly as things went from bad to worse. Nothing spectacularly bad happened, just lots of little things that added up to a grand nuisance. Like every cab company in town receiving crank calls and sending cabs out only to be told that they hadn't been ordered, which resulted in the club being blacklisted so that none of her customers could get a cab unless they walked to the cab offices.

In an attempt to rectify the falling customer numbers, Jenna tried everything. Drinks promotions that lost her even more money – and attracted drunken youths who inevitably disturbed the other customers, which resulted in even more walking out never to return. Door promotions, where girls didn't have to pay to get in one week, men the next, which didn't work at all. She even arranged a themed night, which bombed so badly that Fabian warned her she was turning the place into a joke.

Nothing Jenna did made any difference, and nobody seemed to be able to offer a solution. Fabian had never experienced anything quite like it, so he didn't know what to suggest other than to wait it out and hope it died down when whoever was behind it got bored. And the police were no help either, because they had made it quite clear that they thought she had allowed the situation to develop by attempting to run a club when she didn't have the first clue about the business.

And they were right, because Jenna had come into this believing that she could just pick up where her dad had left off, with nothing to qualify her other than her belief that if James Lorde could do it from scratch so could she. But she'd been so wrong, and she knew that now. There was obviously some sort of secret formula, and you either had the recipe or you didn't. And she quite patently didn't.

But if she'd thought that what had happened so far was bad, worse was yet to come.

Leaving her office late one Saturday afternoon, having spent the day fretting over the appalling accounts books, Jenna waved goodbye to Fabian and Bubba who were doing something with the speaker system down on the club floor. Letting herself out of the back door, she locked it and walked across the yard to open the gate.

It was already fairly dark out, but not quite enough for the security lights to come on when she stepped into their path. Unlocking the gate, she pushed it open, then went to get into her car to reverse it out. But just as she reached for the car door's handle, four figures darted in from the dark alleyway and surrounded her.

It happened so fast that Jenna was too shocked to scream – which was probably a good thing, she quickly realised when she saw the men, because they would no doubt have silenced her in an instant. Anyway, there was nobody in the club to hear her, except Fabian and Bubba, and there was no way they could handle these guys on their own, so they were better off not knowing. She just hoped the infra-red CCTV cameras were picking it up, so at least she'd have something for the police to work on when it was over.

Trying her damnedest to stay calm and collected now, she said, 'I don't have a lot of money on me, but my purse is in my bag. Take it.'

Laughing, one of the men brought his face down close to hers. His breath warm on her cheek, he said, 'I don't want your money, sexy.'

Terrified that she was going to be raped, Jenna held his gaze, determined to remember his face. 'What *do* you want, then?' she asked shakily.

'To make your acquaintance,' he replied, his

voice lightly mocking now. 'This is just a friendly *pre*-visit, so to speak – to let you know that we can get to you, any *time*, any*where*. You've been having a lot of trouble lately, and I think it's time we stopped fucking about and got us a little system going. Understand?' Smiling when she nodded, his eyes glittered like jet in the scant light. 'Good girl, Jenna. Because it winds me up like fuck having to say the same thing twice, so things should be nice and easy next time we meet, eh?'

Jenna's heart felt like a shard of ice had fallen through it. He knew her name!

'For the record,' he went on, stroking a finger down her cheek now. 'If I hear that you've been talking to the police, we'll be paying you another little visit – at that nice little apartment of yours. Ten Clifton Quay House, yeah?' Smiling again as he watched the information sink in, he added, 'Nice plants you got for the balcony last week, by the way. And the new kettle's pretty funky, too.'

Jenna was barely breathing now. They knew her name, where she lived, *and* that she'd bought new plants and a kettle. They must have been watching her. Or, *worse* – been inside her apartment. But how? It was alarmed, and the doors were manned by security, and there were CCTV cameras in all the corridors.

'Bye for now, sexy,' the man said now. 'And don't forget – no police, or you and me are gonna have *real* problems.'

Turning from her abruptly then, he and his friends walked out the way they'd come.

Holding her breath until she was sure they'd gone, Jenna rushed to the gate and relocked it, then ran to the back door, her heart beating furiously in her chest as she scrabbled to get the key into the lock.

'That you, Jenna?' Fabian asked, coming through from the bar with a glass of brandy in his hand when he heard the back door slam shut. Seeing the panicked look on her face, he put the glass down on the table and rushed to her.

'What's happened? Are you all right?'

'Some m-men,' she stuttered. 'They came in when I opened the gate and p-pushed me into the corner.'

'What did they do to you?' Fabian asked, his eyes full of concern as he took her arm and led her to a chair. 'Did they touch you?'

Shaking her head, Jenna sat down. 'Not really.'

Frowning, Fabian went to the back door.

'Don't!' she yelped, thinking that he was going to open it and go looking for the men. 'There were four of them.'

Tugging the bolts across, he said, 'Don't worry

– I wasn't being a hero. I just wanted to make sure they couldn't get in if they came back.' Reaching for his glass now, he handed it to her. 'Take it,' he insisted when she shook her head. 'You need it. You're shaking like a leaf.'

Thanking him, Jenna sipped the drink and exhaled nervously when the liquid burned a soothing path down her throat.

'Tell me what happened,' Fabian said, pulling a chair up beside hers and reaching for her hand. 'What did they look like?'

'Quite big,' she said, squinting as she tried to recall the details. 'They were wearing dark clothes, but three of them had their hoods up so I couldn't really see them. They were white, though, I think. And the main one had short black hair, and brown eyes.'

'Are you sure? It is dark outside.'

'I'm sure. He had a gold hoop earring in his right ear, with a little thing hanging off it – like a boxing glove, or something. And a thick gold neck-chain with a dog on it.'

'Well, that's good. The police should be able to do something with—'

'No!' Jenna glanced up, her eyes filled with fear. 'No police.'

Patting her hand to calm her down, Fabian said, 'I know you've had a shock, Jenna, but we can't just leave this or they'll think they've got away with it and come back.'

'They *are* coming back,' she murmured, sliding her hand free. 'They said they'd be seeing me soon.'

'Why? Are they after money?'

'No, I offered them my purse, but they didn't want it.'

'I don't get it,' Fabian muttered. 'If it wasn't a mugging, and they didn't touch you, what *did* they want?'

'I don't know,' Jenna admitted quietly. 'But they said they'd be coming back to get a system going, or something. I'm not quite sure. Then they said they'd come to my apartment if I talked to the police.'

Bubba had come in while they were talking. Hearing this, he came over and straddled a chair. 'Sorry, but I couldn't help overhearing, and if you want my advice you'll keep zipped about this until you know what they're after, 'cos the Babs won't be able to do nothing but have a word, and that's just gonna piss them off.'

'*Babs*?' Jenna repeated confusedly.

'Babylon,' Bubba said. Then, seeing that she was still none the wiser: '*Five-O*?'

'Police,' Fabian explained.

'Yeah, them,' Bubba said. 'They could really fuck

it up if you send them after these blokes when they haven't really done anything. And you can't be doing with that – not if they know where your pad is.'

'Are you sure they know where you live?' Fabian chipped in. 'They might just have been saying that to frighten you.'

Taking another sip of the brandy, Jenna said, 'They knew I'd got a new kettle. How would they have known about it unless they'd seen it?'

'Did they actually describe it?' Fabian asked, raising an eyebrow. When she shook her head, he smiled reassuringly. 'There you go, then. We had a fair bit of publicity after we opened, don't forget, so most of Manchester probably knows you moved back to take over your dad's club. It wouldn't be too hard to figure out that you'd have bought yourself a new *kettle*, would it?'

Looking up at him, annoyed by his patronising tone, Jenna said, 'So how did they know about the new plants I bought for my balcony last week, then? That's pretty specific, don't you think?'

'They must be watching you,' Bubba said immediately, echoing the conclusion that Jenna had already reached. 'And if they are, it ain't worth trying to second-guess them.'

'So what's she supposed to do?' Fabian argued, irritated that Bubba was contradicting him when he was trying to get Jenna to calm down. 'They're obviously trying it on, seeing if she's scared enough to do what they say. They're probably watching from somewhere right now, waiting to see if she's called the police. If they see a squad car pull up, we'll probably never see them again. But when they don't, they'll know they've got to her, and they'll keep coming back.'

'They'll come back either way,' Bubba said, shrugging as he added, 'that's how these guys work.' Looking at Jenna now, he said, 'What was that you said about getting a system going?'

'I don't know,' Jenna murmured, trying to remember. 'I think he said he'd heard I'd been having trouble, and it was time to stop fucking about and get us a system going.'

'Protection,' Bubba declared. 'They've obviously been behind all the shit that's been happening, and now they're going to charge you to make it stop.'

'If that's true, there's not enough to pay them,' Jenna said wearily. 'The takings are so low that I was just considering closing down to cut my losses.'

'You're not serious?' Fabian gasped. 'You can't do that. This place has been going for years. It's an institution in Manchester.'

'Do you think I don't know that?' Jenna snapped, guilt making her defensive. 'I don't *want* to close, I just can't see a lot of choice. We've lost so many customers recently it isn't even funny.

And you can play spot-the-celebrity these days.'

'Look, let's just calm down and talk this over,' Fabian said, desperate to find a solution. This was his club as much as it was hers. He'd been running it when her father was around, and he'd carried on when Jenna got here. It had been a little more of a challenge to manipulate her as easily as he had James Lorde, but he'd managed, and he liked Zenith just how it was. If she were to close down now, he'd have to find a job somewhere else, and he didn't want to have to go through the hassle.

Sighing, Jenna shook her head. 'I don't want to talk right now, Fabian. I appreciate the concern, but I'm just too tired. I just want to go home and get my head down for a couple of hours, or I'll never make it through tonight.'

'Why not take tonight off?' Bubba suggested. 'I'm sure everyone will pull together and keep it running smooth. You need a break.'

'I can't,' Jenna said, her eyes dark with worry. 'I'd only be wondering what was happening here while I was away. What if those men come back and threaten anyone else? Or hurt someone, even.'

'We'll deal with it,' Fabian said, agreeing with Bubba that Jenna was better off at home.

'I can't,' she said again, more firmly this time. 'It'd probably be even worse at home. I need to be here.'

'Well, you know we've got your back,' Bubba said. 'Anything happens, we're right in there.'

'Let's hope it doesn't get to that,' Jenna said standing up. Anyway I'd better go, or I'll have no time to get ready.'

'Want us to walk you through the yard?' Fabian offered.

Shaking her head, Jenna said, 'No. I'll get a taxi out front.'

'What about when you get home? Are you going to be all right going in?'

'Yeah, I'll get the security guard to come in with me. Stop worrying, I'll be fine.'

'Ballsy lady,' Bubba commented when she walked out.

'Mmm,' Fabian murmured. 'Let's just hope she doesn't try to handle this on her own, or it could get a whole lot worse.'

Going home, Jenna did exactly what she'd said she would and got the guard to come into the apartment with her. She had him check every room, window and door – under the pretext of being concerned about an ex-boyfriend breaking in – thanked him and gave him a ten-pound tip, asking him to let her know if he saw any suspicious men hanging around.

Then, closing all the curtains and blinds, she

turned on every light and took a shower. Feeling a little less tense after that, she poured herself a glass of juice and carried it into the bedroom, locking the door behind her. All she wanted to do was throw her hand in and run away. But she was shackled to the club now, up to her eyes in loan and mortgage repayments, and she couldn't afford to even *contemplate* giving it up with all that hanging over her.

Sighing, Jenna sat down heavily on the bed.

Is this it? she thought, looking around. *Am I going to spend the rest of my life locking myself into rooms, too scared to drive my own car home, having to ask a stranger to check out my apartment before I dare to go in?*

'No, I am *not*,' she said out loud, slamming the glass down on the bedside table and reaching for her handbag.

She might not be able to deal with this alone, but she knew one person who might be able to help.

Taking the number out of her bag, Jenna reached for the phone.

'Hello, Tony? Sorry to disturb you, but I think I need to see you . . .'

14

'Right, first things first,' Tony said, sitting forward with his elbows on his knees. 'You go back to work tonight as if nothing's happened.'

Frowning, Jenna plucked at the corner of a cushion. It was an hour since she'd called Tony, and he had arrived a short time ago with Eddie, and – for some strange reason – Leonard. Sitting with them in her apartment now, Jenna felt awkward, because it was the first time she'd had visitors since moving in, and they were all so big that they made her usually spacious lounge seem small and claustrophobic.

'I don't think I can do that,' she said now. 'What if they come back?'

'Believe me, they won't,' Tony told her with absolute certainty.

'How can you be so sure?' she asked, sincerely doubting it.

'Because I know how these guys work,' Tony said, his voice calm, his eyes reassuring. 'I will personally guarantee that you won't be bothered again.'

'I wish I could believe that,' Jenna murmured wearily. 'These last few weeks have been horrible. I just want to get things back to normal.'

'I hate to say it,' Tony said. 'But I did warn you. Men like that prey on women like you, trying to run a business on your own. There's too much money for them to resist.'

'But that's just it – there isn't,' Jenna said, glancing up with desperation in her eyes. 'If there was, I'd probably pay them to keep them off my back. But there's barely enough coming in now to pay the wages, never mind anything else.'

'That bad?' Tony asked.

'Worse.' Shaking her head, Jenna ran her hands through her hair. 'God, I don't know what I did to deserve this, but I'm in such a mess. I'll be okay for another few weeks, but only because we did so well at the beginning. After that . . .' She shrugged. 'I'm seriously thinking of closing down.'

'Oh, no, you mustn't,' Leonard chipped in. 'Your dad wouldn't want you to.'

'I know.' She sighed despondently. 'But he wouldn't want me to go through this, either.'

'You don't have to,' Tony said. 'Not now, because we're going to help you.'

Glancing up at him, Jenna gave him a defeated smile. 'I hope you can.'

'You *know* I can, or you wouldn't have called me,' Tony reminded her. 'So, now I'm here, you've got to trust me enough to do what I say. And that means going back to work as if everything's hunky-dory, yeah?'

'All right,' Jenna agreed. 'But can I call you if anything happens? Only I really don't want to involve the police.'

'Smart decision,' Tony said, slipping one of his cigars out of the pack. 'D'yuh mind?'

Jenna would have preferred that he didn't smoke in her lounge because the smell would linger for days. But if the alternative was the smell of her own blood when those men came round to 'visit', so be it.

'I'll get you an ashtray,' she said, getting up. 'Can I get anybody a drink?'

'Scotch all round, if you've got it,' Tony said, following her into the kitchen.

Closing the door when they got there, he said, 'You do know I'm going to sort this, don't you?' Holding on to her hand now when she passed him a saucer for his cigar ash, he added, 'And there won't be no comeback, 'cos when I deal with something it stays dealt with.'

Looking into his eyes, Jenna saw the same dark

intensity that she had seen when she'd first met him. She had sensed then that he would be deeply loyal to his chosen few, and deeply dangerous to many others. She was getting a taste of what that actually meant now, because he must consider her a friend or he wouldn't be there.

'Hey, what's the matter?' Tony asked when her eyes suddenly filled with tears. 'Is there something you haven't told me?' Anger in his voice now, he said, 'They didn't touch you, did they? 'Cos if they did, they won't just be dealt with, they'll be—'

'No.' Shaking her head, Jenna bit her lip to bring herself under control. 'I'm just glad you're here,' she said, aware that her chin was quivering. 'I didn't know who else to turn to.'

Pulling her to him, Tony held her, saying quietly. 'Well, I'm glad you chose me, 'cos I got a lot of time for you. You know that, right?'

Feeling safe for the first time in weeks, Jenna rested her head against his broad chest and nodded.

'I told you a while back that you and me would make a good team,' he told her then. 'And I offered to be your partner. Do you remember that?'

Sniffing softly, Jenna gave another nod.

'Well, I'm offering the same thing now,' Tony went on. 'Only I want you to really think about it this time, 'cos I can stop *these* men coming near you again, but what's gonna happen when the next lot decide to try it on and I'm not here to protect you?' Feeling Jenna tense in his arms, he rubbed her back soothingly. 'Hey, I'm not trying to scare you, but you gotta be realistic. You got more than just these guys to worry about, by the sound of it, and I can help you all round. We can help each other, in fact, 'cos I got the money you need, and you got what I need to be able to stay over here.'

Jenna's mind was whirling. She hadn't wanted a partner. Her dad had done without help for twenty-odd years, and she'd wanted to do the same. But the thought of going through more of what she'd been through recently just sapped all the fight out of her. And Tony was right – what would she do if this happened again and he wasn't here to help her? And, as he'd said, he needed her just as much as she needed him. Could she really deny him the chance to make a go of it over here when he was putting himself out for her like this?

'Okay,' she murmured, feeling a rush of relief as soon as the word was out.

'Okay?' Easing her away from him, Tony gazed down at her. 'You said that, right?'

Looking up at him, Jenna smiled. 'Yeah, I said it. I'll let you buy into the club. On one condition.'

'Name it.'

'I keep fifty-one per cent. It might seem petty, but the extra one is for my dad.'

Mulling it over for a second, Tony nodded. 'You got a deal. But I've got a condition of my own.'

'What's that?' Jenna reached behind her for the kitchen roll. Ripping a piece off, she blew her nose.

'That you draw the contracts up in Lenny's name,' Tony said, perching on the back of one of the kitchen chairs now. 'It's my money, and I'll be your actual partner, but that's the way I want it.'

'It's not illegal, is it?' Jenna asked worriedly.

'Hey, come on, now.' Tony drew his head back. 'Do I look like a dodgy guy to you?'

'No, but . . .' Pausing, Jenna shrugged. 'It just seems weird.'

'Granted it ain't the most conventional way to do business,' Tony said. 'But if you knew what I've been through since I got here, you'd understand. I was walking around with a million dollars in my pocket and nowhere to put it before Lenny offered me a helping hand. That's why I want to do this for him now. We both know how bad he wants to be part of the whole club scene, and this is my way of thanking him for everything he's done. With the added benefit of me getting my feet through the door, without the hassle of having to produce papers I ain't got and can't get.'

'Are you sure Leonard *wants* to be involved?' Jenna asked. 'And are you really sure *you* want to do it like this? It's a massive risk handing over that much money and letting him put *his* name to *your* business. What if he decides to cut you out? You'd have no proof that it's got anything to do with you.'

'You kidding me?' Tony chuckled. 'Lenny's a diamond. I'd trust him with my life. You must know how decent he is, what with him and your dad being friends and all.'

'I suppose so,' Jenna murmured. Then, 'Well, I guess if you're both okay with it, there's no reason for me to object, is there?'

'Partners, then?' Tony held out his hand.

'Partners.' Jenna shook it.

'And no one knows about our arrangement, but me, you, Ed and Len. Agreed?'

'Agreed.' Laughing softly now, Jenna shook her head, wondering what on earth she'd let herself in for.

PART TWO

15

Unlocking the door, Tony walked into the larger of the club's two storerooms. It was a vast space, with rough brick walls and a dirty cement floor, situated behind the wall housing the DJ's booth. It spanned the entire width of the club, and had several sub-rooms and alcoved sections. It was also freezing, stank of damp, and was too far away from the back yard and the bars to make it practical for storing alcohol, so all it was used for was storing the cleaning supplies and equipment.

Switching on the light now, Tony held the door open for Jenna to precede him in.

'I was thinking that if we moved all this out,' he said, waving at the boxes of toilet rolls, kitchen towels, soaps and disinfectants that were stacked floor to ceiling along one wall, 'we'd have room for a small bar. And if we take these down –' he indicated the ancient built-in shelves that lined the opposite wall '– we could put in seating. Then we could lay down a small dance floor over here,' he went on, walking across to the back wall. 'Toilets in that section, and a small kitchen in that, where we can get us a chef to do special-occasion dinner parties, and what have you. The rest is just cosmetics – change the overheads to wall lights, give it a good paint job, and it'll be perfect. What do you think?'

'I think we don't need another VIP area,' Jenna told him, repeating what she'd already said before he'd insisted on dragging her in here to take a look. 'The celebrities like to be separated from the general public, but that doesn't mean they don't get a kick out of flaunting themselves in front of them. They *want* to be seen up there in the lounge. It's like a "you can look at me in my castle, but you ain't getting in" kind of thing.'

'Yeah, maybe some of them *do* like being visible,' Tony conceded. 'But there's plenty more who'd rather keep their leisure activities hidden.'

'If we're talking *illegal* activities,' Jenna said, folding her arms now. 'I don't want any of that in my club.'

'*Our* club,' Tony reminded her softly. 'And, no, I'm not talking illegal, I'm talking *private*. Take it from someone who knows, Jenna, there's stars out there who don't want to risk having pictures of them falling over drunk, or taking their mistresses out for dinner and a dance sold to the papers.

They're the real stars – the real money. And there's no one in town accommodating them at the moment, so if we got this off the ground we'd have us some real kudos.'

'I don't know,' Jenna murmured. 'I just think it's a waste of money for something we don't really need – because it would cost a fortune to get it up to scratch. And we'd need permission to open it up as a public area, and that means being inspected by the Planning Department – which I'd really rather not have to get into,' she added, remembering why she hadn't sold the club in the first place.

'Believe me, it won't be wasted money,' Tony assured her. 'And the planning aspect won't be a problem, because Lenny's still got friends in high places.'

'I'm sure he has,' Jenna muttered. 'But I doubt even they could pass this without raising eyebrows.'

'Aw, quit worrying,' Tony said, flapping his hand as if he weren't concerned in the slightest. 'Lenny's already worded up a couple of his guys, and it's practically a done deal, so that ain't a problem. And there's a shit-load of politicians chomping at the bit to get at it. We won't even have to advertise, 'cos these people got an inbuilt radar for safe places to play. All I need is for you to say yes.'

'I'll think about it,' Jenna lied, hoping that he

would be satisfied with that for now. And, knowing him, by the time she got around to telling him no, he'd have already moved on to something else. Glancing at her watch now, she said, 'Right, I'd better get home or I'll never be ready in time. You staying here?'

'For a while,' Tony said, still gazing around, envisaging the private members' club that he *would* set up – with or without Jenna's approval. He liked her, so he'd let her believe that her thinking about it meant something, but he would go ahead regardless.

Jenna was frowning as she made her way across the club floor. She'd been desperate when she'd phoned Tony that day, but he had taken immediate control, telling her that he would sort it all out. And he had done exactly that. She didn't know *how*, and she didn't *want* to know: she was just grateful that it had been so effective. The men who had threatened her hadn't shown their faces again, and there hadn't been a single worrying incident at the club since, apart from the odd little scuffle – which was totally normal and which the security guys were more than able to handle. Now, almost two months into the partnership, the club was well and truly back on its feet, with a full customer turnout and a full VIP lounge every night.

Jenna couldn't have been happier about that, but she was finding the transition from sole owner to partner a little harder than she'd anticipated. She felt dwarfed by Tony's larger-than-life personality, and she had to admit that it peeved her that certain members of staff had jumped so fast onto his side of the new ship. Maurice, in particular, was thrilled to have a male boss again, and Jenna had to battle not to jump down his throat when she saw him sucking up to Tony after he, Maurice, had treated her with barely concealed contempt for so long.

The major problem that she had with the new situation was the way Tony walked around as if it was *his* club. *His* club, *his* rules, *his* way or the highway. Some of his ideas had worked really well, like throwing a party for all of the original New Year's Eve guests, to bring them back into the fold. And the advertising campaign he'd organised, comprising posters being put up all around town, adverts in the press, radio plugs, and even back-of-bus ads, to let the public know they were back on track. But others were just plain annoying. Putting Eddie in charge of security a week after coming on board without even consulting her, for example. That had *really* pissed her off, but by the time she'd heard about it Jacko had already walked out in protest, taking three of the doormen with him. Fortunately, Bobby and Flex stayed and brought in a few of their friends to fill the spaces, so everything was pretty much back to normal on the security front. But it still annoyed her when she thought about it.

Still, Tony was here now and there was nothing she could do about it, so she tried not to let it get to her too much. Jenna reminded herself – frequently – that Tony could think he was in control, but that didn't make it true. She still had the extra one per cent, and everybody knew it was her club really. And, generally speaking, things *were* going pretty well, so she supposed she shouldn't complain.

Letting herself out into the yard now, she forced herself to smile when she saw Leonard manoeuvring his Jag in beside her car. He was here all the time these days, but he wasn't too bad when you cut through the pretentiousness. The only problem Jenna actually had with him was that he was so far up Tony's backside it was difficult to know where the one ended and the other began. And with Eddie completing the triangle of power, she felt a little overwhelmed at times.

'Hello, there,' Leonard called to her now, jumping out when he'd parked and greeting her with a kiss on the cheek. 'And how are we tonight?'

'I'm fine,' she lied, opening her car door. 'You?'

'Grand,' he told her, his smile a mile wide. 'Tony around?'

'Inside,' she said curtly, climbing into the car.

Rushing to the gate to close it after her, Leonard leaned down with his hands on his knees when she pulled up alongside and wound her window down.

'Could you make sure it's properly locked, please,' Jenna said. 'The delivery guys have left the beer crates outside again, and I don't want anybody getting at them. In fact, you'll probably see him before I do, so could you tell Maurice to bring them inside as soon as he gets here?'

'My pleasure,' Leonard said, waving as she reversed out.

Going in through the back door when he'd locked the gate, Leonard made his way through the kitchen into the clubroom just as Tony came out of the storeroom.

'You took your time,' Tony called, dusting his hands off. 'I thought you said you'd be here this afternoon. I was waiting for you to give me a hand.'

'Avril wanted me to take her into Didsbury to pick up some material, then she wanted me to wait for her to get ready so I could drop her at her women's-forum thingummyjig,' Leonard said, going to him.

'And what the good lady wants, the good lady

gets, eh?' Tony shook his head scornfully. 'Well, now you're here, you can help me move these boxes. I don't know where Eddie's got to, but he's getting a bit fucking good at disappearing when I want him nowadays.'

'He's out front having a smoke with a couple of the security chaps,' Leonard told him, slipping his jacket off and looping it over the back of a chair. 'I passed them on my way in.'

'Figures,' Tony grunted, propping the door open with a box and waving Leonard into the room. 'Right, I want all this shit out. We'll put it in the boardroom for now.'

'I take it Jenna's agreed, then?' Leonard asked, rolling up his shirtsleeves.

'Sure she has,' Tony lied, passing one of the boxes to him. 'Did you speak to your guys?'

'Yes, I rang round before Avril dragged me out. They're all thrilled with the idea.'

'And you told them about the membership fee?'

'Yes, and it's quite acceptable. Lord Kimberly had a bit of a grumble, but he'll stump up once he realises that he'll have a place to hide away from Maureen and hang out with the chaps.'

'I don't imagine he'll be too averse when he realises what he's gonna get for his money,' Tony said, grinning.

'Jenna doesn't know about any of that, does

she?' Leonard asked. 'Only I don't think she'd be too happy if—'

'She don't know nothing, and she ain't gonna,' Tony cut him off. 'She might stick her nose round the door when we get up and running, but she won't be interfering, don't you worry about that.'

'And you're sure those girls won't say anything?'

'No one's gonna say a word,' Tony said, getting irritated now. ''Cos they know what'll happen if they do. So quit freaking out.'

'Okay,' Leonard murmured, aware that he was getting on Tony's nerves.

Working on in silence until all the boxes were stacked on the dance floor, Tony glanced at his watch.

'Right, I gotta get back to the hotel. I need to get washed and changed, and check Melody's all right.'

'Oh, dear, is she still sick?'

'Something like that,' Tony grunted, shrugging into his jacket. 'See you later.'

'Bye for now.' Watching as he walked out – the front way, obviously planning to pick Eddie up at the door – Leonard looked at the boxes and sighed. The club would be opening in a couple of hours, so they obviously couldn't stay where they were. Big job for one man, but, oh, well . . . If it shifted another couple of pounds off his waist he wouldn't complain.

Lifting the first box, he'd just reached the office door and was struggling to unlock it when Fabian came in.

'What's going on?' he demanded, looking from Leonard to the rest of the boxes.

'I'm taking them to the boardroom,' Leonard told him. 'Tony wants them out of the storeroom.'

'Oh, does he now? And why's that?'

'Because we're going to be converting it.'

'Into?'

'A, um, private members' club,' Leonard muttered, not sure whether he should be telling Fabian anything but unable to bring himself to tell him to mind his own business. He was the manager, after all.

Peering at Leonard narrow-eyed, Fabian put his hands on his hips. 'Does Jenna know about this?'

'Yes, and she's quite happy about it,' Leonard replied, wondering why the man was giving him such a hard time. He had never been as unfriendly when Leonard had been just a customer, but he'd been decidedly frosty lately and it was beginning to grate.

Giving a grunt of disapproval now, Fabian shook his head and unlocked the door. Propping it open, he said, 'Make sure you stack them neatly, because I don't want them getting in the way. And be quick about it, because we need them off the dance floor before the customers arrive.'

'Well, maybe if you gave me a hand it'd be a lot quicker?' Leonard suggested, but Fabian was heading up the stairs already as if he hadn't heard him. Exhaling loudly, Leonard shook his head. There really was no excuse for such rudeness.

Going into his office, Fabian slammed the door, muttering 'Fucking idiot!' under his breath. He couldn't stand Leonard. Couldn't stand him hanging around all the time. But there was nothing he could do about it, because he was Tony's *friend.* And Tony was *God* – everyone knew that!

Jenna had obviously lost her mind when she took them on, and Fabian was getting seriously pissed off with the lot of them. In fact, he'd have been tempted to walk out like Jacko, but he didn't see why he should have to. This had been his club before any of them came along. He'd run it when James Lorde had been alive, and he'd carried on doing exactly that when Jenna took over – even if she hadn't realised it. But it was getting to be a bit of a joke now that there were three chiefs stoking the fire.

Still, it couldn't last for ever. Sooner or later, Jenna would come to her senses and realise that she didn't want to be involved with a thug like

Tony. All Fabian could do was cross his fingers and wait.

Melody was still in bed when Tony reached the hotel. Walking into the bedroom, he shook his head at her, a glint of disgust in his eyes.

Pulling a sulky face, she said, 'You don't have to look at me like that. I can't help it if I don't feel well.'

'You're a fucking hypochondriac,' he snapped. 'There's nothing wrong with you. You just need to get your ass up out of that bed and quit moaning.'

'I didn't expect you to understand,' she muttered, pulling the quilt up higher around her chin.

Sucking his teeth, Tony went to the wardrobe and took out a suit. Laying it over the back of the chair, he opened the drawer and took out some clean underwear, then went into the bathroom, slamming the door on her miserable face. He didn't know what the hell was wrong with her, but she was doing his head in with all this moping about.

Back in the bedroom, Melody rolled over in the bed as another bout of shivering kicked in. Chase had gone off on his tour of the States a day and a half ago – and she had been counting every single second of every hour in slow motion since, because he had forgotten to leave his stash with her like he'd promised. Or, more likely, he'd accidentally-on-purpose taken it with him – the selfish bastard. He knew that she didn't know anyone else to get it off, and now he was going to be away for months, so not only did she have to put up with Tony again with no relief, she had to face going cold turkey as well. And it was already killing her, so God only knew how she was going to get through the worst of it without Tony finding out.

Chase was such a bastard for slipping that smack into the coke that time.

Thought you'd like it, he'd said. *Thought you'd get off on the different textures of the stone.*

Yeah, right! He hadn't done it for *her*, he'd done it because *he* was a junkie, and like all junkies he'd wanted her to be a junkie with him. Such generous people, these smack-heads, always looking for someone to share the experience with.

Coming back from the bathroom just then, Tony grabbed Melody's dressing gown and threw it at her, saying, 'Get up. I've had enough of this shit. You're coming to the club.'

'Aw, no, Tone,' she moaned. 'I can't.'

'Get the fuck up,' he growled, glaring at her.

Peering up at him over the edge of the quilt, Melody knew she had two choices: get up – or stay put and get battered, and then be *made* to get up.

'Okay,' she muttered, an expression of pure martyrdom on her face as she eased the quilt back and sat up. 'But I'm only doing this for you, so don't expect me to put on a show when we get there.'

'I expect you to get your face on, get dressed up, and get your ass on the dance floor and make like you're having fucking fun, is what I expect,' Tony said, spraying himself with deodorant and reaching for his shirt. 'I own the place now, and you ain't even shown your face there in weeks. Always too busy in the fucking gym, or getting your freaking nails and hair done. Well, enough's enough, 'cos the gym obviously ain't doing you no good, and your hair looks like shit.'

'I take it you approve of my nails, then?' Melody sniped under her breath as she stomped into the bathroom.

Sticking two fingers up at the door as he ranted on behind her, she reached in to turn the shower on. Stcpping bcncath thc hot spray, she winced as it poured over her head and face. It felt like thousands of tiny pins digging into her flesh, and her stomach was tied in a sickening knot of tension. But she couldn't refuse to go to the club again, because Tony would get really mad. Still, it might not be so bad, as long as she didn't have to sit with Tony and his sycophantic fan club. And she hadn't seen Fabian in a while, so that would be nice.

Fabian! Of *course*! Why hadn't she thought of that before, instead of lying in bed thinking that the world was falling down around her. Fabian could get her something to take the edge off. He wouldn't want to see her suffer like this.

Filled with anticipation now, Melody hurried her shower and rushed back into the bedroom to get ready.

Tony took off as soon as they got to the club. He no longer entertained his star friends at his table now that he was the owner, he spread himself about instead, visiting them at *their* tables, making his presence felt in every corner.

Alone at her table, Melody was so busy looking around for Fabian that she didn't notice Leonard approaching. She jumped when he stood right in front of her.

'Shit! You scared the fucking life out of me.'

'Sorry.' Frowning, because he wasn't used to hearing women swear like that, Leonard leaned down to kiss her on the cheek – a habit he'd picked up from Tony, but one which Melody, for one, didn't appreciate, because, while Leonard had undoubtedly lost weight, gained in confidence and regained a little of the once-famous sparkle in his eyes, his weight loss wasn't enough yet to have rectified the excessive sweating. 'Are you feeling any better?' he asked now. 'Tony told me you'd been sick. Nothing too bad, I hope?'

'No, I'm fine,' Melody murmured, glancing pointedly past him, wishing he'd get lost.

'Shame I didn't know you were coming,' Leonard went on, not taking the hint. 'Avril would have loved to have seen you, I'm sure. She was only saying the other day that we should arrange another dinner party. And, you never know, my children might actually be free this time.'

'That would be nice,' Melody lied, getting to her feet. 'Sorry, Leonard, you'll have to excuse me. I'm starting to feel a bit sick again.'

'Oh, dear. Well, off you go.' Stepping back to let her pass, Leonard called, 'Shall I tell Tony you're still not feeling well?'

'No, leave him,' Melody called back over her shoulder. 'I'll be fine in a minute.'

Seeing Tony chatting with Robbie Williams at the bar, Melody made a dash for the stairs. He'd liked Robbie ever since he'd done the Rat Pack tribute album, so he would spend hours with him, given half a chance. And Eddie would be busy doing what he did best – finding people to intimidate in his new role of security chief. Which left Melody plenty of time to find Fabian and get sorted out.

Dashing around the lower floor looking for him now, she spotted him at the foot of the stairs to the DJ's booth and crept up on him.

'Hello, stranger . . . remember me?'

Turning round, Fabian raised an eyebrow when he saw her. Melody hadn't been in much since Tony had bought into the club, and he was a little shocked by how much weight she'd lost. Looking her over surreptitiously, he saw that her voluptuous body was in danger of becoming thin – and that wasn't good, because she'd been perfect as she was. And her face was beginning to suffer, too, he noticed: her cheeks were gaunt, her eyes dull.

'How are you?' he asked, half expecting her to say that she'd been ill.

'I'm all right,' she said, smiling up at him flirtatiously. 'Have you missed me?'

Folding his arms, determined to keep this impersonal, Fabian said, 'I've been too busy. Your boyfriend likes to keep us on our toes.'

'Don't talk to me about him,' Melody grunted. 'I get enough of him at the hotel.'

'Still there, are you? I'd have thought you'd have found yourselves somewhere more permanent now that you've decided to stay.'

'Hey, Tony might have decided, but I haven't.'

'Oh, right.' Fabian shuffled his feet uncomfortably. 'So, what have you been doing with yourself?'

Smiling secretively, Melody said, 'You don't want to know.'

Guessing that she must have found another supplier, Fabian said, 'Ah, well. I'm sure you've been having fun.' Glancing at his watch then, he said, 'Right, well, lovely to see you, but I'd better get moving before your boyfriend complains that I'm not pulling my weight.'

'Is he giving you a hard time?' Melody asked, delaying him because she hadn't hit him for what she really wanted yet.

'Not really. He just makes you feel like he's watching you all the time.'

'Tell me about it,' Melody snorted. Then, smiling again, she said, 'But he's not watching us now. So, how's about we nip up to your office – for old times' sake?'

'I don't really think that's a very good idea,' Fabian said, glancing around nervously.

'Aw, go on,' Melody persisted, fluttering her lashes at him. 'We always had fun, didn't we?'

'Yeah, and look how it ended up.'

'We don't have to do *that*. But I could use a little line, if you've got one. And you know I've never said a word to anyone, so you can't say you don't trust me.'

Inhaling deeply, Fabian thought about it, then

nodded. 'All right, but we'll have to be quick. And if anyone comes up, I'm just going to say I'm showing the new boss's girlfriend around. Okay?'

'Fine by me,' Melody said, already licking her lips in anticipation.

Up in his office, Fabian laid out two lines. Letting Melody go first, he did his, then locked everything away again.

Rubbing his hands together, he said, 'Ready, then?'

'Just give me a minute,' Melody said, pinching her nostrils together because her eyes were smarting. 'Wow, what's in that? It's really tingling.'

'I think it's been cut with something,' Fabian said, shrugging. 'Don't worry. You get used to it after a while.'

'So, you've got quite a bit, then, have you?' Melody asked snidely. 'Enough to spare an old friend some to take away and see her through the night?'

Peering down at her, Fabian frowned. She was acting weird; her tone was wheedling, and a bit pathetic. And she looked awful, he thought again.

'Have you been doing smack?' he asked, the words coming out of his mouth as soon as the thought entered his head.

'No,' she lied, dipping her gaze.

'Oh, Christ, you *have*,' he said quietly. 'What

the hell are you playing at, Melody? That's the worst thing you could possibly do.'

'Don't you think I know that?' she snapped, annoyed that he was preaching and trying to ruin what little buzz she'd got off the line. 'It wasn't *my* fault. Chase spiked my coke with it.'

'Chase?' Fabian repeated. 'Chase Mann? You've been seeing *him*?'

'Well, what was I supposed to do?' Melody retorted accusingly. '*You* didn't want me – you made that perfectly clear.'

'I was *scared*,' Fabian shot back. 'Bloody hell, Melody, did you think it was fun having to look over my shoulder all the time in case your boyfriend was sneaking up on me with a baseball bat?'

'I told you I wouldn't say anything,' she reminded him. 'Didn't you believe me?'

'Not at the time, no,' he replied bluntly. 'You're too unpredictable.'

'I am *not*,' she gasped, looking up at him with pain in her eyes. 'You're making me out to be some kind of idiot, and I'm so sick of being treated like that. Tony talks to me like I'm a piece of shit. Eddie doesn't talk to me at all. *You* turned your back on me. The only one I had left was Chase. And at least he listens to me, and doesn't talk down to me all the time.'

Watching as Melody's eyes filled with tears,

Fabian felt the old stab of sympathy in his gut. She was a beautiful woman, who had, just a few short months ago, had the whole world at her feet. He knew she'd been frustrated about Tony's reluctance to go home, but there was more to this story, he was sure, otherwise she'd have given up on Tony and gone back to Hollywood where she belonged. But she was still here: obviously still frustrated, twice as unhappy as last time he'd seen her, and desperate enough to be taking smack.

'Want to talk?' he asked.

Shocked when she burst into tears, he reached out and patted her on the shoulder, almost falling over when she immediately jumped up and threw herself into his arms. Hesitant at first, because this was what he'd wanted to avoid, he relented after a moment and held her to him.

'I'm sorry,' Melody sobbed, her tears soaking his jacket. 'But it's been so awful. Tony's got my passport, and he won't let me go home. And now my agent's dumped me because he's got a new bitch to push. And Chase went and slipped smack into my coke!'

'All right,' Fabian said softly, patting her back as she wailed. 'Come on, stop crying. You're making a lot of noise, someone's gonna hear you.'

'Sorry,' Melody said again, making little wet choking noises as she tried to quieten down. 'I've just been feeling so bad. I might as well tell Tony everything and let him get on with killing me. At least I'd be out of this misery.'

'Don't talk rubbish,' Fabian said firmly, still holding her as her shoulders heaved. 'You can't tell him anything, because he'll kill you, me, *and* Chase.'

'I don't want to get you in trouble,' Melody cried. 'But I'm so fed up of this. He won't even let me have any money.'

'You've got your own, haven't you?' Fabian said, wondering why she was letting Tony control her like this. 'You must have earned a fair bit from the films.'

'Yeah, but Tony's got my credit cards,' Melody told him. She seemed to be slowing down with the crying at last. 'He took everything off me months ago, because I said I was going home without him.'

'If things are that bad between you, why wouldn't he just let you go to be rid of you?' Fabian asked, rubbing her back soothingly.

'Because he reckons he owns me.' Reaching up, Melody dabbed at her nose with the back of her hand. 'Sorry, I've made a bit of a mess of your jacket.'

'Don't worry about it,' Fabian said, easing her away from him. 'Sit down – I'll get you a drink.'

Pouring two straight brandies, he handed one to her and perched on the edge of the desk.

'So, what makes him think he owns you?' he asked, wondering if he really ought to be getting this involved again.

Shrugging, reluctant to reveal the surgery she'd had at Tony's expense, Melody said, 'He kept me when I was struggling to make it in Hollywood, so now he reckons it's payback time.'

'Why don't you run away?' Fabian suggested. 'You must have friends you could stay with? And once you're safely out of the way, you could send the police to get your things. He couldn't threaten *them*.'

'No!' Melody looked up at him with genuine fear in her eyes. 'You don't know him. He'd kill me if I ever sent the police after him. That's the one thing I wouldn't get away with.'

'Why? What's he scared of?'

'God knows. I don't know *half* of what he gets up to. But whatever it is, Eddie's in on it. *And* Leonard – but they're just using him.'

'How so?'

'Oh, I don't know. But they've got to be getting *some*thing out of him. Why else would they be letting him hang around with them? It certainly isn't because they like him – not if you heard the way they talk about him behind his back.'

'Yeah, I wondered about that,' Fabian said, frowning thoughtfully.

'Yeah, well, don't go saying anything,' Melody warned him, worried that she might have said too much. 'If Tony finds out I've been talking about him, I'm dead.'

'I won't say anything,' Fabian assured her. Glancing at his watch then, he said, 'Subject of, we'd best get moving before he comes looking for you.'

'Before we go,' Melody said, reaching out to stop him when he went to stand up. 'I'm sorry for asking, but is there any chance you could spare a bit more coke? Only that line didn't really do anything. Guess I've built up a bit of a tolerance, huh?'

'Bloody hell, Melody, how much have you been doing?'

'Unlimited supplies.' She gave him a sheepish grin. 'Chase always has loads.'

'And Tony's never noticed?'

'He was too busy working his way in here,' Melody sneered. 'Anyway, he thought I was at the gym, or the hairdresser's, and there's no way he'd ever set foot in a place like that. He hates anything to do with women's things, and exercise is a dirty word to him.'

'Okay,' Fabian said, getting up and going back

to the safe. 'I'll give you some more for now, if it helps. But you need to quit the other shit, or you're gonna be in a real mess.'

'I never wanted it in the first place,' Melody said, her voice glum. 'But I can't just quit without something else to see me through.'

'And coke's going to do that, is it?'

'It's totally different, but better than nothing. Have you never tried smack?'

'Never,' Fabian said, splitting his stash in half and looking in his drawer for a spare bag. 'It wrecks your looks.'

'Not always,' she muttered defensively.

'Don't kid yourself,' he murmured, glancing up at her. 'Come on, Melody, you must *know* you look like shit. And don't tell me it's worth it, 'cos you've just been in floods of tears telling me your life's in pieces.'

'Because of *Tony*,' Melody countered. 'I was coping when I had the smack. And I'm only like this now because Chase pissed off with it and I don't know anyone else to get it off.'

'So as soon as he comes back, you're just going to start all over again, are you?'

'*No*.'

Fabian shook his head. One minute she was saying she didn't want to do it, then she was defending it. But there was no point trying to talk her out of it, because she would do whatever she was going to do, whatever anybody said.

Slipping the bag into her bra when he handed it to her, Melody said, 'Thanks. I'll try and make it last for a couple of days, but do you think you'll be able to get me some more? I've still got a bit of money stashed away, so I'll pay.'

Folding his arms, Fabian sighed. Another lie? She'd just been crying that Tony wouldn't let her have any money, now she reckoned she had some stashed away.

'I'll see what I can do,' he said.

'Great,' Melody said, her voice filled with relief as she stood up. 'And thanks again for this.' She patted her breast. 'You've been a real friend.'

'Don't worry about it,' Fabian said, going to the door and checking the corridor. 'All clear. But if anyone sees us going out, just tell them I've been showing you the offices and the boardroom, okay?'

'Whatever you say.'

They were halfway down the stairs when Tony walked in through the lower door with Brenda Thompson.

'What are you doing here?' he asked Melody, his narrowed eyes flicking from her to Fabian.

'Being shown around, seeing as *you* couldn't be bothered doing it,' Melody said accusingly, giving Brenda the cold eye. 'What are *you* doing?'

'Same,' Tony grunted. 'Brenda's never been backstage before. Thought I'd give her the guided tour.'

'Hardly compares to a *real* backstage,' Melody muttered, folding her arms, wondering if this old bitch . . .

But no. There was no way Tony would touch it. She was about thirty years too old, for starters. And ugly.

Turning to Brenda now, Melody gave her an icy smile. 'You're in for a real treat. I've never been so bored in my life.'

'Yeah, well, you won't want to stick around for a second viewing, then, will you?' Tony said, waving Brenda on ahead. Turning back as they passed on the stairs, he said, 'Yo, Fabian. Make sure she gets back up to the VIP lounge all right, 'cos I don't want no repeats of the last time you was supposed to be looking after her.'

'Absolutely,' Fabian replied evenly, refusing to let show in his eyes the anger that Tony was *still* blaming him for that incident with the men who had hassled Melody, even though he hadn't even been there.

Seeing Jenna at the bar when he had escorted Melody back to her table, Fabian went over to have a word.

Smiling up at him when he reached her, she said, 'I'm just taking a five-minute break. Care to join me?'

'Yeah, thanks.' Sitting down beside her, Fabian waved Kalli over and ordered himself a brandy. Then, turning back to Jenna, he said, 'Can I ask you something? About Tony.'

'Oh, yes?' Jenna said, a flicker of something that Fabian couldn't quite read passing through her eyes.

'Yeah, I was just wondering what's going on,' he said. 'Only, I found Leonard moving stuff out of the storeroom earlier, and he said Tony had told him to because they were converting it.'

'Did he now?' Jenna said coolly. She hadn't known about that, and it pissed her off that Tony was obviously planning on going ahead without waiting for her answer. 'I don't suppose you'd know where he put it?'

'In the boardroom,' Fabian told her, sensing that she might not be as happy about this as Leonard had suggested – if she knew at all. 'He reckons they're going to turn the storeroom into some kind of private members' club.'

'Yes, well, we did discuss it,' Jenna said, not wanting to admit that Tony was walking all over her.

'I see,' Fabian said quietly. 'Well, I guess you

know what you're doing. But I'd appreciate being told when these kind of decisions are made, because it's pretty hard to do what I'm supposed to do if things keep changing. I mean, what am I supposed to say if the staff hear something and ask me about it and I don't know anything?'

Sighing, Jenna gave him a weary smile. 'I understand what you're saying, and I'll try to keep you informed in future. But you might have to bear with me, because Tony's a bit . . .'

She paused to find the right word, and Fabian went through a whole list in his mind that would have fitted the gap perfectly: presumptuous; arrogant; rude; dismissive; crooked; bent; *bastard.*

'Impulsive,' Jenna said. 'He's got all these ideas floating round in his head, and he likes to get stuck in while they're fresh.'

'But the final decisions are still *yours*?' Fabian asked, concerned that she might be losing control.

'Of course,' she said, meeting his gaze. 'My dad left the club to me. I might have screwed up and had to take a partner to keep us afloat, but that doesn't mean I'm going to let Tony take over.'

'Glad to hear it,' Fabian murmured. 'And who knows?' he said then. 'One day, when everything's going great again, you might be able to buy him out and get it back to how it used to be.'

'You never know,' Jenna replied quietly, doubting

that Tony would ever relinquish his share now that he'd finally got it.

'So, this private thingy,' Fabian said now, his expression clearly showing what he thought of the idea. 'Is it actually necessary on top of the VIP lounge?'

Smiling, because he was echoing exactly what she had already said, Jenna shrugged. 'Tony seems to think so.' Leaning towards him now, she added conspiratorially, 'Anyway, I'd have thought you'd be pleased, if it means you seeing less of him and Leonard?' Finishing her drink, she put her glass down and got up.

'See you,' Fabian said, smiling now because she obviously saw more than she let on.

As she walked away, Jenna's smile quickly turned into a tight-lipped frown. She wasn't amused about Tony presuming that she would okay his plans, and she would have words with him when she saw him. Yet again, he'd made her feel as if her opinion counted for nothing in her own club, and she was getting pretty bloody sick of it.

Jenna didn't get a chance to confront Tony until the end of the night. Every time she'd seen him before that, he'd been talking to somebody or other and she hadn't wanted to disturb them. Catching him as he was about to leave, she called him to one side and said, 'So, what's this I hear about you moving those boxes out of the storeroom?'

'Just thought I'd make a start,' he told her, giving her a cheeky grin. 'No point hanging about if you were only going to say yes anyway, was there? And the faster I get the builders in, the faster it's done, eh?'

Looking at him, Jenna sighed. She wanted to reprimand him for going over her head; wanted to say that she still had the extra one per cent, and that he should respect that and wait until she had given him the go-ahead before he put his plans into effect. But she knew that they would be wasted words, because he was obviously hell-bent on going his own sweet way.

'As it happens, I *was* going to give you the go-ahead,' she said instead, refusing to let him think that he'd got one over on her. 'But I expect your builders to keep the noise and mess to a minimum,' she went on, asserting what little authority she had left. 'And they absolutely must not get in the way of the club, so no late nights rushing to get finished. Okay?'

'Oh, absolutely,' Tony drawled, giving her a wry smile. 'They'll be here at eight-thirty tomorrow morning, so they won't be disturbing no one. And the first thing they'll be doing is opening up that back door that's bricked up, so they won't even need to set foot in this side once that's out of the way.' Winking now, he said, 'Chill, partner. I've got it all in hand.'

'Oh, I'm sure you bloody have,' Jenna muttered under her breath as he walked away. There were times when she really regretted taking him on, and this was one of them.

16

As Tony had promised, the building work caused minimal upheaval to the rest of the club. They had unbricked and replaced the old door with a heavy-duty security one, and had used that as their entry point since, so Jenna had barely even seen anyone coming and going. In fact, she'd all but forgotten they were in there when Tony called her down from her office three weeks later to take a look.

'What do you think?' he asked, throwing the adjoining door open and stepping back to let her go in ahead of him. Hanging back in the doorway, he folded his arms. 'Pretty cool, huh?'

Looking around, Jenna's eyebrows crept up. It looked exactly as he'd described it to her that time: small dance floor complete with its own tiny DJ box, gleaming buffed-oak bar, plush seating area, signposted kitchen and toilets. It was classily decorated, too, in subtle shades of scarlet, green, and muted gold, the wall lights adding a warm glow to the whole.

'It looks great,' she said, truthfully. 'But how on earth did you manage it? You only mentioned it for the first time a few weeks ago.'

'Hey, you know I don't like hanging around when I get an idea,' Tony said, shrugging casually. 'I just told the builders what I wanted, and left them to it.'

'Yes, but how did you get them to finish so fast?' Jenna turned to look at him now. 'It took my builders almost two months to finish my office bathroom, and that was already half done.'

'It's a man thing.' Tony grinned. 'You just gotta know the right thing to say.'

'What, like, do it fast or I'll break your legs?' she teased.

'*Now* you're getting it.' Tony chuckled. 'But, hey, don't knock it if it works. And as you can see, it does.' He waved a hand around the room.

Taking another look, Jenna nodded. 'Credit where it's due, you've done an amazing job. So, what's the plan?'

'We open tonight,' Tony told her, relighting the cigar he'd been chewing throughout. 'Lenny's got a load of his old buddies coming in, and I've got some folks lined up, too. It'll be a blast.'

'Do I get an invite?' Jenna smiled up at him.

'Hey, you don't need no invite,' Tony told her, throwing an arm around her shoulder. 'But I don't think you'll like it much, 'cos it's gonna be a lot quieter in here than out there. Just a load of old guys smoking and drinking, and chatting about the good old days, when the jitterbug ruled and women knew their place at the kitchen sink.'

'Oh, so you've aimed this firmly at the ancient MCP crowd, have you?'

'The stinking-*rich* MCP crowd,' Tony said, giving her shoulder a squeeze. 'A grand a year in membership fees,' he lied, knocking a full thousand off the price he had set and already received from quite a lot of his new members. 'And for that, they get their own entrance and exit out of the public glare; a free glass of champagne every visit; and we got us a top-notch chef to dish up the grits. Can't be bad, huh?'

'Hate to admit it, but you could be onto a winner,' Jenna said, gazing around again. 'I didn't think we needed another VIP area, but this is nothing like the lounge.'

'That *was* the intention. No offence, but the decor up there ain't what these folks are used to. They want this posh old shit. And Lenny helped me out on that, so I'm figuring it must be spot on.'

Nodding, Jenna said, 'It reminds me of one of those gentlemen's clubs you see in the old Sherlock Holmes films.'

'Perfect. Just what we wanted.'

'Well, you got it,' Jenna said, walking back out into the main clubroom. 'So, I guess I won't be seeing much of you if you're going to be spending all your time locked away in there?'

'You'll see me,' Tony assured her. 'But locked away is kind of what I wanted to talk to you about, 'cos there's gonna be no access from this side of the club. Once the door's shut, it stays shut till the club's closed.'

'That's a bit impractical, isn't it?' Jenna said. 'What if I need to see you?'

Shrugging, Tony said, 'You'll have to give me a ring and let me know you're coming, so I can get Eddie to let you in round back.'

'Outside?'

''Fraid so.' Tony shrugged again. 'If we open the adjoining door, the Zenith punters will see straight into The Diamond, and that'd negate the absolute privacy guarantee, wouldn't it?'

'The diamond?' Jenna gazed at him blankly.

'Oh, yeah, that's what I'm calling it,' Tony told her. 'Got a nice ring to it, don't it? The Diamond Den.'

'Very original.'

'Yeah, I thought so. Anyway, Eddie'll be doing the security to make sure that no jokers try getting in from this side. And me and Lenny will be in there for the most part, so you'll have to ring if you need either of us. Or we can get some walkie-talkies, or something? Whichever you prefer.'

'How's about I just let you get on with it and I get on with this side?' Jenna suggested, thinking it was all too much hassle. 'I'm not walking all the way around the outside of the club in the dark. If I've got a problem, I'll ring and you can come round here.'

'However you want it,' Tony agreed. 'Before I forget,' he said then. 'I've stocked up the bar, but I'm gonna need to sort out an independent supply tomorrow, 'cos we can't be running round here every time we need a refill. Oh, and I need a couple of the waitresses for tonight.'

'My waitresses?'

'*Our* waitresses. Yeah, I want two for my side. We can spare them, can't we?'

'It's a bit short notice,' Jenna murmured. 'But I suppose we could juggle things for one night. Anyone in mind?'

'Yeah, them two blondes – JoJo and Vanessa.'

'Really?' Jenna was surprised. She'd have expected him to go for some of the older, more respectful girls, given the type of clientele he was catering to.

'Yeah, they'll go down a bomb,' Tony said. 'They're young and attractive enough to please the eye, but sassy enough to fend off any nonsense if the grandads get out of line. And they're friends, so there won't be none of that bitching we get with some of the other girls.'

'Well, it's your choice.' Jenna shrugged. 'I'll have a word with them when they come in, see what they think.'

'If they're all right with it, send 'em straight in to me,' Tony said, glancing at his watch now. 'I want to talk them through my rules before we kick off.'

'Rules?' Laughing softly, Jenna shook her head. 'I don't envy them.'

Tony drew his head back. 'Hey, I'm just a big old softy, you know that.'

'Er, remind me again how you got the builders to finish so fast?' Jenna said, giving him an incredulous look.

Summoned to Jenna's office when they arrived a short time later, JoJo and Vanessa could barely keep a straight face between them when she asked if they wanted to try out working for Tony in the new room. They had known about it for ages, way before *she* had even known that he was planning it. Tony had approached them as soon as he got the idea, letting them know exactly what would be expected of them, and what they could expect to get out of it.

And exactly what would happen to them if they breathed so much as one word about it to anyone – ever.

'I don't mind giving it a go,' JoJo said now, shrugging, as if she really couldn't be fussed either way. 'As long as I can come back in here if I don't like it.'

'That shouldn't be a problem,' Jenna assured her. 'How about you, Vanessa?'

'I'm easy,' Vanessa said, coughing to cover a giggle as JoJo gave her a dig with her elbow.

'Right, well, Mr Allen would like you to go and see him now,' Jenna said, standing up and waving them to the door. 'Just make sure you're on your best behaviour,' she went on, following them out into the corridor. 'Mr Allen's catering to a much older crowd than you're used to, so you need to be respectful at all times – which means no swearing, arguing, or flirting. Okay?'

They both nodded, their expressions suitably chaste, even though they were both thinking the same thing: that Jenna didn't know Tony at all if she thought he was expecting respectful behaviour from them.

'Good.' Jenna smiled. 'Give it a week and see how you get on. If you don't like it after that, come and see me and I'll see what I can do. Oh, and you'd best take your things in with you,' she said, walking into the clubroom and glancing at her watch. 'It's not long to opening, and you won't be able to come back through this side once the club's open.'

'What, so we're gonna be, like, locked in?' Vanessa asked. '*We* can't get out, and no one can get in?'

'That's the general idea.'

'Not even you?'

'Not even me,' Jenna confirmed, not noticing the sly glance that passed between the two of them.

'Girls,' Tony drawled when Eddie brought JoJo and Vanessa in. 'Welcome to a whole new world.' Beaming, he put an arm around the shoulders of each of them and walked them to the bar. 'This is my new barman, Juan,' he said, introducing them to the good-looking young man on the other side of the counter. Juan had glossy jet-black hair, and huge brown eyes framed by lashes that were longer than both of theirs put together.

'Hello, Juan,' they both said, eyeing him with immediate interest.

Nodding, Juan got on with polishing his glasses. He knew they both fancied him, and that he could have taken his pick of either of them, right here and now. But they had the wrong parts to get his engine running. Anyway, just like them – he suspected – when he put out he expected a damn good return for his efforts, 'cos nobody got this hot bod and gorgeous face for free.

'Right, girls, tell him what you want, then I'll show you to your dressing room.'

'Anything we want?' JoJo asked.

'Anything at all,' Tony told her magnanimously.

'Great, well, we'll have champagne, then – won't we, Van?'

Clicking his fingers at Juan when Vanessa nodded, Tony said, 'You heard the ladies.'

'It's really nice in here, Mr Allen,' Vanessa said, gazing around wide-eyed.

'Glad you like it,' he said. 'Because you'll be spending a lot of time in here from now on – depending how you get on. So, what did Jenna say?' he asked then.

'That we should be on our best behaviour,' JoJo told him, smiling slyly. 'She's got no idea what we're going to be doing, has she?'

'None whatsoever,' Tony replied, his voice low as he added, 'and if she ever finds out, I'll know exactly who to blame, won't I?'

'She won't hear anything from us,' JoJo assured him quickly. 'We're not that stupid.'

'Let's hope not,' Tony said, still smiling. Picking the two girls' glasses up when Juan placed them on the bar, he handed them to them, saying, 'Right, follow me. The customers will start coming in at about eleven, so you've got plenty of time to get into your costumes and get your faces on. Oh, and in case you need a boost I've left you a little something in the dressing room.'

'We can't afford to lose two waitresses,' Fabian complained when Jenna brought him up to date. 'The rota is worked out to give us exactly the number we need each night.' Not that he should even have to be telling her this, he grumbled to himself.

'I know. But I imagine Tony forgot in the rush to get finished,' Jenna said, defending him because she'd already okayed him taking JoJo and Vanessa. 'It shouldn't be too much of a problem if we shuffle everyone around.'

'I don't think Maurice would agree with you,' Fabian replied tersely. 'He relies on JoJo when it gets full later on. Patsy's useless when there's a rush on, and this is by far the busiest bar.'

'Right, I'll send Kalli down to help Maurice,' Jenna said, knowing that he was right. 'And tomorrow I'll arrange proper cover. Okay?'

'Not really.' Fabian folded his arms now. 'Kalli's needed upstairs. We can't let that stupid boy run the VIP bar on his own.'

'Austin's a good barman,' Jenna told him, trying

to stay calm – Fabian was annoying her now. 'And he'll have Diane to help him, so I'm sure they'll manage.'

'Neither one of them is good enough to run the VIP bar,' Fabian pointed out, a note of exasperation creeping into his voice. 'Kalli's got to stay up there. If anything, we should send the boy down here to help Maurice and Patsy. But I'm still not happy about it,' he added peevishly. 'You should never have agreed to let him take those girls at such short notice. Anyone would think his stupid room was more important than the club.'

'Okay, Fabian, I get the point,' Jenna retorted irritably. 'But it's too late to do anything about it now, so we'll just have to get on with it. I'll sort it out tomorrow.'

'I sincerely hope so,' Fabian said, glancing at his watch. 'Right, I'd best go and have a word with Maurice – make sure he doesn't start sulking, or we'll be buggered.'

'I'll send Austin down,' Jenna said, heading for the VIP stairs.

'Aw, do I have to?' Austin moaned when Jenna told him he was working downstairs tonight. 'I can't stand Maurice. And that Patsy's a right wimp. Please, Jenna, I'll do anything you ask, but not this. I need to be with my Kalli.'

'It's not a bloody crèche,' Jenna snapped, seriously pissed off that everybody seemed to be arguing with her these days. No matter what she said or did, somebody always had an objection. Or, like Tony, just disregarded her opinion.

'*I* don't mind going downstairs,' Diane chipped in helpfully.

'No,' Jenna said firmly. 'I want Austin down there. No offence, but he can handle a rush much better than you, Diane, and it's the busiest night tonight, so I don't want to take any chances.'

Nodding, Diane stepped back and left them to it.

'Please,' Austin implored, looking up at Jenna through his lashes. 'I really, really hate Maurice. He's a horrible old man.'

Jenna had to fight the urge to laugh. She knew exactly how Austin felt, but she wasn't about to say that, because it was hardly professional. Instead, she gave him a mock-stern look and said, 'Yes, well, just try and stay away from him as much as possible and you'll be fine. If we're still short-staffed tomorrow, I'll think about letting Diane go down. But I need *you* down there tonight.'

Pulling a sulky face, Austin folded his arms. 'Why isn't JoJo doing it? I bet she's skiving.'

'She and Vanessa are working for Mr Allen now,' Jenna told him. 'So get used to it, and stop moaning. I'll get onto hiring some new girls first thing tomorrow.'

'Can't you get boys?' Austin suggested, perking up a little. 'We could do with some fresh blood around here.'

'Don't you mean fresh meat?' Jenna gazed at him knowingly.

'Miss *Lorde*!' he gasped, his eyes sparkling with delight. 'I never thought you'd come out with something like *that*!'

'Yes, well, maybe I'm not quite as stupid as I look, eh?' she replied amusedly. 'There are quite enough boys already, and I'm replacing *girls*, so there we go.'

'Fine,' Austin said, rolling his eyes resignedly. 'Will JoJo and Vanessa be doing whatever they're doing for long?' he asked then. 'Only I thought we were all working for Mr Allen now, anyway.'

'He's got a new project of his own,' Jenna said evasively. 'So they'll be helping him out for as long as he wants them to.'

'New project?' Austin persisted.

'An offshoot club,' Jenna said, refusing to say more, because it was really none of his business.

'In the storeroom?' Austin said, his eyes burning with curiosity. 'I *knew* there was something going on in there. So, what is it? Can I go and see it?'

'Absolutely not,' Jenna told him quietly but

firmly. 'If Mr Allen wants you to see it, I'm sure he'll let you know. But don't be making a nuisance of yourself,' she warned then, her eyes clearly telling Austin that he wasn't to approach Tony about it. 'This is his and Mr Drake's project, and they don't want it to be general knowledge, so keep it to yourself. Understood?'

'Loud and clear,' Austin said, his mind already ticking over, figuring how he could get to know more without The Sopranos – as most of the staff now referred to Tony and Eddie behind their backs – finding out.

Leonard Drake! *He*'d tell him. The man had been following him around for weeks, and Austin was starting to believe that Kalli had been right all along. No, in fact, rephrase that – he *knew* Kalli was right. Leonard had the hots for him, but he was obviously too shy to come out and say it. Whether that was because he'd been in the closet so long that he'd forgotten where the handle was, or because he hadn't even admitted it to himself yet, Austin didn't know. But Leonard definitely liked him, and would probably tell him what was going on if he asked nicely enough.

A little bit of flirting couldn't hurt. And why not? Now that he was finally losing weight Leonard was actually quite good-looking. And he was so nice, too – which was more than could be said for

Xavier. That two-timing little prick – *little* being the operative word! – had bitched and whined and complained and scrounged his way through seven whole months of Austin's precious life. It might be kind of nice to be with an older man for a change.

All depended how forthcoming Leonard was about this secret project. 'Cos you didn't get nothing for nothing in this life.

'Time you got moving, isn't it?' Jenna said, clicking her fingers in front of his face to snap him out of his trance. 'You'll have Fabian to answer to if you don't get your backside downstairs in two minutes flat.'

'Great,' Austin muttered, dragging his feet as he made his way around the bar. 'Maurice *and* Fabian. Can life *get* any better!'

'Ignore him,' Kalli said when Austin had gone. 'He'll be fine once he gets down there.'

'I know.' Jenna chuckled softly. 'That boy should be on stage, he really should. Anyway, will you be all right without him?'

'We'll manage,' Kalli assured her. 'That thing you were just talking about,' she said then, lowering her voice. 'What did you mean by offshoot?'

'I can't really tell you too much,' Jenna said, glancing quickly around to make sure that nobody was listening. 'But Mr Allen and Mr Drake have opened a private members' club, catering to old politicians and reclusive stars. But don't tell a soul, because Mr Allen wants it to be strictly private. And I know I can trust you, but some of the others, I'm not too sure.'

'I won't say a word,' Kalli assured her quickly. 'And I'll make sure Austin keeps quiet, too. And don't worry about this bar. Me and Diane can run it with our eyes shut.'

'I know you can,' Jenna said gratefully. 'And thanks, Kalli. It's good to know I've got a friend in here, because I feel like I'm banging my head against a brick wall sometimes.'

Sensing that Jenna was troubled about something, Kalli reached out and squeezed her hand. 'You sure it's just the club that's bothering you?' she asked, her eyes dark with caring.

'Yeah, course,' Jenna told her, smiling softly. 'It just gets to me sometimes, that's all. Don't worry about me. I'm fine.' Seeing Melody coming up the stairs alone just then, she said, 'If anyone needs worrying about, it's that girl. She's not been herself for ages.'

'I know what you mean,' Kalli said, gazing at Melody. 'I feel really sorry for her sometimes. Mr Allen's not very nice to her these days, is he?'

'Can't say I've noticed,' Jenna lied, thinking it best not to go down the road of gossiping about

Tony. 'But I think I'll go and say hello, anyway. See you later.'

'See you,' Kalli said, watching as she went.

Melody wasn't the only one who hadn't been themselves lately. Jenna was getting more and more irritable, and looked tired all the time, too. Come to think of it, she hadn't been herself since Vibes had left. And she hadn't mentioned him for a while, so he obviously hadn't been in touch, which was probably something to do with her irritability. But there was nothing Kalli could do but be here for her if she wanted to talk. In the meantime, she would do her best to keep the other waiters and waitresses in line while they were understaffed, so that Jenna didn't have to worry about that as well.

Melody was feeling a lot better than she had in a while. And tonight she was particularly upbeat, because Tony wasn't going to be around to keep an eye on her – for a change. He was going to be far too busy with his secret little club – the one that Melody wasn't allowed to go into, because it was a 'man-only zone', according to Tony. She knew he was lying about that, but she didn't give a flying fuck. As long as Fabian wasn't locked in there with him, she didn't care *what* Tony was doing.

Fabian was her favourite-ever man again. He'd

been so good to her since that night a few weeks back, keeping her well supplied with coke to ease the pain of smack withdrawal. She didn't know what she'd have done without him, and she was dying to get something going with him again. He'd been keeping her at arm's length so far, but she understood that. It wasn't just the threat of having Tony on his back that put him off, he'd been genuinely disappointed in her for taking smack. But now he could see that she really meant it when she said she would never do it again, Melody was hoping that he would relax and they could start being honest with each other again. And tonight was the perfect time to talk to him about it, while Tony and Eddie were going to be locked away. It shouldn't be too hard, because she was sure that Fabian felt the same way. And now she wasn't looking so ill any more, and was dressed to kill, how could he resist?

But she'd have to wait before she went chasing him down. Zenith had only just opened, and Tony had another hour before his first night kicked off. Better to give it a bit of time and let him get really rolling before she made a move.

Smiling when Jenna came over to her table now, Melody said, 'Hi, how are you?'

'Knackered,' Jenna said, flopping down onto a chair.

'Already?' Melody laughed. 'You've not been open

two minutes. How are you going to last the night?'

'With difficulty,' Jenna admitted. 'But never mind me,' she said then, flapping her hand. 'I'm just moaning for the sake of it. How are *you*?'

'Feeling pretty good, actually,' Melody told her truthfully. 'I was a bit sick for a while, but it's dying down now.'

'I did wonder,' Jenna said, smiling again. 'We didn't see you for ages, and you didn't look at all well when you did come in. Tony just said you had a bug.'

'Yeah, that's right.' Melody raised a hand to her throat. 'Think it might have been a touch of Mono, or something. Totally wipes you out, that shit. Feels like the worst flu ever.'

'Ah, the kissing disease,' Jenna said, rolling her eyes. 'I caught it when I first went to college. Nasty stuff. Lasted about three months, from what I remember.'

'That's the one,' Melody nodded. 'Still, it seems to be shifting now – fingers crossed. Fancy a drink?' she asked then. 'Or are you too busy?'

Pursing her lips, Jenna said, 'It is going to be a bit busier than usual – thanks to your boyfriend stealing my waitresses. But go on. Why not?'

'I have no ice,' Juan said, walking into the dressing room where Tony was sitting with the girls. They were in costume now, their sequinned bras and panties sparkling beneath the sheer negligee-like gowns, but Juan didn't even look at them.

'You gotta be kidding me?' Tony frowned up at him. 'I put a bag in there myself this morning.'

'There's an enormous bag of water leaking all over the *fridge*,' Juan said, folding his arms. 'I don't suppose that's it?'

'Fridge?' Tony repeated, slapping himself on the forehead. 'Fuck! I thought that was the freezer. So, where's the freezer?'

'In the kitchen,' Juan told him, his tone ever so slightly condescending. 'Next to the sink.'

'Fuck!' Tony said again, glancing at his watch and seeing that they only had half an hour to go before people started arriving. Zenith was already open, so he couldn't send anyone through the adjoining door to get another bag, and the girls definitely couldn't go outside dressed like this. Leaning back, he stuck his head out of the door and yelled, '*LENNY!*'

Rushing out of the toilet, still fastening his belt, Leonard said, 'Did you want me?'

'Yeah, I need you to go round to the big kitchen and get a bag of ice,' Tony said. 'Seems someone forgot to put the last bag in the freezer like I asked, and it's melted.'

'Oh, right,' Leonard murmured, not too thrilled

at the prospect of walking all the way around the outside of the club and down the dark alley to get in through the backyard. But he could hardly refuse if *he* were the one Tony was referring to. He genuinely didn't remember being asked to move anything into the freezer, but his head had been so full of arrangements, he must have forgotten.

'Tonight would be good,' Tony was saying now, a sarcastic edge to his voice that didn't escape the girls, who smirked into their wineglasses.

Blushing, Leonard turned on his heel and walked away. That old nonsense had better not start up again. He'd had more than enough of people smirking at him before he and Tony hooked up, and he wouldn't sit quietly by and watch as people started being disrespectful again. Especially not those sluts in there.

Letting himself into Zenith's kitchen a few minutes later he found himself confronted by the sight of Austin, wearing nothing but his shorts as he stood at the sink, rinsing out his T-shirt.

With his back to the door, Austin didn't see who had come in but he felt the icy draught.

'Fucking hell! Hurry up and shut that,' he complained, turning around, giving Leonard a full frontal of his hairless chest and pudgy little breasts decorated with gold nipple rings. 'Oh, sorry, Mr D.' Raising a hand to his mouth, he giggled. 'Didn't know it was you, or I wouldn't have said that.'

'It's okay,' Leonard said, averting his gaze. 'I know you youngsters have your own way of talking.'

'Hey, you're not so old yourself,' Austin teased, leaning back against the sink. 'How come you came in the back way, anyway? You've not been out there the whole time watching me, have you?'

'God, no!' Leonard yelped, afraid that the boy might think him a peeping Tom. 'I've, er, just come round for some ice.'

'It's in there.' Austin pointed out the chest freezer in the corner. 'Is that for your secret club?' he whispered then, letting Leonard know that he knew. 'Don't worry,' he added, tapping his nose. 'I won't tell. I'll carry the ice round for you, if you like?' he offered then.

'Oh, thank you, but no. Best not,' Leonard said, knowing that Tony would not be pleased, even though Leonard would have liked nothing better than to take a leisurely stroll around the block and have a friendly chat right now.

Austin had been nice to him when he'd been a customer, and a positive delight since he became part of the team. In fact, he was one of the few members of staff who didn't treat Leonard like an interfering intruder when he went into the areas that had previously been off-limits to him. Like

Fabian, some of the others had been rather cool towards him, if not downright offhand. But Austin was never anything less than friendly, and Leonard found himself seeking the lad out more often than was probably decent. But what was the harm, as long as nobody commented upon it – which, so far, they hadn't. And now that Avril seemed to have lost interest in following him around and was content to get on with her own thing, he was free to indulge himself with these friendships that would previously have incurred her scorn, if not her wrath.

'You all right, Mr D?' Austin asked, tilting his head to one side and peering up at him. 'You look miles away.'

'I've, er, got a bit of a headache,' Leonard murmured. 'Best get some . . . Ah.' Spotting the first-aid cabinet, he pointed at it.

Darting in front of him as he headed for it, Austin took out a bottle of paracetamol. 'There you go,' he said, pressing it into his hand. 'That'll shift it. If not, just give me a shout and I'll give you a neck massage. Kalli says I've got healing hands.'

'Kalli?'

'My flatmate. Gorgeous, bossy little thing. Works the VIP bar.'

'Oh, yes, I think I know who you mean,' Leonard said, remembering the pretty little Chinese girl with the highly suspicious eyes. Or maybe that was just the look that came into them when she stared at Leonard, because she certainly seemed to suspect him of something. Though goodness only knew what. 'I didn't realise you shared a flat.'

'Can't afford *not* to on my wages,' Austin snorted.

'Oh?' Leonard raised an eyebrow. 'Are they low?'

'Try limboing under the door, and you'll get an idea,' Austin told him. Then, seeing the concern on Leonard's face, he said, 'Hey, I'm only joking. They're not great, but they're better than at a lot of places. Anyway, I like sharing. Better than going home to an empty place every night, eh?'

'I expect so,' Leonard agreed.

'Don't know why I'm asking *you* that,' Austin said, laughing softly now. 'You've got Mrs D waiting for you, haven't you? She in tonight, by the way?'

'No, she's busy with one of her charity projects,' Leonard replied. 'At least, she was earlier. But I imagine she'll be tucked up in her bed with a book by now.'

'So you're living it up while you can, eh?' Giving him a conspiratorial grin, Austin turned back to the sink to wring out his T-shirt.

Trying not to stare at the tighter-than-tight

shorts, Leonard said, 'Erm, something like that, yes. Busy tonight?'

'*I* am, but I can't say the same for that lazy lot out there. If I had to count the times I've been asked to do someone else's dirty work tonight, I'd run out of fingers, toes, *and* eyelashes.'

'They're not taking advantage, are they? I'll get Mr Allen to have a word, if you like.'

'Hey, *nobody* takes advantage of me,' Austin said indignantly. 'I might look like a pushover, but this boy's got balls – pardon the expression.' Giggling again, he turned to face Leonard. 'So, how about you, Mr D? Reckon anyone could take advantage of *you* – apart from the wife, of course, 'cos that's a woman's prerogative, isn't it? To make our lives as miserable as possible.' Biting his lip playfully now, he said, 'Oops! Me and my big mouth. I shouldn't be saying stuff like that to a happily married man, should I?'

'You're entitled to your opinion,' Leonard said, feeling a little uncomfortable with the subject matter, yet thrilled that the boy felt able to speak so openly to him. 'So, do you have a . . . *partner*?'

'Not now,' Austin said, shaking the damp T-shirt out and pulling it over his head with a grimace. 'I did, but he cheated on me with one of my friends. And one of his. *And* some lad he met on holiday.'

'Oh, dear, I'm terribly sorry.'

'Don't *you* be sorry,' Austin said, reaching for a tea towel to wipe his hands. 'You didn't do anything wrong. In fact, you're such a decent bloke, I can't imagine you ever doing the dirty on anyone. I just wish there were more fellas like you out there. But oh well . . . we can't get everything we want, can we?'

'No, I don't suppose we can,' Leonard said quietly.

'Right,' Austin said, clapping his hands. 'Best get back to work before Fabulous comes looking for blood.'

'Fabulous?' Leonard repeated.

'That's what I call Fabian,' Austin whispered. 'But for *gawd*'s sake don't tell him, or I'll be out on my arse.'

'Wouldn't dream of it,' Leonard assured him, smiling conspiratorially. 'Mum's the word.'

'Jeezus, you wouldn't say that if you'd met *my* mum,' Austin said, shuddering as he headed for the door. 'She scares the absolute *crap* out of me. Bit like your man in there – the big fella.'

'Eddie?'

'Yeah, *him*. He gives me the *right* willies. Doesn't he bother you?'

'I haven't really thought about it,' Leonard said, realising that it was actually true. He'd been so busy focusing his attention on Tony that he hadn't really noticed Eddie. 'I suppose he can be a little intimidating, now you mention it.'

'A *little*?' Austin gasped. 'Wow, Mr D, you're a bigger man than me. Tell you what, you should come out with me some time, only I could use someone fearless like you to put that useless ex of mine back in line.'

'I really don't think I'd be much use to you,' Leonard chuckled.

'Worth a try.' Austin said, rolling his eyes good-naturedly. 'But, seriously, if you ever fancy coming down to one of my clubs, give me a shout, 'cos I reckon you'd get a kick out of it.'

'I don't really think I'd fit in,' Leonard said, folding his arms as his heart picked up speed.

'Rubbish,' Austin scoffed. 'Everyone's welcome down there. Gay, straight, bi. *Curious*.' Smiling when Leonard dropped his gaze, he said, 'No pressure, but I reckon we'd have a laugh.'

'That's very kind of you,' Leonard said. 'I'll keep it in mind.'

'You do that,' Austin said, adding in a whisper, 'only do us a favour, and don't tell anyone, 'cos I don't want them lot out there gossiping. They're too thick to understand that gays and straights can actually be *friends*. And while we're on the subject of keeping things quiet,' he said then, 'any chance of me getting a sneaky peek at this new club of yours?'

'Oh, I don't know,' Leonard murmured. 'Tony – Mr Allen – well, he kind of wants to keep it exclusive.'

'Oh, right,' Austin said, obviously disappointed. 'Never mind.'

'I would if I could,' Leonard assured him, feeling guilty now because Austin had been kind enough to offer to take him out – as a friend. 'Maybe . . .' Hesitating, he shrugged. 'Well, maybe one day, when no one's around.'

'For real?' Austin grinned. 'Cool!'

'But you won't tell anybody I said that?'

'God, no!' Austin promised. 'Right, well, give me a shout when you're ready – for my club, *or* yours. See you later, Mr D.'

'Yes, bye.'

Waving as Austin danced out, letting a loud blast of Kanye West in before the door swung shut behind him, Leonard put the paracetamol bottle back in the cabinet and went to get the bag of ice that he'd come for. Alone now, paranoia reared its mocking head, and he wondered if Austin's invitation had been innocent or if he were playing some sort of game. But surely not, because he'd never been anything but polite, so why would he suddenly turn on Leonard now? And Austin had asked Leonard to keep it quiet, so it was unlikely that *he* would run around starting sordid rumours. But you never could tell, so maybe it was best not to think about it for the time being. Not until he was sure that there was no ulterior motive behind it, because the last thing he needed was for anybody to get the wrong idea.

'What on earth have you been doing?' Maurice demanded when Austin got back behind the bar. 'And what on earth do you think you *look* like?' he said then, looking him up and down with a sneer of disgust. 'This is *my* bar, not some sleazy little dive running a wet T-shirt competition!'

'Keep your hair on,' Austin snapped back. 'I was talking to Mr Drake, if you don't mind. And as for this –' he plucked at the T-shirt. 'Some dick-head spilled red wine all over me, so what did you want me to do? Carry on serving in it?'

'Don't swear,' Maurice hissed, stomping away. 'You sound and *look* like a little guttersnipe!'

'Let's not *mince* our words, eh, Maurice?' Austin called after him, grinning knowingly.

Turning on his heel, Maurice marched back to him and thrust his face into his, spitting, 'Fuck off! I don't want you on my bar.'

'Tough tits!' Austin spat back. 'Jenna *told* me to come down, because *you*'re not capable of running the bar without JoJo, and I'm the next best thing – so there!'

'If you do not get out from behind my bar right this instant, I will not be held responsible for my actions,' Maurice warned, his eyes bulging from their sockets.

'Oh?' Austin folded his arms, his head wobbling like a *Jerry Springer Show* guest. 'And since when was it *your* bar? Did *you* pay for it? No, I didn't *think* so. It's *Jenna*'s bar, and *she* sent me down.' Holding his hand up palm out when Maurice opened his mouth to reply, he said, 'Say it, don't spray it. And, anyway, I'm not interested. I didn't want to work on this poxy bar to start with, so I'm going back to *my* bar, and you can explain to Jenna why *your* lousy bar fell apart without me!'

Flouncing out from behind the bar then, Austin walked away with his head held high until he was sure that Maurice could no longer see him. Then, giggling, he ran the rest of the way up the stairs.

Frowning when Austin came bounding over to the bar, Kalli swiped her hair back from her face with the back of her hand. 'I hope you haven't come to bother me. You might not be busy downstairs, but I'm run off my feet up here.'

'Well, Cinders, you're in luck, 'cos Buttons is

home from the ball,' Austin said, leaping over the bar.

'Pack that in,' Kalli scolded, glancing around in case anyone had seen.

'Oh, don't you start,' Austin moaned. 'I had enough of that off Maurice. I was made up when he kicked me off his bar, but I might as well go back if you're just gonna be miserable.'

Tutting, Kalli pushed him out of the way so she could get at the spirit bottles behind him. 'What happened?'

'I got red wine knocked all over me,' Austin explained indignantly. 'So I had to go and rinse it out, yeah? Anyway, the minute I get back, the ugly cunt starts having a go at me, saying it's not a sleazy club doing wet T-shirt competitions, and calling me a guttersnipe – whatever the fuck one of *them* is. And then he tells me to fuck off out of his bar, or he won't be responsible for his actions. So, *I* said, "Oh, right, so it's *your* bar now, is it? I don't *think* so, matey!"'

'Great,' Kalli murmured, rolling her eyes. 'Just what Jenna needs right now. She sent you down there because she knew they'd struggle, so who'll suffer if it gets out of hand now?'

'Maurice,' Austin declared self-righteously.

'No, *Jenna*,' Kalli corrected him. 'Her bar, her club, *her* profits dropping because her staff are unreliable. And if her profits drop, so will your wages. Remember how bad it was getting before she took Mr Allen on as a partner?'

'Oh, per-*lease*!' Austin groaned. 'Let's not *exaggerate*, or anything.'

'Are you going back down?' Kalli asked, pushing him aside again.

'No, I am *not*,' Austin stated adamantly. 'Even if I wanted to, I couldn't, 'cos Maurice is out for my blood now – the big fat poof!'

'Right, fine,' Kalli said. 'I'll send Diane down. But if you're staying, you'd better make yourself useful, and no messing about.'

'*Moi*?' Austin gasped. 'You know you wouldn't have me any other way.'

'I know I'll be glad when you grow up,' she retorted softly. '*And* when you start taking some responsibility,' she added, giving him a pointed look. 'That electric bill hasn't gone away just because you turned it upside down and shoved it under the bread bin, you know.'

'Nag, nag, nag,' Austin droned, covering a mock-yawn with his hand. '*Bor*-ing!'

'Oi!' Kalli slapped him hard on his bare arm. 'I'm serious.'

'You always are these days,' Austin moaned sulkily. 'Where's my fun little gal pal gone?'

'She'll be in the flaming bin with all our stuff

if you don't get your act together and start paying your share of the bills,' Kalli snapped. 'The landlord came round when you were chasing Xavier around the other day. He said—'

'Yes, I know what he said,' Austin cut in. 'You have told me a million times already.'

'So, what are you going to do about it?'

'Fucking hell, man! I might as well be straight, putting up with shit from me bird, the way *you* go on!' Austin grumbled. 'But if you'd quit nagging for long enough, I *was* about to tell you to stop worrying, 'cos I'm going to sort it all out.'

'How?'

'Never you mind.'

'What are you talking about?' Kalli demanded, peering at him. 'You'd best not be planning to do anything stupid, because you know they've been checking the till rolls every night since Mr Allen came in. If there's a discrepancy, he'll be all over it till he finds out who did it.'

'When you've quite finished, you suspicious little bitch,' Austin said, giving her a mock-offended look. 'I have *not* had my fingers in the till, and if you ever accuse me of it again I'll slap you so hard your eyes will be round in the morning!'

'All right, if it's not that, what is it?'

'Nothing yet,' Austin gave her a mysterious

smile. 'But watch this space, 'cos I'm looking to get me a sugar daddy.'

'Oh, Austin.'

'Never mind *Oh, Austin.* I deserve someone nice after that little prick messed me about. I'm sick of always giving, giving, giving.'

'Stop being such a drama queen,' Kalli scolded. 'And don't you dare go after a rich man from this club, or Mr Allen will skin you alive.'

'Who mentioned *this* club?' Austin said, his face a picture of wounded innocence. 'If you must know, I'm going out after work. And when I find someone, I'm gonna rub him right in Xavier's ugly little mush. You can stand here worrying about bills and landlords if you want, but I've had it with struggling. It's time someone took care of *me* for a change.'

Shaking her head when he flounced away, Kalli sighed. She hoped he was only sounding off after being dumped by Xavier. But if he wasn't, she had a feeling that he would end up with a whole heap of trouble on his hands. Because Austin never did anything by halves; he always had to take everything to the extreme.

'Showtime!' Grinning, Tony popped his head back into the dressing room. 'Are we ready?'

'I am,' JoJo said, jerking her head in Vanessa's

direction. 'Don't know about her, though. She's well sick.'

'Nerves?' Tony asked, his grin slipping.

'Probably,' Vanessa muttered, clutching her stomach. 'I've never done anything like this before.'

'Aw, you'll fly through it,' Tony assured her, coming in and clapping a reassuring hand down on her shoulder. 'Would I have picked you if I didn't think you could do it?'

'No, but—'

'But nothing,' Tony said firmly. 'You're the girls I wanted, because you're the best. Now get yourself up and give yourself a good jiggle about, 'cos I've got twenty-five horny old men waiting to be shown the time of their lives. So get out there, and blow the false teeth right out of their heads!'

'If they give us money, can we keep it?' JoJo asked, giving him a flash of tit when she put her hand into her costume to adjust herself.

'You earn it, you keep it,' Tony told her, thinking that he might just give this one a bit of what she was looking for one of these days. She had something about her. Kind of reminded him of Melody before she turned all Hollywood on him. And her breasts were decent enough. Bit of surgery, they'd be spectacular.

'Hear that?' JoJo gave Vanessa a nudge. 'We earn it, we keep it. And there's some serious money out there, Van. How hard is it gonna be to get them to get their wallets out? They'll probably have a heart attack with a flash of boob, never mind the rest. It'll be a doddle.'

'Attagirl.' Tony gave her an approving wink. 'Leave you to sort her out, shall I?'

'No, I'm all right now,' Vanessa said, taking a deep breath and standing up. 'I'm nervous, but I'm always the same when I get on stage. I'll be fine when I get started.'

'What's that about stage?' Tony asked, only half listening as he cracked the door to look out at the 'crowd'.

'She's a singer,' JoJo told him. 'Lovely voice. Does all that Motown, and old soul stuff.'

'Really?' Tony turned back. 'That's interesting. I reckon we could do something with that. Get you a little rig-up; give the old guys a bit of a cabaret. What do you think?'

'What, instead of the other stuff?' Vanessa asked.

'Maybe.' Tony shrugged.

'Hey, that's not fair,' JoJo complained. 'I'm not doing it by myself.'

'You'll do whatever I tell you to,' Tony told her sharply. 'But we'll stick to the plan for tonight. Talk about the singing tomorrow. And you,' he said directly to JoJo now. 'Come see me later, 'cos we got some things to sort out.'

'I didn't mean anything,' JoJo said quickly, scared by the intensity in his dark eyes. 'I was only sounding off.'

'Yeah, well, we'll talk later,' he said. 'For now, you can get your asses out there and give your audience something to dream about.'

After closing, Austin told Kalli that he was going on to a club and would be home in a few hours. Waving her off in her cab, he waited until she was out of sight and then nipped around to the yard. Standing in the dark alley outside the gate, he hopped from foot to foot, waiting for Leonard to come out and get into his Jag, which was still parked up.

Cursing when somebody walked out of the back door into the path of the security lights, flooding the yard and alley with brightness, he pressed himself back against the wall and waited to see who it was. Luckily, it was Leonard.

Unlocking the gate, Leonard pulled it open and went to his car. Switching his headlights on, he reversed out into the alley and got out again to close the gate. Jumping when Austin stepped out of the shadows, he cried, 'Oh, my good Lord! What on earth are you doing there? I thought I was being attacked.'

'I'm sorry,' Austin said, his fearful eyes

swivelling every which way. 'I was being chased, so I ran down here to hide, but the gate was locked so I couldn't get into the yard. I've just been hiding in the shadows.'

'Are you all right?' Leonard asked, full of concern. 'Who was chasing you?'

'Some men,' Austin told him, shivering visibly. 'But don't worry about it. You get yourself off home to Mrs D. I'll just stay here until I know they've gone.'

'I'm not leaving you in this state,' Leonard said, nervous himself now. 'Get into the car. I'll take you home.'

Folding his arms now, Austin shook his head. 'No, I couldn't ask you to do that. I'll be fine.'

'I insist,' Leonard said, getting back into the car and pushing the passenger door open.

Taking a last look around, Austin got in, saying, 'I'm really sorry about this, Mr D. I wasn't expecting you to do anything.'

'It's not a problem,' Leonard assured him, activating the central locking and easing out of the alleyway onto the road. 'Where to?'

'You can drop me on Kingsway, at the roundabout at the Levenshulme end – if you don't mind?' Austin said, settling back into the leather seat and gazing around. 'Wow, nice car. Is that a DVD player?'

'Yes, but I've never actually used it.'

'How about the CD player? You must have CDs.'

'Probably nothing to your taste,' Leonard said, overly conscious of his size in the confined space. 'I tend to listen to boring old stuff when I'm in the car, I'm afraid.'

'Like what?'

'Oh, you won't have heard of any of them.'

'Try me.'

Shrugging, Leonard said, 'Etta James. Ray Charles. Barbra Streisand.'

'You're kidding me,' Austin yelped delightedly. 'Streisand's an absolute diva; gays *love* her. And didn't you see that film called *Ray* with Jamie Foxx? The man was the *bomb*!'

'You really like it?' Leonard asked, his eyebrows raising with surprise. 'I was sure I was the last person alive who appreciated good music. Avril detests it, says it's too old-fashioned. And people at the club seem to prefer much more modern stuff.'

'Yeah, well, course,' Austin said, opening the glove compartment in search of CDs. 'They go there to dance, don't they? But you'd be surprised what they listen to when they go home. Loads of my friends like trance and techno when they're out zinging off their boxes, but they shove Will

Young and Kylie on when they get in and want to come down.'

'I see,' Leonard murmured, not understanding a word of it.

'Oh, wow,' Austin yelped, finding a Streisand CD and reading down the titles. 'God, I love this album. Can you put it on?'

'Yes, of course,' Leonard said, taking the CD and slotting it into the machine.

'Man, listen to *that*,' Austin groaned, leaning his head back as the first haunting strains of 'The Way We Were' seeped in through the speakers like liquid gold. 'That's some expensive system you've got there.'

'Bang and Olufsen,' Leonard told him proudly. 'I had it fitted when I bought the car. No point settling for inferior quality on those long journeys.'

'You must have some dosh,' Austin said, quickly adding, 'Not that I'm being nosy, or anything. But, well, you can tell you're minted. You've only got to look at your clothes; and you've got a dead posh voice, too. I bet you went to university, and everything, didn't you?'

'Well, yes, I did my time,' Leonard admitted modestly. 'Three years at Oxford.'

'Check the brainbox,' Austin said, laughing softly. 'So, what did you do before you came to Zenith?'

'I was a politician,' Leonard told him, resting

his arm on the door now and driving one-handed as he reached into his pocket for his cigarettes. 'I used to be on TV quite a lot.'

'So you're famous?'

'Moderately so.' Leonard smiled. 'Before your time, though.'

'See, that's what I mean about you,' Austin said, gazing at him admiringly. 'If you look at you, you're just any old posh man – well, not old, but you know what I mean. Then you get talking to you, and find out all this stuff you're into, and it's like, *wow*! I mean, I'd never have guessed you had such cool taste in music. I'd have expected you to be into really boring old white-man stuff.'

Leonard was flushed with pleasure. Nobody had ever described him as *cool* before, and he would never have expected it from a trendy young boy like Austin. Opening the cigarette packet, he offered one to him.

'Nah, I don't do straights,' Austin said, sliding one out of the pack anyway. 'I'll light yours for you, though – seeing as you're driving.'

Taking the lighter, he let his fingers graze Leonard's thumb, smiling to himself when the older man didn't immediately jerk his hand away. Good. Leonard was starting to relax. Handing the cigarette to him, Austin rested his head back again and sang along to 'You Don't Bring Me Flowers'.

'You have a very nice voice,' Leonard commented, admiring the way that Austin did both the male and female parts. 'Have you ever considered taking it up professionally?'

'God, no. Karaoke's enough for me,' Austin said. 'There's a pub in the Village where we all go on a Thursday. It's run by a trannie called Marilyn, and everyone gets up and does a bit. You should come some time, you'd love it. They do all this kind of stuff.'

'Sounds nice.'

'It's *fab*. And everybody's dead laid-back. None of that nudging and winking, and "Ooh, what's he doing in a place like this?" Everyone just goes to have a good time, and your business is *your* business, know what I mean?'

'I think so,' Leonard murmured.

'Well, any time you fancy it,' Austin said. Humming along to the music for a while, he said, 'So, Mrs D does charity work, does she?'

'Yes. Spring and summer are her busiest seasons,' Leonard told him. 'As soon as the sun comes out, you can guarantee that I won't see her for weeks on end. She's invariably already left the house when I wake up in the mornings and, now that I'm involved with the club, she's usually tucked up in her bed by the time I get home, so our paths rarely cross.'

'Ahh,' Austin said sympathetically. 'I bet you really miss her, don't you?'

'Mmm,' Leonard murmured beside him. 'Well, here we are,' he said then, turning onto Kingsway. 'Where would you like me to stop?'

'Anywhere here,' Austin said, sounding disappointed that the ride was at an end.

Pulling up, Leonard glanced out through the window at the deserted street. 'Are you sure you'll be all right? I can take you to your house, if you like?'

'Best not,' Austin said, smiling sheepishly. 'I don't want anybody thinking anything if they see us in the car together. It'd be all over the club by tomorrow that we were having an affair, or something. And I'm sure you don't need that, do you? And I'd hate for you to stop talking to me just because other people can't keep their opinions to themselves.'

Leonard's heart was hammering in his chest. The boy genuinely liked him, and was trying to protect him. There were no games being played; no danger of turning up at the club to find his reputation in tatters. No danger of Avril finding out.

'I, er, have to pass this way on my way home, you know,' he said quietly. 'So, why don't I, um . . . well, I could give you a lift after work, couldn't

I? Save you having to waste your money on cabs.'

'Really?' Austin peered at him as if it was the kindest thing anybody had ever said to him. 'Oh, wow, that'd be great. But what about your wife? Wouldn't she mind having me in the car?'

'Well, actually, now you mention it, she probably would,' Leonard said, tapping his fingers on the steering wheel. 'Probably best if we restrict it to when I'm alone, then. Like you said, we wouldn't want people to gossip, would we?'

Gazing at him, Austin sniffed softly. 'You know what, Mr D, you're one of the nicest men I've ever met. I'd give you a hug, but I don't want to scare you off.'

Swallowing hard, glad of the masking darkness, Leonard said, 'I'm not easily scared.'

'Oh, well, go on, then,' Austin giggled, lurching across to Leonard's side of the car and throwing an arm around his neck, his other hand accidentally-on-purpose landing on Leonard's thigh, high up. Near the groin.

17

JoJo and Vanessa couldn't resist nipping into Zenith to show off before going round to The Diamond on Sunday night. Going in through the kitchen door, knowing that all the other waiting staff would be in there getting changed, JoJo coughed loudly and struck a pose in the doorway before strutting into the centre of the room, calling out, 'All hail Queen JoJo and Princess Vanessa!'

Smiling smugly when everyone surrounded them to admire their new shoes and clothes, all wanting to know how they'd managed to afford them, they would say nothing, except that Tony Allen was the best boss – ever!

They had earned themselves a nice little wedge the night before, and all they'd had to do was lap-dance for a load of horny old men. Vanessa had hated the dancing, but she'd got on with it, knowing that she wouldn't have to do it for long if Tony went ahead with the idea of the cabaret. And she'd been more than happy when they'd hit the shops today and she'd realised that she didn't have to buy the cheapest of everything, because they would probably earn as much again tonight. Plus, Tony had lined up a private session for them with an old judge at a hotel later in the week – a session which, he had promised, would be very profitable.

JoJo had been nervous when Tony had called her into the dressing room after hours. But she'd soon cheered up when she'd realised that he wasn't going to bollock her – even more so when he'd slipped her an extra fifty for one little blow job. If things went on like that, her days of scrimping and scraping on her poxy waitress wages would be long gone.

They were still showing off when Austin came in a few minutes later. Giving their shoes a cursory glance, he sniffed dismissively and plonked his foot on a chair, casually examining his nails as everyone turned their attention to his new trainers.

'Wow, man, they're *bum*!' one of the waiters said enviously. 'I saw them in Foot Locker the other day. They cost, like, one-sixty, don't they?'

'Uh huh,' Austin drawled, as if the money meant nothing. 'But you've got to pay if you want the best in this life.'

Hanging back on the edge of the circle, Kalli narrowed her eyes suspiciously. Where had he got the money to be buying expensive trainers? And if he was that well off, why hadn't he paid the bills instead of treating himself? There was something funny about this. Last night he'd said that he was going to get himself a sugar daddy, but she knew he hadn't been to a club to find one, because he'd got back to the flat just one hour after she had. So he wouldn't have had time.

Pushing the door open just then, Fabian came in and glared at the staff. 'Oh, so this is where you're all hiding, is it? You *do* know we open in fifteen minutes?' Standing back as they trooped out, he raised an eyebrow at JoJo and Vanessa. 'Are you supposed to be here?'

'We're fine, thanks for asking,' JoJo replied cockily. 'Our club doesn't open till eleven, so we can do what we want.'

'Not in here, you can't,' Fabian retorted, looking them up and down, taking in all the new gear they were wearing. And what had they done to get the money for *that*? he wondered. There was no way that Tony Allen was stupid enough to pay them up front – or that much – for waitressing. So what else was going on behind that closed door?

Staring insolently back at him, JoJo said, 'Something taking your fancy, Fabian?'

'It's Mr King to you,' he snapped. 'And no, it bloody well isn't taking my fancy. Quite the contrary, in fact.'

'You can't talk to me like that,' JoJo retorted,

facing up to him in the knowledge that she had powerful friends now. 'I don't work for *you* any more, I work for *Tony*.'

'You work for *me*,' Jenna corrected her, having come in just in time to hear what JoJo was saying. 'Which, in turn,' she added frostily, 'means that Mr King is still your manager – in here, *or* in there. Understood?'

'Yes,' JoJo murmured, dropping her gaze.

'Good,' Jenna said, nodding towards the back door now. 'Off you go, then.'

'Out the back?' JoJo gasped. 'But it's raining. Can't we just go through the club?'

'No, you can't,' Jenna said firmly. 'The adjoining door stays shut during club hours – as I'm sure you've already been told. If that's a problem for you, I suggest you go straight there in future, instead of coming in here bothering people.'

Gritting her teeth, JoJo turned on her new heels and marched out with her nose in the air. Just *wait* till she was Tony's proper girlfriend. See if that pair of dipsticks ever dared talk down to her like that again!

Smiling nervously at Jenna, Vanessa said, 'Sorry,' then followed her friend out.

'Cheeky bitch,' Fabian muttered when the door slammed shut. 'She's lucky you came in when you did.'

'Don't let it get to you,' Jenna told him, guessing that he must be even more annoyed to hear the insolence in JoJo's voice just now than she had been. The girl obviously thought she was onto a good thing working for Tony, but Jenna wasn't having her coming in here rubbing it in everyone's face. And she certainly wasn't going to let her get away with being disrespectful to management.

'Any idea what's going on over there?' Fabian asked now. 'Only I couldn't help noticing what those two were wearing just now. Obviously new, as well, which they certainly couldn't afford on their wages. Doesn't that strike you as odd?'

'I've got no idea what they're doing,' Jenna admitted guardedly, not really wanting to get into any sort of speculation with him – although she was wondering much the same herself. 'I'm just going to grab a quick coffee while we've still got time,' she said then, changing the subject. 'Would you like one?'

'No, thanks.' Fabian glanced at his watch. 'I'd best go out front and make sure everyone's where they're supposed to be.'

'All right. Well, I'll be out as soon as I've had this,' Jenna said, switching on the kettle.

Following Austin when he rushed into the foyer to show his new trainers off to the girl on the pay-desk, Kalli grabbed him. 'I want a word with you.'

'Not now,' he said, wrenching his arm out of her grip. 'I've only got a minute.'

'I don't care,' she hissed, jabbing a finger at his feet. 'I want to know where you got the money from.'

'I told you last night,' Austin whispered, wishing she'd pack in glaring at him in front of everyone like a tiny little monster. 'I found a nice old man to take care of me.'

'Where?' Kalli demanded disbelievingly. 'You weren't out long enough to go to a club. So, unless you picked one up on the street, you're lying.'

'For your nosy information,' Austin told her, 'I *did* meet him on the street, after you took off in the cab last night. I already knew him, but we just haven't *talked* before.'

'And you *talked* last night, did you?'

'We sure did.' Austin grinned. 'And then some.'

'And he gave you money?'

'Enough to buy these *and* pay the bills. Which is exactly what I'm planning to do first thing Monday, so you can stop nagging now, can't you?'

'You are disgusting,' Kalli snapped, her lips as tight as a drawstring purse. 'That's prostitution.'

Widening his eyes, Austin drew his head back. '*Whoa* there, Miss Dynamite! Isn't that a bit kettle-potty?'

'Don't you *dare* compare what you've done to what happened to me,' Kalli warned him, her eyes sparking with hurt and anger. 'You had a choice, *I* didn't!'

Bringing both hands up to his mouth, Austin said, 'Oh, God, Babe, I'm sorry. I should never have said that. I didn't mean it.'

'Didn't you?' Kalli said, still peering at him with pain-filled eyes. 'I wonder sometimes. But, no, you're right. It's got nothing to do with me. You can do whatever you want.'

Reaching out as she turned to walk away, Austin took one of her hands in his. 'Let's not fall out, sugarplum. I'm doing this for you as much as for me. Honest, I'm really gonna pay the bills on Monday. You don't even have to pay me back.'

'I've already got my share, thank you,' Kalli told him curtly.

'Well, keep it. Buy yourself something nice.'

'No, thanks. If I want anything, I'm quite happy waiting until I can afford it.'

'Okay, fine,' Austin said, losing patience. 'You play the martyr if you want, but I've done nothing wrong, so don't think I'm going to grovel. And it's not dirty, because I really like him – so there!'

Watching as he stomped away, Kalli exhaled loudly. She didn't agree with what he was doing, but she sincerely hoped that he did like this new man of his, because it would just be too nasty for words to have taken money off him otherwise.

Opening the door just then, Bobby stuck his head inside and looked around. Seeing Kalli, he waved her over.

'Do us a favour, and go tell Jenna there's a bloke out here asking to see her.'

'Sure,' Kalli said wearily. 'Who is it?'

'Dunno.' Bobby shrugged. 'Some black guy. He reckons he's been told to come and see her about picking up some stuff an old DJ called Victor Brown left here. Can you go now, though? Only we'll be opening in a minute, and them at the front of the queue are gonna get funny about him walking in ahead of them.'

'Won't be a minute,' Kalli said, already setting off.

Jenna had just sat down with her coffee when Kalli popped her head round the door.

'Sorry to disturb you, but there's somebody out front asking to see you.'

'They'll have to wait,' Jenna said, taking a sip of the coffee. 'This is the first cup I've had all day.'

'I think you should come,' Kalli urged. 'I think it might have something to do with Vibes.'

'Oh?' Jenna immediately put the cup down and stood up. 'Why, what did he say?'

'I haven't actually spoken to him, but he told Bobby he's been asked to come and see you about something you're storing for an old DJ called Victor Brown. Bobby wouldn't let him in because we're not open yet, but he told me to let you know he's out there.'

Thanking her, Jenna rushed to the foyer and told Bobby to let the man in. She felt ridiculously nervous all of a sudden, because Vibes hadn't been in touch for months, and their last conversation had been so stilted and short that she hadn't dared ring him in case he'd decided to cut ties with her.

The man was tall and pleasant-looking, and when he spoke Jenna heard that he had the same soft American accent as Vibes. She wondered if Vibes had actually sent him over to get his stuff. Or, worse, had he come, too, and was waiting around the corner somewhere so that he didn't have to see her? Oh, God! He must really hate her. And, what about this man did *he* know her shameful secret too?

'Hi,' the man said, his eyes smiling as he held out his hand. 'It's Jenna, isn't it? I have seen you before, but we didn't actually meet.'

'Oh?' Jenna gazed up at him questioningly.

'New Year's morning. You gave Vibes a lift home.'

Remembering, Jenna said, 'Ah . . . you must be one of the men in the garden?'

'Running around with the Super-Soaker,' he admitted, grinning sheepishly. 'Yeah, that was me.'

Just then Bobby opened the door and tapped his watch.

Nodding, Jenna turned back to the man and said, 'I think we'd best get out of the way. It'll get rather crowded in here in a minute.'

'And I'll probably get lynched for jumping the queue,' he said, looking around as the first people came through the door.

'We'll go to my office,' Jenna said, waving him through the clubroom door. 'Sorry,' she said then. 'I didn't ask your name.'

'It's Kenneth,' he told her, gazing around. 'Hey, this looks great. I came in once, when Victor first started here, but it looks way different now.'

'Thanks,' Jenna said, a confused frown on her brow. 'Sorry, did you just say your name was Kenneth?'

'Yeah, that's right.' He looked down at her with a half-smile. 'Don't tell me Vic's been bad-mouthing me?'

'No, nothing like that,' she assured him, opening the door to the offices. 'I just thought Kenneth was his son's name, that's all.'

'He doesn't have a son,' Kenneth told her quietly as he followed her up the stairs.

'Oh, I see,' Jenna murmured. 'I must have

misunderstood. When he was talking about the baby, he mentioned Kenneth, and I assumed it was another child. Sorry.' Unlocking her office door, she went in, switched the light on and waved him towards the couch. 'Can I get you a drink?'

'A light beer would be good,' he said. 'But I'm cool with whatever if you haven't got any. Neat shot,' he said then, looking at the picture of the tramp on the wall. 'Sure looks happy.'

'Simple pleasures,' Jenna said, pouring him a brandy and handing it to him. 'No beer, I'm afraid.'

Thanking her, Kenneth went and sat down. 'Sorry for dropping in at such an awkward time,' he said when she joined him. 'I came earlier, but I couldn't get an answer, so I thought I'd best try again when I knew someone would be here. I just wanted to set up a time to come get Vic's stuff out of your way. He was concerned that he'd left it too long already.'

'It's not been any trouble,' Jenna replied, her mind whirring with questions. 'I, er, haven't actually spoken to him for a while. I assume he's been busy with his family?'

Looking at her, a flicker of sadness came into Kenneth's eyes. 'He hasn't told you, has he?'

'Told me what?' Jenna asked, aware that she was gripping her glass a little too tightly. Could it be that Vibes's wife had found out about the kiss and was giving him a hard time? She didn't want to be responsible for causing them trouble.

'His family are dead,' Kenneth explained quietly.

'Oh, my God,' Jenna gasped, instinctively putting a hand to the necklace that she hadn't taken off since Vibes had fastened the catch. 'That's terrible. How? *When?* He sounded fine last time I spoke to him. Did something happen after that?'

'It was three years ago,' Kenneth told her, sighing heavily. 'A gang broke into their house while Vic was out playing a gig. They were actually looking for the house next door but got into theirs by mistake. Vic's kid brother must've confronted them, and they shot him. Then they went on to kill his mom, his wife, and his daughter, before going after the guy they really wanted and taking off.'

'So they got away with it?' Jenna asked, her face completely drained of colour.

'For a while.' Kenneth nodded slowly, his eyes dark with painful memories. 'But they got caught a few months ago. That's why Vic went back so fast – for the case.'

'I didn't know,' Jenna murmured, shaking her head. 'I can't believe he's been walking around with this for so long without telling us. It must have been killing him.'

'It damn near did,' Kenneth confirmed softly.

'That's why he came to England in the first place. Me and Gina made him come, because we knew he'd never get over it if he didn't get a break from that place.'

'So Gina's *your* wife,' Jenna said, putting the pieces together. 'And the teething baby?'

'Mine.' Kenneth smiled. 'Not teething any more, though, I'm glad to report. Sleep's never felt so good.'

'I bet,' Jenna said, still reeling from what she'd heard. 'So, how is Vibes?' she asked, thinking that it probably sounded strange to Kenneth because he called his friend by his given name. But she couldn't bring herself to do the same. 'Have you heard from him recently?'

'Yeah, he called this morning. The case has been dragging on because of conflicting witness statements, or whatever, but the prosecution think they've got it nailed now. The jury have been out for the weekend, but they should be ready to give their verdict tomorrow.'

'I hope it turns out the way he wants it to,' Jenna said quietly. 'What will he do after it's finished?'

'I don't think he's really thought about it yet,' Kenneth said. 'But he'll have all the time in the world once this is out of the way. It's always been there in the back of his head, stopping him from moving on. But once it's done, he can start over.'

'So he's not made any plans to come and stay with you again?'

Sighing, Kenneth shrugged. 'He's more than welcome, but it'd have to be *his* decision. No pressure.'

Sensing that he was warning her not to expect too much, Jenna said, 'Do you think it would be all right if I called him? Just to say hello – let him know that we're all still thinking about him. He was very popular here – everyone would be devastated to know that he was going through something like this on his own.'

'I'm sure he'd love to hear from you, but I'd leave it for now,' Kenneth advised, his voice soft. 'Just till they get the verdict.'

'Of course.' Jenna nodded. 'But do you think *you* could let me know what happens?' Getting up, she went to her desk and jotted her numbers down. 'These are my mobile, office and home numbers. I'll always be near one or other of them. I just want to know he's all right.'

'Sure.' Taking the numbers, Kenneth smiled. 'Soon as *I* hear, you'll hear.'

Thanking him, Jenna sat back down. Then she said, 'About his stuff, by the way. When he left it, he said he didn't want to leave it at the house because there wasn't enough room. Is that still an issue?'

'Well, there's no room inside,' Kenneth admitted. 'Especially now Gina's pregnant again.'

'Really?' Jenna smiled. 'Congratulations.'

'Thanks.' Kenneth gave a proud grin. 'Wasn't planned, but, hey . . . God and his mysterious ways, huh? Anyway, I'm gonna make some space in the garage for it. Vic was stressing, 'cos he promised he'd send over for it. But he's been stuck in the courthouse almost every day, and catching up on his sleep when he's not, so he hasn't managed to sort anything out yet.'

'It's not a problem, it being here,' Jenna told him. 'I honestly don't mind. It's quite safe, and definitely not in my way.'

Shrugging, Kenneth said, 'Okay, well, I'm sure he won't mind if you don't.' Finishing his drink, he put the glass down on the table. 'I guess I'd best let you get on, then. I'll give you a call as soon as I hear anything, and I'll tell him you were asking about him.'

'Send him my love,' Jenna said, standing up to show him out. '*Everyone*'s love,' she added quickly, not wanting him to think that she was planning to make a move on Vibes now that she knew his situation.

'I'll do that.' Kenneth smiled. She obviously had feelings for Vic and, if he was any judge, it was mutual. She seemed like a real nice woman, and was probably exactly what Vic needed to put his life back together. But it was too early to tell how Vibes would feel when all of this was over.

Coming back into the club when she'd shown Kenneth out, Jenna went up to the VIP bar to tell Kalli what she'd heard.

Kalli was as shocked and upset as Jenna to think that Vibes had been carrying that burden alone for so long. Her eyes immediately brimmed with tears. 'Please let me know when you hear anything,' she said. 'And give him my love when you speak to him. Tell him he *must* come back, so we can take care of him.'

'I'll give him your love,' Jenna assured her. 'But his friend doesn't want to pressure him into making any decisions, so I won't say the rest. Maybe when he's back on his feet and contacts *us*, we can hint that we'd love to see him again.'

'Good idea,' Kalli said, sighing heavily.

'Everything else all right?' Jenna asked perceptively. 'You seem upset about something.'

Pursing her lips, Kalli shook her head. 'Just Austin doing my head in. Nothing new.'

'Oh?' Jenna gave her a sympathetic smile. 'Want to talk about it?'

'No point.' Kalli shrugged. 'He's an idiot, but he's going to have to learn by his own mistakes –

because I'm sick to death of trying to protect him.'

Just then, a group of Manchester City players arrived. In high spirits because they'd won an important match earlier that day, they came up the stairs arm in arm, singing loudly.

'Looks like you're going to have your hands full,' Jenna said, glancing around as the footballers neared the bar. 'I'll leave you to it. Give me a shout if you want to sound off.'

'Thanks,' Kalli murmured, smiling gratefully. Then, switching on the professional smile for the players, she said, 'Evening, boys. What can I get you?'

Leaving her, Jenna strolled around chatting to people for a while. But she wasn't really in the mood for socialising, so she went to her office to get away from it all.

She seemed to have lost all enthusiasm for the club lately, and she wasn't sure why. They were doing fine financially now, and the customer numbers were better than ever. But the place just didn't feel like hers any more, and she resented constantly having to assert her authority with people like Maurice and JoJo.

Maurice was a perpetual pain in the arse with his supercilious sneers and thinly veiled disrespect, but something was really bugging Jenna about JoJo and Vanessa. Like Fabian, she was wondering where they'd got the money for those new clothes. The Diamond was Tony's project, sure, but the staff wages were still going through Zenith's books, so they shouldn't be getting any more than usual. And if they were, it was totally unfair to the rest of the staff – and totally out of order on Tony's part because Jenna had not agreed to that. She'd have to ask him about it, but she wasn't looking forward to it because he was bound to make her feel like she was making a silly fuss about nothing. She couldn't just say nothing, though, because he'd think he had free rein to do whatever he liked. And they were partners – Jenna more so than Tony, albeit by only two per cent – so every decision should be jointly made.

That said, she didn't want to jump in and start shouting the odds when there was so much other stuff going on in her head that might cause her to overreact. Not least the matter of Vibes.

It had been bad enough walking around with the guilt of thinking that he had cut ties with her because of that kiss. But now that Jenna knew about his family, she felt not just sad, and angry that something so terrible had happened to such a good man, but even *more* guilty that she hadn't seen the pain that must surely have been there beneath his smile the whole time she had known him.

*

Just as Jenna left the room, Leonard came in from the kitchen. Keeping his head down, he made his way up to the VIP bar in search of Austin. They had arranged to meet on the corner by the train station after work, but he needed to see him now, to gauge where his head was at after last night's little 'incident'.

Not a lot had actually happened, but it had been enough for Leonard's heart still to be singing when he'd awoken this morning. Thankfully, Avril had been out already, so he hadn't had to suffer her sarcasm or suspicion, and he had spent the day just waiting for night to roll around so he could see Austin again. He couldn't stop thinking about him, but it wasn't just the joy of what had happened between them that was on his mind. It was the worry of what Leonard had learned about Austin's financial state, too.

They had spoken for some time, and Leonard had been dismayed to hear how much of a struggle it was for Austin just to get through each day. Austin had explained that he wouldn't get better wages anywhere else, given his poor upbringing and education, but his acceptance of his situation didn't make Leonard feel any better. Blessed with a wealthy family, a fabulous education, a well-paid career and a substantial inheritance, Leonard had never really believed that people actually lived like

Austin did. In fact, during his time in politics Leonard and his colleagues had heard the same sob stories many times and had never paid them any mind. They believed that the people who complained of poverty were simply greedy layabouts who were unwilling to get off their backsides and support themselves and the multitude of brats they insisted on burdening the system with.

But the boy had quite opened Leonard's eyes to the inequalities that undoubtedly existed. Austin worked harder than most of the politicians Leonard had ever met, for a fraction of the pay, and all because he had never been given the opportunity to better himself. And Leonard felt that the responsibility for this lay partly on his shoulders, for having been a part of the system which kept Austin down. Not the rest of the spongers, just Austin. And now that Leonard had shown the boy a glimpse of how the other half lived by allowing him into his plush car, he couldn't, in all conscience, refuse to help him out.

Which was why he had driven the lad to the cashpoint last night and given him three hundred pounds from his private account. Small change to Leonard, but the look in Austin's eyes had made it feel as though he had given him a million pounds – and Leonard had never felt so good about anything in his life before.

The buzz had lasted right up until he'd arrived at the club tonight. But it had soon been dampened when he saw the looks passing between the blonde slut JoJo and Tony.

It was obvious that something was going on between them, just as it was obvious from her new attire that JoJo had been well paid for whatever it was. And the thought that she had wheedled her way into Tony's wallet sickened Leonard – almost as much as the so-called 'high-class entertainment' that his friends had been subjected to the previous night.

Tony had assured Leonard that the dancing would be completely tasteful and decent. But it had turned out to be little short of porn as the sluts paraded their naked bodies around the small stage. Leonard had been mortified that his friends – some of whom had been his *father*'s friends – had been tricked into paying for such a disgusting spectacle. He could only assume that the tarts had put their clothes back on soon after he had left the room in protest – given that nobody had actually complained. But he thanked God that Tony had decided to make it a men-only club, because if Avril had witnessed the shenanigans there would have been hell to pay.

Spotting Austin behind the bar now, Leonard approached him cautiously. The small Chinese girl was busy at the other end of the bar, and Leonard hoped that she wouldn't turn around and see him. He knew that his face would betray him if she looked at him with those penetrating eyes of hers.

Austin was equally nervous. Casting a quick glance at Kalli to make sure that she wasn't watching, he whispered, 'What are you doing here? I thought we were supposed to be meeting later.'

'Yes, we are,' Leonard whispered back, glad that Austin didn't seem to have changed his mind. 'I just wanted to make sure you were all right, after . . . well – you know.'

Smiling, Austin said, 'Never better. But you'd best go before someone sees us talking and puts two and two together and makes a porn film.'

'Yes, of course,' Leonard said, reluctant to leave now that he had seen the boy but knowing that he must for safety's sake.

'Oh, before I forget,' Austin said as Leonard was about to turn away. 'When you see JoJo, can you tell her I need to see her for a minute after work? I saw her earlier, but Fabulous chased us out before I got a chance to speak to her.'

'Well, I'm not sure *I'll* be speaking to her,' Leonard said, his tone clearly conveying his disapproval of the slut. 'Is it something I can help with?'

'No, it's just something she owes me that I need to get back before she forgets,' Austin said evasively.

'What's she doing in there, anyway?' he asked then, changing the subject before Leonard could ask what it was that she owed. 'Only she came swanning in here like the cat with the cream earlier, showing off her new shoes and stuff, and I was thinking there's no way she got them on our wages.'

'She's doing the same as she was doing in here,' Leonard lied, aware that he was blushing. Not the best of traits for a politician when lying played such a major part in the game, but he hadn't suffered from it so much in those days. Only now, speaking to people he liked on a personal level, had it become a problem.

'Mmm,' Austin murmured disbelievingly. 'Well, I'd have a word with Mr A if I was you,' he cautioned Leonard now. 'Only I know how secretive he's being about his business, and if she's doing nothing different that ain't the impression she's giving everyone in here.'

'Why, what are people saying?' Leonard frowned.

'That it's a whorehouse,' Austin told him quietly, casting another glance at Kalli and seeing that she only had one customer left to serve. 'Look, you'd best go. Kalli'll be over any minute, and she's too nosy.'

'Right you are,' Leonard said, still frowning deeply. 'I'll meet you as arranged.'

'Yeah, see you.'

Kalli reached Austin just as Leonard went down the stairs. 'What did Mr Drake want?'

'Dunno.' Austin shrugged. 'He was looking for Jenna, but I said I haven't seen her.'

Kalli narrowed her eyes. He was lying, she could tell.

'Are you going to stand there staring into space all night?' Austin asked, nudging her. 'Only there's still two hours to go, and a shit-load of glasses to collect.'

'Start collecting, then,' Kalli snapped, marching away. Whatever he was hiding, she would find out sooner or later.

Outside just then, Phil Dixon had his head down and his collar up against the pouring rain as he approached Zenith's front door. Tony had told him not to come to the club, but after several unsuccessful attempts to reach him on the phone over the last few weeks Phil was so pissed off that he'd thrown caution to the winds and had turned up to see him in person.

Bobby was standing in the doorway, his head barely covered by the arch. Looking Phil over when he reached the door, he shook his head. 'Sorry, our kid, you can't come in here wearing trainers.'

'I'm not a punter, I'm here to see Tony,' Phil

told him, taking a last deep drag on his cigarette and flicking it into a puddle.

'Is he expecting you?' Bobby asked, guessing that he wasn't or he'd have told the man to go to the door of The Diamond, which was around the corner, down the dark, narrow alley between Zenith and the café next door.

'He knows me,' Phil said, pulling his sleeve back and glancing at his watch. 'No offence, mate, but I don't wanna be standing around in this all night. Just give him a shout for us, will you? Tell him it's Dix.'

Telling him to wait there, Bobby went inside. Seeing Fabian passing the clubroom door, he called, 'Yo, Fabian. There's a bloke out here asking for Mr Allen. D'you wanna deal with it?'

Already annoyed because Melody had been sitting with Jay Kay and his mates all night, making it impossible to get near her, Fabian tutted loudly. 'Who is it?'

'He said to say it was Dix,' Bobby told him. 'I'm not letting him in, though, 'cos he ain't dressed right.'

Opening the door, Fabian jerked his chin at the man. 'What can I do for you?'

'Nowt,' Phil said, blowing at the raindrops dripping off his nose. 'I want to see Tony, so be a good lad and go tell him Dix is here, will you? And don't take the piss and forget I'm here, or I'll have to start making noise – know what I mean?'

Frowning, Fabian folded his arms, safe in the knowledge that Bobby was right behind him. 'We don't take kindly to being threatened in here, so why don't you go away and come back when you've found your manners? Oh, and change the gear,' he said then, looking Phil up and down. 'We've got a dress code.'

'Bit of a joker, eh?' Phil sneered.

'Oh, yeah, I'm a regular comedian,' Fabian said, his face dead straight. 'But as the manager, it's my decision who does and doesn't get in, so I'd suggest you drop the attitude.'

'Are you for fucking real?' Phil snorted. 'Just get your arse inside and get Tony before I knock you the fuck out, you cunt.'

Peering at him, Fabian was about to tell him to piss off when he caught sight of his gold earring, which had a tiny boxing glove hanging from it – just like the one Jenna had described when she'd been threatened in the yard. Letting his gaze slide surreptitiously down to the man's throat, he saw the thick gold chain, but he couldn't see if there was a dog at the other end of it because the man had the collar of his jacket turned up. It had to be the same man, but why was he here asking for Tony when Tony had supposedly warned him off?

Suspicions seriously roused, Fabian stepped back and opened the door to let the man in.

'Sorry for being irritable,' he said, forcing himself to smile. 'I've been rushed off my feet tonight. But if you'd like to wait here, I'll have somebody find Mr Allen for you.'

''Bout time,' Phil grunted, brushing past him. Inside in the warm, he shook the rain from his hair and flapped his jacket.

Seeing the gold bulldog clear as day now, Fabian told him he wouldn't be a minute. Going to Bobby, who was back outside now, he whispered to him to make sure that the man stayed in the foyer and didn't go wandering. Then he went into the club-room and tried to reach Tony on his mobile. Getting no answer, he snapped his phone shut and gazed around. There was no point trying the adjoining door because they wouldn't answer it, but there was no way he was walking around to The Diamond in the rain, and the doormen would laugh in his face if he tried sending one of them.

Austin passed just then. Grabbing him, Fabian said, 'I need you to go round to the side door and tell Mr Allen that someone called Dix is here to see him.'

'Like this?' Austin gasped, holding his arms out to indicate that he was wearing shorts and a T-shirt. 'I'll get soaked.'

'Just do it,' Fabian snapped.

Sighing loudly, Austin said, 'Right, fine. But don't blame me if I get pneumonia and can't work for a month!'

'Don't worry, I'll have your cards sent on if we don't see you,' Fabian told him, pushing him out through the foyer.

'He won't be a moment,' Fabian said, giving Phil a tight smile. 'If you'll excuse me, I've got a couple of things to do.'

Letting himself into the pay-booth then, so that he would be able to hear what was going on when Tony came back with Austin, he told the cashier that she could go. Sitting on her chair, he sank down as low as he could in the hope that Tony wouldn't notice him, and started bagging up.

Austin was dripping wet when he came back a couple of minutes later. Shaking himself all over the polished floor, he looked around for Fabian. 'Where's he gone?' he asked Phil in a loud whisper.

'No idea,' Phil said, lighting another cigarette. 'Did you find Tony?'

'Oh, are you Dix?' Austin asked, giving him the once-over. 'Yeah, he'll be round in a minute. Couldn't give us a quick drag on your ciggy, could you?' he asked then. 'Only we're not allowed when we're working, and I'm fucking gagging.'

'Knock yourself out,' Phil said, handing him the cigarette.

Turning away from the clubroom door, Austin took several quick drags and fanned the smoke away with his hand before handing it back to Phil. 'Ta for that; I owe you one. Best get back,' he said then. 'If you see the funny fella, tell him to go fuck himself from me, will you?' Giggling then, he said, 'No, don't! I'll only get the sack.'

Smiling slyly, Phil said, 'Don't worry about it, mate.'

In the pay-booth, Fabian pursed his lips furiously. Just wait till he got hold of Austin. The little poof wouldn't know what had hit him!

Tony came in just then. Seeing Phil, he jerked his head and took him off into a corner.

'What the fuck are you playing at? I told you not to show your face in here.'

'So try answering your phone,' Phil retorted gruffly. 'Look, I ain't come for an argument,' he said then. 'I just want what you owe us, 'cos my lads are bugging me for it.'

'I don't appreciate being hassled,' Tony told him darkly. 'I said you'd get it, and you will.'

'Don't take the piss,' Phil hissed. 'It's been fucking ages, and you ain't been in touch once. Anyone'd think you was trying to avoid us, and that ain't on, 'cos we did our bit.'

Sighing, Tony ran a hand through his hair. 'I've had a lot on, it slipped my mind. Anyway, here, I guess you earned it.' Reaching into his pocket, he took out a thick wad of money. Peeling off several notes, he thrust them into Phil's hand, saying, 'There's a bit extra for waiting.'

Glancing down at the money and seeing how much extra there was, Phil grinned widely. 'Anyone else you want heavying, you know where I am.' Holding out his hand then, he said, 'Nice doing business with you.'

Shaking Phil Dixon's hand, Tony showed him out. Turning to Bobby with a furious scowl on his face when Phil had gone, he said, 'Who sent that waiter round to my club?'

'Fabian,' Bobby told him.

'And did he let that other dickhead in here?'

'Er, yeah.'

'Cunt!' Tony growled. 'I'll break his fucking legs when I get my hands on him.'

Marching inside, he stormed through to the clubroom in search of Fabian. Not finding him on the lower floor, he went up to the VIP lounge and stood at the head of the stairs, peering around narrow-eyed.

'Tony!' Brenda Thompson cried, coming over to him and pulling him into a hug. 'You've been neglecting us. Come and have a drink and let's catch up.' Linking her arm through his, she tried to pull him towards her table.

'Sorry, doll, I've got no time,' Tony said, gently peeling her hand off his arm. 'I'm looking for someone.'

'Who?' she asked, not giving up so easily. 'Maybe I've seen them.'

'Fabian,' he said, his teeth gritted.

'The cutie?' Brenda said, sighing lustfully. 'He was here a few minutes ago. I can never see enough of those toned buns of his. They're so delectable, it makes you want to bite them.'

'Huh!' Tony snorted. 'Probably 'cos they see so much action.'

'Excuse me?'

'He's an ass raider,' Tony elaborated scathingly.

'*Fabian?*' Brenda gave a deep husky laugh. 'Don't be ridiculous, darling. The boy's as straight as a die.'

'Believe me, he ain't,' Tony told her. 'Melody's in showbiz back home, and she's got a nose for that kind of thing. Anyway, you've only got to look at him to know he's got more woman in him than man.'

'My darling, I too am in the business,' Brenda reminded him. 'With a good few years on *your* little chickie, I might add. And I assure you that Fabian is no more gay than you or I. He may take care of his appearance,' she went on, with a theatrical shrug. 'But that, my love, is because these young ones have at long last realised that we girlies like a good-looking, sweet-smelling man in our beds, whose hair is clean enough not to stick to our inner thighs like glue and leave us with a nasty mess to clean up afterwards. Anyway,' she said then, flapping her hand, 'he's had several of my girlfriends, so I know he's straight. And they all gave such *glowing* recommendations that I'd be tempted to go for him myself if my little gigolo wasn't already wearing me out. Worth it, though,' she added with a satisfied sigh. 'So very liberating to pay for what you want and not to have to bother with the tedious endearments. Don't you think?'

Tony wasn't listening; he was too busy mulling over what Brenda had just said. If she was telling the truth – and there was no reason for her not to be – then Melody had either been mistaken or had lied outright when she'd told him that Fabian was gay. And he suspected thc latter, because she'd have known full well that he wouldn't have let her dance with the cunt if he'd known that Fabian was straight. He didn't know what kind of idiot they took him for, but they would both be sorry if they'd been fucking around behind his back.

Filled with white-hot fury now when he spotted Melody flirting with a scruffy pop star whom he vaguely recognised, Tony shook Brenda off and made his way over to her table.

'Yo!' he barked, snapping his fingers at her. 'A word.'

'What's the matter, Tony?' Melody said, her eyes huge with fear when he dragged her over into a quiet corner. 'I wasn't doing nothing. He was just telling me about his tour. They've been in LA, and we were—'

'Shut the fuck up,' Tony yelled, gripping her arm tightly. 'I'm not interested in him. I want to know about the other fella – your fucking dancing partner.'

'Fabian?' Melody gasped. 'What do you mean?'

'What's going on with you and him?'

'Nothing!' she yelped when he tightened his grip. 'You're hurting me, Tony!'

'I'll do a damn sight more than hurt you if you fuck me about,' he snarled. 'You told me he was queer.'

'He is,' she whimpered, petrified now. 'Please, Tony, you're hurting me. And people are looking.'

'I don't give a fuck,' he said, bringing his face down close to hers. 'I've just had it on good authority that your friend is no more queer than *me*. So what's the game, Mel? You been fucking around with him?'

'Don't be stupid!' Melody protested, wincing

when he raised his fist. 'Sorry! I didn't mean that. I just meant don't say stupid things. Of course I'm not messing around. Would I risk doing something like that when I know what I'll get? I swear on my mother's life I thought he was gay. If he's not, I didn't know, hon, I honestly didn't. I'll never speak to him again.'

Sidling past them, Austin ran down the stairs. He didn't think he should interfere, but Kalli was concerned that Mr Allen might start beating his girlfriend up and so she'd sent him to get one of the security guards just in case. Legging it down to the foyer now, he pulled the door open and told Bobby what was happening.

Back upstairs, Tony had decided to give Melody the benefit of the doubt – for now. Shoving her away roughly, he said, 'All right, I'll take your word. But if I find out you're lying, you know what's gonna happen.' Giving her a last warning glare, he turned on his heel and marched back down the stairs.

Shoving past Austin who was on his way back in with Bobby, Tony made his way out and walked quickly back round to The Diamond, deep in thought.

Still hiding in the pay-booth, Fabian was shaking. He shouldn't have sent Austin round there, and now that Tony was gunning for him he'd have to stay out of his way until he forgot about it. Which would be kind of difficult, seeing as they both worked here, but would still be better than having his legs broken.

'You been in there the whole time?' Bobby asked when Fabian came out with the money bag in his hands.

'No, I've been out back,' Fabian lied. 'Why?'

'Good job,' Bobby chuckled. 'Mr Allen's in a right strop with you. Apparently he's just had a go at his bird, 'cos she told him you was gay and he's just found out you ain't. Accused her of fucking around with you.' Laughing now, he shook his head. 'You're a right one, you.'

'Aren't you supposed to be outside?' Fabian snapped, fronting it out even though his knees had turned to water.

Waiting until Bobby had gone out, Fabian walked through the club and out through the kitchen door. He didn't know what had just happened with Tony and Melody but he wasn't sticking around to find out. Jenna could lock up. And she could open up tomorrow as well, because there was no way he was coming back until he knew it was safe. Melody wouldn't dare admit it, so hopefully she would convince Tony that it was all in his head. But until Fabian knew for sure that he was out of the firing line, he was on indefinite sick leave.

And there was no way he was risking telling

Jenna about the man with the boxing-glove earring. Not yet, anyway. Much as she probably needed to know, that would be all the excuse that Tony would need to kill him.

Austin was already changed and on his way out of the door when Kalli caught up with him at the end of the night. Pulling him to one side, she said, 'Wait for me.'

'I can't,' he told her, leaning down to kiss her cheek. 'I'm meeting someone, and we're going to a club.'

'We need to talk,' she persisted, trying to hold him there. 'I'm worried about you.'

'Well, don't be,' Austin said irritably. 'It's getting on my nerves. I don't tell *you* who to go out with, so stop trying to tell *me*.'

'I don't want you to get hurt,' Kalli said, looking him straight in the eyes as she added, 'or anyone else.'

'No one's going to get hurt,' he assured her. 'It's nobody's business but mine and his.'

'And what about his wife?' Kalli asked quietly. Shaking her head when she saw the flicker of surprise in his eyes, she said, 'So I'm right. It *is* Mr Drake.'

'Sshhh!' Austin hissed, glancing quickly around.

'Why?' Kalli asked, pain and anger in her eyes. 'If it's all as nice as you were trying to make out earlier, why wouldn't you want the world to know?'

'Don't be stupid,' Austin snapped. 'It *is* nice, and I really like him. But you know exactly why I can't tell anyone, so keep your nose out.'

'You're making a mistake,' Kalli said softly. 'And I'm your friend, so I'm not going to ignore it.'

'Well, you'll have to, if you want to carry on being my friend,' Austin told her bluntly. 'Don't try and make me choose, 'cos you won't like the outcome.'

'You'd really do that?' Kalli gazed defiantly up into his eyes. 'For money?'

'It's not just the money.' Austin sighed heavily. 'I really like him, Kal. But if you can't understand that, there's nothing I can say.'

'You don't even *know* him.'

'Yes, I do. Don't think last night was the first time we've ever talked. You lot have been treating him like shit since he first started coming here, but I've always talked to him, and he's a really nice man.'

'He's an old *married* man,' Kalli reminded him. 'And he's not your type at all. You like dark and handsome. He's blond and fat.'

'You don't have to tell me what he looks like,' Austin retorted. 'I've seen more of him than you have.'

'Don't be disgusting.'

'If you don't like it, mind your own business.' Shrugging, Austin gave her a take-it-or-leave-it look. 'I like him, and I'm not going to stop seeing him. Not for you, or anyone.'

'Well, I hope it's worth it,' Kalli said sadly. 'When his wife finds out, and you're left with nothing but your fancy trainers to remind you of the job you used to have and the *friends* you lost for him.'

'Whatever,' Austin said glibly. 'See you later.'

Using all her self-control to keep herself from crying, Kalli got changed and made her lonely way home, knowing that things would never be the same between her and Austin again. She'd tried her best, but there was nothing more she could do. When this fell apart, as it undoubtedly would, she just hoped that Austin would learn something from it.

'Anybody seen Fabian?' Jenna asked the security guys as they made their way out.

'Yeah, about an hour ago,' Bobby said, sharing a conspiratorial smirk with Flex. 'He wasn't looking too well. Maybe he's in the loos?'

'His car's not out back,' one of the other doormen said, coming through from the kitchen just then. 'I've just been out there checking that the gate got shut behind the staff, and it's deffo gone.'

Tutting softly, Jenna went back up to her office to get her keys. She'd be having words with Fabian in the morning. He might have let her know if he was leaving early. She could have been waiting all night to lock up.

18

Vibes couldn't settle. Sitting in the bar around the corner from the courthouse, he repeatedly checked his mobile to make sure that he hadn't missed the call telling him that the jury were in.

Sipping his beer, he stared at the screen of the TV above the spirit bottles on the other side of the bar. It was on a news channel, but the volume was down. Vibes was trying to lip-read the female newsreader but was finding it impossible because, like most of the women he'd come across since he got home, she talked way too fast. He'd forgotten that about American women. They got so animated about the stupidest things. Aliya had been no better. Much as he'd loved her, the girl could run her mouth off with the best of them when she got to bitching.

Smiling at the memory, Vibes took a sip of his beer – and almost choked when a still photograph came up on the screen. It looked to have been taken in some kind of nightclub, and showed several men sitting around a table, all grinning at something that was resting on the table between them. The image had been blurred, but it didn't take a lot of imagination to guess what it was, nonetheless.

'Yo! Turn the volume up,' Vibes yelled at the bartender. 'The volume, man! Come on!'

'. . . *Trial of Mafia boss Stelios Zagorakis a.k.a. "Zorba"*,' the newsreader was saying, '*who is charged with a variety of offences from kidnap to extortion to murder.*

'This photograph is one of a set recovered by police from a safe found buried beneath Zagorakis's home on the exclusive Palmira Estate complex, and is believed to show the severed head of a rival Mafia boss, Paolo Vitto.

'Police are now trying to locate the other men pictured with Mr Zagorakis, and have today named them as Raoul Perusa, Anthony Cerrullo, Peter Gossam and Edward Derby. They are wanted in connection with what police are estimating could amount to dozens of murders, dating back as far as 1960 when Mr Zagorakis first arrived in the United States. They are also suspected of involvement in the murders of brothers Martin and Deke Johnson, who were in the custody of the US Army at the time of their deaths, being transported to high-security witness-protection units.

'Anybody who knows the men's whereabouts is asked to contact their local police force immediately, but under no circumstances should the men be approached directly, as they may be armed.

'*Well, those are today's headlines,*' the woman said now, smiling widely. '*We'll keep you updated on these, and all the other stories as they come in throughout the day. But now we go to Frank Highfield for the weather . . .*'

Vibes stared at the screen long after the picture had been replaced by a grinning weatherman who was promising a long-awaited break to the heat-wave being suffered across the country. He wasn't certain by any means, because the photo had been a grainy black and white shot, and was obviously a good few years old, but two of the men around that table had looked just like Tony Allen and Eddie. And could it be a coincidence that two of the names given had been Anthony and Edward?

His mobile rang just then, snapping him back to the present.

'They're in,' Molly, the DA's assistant, told him when he answered. 'You okay?'

'Yeah, I'm fine,' Vibes assured her, gathering his things together. 'I'll be two minutes.'

Judge Mackay looked at the written verdict, his expression giving nothing away to Vibes who was staring intently at him. Nodding, he asked for the jury spokesperson to stand.

Vibes could barely breathe as the spokesman began to give the verdicts, and he could hardly hear above the sound of roaring wind in his ears as his heart raced and pounded. But, somehow, above the storm he caught the word *guilty*.

He sat in stunned silence as the judge picked up the gavel and passed sentence: life without parole for each of the five gang members.

Despite Molly's kind assurances, the forensic evidence and the witness statements, from the very start of this trial Vibes had thought that the jury, with its majority of young white males, would swing in the accused's favour, given that two of the gang were also white. But race hadn't reared its ugly head at all, and Vibes was truly humbled by that. *And* truly grateful.

'Man, it's over!' Tyler exclaimed jubilantly, throwing his arms around Vibes. 'It's *over*!'

Shaking his head in disbelief, Vibes stood up. It really was over. Justice had been done, and he was free to start his life again.

'We're all going to the bar around the corner for a celebratory drink,' Molly told him quietly. 'Are you up to it?'

Looking down into her kind eyes, Vibes shook his head. 'I can't face people just now. I've got to . . .' Trailing off, he bit his lip and raised his chin. 'Sorry, I just need to go.'

'I understand,' she said, reaching up to kiss him on the cheek. 'Congratulations – if that's the right thing to say?'

'Thanks,' he murmured, managing to hold it together as he added, 'for everything. I wouldn't have got through it without you.'

'My pleasure,' Molly said, blushing prettily. Dipping her gaze then, she reached into her pocket and took out a card. 'I, er, don't mean to be presumptuous,' she said, handing it to him. 'But if you ever – you know – want to meet up for a drink, or something . . .?'

Taking it only because he didn't want to offend her, Vibes slipped it into his pocket and thanked her again. Going to Tyler then, who was busy shaking hands with everybody on the prosecution team, he said, 'I got to get out of here, man.'

'No problem,' Tyler said, seeing from his face that he was close to the edge.

Back at Tyler's house a short while later, where Tyler's mom Delores and sister Talisha had laid on a fantastic spread of soul food, Vibes sat quietly in a corner, accepting all the handshakes and kisses and good wishes from his old friends and neighbours. This was home, and these were his people, but he'd never felt so alone in his entire life.

Coming over to sit with him after a while, Talisha said, 'So it's over, huh?'

'I guess.' Vibes nodded, sipping his beer straight from the bottle.

'What you gonna do now?' she asked, stretching her long legs out. 'Planning to stay around – I hope?'

Smiling, Vibes reached for her hand. She'd been a pretty, slightly gawky sixteen-year-old kid when he'd left, with a serious crush on him. Nineteen now, she was a beautiful woman, with a low mellow voice, and dreamy nut-brown eyes. Any man would be proud to call her his own, but Vibes's love for her was the brotherly kind – even though it was plain to see that her crush had developed into something more fiery and adult.

'I wasn't sure until this afternoon,' he said, gazing around the room at the people he had known all his life. 'Part of me wanted to stay and put all the bad stuff behind me, but another part wanted to get up and run and never look back.'

'And which part won?' Talisha asked, her fingers entwined in his as though they belonged there.

Looking at her, Vibes smiled fondly. 'You're a

beautiful girl. Why haven't you got yourself a decent boy yet?'

Biting her lip, she smiled shyly. ''Cos I been waiting on you, Victor. You know that.'

'Don't,' he said softly. 'It's a waste of life to wait around on a dream. You got to get yourself out there and live while you got the chance. You know I love you, right?'

Biting her lip now, her eyes moist with tears, she nodded. 'Uh huh.'

'Then do it for me,' he said. 'Stop kicking it with these idiots, and do what your brother did. Move somewhere nice. Start college and get yourself a future. Do anything, but don't wait on me, 'cos I've moved on and I can't turn back.'

'It's the woman who gave you this, isn't it?' Talisha asked, surprising him with her perception as she stroked her fingertip over the face of his watch. 'You think about her most of the time, don't you?'

Sighing, Vibes nodded. 'Yeah, I guess I do.'

'Do you love her?'

'Mmm-hmm.'

'Then go back to her and be happy,' Talisha said quietly, resting her head on his shoulder. 'She must be some kind of special if you feel that way about her. And I'm damn sure she must love you, too, 'cos she'd be crazy not to.'

'I don't think so,' Vibes murmured softly. 'I left it kind of bad with her.'

'How?' Talisha gazed up at him.

'I kissed her,' Vibes admitted, sighing heavily. 'And I shouldn't have, because she's already got a man.'

'Did she slap you?' Talisha asked. 'Scream? Push you away? Tell you you're disgusting?'

'No. But—'

'She loves you,' Talisha stated with certainty.

Smiling, Vibes put his arm around her and hugged her. 'You're one special sister, Tal.'

'I guess,' she murmured, rolling her eyes. 'And I suppose that'll have to do if it's all I'm gonna get. You'd best invite me to the wedding, though, 'cos I ain't letting go of you for nothing.'

'If it ever happens,' Vibes said, sincerely doubting it, 'you'll be the first to know.'

Putting her arm across his stomach now, Talisha cuddled up closer. 'So, when you going?'

'Soon,' Vibes said, feeling a sudden lift in his heart. 'But I'll have to call first, make sure she ain't mad at me. And I need to let Kenneth know what's happened. But first, I need to get me some sleep, or I won't know if I'm coming or going.'

'You can go to my room,' Talisha told him, smiling up at him mischievously. 'Don't worry, I won't follow you. But Mom's used your room as a coatroom so you won't get near the bed.'

Thanking her, Vibes said, 'I don't suppose you've got a TV in there, have you? 'Cos there's something I really need to check out on the news.'

19

Fabian rang Jenna first thing in the morning, waking her up.

'Sorry for taking off like that last night,' he said. 'I wasn't feeling too good.'

'Yeah, Bobby told me you looked ill,' she said, stretching. 'Anyway, it's all right. I was a bit pissed off, but I figured you must have been feeling pretty bad for it to make you leave like that.'

'I, um, had a bit of an embarrassment,' Fabian told her. 'Dodgy stomach.'

'Nasty,' Jenna said sympathetically. 'I don't blame you for going home. Are you feeling any better?'

'Not really,' he lied, rubbing his stomach as he said it. 'Think I might take a couple of days off, if you don't mind.'

'I'm sure I'll manage,' she told him. 'You just stay in bed and sleep it off. And drink lots of water to flush it out.'

'Thanks, I will. And don't worry about the

takings. I'll keep them safe until I can get in.'

'I'd forgotten all about them,' Jenna admitted. 'But don't worry about it. If it stretches on, I'll pop over and pick them up. Hope you're feeling better soon.'

Hanging up when they'd said their goodbyes, she pushed her quilt aside and got up. It would probably do her as much good as him if he had some time off. The way she'd been feeling lately, she'd all but given up on the day-to-day running of the club. Without Fabian to do everything for her, she'd be forced out of the rut she'd dug herself into.

Getting dressed, she had a quick coffee, then went to the club to let the cleaners in. Seeing Tony's car already parked up, she tutted softly. If she'd known he was coming in early she'd have had an extra half-hour in bed.

Making her way up to the office, Jenna was just looking through her bag for her keys when Tony came marching up the corridor towards her with a face like thunder.

'Morning,' she said, glancing around at him. 'I didn't know you were—'

'Where's the cunt?' He cut her off, the ferocity in his voice and eyes making her jump.

'Who?' she asked, frowning up at him.

'That prick, Fabian!' he snarled, his breath

coming hard and fast as he stood over her. 'Where is he?'

'He's not well, so he won't be coming in for a few days,' she told him, glancing down the corridor to where Eddie was leaning against Fabian's open door. 'What have you been doing in there? That's Fabian's private office.'

'He ain't entitled to privacy,' Tony spat, barely controlled rage flashing from his eyes. 'Not when he's been fucking my girlfriend!'

'Are you sure?' Jenna was frowning now. 'I've never seen anything going on between them.'

'That right?' Tony growled, peering down at her.

Thoroughly innocent, Jenna looked right back at him. '*Yes,* that's right. I've never seen or heard the slightest thing to indicate it. Wherever you've got this from, I'm sure you're wrong. Fabian's a very professional—'

'Oh, don't give me that shit,' Tony interrupted, running a hand through his hair. 'And if you didn't know, you obviously ain't got a clue what's going on under your own fucking nose.'

'I resent you speaking to me like this, Tony,' Jenna said quietly. 'I haven't done anything to warrant it, and I'd appreciate it if you'd stop it – now.'

Tony inhaled deeply. Then he jerked his head. 'Come with me.'

Following him to Fabian's office, Jenna's mouth dropped when she saw the mess. Everything was turned upside down; every drawer opened and emptied; the safe door stood wide.

'What on earth have you *done*?' she gasped. 'This is a complete invasion of privacy.'

'Sit down,' Tony told her, righting the chair that he had minutes ago thrown across the room. 'I'm gonna show you something. But first, take a look at this.' He held up a small plastic bag half full of white powder.

'What is it?'

'Coke. From his safe.' Letting that sink in, Tony held up a pair of panties with a diamante thong. 'Know whose these are?'

'Should I?'

'They're Mel's.' Sneering, Tony crumpled them in his hand and threw them hard at the wall.

Wincing, Jenna raised a hand.

Groaning, Tony squatted down in front of her. 'Hey, don't be scared of me, Jenna. I'm not mad at you.'

Snatching her hands away when he reached for them, Jenna shrank back in her chair.

'Don't,' Tony said, softening his tone. 'I would never hurt you, I swear it. But you've got to understand that I can't let this go.'

'I just don't understand where this is coming

from,' Jenna said. 'I mean, okay, so you've got a pair of panties. But you don't know they're Melody's for sure. They sell stuff like that everywhere.'

'They're hers,' Tony said flatly. 'I bought them myself, back in the States. You don't got that label over here. And they were in his safe.'

'That doesn't mean anything,' Jenna said, knowing it sounded stupid but still convinced that he was wrong, that there had to be a simple explanation for this. 'Melody loves you. She'd never do that to you.'

'You sure about that?' Tony asked, his eyes still too dark for Jenna's comfort. 'Show her,' he said then, clicking his fingers at Eddie.

Slotting the DVD into the machine in the cupboard, Eddie pressed *play* and stood back, his arms folded.

A frown creased Jenna's brow as she looked at the screen and saw a shot of this office. 'It's a CCTV tape.'

'Keep watching,' Tony said quietly, his own eyes riveted to the screen.

Fabian came into the shot, quickly followed by Melody, and Jenna gasped when she saw Fabian lay out two lines of coke on a mirror and snort one. Handing the straw to Melody then, he came up behind her as she leaned down to snort hers and ran his hands over her body. Rocking back against him when he slipped his hand between her thighs, Melody moaned, 'Oh, that's good. Oh, yeah . . . keep doing that.'

'Seen enough?' Tony asked.

Nodding, Jenna lowered her gaze. 'Yes.'

'See,' Tony said when Eddie had switched the DVD off. 'The bastard's been fucking my girl *and* giving her coke, right here in this room!'

Shaking her head, Jenna looked at him. 'I'm so sorry. I had no idea.'

Tony nodded. 'I know. But now can you see why I've got to find him?'

'What are you going to do?' Jenna asked, fearing that she already knew the answer.

'Rough him up,' Tony lied, shrugging. 'Nothing else I can do, is there? He can think himself lucky we ain't in the States, or I'd do a whole lot worse.'

'And Melody?'

'Don't worry about her, I ain't gonna touch her,' Tony said, semi-truthfully. She was going to get the beating of her miserable life when he got back to the hotel, but he needed her alive to finish what he'd started and get his ticket to stay in the country.

'I don't know where Fabian is,' Jenna said now, flapping her hands. 'All I can do is give you his address from the staff files.'

'Good girl,' Tony said, patting her knee. Standing

up, he reached for her hand and pulled her to her feet.

As she went into her office, Jenna's mind was reeling. How could Fabian do something like that? Having an affair with somebody was one thing – but with his boss's girlfriend? And giving her drugs. *Having* drugs on the premises, full stop, knowing that Jenna could have lost her licence at any time because of it – that was unforgivable.

But he didn't deserve to die for it. And, whatever Tony said, she knew exactly what would happen if he got his hands on Fabian while he was in this kind of mood.

Giving him the address, Jenna said, 'Please don't be too hard on him. I know he's done wrong, and I'm going to sack him as soon as I see him, but please don't do anything to get yourself into trouble.'

Kissing her on the cheek, Tony gave her a reassuring pat on the shoulder. 'Quit worrying. All I'm gonna do is warn him off.' Then, turning to Eddie with murder in his eyes, he jerked his head. 'Let's go.'

Jenna waited a couple of minutes, then reached for her mobile. Hands shaking wildly, she called Fabian.

'Come on,' she muttered as his phone rang and rang. 'Pick it up, damn you.'

'Hello?' Fabian said sleepily, answering at last.

'Where are you?' Jenna asked him.

'Still in bed. I'm off sick, remember?'

'Are you at home?'

'Yes, why?'

'You've got to get out of there,' Jenna told him, the urgency in her voice getting through to him at last.

'What's the matter?' Fabian said, fully alert now.

'Tony and Eddie are on their way round,' she told him. 'They've found a DVD of you and Melody in your safe, and some panties that he bought her in the States. They'd ransacked your office by the time I got here, and got your address.'

'Oh, my God,' Fabian muttered. 'What are they going to do?'

'What do you think?' Jenna said sharply. 'Just get out of there, Fabian. And if you've got Melody's number I think you should warn her, too. But get yourself out of there first.'

'Right,' Fabian said, sounding scared and confused. 'Thanks, Jenna.'

'I'm only telling you because I don't want them to do anything stupid,' Jenna told him. 'I know what you've been doing, Fabian, and you had no right to keep stuff like that in my club.'

'Jenna, I—'

'Don't,' she cut him off, not wanting to hear it. 'It's too late.'

'No, you don't understand,' he persisted. 'There's something you should know, about that man who threatened you in the yard.'

'What about him?' Jenna asked, frowning deeply now.

'He was at the club last night,' Fabian told her, breathing hard as he pulled his jeans on. 'He came in asking for Tony.'

'Don't be ridiculous.'

'It's true, Jenna. Ask Bobby and Austin. That's why I went home, because Tony got mad about me sending Austin round to The Diamond to get him. I heard him telling Bobby he was going to break my legs.'

'So, what did the man want with him?' Jenna asked, not sure that she wanted to hear this.

'He said he'd come for the money that Tony owed him. Tony was annoyed with him at first, said he'd told him never to show his face at the club, but the man said he'd waited long enough, that his boys were hassling him for their money.'

'Did Tony pay him?'

'Yeah, and gave him extra for waiting. Then the man said if he ever wanted anyone else heavying, he knew where to find him.'

'How can you be sure it's the one who threatened me?'

'Because he had a boxing-glove earring, and a

gold chain with a bulldog on it.' Pausing, Fabian inhaled deeply. 'I'm really sorry, Jenna, I should have told you last night, but I was worried what Tony would do to me, 'cos he was already mad at me.'

'It's all right,' Jenna murmured, feeling sick to her stomach. 'Thanks for letting me know.'

Hanging up then, she exhaled shakily. If it was true, and it obviously was or Fabian wouldn't have told her to ask Bobby and Austin, it could only mean one thing: that Tony was behind those men jumping her in the yard that day. And if he was behind that, he'd probably organised the other trouble, too. The fights that had kicked off for no good reason; the raids – during which, she realised now, Tony had been conveniently out of town; the taxi firms blacklisting them – everything. Wearing her down, eroding her profits and damaging the club's reputation, then, finally, sending those men to put the fear of God into her, all designed to leave her with nowhere to turn but to him – the one person she'd believed could help her. And all so he could get a stake in her club.

And now that he had it, there wasn't a single thing that Jenna could do about it, because if he was willing to do all that just to get it, he would surely be willing to do whatever it took to keep it. And the police couldn't help her, because Tony's name wasn't even on the contracts. Hiding behind Leonard Drake's respectable name, he would say that she was crazy if she complained that he had conned her.

How could she have been so stupid?

Jenna's mobile began to ring. She switched it off without looking at it, fearing that it would be Tony checking up on her – making sure that she hadn't warned Fabian.

Well, tough: he was too late. Because she *had* warned Fabian – and Fabian had warned *her*. And now she knew where she stood, she had to find a way of getting Tony out of her life and out of her business before he took everything from her.

Getting up, Jenna grabbed her bag and headed out.

Dressed, Fabian grabbed his wallet, cards and car keys and ran down the stairs. Fearing for his life, because Tony and Eddie would surely kill him if they got hold of him, he jumped into his car and took off in a squeal of burning rubber. He didn't know what he was going to do now. Jenna knew about the coke, so he might as well kiss his job goodbye – not that he could go back there anyway, because Tony owned half the business. But at least he had some savings to tide him over while he found a new job. In a new town. Somewhere far away from Tony Allen.

Driving to the old part of Hulme now, Fabian parked up under one of the covered open-ended garages and ran up to Bubba's flat on the third floor of the scruffy block. Bubba would let him hang out there for a while, until he'd figured out where to go.

Hammering on the door, he took out his mobile and rang Melody to warn her while he waited for Bubba to answer.

'Wha's up?' Melody said groggily. 'You woke me up.'

'Tony knows,' Fabian told her quickly. 'Him and Eddie are on their way to my place now.'

'How?' Melody demanded, sitting bolt upright in her bed. 'Don't tell me you *told* him?'

'No, I didn't fucking tell him,' Fabian snapped. 'Do you think I'm an idiot? He must have got it from you.'

'It wasn't *me*!' Melody retorted, her voice panicked. 'He was asking me last night, but I totally denied it. I'd be dead by now if he didn't believe me.'

'Well, he obviously didn't,' Fabian snapped. 'Sure you don't talk in your sleep?'

'Fuck off!' Melody snarled, throwing the quilt back and leaping out of bed. 'Who told you he knew, anyway?'

'Jenna just called from the club. Him and Eddie

have ransacked my office, and they found your knickers in my safe.'

'Which knickers? I haven't left any knickers there.'

'Diamante thongs,' Fabian reminded her.

'Oh, my God,' Melody muttered. Then, 'Okay, that's cool. If that's all he's got, we just say I took them off in the toilets one time, and the cleaners handed them in to you as lost property.'

'That's not all,' Fabian admitted. 'There's CCTV footage of us together in the office. My, er, security camera was still running the first time, but I didn't notice till we were leaving. I meant to delete it, but I forgot.'

'*Forgot*?' Melody yelled. 'How could you forget something like that? What's on it, anyway? If it's just us doing coke, I can—'

'Everything,' Fabian interrupted quietly. 'You can see everything.'

'So you've watched it?' Melody said, stunned that he could be so stupid. 'If you only realised when we were leaving the office, you must have watched it after you went back or you wouldn't know what was on it. So why the fuck didn't you delete it then?'

'I don't know,' Fabian muttered.

'You shit!' she snarled. 'You kept it on purpose, didn't you?'

'It was insurance,' he admitted, getting irritated now. 'In case you did something stupid.'

'Oh, well, congratulations,' Melody shot back sarcastically. 'You've just won first prize in the knob-head of the fucking *century* awards! I never said a goddamn word, but you've dropped us *right* in it, haven't you?'

'I'm sorry,' Fabian murmured, reaching behind him and rapping on Bubba's door again.

'Where are you?' Melody demanded, holding the phone between her cheek and her shoulder as she struggled into her jeans.

'At a friend's,' he told her evasively. 'Where will you go?'

'Tell me where you are – I'll catch a cab over to you,' Melody said.

'No!' Fabian yelped. 'Sorry, Melody, but you said you couldn't get away from Tony because he'd find you and kill you. And I can't risk being with you if he does.'

Melody opened her mouth to call him a bastard, but stopped when she heard another voice in the background say, 'Yo, dude, what's with the rat-a-tat-tatting?'

Staring at the phone when it went dead in her hand, she tried to remember where she'd heard the voice before. But she couldn't quite put her finger on it.

But she'd worry about that later. She had to get out before Tony got back. And as soon as he found out that Fabian had done a runner, he *would* be back for her.

Throwing a jumper and jacket on, she grabbed her handbag, then ran to the closet and pulled the pack of sanitary towels out of her toiletries bag. She had no idea where she would go, but at least, with the money, she'd be able to hide out for a while.

Melody had just reached the door when Tony walked in and knocked her clean off her feet with the hardest punch she'd ever felt in her life. Dazed, she opened her eyes in time to see him running at her. Screaming when he kicked her in the back, she rolled into a ball and prayed that hc would kill her before the beating came to an end.

20

Vibes's instincts were prickling. Something was wrong, he was sure. He'd tried calling Jenna, but she had switched her phone off. And that was odd, because Kenneth had said she was looking forward to hearing from him. She would have seen his name on the screen, so why would she turn her phone off if that were the case?

Taking a chance on her being at work, he tried her on the club phone instead.

'Hello, Zenith. Anna speaking. How can I help you?'

'Hi, Anna,' Vibes said, remembering her as the girl who worked on reception. 'It's Vibes.'

'No way!' she cried, her voice ringing with surprise and delight. 'How are you? Wow! Wait till the others hear that you've called – they'll be so jealous that they weren't here to speak to you!'

'Say hi to everyone for me,' he said. Then, 'Sorry I can't chat, but do you think you could put me through to Jenna's office?'

'Oh, you've just missed her,' Anna told him. 'I can try Mr Allen for you instead, if you like? He went out earlier, but he's always in one door and out another, so he could still be around somewhere.'

'Mr Allen?' Vibes repeated. '*Tony* Allen? Why would he be there?'

'Oh, didn't Jenna tell you? He's her partner now.'

'Her *partner*?'

Chuckling softly, Anna said, 'I forgot how long you've been away. A lot's happened here since you left. We had a load of trouble – fights, and police raids, and all sorts. Then Jenna and Mr Allen went into partnership, and everything got sorted out. It's been great for ages now. He's even opened an offshoot club in the old storeroom, but we're not allowed in there so I can't tell you what it's like.'

'I gotta speak to Jenna,' Vibes said, feeling sick. 'Do me a favour and tell her to call me if you see her before I reach her, will you? It's urgent.'

Cutting the call then, he found Kalli's number and called her.

'Oh, my God!' Kalli said when he told her what he'd found out. 'Jenna's got no idea. She can't have, or she'd never have agreed to let him buy into the business.'

'Any idea where she might have gone?' Vibes asked. 'I know I'm probably overreacting because of what I know about him, but I've got a feeling something's wrong. My friend told me she'd be happy if I called, so I can't understand why she'd turn her phone off if she saw my name. She wouldn't do that, would she?'

'Definitely not,' Kalli replied softly, hoping that he'd get what she meant when she added, 'she really, *really* likes you.'

Completely missing it because he was so concerned, Vibes said, 'I don't suppose you've got Fabian's number, have you? I could call him, see if he's seen her.'

'I haven't got it, but I can get Anna to look it up for you, if you like?'

'Would you?' Vibes said gratefully. 'I'd appreciate it. I'll call you back in ten.'

Disconnecting, he sat down on the bed and looked at the newspaper he'd picked up the previous morning, which had the same photograph on its front page as the one he'd seen on the TV news bulletin. And, having scrutinised it with a magnifying glass, he was positive that the men were Tony and Eddie.

He had considered calling the police, but he wanted to speak to Jenna first, to find out if they were still hanging around at the club. But now that he knew she'd gone into business with the man, he was thinking that maybe he should call them anyway – just to be on the safe side. If Tony Allen – or Cerrullo, or whatever his goddamn name was – could sit and laugh over a severed head, he was capable of anything. And there was nothing Vibes could do to protect Jenna if he set his sights on her, not from all the way over here.

Startled out of his thoughts when his mobile rang, Vibes frowned when he saw Kalli's name on the screen.

'You shouldn't have called me,' he said, answering it. 'It'll cost you a fortune.'

'It doesn't matter,' she assured him. 'I got Fabian's number, but I rang him to save you doing it, and it's switched off.'

'His, too?' Vibes frowned.

'Yeah, and I thought I'd best tell you what happened last night,' Kalli said, her tone grim now. 'Some man called in to the club to see Mr Allen, and Fabian sent Austin round to his *new* club to get him. Mr Allen was really annoyed about it, and came looking for Fabian. Then, apparently, somebody told him something he didn't like about Fabian and his girlfriend, and he started threatening Melody, so I sent Austin down to get security, because he looked like he was going to hit her. Anyway,' she said, taking a sharp, much-needed breath, 'when Anna just went to get the staff file to get Fabian's number for me, she said that his office door was wide open, and the office itself has been turned upside down. And she said Mr Allen and Big Eddie went storming out just as she got to the club today, so she thinks they probably did it. And then Jenna just left without saying a word a few minutes later.'

'I've got to go,' Vibes said suddenly. 'Thanks for that, sweetheart.'

'Do you want me to go to Jenna's flat and see if she's there?' Kalli asked.

'No, stay out of it,' Vibes told her quickly. 'I'll call you later.'

Hanging up, he mulled everything over for a few minutes. There might be nothing going on, but could he really sit here and do nothing if there was even a chance that Tony was posing a threat to Jenna? He didn't think so.

Reaching for the phone, he dialled the contact number listed at the foot of the newspaper article.

Putting the phone down, Detective Bill Martinez stood up and, tucking his shirt in, strolled across the office to his colleague, Matt Knight. 'Just had a call from some guy,' he said, handing him the sheet of paper he'd written the info down on. 'Claims Anthony Cerrullo and Edward Derby are in Manchester, England, staying at some hotel called the Waterford.'

'Sound genuine?' Knight asked, looking at it.

'Yeah. Says he's been working over there, came back just a few months ago. Seems Cerrullo's going under the name of Allen now. Hanging out with an actress called Melody Fisher.'

'Oh, yeah?' Knight said, peering up at him now. 'I wondered where she'd gone.'

'You know her?'

'Nah, the wife was raving about her. Saw her in some movie with Sandra Bullock and rated her. Mentioned that she hadn't heard anything about her for a while.'

'Could be worth looking into, then?'

Grinning, Knight reached for his desk-phone. 'Best let the big guy know. You never know, there could be a trip in it for us. Passport up to date?'

Getting up quietly, Susan DeLornio wandered across the office and put a couple of letters she'd just finished typing in the out-tray. Looking at her watch then, she said, 'I'm going out for coffee, guys. Can I get you anything?'

'Depends what you're offering,' Martinez said, giving her a leering smile.

Tutting loudly, she walked out.

'You've got a hope in hell,' Knight chuckled. 'She's one of the untouchables.'

'Leper?'

'Catholic.'

'What a waste,' Martinez grumbled. 'Why can't they ever get any horny temps in this goddamn place?'

Taking the elevator down to the ground, Susan walked out into the open. Smiling at the security guard who held the door for her, she crossed the square and walked casually around the corner. Then she went into a phone booth and dropped her quarter into the slot.

'Cerrullo and Derby are in Manchester, England,' she said quietly when the call was answered. 'Waterford Hotel, under the name of Allen. They've got Melody Fisher with them.' Smiling when she got her reply, she said, 'My pleasure. But you'd better hurry. The Feds are gonna be all over the place soon as my boss gets the green light.'

21

Leonard's car wasn't in the drive. Pulling up outside the locked gates, Jenna peered at the house, but there wasn't so much as a whisper of movement behind the elegantly curtained windows.

Annoyed with herself for driving all the way over here without calling first, she banged a hand down on the steering wheel. She didn't know what she'd hoped to achieve by coming here, anyway. She supposed she'd just wanted to hear Leonard say that he hadn't known about Tony when he'd agreed to put his name to the contracts. Some reassurance that she hadn't been the only one he'd taken for a ride. If Leonard was in the dark, as she truly hoped, then maybe, between them, they could come up with a plan to get Tony out.

Reaching into her bag, she took out her mobile and switched it back on, intending to call Kalli and see if she was available for a coffee. She didn't want to go back to the club just yet, and she didn't want to go home, either, in case Tony decided to visit her there. Jumping when the phone immediately started to ring, she saw Vibes's name on the screen.

'Jenna, are you all right?' he asked, his voice sounding so concerned that Jenna thought something bad must have happened to him.

'Yes, I'm fine,' she told him. 'Are *you*? Kenneth told me all about the case, and he said the verdicts were coming in soon. Have you—'

'Never mind that now,' Vibes said quickly. 'I don't know what's going on over there, but I think you're in danger.'

'Why?' Jenna asked, shocked that he was saying this when he couldn't possibly know anything.

Explaining everything to her that he'd found out at his end, Vibes said, 'I had no idea you'd gone into partnership with him. I can't believe you did that.'

'Neither can I,' Jenna admitted shamefacedly. 'I was in such a mess, I couldn't see any other way out of it. But I've just found out that he probably set everything up from the start.'

'I'm coming over,' Vibes told her. 'It'll probably take a few days, but I want to be with you.'

'Oh, God, that would be fantastic,' Jenna gasped, aware that she was crying. 'We've all been missing you so much.'

'Have *you* been missing me?' he asked, his voice

quiet and low now. He was dreading a negative reaction.

'More than you'll ever know,' she admitted. 'But I didn't want to call you, because I – well, it doesn't matter now. Kenneth told me everything. Just come back, Vibes. I really need you here.'

'What about Jason?' Vibes asked. 'Is he gonna be a problem?'

'Jason?' Jenna repeated. 'Why on earth would he be a problem? I haven't seen him in almost two years.'

'For real?' Vibes sounded confused. 'But I thought . . .'

'Ah,' Jenna said, remembering when she'd made that slip of the tongue during one of their conversations. 'I said his name in the present tense, and you thought I was still with him. Well, no, I'm not. He lied to me, because he was married the whole time we were together, and I got as far away from him as possible when I found out. I never want to see him again. Okay?'

'I see,' Vibes said, trying to remember that he'd called for far more serious reasons, even though his heart felt like it was busting right out of his chest with joy. 'Okay, well, I'll be with you soon, so we'll talk more then. But right now, you need to be careful.'

'What should I do?' Jenna asked, feeling a little safer now.

'Nothing,' Vibes said. 'If you're not in any immediate danger, don't say or do anything out of the ordinary. Just do what you usually do so you don't raise his suspicions. Let him think everything's fine, so he can't blame you when the Feds move in on him.'

Exhaling shakily, Jenna said, 'Okay, I'll try. But I hope they don't take too long.'

'I don't know what they'll have to put in place to do it,' Vibes said. 'They might have to liaise with your cops, or your government, or something, to get permission to come after him. But if they want him bad enough, they'll get to him. It's just a matter of holding out till they make their move.'

'Right, well, I'll pretend I don't know anything,' Jenna promised. 'But please hurry up and get here.'

'Soon as I can, I'll be there,' he assured her. 'Do me a favour,' he said then. 'Go see Kalli – make sure she doesn't do anything stupid. Not that she'll mean to, but she's seriously worried about you and she might give something away.'

'I was about to call her when you rang,' Jenna told him. 'I was going to take her out for coffee.'

'Do it,' Vibes said. 'I'll call you later, to make sure everything's all right.'

Hanging up, Jenna leaned her head back and hugged the phone to her breast. Swiping the tears away after a moment, she called Kalli and arranged to meet her. Then she turned the car around and set off back to Manchester.

She'd have to act as if nothing were out of the ordinary for the next few days, and it would be hard now that she knew exactly what Tony Allen was really about. But, with luck, then it would be over.

22

The men came out of the airport and paused to light cigarettes. They had one small suitcase each, containing just the essentials for a week-long stay, although they had no intention of staying that long if they didn't have to. Hailing one of the waiting cabs when they had finished their smokes, they climbed into the back with their cases on their laps.

'Waterford Hotel,' one of them told the driver.

'Americans?' he asked, setting off. 'I got a sister lives up that way. You might know her? She lives up in Richmond. Name's Pat Hillman.'

'Maybe,' the man replied, his eyes hidden by dark shades.

They stayed silent for the rest of the journey. Paying the driver when he pulled up around the corner from the Waterford, they got out and walked around to take a look at the hotel. Watching the front doors for a while, they gave each other a nod and entered the foyer.

'Two singles,' one of them said to the receptionist.

'Certainly, sir.' She smiled. 'If I could just take your details?'

Handing their room passes to them when they had been processed, she said, 'Would you like one of our porters to carry your cases up for you?'

'No, thanks, we can manage,' he told her, smiling. 'Have a nice day, ma'am.'

'Oh, I love it when you people say that,' she giggled. 'It sounds just like The Blues Brothers. We've another American gentleman on the third floor who sounds just like you, and it makes me go all weak when he says it.'

'That right?' the man said, still smiling as he walked away.

Melody was asleep on the couch when she heard the knock on the door. Groaning, she picked herself up and hobbled to answer it. It had been two days since Tony had beaten her half to death, and she hadn't set foot out of the room since. Even if Tony had let her – which he definitely wouldn't – she wouldn't have wanted to, because she was too ashamed of the bruises.

Thinking that this would be the room-service boy delivering the painkillers she'd sent down for earlier, she opened the door a crack and stuck her hand out.

Knocked back by the force of the man's

shoulder barging the door, she landed in a heap of agony halfway across the room.

'Who are you?' she screamed when the man and his friend came in, closing the door behind them. 'Don't you fucking touch me!' Opening her mouth, she screamed at the top of her voice.

Pulling a gun out of his pocket, the man slammed it butt-down on her nose. Then, waiting to see if anybody had heard the scream and was coming to investigate, the two men relaxed after a few minutes and set about searching the room.

23

Tony and Eddie found the duty manager waiting for them when they got back to the hotel at four that morning.

'Excuse me, sir, but could I have a quick word?' he said, approaching them nervously.

'Yeah, what?' Tony grunted, hoping this wasn't some stupid shit that could have waited till morning.

'It just that, well, some of the other guests have been complaining about the noises coming from your room while you've been staying with us,' the manager told him, feeling more awkward than he'd ever felt in his life before. 'Now, I realise that people do argue,' he went on, trying to be diplomatic. 'But I'm afraid that this cannot be allowed to continue.'

'What you getting at?' Tony interrupted snappily. 'I ain't uttered a sound in days.'

'With respect,' the manager said, 'the, um, screams were loud enough to reach the guests on the floor below your suite this evening.'

'Screams?' Tony narrowed his eyes.

'Yes, and as it isn't the first time your, um, wife has been heard to scream in that manner, I'm afraid it's fallen to me to ask that you refrain from whatever activity you're involved in that may be causing it.'

'You couldn't just say that in plain fucking English, could you?' Tony snarled. 'I haven't got a fucking clue what you're talking about. I've been out all night. I've just this second got back.'

'Well, then maybe you could speak to your wife?' The manager raised an eyebrow. 'I did try knocking earlier, after the other guests complained of the noise of furniture being moved about up there. I didn't get an answer. But I would have been within my rights to use my pass key to gain entry. It was only the fact that you've been with us for so long that prevented me from doing so. But I would appreciate it if you could resolve the matter so that we don't have to have any more complaints.'

'The furniture being moved about?' Tony said, looking at him with dark eyes. 'Was that before or after the screams?'

'After,' the manager said. 'Which was why I eventually went up there. But I don't really think—'

Trailing off as Tony and Eddie abruptly walked away, he turned to the receptionist and flapped his hands.

*

Taking the stairs at a run, Tony and Eddie came out at the third floor and walked cautiously up to the door of Tony's suite. Pressing his ear to the wood, Tony listened for a minute. Hearing nothing, he took his phone out and called Melody on her mobile. They could hear it ringing inside, but Melody didn't answer. Cutting his phone off, Tony eased the door handle down. Just as he'd expected, the door was unlocked. Cracking it open, he stayed to the side and peered in. Melody was lying on the floor a few feet in, her face a bloody mess, her nightdress pulled up over her bruised thighs, her legs spread wide and displaying her nakedness.

Muttering 'Fuck!' Tony waved Eddie in and told him to watch the door. Then, creeping quietly around the room he checked every corner and cupboard. Then he went into the bedroom and did the same in there and in the bathroom. Satisfied that no one was hiding, he switched the lamp on.

Illuminated, Melody looked even worse. Her tongue was hanging out of the corner of her mouth and her bulging eyes were already clouded. She'd been strangled, raped and, for good measure, shot through the middle of her forehead.

Gazing down at her, Tony shook his head, then reached for the quilt off the couch and threw it over her. Sticking his hand down the back of the couch then, he dragged all his money out.

Stuffing everything he had into one of his cases, he and Eddie left the room, locking the door behind them, and made their escape through the fire exit.

24

'Have you seen the news?' Kalli gasped when Jenna answered the phone.

'No, I'm on my way to the airport,' Jenna told her. 'Why, what's up?'

'Melody Fisher's been murdered. They found her at her hotel, and the police are looking for Tony and Eddie.'

Swerving onto the hard shoulder, Jenna pulled up and grabbed the phone from its hands-free holder. 'You're joking?'

'No, it's all over the news. Big pictures of her, and everything. They reckon she was shot through the head. It's so awful. She looks so beautiful in the pictures, but to think of her shot dead like that, it just makes you feel weird.'

'Right, I'll pick up some papers when I've met Vibes,' Jenna said, restarting the engine. 'Stay at home. I'll come there as soon as I get back.'

'With Vibes?' Kalli asked.

'Of course. He's dying to see you.'

Vibes saw Jenna as soon as she walked through the automatic doors. Swallowing hard, because she looked just as beautiful as ever, he got up and called out to her.

Turning, Jenna saw him and threw a hand over her mouth.

Seconds later she was in his arms, kissing him and telling him that she loved him too.

25

'No, Mr Allen was not my partner,' Jenna told DI Seddon, who was questioning her along with two American detectives. 'He was a customer. Mr Drake here is my partner.'

'Yes, that's right,' Leonard affirmed, aware that Avril was glaring at him, making sure that he didn't get the story wrong. 'As Miss Lorde has already told you, Mr Allen was a customer. Unfortunately, however, I allowed him into my life when I agreed to sell some of my paintings to him. He – Tony, that is – paid for them with a banker's draft, which I deposited in my account. But not long after, he began to call on me for favours, and before I knew it he was demanding money, and threatening to hurt my wife if I didn't pay.'

'And you never thought to report this to the police?' Seddon asked, frowning.

'I'm not the bravest of men,' Leonard admitted, blushing deeply. 'And I'm afraid I took his threats at face value.'

'So, none of this business belonged to Anthony Cerrullo?' Detective Martinez chipped in, looking Leonard over with a scornful sneer.

'None whatsoever,' Jenna told him, drawing his attention to herself to give Leonard a break. He was having a hard enough time keeping it together as it was without these men looking down on him. Getting up, she took the contracts out of her safe and showed them. 'See, just me and Mr Drake.'

'Fair enough,' Knight said, looking them over and handing them back.

'Has anybody come over to identify them?' Jenna asked, afraid that she might be faced with a whole new problem if Tony's relatives tried to stake a claim on his shares. If he'd told them the arrangement, and they were anything like him, they'd be bound to try and muscle in.

'We don't know of any family, as yet,' Martinez replied, giving her a whole different look than the one he'd been giving Leonard. 'But it's highly unlikely that their own mothers could ID them, the state they're in. The ID we found scattered about the canal bank in back of the hotel indicates that they were the bodies of Cerrullo and Derby – or Tony Allen and Eddie, as *you* knew them. We'll go on that for now, see what the DNA turns up when we get them back to the States. Maybe we'll trace family that way.' Pausing, he shrugged. 'Someone's got to bury them, and it sure as hell ain't gonna be at our expense.'

Shaking her head, Jenna exhaled loudly. 'I can't say I particularly liked them, but it's horrible to think of them being shot in the face like that.'

'Typical Mafia execution,' Martinez informed her knowledgeably. 'We deal with this kind of shi—*stuff* every day back home.'

'So, have you any idea who did it?'

'Oh, yeah, and our guys are already onto it,' Martinez told her, puffing his chest out proudly. These English cops were so disorganised, they hadn't even thought to check the hotel register after they found the bodies. If they had, they'd have found out about the two American-Italians who had booked in earlier that day, then disappeared without so much as touching their minibars or beds. And they might then have followed it up, as Martinez and Knight had, and learned that the men had caught an early-morning flight back to New York.

'Right, well, we'd best get moving,' Knight said now. There was nothing worth sticking around for, and Bill looked to be getting a little too friendly with the lady boss. 'Nice meeting you folks. Sorry to put you out with this.'

'It's no problem,' Jenna assured him, standing up to show them out. 'I'm just sorry we couldn't be more help.'

Walking them down to the front door, Jenna shook Knight's and Martinez's hands and wished them a safe journey home. Thanking DI Seddon then, she said, 'You will let us know if you find Melody's family, won't you? I'd hate to think of her being buried with no one to pay their respects.'

'I'll keep in touch,' Seddon promised. Lowering his voice then so that Knight and Martinez wouldn't hear, he said, 'Think yourself lucky you weren't involved with Cerrullo, 'cos I've got a feeling these guys would have been all over your club and your accounts.'

'Well, there's nothing here for them,' Jenna told him, folding her arms. 'And there never will be, because I've got no intention of ever letting anyone worm their way into my club.'

'Good for you,' Seddon said approvingly.

'Do you think they were convinced?' Avril asked when the detectives had left and Jenna had come back.

'I think so,' Vibes said, reaching for Jenna's hand. 'You did good, Princess.'

Gazing into his beautiful eyes, she smiled. 'Thanks.'

Winking at her, Vibes turned back to Leonard and Avril. 'Bet you're glad it's all over.'

'Oh, yes,' Leonard said, sighing softly. 'It's been quite an ordeal, I must admit. I was, um, thinking,' he said then. 'Maybe we should think about having the ownership reverted back to Jenna, now that Tony is no longer around.'

'I don't think so,' Avril chipped in firmly. 'With respect, Jenna, my husband's name is on the contract as a legitimate partner.'

'Yes, and I'm quite happy for it to stay that way,' Jenna assured her. Turning to Leonard then, she smiled. 'I've thought it through, and it seems a waste to let everything slip now. So, if you're willing, I'd be quite happy for you to pick up where Tony left off and continue running your private members' club.'

'Really?' Leonard gasped, hardly able to believe his good fortune. 'Well, of course, I'd be delighted. Oh, but there are a few changes I'd wish to make,' he said then, casting a quick glance at Avril. 'I wasn't too happy with the waitresses, you see.'

Chuckling softly, Jenna said, 'I'm not really surprised. I never thought they'd suit your more *upmarket* clientele, but Tony wanted them, so what could I do? Just send them back in here. I'll put them back on their regular posts.'

'I'm not sure you'd want to do that if you knew what they'd been doing in there,' Leonard told her quietly. 'I'm afraid they weren't very . . . *nice*.'

'Oh?' Vibes peered at him with a smile in his eyes. 'How so?'

'They were lap-dancing and prostituting,' Avril told him bluntly. 'If I'd known, I would have put a stop to it there and then. But Leonard isn't the most forceful of characters, as you've probably surmised, and he went along with Tony Allen's orders not to tell me. Didn't you, dear?' She gave Leonard a spiky smile.

'I'm afraid so,' he muttered, folding his arms.

'Well, I can't keep them on if they were doing that,' Jenna said. 'I'll let them go when they come in tonight. Better still, I'll find their numbers and call them, so I don't even have to look at them.' Sighing, she shook her head. 'Never mind. There's plenty more will be glad of the work. But in the meantime, you'll have to choose some of the others, I suppose.'

'Oh, right,' Leonard said, licking his lips nervously. 'Well, um, if you're in agreement, I wouldn't mind taking that polite girl from the VIP bar.'

'Not Kalli,' Jenna said quickly. 'Sorry, but I can't lose her. In fact, I'm planning to promote her to bar manager. She's been practically running the place anyway, and now that Maurice has decided to retire I think she's the perfect replacement.'

'No, no, not her,' Leonard said. 'The other one – the quiet one. Diane. That's it.'

'Oh, right, well, fine.' Jenna shrugged. 'I'm sure she'd be an asset. Anyone else in mind?'

'Um, yes, maybe the boy who works with her – Austin, I think his name is.'

'I don't think so,' Avril snorted.

'He's very good,' Jenna told her. 'And he and Diane do work well together.'

'No, dear, I don't think he's at all suitable,' Avril said firmly. 'Leonard will take another of the young ladies, won't you, Leonard?'

'Yes, of course,' he murmured, looking down at his hands. She obviously knew. And if she knew, it was over.

Tapping on the door just then, Kalli popped her head in. 'Anybody want anything? Only I'm about to go.'

'Wait a minute,' Vibes said, smiling up at her. 'We'll walk you out.' Standing up, still holding Jenna's hand, he said, 'If everybody's ready?'

'Yes, absolutely,' Leonard said, jumping lightly to his feet, already over Austin because the future looked quite bright without him. 'We shall see you tonight, then.' Turning to Jenna, he bowed. '*Partner.*'

Smiling, Jenna looped her arm through Vibes's and held on tight as they all walked out together. Now that she'd got him back, she was never letting go again.

EPILOGUE

Avril was roused by the sound of rustling in the corridor outside her bedroom door. Opening her eyes, she glanced at the clock. It was only just past two, and The Diamond didn't close until three, so what on earth was Leonard doing home already? And why was he at her door? He surely didn't think that she was going to welcome him into her bed? Oh, no, no, no! It hadn't even been a month yet. He had *far* more grovelling to do before she forgave him his latest indiscretion.

Sitting up when the door handle turned, she was about to call out to him to bloody well forget it when she heard a voice that she recognised all too well.

'It's locked. She's gotta be in there.'

She inhaled sharply. No, it couldn't be. They were dead.

Getting out of bed, she tiptoed to the balcony door.

The wind was high tonight, and a forceful gust

tore the door from her hand when she eased it open. Licking at the curtains, it knocked a jar of cream over on the dressing table, sending it rolling noisily into her perfumes and deodorants.

'Kick it in!' the voice in the corridor hissed.

Bursting in seconds later, Tony saw the hastily vacated bed and the open door and turned back to the stairs. 'She's climbed out. You go look if you can see her, I'll go after her.'

Walking quickly to the balcony, Eddie stepped out and peered over the rail into the dark gardens below.

Holding her breath, petrified that he would hear her, Avril crept out of her walk-in closet with the heavy steel poker held firmly between her hands. Raising it above her head, she came up behind Eddie and slammed it down as hard as she could on the back of his neck.

Letting out a tiny gasp of fear when his knees buckled, Avril hit him again and again on the top of his head, not even aware of the sounds of splintering bone and squelching tissue, just conscious that she needed to make sure he was properly unconscious so that he couldn't retaliate.

'You seen her?' Tony's voice hissed up a moment later. 'Ed?'

Ducking so that she was almost sitting on

Eddie's battered head now, Avril squinted out through the ornate balcony rails. She couldn't see Tony, but she could hear him mooching about in the pitch-dark gardens below. The security lights should have come on by now, but they had obviously disabled them along with the alarms.

Letting out another tiny gasp when Eddie made a sighing sound, she reached down to steady herself, and almost fell over when her hand landed on the gun he was still holding.

Bringing her hands up to her mouth in shock, Avril recoiled when she felt and tasted the blood on her lips.

'Yo!' Tony hissed. 'What you doing up there, man? I can't see her. I'm coming in.'

Heart hammering in her chest, Avril wrenched the gun out of Eddie's hand and stumbled back into the bedroom. Running back to the closet, she crouched on the floor inside the slightly open door so that she could see Tony when he came in. She felt sick, and every nerve in her body seemed to be sparking, every muscle taut with terror.

Running into the doorway a minute later, Tony made his way to the balcony door in search of Eddie. Pointing the gun at his back through the crack, trying desperately to still her wildly shaking hands, Avril closed her eyes and squeezed the trigger.

There was a slight popping sound, followed by

a grunt and the sound of something falling heavily to the floor.

Hardly breathing now, Avril opened her eyes and looked out.

Tony was lying in a heap a few feet away. Standing up, Avril ventured out warily. Screaming when he moved, she shot him again, not even sure if anything had happened because she couldn't hear anything at all this time – she just saw the flash of light that illuminated Tony's darker than dark eyes.

Turning, she ran for her life.

Mandasue Heller's next novel

SHAFTED

will be published on September 20, 2007

Turn over for an exclusive preview . . .

I

'*Aaaand* cut!'

'Thank fuck for that!' Larry Logan muttered, pulling a tissue from his pocket and wiping his handsome face. Tossing it onto the floor, he said, 'I thought there was supposed to be flaming air con in here?'

'There is,' the floor-manager replied curtly, sick of his moaning and whining - like *he* was the only one suffering. Snapping her fingers at one of the runners now, she barked at him to dispose of the tissue properly, then strode out onto the studio floor, yelling, 'Quiet in the audience, please! We're back on air in ten minutes, so no clever ideas about nipping to the toilet or opening noisy sweets, or you're out!'

Sticking two fingers up at her back, Larry side-stepped the make-up girl who rushed forward to repair his face and made a dash for the heavy, soundproofed studio door. Yanking it open, he stepped out of the stifling heat and shivered as the contrasting iciness of the corridor bit into him.

Heading towards his dressing room, he glanced back to see if anyone was following, and groaned when he saw the assistant director barrelling out of the studio door.

'Christ's sakes, Gord,' he complained, knowing full well that he'd come to keep an eye on him. 'I'm only going to the fucking loo.'

'I'll come with you,' Gordon told him firmly. 'You know what Jeremy said.'

'Tell him I gave you the slip,' Larry flipped back defiantly, walking on.

'No can do,' Gordon said, catching up.

'Give me a break,' Larry moaned. 'I've got the trots, man.'

Stopping in his tracks, Gordon frowned. He'd been ordered to watch Larry like a hawk to stop him from getting his hands on any booze, and that's exactly what he *had* been doing - all bloody day, despite having a heavy workload of his own to be getting on with. But there was no way he was standing outside the cubicle while Larry took a dump. That was *way* above and beyond.

Nodding, he said, 'Okay, go on then. But I'm waiting here. And if anyone asks, I was with you all the way.'

'I'll tell 'em you wiped my arse, if you want?' Larry quipped.

'Fuck off! And hurry up. We've only got a few minutes.'

'Thanks, mate. I owe you one.'

Taking off again, Larry turned the corner, and ran straight past the toilets. Letting himself into his dressing room, he closed the door firmly and dragged his holdall down from the top of the cupboard. Taking out the bottle of Scotch that was stashed at the bottom, he twisted the cap off and took a long drink, exhaling with pleasure and relief as the liquid seared his parched throat.

Taking another long slug, then another for the road, he stashed the bottle away again and gave himself an approving once-over in the mirror before heading back to set.

Concerned that Larry wasn't going to make it back in time, Gordon was just contemplating going to get him when he came hurtling around the corner, making an exaggerated show of zipping up his fly.

'Sorry, Gord . . . took a bit longer than I expected. And there was no paper in my cubicle, so I had to run down the line with my kecks round my ankles. Thought I was gonna have to mop up after myself, as well. Still, better out than in, eh?'

'Too much information,' Gordon grunted, yanking the studio door open and waving him back in. 'Better hurry up,' he warned then, nodding towards the floor-manager who was standing in the middle of the stage, hands on hips, tight-lipped scowl on her face. 'Looks like she's on the warpath.'

'Fuck her,' Larry scoffed. Then, laughing, he nudged Gordon in the ribs and said, 'Then again, maybe not, eh? I mean, you wouldn't, would you?'

Getting a full blast of Scotch fumes, Gordon grimaced. But it was too late to say anything, because Anne was already waving Larry over, hissing, 'Get a move on! We've got exactly twenty seconds.'

'Keep your knickers on,' Larry called back, blithely strolling towards her - and infuriating her some more, when he decided to waste a few more seconds saying hello to the pretty girls on the front row.

Biting down on her irritation, Anne held up her hand when Larry finally sauntered into position.

'Three . . . two . . . one . . . *aaand* action!'

Back under the blistering heat of the lights, the Scotch began to kick in, and Larry swayed slightly as he turned to camera six to welcome the viewers back. Burping loudly when he opened his mouth to speak, he gave the audience a mock-sheepish grin.

'Oops! Pardon me for being rude, t'was not me it was my food.'

Up in the editing suite, watching the action on

a high-tech bank of monitors, Frank Woods gave Jeremy Hislop an accusing look, hissing, 'He's pissed! I thought you said Gordon was watching him?'

'He was.'

'So, how the fuck did it happen, then?'

'I don't know,' Jeremy admitted, frowning as he studied Larry's face on the monitor. He was definitely under the influence; cheeks flushed, eyes beginning to glaze over.

'Idiot!' Frank snarled, slamming his fist down on the console. 'How could you let this happen? It's *The Kiddie Kare Telethon*, for fuck's sake. You knew how important it was to keep him in line. You should have handcuffed yourself to him.'

'You wanted me up here with you. I can't be two places at once.'

'You won't be *any* bloody place if he cocks this up, I can promise you that.'

'I *warned* you this would happen,' Jeremy argued, swivelling his chair around to face Frank now. 'But you ignored me, so . . .' Leaving the rest of the sentence hanging, he shrugged, his meaning quite clear without having to spell it out.

Annoyed as much by the intimation of blame as by the knowledge that it was rightly placed, Frank said, 'What choice did I have? It's the first time they've put a gameshow in the line-up, and they chose ours. I'd have been crazy to turn it down.'

Crazy to agree to it, more like, Jeremy thought scathingly, shaking his head as he turned his attention back to the screens. Only a fool would let a loose cannon like Larry Logan front a live show. He might be Mr Gorgeous, with the ability to charm the knickers off any woman at fifty paces – as he seemed intent on proving, going by the number of times he'd been papped coming out of clubs with different tarts hanging off his arm. But for those who had to suffer him on the dark side of the screen, he was rude, arrogant, and completely incapable of sticking to the format, and working with him had been the longest, most stressful six months of Jeremy's career to date.

And it didn't help that *Star Struck* was the biggest piece of crap TV Jeremy had ever been unfortunate enough to direct. But a job was a job, and this one paid well enough for Jeremy to bury his personal opinions - for the most part.

Back on set, Larry was taking the two surviving contestants into the final head-to-head. They were both female, but while one was middle-aged and plump – and, therefore, of no interest to Larry whatsoever; the other was young and pretty, with small, pert breasts, full glossy lips, and a sleek, jet-black bob. Just how he liked them!

'The Bat' – as Larry had mentally been referring to the older woman throughout the show – was first up. Making a concerted effort not to stare at the mole on her cheek that was beginning to look suspiciously like a couple of money-spiders mating, Larry cleared his throat and peered down at the question card in his hand.

'Right, Elaine . . . for a chance to win tonight's jackpot . . . can you tell me the real name of the former girl-band member known as Baby?'

'Oh, I really didn't want a pop question,' Elaine moaned, biting her lip. 'Oh, damn! I can't think of *any* girl groups.'

'Gonna have to hurry you along, there, sweetheart.'

More lip biting and frowning. Then, shrugging hopelessly, 'Is it The Supremes, Larry?'

''Fraid not.' Mock-sympathetic smile. 'I was looking for Emma Bunton from The Spice Girls.'

Turning to tonight's shag now, Larry gave her a conspiratorial wink and slipped an arm around her slim waist.

'Okay, Cindy, my darling, get this right, and you'll steal the money. Ready?'

'I think so,' she gasped, her heart thudding in her chest as his hand slid from her hip to the curve of her buttock. She'd loved him from the moment she first laid eyes on him, and couldn't believe that she had finally made it onto his show. And not only was she in with a real chance of winning, but she just knew that he fancied her, because he'd been winking at her all day, and giving her that super-sexy grin of his. And now he was actually touching her bum!

Stumbling slightly as an alcohol rush threw his head out of whack, Larry dropped his question cards. Muttering, 'Shit!' when they landed question-side up on the floor at Cindy's feet, he reached down and snatched them up. 'Sorry!' he said, waving them at the camera. 'But don't panic, she didn't see them . . . You didn't, did you, darlin'?'

'No.' Cindy shook her head innocently.

Feigning a cough to bring himself under control as he felt a sudden urge to laugh, Larry said, 'Sorry, folks, frog in the throat . . . better than *cancer*, though, eh?'

Waiting for the smattering of nervous audience laughter to die down, he turned back to Cindy.

'Right, then . . . for a chance to win ten-thousand pounds, can you tell me the name of Britney Spears' last husband, Kevin Federline?'

'Moron!' the floor-manager hissed, standing in the shadows beside the camera. Stepping forward now, she waved her arms to attract his attention.

Frowning when he saw her, Larry shrugged, and mouthed, '*What*?'

'*You gave her the answer*,' she stage-whispered, jabbing a finger at the question card. 'Ask her another! Ask . . . her . . . *another*!'

'Oh, right,' Larry murmured. Then, giving a cheeky grin to camera, 'Sorry 'bout that. Seems I made a bit of a boo-boo. But s'all right. Just gotta ask another question.'

Rifling through the cards now, he pulled one out at random and looped his arm around Cindy's shoulder.

'Okay, my darling, for ten thousand pounds, can you tell me . . . why the hell Madonna picked Guy Ritchie over me?'

Cindy peered up at him confusedly. Then someone in the audience started laughing, and everyone else quickly followed suit - Larry included.

Alan Corbin, Oasis TV's Head of Light Entertainment was far from amused. Storming into the editing suite, he yelled, 'Get him off! *NOW*!'

'He's on the last question,' Jeremy said, trying desperately to remain calm even though he knew it could only get worse. 'If we just -'

Corbin wasn't listening. Eyes bulging from their sockets, he stared at the monitor screens and yelped, 'What the bloody hell's he doing *now*?' in a voice several octaves higher than was healthy for a man of his age.

Down below, Larry had totally lost it. Clutching at Cindy with tears of laughter streaming down his face, he'd managed to snap one of her flimsy shoulder straps, revealing one of her bare breasts.

'Oh, my God!' Corbin croaked as the studio audience erupted with male approval and female disapproval. Shoulders slumping, he sank down on a vacant chair and dabbed his handkerchief over his sweat-slick face. 'We're fucked!'

'Not necessarily,' Jeremy muttered, pushing sliders and pressing buttons on the master control panel. 'We've still got time-delay on our side. Any luck, we'll black-screen before anyone spots the tit.'

'Bit late for that,' Frank interjected bitterly. 'They've been watching him for the last half hour.'

Ignoring him, Jeremy carried on with what he was doing. Then, sighing with relief after a moment, he said, 'We're off air.'

'What about the tit?' Corbin wanted to know. 'Have you caught it in time?'

'Soon know,' Jeremy told him, turning his attention to the live-stream monitor.

Everyone in the editing suite held their breath as, on screen, Larry reached the point where he'd dropped the question cards. Snatching them up again, he started to ask the Britney Spears question, but just as he reached the point where he unwittingly supplied the answer, the screen went blank, and seconds later a 'Technical fault' warning flagged up, followed by the help and appeal-line numbers, and a pre-recorded voice-over by Matty Kline, the comedian who was compering the telethon, urging people to "*Keep ringing in those donations, guys, 'cos every little helps!*"

Excusing himself now that the worst of the disaster had been averted, Jeremy rushed down to the set to try and salvage what was left of the show. Grabbing Larry, he frog-marched him to the studio door and ordered him to go and get himself sobered up. That done, he asked Matty Kline to stand in and wrap *Star Struck* up.

Frank Woods and Alan Corbin were in the middle of a hushed, but obviously heated discussion when Jeremy got back to the editing suite; Corbin telling Frank that Larry had to go, but Frank in no mood to be dictated to. Bad as it had been today, *Star Struck* was his baby, and he was proud of its success. And he wasn't about to risk a drop in the ratings by replacing Larry - not on Corbin's say-so, anyway.

'You're over-reacting,' he told Corbin now. 'The viewers love Larry, and they won't hold this against him. We'll just issue a statement saying he was doped up on flu medication, or something.'

'Don't be ridiculous,' Corbin snorted contemptuously. 'Any idiot can see he's steaming. And, to be honest, he's not good enough that I need to be putting myself through this kind of stress every time he hits the screen. He's goes – that's my final word.'

'With respect,' Frank replied with measured calm. 'This is my production company, and *I* decide who goes and who stays on my shows.'

'And *I* decide which programmes to commission for my station,' Corbin reminded him firmly. Exhaling wearily then, he said, 'I don't want to fall out with you over this, Frank, but if you can't see what a liability Logan is, you're not the man you used to be.'

Frank knew that Corbin was right. Logan was a liability. But the public didn't know that, and if Frank had his way, they never would.

'I know what you're thinking,' Corbin said perceptively now. 'He draws the viewers, so we should give him leeway. But *The Kiddie Kare Telethon* is *sacred*, and I paid too much for the broadcasting rights to let one man – who, incidentally, I don't even *like* – jeopardise its future. And you're very much mistaken if you think the public won't hold this against him. Jokers, they accept; piss-heads who make *sick* jokes, they do not.' Standing up now, he shrugged. 'Take my advice, get shot of the dead wood and bring in someone reliable like Dennis or Monkhouse before it's too late.'

'Monkhouse is dead,' Frank reminded him, his flat tone disguising the anger simmering beneath the surface.

'So he is,' Corbin conceded. 'Oh, well . . . Dennis, then. Or how about Richie? He's a good-looking lad with a bit of spark about him. And the viewers adore him.' Nodding now, pleased with his vision, he said, 'Get Shane to front it, and we'll talk about keeping *Star Struck* in the schedule.'

'That's blackmail.'

'Call it what you like, but I don't want to see Logan's face in my station again – *ever*.'

'Bastard!' Frank snarled when the door swung shut behind Corbin. 'Who the hell does he think he is, telling me how to run *my* show? His station was on its bloody arse when I gave him *Star Struck*!'

'You've got to admit he's got a point,' Jeremy said. 'You don't realise how bad things actually are, because we've always smoothed everything out by the time the show airs, but it's murder trying to get a good take out of Larry these days.' Shrugging now, he added, 'Might be worth thinking about a replacement - even if it's only temporary; until he's been through rehab, or something.'

'Bollocks!' Frank shot back dismissively. 'Logan doesn't need rehab, he just needs a damn good kick up the arse.'

'If you say so,' Jeremy said, casually easing up the volume on the monitor so that Frank could hear how good a job Matty Kline was doing as a stand-in for his golden-boy right now. 'The audience really likes him, don't they?' he commented as the sound of cheering filled the suite.

'They liked the flaming singing *gerbils*!' Frank reminded him caustically. Then, shaking his head, he muttered, 'All you had to do was keep him in line, but if you're not up to it, just say the word, 'cos there's plenty more directors where you came from.'

Biting down on the angry reply that sprang to his lips, Jeremy folded his arms. There was no point arguing with Frank when he was in this kind of mood; he would just dig his heels in deeper and lash out at whoever was closest.

Pushing his chair back with a scrape now, Frank stood up and headed for the door, barking back over his shoulder, 'Find Larry and tell him I want him in my office in five minutes. And, while you're at it, sack Gordon!'